BEST OF TOMES OF THE DEAD VOLUME III

# THE SECRET ZOMBIE HISTORY OF THE WORLD

WWW.ABADDONBOOKS.COM

An Abaddon Books™ Publication
www.abaddonbooks.com
abaddon@rebellion.co.uk

First published in 2013 by Abaddon Books™, Rebellion Intellectual
Property Limited, Riverside House, Osney Mead, Oxford, OX2 0ES, UK.

10 9 8 7 6 5 4 3 2 1

Editor-in-Chief: Jonathan Oliver
Commissioning Editor: David Moore
Cover Art: Pye Parr, with thanks to Molcher, David-Eliot Cooper
from Histrionics (www.allthehistory.com) & Rob Temple
Design: Pye & Sam Gretton
Marketing and PR: Michael Molcher
Publishing Manager: Ben Smith
Creative Director and CEO: Jason Kingsley
Chief Technical Officer: Chris Kingsley

ISBN: 978-1-78108-160-0

Printed in the US

# INTRODUCTION

IT'S SOMETIMES EASY to forget how recent a creation the zombie really is.

Okay, so the *word* comes from a West African (via Afrocaribbean) tradition dating back at least a couple of centuries, but the *zonbi* of Vodou belief is usually represented as reasonably conscious, or (if mindless) a harmless slave of a bokor's will, obeying orders without complaint. And while Richard Matheson's *I Am Legend* – the main inspiration for the zombie genre – drew on an existing mythic template, his monsters are rightly *vampires*; the infected are entirely conscious, a fact that drives the main plot of the book.

Your actual *zombie*, the mindless, shambling, nigh-unstoppable, flesh-eating and above all *infectious* monster of Hollywood, stepped fully formed and cold-blooded out of the screen in George Romero's 1968 classic, *Night of the Living Dead* (although the word "zombie" didn't attach itself to the creatures until later). Strictly speaking, the poor things don't belong in history at all; they're fiends of the atomic age, shambling reminders of the implacable and ineluctably democratic nature of death.

And yet. There's something terribly old-school about them, isn't there? With a zombie, all the grey areas of life go out the window. It can't be reasoned with; it attacks without provocation; it's a terrible danger, not just in itself, but through the infection it spreads. It's even, conveniently, already dead! Killing it is a kindness, a merciful end to an indignity no right-thinking man or woman would tolerate. And zombies are so often associated with apocalypse, with the breakdown of society's rules. So, what the hell; as long as we're going on a legitimised killing spree, we may as well go the whole hog. Strap on some armour, pick up an axe or club. Get medieval on their asses.

And I suppose they don't fit so badly in history after all. If the walking dead of the past aren't actual *zombies* as we know them, then there are plenty of different takes on the idea of living corpses to be found in other cultures that fit the bill: the *ghuls* of Arabic myth, the *draugr* of Viking belief, the Greek *vrykolakas*, even the dead revived by the Pair Dadeni in Welsh belief offer places to find stories of the rotting hordes.

This was actually the original brief for *Tomes of the Dead*; stand-alone stories from throughout history, showing the grey hand of our non-vital cousins at work. It was even going to have a single continuity, with events from books earlier in the timeline potentially impacting later stories. We diverged from both the single-world idea and the emphasis on history pretty early on, with the second title *The Words of Their Roaring* set in modern London, but we've returned to it fairly frequently through the series, from the ancient Rome of Rebecca Levene's *Anno Mortis* to the English Civil War of Mark Beynon's *The Devil's Plague* and beyond.

THE THREE NOVELS collected in this omnibus are presented in reverse order of publication, so as to give you a chronology of sorts, from the earliest – Toby Venables' *Viking Dead*, set in the year 976 – to the most modern – Matthew Sprange's *Death Hulk*, set at the height of the Napoleonic Wars.

*Death Hulk* was one of the first novels we commissioned, for the August 2006 launch of the Abaddon imprint. Matthew Sprange of Mongoose Publishing had been working with us on the *Judge Dredd* roleplaying game, and we approached him about kicking

4

off one of our initial series. *Death Hulk* is a rollicking high-seas adventure tale in the spirit of Patrick O'Brian, with the cursed Captain Havelock standing in as a singularly tragic Jack Aubrey, accompanied by a veritable rogues' gallery of salty mariners.

Retired police officer Paul Finch is an old hand on the UK horror scene; a long-standing fan of his writing, Jon asked Paul to submit what turned out to be *Stronghold*, a tense, bloody siege tale set against the backdrop of Edward I's Welsh wars. Paul has a fascination with English culture and history, which shows in the gritty reality of the meticulously researched Grogan Castle. *Stronghold* has since been option by a movie studio, Amber Entertainment, who intend to release it to film in the next few years.

Toby Venables is a journalist, screenwriter and academic (with an award for an essay on the poetry of the Romantics). We dug up his *Viking Dead* pitch from the bottom of a slush pile; we weren't even sure it was still on offer, and were relieved and pleased to publish his debut. I particularly enjoyed the beautifully realised and lovable (and surprisingly international!) Viking crew, and Toby's use of point-of-view, switching between the seasoned captain Bjólf and his fish-out-of-water farmboy recruit Atli, all the better to round both men out.


HERE, THEN, WITHOUT much further ado, are three of the best historical novels from the *Tomes of the Dead* series. Follow Toby Venables' Viking captain Bjólf Erlingsson, Paul Finch's English knight Ranulf FitzOsbern, and Matthew Sprange's British Captain James Havelock as they lead the battle against the raddled, rotting, bone-gnawing, flesh-eating blank-eyed hordes of the dead across nearly a thousand years of the past.

Enjoy.

David Thomas Moore
Oxford, 2013

# VIKING DEAD

TOBY VENABLES

# PROLOGUE

SKALLA SAT, HIS hand resting on the pommel of his sword, his chin resting on his hands, staring at the pile of bodies.

The still-warm corpses steamed in the cool air of the clearing. Behind him, his black-clad men, done cleaning their weapons, stood in silence, waiting – for what, they knew not. Some, perhaps, suspected. But only Skalla knew for certain.

To his right, he heard feet shifting nervously among the damp leaves. That would be Gamli. Like the others, he was impatient to get out of this place. But there was more to his restlessness than that. Skalla had had his eye on Gamli for some time, aware that he had started to lose faith in their masters. More than once he had questioned their orders. It took a brave man to do that, or a stupid one. Skalla knew Gamli was no fool – but he also knew the man's boldness hid deeper fears. Fears that could spread, infecting the others, contaminating them with doubt. That, he could not allow. It threatened everything they had built here.

He ran his fingers through the black bristles on his chin, then up to the scar that passed through his left eye. It ran from his forehead down across his cheek, and had left the eye sightless – milk-white and dead. He pushed at the edge of his helm, relieving the pressure on his forehead for a moment. The scar tissue itched badly today. It always did after combat – the result of the heat and sweat. Not that what had just passed could truthfully be termed 'combat.'

There had been six in all. Perhaps seven. He couldn't remember. They were the ones who had been locked up the longest, those meant to be forgotten. The ones who ran, who broke down, who refused to work, who fought back. The biggest heroes and and the biggest cowards. All the same, now. They had also been kept separate all this time – well away from the various wonders and horrors that had been unfolding. That, Skalla suspected, was one of the real reasons for this little outing to the woods. True, his masters had no desire to waste further food on these lost causes. But they were also wise enough not to waste an opportunity. They would make some use of them, even in death.

And so, they had marched them to this lonely spot, shackled and at spear point, and forced them to cut logs for firewood. They had performed the tasks well, considering their chequered histories – some, almost with gratitude. Perhaps, thought Skalla, it simply felt good to have a purpose again. He had not told them they were gathering wood for their own funeral pyre.

The killing had been quick. Regrettably, the kills were not as clean as he'd hoped. There were struggles, cries, prolonged agonies, repeated blows. From the start, it had not been the most straightforward task. His men had been reluctant to venture into these woods, even during daylight. Then there had been the orders themselves. No damage to the head or neck – that's what their masters had specified. The order had bemused Skalla's men, and in the heat of the slaughter – one could hardly dignify the killing of these unarmed, underfed wretches with the term 'battle' – he could not be sure how closely they had adhered to it. At least one had taken a glancing sword blow across the top of the head – protruding from the heap, Skalla could see his hairy, blood-matted scalp, flapped open like the lid of a chest, the yellow-white bone of the skull grinning through the gore. But it didn't matter now. It was done. They would see soon.

"We're done here," said a voice behind Skalla. It was Gamli. He had stepped closer to where Skalla was sitting. Clearly, he was itching to leave. Perhaps he understood more than Skalla had realised.

"We wait," said Skalla.

"For what?"

"Until we are sure."

"Sure?" Gamli's voice was edgy. As always, he tried to cover it with a kind of swagger. "What is there to be sure of?"

"That they're dead."

Gamli laughed emptily, his throat tight. "Then why not burn them now and have done with it?"

"Are you questioning me, Gamli?" Skalla's eyes remained fixed on the corpses.

A kind of panic entered Gamli's eyes. "Not you. I would never... but the masters. There are doubts about them." He looked around as he said this, as if expecting support from his fellows. None came.

Skalla did not move. "I pledged my sword to them," he said, "and you swore an oath of allegiance to me. You do not question one without also questioning the other."

Gamli stood motionless, robbed of speech.

"Step back into line," said Skalla.

Before he could do so, a sound came from the heap, and an arm flopped out of the tangle. The men's hands jumped to their weapons. The arm hung there, motionless – quite dead. Olvir – one of the three crossbowmen – broke the silence with a nervous laugh. "For a moment, I thought..." He was interrupted by a low groan from the centre of the heap. Skalla stood slowly, hand still upon his sword, and, stretching to his full height, slowly flexed his shoulders. It was part of his ritual before combat.

"Gas. From the bodies," said another of the men, nervously. "They can do that." Olvir began to cock and load his crossbow. The others followed suit.

From deep within the pile came a weird, semi-human grunt, and the whole tangle suddenly shifted. As one, the men drew swords and raised crossbows. The uppermost body – a skinny man, whose abdomen was split open, and whose right arm had been all but severed – slithered from the top of the heap. The hand that had loosed itself from the pile twitched, its fingers inexplicably starting to straighten.

"It's beginning..." said Skalla. The hollow moan repeated itself, and was joined by two more in a kind of desolate, mindless chorus. As they watched in horror, dead limbs moved, arms flailed and grasped, lifeless eyes flicked open.

"This can't be happening," said Gamli. "Not to *them*..." From the heap, one of the men – a solid, muscular fellow who had taken two crossbow bolts through the chest, one of which had pinned his right hand to his sternum – staggered unsteadily to his feet. For a moment, he seemed to sniff the air, then turned and lurched towards them.

Skalla spat on his palms and raised his sword. "Aim for the heads," he said, and swung the blade with all his strength at the dead man's neck. Such was the force of the cut that it sliced clean through, knocking the attacker off his feet and sending his head bowling into the bushes. Already two more were on their feet – the skinny man, his right arm hanging by a sinew, his glistening guts dangling between his legs, and the scalped man, his cap of hair flapping absurdly to one side like piece of bearskin, who Skalla could now see had been killed by a heavy sword blow to the left side of his chest, the upper and lower parts sliding against each other gruesomely with each lurching step. A crossbow bolt hit the skinny man in the shoulder, spinning him round. "In the head!" barked Skalla. As the skinny man resumed his steady progress a second bolt thudded into his eye, knocking him flat. A third flew uselessly past the scalped man's ear. His arms reached out, grasping at Skalla, as another three grotesque figures rose stiffly behind him.

The rest of Skalla's men, momentarily mesmerised by the scene unfolding before them, now threw themselves into the fight. Gamli stepped forward first, grasping the scalped man's outstretched arm and hurling him to the floor. Drawing a long cavalry axe from a strap at his back, he flipped it around and with one blow drove its long, steel spike through the exposed skull. As his other men hacked mercilessly at two of the remaining ghouls, Skalla advanced to finish off the third – a once-fat man with folds of saggy skin beneath his ragged, filthy tunic. Skalla recognised the stab wounds in his chest – wounds that he himself had delivered with his knife. The fat man's left arm – bloody and slashed where he had attempted to defend himself from Skalla's blade – waved before him, his right – bloodier still – hanging crippled and useless by his side. Skalla raised his sword steadily, waiting for the right moment. The man's hand, formed into a claw, swayed and snatched at Skalla, his jaws opening and closing like those of an idiot child, dribbling bloody drool down his chest. Skalla began to swing – but something caught his foot, pulling him off balance. He stumbled and fell heavily onto the damp earth.

Looking at his feet, he saw that the seventh prisoner – his spinal cord severed, his legs useless – had dragged himself along the forest floor, and now, teeth bared, Skalla's ankle gripped in both hands, was gnawing at his leather boot, his blue-tinged jaws opening and closing mechanically like a landed fish gasping for air. Skalla recoiled in disgust, kicking at the ghoul's slavering, gap-toothed mouth – but the tenacious grip held, and over him now loomed the fat man, moaning and clawing at his face. Too close for an effective blow, Skalla abandoned his sword and scrabbled for his knife – but, before he had time to draw it, another sword blade was driven hard into the fat man's mouth, sending him choking and tottering backwards, his teeth grinding horribly against its metal edge. Skalla recognised the hilt: Gamli's sword. Skalla swiftly regained his feet, took up his own weapon once more and brought it down with a crashing blow, cleaving the skull of the crawling man in two. He gave a nod of acknowledgement to Gamli, and scraped the man's brains off his black boot with the point of his blade.

It was over. And his men, thankfully, had escaped unscathed.

"So it's finally happened," said Gamli, surveying the carnage that surrounded them – the men they had hacked down for the second time that day. "Our worst fear has come to life." The others exchanged anxious glances.

Skalla ignored him, wiping clean and sheathing his sword as he hunted around for the head of the first corpse-walker. He would take that back to his masters.

"I'm sorry," said Gamli, bowing his head. Skalla turned to face him. "I will not question you again."

"No," said Skalla. "You will not." And without blinking he stabbed Gamli in the side of the throat with his knife, severing both carotid arteries, then pulled the blade forward through his windpipe. Gamli collapsed in an eruption of blood, his last cry turned to a choked gurgle of air bubbling and frothing from his neck.

As he pumped crimson onto the forest floor, a contorted expression of disbelief frozen upon his face, Skalla looked upon him for the last time. "I did not kill you before only because I needed your sword," he said matter-of-factly, and stepped over the body. The other men drew back as he approached. He scanned their faces one at a time, then sheathed his knife.

"Burn them," said Skalla, the still-living Gamli convulsing behind him. "All of them."

# PART ONE

*VIKINGR*

# CHAPTER ONE

## FOG

ATLI SHOULD HAVE been home hours ago. Clutching the bundle of gnarled sticks tight to his chest as he emerged from the trees onto the broad curve of the riverbank, he looked south towards the distant, looming shadow of the Middagsberg. His heart sank. It was even later than he'd thought. The low sun, a watery smudge of light in the late summer mist, had long since passed the cleft in its summit, and was already half-way to the mid-afternoon daymark – the ragged edge of tall pines puncturing the horizon on the mountain's shallow western slope. For a moment he imagined his father looking up at the same line of trees, his face livid with anger, cursing his son's name.

He would get a beating again. It was part of the routine.

He shivered, turned his eyes resignedly to the ground, and kicked idly at the wet, grey stones that littered the bank, the smell of the damp wood in his nostrils. The threat of his father's stick across his back should, he knew, be sufficient incentive for him to head back home in good time. That was certainly the intention. But it just made him all the more determined to stay away. And the longer he put off his return, the more severe became the inevitable punishment – and the more gloomily reluctant he became. A vicious circle. "Like a dog chasing its tail," his mother used to say. It had been eight winters since she'd passed, when Atli was barely five years old, but he still recalled her words from time to time, although her face was now lost to him.

It had been this way almost as long as he could remember. He often wandered by the water now, dreaming of change, escape – something, *anything* – but where that change might come from, even he could not imagine. And as he dreamed, and his father fumed – increasingly at odds with the world, as well as his own son – each grew more distant from the other, more stubborn, more deeply entrenched, until Atli had begun to fear where it might ultimately lead.

He flicked a loose stone with his foot so it tumbled and splashed, coming to rest in the shallows at the water's edge – the edge of his world. These waters were their protection. That's what his father always told him. To Atli, however, they seemed more like a prison. To the north, through the woods and beyond the village, was the river Svanær. South of the village – and on whose banks Atli now stood – the wider, meandering Ottar. Each provided them with plentiful fish and formed a barrier against overland raiders and outlaws. To the west, on the spur of land that dwindled to a point where the two rivers met, was thick forest with good hunting – accessible only from their village. To the east, the fertile land and rich pasture upon which they'd built their farms rose to distant, rocky fells – a natural discouragement to any who did not already know the paths, and which had long proved its worth. As his father had said so often, it was the land that supported them, and the land that kept them from harm. Atli thought of all the times he had sought solace down by the water's edge, and wondered how often, had the river not been here to protect them, he would have kept on walking until that familiar landscape were left far behind.

There was one threat the land did not keep them safe from, however; a danger that tormented his father's mind and had become the subject of repeated, dire warnings. River raiders. Pirates. *Vikingr*. "If you see *vikingr*," his father said, "you must *run*. Run as fast as you can. They are bad men. Desperate men. They will cut a man's throat for the fun of it – and much worse. They steal everything that isn't nailed down. Even the animals. They dishonour and kill women. They eat children. I have heard it! Remember, you must *run* – and warn the village. But make no sound!"

"How will I know them?" Atli had asked.

"You will know them." His father had nodded with a kind of portentous unease. "They will come from the river. And you will know them..."

There hadn't ever been a raid in these parts. Not even further downriver was such a thing heard of these days – at least, not as far as Atli knew. And anyway, if he did encounter *vikingr*, the one thing he wouldn't do was run. He would beg to be taken with them.

He sighed and gazed longingly across the still water – or, at least, as far as it would let him. In the last few hours a thick shroud of fog had rolled in from the estuary. Following the course of the river upstream with eerie precision, it hovered silently over the river's surface now, mocking its shape, obscuring the tall trees of the opposite bank as it thickened the air. Dead. Impenetrable. Ungraspable. *Like a ghost,* thought Atli. *Like the creeping ghost of the river.* Images crowded his head from old stories his father had told – of whispy spirits escaping from the bodies of the dead, of glowing smokes and fogs seeping out of mounds and barrows and taking terrible, half-recognised shapes that sucked the life out of the living. Another chill ran through him. He kicked at the stones with a sudden anger, as if to banish thought with physical action – any kind of action – to kick his childish night-terrors away. He refused to succumb to the anxieties and superstitions that had taken over his father's life. He refused to live in fear. Every day now he saw it in his father's eyes, and it made him ashamed.

Superstition had been the other half of Atli's upbringing. When he was young, the stories had seemed magical – dwarves and elves that lived in the earth and forged great gifts of gold, spirits and serpents that lived in the woods and the water, gods who turned men's fortunes, playing cruel tricks on the proud and bestowing blessings upon the brave. Although, in his heart, he had never quite believed in their literal truth, as others seemed to, they nonetheless had their own reality – one that he loved. They existed in another world. And they were an escape from his own.

Then, after his mother died, the tone of the stories changed. Each one became a warning. Another stick to beat him with.

All manner of irrational fears seemed to take over his life. His father became obsessed with death. At wakes – where most were content to drink and share good memories – he cut a gloomy, troubled figure, repeatedly warning those present to take precautions against the corpse's potential return. He would insist upon an open pair of iron scissors being placed on the chest of the deceased, and always afterwards could be seen sprinkling salt along the threshold. It was protection, he said, against the *draugr* – the undead – who returned to inflict untold horrors upon the living. In regions to the south, there was talk they were on the rise. He'd heard it from a merchant who refused to go near the place.

Privately, many scoffed at him for wasting such precious commodities. Others simply laughed at his ways. Once, when he was too young to know better, Atli had asked his father if it wouldn't be a *good* thing for his mother to come back. Wasn't that what they all wanted? A weird terror burned in his father's eyes. "Try to understand," he said, his voice trembling. "It is not *they* who come back, but something else. Something terrible." His eyes widened. He spoke in a hoarse whisper, as if afraid of being overheard. "You would wish to see her again. You would welcome her in when she came knocking at night. But it would not be the mother you knew. Imagine a lumbering, soulless mockery – heavy with the stench of decay, her body bloated, distorted, monstrous in proportion, her heart empty of feeling, her head a foetid shell, her eyes dead as a fish's, her only emotion a blind envy for the living whose flesh she is driven to devour, crunching the bones, drinking the blood in great gobbets..."

The image haunted Atli's nightmares for years.

Then, in his eleventh year, he had come to his current realisation. It was fear, not anger, that drove his father. And that, ultimately, was why he hated him. It was not because he was a bully, (not only was he bigger than Atli was, but bigger than most of the men in the village), nor because he thrashed him on a regular basis. He hated him because he was a coward. Atli knew that he bore the brunt of the man's frustrations only because he could not offer any resistance. His father beat him not just because of what he did or didn't do, but because of all the other people and things in life that he was too afraid to confront – chief among them, Atli had begun to suspect, himself. His own weakness. The weakness to which the father knew his son's eyes were no longer oblivious. The weakness which Atli doggedly refused to inherit.

He trudged to the edge of the river and stared momentarily at his own indistinct reflection in the water, then kicked another pebble and watched the ripples break it apart.

Vaguely he wondered what was going on back at the village. Not long ago there had been a distant clamour of shouting from that way – some sort of argument that was best avoided, probably. Recently, a fight had broken out over a pig which had wandered into a neighbour's house and eaten a cabbage that had been cut for dinner. Bera, the woman of the house, had demanded compensation for her loss. Yngvar, the pig-owner, had countered by accusing Bera of trying to steal his pig. After a lot of shouting, during which Bera had cracked Yngvar across the temple with a wooden ladle, it ended with a rather fearful Yngvar conceding that his pig had probably wandered of its own accord and Bera accepting a quantity of pig dung – some of which had already been deposited in her house – in payment for the cabbage. Such were the heady thrills of farm life.

Now, Atli could see there was also a thick column of dark smoke coming from that direction. Perhaps they weren't so desperate for his kindling after all. Gripping his bundle under one arm he crouched down to pick up a smooth, wet pebble, and hurled it at the water. It was swallowed instantly with a loud plop. He screwed up his face in frustration, grabbed another, flatter stone and, crouching lower this time, aimed it at a shallow angle. It skipped once, twice, three times.

Good. But he knew he could do better. Seven was his record. It needed a certain kind of stone, though. His eyes darted about the shore by his feet, among the wet pebbles and grit and occasional patches of green weed that waved in the lapping water. A perfect stone caught his eye – nicely smooth and flat, with a notch in its edge for his forefinger. He snatched it up, aimed, and let his arm sway back and forth for a moment, rehearsing the arc of the throw. Then... Snap! Cracking his whole body like a whip, he let the stone fly. He knew from the moment it left him that it was a perfect throw. The shimmering stone skipped across the smooth water, dipping like a dragonfly, weightless – three, four, five – until finally enveloped by the fog. In the stillness of the afternoon he could still hear its sound: six, seven, eight, nine... ten?

That couldn't be right. Yet still it kept going. He'd lost count, but stood, holding his breath, ears on stalks. He could still hear the surface of the water being broken. A fish? No. A steady rhythm. He'd swear to it. But different now. Surely the fog must be playing tricks? No, there was definitely something. Another sound, that had at some point merged with the first. Slow and steady. And not receding, but coming closer.

Atli fought against the images of wraiths and phantoms that suddenly flooded his mind. His father had warned him the fog brought terrible things. It was the cold breath of Niflheim – of Hel itself. Who knew what horrors travelled within it? Atli got a grip of himself. Such things were not real – or, if they were, they were not part of his world.

But the sound kept coming all the same.

A sequence, continually repeating, echoing weirdly in the dull air. A splash of water. A hollow clunk, like wood against wood – but somehow multiplied. A creak. Then again. Splash. Clunk. Creak. Over and over. He bit his lip, frowning hard, straining to penetrate the grey murk. He knew this sound – but couldn't place it. It grew closer. His mind raced. The hairs on his neck prickled in slow recognition. Involuntarily, he began to take slow steps back from the water.

Then a great shape loomed out of the fog.

The head and neck of a dragon.

Gliding straight at him in a moment of surreal silence, the dragon's huge bulk bit into the grit and pebbles of the shore and drove part way up the bank with a crunching of wood, stone and water before coming to rest just yards from Atli's astonished face. He was dimly aware of the loose bundle of twigs falling one by one from his enfeebled hands. High up and to the left, a figure emerged from nowhere and landed heavily on the rocks and shingle. A tall man, broad-shouldered, beardless, but spiked with blond stubble, ice-blue eyes glinting behind the eye-guards of a steel helm.

*Run*, said a voice in Atli's head. *Run as fast as you can*. But he could not move.

The man took three steps towards him – mail-coated, rings shimmering in the feeble light, circular shield strapped to his back, gold-hilted sword drawn and ready – so close that Atli could make out the pattern-welding on the gleaming blade. A hint of a smile flickered across the man's face, his sword point hovering barely an arm's length from Atli's chest.

Another figure – a giant of a man – heaved itself over the right side of the ship, making the ground shudder as his feet sunk into shore. This one was equipped much like the first, but for his simpler helm whose rim rested on his heavy brow, and the dew-damp fur of some grey creature wrapped across his shoulders and tucked into a wide leather belt. Dark, deep-set eyes peered from amongst unruly black hair and beard, fixed intently on the boy. He spat in his palms, and, holding Atli's gaze, reached over his left shoulder and drew forth a broad-bladed axe.

Behind him, another man landed on the shore. And another...

One by one they spilled over the sides and crunched and splashed down onto the riverbank – twenty, thirty, more – until the grey stone beach and misty shallows around the dragon's oaken hull were filled with men, some trudging shoreward from the deeper water, emerging from the fog like ghosts – grim-faced, steel-helmed, girt with hide and mail, until, finally, it seemed the whole river's edge shimmered with the glint of weapons.

Though he had never seen such a thing in his whole life, Atli recognised them instantly.

Not ghosts.

Worse.

*Vikingr.*

# CHAPTER TWO

## THE CREW OF THE *HRAFN*

BJÓLF ERLINGSSON TOOK another step towards the boy, eyes fixed on him, sword steady. He gave a nod towards the ground. "You dropped your sticks, little man."

A rumbling laugh ran through the assembled men as the lad crouched and began to gather up the scattered firewood. Bjólf watched the farm boy with amusement as he tied up his bundle – stick-thin legs and crude, ill-fitting clothes, no doubt cut from the roughest, itchiest, shittiest blanket in the place; the blanket even the dogs rejected. The look of it, the smell of it... It all seemed so familiar. It was at times like this he was reminded exactly why he'd left that life behind all those years ago. True, the plundered cottons and silks to which he had since become accustomed may have meant him facing danger and death on a daily basis, but it seemed a fair trade. Hel, how those bloody blankets had itched!

"Are you from the village?" he demanded. The boy nodded hastily, jumping at the sound of the man's voice. Bjólf rested his sword casually over his shoulder – looking momentarily like a wayfarer with his bundle of belongings – and scanned the treeline ahead, taking note of the path that disappeared into the wood. He nodded towards it. "How far?"

"Six hundred paces..." In spite of his obvious efforts, his voice sounded thin and reedy.

Gunnar Black-Beard shifted his axe from one hand to the other. "Hm. The boy can count."

*Fisherman*, thought Bjólf. *Counts the fish for his father.* He knew all about that. Most of his men knew it, in one way or another. And those who denied it most perhaps knew it keenest of all. Bjólf turned back to the lad. "You have animals there? Food? Valuables?"

"Animals... and food. Not the other."

"We'll have to make do with that," sighed Gunnar.

Godwin snorted dismissively, resting his hands and chin on his massive axe. "Everywhere the same. You'd think there was no decent treasure left. How's a man to make a living?" A few of the men muttered at his words.

"Have I ever let you down, Godwin?" Bjólf shot back. He didn't give him a chance to answer, but turned to the boy again.

"Any weapons there?"

He shook his head.

"Then we go," said Bjólf. And with that he made a sudden move towards the boy, his sword raised threateningly over his shoulder.


I'M DEAD, THOUGHT Atli. *I've told him what he needs, and now he's going to kill me.*

In the moment that followed, he involuntarily pictured the heavy blade slashing downward and across in one movement, the catastrophic moment of contact stretched out into a slow, dreamlike sequence – the sword's edge striking his left shoulder, parting the flesh, shattering the bone and not stopping until it had come clean through to the opposite side of his chest, severing his head, shoulder and right arm in one continuous action.

Curiously, it was not fear that took hold of him in that weirdly suspended moment, but a kind of anger. With tears suddenly stinging his eyes, he inwardly cursed his own inability to act – cursed this last, lost opportunity – and wondered abstractly whether he would remain conscious long enough to gaze up at his own lopsided, headless corpse, its insides still pumping, and see it sway and fall.

Without warning, the beardless warrior thrust out his left hand, ruffled his hair with a gruffly dismissive laugh, and gave a nod to the giant alongside him. Then, to Atli's great surprise, the entire party of men began to move rapidly up the shore, the ring of metal against metal filling the damp air. Slowly, the realisation dawned that the man had no intention of spilling Atli's blood on the dull, grey stones of that lonely beach. There was, as far as Atli was concerned, a far more terrible fate in store.

He was going to ignore him.

Atli couldn't stand it. With a mixture of anger and desperation, he whirled around to the rapidly receding throng and called out: "I could lead you!"

As one, the group stopped. The captain turned and stared at him. There was a chuckle and a murmur among the men. "And why would you do that?"

Atli felt his face flush red. He strove to find an answer, but under the hard stares, no words came. Then one among them spoke up – his voice little more than a hoarse whisper, his words clipped and strange. The men fell silent at the sound of it.

"My people tell a story of a boy who offered to lead raiders to his village..." The owner of the voice stepped forward, drawing a long, curved knife from a fringed leather sheath on his belt. His general shape was unremarkable – a little shorter in stature than the majority of the men, perhaps – yet his appearance was unlike anything Atli had encountered; his clothes and cap made of skins from no animal Atli had ever seen, and his dark body-armour – like the segmented carapace of a cockroach – formed from toughened strips of hide sewn together in wide bands. The man's hair was dark, his nose upturned, his hairless face broad and flat with skin the colour of beeswax. The wide eyes that now bored into him seemed permanently narrowed, as if in the glare of the sun, and, as the figure loomed closer, the complexion that had appeared smooth from a distance revealed itself to be so covered with spidery creases that Atli could not honestly tell if the man was twenty summers old or a hundred. Something in his otherworldly aspect caused Atli to shudder. As the thin blade swayed near the boy's pale, exposed neck, the man bore his teeth in a strange smile. "He led them to their deaths..." The breath stopped in Atli's throat as if it were held in the man's fist.

"Enough!" called the captain, giving an abrupt flick of his head. Wide-Face acknowledged it with a sly grin and turned slowly away, silently sheathing his blade. Atli, suddenly able to breathe again, gasped, his head swimming.

The beardless warrior stared at the boy for a moment, his eyes seeming to narrow behind his eye-guards, then turned back to his companion. He didn't need to speak. They'd known each other too long for that.

"Personally, I'd sooner have him where I can see him," said the giant, shrugging.

The captain nodded slowly, then made a sudden, exaggerated half bow, and extended his arm dramatically towards the woods as he did so. An invitation. Atli stared at him for a moment, incredulously. "Lead on, little man."

At their captain's gesture, the men parted. It was true. He really meant for him to lead them. Atli stumbled nervously past the silent ranks, his bundle of sticks still tucked under his arm – all eyes again upon him. As he advanced, he was now able to take in the grim array of figures for the first time; no longer the shadowy, grey shapes that had emerged from the fog, but distinct, real. Faces that were scarred and weatherbeaten and spoke not only of years lived, but of miles travelled, of things seen, of battles fought. All men who worked the earth and the sea were hardened to life, with muscles like twisted rope and faces carved from aged applewood – but these had something else, something that Atli had not seen.

They had no fear.

Those closest now stood out to him, startling in their detail. There was, of course, Long-Axe – the one they called Godwin – bare-chinned and impressively moustached, his blackened helm with long bronzed nasal and cheek-guards, and his mail coat almost to his knees; and the unnerving Wide-Face, the ageless one, dressed head to foot in animal hides, still fingering his knife, his eyes glinting darkly. There was Curved-Sword – a slender, fine-featured man in long robes and armoured hauberk like the scales of a fish, his helm pointed, his short hair black, his skin dark, his sword long and thin and curved like a scythe, and near him – in utter contrast –

One-Ear, wearing quilted body armour reinforced with leather and no helm at all, his face and head shaved to stubble, his lips scarred, his shield rim battered, his spear notched, and his left ear missing its top third, looking for all the world as if someone had taken a bite out of him. Opposite them, Red-Hair, his rust-red mane and beard standing out sharply against his thick cape of green wool, clasped with an ornate bronze brooch, his helm and breastplate of dark, hardened leather, a spiked mace slung over his shoulder, and near him, Two-Axe, barely taller than Atli, but at least three times as wide and built like an ox, his face entirely obscured by a masked *grimmhelm*, his armour of tarnished metal plates joined with leather thongs, and, unlike all the others, no shield – just a heavy axe hanging from each large, calloused hand. And, perhaps weirdest of all, there was Grey-Beard, a gaunt figure of a man in heavy, brown, hooded robes, simple conical helm on his head, from his belt hanging not only his sword but such a variety of knives as Atli had never seen in one place, in his hands a long ash spear, in his face a dark, puckered hole where one of his eyes should be – a vision, it seemed to Atli, of Odin made flesh.

They formed a terrifying company. Yet, as Atli walked, a confidence grew in him – increasing with each step. *They trust me*, he thought. *I have their respect...* It was the first time he had inspired such a thing in any man, let alone such men as these. But as he reached the head of the troop, there was a sound of movement immediately behind him. Before he had time to react, he felt something whip around his neck and pull tight. Clawing at it, he turned in shock.

With his free hand, the captain was twisting the decorated scabbard of his sword, from which issued a thin, looped leather strap – the baldric from which both sword and scabbard, until recently, had hung – now taut like a ship's rope.

Atli was tethered like a dog.

"My apologies," the man said with a smile. "But you know these woods, and doubtless can run a good deal faster than us in your attire..." The men laughed once again, and once again Atli felt the blood rush to his face. "Now, lead on. Where you go, we follow."

And with that, he gave the strap a sharp flick. "*Hyah!*"

Atli staggered forward in a daze, his mind only now starting to grasp the grim reality of what was about to happen.

# CHAPTER THREE

## THE VILLAGE AT TWO-RIVERS

As THE COMPANY moved swiftly up the beach toward the trees, Atli looked back to the river. The swirling mist was creeping onto the shore now. From it, the tall slender prow of the longship stood like a lonely sentinel.

Feeling strangely numb, he pulled at the strap around his neck as a sharp prod from the captain's sword urged him on. He spoke without thinking. "There's no-one guarding your ship."

The big one laughed. "Everyone knows what a dragon-ship means. No one who values their life will go near."

"But what if they have no fear? What if they are stronger?"

"Then we don't want to meet them, and they're welcome to it!"

It seemed these men even approached the prospect of failure with a kind of boundless confidence – certainly far beyond anything the people in his village possessed. Except, possibly, Bera. Now, that was a revelation... Atli had always found her a cantankerous, difficult sort, her stubborn ways typical of the old folk hereabouts.

Yet, he began to realise, she was as different from her fellow villagers as a wolf from a goat. She had no fear – of others, of the world, of herself. Yes, that tough old widow was was more like these *vikingr* than most of the surrounding menfolk could ever hope to be.

Whether she or anyone else would live to see tomorrow was the one question Atli was now trying to put out of his mind.


THE MOMENT THE men entered the shade of the trees, they fell silent. Shields were hurriedly hoisted off backs, helmet straps pulled tight and empty hands filled with weapons. All knew this was the most hazardous part of the raid. Forty *vikingr*, armed to the teeth and with the advantage of surprise, were more than a match for any village, no matter how bold its population. But there was always the unknown, the unpredictable. Regardless of careful planning and advance information, none could be completely sure what they would find, nor who or what they would encounter first. By chance they might run into another from the village, as they had the farm boy – but this time, perhaps, the stranger would scream or shout, or run from the attackers and raise the alarm. In this way, even the smallest child could treble their casualties.

The path narrowed as they drove deeper into the forest. No one spoke. Only the scratch of branches and brambles against wood and metal and the rhythmic pounding of their feet – made heavy by arms and armour – accompanied their swift advance. The sharp smell of damp pine and bruised bracken filled the air. All knew that being forced to move in single file by tangled bush and shrub made them vulnerable. From beneath the eye-guards of his helm Bjólf's eyes instinctively scanned every tree and shadow, calculating where he would place archers, a trap, men with spears. Hemmed in and spread thin as they were, they would be easy prey for an enemy who was prepared.

But Bjólf knew they would not be.

There was to be little finesse about this attack. No sophisticated strategy, no circling around to seal off escape routes. Bjólf knew there was nowhere – and no one – for the villagers to run to. Today, it was about speed. They would hit hard and fast, taking what they could while their quarry was still reeling from shock. A single hammerblow. He was proud of the fact that, in the past, they had often achieved this without a single casualty.

Looking ahead, he gave a tug on the lad's lead and spoke in a cautious whisper. "Little man... six hundred of your paces or six-hundred man-paces?"

"M–my paces."

"Then we're close."

Up ahead, the trees were already beginning to thin out and, beyond, Bjólf could see gaps of light where the forest gave way to a clearing. For an instant, a light breeze brought the unmistakable scent of smoke and pigs to his nostrils. He pulled at the strap around the boy's throat, jerking him to a sudden halt, and raised his sword. As one, the rest of the company stopped.

Listening carefully, but hearing nothing, Bjólf gestured them forward slowly. They spread out in the dappled light as the close undergrowth gave way to a more even covering of ferns and wild garlic, its thick aroma filling the air. Here and there, a few plants still in flower dotted the forest floor. They paused again, their target now visible from the cover of the trees.

"Fjölvar!" hissed Bjólf. The lean, thin-faced young man came forward. He was one of the least armoured of all Bjólf's crew, with no more than a hide coat upon his back and a soft leather Phrygian cap upon his head. From his back, he unslung a bow, ready strung and almost as long as its owner. From his belt hung a quiver thick with arrows, some fletched with white goosefeathers and some with the mackerel-striped brown of a pheasant. The man's eyes – close together, and peering from either side of a narrow, beaky nose – remained firmly fixed on the boy.

Bjólf turned to Atli. "We'll take things from here," He removed the strap from around their guide's neck and slung it back over his shoulder. "Don't run." As he said this, Fjölvar placed a white-feathered arrow with a barbed iron tip on his bowstring.

Crouched behind the abundant tangle of grasses that marked the edge of the trees, Bjólf and Gunnar looked out upon the village. Ahead, speckling the gentle hill that rose before them, was a scattered collection of thatched houses and barns, each accompanied by small, crudely constructed, but sturdy animal pens. Beyond, across the undulating landscape, stretched acres of lush pasture and growing land, some patterned by rows of cultivation, age-worn paths and the occasional, winding fence. From each dwelling curled a peaceful whisp of woodsmoke, and, between them wound a muddy, heavily-trodden track which disappeared over a rise, beyond which lay the rest of the settlement, ultimately bounded by the northern river. It was an idyllic scene – but for the thick column of black smoke coming from over the rise, and the complete lack of any signs of life.

"Where is everyone?" said Bjólf.

"And where's their livestock?" replied Gunnar. "I can't even see a chicken."

"Do you smell pigs?"

"I *smell* them. I just don't *see* them."

Over to their left, just beyond the nearest dwelling, a muddy hog pen lay empty, its gate tilted and broken. Up on a distant slope, in a far corner of an enclosure, a single sheep stood, the only fleck of white upon the hillside. A living thing, at least. To its lonely, urgent bleating, nothing responded.

Gunnar grabbed the farm boy by the shoulder and gave him a shake. "What's going on, boy?" The boy looked at the weirdly empty village, then back at Gunnar, bemused and speechless. The baffled, anxious expression on his face did not reassure them. Gunnar narrowed his eyes, surveying the unnervingly still scene.

"I don't like the look of that smoke." A gust brought the smell to their nostrils again – but there was something else detectable in it; something acrid. From somewhere, caught on the same wind, came the sound of a woman wailing. "You sure about this?"

Bjólf wasn't sure. But what was certain was that they needed supplies of meat, drink and grain at the very least if they were to continue on. He pursed his lips. "Go in fast. Get what we need. Get out."

Gunnar nodded. Bjólf hefted his shield – red-painted – off his shoulder and spoke without turning to his men.

"Finn – you take the left." Wide-Face face nodded. "Godwin you take the right. Gunnar, Thorvald, Kjötvi, Magnus and Úlf – you're with me." Two-Axe, One-Ear, Grey-Beard and another huge man with blond plaits and arms like hams strapped into leather arm guards moved in to join Bjólf and Gunnar.

There was a moment of silence, all muscles tensed, then at a signal from Bjólf, they broke from the trees.

# CHAPTER FOUR

## BLACK SMOKE

SWIFTLY, SILENTLY, THEY moved on the village. Finn and Godwin's companies took each flank, and, as they approached the knot of buildings, the two bands began to disperse, pairs of men splitting off and bursting into each dwelling, while Bjólf and the others headed straight for the heart of the village, weapons raised, eyes alert.

The men moved swiftly from house to house, their passing accompanied by the sounds of crashing from within as beds and chests were overturned. "Nothing," called one, emerging back into daylight. They moved on to the next.

"Nor here..." called another.

"Try the barn," called Gunnar.

"Empty."

"The chests have been broken open..." spat Finn, striding out of the nearest house.

"There must be someone here," said Gunnar. "I smell cooking." So

33

did Bjólf. But there was something about it, different from the honest smells of stew and woodsmoke.

"Keep looking!" barked Bjólf. But his sense of unease was growing.

"Blood," said Kjötvi. Bjólf followed his gaze and saw a trail of fresh gore, and signs that something had been dragged. An animal?

"Rich pickings, you said..." hissed Gunnar, as more men emerged empty handed.

"It was a reliable source," Bjólf shot back. "He's never failed us before."

"Bjólf!" came a voice. It was Finn, emerging from one of the farthest dwellings. In his outstretched hand he held his sword. From it, hooked over the blade, hung a small iron scythe. And, still gripping the scythe's crude wooden handle, a severed hand.

Gunnar scanned the empty village and sniffed the air again in agitation. "There's something very wrong here."

Up ahead, Bjólf suddenly became aware of a single figure, right in the middle of the muddy track. A big man, ragged, staggering slightly, eyes and nose streaming, a mixture of blood and soot smeared across his forehead. He stopped dead when he saw them.

Without hesitation, Bjólf marched up to him, sword raised. But before he could do or say anything, the man collapsed to his knees, sobbing.

Bjólf stared at him. "Get up!" he shouted. "Get *up!*" Slinging his shield on his back, he grabbed the man's torn tunic and hauled him to his feet, his sword blade against his throat. "Answer me quickly. Where are your valuables? Your food? Your animals? Don't think you can hide them from us. We know all the tricks – and trust me, you *will* give them up."

Inexplicably, the man began to laugh.

"We have nothing!"

"They all say that," growled Gunnar.

"No, you don't understand..." He choked out the words between bouts of sobbing laughter. "There's nothing left! They took it all!"

Bjólf's blood ran cold.

"'They'?"

The man frowned and looked from one to the other. "Moments ago. *Vikingr* like you." He pointed a shaky hand towards the far end of the village. "You just missed them."

Bjólf and Gunnar stared at each other in disbelief.

"Regroup!" shouted Bjólf, a note of unease in his voice. "And stay close." He grabbed the man roughly by the shoulder, spun him round and shoved him onward.

As the party of men followed the curve of the wide track, adrenaline still pumping, a group of ragged women and children came into view. Several of the women were on their knees. One pulled at her own clothes and wailed hysterically at the sky. Beyond them, a great fire raged. At first, Bjólf could not make out what it was about it that brought back buried memories. Then the wind gusted, carrying a smell of burnt meat and tallow. And he realised. What he had first thought to be thick branches in the huge pile of wood were the twisted limbs of men. Bodies were heaped one upon the other, crackling, spitting, bubbling. Sizzling fat dripped into the earth, bones cracked, body parts popped and spat and sent jets of steam into the smoky air.

"Gods!" breathed Gunnar. "What happened here?" But it was plain to see. Whoever had raided the village had hit them hard and fast. Efficient. Seasoned. Merciless.

On the pyre, something moved – still alive. Bjólf shuddered.

"Is this how you treat your dead here?" said Godwin, barely able to hide the revulsion in his voice. "You should show more respect, give them the proper rites, or they will surely come back to haunt you."

"No! We have to burn them." said the big man. He gesticulated wildly as he spoke and clawed pathetically at Bjólf's sleeve, a hysterical tone to his voice. "We must send them up quickly. To *stop* them coming back. It can happen. I've heard of it! It's the only way to be sure..."

Some of Bjólf's crew – battle-hardened though they were – were visibly unsettled by the man's words and the weird, grisly scene. But Bjólf knew it was not fear of death or physical threat that got to them. It was something much worse. Something harder to fight.

"This is a bad omen," said Finn.

"Ah, he's lost his wits," said Bjólf dismissively, and spat in the mud. "Do you blame him?" He was well aware there were superstitious men among his crew – warriors and sailors were the worst for that. But he needed to keep them focused. He turned to Gunnar, speaking now so the others could not overhear. "Can you believe this? No raids for years – no one even knowing it was here – then two at once! This is not turning out to be a good day."

Gunnar sighed heavily, surveying the chaos. He could tell by the damage to the bodies that those who hit this place knew exactly what they were doing. And that was not all. "Could've been worse," he said wistfully. Then, after a thoughtful pause, added: "We might've run into him ourselves."

Bjólf eyed him for a moment. "Then you're thinking what I'm thinking..."

Gunnar nodded.

"Grimmsson." Even uttering the name made Bjólf's teeth clench.

"Looks like his work."

"It couldn't be anyone else." Bjólf waved his sword in frustration at the bodies heaped on the crude funeral pyre. "Look at this mess! These peasants are not the sort to resist. But killing five or six straight off as an example... That's his way." Gunnar nudged the big man with his axe. "You! How many were there?"

"More than I've ever seen. Seventy or eighty at least."

"And the sail of their ship – what colour?"

"Red!" wailed the big man, a bubble of snot bursting beneath his nose as he whimpered at the memory. He flung a wild arm past the fire and smoke, where the village broadened out and dipped down to the bank of the northern river, whose waters were clearly visible. "That's where they came... Took everything. Then off upriver. Just like that. They've ruined us!" He fell quivering to his knees.

There was no doubting it, then. For Bjólf, it was yet another reason to detest his rival. Not that he needed one. He hated everything about him. His brutality, his arrogance, his massively inflated ego. And, most of all, that *fucking red sail*... Only Helgi Grimmsson was possessed of the kind of vanity – not to mention bad taste – to have an entire ship's sail dyed red. The man had too much money and no honour. Unfortunately, he seemed to attract an exceptionally large number of men – all of whom were as dishonourable, foolhardy and dangerous as him. And with the opportunities for freelance operations dwindling as more regions came under the sway of kings, it was becoming increasingly likely that they would run into Grimmsson's sadly far larger vessel. And that, Bjólf knew, was a confrontation that he could not win.

"Got the same tip as us, I reckon," muttered Gunnar.

"And got to it first..."

"Payback for Roskilde..."

Bjólf stared dejectedly. But, in spite of everything, he was counting his blessings.

As THE VIKINGR launched their attack, Atli had crept cautiously from his hiding place at the edge of the trees and made his way into the village. Everything that had been so familiar for so long – for his whole life – suddenly seemed strange. A kind of panic gripped him. There was no sign of Yngvar's pig, nor of his fowls. Tools lay here and there, as if suddenly abandoned. He had seen the warriors advance ahead of him, and heard their shouts to one another, seen the disarray as he passed dwellings with their doors swinging open. But nothing had prepared him for the sight that finally greeted him: the spitting flames, the acrid smoke, and the stunned looks on the faces of all gathered there. What had happened here? As he approached, a pair of cowed figures appeared on the track. Bera, her face set in a grim expression, and a younger woman who Atli knew as Úlfrún, her features deathly pale and weirdly blank, as if suddenly deprived of the ability to show emotion. They were dragging something between them on a blanket. A body. As they struggled past dejectedly, the head flopped out from its wrappings, its lifeless eyes seeming to gape at Atli. It was a horrific sight: the right cheek purple and swollen almost beyond recognition from some massive blow, and the lower jaw hanging completely off, swinging horribly as they plodded along.

It was Yngvar.

Atli watched as the women shuffled on towards the fire, Bera's gaze catching his. It seemed to cut through him. He felt sick and confused, not understanding what had happened. As he drew closer to the pyre, through the wafting, bitter smoke, he saw, near to the captain and his big companion, a pitiful figure crouched upon the floor. The man had his head in his hands, but Atli recognised him immediately.

BJÓLF WATCHED BERA and Úlfrún heave the limp body onto the fire, sending a shower of sparks into the air, their faces red from its fierce heat. A blackened skull rolled out of the heap, smoke billowing from its eye sockets.

"Old woman," said Bjólf, a note of pleading in his voice, "why are you doing this? It's madness."

Bera stared back at him and shrugged. "What else can we do?"

He regarded his men, then the villagers. "Well, we'll take some firewood at least. It's better keeping the living warm than the dead."

The big man on the ground looked up, a slightly crazed expression upon his face. "Oh yes, why not?" He laughed, and stood up. "Take it all! Take our homes!" And with that he rushed to the nearest house, trying to pull pieces of wood off it in a frenzy. "Take this! We've no need of it now! Yes! Burn it! Burn it all!" Clawing hopelessly at the solid door and frame, sweat flying off his fevered brow, he succeeded only in tearing off a few meagre strips and several of his fingernails before finally collapsing once again in a sobbing heap. Bjólf and Gunnar watched with a mixture of pity and contempt.

"You can have mine."

Bjólf turned to find the farm boy, standing, arms outstretched, holding his bundle of sticks towards him. The big man on the ground gawped up at the boy in shock, struck dumb. He returned his father's gaze in silence. As boy and man faced each other, the resemblance was suddenly clear. Both Gunnar and Bjólf noted the look that passed between them, and understood.

Bjólf nodded slowly, a flicker of a smile creeping across his face. "Take it back to the ship," he said, packing the boy off with a slap on the shoulder. He looked back once, then ran headlong towards the forest, the bundle under his arm. The boy's father raised his head slowly, tears welling up in his reddened eyes, and held Bjólf's gaze. "A curse on you and all your kind," he said in a hoarse whisper. "May all you've killed return to claim you." And with that, his head fell again.

Bjólf watched him in silence for a moment, then turned to his men, determined to make the best of the dismal situation. "Let's see what we can salvage from this mess and get out of here..." Then he muttered to Gunnar, with a nod towards the father: "... before we all end up as crazy as him..."

Gunnar shrugged. "Maybe he's not so crazy."

Bjólf stopped in his tracks. It seemed Gunnar, for all his old-fashioned ways, still had the capacity to surprise him. "He's throwing his neighbours on a bonfire to prevent them rising from the grave. These are hardly the actions of a sane man. Someone of your religious convictions should at least deplore the lack of ceremony."

"Maybe there's something in his stories."

"Or maybe," said Bjólf dismissively, "he's suffered brain sickness as a result of a serious blow to the head." He turned away once more.

"I'm just saying I've heard of such things, that's all. The dead coming back, I mean."

Bjólf stared back at his friend.

"It was from a merchant..." began Gunnar defensively, his face reddening. "Last time in Hedeby." He raised his hands in an apologetic gesture. "I'm only telling you what he said." Bjólf looked from Gunnar's face to those of his men in amazement. One or two gruffly acknowledged Gunnar's words.

"I met a man last month who said he'd seen it with his own eyes," said Godwin. "South of here. Dead men walking. Refused to put ashore, even though his crew was parched. Face was white as a swan's back when he told me."

"Everyone's heard tales of *draugr*," added Úlf. "And more often, of late."

"Tell me you don't believe all this," said Bjólf. "Stories to scare children!"

"The people there told of fire-drakes flying in the air, and the sea boiling – terrible portents." Godwin added.

Magnus stared at the pyre, its flames glinting in his eye. "The gospels tell of such things." A few men murmured in agreement. "They say that when the dead return, it is a sign of the coming Apocalypse. The end of all things."

Gunnar nodded solemnly. "Ragnarók."

Bjólf looked from face to face in silence. "Horseshit! Will you listen to yourselves? The dead coming back! You sound like old women! One bad raid and suddenly you're doubting everything." They stood, heads hanging, like chastised infants. He pointed at them with his sword, sweeping it slowly from one side to the other. "We've seen more death than most. Never yet has someone I've put down with my sword got up again." He fixed his steely eyes on each one of them in turn. "So, tell me, has any one of you, ever, in your whole life, and with your own eyes, seen a dead man walk?"

Magnus shuffled his feet uncomfortably. "I know it's in your bible-book, Brother Magnus..." said Bjólf irritably, not looking at him. "But *actually seen...*"

None spoke, their eyes cast down. Bjólf turned on Gunnar.

"And you, of all people, should know better than to listen to merchants' tales. They spend half their time going to places that are just like everywhere else, and the other half inventing things designed to make them sound more exotic."

"Like 'rich pickings' you mean?" grumbled Gunnar.

Under normal circumstances, Bjólf – rarely at a loss for words – would have countered Gunnar's comment with an even more withering reply. It was the kind of exchange upon which their relationship was largely based – a relationship only made possible by an underlying, mutual respect. But just now, he seemed not to have registered Gunnar's words. His mind was elsewhere, his expression changed, distant. Beneath his helm, a frown creased his brow. "Coming back..." he muttered to himself. Gunnar looked at him, puzzled.

"You say the raiders who came before us went *upriver*? What is upriver?" Bjólf shook Atli's father roughly by his shoulders. The man just stared at him, vacantly. "They went upriver to see if there was anything more worth having. Is there? *What is upriver?*"

"Nothing." Bera stepped forward, her head raised, her gaze unwavering. "Water. A bend in the river. Then rocks."

"Rocks?"

"A ford. Beyond the fells." She waved her hand vaguely at the eastern horizon.

"Deep enough for a ship?"

"Only if you have a crew happy to drag it."

Bjólf and Gunnar looked at each other.

"It's fully-laden," said Bjólf. "They won't be dragging that ship over any rocks."

Gunnar's expression became one of slow realisation. "They're coming back..."

"We have to get out of here."

In haste, they turned to leave, Bjólf rallying his men to him. As they did so, Gunnar glanced back towards the river. His face fell.

"Too late."

# CHAPTER FIVE

## HELGI GRIMMSSON

No sooner had the distinctive, spiked prow of Grimmson´s ship loomed into view between the banks of dark trees than his men were pouring ashore, spilling over the garishly-painted gunwales and swarming up the grey, stony bank. They pointed and shouted, some shaking their weapons with movements that, from a distance, seemed wildly exaggerated – almost absurd. For a split second, Bjólf and his crew stood stunned – then, instinctively, and as one, tensed and tightened, locking shields, shoulders hunched, weapons gripped, muscles set, as their fate flung itself headlong towards them.

"Orders?" barked Gunnar.

Bjólf hesitated.

"It's two to one at least," came Kjötvi's voice.

"If we stand, we die," added Godwin.

"I thought we all returned from the dead nowadays," said Bjólf, tersely. Still he did not move.

Godwin gave a grim smile. "Let's not put that to the test just yet, eh?"

"Nothing focuses the mind like a blade in the belly," said Gunnar, then added – more urgently this time: "Orders?"

Bjólf knew there was only one choice. But the thought of showing his back to Grimmsson – of running... It stuck in his craw. Anger welled up and pride gnawed at him. His teeth clenched until he felt they would crack, the paralysing knot of indecision burning in his chest.

Grimmsson's men – many with their clothes awry and bereft of armour – were now pounding up the track, red-faced, the fire from the previous raid still in their eyes and the new fury on their faces clearly visible, their hurled insults already striking the ears of their quarry, their footfalls shaking the earth.

An arrow glanced off the rim of Úlf's shield and was sent high into the air. It was now or never. Steeling himself for the inevitable humiliation of retreat, Bjólf raised his sword and took the breath to give the command, when... A harsh cry from the depths of the advancing army brought the thundering horde to a shuddering halt. Bjólf froze, holding his breath, sword aloft, every sinew taut. From either end of the rutted village track the two sides eyed each other in a tense, eerie silence. For the first time, Bjólf became aware that the villagers had disappeared – no trace of them remained, except those whose corpses still crackled and spluttered upon the fire. Then the ranks of the opposing army parted, and from them stepped Helgi Grimmson himself.

He stopped a few paces from his men. Built like an ox – and, Bjólf knew, with a personality to match – Grimmsson stood, stripped to the waist, his shirt tied loosely around his middle, looking for all the world like a man called forth in the middle of a wash. He was armed only with a long, grey throwing spear and, like the majority of his men, had neither helm upon his head nor mail upon his body. Clearly, this encounter had caught them by surprise, with their guard down, basking in the glory of a successful raid. Equally clear was the fact that they had not had the time – or the inclination – to equip themselves before confronting Bjólf and his crew.

"He wants to talk..." muttered Bjólf, barely able to conceal his own disbelief.

Gunnar frowned. "But why?"

"I could take him," said Fjölvar, a white-fletched arrow ready on his bow.

"No!" said Bjólf, and, lowering his sword, took two steps forward. "Let's see what he wants."

For a moment the pair stood face-to-face across the yards of hoof-churned mud, behind one a knot of armoured men in tight formation, behind the other a steaming, panting horde. Bjólf debated within himself how best to approach this previously undreamt-of dialogue. Open with a joke? Grimmsson had no sense of humour. An expression of defiance? Unwise, under the circumstances. Keep it simple, perhaps. Firm and direct. Polite.

No sooner had Bjólf settled on a form of words than Grimmsson flung his arms wide and bellowed to the sky at the top of his lungs. "ODIN!" The sound echoed off the distant, mist-wreathed mountains. Rooks croaked in alarm in the far treetops. "To you, I dedicate this... my enemy's DESTRUCTION!" And with a great, bestial grunt he hurled the spear high over the heads of Bjólf and his men.

There was to be no hesitation this time. "Run..." hissed Bjólf – and as they turned, a great roar rose again from the throats of their foe.

What followed was chaotic and confused. With the slope in their favour as they pounded over the rise and back towards the trees, Bjólf's crew made good headway against their pursuers. But as Grimmsson's men charged down the same incline, unencumbered by mail and equipment, the gap began to close. When Bjólf and his men hit the trees, arrows, axes and other projectiles were already thudding around them. There was no time to look back. Bjólf flew along the path, lashed by branches, occasionally catching glimpses of members of his crew ahead of him, and dimly aware of others crashing through undergrowth to his left and right. The forest muffled the savage cries of their enemies. It became impossible to judge distance. Bjólf could no longer guess how close he was to capture or death. He only knew to keep running.

As the path widened and the trees became more scattered, he knew at last that he was nearing the south river – and the safety of their ship. Up ahead and converging on either side of him he could now see dozens of his own men. From the left, Fjölvar flew out from a tangle of brambles and overtook Bjólf with incredible speed, face scratched and bleeding. A long-bladed spear whizzed after him as he hurtled past, missing by an arm's length and sending a chunk of bark flying as it caught the trunk of a beech tree. To the right, Kjötvi – running full tilt – suddenly cried out and fell with a heavy thud, bowling over and over in an eruption of leaves and pine needles. From behind, crunching through the forest like a giant, came the hulking figure of Gunnar who, without stopping, grabbed Kjötvi's padded tunic, hauled him to his feet and set him back on course for the beach before Kjötvi had time to realise what had happened.

Finally, his lungs bursting, Bjólf broke out of the trees. Ahead, a few were already at the ship, their shoulders to the prow. More joined them, heaving at the old, heavy timbers. The final stretch down to the water's edge seemed to expand like a bad dream. Bjólf felt his feet – made clumsy by exertion – stumbling over the uneven stones, then sinking into the rough, grey shingle as he grew closer to the shore. Finally, close to the water, the ground firmed up; he put on a burst of speed and cannoned into the ship with his shoulder. It shifted against the grit. Gunnar slammed into it with a great roar, and the ship slid another five paces. With the cries of their pursuers ringing in their ears, the gathering men heaved at the hull. It began to move easily now, further with each effort. Turning, Bjólf saw that the first of Grimmsson's men would be upon them before they made clear water: at least five – the youngest and fittest – were already half way down the beach. But these few had run so swiftly, with such eagerness, that they were now alone – unsupported by their slower comrades. And they were without shield or armour.

As his men splashed deeper into the river, heaving the ship away from the shore, Bjólf did something his pursuers did not expect. He turned and ran at them. Bjólf barely had time to register the lead attacker's shocked expression before delivering a devastating punch to his face with the iron boss of his shield, knocking him flat and sending his axe flying. Without pausing, Bjólf swung round with the full weight of his sword and caught the second attacker across the face, his blade smashing through his teeth. He felt hot blood splash across his cheek and bits of tooth rattle off his shield. The man's momentum carried him forward, and he careered drunkenly for several more paces, his smashed, almost severed head gurgling and gushing as he finally collapsed face-first onto the rocks. He was dead before he hit the ground.

A third had gathered his wits and was on Bjólf before he had time to prepare himself, aiming a huge swing of his short axe at Bjólf's exposed shoulder. Instinctively, his head turning in anticipation of the impact, Bjólf punched upward with his shield and caught the full force of the blow. The axe blade cut through the wood of the shield, narrowly missing his left forearm, and was firmly wedged, gripped by the grain. Without stopping to think, Bjólf heaved violently with his shield, giving his assailant two choices: keep a grip on his axe and be pulled to the ground, or let go and lose his weapon altogether. The man – a wiry character with a spiky, brown beard and a missing front tooth – surprised Bjólf by immediately letting go. The man was now unarmed, but he had his feet and he was alive.

At once, Bjólf sensed he had a bold and unpredictable opponent. Without hesitation, knowing the urgent need to end this, he aimed a killing blow at the man's exposed head, but as he did so, the man surprised him again, charging at him, grabbing at the embedded axe and almost wrenching both axe and shield from Bjólf's grasp. The sword blow came down wildly but with full force, missing his opponent's head but finding another target. As Bjólf struggled to steady himself, he saw the man stagger back, staring with a strange, blank expression at the cleanly cut stumps where his hands had been, his thumping, battle-charged heart pumping the lifeblood from him, a splash of steaming red upon the dull, grey stones.

Now Grimmsson's men were coming in their droves. Bjólf turned and, not daring to look back, ran headlong for the ship – now floating free of the beach, hastily deploying oars like the struggling legs of a great insect. As he neared, splashing into the water, his throat and lungs on fire, he saw Fjölvar perched on the dragon prow, bow drawn, and aimed directly, it seemed to Bjólf, at his head. The bowstring sang. The arrow hissed past – so close, Bjólf felt the wind from it brush his right cheek. Behind him was a stifled cry; something heavy fell, catching his heel, and the sword that had meant to cleave his skull clattered past him into the rocky shallows. With moments to spare before Grimmsson's men overran them, Bjólf flung his shield over the bow of the ship and Gunnar' reached down, grabbed his hand, and hauled him aboard.

Panting heavily, his head throbbing, Bjólf lay flat on his back on the deck as the ship headed into the safety of deeper water. Bathed in sweat, his armour weighing upon him, he watched as more men joined Fjölvar at the prow to pick off Grimmsson's men with their bows. Then, as the ship turned slowly downriver, he stood, threw off his helm and surveyed with relief the receding mob left behind on the riverbank. Nodding wordlessly, he slapped Gunnar on the shoulder.

Gunnar nodded back. "I see you had to go back for a souvenir." Bjólf followed his gaze. Upon the deck was his cloven shield, the axe still embedded in it, and, still gripping it, one of the pale, lifeless hands of its owner.

He looked back over the heads of his crew, now settling into an even rhythm as Úlf, who had taken the role of *rávordr* – the watch position by the mast – called the strokes. Bjólf's eyes darted from man to man, only now realising that not all were on board.

"Hallgeir?" he called.

"Spear in the back," panted Finn.

"And Steinarr?"

Magnus Grey-Beard answered him. "I saw him fall on the rocks as the shore was overrun. He was last out of the trees."

Bjólf cursed under his breath. It was not their way to leave others behind. He remembered that, before the raid, Steinarr had been complaining about a loose shoe. Quite likely, it had been the death of him. Bjólf gazed through the mist towards the ugly horde on the stony bank, wondering at Steinarr's fate. Then, another distant cry went up, and before they were finally swallowed up by fog he saw Grimmsson's men turn again and make for the trees.

It wasn't over.

# CHAPTER SIX

## THE WHALE ROAD

GUNNAR IMMEDIATELY SENSED something was wrong. "You hurt? Apart from your pride, I mean..."

Bjólf, still staring back upriver, ignored his question. "I need you to take the helm."

"Thorvald has it."

"It's going to need more weight behind it..." Gunnar frowned. Bjólf spoke without turning. "They were heading back to their ship. In haste. The north river joins us up ahead – and it flows faster than this one." Without another word, Gunnar turned and hurried towards the stern.

Bjólf climbed high in the prow, arm wrapped around the dragon's neck. "Úlf! Full-stroke on the oars!"

Some of the men – until now joking with relief, blood still fizzing in their veins – looked at one another in concern. A silence fell.

"We're not out of this yet," added Bjólf, a sense of foreboding in his voice.

With a terse nod, Úlf changed to a new chant – a song, this time, slow to begin, but gradually picking up the pace, from short-stroke, through steady-stroke, until the men were rowing at the limit of their abilities. The ship creaked and cracked, lurching forward as each pull on the oars ploughed its timbers on through the water. The song told of sailing north to Tronhjem – a cheerful song of homecoming. It was the one Úlf always used when speed was required. They needed a cheerful song then; rowing at full-stroke meant they were rowing for their lives. At other times, when the rowing was more leisurely, the men would often raise their voices together, but this song was always sung alone.

Leaning hard into the steer-board, praying to Thor that the old leather of the rudder-band would take the exertion, Gunnar steered the straightest possible course through the bends of the river, taking the ship as close to the banks as he dared. Magnus and Godwin, not needed at the oars, positioned themselves amidships to port and starboard, signalling to Gunnar at any sign of rocks or sandbanks, while Thorvald, relieved from his position at the helm, had taken up a section of planking just behind the mast-fish – the huge block of oak that held the mast – and stood waist-deep below the deck, wooden scoop in hand, ready to bail when they hit wilder waters.

None spoke. Only Úlf's voice rang out, strangely muffled by the fog, its beats matched by each dip of the oars.

His eyes straining as they struggled to penetrate the fog, Bjólf could finally make out the swirling waters where the north river joined immediately ahead. They would pick up some speed here, but would also find out if they had escaped the wrath of their pursuers. If they could not see each other in the mist, Bjólf knew they were safe.

As the ship pulled past the dwindling promontory of land separating the two rivers, the current caught the ship and turned its bows away from the mouth of the north river. Looking upstream, struggling to see past the mast and stowed yard and sail, Bjólf could see nothing in the grey gloom. He breathed a sigh of relief. But as Gunnar pulled against the steer-board, straightening the line of the ship, he heard a faint cry in the distance, and – as if from nowhere – the gaunt shadow of Grimmsson's ship hove into view. Up by the stark dragon's head, holding aloft a burning torch, the unmistakeable figure of Grimmsson himself. Before him, just visible on the front edge of the prow, thick iron spikes projected forward like great thorns, a gesture of contempt – and a hint of what was to come – for any vessel that got in their way. Another of Grimmsson's affectations. Another reason to detest the man. Yet Bjólf could not deny the tenacity of his crew. How they had made up the distance so fast, he could not imagine. But there was no time to think about it.

"Row! Everything you've got!" he roared. Similar cries went up from Grimmsson's ship. It would be a race all the way to the estuary and the open sea.

A pair of arrows, their tips aflame and sticky with pitch, flew towards them, falling short and hissing in the water near the rudder. "They mean to make a fire-ship of us." bellowed Gunnar. "We need to stay out of range!"

"I'm not ready for a funeral just yet," roared Bjólf, and leapt down from his position on the prow. He raced the length of the vessel, eyes wide, willing on the straining muscles of his crew as he passed. "Come on!" he cried. "Leave the bastards standing!"

Úlf had abandoned his song and was now shouting the strokes, pushing them faster, faster.

Bjólf stood by Gunnar, looking back from the stern at their dogged pursuers with a deep frown, the defiance from seconds before now turned to consternation. "How did they do that? Fully-laden, with a poor start and a crew that ran over twice the distance, and still they're right on our tail."

"They must really hate us!" cried Gunnar, leaning hard into the rudder.

Bjólf turned an eye to the bronze weather vane on top of the mast. He knew they could easily outrun Grimmsson's ship under sail. But, in such weather, a decent wind was a remote hope. Up above, the bronze vane swung loose, the black ribbons tied to its edge flapping limply.

With thirty-two oars and now only thirty-eight men – including himself – there was no chance of respite for any but a handful of his crew. Each man could normally manage around a thousand strokes before needing rest, but at this pace, their backs would start to break at six hundred. He only hoped it was enough.

As they pulled away from the mouth of the estuary the fog thinned, the jagged coastline curving away into the murk on either side of them. "This is where it begins," said Bjólf, and turned towards the bow again.

"Which way?" called Gunnar.

Bjólf pointed straight ahead. "The open sea." He swung past the mast and headed back to his position at the prow.

Gunnar stared after him in alarm. Ahead, the flat, leaden grey swell of the ocean heaved beneath a shroud of luminous mist.

"In this? It's madness!"

"Let's hope they feel the same," called Bjólf, and gave a disconcertingly wild laugh. Somehow he seemed to thrive in such moments of desperate adversity.

As they left the protection of the estuary, the ship began to rise and fall on the swell, every timber protesting at the conflicting pressures of oar and ocean, salt spray stinging hands and faces. At the crest of the first steep wave, several of the men in the bows failed to connect their oars with the water and missed a stroke, falling into the men behind them. Hastily they regained their positions, slotting back into the rhythm. Bjólf could not hope for a better crew. But it unsettled him to be heading out from shore into such deep, rolling seas – he'd seen a longship break its back on the swell once, out on the merciless waters of the North Sea. Light and flexible as they were – shallow of draught and slim of build – longships were not at their best in the open ocean. He knew that Grimmsson, with his larger ship and heavier cargo, was at far greater risk. Yet Grimmsson also had more fresh men to relieve his rowers. It would be a battle of wills now. A game of bluff. Bjólf had only one chance, but it meant gambling everything they had.

As the ship rode up the swell, Bjólf looked down onto the pursuing vessel as if from the side of a great valley. They were riding the seas more heavily than Bjólf and his crew, it seemed. The distance between them was growing. The hull of the ship creaked and gave an agonised groan as it tipped again over the peak of the swell, making Grimmsson's ship disappear completely before rising once more above them. The spray cascaded over the bows; Thorvald bailed ceaselessly, the seawater slopping past his feet, keeping time with the rowers – and, amazingly, given the circumstances, humming Úlf's tune to himself. Bjólf felt the timbers shift and twist against each other once again and gritted his teeth. He knew this ship better than any man alive – it was the vessel left to him at the age of only twenty, given to his uncle Olaf years before in recognition of his services to Haakon the Good of Norway. Bjólf never knew the full story, nor the nature of the services (it was the one thing of which Olaf never spoke); all that was certain was that they had earned Olaf the undying hatred of no less than Eirik Bloodaxe, doomed king of Jorvik.

This, then, was one of the great old ships – but for the mast, and a few repaired strakes on the starboard bow, built entirely of oak, and shapely as a swan. She had journeyed to the kingdom of the Rus in the east, and south as far as the Arab lands. She had sailed into Constantinople, and made landfall in Ireland, Normandy, England, the Orkneys and the kingdom of the Franks. She had proved her worth in battle against men, wind and sea, and been Bjólf's true home for the past ten winters. But even he could not be certain of her limits. He would only know them when she finally tore herself apart. Gazing up pleadingly at the dragon's head, he slapped the thick timber of the prow. "Keep it together, old girl. Just a little longer..."

His crew were close to the limit of their endurance now – arms and backs straining, veins and muscles standing out like whipcords, teeth clenched, breaths coming hard and fast. Most had not had time to remove their armour before the chase. Sweat poured off their brows. But, by some miracle – a miracle of muscle and grim determination – they were continuing to pull ahead.

"We have them!" hollered Bjólf. "A few more strokes, and they're dead in the water." The words seemed to drive his men to even greater exertion, a last burst of defiance. Yet, no sooner had he uttered them than one of the men – fourth rower from the port bow – collapsed.

Kjötvi.

As he fell forward, limp and strangely pale, he hit the man in front, knocking him off his stroke. His own oar flailed uselessly, clashing with the two behind. Other oars down the line clashed and faltered as the rhythm broke on the port side. The ship heaved and rocked alarmingly as the uneven pressure of the oars began to turn her. Gunnar fought with the tiller. If they hit the swell at a bad angle, they were in trouble.

Bjólf leapt forward and, as Magnus hauled Kjötvi clear, took control of the oar. Around his feet, the deck was dark and sticky, the froth from the sea spray stained red. Kjötvi's blood. "Pull!" he cried, as the men fought to re-establish the rhythm. "*Pull!*"

The ship straightened. Bjólf heaved on the oar until he felt it would crack, driving his men on, spurring them to one last effort. After what seemed a lifetime, the waters broadened and smoothed, and Grimmsson's ship gradually receded into the fog, until, finally, only the distant glimmer of the torch remained as evidence of its existence.

"Rest!" called Bjólf. The men collapsed over their oars, gulping at the air. A few whooped and cheered in triumph. Bjólf hushed them. Moving astern, he squinted at the faint orange glow in the fog. Bjólf spoke to his expectant crew in hushed tones. "Keep it quiet. And nothing over the side – you can bet Týr's right hand they'll be on the lookout for that. If you have to piss, you piss in a pot." There were nods all round. Some were only now able to throw off their armour, groaning at the pain in their exhausted limbs. He broke into a smile, allowing himself to feel a glow of satisfaction for these men who placed such trust in him. "Good job."

With that, he kicked open a long, rather battered sea chest, flipped his own mail shirt over his aching shoulders and bundled it inside. Pulling out a thick blue cape, he fastened it around him with a bronze brooch, and, slamming the chest shut, gazed at the lid for a moment, lost in thought. In the surface of the wood – once the colour of a fresh horse chestnut, now bleached by sun and scoured by salt – were delicate carvings of the hero Sigurd slaying the dragon Fafnir. They were in the old style. The chest had once belonged to his uncle, and – despite his father's efforts to keep his eldest son focused on the farm, and the wayward brother at a safe distance – had always inspired him as a child, whenever his uncle came visiting from his voyages. Bjólf had imagined himself as the dragonslayer, travelling the world and doing great deeds; a proud and noble warrior. While the reality of adult life had proved a little more complicated, there were fleeting moments when that childhood dream seemed once again to flicker into life. Despite the terrible misfortunes of the day, this was one of them.

"Is there a plan?" said Gunnar, breaking the spell.

"We gather our strength. Then we row with a half-crew, taking shifts of five hundred strokes, until we lose that..." He pointed toward the stern, where the flame of Grimmsson's ship was still dimly visible.

"And then?"

Bjólf surveyed the blank, still greyness that surrounded them on every side. "One thing at a time."

# CHAPTER SEVEN

## KJÖTVI THE LUCKY

KJÖTVI LAY ON the raised deck at the prow, deathly pale, his lips tinged with blue, but for the flickering in his eyelids, the very image of a corpse.

"Will he live? asked Bjólf.

"He's lost a lot of blood," said Magnus. "His skin is clammy." That was a bad sign. Magnus had propped Kjötvi's legs up on a chest to slow the flow of blood and, using a small collection of delicate iron tools spread out on their leather wrapping, was now engaged in cutting open the ragged, blood-soaked material to reveal the wound on the lower part of Kjötvi's left leg. As he carefully snipped and peeled away the wet, sticky fabric, a flap of flesh fell open, spilling thick gobbets of half-clotted blood on the deck. It looked for all the world as if someone had tried to carve a neat slice from Kjötvi's calf, mistaking it for a roasting joint. "A blade caught him from above," said Magnus, indicating the line of entry with the flat of his hand. "Very sharp. Very deep. But the battle-fire was in him. Probably didn't even feel it."

"In the woods...." said Gunnar, nodding. "A throwing axe flew past my ear and bounced off his leg. I helped him up."

Magnus examined the angle. "Stopped against the bone. He's fortunate to have kept his foot."

"Kjötvi the Lucky," muttered Gunnar. He did not appear so lucky just now, lying there, half dead. But then, mused Gunnar, half dead was better than all dead.

With delicate movements, compensating for the slow rise and fall of the ship, Magnus peered into the depths of the wound, tentatively opening up the sliced muscle tissue. He squinted hard with his one good eye, a pair of iron tweezers between his steady fingers. "There's something I need to..." Before he could finish his sentence, blood suddenly began to flow again, dripping through the fingers of Magnus's supporting hand. "Ach! We could do with more light here."

"We could risk it, for Kjötvi's sake," said Bjólf.

"Wait..." said Magnus. He knew time was not on their side. Holding his breath, he reached deep into the wound with the tweezers, then emerged with a short, yellow-white sliver of bone between its tiny jaws. "That's where the axe stopped," he said, exhaling heavily. "At least that won't stay rattling around inside him." Without further delay, he pressed the sticky halves of the wound together and, gesturing for Gunnar to place pressure upon it, began to bind up the leg with strips of linen.

Gunnar looked thoughtful. "That could have been my head."

"His bad luck was your good luck," said Bjólf.

Magnus sighed. "Were we ashore, I'd seek herbs to aid the healing. As it is... It's in God's hands now." He silently blessed his patient, kissed a small wooden cross hanging from a thong of leather around his neck and tucked it back into his brown robe.

Stooping, Gunnar picked up the small shard of bone, chipped off Kjötvi's leg like a piece of whittled wood. Studying it between his great thumb and forefinger, he shuddered inwardly, wiped it clean on his sleeve, then tucked it in the small leather bag hanging from his belt. He looked up to the featureless dark sky and muttered to himself. "Gentle Eir – listen to the pleading of this faithful old fool and care for our battle-weary friend." Drawing his knife, he pricked his thumb and let a drop of blood fall onto the deck.

Bjólf placed a hand on Magnus's shoulder. "Do what you can," he said, straightening up. "And do not trust too much to gods, or miraculous resurrections."

He walked with Gunnar, picking his way past the men, huddled between their sea-chests, wrapped in thick woollen capes and furs. After their momentary victory, the fall of Kjötvi had put them in a melancholy mood. The fog clung to them, making everything damp with beads of moisture. At the small steering deck, Bjólf relieved Finn at aft watch and stared with Gunnar out across the darkening sea. For a long time they stood and watched in silence, the only sounds the lap of the water, the creak of the timbers and the occasional isolated cough from a member of the crew. The swell was longer and more even now, and night was almost upon them. Of Grimmsson there was no sign. Not even a glimmer in the failing light.

"Must've given up," muttered Gunnar.

"Can you blame them?" said Bjólf, blowing through his hands, his breaths turning to fog. "They'll be feasting on roasted pork and lamb tonight. On dry land. And where are *we*?"

"Hey, we're alive, aren't we?"

"No, really..." said Bjólf squinting at the featureless gloom surrounding them. "Where *are* we?"

"No sun. No stars. No moon." Gunnar sniffed the cold air, then licked his finger and held it aloft. "No wind... No land in sight. Not even a horizon. No creatures in the sea, nor birds in the air." He shrugged. "It's anybody's guess."

"And what would your guess be?"

"My guess would be no better than yours," he said, then, after a moment's hesitation, added: "But Kjötvi would know."

Kjötvi the Lucky was *kentmand* – one who had a deep knowledge of the seas. He was also the unluckiest person Bjólf had ever met; one of those for whom fate seemed to deliver ten times the misfortune of ordinary men. It had become a standing joke among the crew. In the past, some had expressed reservations about even having him on board. In the course of their current voyage, he had lost his father's helmet in a well, his mail coat overboard, his sword and half his ear. But the one thing Kjötvi had never lost was himself. He knew the currents of the air and the water – and perhaps others yet more subtle – better than any man. 'Wayfinder,' they called him, and it was this uncanny ability that persuaded even the most superstitious of the men to accept him. If Kjötvi could not find a way, they would say, there was not a way to be found. Others said the gods had played a cruel trick, granting him exceptional powers of foresight and sensitivity to the ebb and flow of the world, but taking half of his luck in payment.

"Kjötvi..." said Bjólf with a sigh. And then there was Hallgeir and Steinarr. "This has not been a good day." He dug absent-mindedly at a large splinter in his left palm – where and when he'd got that, he had no memory – then, with a deep sigh, pulled his cloak tighter and stared out again into the nothingness that surrounded them.

"You know what's hardest to take?" he said dejectedly. "Grimmson's men didn't even bother to put their armour on. Do they really have such a poor opinion of us?"

"I think it's more a measure of their blind hatred."

Bjólf looked sideways at him.

Gunnar shrugged. "Basically, you pissed them off so much, they didn't even stop to think."

"Well, that makes me feel better."

"If you were so worried about feelings, you probably shouldn't have taken their plunder right from under their noses that time at Roskilde."

Bjólf couldn't resist a smile at the thought of it. Now *that* was a good day.

"I don't like to run, Gunnar," he said. "What is it the *Hávamál* says? 'The fool believes he'll live forever by running from battle – but old age gives no peace, even though spears might spare him."

"No one likes to run at the time. You'll be glad of it tomorrow." Bjólf looked unconvinced. "And anyway, you did for... what? Two of them?"

"Three."

Gunnar looked at him thoughtfully. "The thing is, I know you're not really angry because you ran. You're angry because you hesitated. But that proves it, you see?"

"Proves what?"

"You didn't run to save yourself. You ran to save your crew. Left to your own devices, I have no doubt you'd be lying hacked to bits back there, your blood feeding their crops – most likely having taken Grimmsson and several others with you."

"That hesitation cost two lives."

"Steinarr most likely lost his shoe. Hallgeir let himself get fat. Their time was up. And they died fighting."

"And Kjötvi?"

Gunnar shrugged again. "The *Hávamál* also says: 'Better blind or crippled than burning on a pyre.'"

"Better still to be in one piece."

"Ah!" Gunnar threw up his hands in disgust. "Your problem is you think you can change everything. Bend it to your will. Me? I know perfectly well I can change nothing. I follow the thread of my fate, knowing it was set down long ago."

"I cannot believe that. A man's life is his own."

"And that, my friend, is why you are our captain." Gunnar laughed and clapped his huge hand on Bjólf's shoulder. "Maybe that's your fate. To give *them* something to think about." He thrust a thumb out towards the surrounding emptiness as he spoke, at some vaguely-situated dwelling place of the gods.

Bjólf allowed himself another wry smile. For some reason – he had no idea why – the mood of one of them was always unfailingly up whenever the other's was down. He was glad there was one thing that could be relied upon. But as he continued to look out into the nothingness, some words drifted back to him. '*May all you've killed return to claim you...*' He wondered at the curse, and the broken man who had uttered it.

"How many do you suppose we have killed over the years?"

"Hmph! A small army."

"It has not always been something to be proud of."

Gunnar sighed deeply. "That, I grant you."

"Ever feel we're getting too old for all this?"

"All the time. For this life you're always too old or too young. Never exactly the right age."

"It was easier in the old days. Now there are too many earls and kings taking over, pushing people around. Hardly any opportunities left for free enterprise."

Gunnar stared into the dark water. "Norway and Denmark under one king. The White Christ replacing the old religion. The world is changing – everything being drawn to one centre. Even Harald the Blue-Toothed gives up on the ways of our ancestors. And Hedeby and the Danevirke overrun with Germans! I can't help but feel that a great age is coming to an end."

"Maybe it's time we got out."

"I must admit, the prospect of a quiet farm somewhere is starting to look increasingly attractive."

"I never thought I'd find myself thinking that. Or agreeing with you. Maybe after this, one more, then we quit. Agreed?"

Gunnar nodded slowly. "Agreed."

Bjólf spat in his palm and slapped it against Gunnar's. "Our fate's our own, old man." He waved vaguely in the direction of the gods, mocking Gunnar's gesture. "Let *them* concern themselves with someone else for a while." Gunnar grinned and shook his friend's hand heartily.

As he spoke, Magnus approached, an urgent look in his eyes. For a moment, Bjólf feared the worst. Magnus waved away Bjólf's concerns.

"He wakes from time to time," he said. "This is good. But he drifts between this world and the next. And he has no warmth in his body, for all the blankets and skins we pile upon him. Hot food or drink is what he needs now."

"We could all use some of that," said Gunnar.

Bjólf looked out again at the blank, grey night. "What we need is land. Gunnar – tell me straight: what are our chances?"

Gunnar shrugged. "If a breeze comes up, it might be enough to take us southwest. Then we hit the coast of the English and get slaughtered like pigs. Or, perhaps, the current will be stronger and carry us north. Then, potentially, we miss landfall altogether and end up frozen to our oars for all eternity."

"And the bad news?"

"Well, if we row..."

"We're rowing blind..." said Bjólf, nodding.

"... and, at worst, we run straight back into Grimmsson. There's a chance he may yet be out there somewhere."

Bjólf sighed again. "So we have no choice but to sit tight until this fog clears and we can get our bearings." He gave Magnus a grim smile. "Looks like it's going to be a long night, brother."

Gunnar clapped him on the shoulder again, and gave a cheerful smile. "Don't worry! Thor loves the foolhardy!"

"Fjölvar!" called Bjólf. "What's our food situation?"

Fjölvar stirred, heaving himself stiffly to his feet, and, weaving past his hunched shipmates, pulled up the loose planking of the deck before the mast-fish. Immediately below was a small collection of barrels and caulked chests, lashed to the mast-beam below to prevent them shifting on the swell. He dug around, half buried below the deck.

"Some barley meal, a little dried meat, salt fish, two barrels of water, several rotting onions..." He dragged a small sack from a chest, peered in, sniffed tentatively, and recoiled. "And I think these once were mushrooms."

Gunnar sighed. "No fresh meat. No butter. And nothing to drink but water."

"It'll do, for a start," said Bjólf. "Thorvald! Finn! Throw the lines over, see what we can catch. There must be something alive out there." The two men set about the task, while Bjólf, striding past Fjölvar to the prow, dragged a bulky, heavy bundle from beneath the fore-deck and undid its wrappings. It clanked as he did so. Kjötvi stirred, his eyes flickering open for an instant.

"Sorry, my friend," said Bjólf. "But you'll thank me for it later." He unfolded a sturdy, black iron tripod – as tall as a man – pressed its clawed feet until they bit into the deck, and anchored each foot with a sack of sand. Then, drawing out a wide, charred metal dish – almost the size of a small shield – he suspended it by three long chains from the apex of the tripod. Above that, from three similar chains, he hung a large, fire-blackened cauldron.

"Now... Firewood." He scanned the length of the ship, a vague memory stirring as he caught sight of a familiar bundle of sticks tucked into the gap under the steering deck. He frowned. "Firewood..." As he looked, taking in the distribution of his men on the deck, he noted a slight list of the ship – so subtle, that another eye could not have detected it.

"Thorvald, are we taking in water?"

Thorvald looked up from baiting the lines with a frown. "No. She's sound."

Pulling his knife, Bjólf strode toward the stern, looked around for a moment, then hauled up a section of loose decking on the steer-board side, barely a pace from where he and Gunnar had been standing moments before. From the cramped, dark space below the deck, a shivering, white face peered back up at him.

The farm boy.

# CHAPTER EIGHT

## THE THING IN THE WATER

Bjólf REACHED IN with one arm and hauled the skinny wretch to face height, then deposited him roughly on deck, still clutching the front of the boy's scruffy tunic in his fist, his knife at his throat. His eyes burned with anger.

"What do you think this?" He shook the boy violently. "Just hop aboard and it's a-viking we will go? Well?" With that he pushed him away.

The lad looked at him in pale-faced shock for a moment, then vomited violently over the gunwale.

Bjólf raised his hands in despair. "This is all we need." The stowaway, recovering himself – though still slightly green – wiped his mouth, and stood swaying awkwardly on the shifting deck, every eye of the crew upon him.

"I... I thought..."

"You thought!" roared Bjólf, pointing at his face with his knife. "This is not a child's game!"

Gunnar put a hand on Bjólf's arm. "Go easy. I seem to remember you starting out much the same way."

"That was different," spat Bjólf. But he could not hide the note of defensiveness in his voice. He had been twelve when he stowed away on his uncle Olaf's ship. It was the only time he saw Olaf get really angry with him. The storm blew over quickly – but the voyage that followed was tough on the boy, and Olaf spared him none of its hardships. Upon his return, Bjólf's father met him not with with the expected fury and platitudes, but merely silent disapproval. Secretly, he thought the experience would turn his son against the viking life, and back to more serious application on the land. It did exactly the opposite. He thought now of the wrecked village the boy had left behind – the crazed, snivelling man on his knees in the mud – and his anger began to subside.

"Well, this solves the food problem, at least," said Fjölvar. The farm boy looked at him in alarm. "What do you say? Throw him in the pot?"

Bjólf looked the boy up and down slowly and shook his head. "Too scrawny."

"I'll have a leg!" called a gruff voice from the dark. There was a chuckle beside him.

"Save me the liver," said Finn with a smile, tapping the blade of his knife against his knuckles.

"Nah," said Njáll Red-Hair, matter-of-factly, "if it's a young lad, the buttock's the best part." A few of the men snorted with a mixture of amusement and incredulity. Njáll threw his hands apart in mock innocence. "Don't blame me, lads. I heard that one from a Christian bishop." There was an uproar of laughter among the crew, during which Njáll threw a brotherly arm around Magnus and planted a kiss on the side of his head. "And if a Christian man said it, it must be true!" Magnus responded with a sardonic smile. For many of the men, those Christian jokes just never wore thin. Although Magnus was far from the only member of the crew who claimed to follow the White Christ, he was the only one to worship him exclusively, or with any real dedication. For most, he was simply another god to add to the extended family – an additional insurance policy against the perils of the world, and an uneasy bedfellow of Thor, Týr and Freyja. Even for Odo of Normandy – the only other crew member who could justifiably be termed 'Christian'– the faith had been born more out of the pragmatism of politics than of personal conviction.

Bjólf had by now regained his sense of humour, but when he turned to face the lad again, his face was sombre. He raised a hand, and the crew fell silent.

"I don't like people coming aboard my ship uninvited, large or small," he said, gravely. "But since you're here, little man, you now have a choice to make. On this ship, you're either crew, or you're cargo. If you're crew, you work, you follow my rules, and you live and die for this vessel and the men aboard it. If you're cargo... Well, let's just say that the only cargo we find ourselves interested in at the moment is the edible kind."

The stowaway looked nervously from face to face. From somewhere came the sound of a knife blade scraping slowly on a whetstone.

"C... crew..." he stammered.

"Good choice!" said Bjólf, clapping his hands and breaking into a broad smile. "Now we will throw you overboard." And with that, several of the men hoisted the boy like a sack by the hands and feet, manoeuvred him to the port side, swung him twice over the gunwale, and on the third, hurled him far out into the heaving sea.

THE COLD HIT Atli like a stone. The world turned blue-black, the distant sounds of laughter deadened by the icy water that enveloped him. He thrashed helplessly as if in a dream, ears ringing, silver bubbles bursting from him as the pressure crushed against his aching chest. He felt a sickening panic at his sudden inability to breathe, then deeper, existential dread at futility of his situation, at the terrifying scale of the surroundings, as if momentarily aware of himself as a tiny, insignificant speck in the vast, black, implacable ocean. He tried desperately to swim, to reach air, but could no longer tell which way was up or down. The strength drained from his limbs. He flailed uselessly. Then, as shock and disbelief subsided, it was replaced by a kind of detached numbness. A strange calm descended. He seemed to withdraw from his body; it felt insubstantial – nonexistent. For the first time in his life, he knew, with absolute certainty, that he was going to die.

Then, in those last moments, at the point where life and death met, a weird vision came to him. Looking down at his own body, as if from outside it, he became aware of something in the dark water below him. A pale shape, coming closer. A face. At first – such was his disorientation – he had the strange idea that it might be his own. But as it loomed nearer, its features resolved into those of a corpse, its skin and eyes as pallid as a cave fish, its flesh drawn and bloodless, lips and gums shrunk back from its jagged, broken teeth, its long, tangled hair, flecked with the whorled shells of sea snails and silver with their slime, fanned out like lank, oily weed. All over its grotesquely bloated belly and sunken chest, strange eel-like creatures clung and writhed, while pale, lifeless fish-eaten organs lolled from a ragged black cavity in its side. Out of the black water – impossibly – its dead, skeletal arm, almost stripped of tattered flesh, reached towards him, the fingers of its ghastly hand – thin and sharp as bleached fishbones – clawing convulsively at his leg.

A tug on his wrist brought him back to life. He felt a sudden, rapid motion through the water. A rope burned him. Then the distant sounds of laughter and shouting gurgled back into his head, and, as the weight of the world returned, he was heaved back onto the deck, retching and coughing up salt water, and finally lay quivering and spluttering in a pool of his own making like a helpless newborn. With one swipe of his thin knife, Wide-Face – Finn – cut the line that had been lashed to his wrist as the crew had readied him for the plunge.

Atli looked up to see the beardless captain's hand extended towards him. "Welcome aboard the *Hrafn*."

As the cheers and laughter rang around him, muffled by fog, he stood unsteadily – ears popping, water dripping in a pool at his feet. His toes were so cold now he could no longer feel them. He shivered, shoulders hunched, teeth rattling noisily in his head – a sensation he felt rather than heard – staggering awkwardly with every heaving movement of the ship, movement to which the forbidding, sturdy figures before him seemed utterly oblivious. For a moment, in a kind of abstract trance, his ears ringing from the cold and the water, his head battered by the dull thunder of their disconnected voices, he marveled at it – at the way they moved with the ship, as if part of it. Somehow, in this strange state in which he now found himself, they appeared to inhabit a different universe altogether, one in which the laws he knew – those which weighed him down, chilled him to the bone, hauled him off balance – did not apply.

He struggled to process all that had happened to him, but could hardly summon the strength. Somehow, as they had actually been happening, he had taken the day's extraordinary events in his stride, even with all their horrors and hardships. He had held on, kept going. He'd felt proud of himself over that. Strong. But now, just when it seemed he had achieved his long-held dream, now that he was once again safe – or as safe as he was likely to ever be – they threatened to overwhelm him; images and sensations flooding into his brain as if the dam holding them in check had finally burst. His dream had turned to nightmare. He felt weak and alone. Tears stung his eyes, lost in the rivulets of seawater coursing down his face. All he wanted now was to go home, and to sleep.

Back at the village, his resolve had been clear. Leaving behind its bafflingly surreal confusion – so strange and unfathomable that it had seemed to barely touch him – he had made his way back through the trampled, fragrant forest to the longship. There was nothing left for him there, no reason now to stay. He was a victim in a village of victims. But he would be that no longer. If he was to die, let him go down fighting like these bold warriors.

Splashing into the shallows along the ship's port side, to which the beached vessel now gently listed, he'd hurled his bundle of wood over the battered, grey-brown gunwale, and hauled himself after it. It was the largest ship he had ever seen, yet once aboard he'd found himself marvelling at how so many men could be accommodated in so cramped a space. From the tall mast – a single trunk of pine – a complex system of ropes stretched all around, some, he could see, wound around wooden cleats at key points along the ship's elegantly curving hull. The central portion of the vessel was dominated by the lowered wooden yard and heavy, furled sail, resting the length of the ship on three supports. Almost as tall as Atli himself, the sturdy posts were topped with horizontal crosspieces shaped to carry the yard and sail – like perches for impossibly large hunting birds.

The main part of deck seemed a chaotic mess of obstacles. Scattered at regular intervals, forming two rows along each side of the ship, were at least thirty long, low chests of various designs, interspersed with numerous boxes, coiled rope, tools and weapons. In the very centre, some distance before and behind the mast, were thick bolts of heavy, folded, striped cloth, tied roughly together with carved planks and poles: tents, for the crew's accommodation when ashore.

At either end, some brightly painted shields – several battered and badly split – stood stacked together, with space for many more. On top of it all lay the shipped oars, hastily hauled aboard through the oar holes and laid at an angle towards the stern, ready to be rapidly deployed upon the crew's return. At first, it seemed there was hardly any deck visible, let alone available to walk on. But as Atli picked his way through, it became clear that there was order to this chaos; everything had its place, every bit of space used to best advantage, and – although it was not immediately apparent beneath the abandoned oars – every chest carefully positioned to allow access to any part of the ship, leaving clear pathways down the centre of the vessel for any with a keen eye.

As he passed the length of the furled sail – a vast sausage of dirty, pale, heavy material, criss-crossed with strips of leather – he could just make out glimpses of what appeared to be a dark motif painted or dyed in black upon parts of its surface. An unpleasant, acrid smell of damp rose from it, like wet clothes, mingled with the rank odour of old animal fat. They joined the various other smells that seemed to emanate from the timbers as he negotiated his way aft – fish, rotting seaweed, wet animal skins and stale sweat.

He had to think quickly now. His plan, such as it was, had not extended beyond this point. It was clear that if he was to make good his escape, he would have to hide from his unwitting hosts at least until the ship was in open sea. But where? He stood at the stern, near to the steering board, looking back over the deck, mentally probing every nook or cranny he could find. It seemed hopeless. On this crammed deck there was barely space to hide a rat.

Panic was starting to rise in him. What if there was nowhere? What if the returning *vikingr* were to find him there, and, laughing, simply deposit him back on the shore, back in his everyday life, and leave, never to be seen again? He could not bear the thought. Then, as he stepped back, he felt a portion of the deck shift under his weight. Crouching to examine it, he noticed a small hole cut in the planking, just big enough for a forefinger. He poked one in, and pulled.

A section lifted like a hatch, opening into a dark confined space below, among the ship's ribs. It was damp and dark with tar and smelt like urine. But it would do. Partly filling the space was some sort of bulbous cage made from withies, broken and useless – a bird or animal trap of some kind, he supposed. Further over, a tiny carved effigy of a god, wrapped around with twisted straw, had been nailed to the inside of the keel. Atli abandoned his bundle of sticks, climbed in, and, shoving the trap further under the deck with his feet, nestled against the clammy timbers, pulling the hatch back over him.

He couldn't tell how long he had waited in darkness, listening to the lap of the water. He had been aware, at some point, of shouting in the distance, and the pounding of feet on shingle. Then, quite suddenly, the deck above him had burst into life with the hasty, heavy tread of the crew, and the rumble of oars being thrust into position. There had been urgent cries all around – some so close, he could hear them swear under their breath. The planking creaked and shifted. Further away, the shouting grew to a roar. There was the clash of metal against metal, and the space around him suddenly reverberated with the grinding of wood and gravel. The ship was moving. Then the vessel freed itself and began to heave to and fro, pitched forward with each pull of the oars. There had been laughter. For a time the motion had even seemed leisurely. Then another shout had gone out, and the ship had begun to lurch more violently, the rhythm of the oars building in speed until everything around him creaked and cracked as if the ship was about to break itself apart. Somewhere to the right of him, the heavy wood of the steer-board had clunked and groaned against the outside of the hull. Amongst it all, inexplicably (at first, he thought he had imagined it) a voice had begun to sing. Suddenly, up ahead, he had seen daylight. Someone further down the ship had raised a section of planking. Surely they could not know he was here? He had gripped the ship's ribs tightly, then, holding his breath against imminent discovery.

But no discovery came. And, as the rise and fall had grown greater, a more urgent fear began to grip him. In the darkness, with each inevitable plunge leaving his stomach behind, he had tried to brace himself against the relentless, increasingly violent motion, clinging to the slimy timbers until he felt his knuckles would burst, repeating over and over the prayer for protection that his father had so often used when they were fishing out in the estuary, and which Atli had never before believed.

It had got significantly worse after that.

The torment that followed had seemed endless; the heaving of the ship so extreme – the inexorable climb on the swell, the sudden drop like a stone, the shuddering and cracking and groaning of the timbers, like howls of agony – that he felt sure he could not survive it. He could not understand how men could go to sea in such conditions. Even in his terrified state, it had made him angry to think of it. Surely, he had thought, whatever was going on outside his wooden prison must be the most treacherous, the most violent of storms? It was only the onset of seasickness that had finally taken his mind off the danger. He had spent the rest of the journey not so much fearing for his life, as wishing for death.

Time had blurred, then. He only remembered becoming aware, somehow, that the swell had diminished – and then, without warning, the scowling face of the ship's captain had appeared, framed in the dim rectangle of the open hatch. Then he had been quivering on deck, facing the stares of the crew – and before he knew it, engulfed by the numbing cold of the sea.

And then there was the thing in the water.

The memory came back, chilling him to the core. He could no longer judge whether it had even been real. As he swallowed, his ears popped and crackled again. Water ran from them, and the sounds of the ship, the sea and the men – now busying themselves with the fishing lines – returned with a disconcerting clarity, sharp and bright in his aching head. He felt himself fully back in their world, stunned and helpless, and only dimly aware of a throbbing pain in his calf where four rows of parallel scratches stood out, angry red weals against the white flesh.

# CHAPTER NINE

## THE NAMING OF NAMES

STANDING SILENTLY AT the stern, the captain kicked open a chest and rummaged inside, pulling out a worn leather belt and short blue tunic embroidered in red and white at its edges. He looked at them, thoughtfully, then back at Atli in his soaking, sagging excuse for a garment. "These were Steinarr's. They would pass to his family, but he has none, so they pass to me. And I am lending them to you." He threw them at the boy. They were soon followed by some brown leggings, and finally an old pair of fur-lined boots which Atli, arms now full, fielded clumsily with his feet. Still shivering, too weak and cold to question it, he immediately changed into them, heaving his old, sodden tunic over his head. It slapped in a heavy, soggy pile on the deck. The new clothes were warm against his skin, more comfortable than anything he had ever worn. The boots, incredibly, were a good fit. Steinarr, whoever he was, must have been a small man. Atli felt the life returning to his toes, to his whole being. It wasn't just the warmth, he realised. It was something else. These were the clothes of a warrior. It was as if they were giving him new strength, new purpose. He felt like a king. For the first time in his life, he was somewhere he belonged.

Bjólf looked him up and down, critically. "A little long, and a bit baggy here and there, but more fitting for a member of this crew." Atli pulled at the belt, fastened as tight as it would go, but still falling about his waist. Steinarr clearly had been a rather slender fellow, but nowhere near slender enough.

"Do you have a knife?" Atli said.

The captain stared back at him in amusement. "Slow down, little man. You're not quite ready for battle just yet."

Atli felt himself blush. "It's for the belt. To make holes."

The warrior laughed and rummaged in the chest again, unearthing a small, sheathed eating knife, which he tossed to Atli. "Don't lose it. It's valuable." Atli gazed in wonder at the ornate handle. He had never seen such a common implement made with such care and skill. It was carved with an intricate, interweaving knotwork pattern in what he assumed – never having encountered walrus ivory before – was some kind of bone. He drew the knife slowly from its simple, brown leather sheath and marvelled at the blade; thin and slightly curved, with a very fine point. It had, at some point in its life, acquired a notch in its edge, close to the handle (what story lay behind that, he wondered?) but otherwise, the smooth metal had all the appearance of having been lovingly cared for, polished, sharpened and re-sharpened over many years. He immediately set about his belt, twisting its sharp point into the tough, brown leather.

"Ah, give the boy a proper weapon," called the giant with a laugh. "He's one of us now!" The words gave Atli an instant glow of pride – so much so that in his distraction he almost drove the knife into his palm. He hoped no one noticed.

"The captain considered his words, then slammed the chest shut and rose to face Atli once more. "First things first. Swords must be earned. For a sword to be given, an oath must be made, and for an oath to be made, one must first have a name."

Atli stopped fiddling with his belt and stared nervously at his new captain.

"Bjólf, son of Erling." He pressed his palm to his chest as he spoke. "And this" – he slapped his hand against Gunnar's shoulder

– "this is Gunnar, son of Gunnar. Imagination was not his father's strong point."

Gunnar snorted in gruff acknowledgement. A few of the men nearest them chuckled.

"He is *skipari*," continued Bjólf, "first mate of this ship. Make sure you stay on the right side of him, and do whatever he tells you."

Atli had no idea what to do when meeting a fellow warrior – should he make some kind of greeting? Grasp the man's hand? – and instead just stood uselessly, tongue tied, shifting from foot to foot.

"I'm guessing you've not strayed far from home before, little man," said Bjólf. "Am I right?"

Atli nodded, while trying to exude an air of confidence. He did not wish to admit that he had barely been out of sight of his village.

"Well, your travels begin today." He turned and began to pick his way between the men, several of whom were now occupied with catching whatever vaguely edible creatures the ocean was willing to give up. Atli hurried after him, staggering awkwardly with each movement of the ship and trying not to trip over men, ropes, and the vast array of strewn objects upon which he constantly threatened to bark his shin or impale himself. All around, the crew – each seeming to know their purpose on the vessel without the need for communication – busied themselves with all manner of tasks, most of which Atli could only guess at.

"Half the world is right here on this vessel," continued Bjólf. He gestured to a tall, clean shaven man with black hair and olive skin, the one Atli had called Curved Sword. "Filippus, from Byzantium. You know of it?" Atli, not wanting to admit he had not, made a non-committal kind of sound. "A great city. Many *sjømil* from here. Perhaps you'll see it one day." Filippus gave an elegant nod of his head. Bjólf raised his eyebrows and puffed out his cheeks. "He has a father, so we're told, who has a name, but none of us can pronounce it." There was a hearty laugh from a thick-set man with short-cropped hair nearby.

"Odo, son of Theobald," said Bjólf, clapping the laughing man on the back. "From the land of the Normans. Good fighters. Bad haircuts." Odo half smiled, half scowled back at him, his fellows – Filippus among them – now laughing at his expense.

Bjólf continued to call out names left and right – Thorvald, Úlf, Njáll, Egil, Kylfing – more than Atli could hope to remember. Bjólf gave a friendly kick, in passing, to a lean figure of a man who was crouched at the foot of the mast, seemingly trying to untangle a fish line with his teeth. "Skjöld, son of Jarl. He's an Icelander." Skjöld made to grab Bjólf's foot, but the other was too fast for him. "He'll tell you all about that forsaken place. Just don't ask him to recite any poetry unless you've a couple of days to spare."

At that, a smelly, wet rag flew past Atli and slapped Skjöld full in the face, raising a cry of disgust from the victim. Bjólf rounded on the culprit. Atli recognised the grinning, thin-faced man as the bowman from the forest. "That's Fjölvar, son of Mundi. Don't upset him. He's the cook."

Bjólf moved swiftly onwards, a further cascade of names flowing from him as he picked his way past men of every size, shape and demeanour – Lokki, Odvar, Salomon, Gøtar, Farbjörn, Hrafning, Arnulf, Halfdan, Ingólf, Áki, Eyvind – all with father's names and, more often than not, a less than complimentary nickname too – Ham-Fist, Flat-Nose, Hairy-Breeches, Crow-Foot – the list went on until Atli felt his head start to spin.

Bjólf then came to one Atli remembered. Long-Axe was sat on his sea-chest, running a whetstone along the blade of his axe. Passing behind him, Bjólf placed his hands on the man's shoulders. "And this is Godwin, son of Godred. From England, no less. Nice place. Good growing land – though I don't think he'll be returning there any time soon." Godwin gazed back at Atli, implacable as ever. "He had a slight misunderstanding with some of his kinsmen..."

"They are no kinsmen of mine," said Godwin flatly. Atli felt the man's hard eyes bore into him.

"A good man to have at your side in a tight spot," said Bjólf, back on the move. Before Atli turned away, one of Godwin's eyes winked, and he even fancied he saw a smile flicker beneath the great, sandy moustache.

"And this is Finn," said Bjólf, pulling the man's fur hat roughly over his eyes. Wide-Face said some words of protest that Atli did not understand and pushed it back where it belonged, then returned to baiting his line with what looked to be thin strips of dried fish skin. "He's from Finnmark, in the far north, and his real name is more of a mouthful than raw reindeer balls."

"Lávrrahaš Hætta!" protested Finn. "Even our littlest children can say it!"

Bjólf shrugged. "'Finn.' But of course – you've met already..."

Finn eyed the boy with a smile, skewering the dried fish on a hook. Atli edged around him cautiously, bumping into a great iron dish hanging from a tripod of metal, which rocked and clanged as it swayed on its chains.

They were almost at the bow now. As at the stern, the long, slow pitching of the ship was more extreme here, so much so that Atli struggled to keep his feet, even though Bjólf seemed immune to its influence. Ahead, crouched over a pale, lifeless figure, squeezing a dribble of water onto the blue-white lips, his head partly hidden by a cowl and his thick brown robes draped in folds around him, was Grey-Beard.

"This wise man is Magnus, son of Ingjald. Doesn't fight much. Good healer, though. A Christian man, but we don't hold that against him." Magnus looked up with a half-amused grunt. Atli stared back, his eyes drawn inexorably to the dark, empty socket where the man's left eye had once resided.

"If you are injured, Magnus will put you back together. He was once to be found rotting in a monastery in the middle of nowhere, but he grew tired of the reclusive life. And I know what you're thinking." He whirled his index finger in front of Magnus's face and mouthed a word: "Odin..."

"Ah! Not that again!" Magnus waved his hand dismissively and turned back to his patient.

It was, indeed, exactly what Atli was thinking.

"It's a curious irony, to be sure," said Bjólf. "The Christian man who is the very image of the All-Father."

Magnus turned to look at Atli, and a smile creased his brown, whiskered face. "Well, you look a little more presentable than you did."

Atli had thought Magnus a startling presence back on the riverbank, in the shadow of battle, but now he saw him like this, smiling warmly, it seemed hard to believe he could inspire anything approaching fear. Atli cursed his own stupidity. What use would he be to the crew if he let such childish superstitions get hold of him?

"And this," said Bjólf, crouching, his knees cracking, "is Kjötvi, son of Björn. A finder of ways. We call him 'The Lucky.' Not so lucky today." His face became suddenly grave. He looked up, staring distractedly at Atli's new clothes for a moment, lost in thought. "But luckier than some."

The approach of Gunnar broke the spell. "The fog is thickening. Maybe rain later. Could make for better light tomorrow."

Bjólf nodded, and gazed at the flat featureless sky. He stood suddenly, addressing Atli. "Now you have our names, we should have yours."

"Atli."

"Son of...?"

"Just Atli."

From where he stood, Gunnar saw again the tightening of the boy's jaw at the mere memory of the parent he had left behind, the anger contained within his refusal even to name him. His mind went back to his own childhood – to the harsh words and harsher blows he had suffered from his own father. One day, when he was big enough, he had turned on the old man, wrestled him to the floor and held a knife at his throat. To his great surprise, the old man had broken into an uproar of laughter, and insisted on them both breaking open the mead he'd been saving for Yule. Things were much better between them after that.

"Well, Atli Just-Atli," said Bjólf. "I have a job for you."

# CHAPTER TEN

## NIGHT, WOOD AND FIRE

ATLI PULLED THE stick against his bent knee and felt the satisfying snap as it yielded to the pressure. Placing both halves on the deck, he rested the end of one on the middle of the other, then gave the raised half a sharp whack in the middle with the hand-axe he had acquired earlier that evening. It immediately cracked in two. He fed the two smallest parts into the fire that was now crackling away in the broad, blackened metal dish and watched them catch and spit in the glow, relishing the warmth. The cauldron of water swaying on its chains above was at last starting to steam.

All along the ship, the men were hauling up lines to examine their catch. Now and then one wrestled with small fish – haddock, Atli thought – some of which flipped and slapped on the deck. High on the prow, a man with no front teeth whose name Atli could not remember stood looking out to sea. *Sundvordr*, had Bjólf called it – bow watch. Below him, on the forecastle, Kjötvi lay, tended now and then by Magnus, while closest to Atli, now wrapped in a smooth

74

skin coat lined with thick fur, Finn scanned the dark water silently, the finger of his right hand tucked under the taut fishing line that disappeared over the side and into the inky black swell, sensitive to the slightest movement. Atli found his own gaze continually returning to this strange figure. He was Sami – so Gunnar had told him; a reindeer herder from the far north, where there were year-round snows. This one had been a shaman of his tribe before the lot of them had been killed by raiders. Somehow, he alone had survived. Powerful with magic, Gunnar said. Atli had already noticed that the attitude of the other men was different towards this one. Though jovial and direct, as they all were with each other, they kept more of a distance from him. There seemed an unusual kind of respect, or perhaps fear. Despite his continuing efforts to fight the superstitious dread that had made his family life so miserable – efforts bolstered by the welcome pragmatism of his new captain – something about this man made Atli edgy. Something unnerving, dangerous – like a feeling half remembered from a dream. Or perhaps it was just Gunnar's story that had disturbed him. He poked the fire, and set about the wood again with his axe. Never mind. At least there should be some proper food soon.

Not long before, Atli had watched as Bjólf had set the fire. It was a familiar ritual – one he had seen perhaps a hundred times before as part of his father's regular routine – yet here performed with such elegance and efficiency that it was somehow rendered fascinating again, as if seen entirely anew.

First, Bjólf had snapped one of the thinnest of the dry sticks into short lengths, then, smashing one of its ends to splinters with the flat back of an axe, placed it in the charred middle of the great metal dish, on top of a handful of straw Fjölvar had brought from a box beneath deck. On top of that, he had piled more small, kindling-sized pieces of wood, then, from the bag on his belt, he had drawn a small pouch, from which he had pulled a tuft of what looked like wool – flax, Atli thought it was – and tucked it into the straw. Rummaging further in the pouch, he had then produced a lump of flint and an elegantly shaped metal tool whose purpose Atli did not recognise – smaller than a palm and something like half a belt buckle, it was completely flat along one edge, the other delicately fashioned with intertwined dragons, the long, snaking necks curving outward and back towards the centre so their heads met in the middle. Its purpose was soon to become clear. From the pouch, Bjólf had taken a small piece of what looked like black felt – Atli recognised it as *hnjóskr*, or 'touchwood,' something his grandfather had once been renowned for making – and, gripping the flint in the upturned palm of his left hand with the touchwood held between his fingers, began to strike the exposed surface of the stone with the flat edge of the tool. Sparks flew. A firelighting steel. Bjólf repeated the blow over and over, moving the touchwood around in relation to the flint, altering the angle of striking to direct the now steady flow of sparks towards it. Wisps of smoke and the sharp tang of flint filled the air. Within a few moments, Bjólf had cupped his hand around the strip of touchwood, and Atli could see that its rough edge was glowing. Transferring it swiftly to the flax tuft, he blew gently until the glow caught the flax fibres and, with the nurturing of another few breaths, made a tiny flame. The flax flame caught the straw, the straw the wood splinters, the splinters the kindling, and, before long, a respectable fire was flickering and swaying before Atli's eyes. Bjólf had stood then, saying: "Keep this fire going, no matter what." Then, as he had turned to go, added: "And don't set fire to the ship."

As he was leaving, Fjölvar had returned with the big cauldron, now full of water, and hooked it back onto its chains above the fire. For a moment it had rocked and swayed dangerously, its contents slopping about above the still-meagre flame. Fjölvar tapped the cauldron with his knuckle. "Every man aboard is depending on you," he said, encouragingly, then, with a single slap on Atli's shoulder, had made off, back to a small area near the mast that he was now using for food preparation.

The first thing Atli had realised, once things had settled down, was that he was faint with hunger. Somehow, the events of the day had managed to keep his mind off his stomach, but suddenly, he felt his head swimming. His hands shook as he fed wood into the fire, his stomach tightening as if it were about to cave in. The mere mention of food had brought him crashing back to the reality that not a morsel had passed his lips since early morning. It had been a rough meal porridge with some dried fish in it. The fish had had a particularly rank taste today – it could get like that when the weather wasn't good for drying – but right now Atli would have given anything for a bowl.

"Here." Atli had jumped at the voice beside him. It was Gunnar.

He set down a bowl of drinking water, and then, reaching into a black leather bag – of a type that all the men seemed to wear at their belts – he drew out his huge fist and held it towards the boy. Atli offered his cupped hands, and into it was deposited a huge handful of hazelnuts, shrivelled berries and small pieces of what looked to be dried meat. "Keep your strength up," said Gunnar with a curt nod. He stood awkwardly for a moment, scratching at his black beard, then, with a grunt, turned and went.

At first, Atli had simply stared at the small feast, almost too exhausted to eat. Then a wave of hunger overwhelmed him again. Having no hands free, he simply shoved his face into the mix and chomped on it like a hog. The sweet bitterness of the hazelnuts and sharpness of the berries made his saliva run like a dog – his cheeks ached with it. Then came the pungent, deep flavour of the meat. It was the most delicious thing he had ever eaten. Its effect was like magic. Within moments, he felt his strength and his resolve returning – enough to realise that here, now, food was a commodity too valuable to squander. Half the mixture remained in his cupped hands; it would be wise to pace himself. But, as he looked up, he realised the fire was already dying. Scooping the remaining half of the mixture into his left hand, he shoved a stick into the dwindling blaze then looked around for somewhere to put his precious food. He eventually drank the bowl of water, put the dried mix into it, then turned his full attention back to the fire, piling up the embers with another stick and coaxing it back to life with his breath.

Bjólf, who had been watching from a distance, smiled at the boy's ingenuity. He'd be alright. They could adapt to anything at that age – it was the best time to go to sea. Or maybe he was just getting sentimental in his old age.

A thought struck him. Returning to Steinarr's chest, he pulled something from it and made his way back to the prow.

The sudden slap of leather on the deck had given Atli another start. At his feet lay a bag that had been repaired in one corner, with a bronze clasp and two straps that had been designed to fit neatly over the belt now at his waist, and of the same brown leather. "You'll be needing that," Bjólf had said, towering over the crouching boy. "Unless you want to keep all your possessions in a bowl."

Atli had wasted no time in putting the bag where it belonged – on his belt, next to his shiny new knife. And it had not been the last gift of the evening. Later, when he had been struggling to break some of the thicker pieces of wood, another of the crew – the one called Thorvald; a short, stocky fellow – had taken pity and given him the axe. Its owner, he said with a laugh, had no further use for it; a trophy of their battle on the beach. But before Atli could ask him further about that, he had gone. It had made his task easier, that much was certain, but, more importantly, it had made him feel trusted, one of them. A warrior. When not in use, he tucked the axe proudly, if a little awkwardly, into his belt, and became all the more determined to make this the best cooking fire the crew had ever seen.

Atli's great worry now was his supply of wood. He had tried to make it last, while getting the best blaze he could to heat the water as quickly as possible – for his hunger, and, he supposed, that of the others, demanded more than dried fruit and nuts – but already, half of it was gone. How long did they want him to keep this going? Until the cooking was done, certainly. But how long would that take? And how much longer after that? An hour? Two? All night?

Emboldened now– and realising he must act before the need made itself too keenly felt – he built up the fire as much as he dared and set off on a foraging mission about the ship. As the men worked around him, sometimes ruffling his hair or making a quip about his size, his eyes darted about in the darkness, searching for anything – anything at all – that might keep the fire going. He found the shattered remains of a shield – Godwin indicated with a stern nod that he could take the boards from it – and then, remembering the broken trap below the boards, in his old hiding place, sought permission to drag it up and put it to better use. As word spread about his quest among the crew, more offerings came – an old broken chest, a pail that had rotted through, a couple of warped spear shafts, an oar that had split its blade and been sitting below deck ever since. Up in the bow, Atli had seen a choice piece – a big, roughly conical chunk of oak, about the length of his forearm, tucked into a gap at the edge of the planking, beneath the prow. He had pulled it out and was about to add it to his hoard when he saw Magnus shaking his head discreetly.

"That's part of the ship," the old man whispered.

Atli returned it without a word.

# CHAPTER ELEVEN

## A GRIM CATCH

By the time he was done ferrying his spoils to the fireside, Atli had fuel enough to last a night and a day at least, and plenty of work for his axe. Breaking up the wood proved an arduous task, but it was one that his mind and body welcomed; his limbs ached with it, but it was a good ache. He felt somehow connected. Focused. Useful. Before he realised where it had come from, a saying of his father's drifted into his head: "Good firewood heats you up twice – once when you chop it and again when you burn it!" Atli attacked the wood harder and tried to shake the memory from his head.

He had saved until last what he knew would be the most difficult – the tough, thick wood of the broken oar – and had only just begun the painstaking task of chopping it into usable lengths when a sudden movement nearby caught his eye. For nearly the whole time he had been working, Finn had been sitting practically motionless astride his sea-chest, chewing silently on a strip of dark, unidentifiable dried meat, the taut fishing line that stretched over the gunwale tied to the nearest of the three upright bird-perch-posts behind him. Some time ago, he had removed his right boot, and for the past hour had sat with his bare right foot propped up on the long chest, and the line between his toes, waiting, Atli supposed, for the twitch of a fish. Now, something had Finn's full attention. He was sitting bolt upright, his mouth stopped mid-chew. For a moment he remained utterly frozen, his gaze focused somewhere out there, where the line met the sea. Then, never once taking his eyes off the line, he eased his foot off the chest, stood up and carefully replaced his boot. Atli saw the line slacken for a moment, then suddenly tighten again. Finn gave it a gentle pull. It responded, pulling so tight, so fast, it reverberated like a bow-string.

"Something here…" he called, still chewing. Close by, two other men – Thorvald, and the one called Njáll Red-Hair – stood; a third – Eyvind – abandoned the tub of water in which he was meticulously washing his neck and shoulders and moved to join him.

"It's big," said Finn.

Eyvind tested the tension of the line. "Cod, maybe. Good eating. I've seen them as big as deer."

"Bigger," said Finn.

Eyvind laughed. "It's not a fishing contest, north-man!"

Finn's eyes remained fixed on the point where the line disappeared below the surface of the water, a frown creasing his heavy brow. Reaching down, he flipped open his sea-chest, dug out a pair of tough, reindeer skin gloves and pulled them on. "Not fish," he said.

Eyvind chuckled again. Thorvald and Njáll looked at each other in bemusement.

"Well, what else is it going to be out here?" asked Eyvind, spreading his arms wide and surveying the blank desolation that surrounded them. "Sea serpent?"

Finn said nothing.

"Whale?" muttered Thorvald, squinting at the slowly heaving sea, trying to penetrate the thick fog.

"Seal maybe?" ventured Njáll.

"Not seal. Or whale," said Finn. Then, after a pause, added: "Nothing I know."

Thorvald and Njáll exchanged anxious looks. "But there's nothing in the sea you don't know," said Thorvald.

"Something different here."

By now, the small knot of men had attracted Bjólf's attention. "If it takes four of you to haul it in," he said, approaching them, "I'd be more worried about it eating us." But the looks on the faces of Thorvald, Njáll and Finn immediately killed the humour in his voice. "What is it?"

"Something out there," said Finn, nodding towards the black waves.

Bjólf frowned deeply.

"Before you ask," said Njáll, "he doesn't know what." Bjólf looked uneasy at his words.

"Well, let's just wind it in and have a look," said Eyvind matter-of-factly. He picked up the winding frame, and, leaning forward, went to hook it into the line, but, at that moment, as if responding to his words, it fell slack at his feet. Eyvind tugged on it gingerly, and met no resistance. He pulled harder. It kept coming.

"So much for your prize cod!" said Eyvind. "That'll be more hooks lost." And, taking up the limp line he started swiftly reeling it in by hand, letting it fall in a wet heap at his feet. "Just got caught on something, that's all. Some old bit of flotsam or..."

Before he could finish the sentence, the line whipped through his hands with such speed it sent a mist of salt spray into the air. Eyvind howled in agony as the line sliced through the flesh of his palms. As it snapped taut, his body jerked violently forward and he collapsed to his knees, blood coursing from his right hand, the trembling arm stretched out awkwardly before him in a curious, twisted gesture. For a moment, the stunned onlookers struggled to make sense of what had just happened. Then it became clear. Without thinking, Eyvind had wound part of the line around his right hand; now, pulled tight, hauled seaward by whatever lay below the surface, it had him caught like a rabbit in a wire trap, suspended between post and gunwale, cutting him to the bone. If the line were to break now on the seaward side, he would be saved, but if it snapped behind him, he would either he dragged into the sea or have the flesh stripped from his hand. Finn was the first to act, flying past Eyvind, grabbing the line with his gloved hands and pulling with all his strength, his feet braced against the gunwale. The line slackened. Eyvind fell back. Thorvald and Njáll leapt forward in an effort to free him, desperately trying to untangle the line from the afflicted hand.

"Cut the line!" called Bjólf. Thorvald pulled his knife, but before he could act the line whipped through Finn's gloved grasp, sending the smell of salt and burning hide into the air as it snapped taut again and sent Thorvald's blade flying. Eyvind fell forward once more, screaming with the pain like a trapped animal, desperately trying to pull with his free hand as Finn fought to get a grip and, baring his white teeth like an animal, tried to bite through the line.

"Cut it!" bellowed Bjólf, searching urgently for a blade, any blade. The commotion had caught the attention of the entire crew now.

Atli, stunned and horrified by what had occurred in the past few seconds, stood helpless. Only when Bjólf called out for the second time did he realise that he alone, of all those within reach, had within his grasp the means of Eyvind's salvation. The axe hung idly in his hand. With everything seeming to slow as if in a dream, he stepped forward, and raised his axe.

Without warning, as if a spell were suddenly broken, Eyvind and Finn fell back with a crash onto the blood-soaked deck. The loosed line whipped backwards over the gunwale, and something – still attached to its end – flew from the water, arced high in the air with a trail of salt spray, and landed with a wet thud on the deck next to them.

Atli glanced at the axe – still in his raised right hand – then, in the moment of stunned silence that followed, at the dumfounded faces of the crew. Bjólf stared at the thing on the deck, a look of disbelief on his face. Behind him, Gunnar looked on, his characteristically stern features now fixed in an expression of horror. Njáll took a step back. On the deck, Eyvind, nursing his hand, shuddered, and scrabbled to get away from it.

Atli looked. At first, he struggled to make sense of the weird, white shape in the gloom. It was like no fish he had ever seen, and certainly did not seem large enough to have put up such a struggle. Then his reeling brain saw it for what it was. The hand and forearm of a man – or what had once been a man – its grey flesh bloodless and nibbled by fish, its skin bleached by the sea and barely covering the extent of bone and wasted muscle beneath, its elbow ragged with gristle and tendon as if freshly wrenched from its joint. Wrapped around its length was the remainder of the tangled, hooked fishing line.

The first wave of recognition was followed by another, but

of a worse kind. With all that had happened, Atli had had little trouble consigning the ghoulish apparition in the water to a place somewhere in his imagination, a place of safety. But now, he knew for certain it was real. It was out in the world – here, on the ship, amongst them.

Bjólf pushed past Thorvald and Njáll and knelt over it. "Give me the axe, boy."

Atli passed the weapon haft-first over their grisly catch, never once taking his eyes off it, then hopped back again, putting as much distance between him and it as honour would allow. Bjólf prodded the skeletal limb, turning it over slowly. A length of limp, green weed entwined its white, bony fingers, now curled skyward like the legs of an upturned crab. A putrid smell rose from it. Around its wrist, Bjólf now noticed, was a twisted bracelet, tarnished green at the ends, its plaited strands coloured black and red.

"Gunnar?" called Bjólf. The big man stepped forward. Bjólf looked at the axe for a moment, turning it around in his hand. "The former owner of this... he left something else behind. What did you do with it?"

"Over the side. Back in the estuary."

"Could this be it?" Bjólf prodded the forearm again.

Gunnar shook his head. "It is... different. This one, there's more of it. And anyway, this has been in the water longer."

Bjólf nodded. "A drowned sailor then? The rest of him down there somewhere?"

"Must be."

"A drowned sailor who pulls," growled a voice. It was Finn. "I felt that line. The dead do not fight back." A few of the men muttered, unsettled at his words.

"This is bad," said Úlf, shaking his head. "The raid. That madman at the village. Steinarr. Hallgeir. Kjötvi... And now this."

"Enough!" Snapped Bjólf, rising to his feet. "We've all seen dead flesh before. Enough to know we should thank our lucky stars we're better off than this wretch." He gave the limb a kick. "He's half eaten by fish. That's what pulled at your line."

Several among the crew nodded or exclaimed in agreement as he spoke, some nudging the more superstitious among them. But, in the very next moment, a gasp came from all their throats. Expressions fell in horror.

Bjólf followed their gaze, and recoiled. The thing on the deck was moving.

Its fingers twitched, writhed, then slowly curled into the palm, its forefinger last to join its fellows, as if beckoning to all those who beheld it. Atli backed away involuntarily, suddenly aware, once again, of the angry scratches upon his calf.

Bjólf raised the axe and brought it down hard, cutting the line. Without a word, he picked up the limb and hurled it out to sea.

"Haul in all the lines," he said, his face and voice grim. "Let's eat."

# CHAPTER TWELVE

## THE CORPSE-PICKER

IT WAS NOT long before Fjölvar was serving up steaming portions of fish stew from the cauldron over Atli's fire. The catch had been fair. The fish was sweet and tender, some barley meal and dried cod had gone into the pot to add substance, and Fjölvar had even managed to rescue enough of the onions to give flavour to the broth. And, most of all, it was hot. Atli had lapped it up hungrily, burning his mouth in the process, but unable, for the moment, to think of anything else. Magnus, meanwhile, had succeeded in spooning some of the hot liquid between Kjötvi's lips, and the stricken man was soon eating as hungrily as his fellows, miraculously returned to life by the brew. Eyvind's wound had been bound, and by great good fortune he had escaped permanent damage. He would be left-handed for a while, but it would heal, and he would still have the use of his fingers. Only Gunnar had had the nerve to grumble.

"Needs salt," he'd said.

Thorvald laughed and gestured to the surrounding sea. "Help yourself!"

Gunnar gazed out at the dark water that hid the rotting, drifting remains of their mysterious visitor, then back at his fish. He said nothing. Despite the welcome luxury of a hot meal, there were few among them who, while swallowing the white flesh, had not thought of the pallid corpse that, until recently, had shared the same domain as their dinner.

After that, the atmosphere remained subdued. The fog hung about them still, like a thick, blank shroud; a physical manifestation of the depressed mood. The ship heaved slowly on the swell as if rocked by an invisible hand. A fine rain fell for a while, and there was not a single one among them who did not yearn for dry land beneath his feet. Men exchanged short words now and then as necessity required, but otherwise kept their thoughts to themselves. No one spoke further of the thing in the sea.

Atli ran his fingers gently over the weals on his leg and thought over and over of the ghoulish nightmare that he now knew lay somewhere beneath them. Not far away, Bjólf sat hunched against the gunwale, a thick sheepskin around his shoulders, his head bowed in dark meditation. Atli wanted to go to his captain and tell him that he had seen it, that it had been real. But he did not have the nerve to penetrate the heavy silence that had descended. Instead, he concentrated on keeping his wood store dry, and feeding up the cheering, crackling flames.

His mind began to drift. Already drowsy from the meal and the glow of the fire, wrapped in a damp but warm woollen cape – another posthumous donation from Steinarr – he allowed his lids to droop and close. The minute he did so, exhaustion washed over him. He tried to fight it, forcing his eyes open, telling himself of his responsibility to ship and fire. But again his lids became heavy, sinking once, twice... The third time, he gave in to it. *Just for a moment,* he told himself. *Just a few more seconds...*

Immediately, fevered images began to swim through his tired brain – images of the thing in the water – lifeless but moving, suspended in icy darkness beneath the hull, grasping at him. In a world somewhere between nightmare and daydream, he imagined it clawing its way up the side of the ship, its sodden, ragged, wrecked form slithering and rattling over the gunwale and onto the deck, squirming in the wet like some ghastly newborn, then tottering unsteadily to its feet, staggering towards him while the crew slept on, oblivious.

Sounds came to him too. Somewhere between asleep and awake, beyond the lapping water and the creaking of the timbers, he thought he detected another sound. Like something scratching slowly, repeatedly against the hull. Like nails dragged against wood.

A sudden movement nearby shocked him awake. He looked around, dazed, unsure how long he had slept. The fog had thinned considerably. The fire was low, its light barely penetrating the gloom. He tucked some kindling into the embers and, as it began to catch, threw on a few more chunks of wood. As he did so, he heard a movement behind him. A strange kind of movement – the same, he now understood, as the one that had jolted him awake. It was a sort of shuffling, flapping sound, something at once utterly alien, and yet uncannily familiar. It sent chills through him. For a moment, he did not dare move. Then came a horrible exclamation, something between terror and disgust. He whirled around. A pale face hovered in the dark extremity of the prow. Near it, an unidentifiable black shape flopped and scratched. For a moment, Atli's eyes – fresh from the fire – struggled to adjust to the shadows.

Then he saw it.

Kjötvi, his face as white as a ghost, his eyes wide as shield-bosses, was staring in horror at a big, black shape that was pulling at his leg. His bandages lay unravelled and strewn about the deck, and a great bird – black as soot and big as a cat – was holding a red, wet length of... something... in its beak, something that was still attached to Kjötvi's calf. It was the flap of flesh that the axe had failed to remove, far too great a prize for a meat-hungry raven to leave behind. It yanked at it repeatedly, each time eliciting a stronger cry of pain and revulsion from its victim, while Kjötvi swiped at the creature weakly, as if trying to swat a gigantic fly.

By now, Bjólf and several of the crew were on their feet, the growing flames of the fire illuminating the bizarre scene, shadows flickering and dancing like ghosts against the timbers of the bow. Fjölvar had strung his bow and already had an arrow upon it, the bird in his sights.

"No!" said Bjólf, shoving Fjölvar's arm roughly aside. The arrow loosed, hissing over Atli's head and disappearing far out into the foggy ocean. Fjölvar glared at Bjólf with a mixture of anger and shock – then suddenly understood. No one moved.

The raven hopped and loped and flapped about, clinging doggedly to the precious bit of meat, the blue-black sheen of its feathers reflecting the flickering light of the fire. Kjötvi, wide awake now, kicked at it desperately with his good leg, looking to his shipmates for aid, not understanding why it would not come.

"To oars!" whispered Bjólf, not once taking his eyes off the black, ravenous creature. "Quickly."

The bird momentarily lost its hold, then flapped and jumped as Kjötvi's foot tried to connect with it again, its hunched form croaking angrily at him. He flailed again and missed – then, seeing another opportunity, it darted back in. It snapped and pulled. Kjötvi cried out. Then again. The creature suddenly tottered backwards and flapped off, up onto the figurehead where it perched victoriously, teetering against the swell, a glistening red strip of Kjötvi's leg in its bloody beak.

The crew, meanwhile, had snapped into action, swiftly deploying the stacked oars. The tips of the port set, Atli now saw, were painted red, the starboard oars tipped with yellow, and each one – slightly different in length from its neighbour to compensate for the curve of the ship – carved with one of sixteen runes to indicate its position. Within seconds, the oars were out over the water, the crew ready.

Bjólf, surveying the scene with growing satisfaction, and turning back to the prow, ran suddenly at it, clapping his hands noisily. "*Hyah! Hyah! Hyah!*" The raven took off and swooped ahead and to port, while Bjólf leapt past Kjötvi, up into the ship's prow and pointed triumphantly after the flapping black shape. "Follow *him!*"

The ship lurched forward as Gunnar called the strokes, Thorvald at the helm guiding the ship along the raven's path. Bjólf noted with satisfaction the faint glow of dawn on the horizon, off the starboard bow.

"I didn't feel it," gibbered Kjötvi, looking up at Bjólf. "I didn't feel it. I just woke up and it was there..."

"We're just glad to see you alive again," laughed Bjólf.

Kjötvi shuddered as Magnus set about binding his wound again. "It's not right, to still be alive and to have part of you pass through a raven!" He looked at his leg. "I'll never get that back!"

"Your sacrifice was not in vain, my friend," said Magnus.

"You saved us," said Bjólf, beaming. "Trust Kjötvi to find the way!"

The raven, much faster than its sea-going namesake, soon disappeared from sight. But such birds would not stray far from land, and now they had a bearing from the distant glimmer of the sun too. Nevertheless, a tense silence fell as Bjólf stared intently into the eerily glowing fog, trying to read shapes within it. For the space of about sixty strokes, nothing appeared. Then, quite suddenly, a half imagined band of dark, ragged forms emerged dead ahead. Rocks. Grey cliffs. A coastline.

The cliffs were precipitous and inaccessible, but, to port, were broken by a wide, sheer-sided inlet.

"There!" called Bjólf. The oars pulled in steady rhythm. Thorvald heaved on the creaking rudder.

Leaping down from his vantage point, Bjólf bounded past Atli, then snatched up a pail and hurled its contents over the fire, extinguishing it immediately. A hiss of steam shot up as the water hit hot metal. Atli stared at the sodden ruins in utter disbelief, the wreck of the fire that he had nursed through the night.

"Wh-why did you...?" he stammered, wide-eyed.

"We don't want to announce ourselves until we're ready," said Bjólf, weaving his way back towards the stern. "Don't look so downcast, little man," he called as he went. "The long night is over. And tonight we eat and sleep on land!"

As one, the men cheered, relieved that the worst of this ill-fated raiding trip – and the dark matter of the previous night – was at last safely behind them.

# PART TWO

*DRAUGR*

# INTERLUDE

THE RELENTLESS SUN beat upon Bjólf's back, making his tunic sticky with sweat. It was low in the evening sky now, but still ferocious. In the three weeks that had passed since embarking on their southward journey the heat had been steadily increasing, and the past few days had been the hottest he had ever known in his short life. Like standing over a forge night and day, his uncle Olaf said. Bjarki, Olaf's trusted *skipari*, claimed that further south the sun was fiercer still. He had seen lands where everywhere the soil had turned to dust, where there was no rain and not a single leaf of green. How people lived in such conditions, Bjólf could not imagine.

The voyage had been hard. By the end of the previous week the sun had burned Bjólf's skin raw, and the wind had rubbed the salt spray into the worst afflicted parts of his face, leaving his lips cracked and blistered. He was healing now – his skin unevenly brown and peeling – but for a while had been delirious with it, feeling as if his skin were on fire. One night, just as Bjólf's fever was hitting its peak, they had put ashore at a small, dusty port where the houses appeared to have grown out of the dry earth like anthills and the bustling throngs of merchants seemed to be perpetually shouting; words that were harsh and alien to his ears. He remembered the sights, sounds and smells like disconnected images from a dream: dark faces lit by the flicker of firelight; cries in a dozen unknown tongues; the smell of hot coals, raw fish, stale sweat, fresh garlic, spices and vinegar; drums and wailing pipes and voices raised in song. He remembered strange loping creatures that snorted and stamped and dropped their dung, or capered and flapped at the end of a chain: a dwarf-like creature covered in hair with arms and hands and a face like a shrivelled man; a squawking bird that spoke whole words, all colours of the rainbow; a black bat hanging from a perch, as big as a seagull. His uncle bought him wine, some skewered, charcoal-grilled meat, and black berries that looked to Bjólf like the small plums his mother used to gather, but which were hard and oily and bitter-tasting. The wine – his first taste of this great, southern luxury – was good, and he wolfed the food down, ravenously hungry, but nonetheless also strangely disconnected, and no longer entirely able to tell what was real, and what the creation of his fevered imagination. He had lain awake all night, sweating and shivering and drifting in and out of maddening, repetitive dreams, desperate for the clear, cool air of the open sea.

Now that the fever was past, the burning flesh calmed, he stood at the prow of the ship under full sail, feeling the cooling air and the fine salt spray on his skin, able at last to appreciate the beauty of this ocean that held such a fascination for his otherwise unsentimental uncle. In these waters, it seemed, one barely had to lower a net into the waves for it to be blessed with creatures that made good eating, and never had the sea and sky seemed so blue, nor the shore glowed with such colours as they did in these long, late evenings. At moments like this, even the crushing heat did not seem so bad.

But there was another, deeper kind of contentment. Although his frame had yet to fill out with muscle, Bjólf was tall and broad for his thirteen winters, at least on a par with the shorter members of the *Hrafn*'s seasoned crew – none of that stopped jibes about his size, of course. But, as he stood shoulder to shoulder with Svein, on watch at the bow, he felt that he had grown in other, more important ways upon this journey. Ways that could not be mapped or measured.

Yet, despite everything that had happened to him, there was one more experience, one more milestone that this trip had to offer. It was something that he had long known would come, but he anticipated it with increasing dread.

"Sail!" called Svein, snapping Bjólf out of his reverie. Olaf stepped up to the prow and curled a hand around his right eye.

Bjólf looked. At first, he could not be sure what he was looking at – just a flash of brilliant white in the far distance off the port bow – but as his eyes found their range, the dark smudge beneath resolved into a distinct shape. As they cut through the waves in their steady advance he could make out a vessel; compact, with one – no, two – square, white sails. It bobbed in the water, apparently without direction, both sails flying in the wind.

He saw his uncle's face crease into a frown as he squinted at the horizon.

"What're they playing at?" muttered Bjarki behind his shoulder.

Even with his limited experience, Bjólf could tell something was wrong. He could see now that one of the sails was only partially secured, flapping limply at one of its corners in the steady breeze; the other had seemingly come completely adrift of its sheets and billowed uselessly from the yard, occasionally catching the sun as it did so.

"Who are they?" asked Bjólf.

"Arab traders," said Bjarki. "From the East." He nodded directly ahead.

Bjólf could now just make out figures on the deck – dark-skinned faces and arms, heads and bodies garbed in white – waving in their direction.

"Arab traders in trouble," snorted Svein, dismissively. "Either their fathers never taught them how to sail, or they have worse problems on board."

Distant raised voices now carried across the water as the westerly wind ebbed. Although Bjólf could make out none of the words, there was no doubting the tone. They were cries for help.

"What do you think?" said Svein.

"Attacked, maybe," ventured Bjarki.

Olaf narrowed his eyes, rubbed his thick beard and gave a grunt. "That's what they want us to believe."

Bjólf frowned at his uncle. Olaf seemed to sense his question without once taking his eyes off the horizon.

"They're no merchants," he muttered.

"Who then?"

"Pirates."

Svein nodded. "A trap." Without a word, he reached down beside his sea-chest and began to strap on his sword. Olaf gave a curt nod to Bjarki, who turned and gave a shrill whistle towards the helm. The tanned and weather-beaten faces of the crew looked up to see him make a concise gesture – a single slap of his clenched fist against a flattened palm. It was a signal Bjólf had seen only twice before, when arming for a raid. There was a creak deep in the timbers of the ship as it changed course directly for the Arab vessel. Olaf made a sudden turn and headed back along the length of the ship.

"But, how can you be sure?" said Bjólf, hurrying after.

"If they'd been attacked, they'd be dead. But since they have a good many able-bodied men on board, alive and well, one has to ask how they got this far if they can't even secure a line."

Bjólf, alarmed, gawped at his uncle and then towards the nearing vessel. "They intend to trap... *us?*"

Olaf gave a deep, rumbling laugh. "No! They don't intend that." He stopped and stared back at the other ship for a moment. "They don't yet realise what we are."

His uncle gave another hoarse grunt, then resumed his purposeful march.

"The sun is behind us," he continued, stopping at the place where his sea-chest stood. "They see only a silhouette of a square sail. They assume we are a trading ship returning to the East – exactly what they are pretending to be." He hauled out his coat of mail "Fully laden. Easy prey, especially when coming to the aid of another we believe to be in distress."

"So, what do we do?"

Olaf shrugged matter-of-factly. "We go to their aid." He flipped the mail coat over his head, shook it down over his huge body and began strapping his wide belt around it. "No reason to disappoint them." In a few swift moves he had slung his sword over his shoulder and tucked his axe into his belt. All around, without a word, men were doing the same, checking blades, passing out shields and tightening helmet straps. "Better arm yourself, little man," said Olaf. And with that, he took up his battered helm and headed back towards the prow.

Bjólf hastily grabbed his weapons and scurried after, struggling with belts and straps as he went. He recalled the words of his uncle a few days before, when they had first entered these calm, blue waters: "Take care," he had said. "Our people inflicted great damage upon these regions in past years, and some hereabouts have long memories."

"But... What happens when they realise who we are?" Bjólf called nervously. Olaf stopped next to Svein at the prow.

"They just have..." said Svein.

Bjólf looked again towards the Arab ship. The urgent babble of voices was clear now, but the pattern of movement on board had entirely changed. Instead of waving in distress, their attention had now turned inward. One of the sails had already been secured, and the rest dashed about in a bustle of frantic activity, some shouting impatiently at each other. Just one man – their lookout – was completely motionless; a strange, still point amidst the mayhem, staring silently back at them. Bjólf could just begin to make out his features. It seemed to him the man wore an expression of barely concealed horror.

"Hoy!" called Olaf, standing high on the prow. Despite the Arabs' haste in securing the other sail, it was clear the longship would be upon them before they could get underway. Some turned and began more wild gesticulations. Voices called out urgently. Olaf's booming voice answered in what, to Bjólf, seemed disconcertingly friendly tones.

"What's going on?" he asked. He thought he had caught odd words – it was not the Latin his uncle was teaching him, but the Byzantine Greek that was spoken so widely in this region.

"They are saying there is plague of some sort on board, that we should stay away," said Svein.

"Then, should we not just go around?" said Bjólf. Svein said nothing.

There was barely any distance between the two vessels now. Olaf called out again, even more cheerily this time. Svein chuckled at his words. "Now he's saying we have many healers on board, who can release a man from his sickness."

"Do we?" said Bjólf, bemused.

"Oh, yes," said Svein. "Though it may not be quite the release they are after."

Bjólf frowned. But before he had a chance to even ask the inevitable question, Svein had drawn his sword.

"Better get ready," he said, bracing himself against the gunwale.

With that, the helmsman leaned hard on the rudder, bringing her right alongside the Arab ship. The crewmen on the halyards dropped the yard, several more on the deck reefed the sail in one rapid, fluid motion, and the hull of the dragon ship butted violently against the Arab's bow. As it did so, to Bjólf's utter amazement, Olaf launched himself from the gunwale and landed heavily with both feet upon the enemy deck. A space instantly cleared around him, like a stone dropped among swarming ants. For a moment the man stood, regarding them in silence on the swaying deck, towering over all around by at least a forearm's length. Bjólf could make out their faces now – gnarled and seasoned, much like Olaf's crew, but with skin of every hue from the palest brown to the darkest black – what some of the older Norse crewmen referred to as 'blue men.' Among them were expressions ranging from nervous dread to simmering defiance. One stepped forward, speaking rapidly, and, Bjólf thought, with barely contained agitation, despite a fixed smile, gesturing repeatedly at something on deck, something Bjólf could not see.

"They are telling him to return to his ship, that it is too late for healing," said Svein. Then, craning his neck, added: "It appears the Nubian fellow at their feet is already dead."

Bjólf raised himself as far as he dared, high enough to glimpse a long body in robes of white and tan, stretched out and motionless on the Arab's deck, the dark skin of his face tinged with a deathly, ashen pallor. But already hooks had been thrown over the side of the Arab ship, pulling it tight alongside, and other members of Olaf's crew were now clambering over, while Olaf himself continued to smile at the increasingly nervous Arab sailors.

"Stay close, young cub," said Svein. "I promised your uncle I would keep you alive." And with that, he too slipped over the side. Bjólf followed, his hand on the old sword his uncle had given him and which, as yet, had not shed blood, his eyes nervously scanning the rows of faces that greeted them. Their fingers twitched towards weapons, their tense bodies edging back and forth, keeping their distance from the silently invading Northmen.

Bjólf felt his knees shake. Cold beads of sweat trickled down his sides. Now, with his ship behind him and his feet on this unknown vessel, he had never felt so exposed. He wished to turn – to check his ship was still there, at least – but did not dare.

Looking around slowly, still smiling, Olaf picked up a pail from the deck, and took two steps toward the dead Nubian, ignoring the shouts of the Arabs' leader. Others inched away at his approach. Then, as he looked back at the dead man, Bjólf happened to notice that the deathly pallor of his face was entirely absent from his hands. Finally, he understood, and knew for certain what was to come.

"Time for the cure," muttered Svein. Olaf hurled the contents of the bucket over the Nubian's face. The man roared and leapt to his feet in a fury, easily matching Olaf for height, shaking his head violently, white powder running off his face, his gold-ringed hand grasping a huge curved sword that had been concealed beneath his body. Eyes blazing, he lunged forward, and as one the Arab crew flew at the invaders.

Several fell in that first moment. Less armoured than their Norse opponents, with no helms upon their heads, a few among the Arab pirates succumbed immediately to well-aimed blows. A single strike of a sword or axe to the head was usually enough to settle the matter, but many of the viking's body blows were turned by concealed armour. The fighting that followed was intense and bitter. For Bjólf, it lived as a confused memory, the details of which were fractured and blurred. He remembered men wrestling for their lives all around him, falling in spilt blood, the white robes stained red. He saw Olaf dispatch one with a swing of his axe, catching the small wiry man with the flat of the blade against the side of his head with a sickening crunch and propelling him clean overboard. Near Olaf's feet was the big Nubian, motionless, blood on his head. Then Bjólf was buffeted by something – other men, struggling in each other's grips – throwing him off his feet and knocking the wind out of him. Someone stepped on his left hand with all his weight. He felt a bone crack. Through the pain, he recovered his senses and looked up to see the Nubian, somehow up again and almost upon him, staggering, his blade raised. As it swung wildly at him, Bjólf scrabbled desperately backwards. Something caught his forehead a glancing blow. He crumpled, his head swimming. Afterwards, he remembered being suddenly on his feet again – how, he had no idea. There was a ringing in his head, and he was blinded in his left eye, but he was up, alive and alert, his sword still in his hand. The chaos continued all around, and the Nubian swung at him again. Having no shield, Bjólf parried with his sword. The two blades met with a jarring crash, sending both singing out of the their owners' hands to clatter on the wooden deck. Bjólf staggered back as the Nubian went at him again, hands reaching out towards him, grabbing his throat. He could smell the man's sweat. To his left, he was dimly aware of Svein, sword drawn, trying to fight his way towards them, but suddenly blocked by a small man with a halberd, screaming at the top of his lungs. No help was coming. Without thinking, Bjólf unsheathed his knife and lashed out blindly. The Nubian's eyes suddenly widened, his grip on the boy's windpipe loosened, and with a horrible, rattling groan he slid to the floor, taking Bjólf's knife with him, stuck fast between his ribs. Bjólf stared into the man's face as he gasped his last breath, the life leaving his eyes.

In minutes it was over. Every Arab pirate was dead. The deck swam with blood. In a daze, Bjólf watched it wash back and forth with the roll of the ship. He felt the gash on his left brow from the tip of the Nubian's sword, realising now that it was only the blood in his eye blinding him. A lucky escape. Olaf's men relieved the hold of its plunder, which was considerable. His own crew had got away with only minor injuries. Tonight, they would celebrate. Bjólf would be singled out for special treatment; he had made his first kill. And he was alive. They would drink mead, and sing songs, and make oaths. Olaf would honour him with a new sword – the sword once meant for the son he never had.

The memory faded, but some things remained. Through the middle of Bjólf's left brow there would now always be an angled scar where no hair grew. His right hand would ache in cold weather. And for years he would dream of the face of that Nubian, rising from the dead to kill him.

# CHAPTER THIRTEEN

## THE GREY LAND

As THE SUN rose, the *Hrafn* made its slow, steady progress inland, a half-crew keeping a slow stroke on the oars. The grey walls of the deep fjord towered above them on either side, shrouding them in shadow, and, despite what the raven had promised, offering no place to make a landing, and precious few signs of life. Save for some smears of slimy green algae close to the water's edge, no growing thing seemed to have gained a foothold on the steep, forbidding crags. Occasionally, a large bird flapped and cried out at the brow of the cliff, and the eyes of the men flicked nervously upward, scanning its broken edge. Weapons were kept ready for fear of other eyes watching, but mostly it was the unnerving, dead stillness of this place that made them tense, and kept them keen. Even Kjötvi, though still weak, was awake and alert. Then, after a while, just when it seemed the sun might break into the depths of this lifeless chasm, another thick fog rolled in. Different, this time, seeming to come not from the sea, but to creep out from the landward side, to seep out of the rock itself, heavy and tinged with sickly yellow. It clung to their clothes and made all aboard shiver.

For a long time, no one spoke. Only the sound of the oars accompanied their progress. They hugged the shore on the port side, close enough to keep it safely in sight, but just far enough to keep their oar-tips clear of the rocks. The surroundings were beginning to have a strange effect on all aboard, making them sullen and listless. The lack of any other sound save those of the ship itself had a curiously disorientating effect. Bjólf could not even judge the passage of time with any certainty, and found himself counting oar-strokes in an effort to combat the sense of disconnection from the world.

Gradually, the terrain began to change. The cliff wall became less sheer, more broken. Here and there, in the few, tiny bays where life had at some time taken hold, twisted roots wound their way through fissures in the rock. Occasionally, there were spiked, leafless limbs of trees – grey as the stone to which they clung – that reached out and trailed the tips of their warped, gaunt branches in the water, some choked with the sinewy remains of old, colourless ivy. At the port bow, Bjólf scanned the forbidding land for even the slightest offer of a place to make landfall. But everywhere the cliff was too sheer, the rocks too treacherous. He heard a grunt at his shoulder.

"This is bad," said Gunnar, speaking in a whisper.

"We'll find a place," said Bjólf. "It's just a matter of time."

Gunnar shuddered. "You follow a raven, you should not be surprised that he leads you to a land of the dead."

"That bird saved our skins, Gunnar." He turned to his old friend, frowning. "What's wrong with you?"

Gunnar could not place the feeling. He shrugged. "Maybe it was a bad omen. Coming from nowhere, out of that fog."

Bjólf sighed. "Gunnar, this ship is called 'Raven.' We have a raven on our sail. The weather vane atop our mast is shaped like a raven's wing. If you're really so superstitious about that particular bird, you joined the wrong ship."

"They're different! We all know what the raven is. A Corpse-Picker. A Death-Follower. And he doesn't just follow death; he casts death's shadow. It's no coincidence the All-Father has them in his service." Gunnar pointed discretely towards the heavens once more as he spoke, as if afraid someone out there might notice."

Bjólf laughed. "Gunnar, I can't believe the Old One sends his personal ravens to earth just so they can have a peck at Kjötvi's leg."

"Ah, you're mocking me!" barked Gunnar. "You don't know what schemes are being played out, what fates we may have spun for us." He shook his head in dismay. "You never did have respect for the old religion."

"What faith I have is in these two hands," said Bjólf irritably, raising them before Gunnar's glowering brow. "And I have no time for omens." He turned them, then, in a conciliatory gesture. "I've no greater respect for any man, Gunnar. You know that. But... It's just a bird."

"It's not *just* –" began Gunnar, but thought better of it. He had never won this argument, and never would. "I'm just saying. One should not tempt fate."

"Fate will come whether I tempt it or not," said Bjólf, his voice as hard as steel. Gunnar kept silent. Upon this one point, at least, both could agree. Bjólf thought for a moment, then added: "Anyway, it was a crow."

Gunnar growled, doggedly refusing to crack his face at the joke.

"Hoy!" hissed a voice.

In his position high on the prow, Fjölvar was pointing up ahead. As Bjólf peered into the murk, he could just make out the beginning of a long bend in the waterway off to the starboard side, and with it another change in the landscape. The sheer cliffs – whose dominance had evidently been diminishing for some time behind the fog – were finally giving way to a gentler shore, the dead rock to ever more thickly tangled forest, whose boughs and thickets overflowed and tumbled into the water. Up ahead, the overhanging foliage – as dense as Bjólf had ever seen – still presented an impenetrable barrier to their landing. Yet here and there, where the knots of vegetation occasionally thinned, there were glimpses of a swampy land beyond, bringing the hope that landfall could not be far away.

"There!" said Fjölvar. His eyes were sharper than most, but finally Bjólf saw it: a tiny sheltered bay, little more than the length of their ship, where the small closely-knit trees stood back a little from the water's edge and presented a thumbnail of solid ground – albeit covered in thick tangles of bramble, hawthorn and mossy roots. At the nearest end, half in the water, was a huge boulder that seemed to bear no relation to its surroundings, as if dropped there by a passing giant. Bjólf gave the signal to Úlf, at the helm, to take them in.

"This forest is old as the hills," he said to Gunnar. "Must be teeming with game."

"I'd feel better if I could hear it," said Gunnar, still evidently unnerved. He turned and hauled up a length of rope from the deck, at the end of which was a large iron hook, and slung it over his shoulder. "Nevertheless, I volunteer to go ashore, if only for the forgotten pleasure of relieving myself on dry land."

Úlf steered the ship into the tiny, still cove as Bjólf's crew shipped their oars. Gunnar made ready at the gunwale, and as the hull rasped and crunched against submerged stones and roots, he made a jump for the strip of shore. It was not the most elegant of landings. He came down short, his feet splashing in the filthy, green water hidden beneath the mesh of roots and creepers, then, in trying to step forward to steady himself, snarled his toe in the tangle and pitched forward, landing heavily on his front and barking his shin on a tree root. The crew guffawed.

"Dry land, Gunnar!" called Bjólf.

Gunnar struggled to his feet, hauling the ship's line back over his shoulder and muttering to himself as he fought through the knee-high web of foliage to firmer ground. Finally, he rose up onto what was evidently a solid bank, veined with thick, tuberous roots, made a great show of stamping his feet upon it, then turned and raised his arms in triumph. All aboard the ship gave a cheer.

Suddenly aware of the uncertainty of their surroundings, Bjólf turned and gestured for quiet. The laughter died down, the occasional lingering chuckle echoing away to nothing in the still air. "Now, just get on with it!" he called.


"First things first..." replied Gunnar, throwing the grappling-hook and line on the ground and hitching up his tunic. The foliage steamed as he emptied his aching bladder. "Ah, that's better. You can't beat a good piss in the open air with the earth beneath your feet!" He shuddered as he finished, the muffled sniggers of the men behind him and the splash of his own water before, and another sound caught his attention.

It came from within the trees.

At first, he thought it must be the groan of the ship's timbers, somehow cast ahead of them by the strange nature of this rocky fjord. Then, he heard a distinct movement directly ahead. He stared hard into the dark shadows of the forest, trying to penetrate them, but could see nothing. Fastening his clothes, he stepped forward gingerly, pushing apart the thorny outer branches at the forest's edge.

"Gunnar?" The voice was Bjólf's.

Without looking back, Gunnar raised his hand in acknowledgement, but it was a gesture that also called for silence. If there was game here, he didn't want to scare it off. What he wanted most was to sink his teeth into it. His mouth watered involuntarily at the thought of its succulent flesh. As he took a step forward into the woods themselves, he frowned deeply, his eyes becoming slowly accustomed to the gloom. There was a dead, still atmosphere amongst these trees – like none he had ever encountered – the boughs of the trees, where they were visible at all, covered in clumps of ancient moss, dusty, crumbling layers of lichen and the choking, skeletal remains of old ivy. A sudden, sickening stench of organic decay wafted over him. Some stinking bog in the forest's interior, he supposed. He shuddered again. A twig snapped to his right. Whatever it was, it was near, but the vegetation was so close, so dense and dark, he was barely able to glimpse anything beyond a couple of paces. *Stupid*, he thought. *What can I do about it now, anyway, with no spear and no bow?* He was about to turn back when something big crashed unsteadily through the thicket with a great, unearthly groan, its face suddenly emerging from the mass of thorny suckers and grey leaves, barely an arm's length from his own. Gunnar, who had seen every terrible thing that deprivation and savagery could deliver, reeled in sickened horror at the sight of it, staggering backwards through the bushes and clear out of the woods to the thin, tangled strip of shore.

He had only a fleeting moment to take in what he had seen.

It was the face of a man – or what had once been a man – its skin quite gone, like something flayed alive. But he could hardly believe that what lurched towards him in those woods was actually alive. The veins, sinews and musculature were not only uncovered, but bloodless, misshapen and eaten away like rotten, wasp-gnawed fruit. It was – he could not doubt it, for he had seen enough of them in his life – the face of a long-dead corpse. Beneath it, hung in limp, wet rags, was a body so ravaged that the impression was of a skeleton barely held together by its liquifying gobbets of grey, slimy flesh, its extended right forearm so stripped of meat that he could clearly see between the exposed bones. Yet its hand grasped, its yellowed eyes without lids twitched in their sockets, staring madly at him, and its lipless mouth snapped, the blackened, loose teeth clattering horribly against one another. Gunnar had hesitated just long enough to see it take two quivering steps towards him.

GREETED BY THE comical sight of the big man tottering wildly backwards out of the undergrowth, Bjólf broke into a laugh. "Gunnar?" His old friend stopped dead. Bjólf's smile faded. "Gunnar...?"

"We have to get out of here," said Gunnar in a monotone, then resumed backing away, his eyes fixed on the trees.

"What is it?"

"Something bad here." He was ankle deep in the water now, stumbling against roots.

Bjólf scanned the treeline, but could see nothing.

Gunnar splashed towards the ship and heaved himself up and over the gunwale, his face pale. He spoke in short, urgent bursts. "Some... pestilence... a man. Half dead. More than half..." He fixed Bjólf's eyes with his own. "We have to get out of here."

Bjólf had never seen Gunnar like this. He turned back to the tangled wood, thinking of his crew's desperate need for fresh food and water. "Are you certain?"

"I saw it, this close" said Gunnar, grasping Bjólf's arm. "It was a man. Eaten away. Dead. But alive... I saw it, up close."

Bjólf stared at his friend, then back at the trees.

"I saw it too." The voice came from behind him. It was Atli. So quiet had he been these past few hours that Bjólf had almost forgotten he existed. Now, the eyes of the entire crew were upon the boy. He spoke confidently this time, as if relieved to unburden himself of the matter. "Not here. Back there. In the water. A man. Dead... and alive." Several among the tense crew shifted nervously, recalling the thing pulled up on Finn's line.

Bjólf eyed the lad with a mix of concern and anger. When it came to their survival, he trusted Gunnar beyond all men. But he had no patience for superstitious talk. He gestured towards the blank wall of foliage. "But there's nothing..."

His voice trailed away as a weird, strangled cry – neither human nor animal – rose from the depths of the forest. Then another, off to their left, like the wheezing of broken bellows. The whole crew tensed, hands on their weapons, eyes scanning the trees. A third, baleful groan came – close by, this time. Then the sound of movement in the undergrowth; something moving clumsily, not caring whether it was heard. Not the way any animal moved.

And another, deeper in the trees.

And more, to the other side.

"Get us out of here," said Bjólf.

The men snapped into action, extending the oars and pushing the ship away from the bank – slowly, slowly – all eyes on the dark trees, no sound but the creak of the ship and the unidentified groans echoing in the dead air.

"D'you see them?" Gunnar asked Fjölvar, his eyes frantically searching for signs.

"I see nothing," said Fjölvar. At that, the leaves shook, and something crashed in the thicket. Bjólf's men heaved on the oars to pull them into clear water.

"Let's hope they can't swim, whatever they are," muttered Fjölvar. But there was hardly a man aboard now who was not thinking of that thing in the water.

"The line!" called Thorvald. Bjólf looked. He could just make out the rope Gunnar had abandoned on the shore, its outline snaking through the water from the ship to the forest's edge. It was drawing tighter as they moved. Thorvald, at the port bow, tugged hard upon it, sending a line of spray into the air. "Hook's caught fast on the roots."

Without a word, Gunnar took the coil of rope from him and threw the whole lot overboard. "Go!" he said. A few of the men looked questioningly from Gunnar to Bjólf.

"Do as he says!" barked Bjólf. He gave Atli a hard look as the oarsmen settled into their rhythm, then stalked off towards the stern.

Atli was glad to have said what he did. He felt a closer bond with Gunnar. But he had not liked the look Bjólf had given him. Turning away from the ill-fated shore as Úlf took the ship out at a sharp angle, he looked across the starboard gunwale, into the yellow fog, one arm wrapped around the thick mast.

Then, for the second time in as many days, he saw the towering head of a dragon charging out of the fog towards them, the iron teeth on its prow just moments from biting into their hull.

# CHAPTER FOURTEEN

## THE DRAGON'S TEETH

WITH A DEAFENING crunch the bows of the oncoming craft hammered into the *Hrafn,* striking at an oblique angle just ahead of the steer-board. The battered vessel tipped violently, her starboard side lifting crazily, her port side almost driven below the waterline, the mast whipping through the air as every timber and rivet cracked and groaned in protest. It was only Atli's grip on the mast that saved him from being hurled against the port strakes. The shuddering impact had thrown three of the crew clean off their feet, and as she righted herself, Grimmsson's ship – fully laden, and far heavier than Bjólf's even when empty – ploughed on inexorably, its ironclad, brightly-painted prow raking along the *Hrafn's* side, shearing two oars outright, the splintered shafts flying from the hands of their owners and smashing into the backs of the oarsmen before them, crushing one – Gøtar the Swede – hard against the gunwale. He gave a short, stifled cry as the air was squeezed out of him.

What happened in the next few minutes was to shatter any

remaining illusions Atli may have had about the realities of life among the *vikingr*. Men on both sides scrambled for any weapons that came to hand, while Grimmson's crew – looking every bit as confused by the collision as Bjólf's – reached out to the rival ship, grasping over the gunwale. It was clear to Atli that they intended to board. Then he heard Bjólf, who had been standing at the stern and was one of the closest when the two ships clashed, suddenly roar with terrifying ferocity, flying at the invaders with a huge axe, which he swung in great arcs around his head. The battle-cry set a fighting spirit spreading like fire through the men, and they surged forward to meet their foe. This time, they would not shrink from battle.

It had taken some moments for Bjólf to recover his senses after the shock of the impact. But the instant he understood what had happened, he had thrown himself into the attack. The thoughtful, circumspect man who Atli knew was quite gone. Bjólf launched himself at the first of the invaders – a huge fellow with food in his beard, who was fearlessly straddling the gap between the vessels and already had one foot on the *Hrafn*'s deck. It was a gesture for which the man would pay dearly. Bellowing like thunder, driven by a burning anger, Bjólf swung the axe high above his head and brought it down with every ounce of strength, severing the man's leg above the knee and embedding the blade in the boards. Without hesitation, he heaved it free, hefting its bloodstained blade in great wheeling curves, as the man – pale as a ghost – tottered backwards aboard his ship, leaving his leg behind, his face contorted in utter disbelief. Flying so fast at the end of its shaft that the air hummed around him, Bjólf's blade caught another square under the chin, then cut straight through and around to take the head of a third, each exploding in a spray of gore. The head bounced and rolled on the deck, leaving a crimson trail in its wake.

The rest of Bjólf's crew, meanwhile, had not stood idle. They knew well that once aboard, the invaders would have the upper hand, and had grasped anything they could to fend off Grimmsson's men. Led by Gunnar, who had driven his spear into two men before Atli had time blink, and spurred on by the shouts of Godwin the Axeless, a solid row of defenders had formed rapidly along the gunwale where the two ships touched, each one wielding a weapon to keep the attackers at bay: spears, boat-hooks and oars – even an iron anchor, swung wildly by a Norwegian called Háki the Toothless, who struck one man a terrible, crunching blow across the jaw. All these weapons were thrust mercilessly at the enemy crew, inflicting horrible injuries on the invaders. This was no time for chivalry. Behind them a second rank of men had formed; led by the short but formidable figure of Thorvald Two-Axe, who cast colourful insults above the clamour. They armed themselves heavily with helm, shield and blade. Magnus Grey-Beard, meanwhile, scurried the length of the ship, tending wounds as best he could, while Finn and Fjölvar, perched on the prow, picked off the loftier among their opponents with their bows. As the battle raged around him – so close that flecks of the blood of their foes splashed upon his face – Atli stood sweating, rooted to the spot, still hugging the mast and gripping his hand-axe in terror, the shouts of pain and fury ringing in his ears.

In the fight that followed, it was the aggressors' own impatience that proved their greatest downfall. In their hunger to engage the enemy, and with an arrogance known only too well to Bjólf and his men, they had armed themselves for attack, taking up swords and axes: weapons suited to close combat – close combat that they were now denied. They struggled to raise spears, shouting bitter obscenities at their foes. In frustration, some threw axes and clubs, one of which sent Kylfing sprawling on the deck. But the place where the prow of their ship overlapped the *Hrafn* was small, and in their eagerness they had become crammed against their own gunwale, with those behind unable to wield their weapons to any effect, and those in front trapped between their fellows and the vicious, thrusting points of Bjólf's men.

AT THE STERN, finding his opponents' resolve had mysteriously melted away, Bjólf took up the huge, sweaty, severed leg of his first victim by its blood-soaked bindings and heaved it back at his attackers in contempt. It crashed into the chest of a broken-nosed man with a braided beard and then fell at his feet; he staggered unsteadily and promptly vomited over it. Among the attackers, Bjólf realised, a space had cleared where he stood. None now dared to face him, filled with fear at the mere sight of this man, his body bathed in their blood. Up at the prow of the enemy ship, in the midst of the melee, he finally caught sight of Grimmsson. Spying his rival, his sword held aloft, Grimmsson turned and fought to make his way towards him, keen to settle the score, but his own men hemmed him in, he shoved and struck at them in exasperaton.

Bjólf saw his opportunity. Grimmsson's men had not been given the chance to get their hooks into Bjólf's ship, and already the gap near the *Hrafn*'s stern was widening as the two vessels drifted in the current. Grabbing an oar he shoved hard at the hull of Grimmsson's ship. "Come on!" he cried. Several in the second rank of defenders – including Thorvald and Finn – immediately lowered their weapons and took up oars to push.

UNDER THE SUDDEN exertion the ship slid away from the attackers, and as the gap widened, Gunnar and his men joined the effort, planting their oars and spear-shafts against the side of Grimmsson's ship and heaving with everything they had. Grimmsson's crew, furious that their quarry were breaking free, hacked and hammered at them, trying to dislodge the forest of poles that were pushing them apart. But already, in the fore section of the *Hrafn* where there was clear water on both sides, Úlf had hastily mustered the men, and under the power of almost half their oars, they were now pulling steadily away.

At the enraged bellowing of Grimmsson – red-faced and streaked with sweat – part of Grimmsson's crew scrambled to their own oars, while the remainder, fuming and outraged, sent all manner of axes, arrows and other missiles raining down upon the deck – even a boot bounced off the yard. On this occasion, however, his crew – less disciplined than Bjólf's men – were far slower off the mark.

"Give it everything you've got," called Bjólf as they began to pull away from their pursuers. Gunnar heard him muttering under his breath, then he seemed to spy something in the water, and in the next moment was kicking off his shoes and throwing off his bloodstained tunic.

"What is it?" said Gunnar. He scanned the water where Bjólf had been looking, but could see nothing. "This is a Hel of a time to change your clothes..."

Bjólf simply smiled and threw off his shirt.

Gunnar gawped at him. "What in Frigg's name are you doing?"

"Going for a swim," said Bjólf, then added: "Don't wait for me."

Without another word he slid over the port side, hidden from Grimmsson's ship, and disappeared under the water. Dodging down as a fresh volley of arrows hissed past, Gunnar stared after the dwindling trail of bubbles in astonishment.

Grimmsson's crew were getting into their own rhythm now, but already there was a full length of clear water between the vessels, and the *Hrafn* was gathering speed. For what seemed an impossibly long time, an increasingly anxious Gunnar saw no sign of Bjólf. He had no idea what his captain could have in mind. He only hoped it wasn't some stupid, final act of defiance. A hero's death and an eternity in Valhalla were all very well, but on the whole he'd rather that his old friend lived, to drink and laugh and fight another day right here on Earth.

Then he saw him. In a dangerous and unexpected move – to which their pursuers were entirely oblivious – he had emerged right in front of the toothed prow of Grimmsson's ship, and, as it advanced toward him, flung his right arm up and caught hold of the lowest of its iron spikes. For a second he clung there, just above the waterline, a rope held fast between his teeth. Hurriedly, he wrapped the rope around the spike and knotted it tight. And finally Gunnar understood. His eyes at last picked out the slowly tightening line, stretching from the prow of Grimmsson's ship back to the root-snarled shore from which he had only recently fled.

Bjólf waited for the next thrust of the oars and flung himself forward, his powerful arms plunging into the water, legs kicking for all they were worth. Gunnar knew Bjólf was a strong swimmer, and with his first great spurt was even pulling away from their pursuer, but it couldn't last; within a half-dozen strokes they would be upon him.

Bjólf was caught between the two vessels now, his enemy starting its creeping advance toward him with each pull on the oars, his salvation drawing further from reach. A shout went up from Grimmsson's ship. Several arrows zipped through the water, narrowly missing their new target. On the prow Grimmsson himself appeared, and grabbed the bow from the archer there. He wanted this pleasure to himself.

"A line!" called Gunnar. "Get me a line here!"

Eyvind hurried to him, a wet length of rope coiled around his shoulder, which Gunnar grabbed and hurled out into the water as far as it would go, wrapping the rest around his arm and waist. Bjólf spied it as it snaked out from the stern. But, fast as he was, Gunnar could see it would be two or three strokes at least before he would make the rope. And that would be too late. They were picking up rhythm and speed now, bearing down on Bjólf, and by some great effort even gaining on the *Hrafn*. Another arrow flew from Grimmsson's bow and shot into the water a hand-width from Bjólf's head – so close that Gunnar caught his breath.

Then, just moments before the barnacle-crusted keel would have driven over him, the vessel made an inexplicable turn to port. Grimmsson looked around in confusion and alarm as the helmsman fought with the tiller. The line was now pulled tight, the ship's momentum pulling it round in an arc towards the shore. "Hold fast..." muttered Gunnar through clenched teeth, a prayer for the resilience of the rope going out to Thor. "Hold fast..."

It was all Bjólf needed. In the next moment, he grasped the line, wrapping it around his wrist, and Gunnar hauled upon it, and he and Eyvind heaved him up out of the water. "What kept you?" said Gunnar.

Bjólf looked back, just in time to see Grimmsson's ship – nearly broadside-on now – crash into a knot of overhanging branches, both Grimmsson and its prow disappearing into the jumbled, prickly mass as it finally struck the shore and shuddered to a halt.

There was a roar of fury and a final hail of arrows and other missiles, most of which now fell far short. But just when it seemed they were out of range, Oddvarr, who had taken up his oar near the stern and was in the process of cracking a joke at Grimmsson's expense, caught a spear clean through the shoulder. Hurled with what must have been exceptional force, it passed out the other side and stuck in the deck, pinning him in place at his rowing station until Magnus and Eyvind were able to break the shaft and free him.

In response, his eyes blazing with anger, Bjólf picked up by the hair the head of the man he had felled and hurled it with all his strength at the receding vessel. Atli heard it thud sickeningly upon Grimmsson's deck – a grim reminder to all who would seek to take this ship from its captain.

He stood in silence for a moment, dripping on the deck, his lungs aching with the effort. Once again, they had prevailed. But as he and Gunnar watched the other ship melt into the fog, a curious change came over its crew. New cries went up. A kind of panic seemed to take them. And, just before it finally disappeared from view, it appeared to both men that the crew had turned savagely upon each other, as if gripped by a kind of madness.

# CHAPTER FIFTEEN

## WAR TOKENS AND WOLF'S FOOD

"A FAIR FEW rivets rattled loose along the steer-board side," said Úlf, half hidden below the planking. "Caulking's gone in places. We'll need to get some tar on that."

Crouched at the edge of the raised planking, Bjólf looked on anxiously as the big, heavily muscled man – the ship's *filungar*, learned in the ways of ship-building – continued his examination of the hull, ankle-deep in water. Behind him, Grimm the Stout, who fully lived up to his name, and Áki Crow-Foot, a lanky Dane from south of Ribe, bailed water steadily, while all around a three-quarter crew kept up a brisk pace at the rowing benches. Having no replacements for the two lost oars had meant moving one from port to starboard. They would be fine rowing that way for the time being, fifteen oars a side, although Bjólf knew there was not a man aboard who was not praying for a breath of wind.

"The timbers?" he enquired.

Úlf frowned and ran a huge hand along the point of impact. "Ribs and thwarts are sound..." He grunted and nodded to himself. "Top two strakes are cracked, but they will hold."

Bjólf sighed with relief. He was still master of his own vessel, they were not sinking, and compared to the terrible damage inflicted upon their impetuous attackers, their casualties had been light. Bjólf had often had occasion to curse his acute sense of caution – a trait reflected in his crew. But not today.

Úlf stood and slapped the gunwale where Grimmsson's ship had struck. "We picked up a souvenir, though..." Above the water line, projecting through one of the oak strakes and held so tightly by the wood it had completely plugged the hole it made, was the sharp tip of a rough iron spike, snapped off Grimmsson's prow. "He bit off more than he could chew this time!" chuckled Úlf.

"Well, I hope the raven left a bitter taste in his ugly mouth," quipped Grimm, and patted the deck affectionately.

"Was it his intention to ram us, do you suppose?" said Gunnar from the helm.

Bjólf straightened and shook his head, moving to join him. He stared back out into the fog. "If it had been, we would not have got off so lightly. I think they were as lost as we were." He shrugged. "Pure chance."

"Some chance!" scoffed Gunnar. "I don't believe in chances. Not like that, anyway. Across that expanse of ocean, in all that fog..."

"Please, Gunnar," Bjólf raised a hand in protest, "don't give me the 'destiny' speech."

Gunnar merely shrugged and raised his palms and gave a familiar smirk that said: *As if I would...*

Magnus approached then, his face strained and tired. He spoke in low tones.

"Mostly small wounds. Gashes and broken ribs. Two were struck by arrows, but the damage was small. And Kjötvi lost a finger in the fight." Bjólf and Gunnar exchanged looks of disbelief at the man's singular misfortune. "He is well – he rallies," said Magnus. "But three others will not see home..."

Kylfing had taken a club full in the face, and though he had at first had fought back despite his entire visage having swollen up like an inflated pig's bladder, he soon after became suddenly dizzy and slurred of speech, and fell into a sleep from which he would not awaken. Then there was Oddvarr, who had taken the spear, and his fellow Swede, the big Gøtar, who had been crushed behind one of the oars as the other ship struck. For one, the fight was already over. The other's breathing was laboured, and periodically he coughed up blood – each bout worse than the one before, and causing such pain that the colour drained from his hands and face when the fit was upon him. A broken rib had pierced his lung. Magnus hung his head as he described what each sensed was inevitable.

"There is no remedy within man's power," he said. "But, I can give dwaleberry to ease his passing."

Bjólf nodded. There was nothing to be said.

Magnus shrugged. "They are beyond my help now." Then he nodded in the direction of the mast. "It's him I'm worried about…"

Bjólf followed his gesture and saw young Atli: pale, trembling, his white knuckles still gripping the shaft of his axe, his other arm still clamped around the mast. He gave the briefest of laughs at the sight of it. "We'll sort him out. Just see that Oddvarr, Gøtar and Kylfing have what little comfort we can give."

Magnus nodded and left Bjólf and Gunnar to their thoughts.

"We must do right by them," said Gunnar. "Give them a proper burial."

"And we shall," said Bjólf. "But we must put more distance between us and Grimmsson first. Just to be certain. Although…" He looked back into the fog.

"You're thinking about what happened on that ship after it hit the shore," muttered Gunnar. "Do you think they turned on each other, or…?"

"Or?" Bjólf looked at Gunnar. Gunnar said nothing. But each knew what the other had in mind. "I need to hear from you exactly what you saw in this forest," said Bjólf. "And to talk to the boy, too. Away from other ears – for the moment, at least."

Gunnar nodded in silent acknowledgement.

"First," said Bjólf with a sigh, "let me see if I can prise our young recruit from the mast."

# CHAPTER SIXTEEN

## *STEINARRSNAUTR*

"LITTLE MAN?"

The words caused Atli to start violently, snapping him back to the present. For some time – he did not know how long – he had been unable to tear his gaze from the places along the gunwale where the battle had raged, marked by the dark stain of blood. Now he stood, hunched, feeling small, and stared at Bjólf, his eyes filled with confusion and fear.

"Are you hurt?" asked Bjólf.

Atli shook his head.

"Do you wish to leave us? You're free to go your own way."

Atli, not needing to look at the uninviting shore to arrive at an answer, shook his head again, though less vigorously this time.

"I have never seen a battle..." he said.

"As you see, it is not all adventure and glory. Not even in victory."

Atli frowned, felt sick. "Is it always... like this?"

"You do what you need to."

An sob suddenly escaped Atli's lips. This was not the life he had imagined. He tried to contain himself, embarrassed before the other men, tightening his grip on the axe in an attempt to stop his hand shaking.

Bjólf nodded. "You think this might have been avoided. The bloodshed..." His voice suddenly changed, becoming stern, charged with the same steely defiance Atli had seen during the fight. "Understand, boy, they meant to kill us, and to take this ship. They had no mercy in mind, and expected none in return." Atli knew he spoke the truth. Yet, as he spoke, each blow of Bjólf's axe blade replayed itself in Atli's mind – a parade of faces at one moment filled with passion and vigour, and the next... His face drained of blood, and for a moment he felt he would vomit.

Bjólf slapped his hand suddenly against the mast, making Atli start once again. "This ugly pile of wood... It is no mere chattel. This ship is my livelihood, my home, my family. And these men are my kin, for I have no other I value as much. I am bound to them, as they are to me. Who threatens them, threatens me. And who does so incurs my wrath."

Atli nodded, saying nothing. Tears stung his eyes; tears of anger, now, at his own feebleness.

Bjólf took a deep breath then, and, leaning in, spoke in softer tones: "You may not believe it, but I know what it is you are feeling. I have felt that fear in my own stomach, and on this very ship. There is no man here who has not, and none will think the less of you for it."

"I will do better. I will learn."

"Yes. You will." Bjólf slapped the boy on the shoulder. "And I have just the thing to help you in your quest." With that he made towards the stern, stopped after a few paces, turned and looked back at Atli. "Well? Are you coming or not?"

Atli slipped his aching arm from around the mast and followed.

At the stern, just below the steering deck where Gunnar still stood at the helm, Bjólf had several long chests, at the centre of which was his own; the fine, carved box adorned with dragons that he had inherited from his uncle. To the left was Steinarr's, from which Atli had already gained much, and to the right another of exceptionally dark wood, polished and left plain, but with ornate, green-tinged bronze hinges. All stood open.

Bjólf reached into the black box. "First," he said, rummaging noisily inside, "something to keep you alive." And as he straightened up, Atli saw his hands were filled with bunched swathes of linked mail. "This was Hallgeirr's. He would not mind me lending it out."

"He never liked that shirt anyway," grunted Gunnar.

Ignoring him, Bjólf held it aloft. "Belt," he said to Atli, nodding in the direction of his waist. Atli took a moment to realise what Bjólf meant. "As soon as you are ready, little man, this stuff is heavy..." Hurriedly, Atli undid the buckle and let it fall to the floor. "Arms," said Bjólf. Atli raised them. Bjólf heaved the mail over the boy's hands and let the gathered folds of linked metal fall down over his body to just above his knees.

Atli felt his legs bow at the weight hanging on his shoulders. He had never imagined a garment could be so heavy. But then, had he never seen mail so close up, let alone dreamt he would one day be wearing it himself. Where he came from, you only had such stuff if you were wealthy, and nobody was.

"It was always short, but Hallgeirr was taller..." Bjólf looked him up and down. "I think we have a fair compromise. Good?"

Atli nodded, and even managed a smile. "Why did Hallgeirr not like it?"

"Cheap stuff," said Gunnar dismissively, his arm wrapped around the tiller. "Always complained the links were too large. Said it was too noisy."

"Noisy?"

"Bad for sneaking up," explained Bjólf.

"But what if I need to sneak up?"

"One step at a time, little man," frowned Bjólf. "A moment ago you had no mail at all. Now you're getting picky."

Gunnar chuckled.

Atli looked thoughtful for a moment. "Does mail make you..." – he struggled to find the word – "invincible?"

Gunnar laughed. "No, nothing can do that. Everybody dies."

"And, in case you didn't know, Gunnar is the man responsible for morale aboard this ship – if you can believe that," sighed Bjólf. "But there is one more thing." He looked down into Steinarr's sea-chest. "The other half of the story. Something to make you a true warrior." From the chest, he lifted a long, fine-hilted seax, sheathed in red-stained leather. Drawing it for Atli to see, he held it across his outstretched palms. It was sharp on one side only, like a knife; a narrow, straight, fullered blade, but thick and strong at the back and angled at the end to a sharp point. The grip was girt with black leather, the bronze hilt plain, the matching pommel lobed in three. Along the blade, before the fuller, a repeating diamond pattern had been etched, and close to the hilt the bright blade was marked with runes. Though the whole thing was barely the length of just the blade of Bjólf's sword, it was a handsome weapon. Atli's eyes glittered at the sight of it, all thought of the bleakness of battle, for the moment, quite gone.

"One does not lend swords," said Bjólf. "One can only give them. I therefore give this sword to you, but in doing so, call upon you to make an oath, if you are ready to do so."

Atli nodded.

"Kneel and place your right hand upon the blade," said Bjólf solemnly. Atli did so. "Do you swear on this blade the unbreakable oath of kinship and loyalty to this ship, its crew and its captain, Bjólf, son of Erling, to use this sword in its service and for its protection, and never to spill the blood of your kin?"

Behind Bjólf, Atli saw Gunnar mouth the words: "'I, Atli, do swear it...'"

"I, Atli..." he began. He hesitated, a dim thought coalescing in his mind. Then he raised his voice again, stronger this time. "I Atli... Son of Ivarr... do swear it..."

Gunnar smiled at the words.

"I call this blade *Steinarrsnautr* – Steinarr's gift," said Bjólf, passing him the sword. "Remember the name, and never put yourself more than two paces from it."

"Something we could all do to remember," muttered Gunnar, recalling Bjólf's use of Godwin's axe.

"Now," said Bjólf in hushed tones. "We must talk, you and I, about this thing you saw in the water."

# CHAPTER SEVENTEEN

## THE ROAD TAKEN

IT WAS ONLY gradually that Atli realised what his new treasures meant. As they talked, the weight of his situation began to bear down upon him as palpably as his new mail-shirt. But now, like the mail itself, there was something oddly comforting in the burden, and while he felt a rush of sheer terror each time he even thought of putting his sword to use, its presence also reassured him. In this company, dressed as he was, he felt himself speak a little more assuredly, move a little more naturally with the ship and stand a little taller.

"Then we are agreed. There is some pestilence in this land," said Bjólf.

"I have no need to agree anything," said Gunnar, his patience wearing thin. "I saw it with my own eyes."

"But some *pestilence*. That was what you said. A plague of some kind?"

"I suppose," shrugged Gunnar. "But unlike any I've seen. And we've seen many, you and I."

Bjólf nodded gloomily. "And you are certain of what you saw?"

"Odin's beard! For the last time... It was like something yanked out of a grave; a puppet of rotten flesh and bones! Just as the boy describes. And don't forget those moans, you yourself heard those."

"Could they have been something else? An animal of some sort?"

Gunnar threw up his hands. "If that was an animal then you can drop me in a cauldron and call me a Celt."

"Well, this makes sense of the merchant's' tall tales."

"And perhaps, too, of our old friend back in the village." Gunnar gave Atli a swift sideways glance as he spoke, then added: "Of Ivarr..." Atli felt mixed feelings at the vindication of his father's actions. He chose to remain silent. But he was glad, at least, that Gunnar had chosen to honour his father with a name.

"There's one good thing to come of it," sighed Bjólf. "If the poor wretches you saw did stray onto Grimmsson's ship, then that crew will have more pressing things to worry about than us."

"It seems the bad luck was in our favour."

At that moment, the voice of Finn called out from his position at the prow. "Hoy! Up ahead – a fork in the channel."

Bjólf hurried to the bow, with Atli close behind, as the steady rhythm of the oars drew them through the fog, closer to the place where the waterway branched off, off to port. Splitting off at an angle and heading back in the opposite direction from that in which they were now travelling, it was far narrower than the fjord in which they now found themselves – but still a good size for their ship. It was also considerably more inviting. The banks were greener, it even seemed the sky beyond was lighter, and they could see slight eddies around the confluence – signs of the gentle current against which, thus far, they had been rowing.

"So," he said. "It seems we have a choice. Keep on inland within this fjord, or turn back down this tributary, and perhaps on to the sea. What say you, little man?"

Atli looked ahead at the forbidding, indistinct gloom of the fjord, then back at the leafy, gently sloping banks that lined the waterway to port. "This is like the rivers of my home. Its forest has a kindlier look than hereabouts. More the kind of place I would wish to be if I wanted fresh meat and game."

Bjólf nodded. "More hopeful of a landing place, too. And everyone has had a bellyful of rowing, and it's easier to roll a stone downhill than up. Bring her about!"

Slowly the *Hrafn* was turned into the gentle current, and the men, every one of them glad at the boy's decision, were finally able to ease up on the oars. "Don't let her drift!" called Gunnar. "I can't steer her if you drift!" All jeered at his protest, but Úlf, relieving half the rowing crew, made sure the remaining men kept up a gentle pressure on the oars.

It was not long before all spirits were lifted. The surrounding banks, though swampy, were green and verdant, the fog was clearing with every stroke of the oars, and soon the haze was pierced by glimmers of sunlight and the sounds of birdsong. Finally, there began to appear subtle signs of human habitation: a thick wooden post among the branches at the water's edge, once a mooring for a boat; a long wicker basket, abandoned now by the side of the river, but meant for trapping eels; in a stark, half-dead ash tree, old sacrificial offerings to the gods – skeletal remains of pigs, sheep and birds nailed to its mossy boughs.

Bjólf stepped up to the prow then, and, taking up the thick, conical wedge of wood that Atli had once thought to put on his fire, climbed up past Finn to the dragon's head and knocked out two pegs from the point where the neck joined the prow. For the first time, Atli realised that the head – intricately carved, and once painted in bright colours, though now faded and chipped almost down to the dark, bare wood – was an entirely separate piece.

To Atli's great surprise, Bjólf then tilted the dragon's head backwards until it came away completely in his hands. He paused for a moment, patted the dragon's forehead affectionately and muttered "Sorry about the 'ugly pile of wood,' old girl..." Then he kissed his fingers, pressed them on the dragon's head, wrapped it carefully in sacking and laid it gently in the crook of the prow. "We are not on a raid today," Bjólf explained, seeing the questions creeping across Atli's face. "So, we take her down to show we have no warlike intent. No point making enemies until we know what we're dealing with."

As he was speaking, Finn, looking ahead, had spied something. He nudged him, and gestured downriver. Just visible in the distance, on the river's left bank, was a clearing around a muddy bay, and beached in the mud several small boats.

"However," Bjólf continued, "there is no advantage in appearing weak."

He turned and gave a shrill whistle to the crew. All looked to him. And without another word he raised his arms to head height and struck a clenched fist against the flattened palm of his left hand.

As Bjólf strode astern to arm himself, all around threw open chests and set about the same task. The air was filled with the chink of mail and the glint of helms and blades as hauberks were thrown over heads, straps tightened and quivers filled. Shields and spears were passed out from their places on the deck, while amidst the clamour came the sound of whetstones honing sword and axe.

Among the men, Gunnar spied Kjötvi, up and about and making his own preparations, despite a near total lack of armour with which to prepare. His leg was bound, his left hand wrapped in a bloody bandage so he struggled to buckle his belt, yet it seemed to Gunnar that, aside from the obvious injuries and the near permanent look of consternation upon his face, that he was the very picture of rude health. That was just the way of things, he supposed. Some men could trip on a bucket and that was the end of them. Others could be trampled by a dozen horses and get up afterwards. Kjötvi, uniquely among men, seemed to combine the worst of one and the best of the other. It was certainly a strange kind of half-luck that he had.

Gunnar approached him. "Sorry about the, er…" He nodded in the vague direction of the place where Kjötvi's left index finger had once been.

Kjötvi shook his head in disbelief. "I put my hand on the gunwale for one moment. The two ships' hulls clashed, and…" he shuddered at the memory.

Gunnar reached into the bag on his belt and pulled out a small, yellow-white sliver. "I have something. Something to return." He handed it to a bemused Kjötvi. "The shard of bone that Magnus removed from your leg," explained Gunnar. "I kept it safe. It's not much, but it seemed to me you'd already lost enough for one trip."

Kjötvi took the bone fragment, and, closing his fist around it, gave a smile of deep gratitude.

Atli – already kitted out with mail and sword – had meanwhile hurried back to his small heap of belongings at Bjólf's command. As he fastened his belt, from which hung his leather pouch, eating knife and axe, Magnus approached, in his hands a simple steel helm with a straight nose-guard. He held it out to Atli.

"Gøtar asked me to give you this," he said. Atli took it from him, momentarily lost for words. Like the mail, it was far heavier than he had imagined. Responding to Magnus' encouraging nod, he lifted it and placed it carefully over his head, uncertain how he was supposed to tell whether it was a good fit or not. His head rattled around inside the metal casing like a clapper in a bell. Magnus raised a finger, then reached inside his tunic and pulled out what looked like a woollen cap. "Here," he said, "you need one of these." And with that he took off the helm, then, having pulled the tight-fitting cap onto Atli's head, put it back over the top. Atli shook his head from side to side again. It was a snug fit now. Magnus smiled and rapped a knuckle on the front. "Better!"

Atli beamed. "I should thank him..."

Magnus shook his head solemnly. "He has passed. But this was his last wish."

Atli's face fell at the words.

"He knew the life was leaving him," said Magnus. "The helm was no protection when his time came. But he hoped it might help you live out longer days."

And without another word, he turned and left Atli standing in silence. The boy could not put a name to the feelings he felt at that moment. Never had he experienced such a mix of pride and sorrow. That a man who he barely knew – a warrior – had spent his last breath upon him... As he thought of the lives these many forge-fashioned works of metal had known – these things, everything he owned, that now were part of him – his feelings resolved into a steadfast determination, a decision about how his own life should be. Whatever he did, wherever he went, he would strive to honour them all – Steinarr, Hallgeirr, Gøtar and the rest.

# CHAPTER EIGHTEEN

## LANDFALL

"MAKE READY!" CALLED Bjólf. He, too, was fully fitted out with war-gear now, more than Atli had ever seen: fine mail-coat gleaming, gold-hilted sword at his side, short seax hanging cross-wise beneath his belt, a bright blue cape over his shoulders and clasped by a gleaming gold brooch, and over that, at his back, a red-painted shield with bronze decorations on its face, and a bearded fighting axe. In his right hand he held an ash spear, its long, leaf-shaped point glinting in the sunlight. Only his helm hung from his belt, to show his intentions were not hostile.

Every one of the other men was similarly attired, each in their own fashion, but all contrived to invoke awe in those who confronted them. In the short time this had taken, the ship had closed upon the boggy harbour, and half the crew kept up the pressure at the oars as Thorvald, who had taken the helm, guided her in. Gunnar now stood alongside his captain at the prow, his great, grey wolfskin across his shoulders.

"Ymir's breath..." he muttered, looking out at what greeted them. "What is this?"

Atli moved forward to get a better view. In many ways, what he saw still greatly resembled the river approach to his own village: there was the natural harbour, the gently sloping shore leading up from the water, providing a good landing place for boats, the protective banks of trees and foliage on either side. But where his home was all pebbles and shingle, here the bay was lined with dark estuary mud giving way to thick grass that, but for a worn yet oddly neglected path, swathed the long, gentle slope far inland to the boundaries of the forest, only occasionally punctuated by an outcrop of jagged, grey, moss-covered rock. And, where the woodland around his village was, he now thought, welcoming in character and pleasing in scale, the forest here was massive, thick and brooding, its gigantic forms seeming to pile up and press in on either side, ancient boughs that hung so far out over the edges of the water that one could hide a whole army beneath them. Dotting the muddy shore were five small boats – one filled with greenish water, and one so old and uncared for it had rotted through to its ribs and sat, half sunk, like a forgotten carcass. And there, way ahead up the slope, at the far end of the untended path, the first sign of human settlement; a towering rampart of whole pine trunks, higher than a house, curving away on either side until it disappeared behind the screen of trees, at its centre a crudely constructed but formidable pair of gates hanging between rough wooden watchtowers, the whole length of its top edge lined with thick, sharpened stakes.

The men shipped the oars and, in silence, the ship slowed and came to a gentle stop as its keel eased into the mud, its prow sliding part-way up the marshy bank. Four men hauled up a long section of the deck that served as a gangplank and rapidly extended it from the port bow to more solid ground.

"Úlf," called Bjólf. "Take Eyvind, Guthmund and Ingólf and form a watch. We do not leave anything unguarded here."

"And keep vigil over our fallen brothers," added Gunnar gruffly, his eyes scanning the sky. "We've fed enough ravens today."

"Amen," muttered Magnus under his breath.

With their captain at their head, the party tramped down the gangplank and gathered on the shore, Atli making sure he was close behind Bjólf and Gunnar. It had only been a day and a night since he had first trod the deck of the dragon ship, yet now it was the solid ground that felt unfamiliar beneath his feet. He staggered unsteadily, unconsciously anticipating its rise to meet him. Even in this sodden state, it seemed strangely unmoving and implacable – a memory from an age ago that already his body had forgotten. As he moved across the muddy ground with the other men, he felt the full weight of arms and armour pull down upon him – the warrior's burden.

THE ASSEMBLED MEN made an imposing sight – something no foe, no matter how fearsome, would wish to tackle lightly. Yet Gunnar surveyed the scene with trepidation. There was a strange air of abandonment about the place. In the mud, near the waterlogged rowboat, a familiar, grisly shape caught his eye. A human skull, bulging out of the dank-smelling mire. Nearby, the same colour as the mud in which it lay, the stark, curled claw of a ribcage. Gunnar nudged Bjólf, but Bjólf had already seen them for himself.

"What in Thor's name is this place?" whispered Gunnar. "Is it deserted, do you think?" Thoughts of plague and pestilence still played on his mind.

Bjólf said nothing, but simply pointed to a patch of sky immediately above the stronghold's wall. A thin column of grey smoke curled upward from its interior. Gunnar hardly knew whether to be glad or sorry.

"We go!" Bjólf called, and they began the march to the gates, mail and war-gear clashing as they went.

"So," said Gunnar, close to Bjólf's ear. "How do you want to handle this?"

"Carefully. Does that meet with your approval?"

"Does Idun have apples?"

"Remember the old saying: where we can't raid, we trade."

"Trade? With what?"

"Our hands. Our wits. Our swords." Gunnar looked skeptical. Bjólf merely picked up the pace. "We have few choices, big man. Let's see what we can make of it."

"What we can make of it..." he grumbled, then nodded towards the stockade. "What do you suppose inspired someone to make *that*?"

"Perhaps a need for men just like us."

Great, grey clouds had begun to move rapidly across the sky, casting huge, solid shadows that rolled across the landscape like striding giants. Gunnar felt the wind on the side of his face. "Hmm! *Now* we get a breeze!"

Picking their way up the path, making no effort to conceal their approach, they saw no signs of life besides the trail of smoke. The path itself had been used over years, that much was clear – and here and there it seemed the damp, overgrown grass may have been trodden or parted by something – but whether any man had come this way in recent days was impossible to tell. They pressed onward without a word, crushing the covering underfoot, the grass giving up its sweet, moist scent.

Finally, the great stronghold, an endless row of stout pine trunks, loomed above them. Still nothing stirred. Bjólf halted before the bulwark.

"What now?" said Gunnar.

"We do what any well-mannered man would do," said Bjólf. "We knock."

And with that, he strode straight up to the gate and, raising the blunt end of his spear, hammered hard upon it five times.

He stepped back. Then, at the lookout point atop the left of the two watchtowers, a face appeared.

"Who are you?" snapped a voice.

"Well, at least he speaks our language," muttered Gunnar.

He was an old man, bearded and grey, his rheumy eyes squinting and blinking ceaselessly behind his quivering bowstring. Not the most obvious choice of lookout, thought Bjólf. Little wonder their approach had not been spied earlier.

"I am Bjólf, son of Erling, captain of these men."

"State your purpose!" Even from here, Bjólf could hear the old man's wheezing.

"Please, friend, lower your bow. Only I'm afraid you might let go and accidentally kill one of us."

The man's bow dipped and trembled, his grip on the arrow faltering. Several men in the front rank of Bjólf's company winced as it wavered in their direction. "We require provisions," continued Bjólf. "Grain, meat and ale..."

The bow drooped immediately. A look of terror had passed over the man's face. "You are Skalla's men?"

"No." Bjólf noted the look of relief that transformed the

watchman's features. "But perhaps there is something with which we could help. A trade..."

The old man frowned. Other voices could be heard behind the stockade: one harsh, one less so, both female. The old man responded to them, then disappeared from view. The tone of the discussion turned to one of bickering, in which the watchman seemed to be coming off distinctly the worst.

"They must not get many visitors," said Gunnar.

In another moment, the face of an old woman, well-dressed, her hair in a fine linen hood but her expression sour, bobbed up and glared at them, then after another bout of babbling, another female figure appeared, and stood for a moment studying them, silent and unmoved, framed by the timbers of the watchtower.

The second woman had quite different qualities – qualities which Bjólf and his men were quite happy to regard at greater length. Her neck was pale and slender, her features fine and well-proportioned, her dark chestnut hair drawn back in two elegant plaits which were wound at the back, a slim band of green and gold brocade across her forehead. From a belt about her slim waist hung a bunch of iron keys. No peasant, this one, thought Bjólf. Though little more than twenty summers, he would guess, she held her head like a queen, and looked down upon this daunting band of men with no hint of fear, a hard frown upon her face.

"What do you want?"

"We have travelled a great distance, my men and I. We wish to speak with the lord of this noble place."

"There is no lord," she said. "I am mistress of its hall."

A few of the men murmured in amazement. Bjólf tried not to show his surprise.

"Then... we throw ourselves upon your hospitality," he said, pressing his hand to his breast, "and hope that we may offer something in return."

"Don't offer too much..." hissed Gunnar.

A frown crossed her face. Urgent, whispered words were uttered somewhere behind the stockade. "What is it you bring?"

Bjólf spread his arms and gestured either side at the fearsome company that surrounded him. "As you see... No more. No less." Then, acting on a gut instinct – the instinct of an opportunist pirate – added, "This 'Skalla' you speak of..."

The woman's expression turned to one of sudden realisation. "Then at last you have come," she gasped, and disappeared from view.

Bjólf stared up at the empty space and, leaning towards Gunnar, allowed a puzzled frown to cross his face. "What did she mean, 'at last you have come'?"

Before Gunnar had the chance to respond, there was a sudden uproar behind the gates, followed swiftly by a great grinding of wood against wood, a chorus of voices joined in effort, and a heavy thud that shook the earth beneath the warriors' feet. And with a deep, sonorous creak, as of something unused to movement, the gigantic gates swung inward. From its opening crept a slender figure robed in green – a two-part dress of exquisite handiwork with fine clasps of gold above and below the breast. She flew forward suddenly, and flung her arms around Bjólf's neck, grasping him tightly to her. In her wake came the old woman, arms aloft, exclaiming tearfully as she threw her own arms about an astonished Gunnar, then, upon her toes, planted kisses on each black-bearded cheek.

Both men stood, disarmed and dumfounded, as behind them the whole company of men struggled to contain their mirth. With the fine scent of the woman's hair filling his nostrils, the soft green fabric of her dress pressed against the unyielding grey metal of his mail shirt, Bjólf turned his head and beamed at his comrade. Gunnar, the old woman's face buried in his chest, glowered back, daring him to speak.

# CHAPTER NINETEEN

## HALLBJÖRN'S HALL

THOUGH HE HAD never encountered her like before, Atli knew at once she was of noble blood. It was not just the fine weave of her clothes, the softness of her skin and the glittering adornments of gold. It was her whole being – the way she spoke, the way she moved. She was also one of the most beautiful women Atli had ever seen, though perhaps, he thought, that was not saying much. There was, above all, a kind of dignity contained within her young frame by which one could hardly fail to be impressed. All the more odd, then, that she should fling herself at Bjólf with such abandon. Had she thought he was someone else? Some long-lost friend? Atli could not fathom it.

As soon became clear, it was not only he who regarded the scene with puzzlement. Looking around at the faces of the others, he read in them all varying degrees of amazement. And so, bemused or not, he found himself able to chuckle along contentedly with his new-found fellows.

"Please, forgive me," she said, releasing her grip on Bjólf, her face flushed, her head bowed, as if with sudden embarrassment. "We had given up hope..." She smiled and wiped away a tear.

As she withdrew her hand, something caught Bjólf's eye. He caught her hand in his. Around her pale, slender wrist was a thing he had seen only hours before, in the grim, fog-bound delirium of that long night on the heaving ocean. It was the simple, solid band of a bracelet, formed of two interwoven strands plaited carefully together – each no thicker than a barley stalk – one blood-red, the other crow-black. For the space of two breaths he stood with her small, delicate hand held between his rough fingers, scrutinizing it intently, a frown spreading across his forehead. "Where did you get this?" he said.

The woman's face reddened. "It was a gift," she said, seeming suddenly downcast.

"It is very distinctive," said Bjólf. "Are there... many like it?"

"One other. But it is lost. As is its owner..." – she struggled to recover her composure, her voice wavering – "my husband."

The old woman, who had now released Gunnar from her clutches, clasped her hands together and gazed tearfully at her mistress. Turning the band around her wrist, momentarily lost in thought, the young woman looked up at Bjólf, cocking her head quizzically. "Why do you ask?" she said. A look of vague hope then lit her features. "You have seen its like before?"

Bjólf slowly shook his head. "No. Never."

Her eyes lingered on him for an instant, then she gathered herself, standing straight and smoothing her hands down her dress. "I welcome you to Björnheim. I am Halldís, daughter of Hallbjörn, jarl of this land."

"Bjólf, son of Erling," responded Bjólf with a bow of his head, then gestured towards Gunnar. "And this..."

She held up a hand, silencing him. Atli was impressed.

"You and your men are surely tired and in need of refreshment after your long journey. And we should not linger longer than necessary outside."

Indicating for them to follow, she turned and moved swiftly towards the narrow opening from which she had come, the old woman scuttling behind. Bjólf and Gunnar registered her nervous glances towards the dark edges of the forest that surrounded them. They exchanged a silent, questioning look – then led the band of warriors between the great, rough-hewn wooden gates to the interior.

What met their eyes as they entered was a bizarre mixture of sights. Within the colossal stockade lay a wide, open space of grass and beaten earth in which were arrayed a great variety of sturdy, wooden buildings, of considerably greater age and quality than that surrounding wall. Up ahead, at its centre, past houses, barns and a forge and dominating the view, stood a huge hall, its great roof curved along its length like an upturned boat. The thick timbers that supported it were sturdy and of exceptionally fine craftsmanship, the gable ends delicately carved with intertwining patterns of branches and vines, all filled with stylised representations of birds and beasts, the richly decorated boards crossing at the peaked roof and finished with the elegantly sculpted, curving heads of horned stags. Rarely had Bjólf seen a hall of such scale and grandeur.

Yet all about, the haunted, hollow-cheeked faces of the rag-tag band of villagers that silently greeted them seemed to tell a quite different story. For the size of this settlement, they were  pathetically few in number and curiously devoid of vitality. Ragged, thin and baffled of expression, they were composed of the leavings of society: the old, the crippled, the infirm, the weak of body and mind. Among them, Bjólf counted less than half as many men as women, and of those, barely a single one between the ages of twelve and forty. Halldís' limited retinue – the nobility among the population – were also few in number, and, despite the few trappings of wealth and the healthier disposition that came with it, seemed ill-equipped to protect even this sorry crew. Of them, only Halldís and her companion – the old woman, Ragnhild – seemed to stand out as still stout of heart, undefeated and indefatigable.

Gunnar had been wrong – the place was not deserted. But the dead, stultifying air of emptiness and desolation hung about its neglected beams and rafters as surely as if it had been left in the keeping of ghosts. A deep, portentous thud sounded behind their backs as the gates were pushed shut, and a huge bar of wood was heaved into place by its weary-looking custodians. For good or ill, Bjólf, Gunnar and the rest were now captive within this strange, necrotic netherworld.

Yet, as they ran the gauntlet of these blankly staring spectres, both sides stunned into an eerie silence by the sight of the other, a change seemed to come over them. Slowly, as if waking from sleep after taking a draught of bitter wormwood, some of the spectators seemed to come to their senses, a light returning to their eyes. They began to murmur to one another as they watched the men march past. Their limbs, too, seemed to stir into life, and some hurried alongside as the party advanced, expressions of excitement creeping across their tired faces as, bit by bit, they realised what this awesome band of fighting men might mean to them.

At the near end of the hall, as they approached, stood a lone, hunched figure, whose gloomy presence, in the space of a moment, seemed to suck the life back out of the party.

Dressed in clothes of once fine quality, topped with a cape of charcoal grey, the man nonetheless seemed an ill fit for his clothes, as if he had somehow shrunk inside them, like a piece of air-dried meat. Yet his skin was so pale that it hardly resembled anything that had ever been alive, and his tiny eyes seemed themselves so devoid of colour that they hardly seemed composed of a distinct kind of matter from his face. This was long and lean with high cheekbones. His thin nose projecting from his pallid, bony face like a blunted axe blade. On either side of it hung curtains of long, lank hair – strikingly blond. His thin beard seemed to sprout only from the end of his chin, and hung beneath in straggly tendrils like the roots of an onion.

The only man in this place who appeared of useful age – around thirty summers, Bjólf would guess – he and he alone appeared unimpressed and unmoved by the sight of the warrior band. In fact, it seemed to Bjólf there was brazen hostility in that peevish scowl. He glared dismissively at Bjólf's crew, looking them up and down with as cold and unsympathetic an eye as a slave trader judging a potential purchase, then cast Halldís a similarly hard and sneering stare. Then, without a word, he turned with a brusque and petulant flourish of his cape and stalked off into the shadows.

Halldís turned to face Bjólf and his men apologetically, her confidence somehow shaken, as if mere sight of the pale man had brought doubts to mind. "I am sorry. What am I thinking? The hall is not prepared. There is no fire in the hearth. It has been closed up for some time and is disarrayed – more a meeting hall for mice and spiders than a fitting place to welcome men." She laughed awkwardly, then looked downcast. "It would shame me to show you into my father's hall in such a condition."

"The sky is hall enough," said Bjólf, with a shrug. He looked about him, at the great open space that extended north of the great hall – evidently a gathering place – in its centre a stone well, richly bedecked with all manner of wild blooms. He gazed up at the sun, a hand shading his eyes, fleetingly catching the scent of the flowers on the breeze. A sense of wellbeing washed over him for the first time in many days. "We're men of the outdoors. The air is fresh and the weather is fine. Better to enjoy it than lurk in the dark." He cast a fleeting glance after their skulking friend, now lost in the shade cast by the hall.

Her face beamed with a smile. "Ragnhild, have benches brought out. And prepare the hall." She turned back to Bjólf. "This evening we honour you with a feast!"

A great murmur of approval rose from the men. Ragnhild clapped her hands with glee before hurrying to her task, and a rush of excitement spread through all about as if the villagers were finally awoken from their torpor. "Food..." muttered Gunnar in grateful anticipation, then rolled his eyes skyward. "Thank you, old Troll-Beater, for looking after our needs." And he raised his Mjollnir hammer pendant briefly to his lips.

# CHAPTER TWENTY

## BREAD AND BEER

FOR SOME TIME they sat as the great clouds hurtled overhead, eating the bread and beer that was brought by willing hands. The bread was gritty and tough – poor flour, thought Bjólf, adulterated with acorns or who-knows-what to make it go further – but the butter was sweet, and the beer, though thin, was welcome relief for their parched throats. Ragnhild and Halldís passed amongst them with great flagons of the stuff, raising spirits wherever they went, broad smiles upon their faces.

"So, have you found out what all this is about yet?" said Gunnar.

"Enjoy the moment, old man," said Bjólf dismissively. But Gunnar knew only too well when his friend was avoiding the issue.

"It's plain they think we have come to fight for them," he said. "It seems we may have survived a battle only to get involved in a war."

"Let's see how this unfolds," said Bjólf. "Perhaps it's in our favour. And if not, well, we restock, make our excuses and get on our way." Despite his cheerful tone, he did not look entirely convinced by his own words.

"At the very least, she should know that we're not the army she thinks we are."

Bjólf looked him straight in the eye. "So, do you want to tell her before the feast, or after?"

Gunnar looked into his beer, then back up at Bjólf, and grunted in assent. He took a great swig, then passed his hand across his wet mouth. "There is something strange here. No young men. The remainder looking like the walking dead, in spite of rich land all about. A wall penning them in like frightened cattle. And a woman lord of a hall!"

"It's not natural!" laughed Bjólf.

"Well, it isn't!" protested Gunnar. He looked about him at the inhabitants of this stronghold, at the haunted expressions behind their smiles. "Are they under siege from the pestilence we witnessed, do you suppose?"

"Maybe. But that doesn't quite follow. You don't fight plague with an army."

"Unless it gets up and walks," said Gunnar.

Bjólf said nothing in return, but simply sat, chewing on his bread, frowning at his own thoughts, and watching Halldís weave to and fro between the benches. He found himself captivated by her. Not that she was the most beautiful woman he had ever seen, but there was... something. A curious mixture of strength and vulnerability that he had not encountered before. As she laughed with the men – at the unashamed joy they took in her company, at their gentle flirting – he nonetheless saw a kind of fragility, even sadness, behind the confident persona she presented. And yet, when she drew apart from them to the heavy wooden table upon which the ale had been set, standing lost in her own thoughts and for the moment distant and melancholy, it seemed that it was quite the other way around – that somewhere beyond that sad demeanour lay a core of defiance and courage. She caught him watching and looked away hastily, busying herself refilling the flagon with ale. He stood and moved to join her.

"We're grateful for your hospitality," he said.

"It is an honour," she replied.

Bjólf smiled, sipping from his horn-cup. "Perhaps you have slightly too high an opinion of us."

"It is not matter of opinion," she said, not meeting his eye. "It is my duty. High-born or low, you are our guests, and deserving of every courtesy. That's what my father raised me to believe."

"A man of ideals. That's a rare thing these days."

"He was a good man," said Halldís, hanging her head, "until this loathsome conflict destroyed him."

"The feud with Skalla?" probed Bjólf.

His words seemed to sting her. She dragged the heavy flagon to her hastily, causing some of the ale to slop out on the tabletop as she did so. Frowning, she mopped at it in irritation. "I do not wish to speak of it." Her voice was hard, angry. "Nor will I have his name mentioned here. It is an obscenity among the people of Björnheim." Then, after a moment, she seemed to relent, and for the first time a look of gloomy resignation came over her. A deep sigh escaped her lips, and she began to speak in slow, measured tones. "They came in black ships from a dark fortress in the fjord, and have grown in strength as we weakened." She looked at Bjólf almost apologetically. "We are far from kings and their laws." She looked away again, troubled by memories. "Unimaginable horrors came in their wake. For five years they have taken our crops and livestock. They have enslaved our men and dishonoured our women. It is more than a feud. It is a curse they have brought down upon us."

"But you sent for help..."

"More often than I can remember. None of our emissaries escaped this valley. Each time the bodies of our people – or parts of them – were sent back to us. They were the lucky ones." She shook her head, as if trying to rid it of the dark thoughts that rattled inside. "Those men... they are few in number, but their masters command a dark magic. And so, as you see, we cower in this prison of our own making."

Bit by bit, Bjólf was beginning to build a picture of this place – of this woman – and their desperate history: the oppressed community, the fallen jarl, the lost spouse. Yet each new piece of information he gleaned, illuminating as it was, seemed only to lead back to the same inevitable question. He thought of the bracelet upon her wrist, and of its twin upon the ravaged body in the sea. The body of the husband that he alone knew was dead. The body that was dead and yet still moved. "I had wondered," he began, "if these walls were measures against the plague we had seen hereabouts."

Halldís stared at him, wide-eyed. "I should not have brought you here," she whispered, and hurried away.

Bjólf gazed after her, more bemused and troubled than ever.

# CHAPTER TWENTY-ONE

## A BOAT

TIME PASSED SWIFTLY for the rest of the crew. Halldís buried herself in her duties as hostess, the beer flowed freely, and all had begun to be lulled by the general good cheer of the occasion when a shrill shout brought them suddenly to their senses.

"Boat! Boat!" It was the reedy voice of a boy waving frantically from the watchtower. Bjólf and his crew were immediately on their feet, heading to the gate, weapons ready. The local people's reaction to the cry was equally swift, but their sense of urgency took them in quite the opposite direction. As Bjólf's crew raced past, mail and weapons ringing, they retreated rapidly, melting away into their homes, terrified.

"Look at them!" said Godwin in disgust. "Like frightened sheep!"

Arriving at the gates, Bjólf hurled himself up the uneven ladder to the covered platform of the watchtower where the young, skinny lad still stood, spotty beneath his straggly blond hair and red-faced, pointing down towards the water's edge.

Before he had even made the top of the tower, Bjólf had heard Úlf's distinctive whistle fade in and out on the stiff breeze that now blew at his back. It was the signal indicating another vessel, yet Úlf had not raised an alarm. Bjólf narrowed his eyes, looking down towards the harbour where his ship sat – at an angle now on the mud, where the tide had left it stranded. At first he did not see it. There was no sign of his men on the ship – they would have concealed their numbers, he knew – but beyond that, there seemed to be nothing unusual about the scene, just his ship, and a few small boats... Then he realised. Out in the water, almost obscured by his own craft, a small boat, sitting low in the water, drifted gently past, apparently brought by the current, its upper strakes and curving bows gaudily painted in a familiar style. He could see no sign of life, but within it was a curious shape, partially covered by a large swathe of dark red cloth. Another whistle went up – the sign that all was clear – and Bjólf saw the characteristic shape of Úlf Ham-Fist stir in the stern, his big forearms reaching out to the water with a boat hook to catch the passing craft.

"Open the gate!" called Bjólf as he threw himself back down the ladder. The gatekeepers hesitated, looking timidly from him to Halldís, who had herself just arrived at the rampart.

"Do it!" she cried.

They set about the task, hastened by several of Bjólf's men who lifted the weighty oak beam clean out of their hosts' hands and tossed it aside. Atli jumped back as it crashed at his feet, then joined them as they heaved on the creaking gates.

Within moments, Bjólf and his band were striding into the harbour mud, where Úlf had hauled the small boat up onto solid ground. The decoration upon it was unmistakable now. It was the row-boat from Grimmsson's ship. As he approached, he saw the big man – who was afraid of nothing on earth that Bjólf knew of – staring down into it, quite motionless.

"What is it?" said Bjólf as he came up alongside, breathing heavily. But he could see for himself now. Inside Grimmsson's boat was a single oar, a large wooden chest girt with black bands of iron, wrapped around with a heavy chain, half-draped with a cape of fine manufacture, and an expertly-wrought Frankish sword, its blade slicked with something black and sticky. Nothing else. It was immediately clear, however, what had caught Úlf's attention. On

142

the top of the chest was a single, clear handprint of blood, still glistening in the early afternoon light.

The other men crowded around the boat, each staring at the strange sight.

"Things did not go so well for Grimmsson, then," said Gunnar. He prodded the abandoned sword-blade tentatively with the tip of his spear. "What is that? Is that blood?"

"If it is," said Godwin, "it's like none I've seen."

"Not from a living man, anyway," said Njáll.

Atli, catching only the occasional sight of the boat between shifting bodies of the other men, shuddered.

"Open it," said Bjólf.

Úlf stepped forward, his mace raised, and gave the iron lock a crashing blow. Bits of metal were sent flying. Bjólf threw off the chain and heaved the heavy lid open. The men murmured in awe at its contents.

Atli at first struggled to get a glimpse of what so impressed them. Then, as they moved, he caught sight of it, glittering in the sunlight. A precious hoard such as he could not have imagined.

Njáll whistled. "Arab dirhems, English silver pennies, Byzantine gold... this is the cream of their booty."

"Such valuables would only be in this boat if someone had been trying to make off with them," said Thorvald.

"Or more likely if the ship was lost, and they were trying to make an escape," added Godwin.

"So, what became of those who loaded it into the boat?" asked Njáll.

"The greater question must surely be what happened to the rest of the crew," said Godwin.

"Dead," said Bjólf.

Thorvald frowned at him. "All of them? The whole crew?"

"Or they fled for their lives. From a threat greater than the lure of this booty."

"Grimmsson's crew doesn't run," said Gunnar.

"And no one lets go a sword like that while they have breath in them," added Njáll.

"Then that leaves only one possible fate," said Bjólf.

"But what could wipe out an entire crew like that?" said Atli.

Gunnar looked about at the dark, blank walls of forest that

surrounded them. "There's something out there. Worse than plague."

For a moment all the men looked around them, shifting in anxious silence. The thickening, mountainous clouds finally succeeded in obliterating the sun, casting a chilling pall over the company.

"Looking on the bright side," announced Fjölvar, attempting to dispel the gloom, "in the space of a day we have gone from being poverty-stricken victims of that dishonourable bunch of inbreds to having the greater part of their plunder."

"Perhaps we should quit while we're ahead," mused Thorvald.

"I vote we take what food we can and get out," said Godwin. Several nodded and muttered their agreement.

"We cannot leave," said Bjólf. The men fell silent.

Gunnar frowned at him. "One more successful raid, we said, remember? We have that now. Grimmsson finally destroyed and enough plunder to set us all up for life."

"I am sick to my stomach of running," said Bjólf. "We chose this life to be free from tyranny. Now here we are retreating from it."

"This is not our fight, my friend." Gunnar said. "And it is not tyranny we have to worry about. There is something different here. Something deadly... That wiped out eighty warriors like *that*." He snapped his fingers.

"The people here expect it of us," said Bjólf. Then, after a moment's hesitation, added: "She expects it."

Gunnar's voice hardened. "We made no deal. There would be no shame."

"There would," said Bjólf, tapping the side of his head, "In here." For a moment the two regarded each other, deadlocked. Finally, Bjólf pulled himself away and raised his voice to the rest of his men. "It is your decision. Stay or go?"

For a moment there was silence. Few could honestly say they were for staying, but none wished to speak out openly against their captain.

"Stay," said Atli. The men parted, turning to him.

Gunnar stared in surprise. "*Now* I feel shame. You have an uncanny knack of complicating matters, boy!"

Godwin gave a heavy sigh, nodding in reluctant agreement. "This little man is making us look bad."

"While you ladies are deliberating," interrupted Úlf, giving the hull of the *Hrafn* a slap with his huge hand, "allow me to point out that there's no way we're shifting this out of the mud without nature's help."

Bjólf looked at his beloved ship, held fast.

"How long until next high tide?" he asked, squinting at the edges of the mudflats.

All then looked at Kjötvi. He leaned heavily on his spear, looking back at them awkwardly. Gunnar noticed that he had bored a hole in the sliver of leg-bone and now wore it on a thong about his neck like a talisman. Kjötvi shrugged. "Tide's at its lowest. It'll be another quarter day until it's at its peak again. Around nightfall. Then again in the morning, when it will be high enough to get us off the mud for nearly half the day. But if we are still here at midday tomorrow, we'll likely be stuck again."

Bjólf nodded. "Then the decision is made. For now, at least. We stay put and take stock in the morning. See what another night brings. Which means, gentlemen," his voice rose with enthusiasm and not a little relief, "that tonight we feast!"

There was a mutter of assent from the men, mingled with muted approval. If they were forced to stick around to partake of a feast, well, maybe that wasn't so bad. Catching Atli's eye for a moment, Bjólf gave the boy a smile. He had earned the respect of many of the men today, men not easy to win round.

"We must prepare," Bjólf said. "Bring all weapons from the ship. Everyone is to stay armed." He pointed at Grimmsson's chest of silver and gold. "Stow that aboard, out of our hosts' way. Thorvald – take Einarr, Grimm and Eldi and relieve Úlf's watch here." The men snapped into action, heaving the chest from the boat and clambering aboard the ship. "Godwin?" The Englishman stood at his captain's shoulder. "I want a man up on the ramparts. Keep the ship in clear sight at all times. And have four more men on hand below. I want to be able to open those gates at a moment's notice if need arises, whether we have our host's permission or not."

"One more night, Gunnar," he said, slapping his friend on the back. "Then we see."

Gunnar looked up from beneath creased black brows, his eyes scanning the slowly darkening sky. "A storm is coming," he said.

# CHAPTER TWENTY-TWO

## A FEAST

THUNDER RUMBLED AROUND them as they sat in Halldís's hall, arrayed along the mead benches with as many as would fit in the place. It had turned to a dreary night, with rain rattling on the great curved roof all around them. But the heat from the flames of the great log fire that crackled and popped in the central hearth set all their faces a-glow, swiftly driving out the damp and musty smells of neglect, restoring to life some of the grand and noble feelings of the past – feelings all too many had forgotten.

Their nostrils now were filled with the welcome, warming smells of bubbling stews and roasting meats, Sweet, heady mead had been brought forth, too, served first to Bjólf by Halldís herself. The doughty captain had drained the long, curved drinking horn in one, as tradition demanded, to the enthusiastic claps and cheers of his men. Even Halldís – presiding over the rest of the feast from the high seat at the centre of the hall, her cheeks flushed in the heat – had regained her former poise, and seemed, at last, to appear as one who sat at the heart of a proud community, the worries of the outside world, for the moment, completely banished.

The road to the evening's celebration had not, however, been without its obstacles. There had been a tense moment at the very start, when Frodi – the reeve of the village since the time of HallBjörn, and one of Halldís's most dependable supporters – had thrust himself in front of Bjólf's men just as they were about to troop in and reminded them, politely but firmly, that no weapons were to be carried into the hall. "We feast in friendship and trust," he said, "or not at all." All were perfectly well aware of the rules of hospitality, and the banishment of blades from the feast, but few gave them up willingly. Njáll, the Irishman, who claimed to have seen this very rule exploited to treacherous ends, even squared up to the old man, who nonetheless refused to budge. It fell to Bjólf to resolve the matter to the satisfaction of both sides. All weapons were left outside, but within easy reach, and under guard by one of his own men. Frodi eyed Njáll with some suspicion after that.

When the food was brought, that, too, fell a little short of expectation; a single roast pig, a few scrawny fowls, a leg of ham and – much to Gunnar's displeasure – a fish stew with mussels that was uncomfortably similar to their makeshift meal the night before.

"Mmm. Seafood," said Gunnar, sniffing the stew. Bjólf glared at him. The fare was certainly meagre, even by the standards of the average farmstead, but he had no wish to embarrass their hosts. Although one or two among the crew seemed to take the poor quality of the food as a slight, he understood that this, in all likelihood, represented the very best they had to offer.

"The mussels were gathered today," said Halldís, adopting a cheerful air. "They are at their sweetest now." But Bjólf could see that she, too, was aware that their offerings fell far short of what they would have wished.

"We rarely hunt game in the forest," added Ragnhild. "Not unless forced to do so." Halldís silenced her with a look.

Bjólf stood, then, and raised his mead-cup. "To the mistress of this hall, who honours us with this feast, and to new friendships..." All raised their voices together in the toast. He thought he detected a flicker of a smile upon Halldís' face.

"Thor!" added Gunnar, tipping a drop of drink upon the beaten earth floor before taking it himself – a small offering to the gods. Many about him did the same.

Soon, as bellies were filled, faces warmed and the mead hit its mark, the conversation blossomed, and the laughter grew. A harper struck up and sang a song of the adventures of Sigurd, and then Skjöld the Icelander, very drunk but all the better for it. Before long, crew and hosts were laughing uproariously together like the oldest of friends: Njáll was slapping a smiling Frodi on the back, forcing more drink into his already overflowing cup, Ragnhild was hooting and flapping her apron whilst eyeing up Gunnar with ever-decreasing subtlety, and Fjölvar was engaging the old man from the watchtower in some kind of drinking game at which he himself was very obviously cheating, much to the amusement of his neighbours. Finally, Halldís too, who at first had tried to keep a sense of decorum by pretending not to understand the jokes at Skjöld's expense, gave in to fits of laughter, wiping tears from her eyes. Bjólf was gladdened by the sight of her, feeling, at last, that there was something here worth fighting for.

Among them all just one sat apart, disdainful and humourless. In a far corner, the pale man sipped sparingly at his drink, watching Bjólf intently.

"Who *is* that sour-faced fellow?" asked Gunnar, slamming down his cup in irritation.

"Ah, now," said Fjölvar, perched on the edge of their table. "I have the story on that one, from Klaufi, our short-sighted friend at the gate. Remember?"

"You trust that old fool?" asked Bjólf.

"His wits are still sharp, even if his aim is not."

"It's not his wits I question," said Gunnar. "It's his eyesight. He called Filippus 'Miss'."

"I always said he should grow a beard," quipped Bjólf.

"Fortunately, what he lacks in one faculty, he gains in another. He may have all the visual acuity of Odin's missing eye, but he is blessed with Heimdall's hearing." Fjölvar bent forward, adopting a confidential tone. "It seems those ears of his take in far more than any around him would imagine, and fortunately it only requires a few ales to get it out of him again."

Bjólf and Gunnar both leaned in closer to hear Fjölvar's findings.

"The lonely man is Óflár, son of Hallthor. He is cousin to Halldís, but while he is very much the son of her uncle, he was not born of Halldís's aunt..."

"Ah, the old story," sighed Gunnar. "One foot in the family, one foot out."

"Well, that matter has long since been forgotten. But it seems that, being the acknowledged son of Hallbjörn's brother, he believes he has been cheated of his birthright by the fair Halldís."

Bjólf nodded. "In other words, he thinks it should be his scrawny arse upon the high seat of this hall."

"I think Halldís graces it rather more agreeably," mused Gunnar.

"No wonder he looks so bloody miserable," said Bjólf.

"He failed to act when the time was ripe, and Halldís, knowing that the hall should not fall empty and feeling her father's loss keenly, stepped forward to assert herself. A popular move, by all accounts. Now he fears that popularity."

Gunnar frowned in exasperation at this pathetic tale. "So what is he doing now? Waiting for her to give up the ghost?"

"He could be in for a long wait," said Bjólf. "The girl is slight, but what she lacks in brawn she makes up for in spirit."

"She had more supporters back then," continued Fjölvar, "men who would fight for her cause, if need be – including Hunding, the one became her husband. But Hunding is lost, and they have since dwindled. And so Óflár bides his time."

Bjólf snorted. "If he intends to wait until all opposition fades away, then all he stands to inherit is a ghost town."

"It is nearly that already," grumbled Gunnar.

"This husband of hers, Hunding," Bjólf said, "what is his story?"

Fjölvar shrugged. "He took a ship to seek aid from the king. Its charred bones were found washed up two weeks later. Of the crew there was no sign."

Bjólf nodded solemnly.

"Soon after," added Fjölvar. "Óflár made a generous offer of marriage to Halldís."

"Clearly a man of tact." Gunnar said.

"She roundly, and rather publicly, rejected him," said Fjölvar, spinning a knife idly upon the table. "He has not forgotten it."

As Godwin approached to join them, Bjólf looked up and, glancing beyond him, caught Óflár's eye with his own. He held his gaze until the other weakened and broke away. "You notice he is almost the only man here isn't either too old or too young to take a wife. Why is that?

Fjölvar looked across at him, too and frowned. "Why, indeed."

"Watch him," said Bjólf.

"Who is this 'Skalla' anyway?" asked Godwin, throwing his leg over the bench and slumping astride it heavily. "Has anyone found that out yet?"

Gunnar grunted as he lowered his mug, dripping beery froth from his moustache. "Hmm! Sounds like a girl's name."

"An *ugly* girl's name," added Godwin.

"None will talk of him," said Fjölvar. "Not even Klaufi." He threw up his hands. "I tried everything."

"I found the same," nodded Godwin. "As soon as the name is mentioned, the gates are shut and bolted."

"All I know is he is the captain of the clan with whom they have their feud," said Bjólf. "A river-raider. But he must hold some terrible power over these people that they will not even talk of him."

"I assume he is the reason for these fortifications," ventured Godwin.

"Perhaps," said Bjólf, staring into the flames that leapt in the hearth. "But if the threat comes only from the river, why does this stockade surround them on every side?"

All four men looked at each other in silence.

"I trust Halldís," said Bjólf. "But there is something they're not telling us. Stay on your guard."

With that he stood and crossed the earthen floor to where Halldís sat. She saw his approach and smiled.

"With your permission, I wish to send some food out to my men on watch," he said.

"Upon the rampart?"

"Aboard my ship. It has been a long, cold night for them, and..."

"You left men aboard your ship?" interrupted Halldís. Her voice and her expression were suddenly changed, her face registering shock at his words.

"Of course."

"It is not safe."

He frowned. "That is precisely why we guard it."

"Your ship is not in danger so long as your men are not on it."

He puzzled over the words. "It is not only our ship that needs guarding. They keep watch over our dead."

Halldís stood in alarm, the colour drained from her face. "You have dead aboard your ship?" Several about her, Frodi included, fell silent, turning to face Bjólf, their expressions grave.

"Three of us fell in conflict with some common sea-pirates."

"Why did you not tell us of this?"

Bjólf stared at her, utterly bemused. "What need was there? They lie, wrapped in linen, bothering no one. And then we will bury them."

"How long has it been?"

"What?"

"How long have they lain dead?"

"Half a day. Three-quarters at most." Bjólf was losing patience now. "But what concern is that of yours?"

"They must be removed and burned," said Halldís. She turned away. "Ragnhild – fetch men and see to it immediately."

Ragnhild made to stand, but before she could move Bjólf stepped forward, grabbed Halldís by her shoulder and spun her back round to face him. "No! You will not touch them."

Halldís glared at him, outraged. Frodi stood, his cool, grey eyes blazing. Godwin and Njáll were instantly on their feet, followed slowly by Gunnar, who towered over them all.

"Three days we let them lie," rumbled Gunnar in the tense silence. "To show respect. That is *our* way, whether it be yours or not."

"Believe me, it is not from lack of respect that I say these things," replied Halldís.

"We have seen how you show respect to your dead," said Bjólf, "from the bones left rotting in the estuary mud."

"You do not understand," she protested, tears welling in her eyes.

"No, I do not! And you have done little to remedy that lack of understanding. We ask about Skalla and your lips snap shut like an oyster. I make mention of the pestilence that we know afflicts this land and you run from an explanation. If I am ignorant, if I am ill-informed, it is only through want of answers – answers that only you in this hall can give, but will not."

For a moment they stared at each other, the great, shadowy spaces of the hall filled only with the hiss and crackle of the fire, and the thrash of rain.

Halldís let her head fall, then began to speak in a quiet monotone.

"When they first came in their black ships, their cruelty knew no bounds. But they were just men, and were as strong or as weak as men ever are. At first, we resisted. They were few in number, and though unused to war, we were a proud people. We forced them to an uneasy truce."

"Then... *Skalla*..." she forced herself to utter the name, "unleashed a new abomination. One day, after many weeks respite, the black ships appeared again. Our men rode to face them. Skalla's crew dragged seven great, long boxes from their ships, and upon prising off the lids, revealed inside bodies of men – or what once were men; huge, bear-like warriors, their flesh grey, the stench of decay about them. Some had once been our own warriors. What this meant, our warband could not guess. Skalla threw a liquid in their faces and his men hastily retreated to their ships. The bodies stirred, staggered to their feet – moving, but the light in their eyes quite gone out. They were *aptrgangr* – death walkers; like the *draugr* in stories of old. But no story could have prepared us. Like ravening beasts they attacked – tore with hands, with blades, with blood-drenched jaws. Our weapons would not touch them. A terrible havoc was wrought that day. Then, when their masters were at last satisfied with the quantity of corpses their hideous progeny had heaped up – the limbs wrenched from sockets, the bones bitten, the flesh devoured in great gobbets, the mud made red with gore – they once more crept forth from their ships. Skalla threw a powder in their faces. Lifeless, they fell to earth. Nailing them back into boxes, they dragged those monstrous berserkers back aboard their ships. Thirty men lay slain. One survived the butchery, his arm left somewhere in that charnel heap. From that day, we did not resist.

"One might think this suffering enough. But the gods, in their wisdom, did not deem it so. We have since become a cursed people, whose dead the earth will no longer hold. Our own land rejects us, as a dog vomits up bad meat. First, the curse was merely passed from one to the other. That, we could control, though the methods were harsh. We were forced to retreat within the walls of this stockade, to abandon the outlying villages and farmsteads to their fate, even the burial grounds of our ancestors. They walk the forests now. But then it began to afflict all who died here. We have returned to the old ways, burning our dead, but in unseemly haste, else they are spat from their graves to wander as restless, mindless monsters, no longer knowing loved ones, driven only by the need to feast on the flesh of the living. This fate awaits us all. And so all of Björnheim cowers in its shadow – doomed, defeated, already dead in life."

Bjólf's men could only stare at her, incredulous. Yet not one could shake the creeping sense of inevitability that hung about her words, the way they seemed to give horrid meaning to the grim details of past days. Even Bjólf himself, still searching for earthly explanations, could see in her eyes that she spoke the truth, or, at least, what she believed to be the truth.

Halldís relieved the silence. "Tell, me, if you had known this, would you have come, or simply thought us mad?"

Bjólf, briefly wondering whether it could indeed be a kind of madness that afflicted this place – and perhaps infected him and his own men too – resolved there and then to reveal his own secret; that they had not come in response to a call for aid – that, in all likelihood, no message had got through, and no aid would ever come. And that her husband Hunding – for whom she still held some hope – had succumbed to some ghastly fate, his body tossed and battered by the eternal churning ocean out beyond the fjord. But, as he drew breath to start his speech, a great crash turned every face to the door. It had been flung back on its hinges; leaves and rain now swirled on the wind, and in the doorway, soaked to the skin, his sword drawn, stood Atli, eyes wide, his face pale as a ghost.

# CHAPTER TWENTY-THREE

## DEATH WALKERS

IT WAS A flash of lightning that had first revealed it, standing stark and pallid against the endless black of the forest's edge. For an instant, the white, forked shape had burned and flickered – and then was gone. At first, Atli had simply blinked back at the featureless night into which he was immediately plunged, uncertain of what he had glimpsed, the intense but indistinct image still seared into his brain, blinding him not only to what he could now see, but also to what he had seen. Then, just as the deep, rolling rumble of thunder had followed the lightning, so the realisation of what he had witnessed gradually grew clear in his mind.

A figure, deathly pale, its ragged clothes offering scant protection against this cold, rainy night – or any night – standing, motionless, half way between the stockade wall and the brooding immensity of the trees. Atli's eyes now strained to see anything in the pale moonlight, which came and went through the heaving cracks in the violently rent sky. But in his mind, the fleeting image slowly asserted itself in all its details, like the blood that comes gradually to a fresh wound. Chief among them was a face. Or that was the best word Atli had for it, at least. For while it had the familiar arrangement of physical features, it was yet lacking something in every one of those details. Its eyes were dark pits, its nose withered and collapsed, its mouth lolling open, devoid of expression. Like a blind, idiot child it stood, its limbs like a doll's, its grey, lifeless visage now seeming to him a kind of horrible mask, behind which was nothing.

It was only then he had realised that the beacon on the *Hrafn*, his only link with the handful of men still aboard the ship, had disappeared.

Moments later he had been stumbling headlong through the wild, rain-lashed night towards the great hall, his mail and weapons weighing heavily upon him, his limbs seeming to move with the agonising inertia of a tormented dream.

As the invaded hall now emptied into the hectic night, Bjólf's men, still dazed with drink, grasped weapons and torches in a chaos of urgent movement, and for the second time that day found themselves hastening towards the gates and the harbour beyond – to face what, none yet knew. Even Atli himself could not be certain. His breathless, fractured exclamations at the door of the hall had been sufficient to raise the alarm and get every man on his feet. Now, as he struggled to keep pace with Bjólf, still gasping from his run and having to shout above the wind and clamour, Atli fought to give an account of the sequence of events that had led to his dramatic intrusion.

While Bjólf and the guests at the feast had been carousing in the mead-glow of the fire's flames, Atli had been stationed upon that lonely rampart, huddled in the icy downpour, helm rattling in the rain, his woollen cape pulled tight against the wind.

The task with which he had been charged was simple – to keep in sight at all times the beacon that had been lit upon the ship. At regular intervals, this torch – mounted upon the prow – was raised and waved from side to side six times by a member of the first night watch. Should it disappear, or fail to move at the appointed time, Atli was to alert those of Bjólf's crew who who manned the gate below. Of these there were four.

On occasion, one or other of the crew would call up to the

watchtower, or come to see how Atli fared. Later in the evening, Salómon had even brought up some mead that had been smuggled out of the hall. Atli supped the sweet liquor, and felt its satisfying warmth seep into his bones. Supposedly these things were done out of simple fellowship, to ease a long and lonely watch. But they were also, he suspected, to ensure he was awake. Either way, he was grateful.

Atli spent long periods leaning on the log parapet, at first gazing toward the ship, where a second, dimmer fire could sometimes be seen – a sign of Thorvald's work, applying pitch to the ship's damaged hull – and then staring out towards the dark trees. Something about them pierced him through with a kind of primeval dread. Though he could barely make out their shapes – or perhaps because of it – his mind swam with restless thoughts of the unnameable horrors that lurked within those deep, ages-old shadows. And yet he kept his eyes resolutely, defiantly upon them. It became a challenge, a test of his mettle, to look upon them unflinchingly, to conquer them and the demons they loosed in his imagination.

It was then that the ghastly apparition had appeared.

For a moment, he had been paralysed with shock. But, slowly, his mind began to rationalise what he had seen. Perhaps the weather had put out the torch, and perhaps the figure he had seen was one of the crew, come to fetch fresh fire from the stockade. Then something happened that he could not explain. He saw a glimmer of orange light dart about near the ship, then suddenly erupt into a great column of flame. And, blinking away the drops of rain that coursed from his helm down onto his face, he began to realise that it had not only the leaping, shifting patterns characteristic of a fire, but a distinct shape. The shape of a man.

As he watched the form with growing horror, he saw that it was moving. It advanced slowly, steadily, with a kind of staggering gait, its arms reaching out before it. Then, flame leapt up again just within their reach, as if a second creature of fire had been spawned by the first, its shape more wild and disordered this time, and a horrible, agonised shriek tore through the night.

Atli flew to the top of the ladder. Below, his fellows had already registered the scream, and he met a cluster of pale, upturned faces. "Fire!" he shouted, his voice coming feebly and getting lost on the wind. Then again, with more urgency as he pointed over the rampart, *"Fire!"*

Lokki, frozen in the middle of a trick involving three walnut shells, dropped everything and leapt at the bar upon the gate. The others, slower off the mark, were soon upon it, hurling the beam away into the mud and squeezing out through the gate the second it was wide enough for them to pass, torches in their hands.

"Get the others!" called Halfdan. They pounded off into the night as Atli scrambled and slipped down the rain-soaked rungs of the ladder.

When the party of men from the feast finally reached the gate they found its keepers, leaning against the gates in desperation, like children pressed against a door, as if such efforts were capable of preventing anything but the most feeble intruder. Godwin and Gunnar thrust the men aside and hauled the gates open. Beyond, no light could now be seen. The fact alarmed Atli. For a moment, he feared he had been somehow mistaken, that he had thrown his new shipmates into confusion for nothing. But at least the ship was not ablaze. Then, with an icy chill, he remembered Lokki, Halfdan and the others. Where were the lights of their torches?

"Farbjörn, Arnulf, Hrafning," barked Bjólf. "Stay and guard the gate." He glanced back towards the hall, where, in the semi-darkness, a lone figure was hobbling, resolutely. "And when Kjötvi gets here, tell him to join you."

With that, weapons drawn, they advanced into the raven-black, cloaks flying, their own torch flames roaring as the wind whipped and pulled at them. Atli could not suppress a shudder at the sound of the gates thudding closed behind them.

The band moved swiftly down the path, long wet grass soaking their legs as they went. They were lighter on their feet without their armour, and emboldened by drink, but each of the two dozen men also had Halldís's words echoing in their ears. Torches aloft, they wheeled around at the slightest sound or movement on either side.

"You say they all followed, boy? All four?" demanded Bjólf. Atli reluctantly affirmed it.

"There should be eight men out here," called Gunnar over the sounds of the storm. "They cannot simply have disappeared."

"Spread out," ordered Bjólf. "And stay sharp."

As grass gave way to mud, another silent, searing flash cracked open the night sky, illuminating the harbour for an instant and throwing out stark shadows: the eerie, slender prow of the ship standing like a lone sentinel, its shape reflected in the shallow water.

"There!" shouted Finn, and surged ahead as they were again plunged into darkness.

They followed Finn's flame as the thunder boomed and wrenched the air. Near the edge of the water, half-lit by Finn's torch, was an irregular shape from which a choking smoke was rising. Finn crouched over it, then recoiled. As the others approached, their light showed it to resemble a body, lying on its back, its arms held before it in twisted, horribly contorted gestures. Every part was burned down almost to the bone, blackened and crusted with what now passed for flesh, smoke still billowing from its cavities.

"Is that a man?" muttered a horrified Gunnar.

"Another here!" called Njáll, splashing into the water, close to the ship. Bjólf, Atli and several others followed. As with the first, whisps of smoke were tugged and whipped from it by the wind, the hiss of heat that issued from it audible even above the storm. Yet this one was far less destroyed – presumably because the water into which it had collapsed had quenched the flames. The lower legs were virtually untouched by fire, the upper body still partly protected by the blackened metal of its hauberk. The helmed head, however, had borne the brunt of the burning. Crouching, Njáll turned it over in the water, cursing as he scalded himself on the still-hot metal of its mail. Magnus knelt by him. The face was blistered and blackened to a crust, the hair quite gone, a steady smoke coming from the helm like steam from a hot cauldron. But there was no doubting its identity now. With sinking heart, Atli recognised one of the crew. "Eldi," confirmed Magnus.

"Hoy!" All turned in alarm at the voice. There, aboard the ship, dimly visible in the feeble light, a figure was clambering over the gunwale. Advancing to meet him, they could see now it was Einarr, one of the ship's watchmen, his eyes wide, his face white and stained with blood. He had lost his helm, and his dark hair – normally in thick plaits – had come loose, its wet strands flying about in the wild air. In his right hand, his sword – gripped as though his life still depended on it – was blackened along the blade by some oily ichor. He staggered. Godwin ran to support him.

"The others?" demanded Bjólf.

Einarr shook his head. "I am alone," he panted, his voice strained. "I stayed with the ship... they went after them. Those things... We threw them off... they could not climb back aboard. But more came... I was the lucky one."

"They?" said Bjólf. "Who? You were attacked?"

At that, Einarr, to the bemusement of his fellows, began to laugh. It grew in volume and intensity, strange and hollow, until finally the moment of hysteria passed and he seemed to gain some measure of control. "By our own men..." he chuckled drily. "The fallen..."

Fjölvar and Finn had meanwhile climbed aboard the ship, looking it up and down.

"You won't find them!" called Einarr. "They've fled the nest!"

Finding little sense in his words, Bjólf looked to Fjölvar and Finn. "Anything?"

But where the bodies of their three dead comrades had been, there now was nothing but a single length of ragged linen, someone's funeral shroud. Fjölvar held it up for Bjólf to see, and simply shrugged, his expression baffled.

Bjólf turned back to Einarr, a deep dread now gripping him. "Where are they? The fallen men? Someone took them?"

"No! *They* attacked us. Our dead." Einarr's eye suddenly caught sight of the blackened, smoking skeleton that lay in the mud, and he fell silent. Staring, wide-eyed, yet half averting his gaze as if not wishing to acknowledge it, he extended his arm slowly and pointed at the thing. "Kylfing."

Bjólf glared at him. "But Kylfing was a corpse," he said. "His flesh grey. The flies on him... we all witnessed it."

"I saw him. And the others too. As clear as I see you now." He turned and looked around as if reliving the nightmarish events. "Oddvarr rose first. We did not see him. He got Grimm from behind, sank his teeth into his neck. Grimm struggled, took both of them over the starboard side, and the beacon too. We heard shouts, running, splashing of water. Thorvald... he went after them, into the darkness towards the trees. Told us to stay with the ship. Then Gøtar came... his eyes were empty, his teeth..." Einarr shuddered at the memory. "Eldi and I fought him – gave blows that should have felled a mortal man. With a spear I thrust at his neck, pushed him over the side. Still he was not dead. We heard him moving in the darkness. Thorvald called to us in the distance then, and it seemed the movements we heard went off towards the sound. Then it was Kylfing's turn, his face swollen, grotesque..."

He moved toward the ship, making wild gestures as he continued his description. "Eldi had a plan. I fought with Kylfing, could not stop him, but forced him over the port side. Eldi was waiting there. He had the pail of pitch that Thorvald had been using, and a brand from the fire beneath. He lured Kylfing a safe distance from the ship, then hurled the pitch over him and set the body afire. But he must also have spilled pitch upon himself. Kylfing did not stop – came at him even as the flames consumed his flesh. The fire caught. Eldi burned as I watched.

"Then there was fighting in the darkness. Out there, the others from the stockade. More of the creatures had come. They showed no interest in the ship. But I could hear them moving. I stayed quiet."

A sound made them all turn, weapons drawn, limbs tense. A splashing of water followed by a kind of grunt. Somewhere, off to the left of the ship, close to the trees, something was approaching. Bjólf strained to see past the torchlight. As the moon broke briefly through the clouds, a pale shape loomed dimly, staggering out of the night. It was weird – unrecognisable. Then a familiar voice called out. Halfdan. As they watched, he came splashing heavily along the edge of the water, sword in one hand, the other struggling to support the stocky, flagging figure of Thorvald. Halfdan raised his sword hand in greeting. "Don't kill us," he called, somehow managing to cling to a grim kind of humour. "We're friendly." Others rushed to their aid. Thorvald was shivering and bloody, but both seemed to have escaped serious harm.

Sheathing his sword, Bjólf placed his hands on Thorvald's shoulders, looking hard into the scratched and bloodstained face he knew so well. He knew if anyone could give a rational account that would dispell Einarr's mad ramblings, it was Thorvald. "Salómon?" Bjólf demanded. "Lokki? The other men..?"

Thorvald, breathing heavily, looked across at Einarr. Something seemed to pass between them then. Thorvald simply shook his head. Halfdan, too, cast his eyes down into the black muddy water, his humour quite gone. "We found Salómon back there, near the trees." Magnus grabbed a torch from Finn and made to move in that direction, but Halfdan stopped him with the flat of a hand upon his chest. He shook his head solemnly. "What is left is beyond help."

"Burned?" asked Gunnar.

"Eaten."

The men stared at each other. Thorvald looked about for a moment, frowning at the silent, sickened faces, as if unable to believe his own words. "I would blame it on wolves or some other beast if I could. But it is not so."

Bjólf scanned the dark edge of the forest, squinting through the rain, trying to make sense of this nightmare. "What of the rest?" he insisted. "Grimm? Hrolf?"

"I searched as best I could..." Thorvald could only shake his head again, then let it fall.

"I saw a body taken off by the river, too far out to reach," said Einarr. He shrugged. "It could have been Grimm."

"Two dead. Three missing," said Bjólf. "And for what?" He glared into the surrounding faces of his fellows. "Whoever this enemy may be, they will pay for the outrage they have visited upon us this night."

There was a grunt of steely defiance among the men. Thorvald looked at him pleadingly. "Swords do not stop them. We have not seen a foe like this before." He placed a hand on Bjólf's shoulder. Bjólf shook it off irritably.

Einarr spoke then, his voice now clear and grave. "You have fire in your blood – the fire of revenge. But know this: death stalks around us. And it will take us all unless we leave this cursed place."

Suddenly the sky was rent by a lightning flash – so close that it set the air crackling, the roar of thunder rolling immediately behind.

"We have company," said Godwin, swinging his axe over his shoulder. Following his line of sight, Bjólf could just make out a random scattering of shadows between them and the torch flames upon the distant rampart – a dozen or so slowly moving forms. He scowled at them, unblinking in the flickering, wind-lashed torchlight, the rain coursing down his face.

Without breaking his gaze he addressed this crew, his voice stern – measured but simmering with fury. "We did not seek to fight these men, but they have chosen to make a fight of it nonetheless. So be it. I know nothing of ghosts and trolls, but whoever, or whatever, these men are, they look to be locked in flesh and bone, just like the rest of us." He drew his sword. "And bone is not as hard as steel."

All around, men readied themselves.

"Forget the ship," said Bjólf. "Let's see what these death-walkers are really made of." And with that, his wind-blown hair whipping in his face, he moved swiftly toward the lurching shadows.

# CHAPTER TWENTY-FOUR

## STEEL AND BONE

AS BJÓLF ADVANCED, the men following in his wake, his speed quickened. The stride became a jog, and the jog a run, until Atli found that he was struggling to keep pace. The *vikingr* captain flew forward, eyes fixed, head low, sword held wide and ready. It was with sudden alarm that the boy realised he was now hurling himself headlong towards his first battle, unprepared, in rain and darkness, and against a foe who, without the benefit of weapons – for he could see none among their silhouettes – had utterly destroyed several of the hardest men he had ever encountered, and left the survivors with their nerves, and perhaps their sanity, shaken to their roots. He could not yet understand how Bjólf – careful, thoughtful Bjólf – could so hurl himself towards potential destruction. And yet he ran, caught up in the impetuosity of the moment, forcing the fear that gripped him into the straining tendons of his fingers, tightening them around his shield grip and seax, and thanking fate for having this happen while he was on that rampart, in full armour.

\*　　\*　　\*

FOR GUNNAR, SQUELCHING heavily behind, sword in one hand and axe in the other, Bjólf's behaviour was no longer cause for surprise. He had often joked, over the years, that there were two Bjólfs. There was Bjólf the Careful, the cautious sea captain, the thinker and planner – even, he sometimes thought, the politician. And then there was Bjólf the Reckless. The fighter. The killer. Most of the time, the former held sway. But then, every once in a while, he was pushed by circumstances beyond some invisible limit. That was when the other burst forth. There was no gradual transition. The change was sudden, absolute, devastating. The man became a whirlwind of violence: merciless, unstoppable, and knowing no fear. Gunnar felt a pang of pity for any whose fate placed them in Bjólf's way when the battle-fire was in him. Whether even this would be enough against this new, weird enemy, however, he could not begin to know.

AS THE SWAYING figures loomed out of the darkness, the flickering, uneven light from the crew's torches finally struck the faces of the first few. Several of Bjólf's men faltered, shocked at what they saw – pallid, lifeless flesh, dead, dry pits for eyes, cavernous, hollow cheeks, gaping, shapeless mouths – some with the meat rotted to black, oily pulp, others little more than dry skin stretched over bone. But they had only moments to process the information before the inevitable, bloody clash.

The nearest, directly in Bjólf's path, appeared in most respects surprisingly presentable; his clothes, although bloodstained and muddy, were unworn and of fine quality; his hair and beard neatly braided into plaits in fashionable style, fastened at their ends with short, neat lengths of coloured material. For an instant Atli convinced himself this must be someone come down from the village, that this whole attack was perhaps a mistake. The belief was short-lived. As the flames burned closer, his gaze fell upon the man's half-illuminated face.

One whole side of it was missing – torn away, as if savaged by a wild animal. His left eye hung out, the flesh from forehead to chin scraped off, as if by a great claw. The hair was matted with blood, forming a stark contrast to the still neat coiffure on its opposite side. Below, the left arm was half missing, wrenched away at the elbow, from which clot-strewn shreds of flesh hung, trembling as the creature moved.

In a fleeting moment of incongruous recollection, Atli realised had seen something like it before. Once, the people of his village had found a stranger – they never knew who he was, nor from where he had come – who had blundered too close to one of the bears that lived on the mountain. Felled by a single blow which had ripped through his face and shoulder, he was hauled away by hunters who had warned the creature off its meal. But that man had been stone dead. This man, impossibly, stood before them, gesticulating weirdly with his remaining arm like an uncoordinated infant, a strange, hissing grunt escaping his half-mouth.

BJÓLF ALLOWED HIMSELF a split second of doubt before striking. Why had this man not drawn his weapon, or made to defend himself? He had never encountered so unflinching a foe. Was it the sickness that so disordered this creature's mind?

Seeing the ghastly half-grin of the face, he did not stop to question his advantage. Using all his momentum, he swung his sword in a steep arc, bringing it down on the base of the neck with such force that its bones snapped and sprang apart either side of its edge, leaving the body sliced across to the edge of the ribcage. He drew his blood-slicked blade from the cleaved flesh without pause, the nauseating sound of metal scraping bone echoing in the chest cavity. The momentum spun the hapless victim around as he did so. The man's head, right arm and shoulder teetered away from the rest of the body for a moment, revealing a sticky mess of black, half congealed gore, then its legs buckled and it collapsed in an ungainly heap with a horrid, sickening crunch.

Bjólf looked back at his men, sword extended, crumpled body at his feet. As if in response to the sound of the impact, a chorus of groans had come from the throats of the other staggering figures, and they had started dragging their half-dead limbs towards him, clawed hands outstretched, as if seeking revenge for their own lost brother. But Bjólf's men, seeing the fall of the first of them and their captain's expression of defiance, were suddenly spurred to greater boldness.

The night-stalkers were real, but they were not immortal. Nor were they immune to the bite of the sword's blade. With a great shout, swords and axes flying, the first rank of warriors hurled themselves at their expressionless opponents.

As his men engaged the enemy with a clash of steel and bone, something cold gripped Bjólf from behind, throwing him off balance. A putrid smell filled his nostrils. Staggering back, reeling at the sickening stench, he grasped at the thing about his throat, the grip of his fingers slipping against its cold and yielding surface. It was an arm, but so rotted as to resemble little more than bone dipped in oily grease. A horrid, hollow moan sounded in his ear like a cold wind blown through an empty skull. He could hear teeth gnashing and rattling together like a bag of shaken runestones. Tearing desperately at the ruined limb – astounded by the strength still in it – he felt the crack of bone and the snap of shrunken sinew as he heaved it away from him, nearly retching at the proximity of it. For an instant, as he struggled to regain his balance, its clawed hand twitched and grasped convulsively before his face. Another horrid groan assailed him. Then, feet planted firmly, he twisted hard and suddenly, flinging the half-dead thing off him. He whipped around, striking instinctively with his sword. The thrusting blade met little resistance, passing right through the ribs and skewering the man like a pig, through the heart.

For a moment, they regarded each other from either end of the weapon.

Man? Bjólf looked on in appalled disbelief. This was no man. Not any more. The bones – completely exposed where the rotted, colourless rags of his clothes no longer clung – were held together by shreds of gristle and sinew, withered like whipcords, the flesh so advanced in putrefaction that it was now no more than a covering of slimy, stinking jelly. The face grinned perpetually like a mask, its jaw clacking up and down. Within the ribs and body cavity, dark, glistening, shifting shapes lurked; in death this creature seemed to have given rise to whole new forms of writhing, wriggling life whose nature Bjólf had no desire to know. Finally he understood Gunnar's words. It was absolutely as he had described; a puppet of rotten flesh and bones.

The figure advanced towards him. It was not falling. Not collapsing. Not even flinching at the wound – a wound that should have been instantly fatal to the healthiest of men, let alone such a wretched, degraded body as this. As it came, it impaled itself further upon the blade, with no more care than a living man might show pushing through a thicket.

The undead thing before him shifted forward another staggering step, and he felt his blade scrape against its backbone. He was now, he realised, faced with an intriguing philosophical problem. How do you separate a soul from its body, when the body has no soul? There was no time for such conundrums. Drawing the sword rapidly, he swung around and aimed low, at the creature's left leg. Bone shattered. The creature fell at his feet. As it continued to grasp and crawl, as if the injury were no more than an irritation, he stood over it, then brought the blade crashing down upon the skull, its black, oily contents splattering the wet grass.

It did not move again.

"Get them in the head!" he called out. "Do not rely on anything else!"

Then he spat, in an attempt to rid his mouth of the all-pervading tang of festering death, and looked back up to the wooden rampart. Emerging from out of the right-hand bank of trees were another two dozen death-walkers, creeping towards them erratically like damaged beetles.

ELSEWHERE, THE FIGHTING had been no less chaotic. At first, it seemed all too easy. The foe was slow moving, and even the few who had weapons made no move to use them. Flailing both sword and axe before him – making up in sheer brute force what he lacked in style – Gunnar had cut a swathe through the rag-tag group of figures, knocking three of them flat with as many blows. Others around him had similar success. Only Atli was hesitant, stopping where Bjólf had felled the first of them and staring, horror-stricken, at what remained. But it wasn't so much the battle-carnage it had suffered that horrified him. It was the fact that the elegantly coiffured half-face was still swivelling its one good eye and snapping its jaws.

"Hurry up, little man!" called out Gunnar. "There'll be none left!"

Then came the slow realisation. Only gradually did they discover that, of those they had struck down and left for dead, more than half were regaining their feet. For some, that knowledge dawned late. Both Fjölvar and Jarl were attacked from behind by men who should not have survived their assault. One – a stocky peasant of a man, whose grey, shapeless face looked as if it had slid out of connection with his skull, and who Fjölvar had taken down with an arrow to the chest – grappled him to the floor, then fell on top of him, the fletched end of the arrow catching Fjölvar in the throat. Scrabbling for his knife, choking at the wound, Fjölvar stabbed the man in the neck, then hurled him off and fired another arrow point blank into his eye.

Jarl was not so fortunate. A horrid apparition of a woman – once beautiful, perhaps, but now a ragged, bony wraith with milky, staring eyes – grabbed from behind at his head, catching him around the face with the talons of her flesh-stripped fingers and driving her long, bared teeth into his exposed neck. He cried out, temporarily blinded and trailing blood, while another of the ghouls, utterly destroyed from the waist down, reached up and, biting to the bone, chewed noisily upon his hand. Crashing blows from Gunnar's axe saw both of them off before Jarl succumbed.

It was those with stabbing weapons and arrows who came off worst – and of those, many fell victim to their own shock at their fallen enemies' sudden resurrection. But then Bjólf's cry had gone up, and those with axes – and especially Úlf with his mace, which was rarely aimed at anything but a skull – made quick work of those remaining. Atli, who had not struck a single blow, breathed a sigh of relief.

Then, with sinking heart, he saw the second, larger force of ghouls lumbering between them and the gates. The men drew together again, weapons readied.

"Gods! How many of them are there?" exclaimed Gunnar.

"How many have died here?" muttered Godwin.

"It's the noise," came a voice. It was Einarr. "The noise of battle draws them."

"There will be more of that before the night is out," said Bjólf grimly, staring through the rain at the broken line of silhouettes that swayed slowly, relentlessly towards them. He drew a whetstone from the bag on his belt and ran it along his sword blade, drawing sustenance from its sharp, clear sound. "Take down all in your way. Protect your fellows. Ignore the rest. We'll lose no more men tonight. And remember, aim for the head."

What followed was horribly confused and disjointed in Atli's mind – a nightmare of flickering shadows, teeming rain, roaring torch flames, groaning, leering faces and the sickening crack of steel against skull and jaw. And everywhere the stench of the grave.

At first, the men had formed into a tight group, in which Atli was more than happy to hide from harm. But as the mindless creatures clustered around like pigs at the trough, pressing in at them, surrounding them, the need to disperse became clear. The group broke, scattering the disordered ranks of the enemy as they drove forward, taking them down wherever they could. Here and there, torches were swung with a great roar of fire and a cascade of sparks as they struck their targets. Sometimes, the undead burned briefly in the downpour, flailing, blinded by flame. It did not kill them. But it did provide precious time and a clear target for the decisive blow.

Atli, meanwhile, had decided to skirt around the death-walkers where they were thinnest, far out on the right side. One of the few to have a shield as well as a sword, he was at least comforted by the knowledge that there was some solid linden wood between him and the gnashing teeth of these monstrous creatures. What he lacked, as soon became abundantly clear, was any fire to light his way. In the darkness, the uneven ground between the path and the edge of the trees rose up to meet his feet in every kind of unexpected way, jarring his knees and turning his feet as he stumbled across the rough grass. Cursing his lack of light, he clenched his teeth, held his weapon tight, and kept the torches upon the watchtowers fixed firmly in his sights – beacons he knew would see him back to safety.

As he went, he chanced to look to his left, across the ragged line of men, their torches dimly visible in the thrashing rain. Only then did he understand how fortunate he had been.

At first, he thought it an optical illusion – an exaggerated impression caused by the light thrown from the torches, making their surroundings more immediately visible. But no... there was something else. As his eyes adjusted to the gloom, it became clear from this distant perspective that the crew's torches were actually serving as beacons for the corpse-creatures – that they drew the mindless foe to their intended victims as a candle flame draws a moth. He smiled to himself, then, as he pounded closer to his goal, suddenly thrilled with his own shrewd judgement, and thankful for the fortuitous lack of light which, just moments before, he had so ardently wished.

Suddenly, he barrelled straight into something large and solid.

Losing his footing, he bowled over heavily, barking his shin on a rock and thudding onto the sodden ground, his front tooth cracking against his shield, his seax flying off into the dark. The fall, made worse by the weight of his mail coat, had knocked the wind clean out of him. For a moment he lay, crippled and wheezing, trying to get his bearings. There were no lights visible now, and only gradually did he realise that the sticky wetness on his face was not just from rain or mud. He put his hand to it. It was slick and viscous. Had he done himself some injury? Apart from his throbbing shin and chipped tooth he felt no pain. Then a foetid smell stang his nostrils. He felt sick, suddenly struck by the horrible feeling that he had fallen headlong into the rotting carcass of an animal, or worse.

Then the dark object let out a low, half-human groan, and took a faltering step towards him.

As Atli scrabbled to his knees the cloud cover began to break, and the watery light of the half-moon illuminated the scene.

To one side of him, and just a body's length away, towered a massive figure. Broad shouldered and thickly muscled, it was dressed in a simple, plain tunic – white in the moonlight – which the downpour had so completely soaked that it was plastered to its body. From its foot, a long length of muddy cloth dragged, while upon its chest was a great patch of congealed, blood – blood which, Atli now realised to his horror, had left the thick, stinking residue upon his face. He retched, frozen to the spot. Then the clouds cleared further to cast a less broken light upon the pale monster's shadowed visage, and a new kind of horror gripped him.

Long hair hung in lank shreds to the shoulders, a horrible vertical wound made the mangled neck gape open like badly butchered meat, the forked beard was stained with blood which had streamed from the mouth, and now hung from it in quivering clots. But it was the face itself that struck him through like a blade. Though handsome and well-proportioned, it had been rendered gaunt and ugly by death, its flesh as grey as ash, its lifeless, unblinking eyes expressing nothing. But Atli recognised it, nonetheless.

It was Gøtar.

Atli was struck by the insane thought that the man had returned to reclaim the helm that now sat upon his head, to mete out a horrible revenge on the foolish, arrogant boy imposter who dared to dress in the garb of a warrior. It was action that pulled him past that paralysing fear. The hulking mockery made a sudden lunge for him with its huge, muscular arms, a ghastly wheezing cry rising from its ruptured throat. With shock and alarm, Atli was awoken from his horrified trance to the reality of his surroundings. He dodged and looked about him, desperately aware that if others heard the sounds, they would be drawn to him too.

And then he realised he had no sword.

He did not even think about drawing his axe. Instead, some other instinct caught hold. As the creature lurched toward him again, he raised his battered shield and charged at it with every ounce of his strength. The iron shield boss crunched into the death walker's chest; with all the weight of body and mail behind him, Atli slammed his shoulder hard against its wooden boards. To his surprise, he did not stop dead against that great column of flesh, but kept on going. Stumbling clumsily as the obstacle gave way before him, he fell, rolled over in the dark, wet grass, righted himself and, unharmed, scrambled to his feet. The great figure crashed backwards onto the ground with all the crushing force of a felled tree, its limbs flailing and twitching like a freshly slaughtered ox. Panting with the effort, his head spinning, he tried to think what his next move should be. Dozens of disordered thoughts – incomplete or too fast to properly grasp – cascaded through his mind. Out of the chaos, one clear, urgent thought came. *Run*, said a voice in his head. *Run, run, run!*

He fought to stir his trembling, leaden limbs, unable to take his eyes off the stirring, groaning thing that he knew would be on its feet in moments, its head wobbling, turning toward him. He finally broke the paralysis, took a step backward, and his heel met something hard and sharp in the grass.

*Steinarrsnautr.*

Once again, something swifter than thought took him over. In the next moment he found himself poised over the great beast, sword raised high above his head, hardly knowing how he got there. He had one final, chilling look into the hollow, empty eyes of the man whose dying thoughts had been of generosity towards him. Then, with a force that left Atli shocked, as if it somehow came from outside of him, the heavy blade crashed down upon the creature's neck, chopped through the throat and jarred against breaking bones. Black blood spilled.

Such was the second passing of Gøtar, son of Svein.

When he thought back on it later, Atli could remember nothing of the journey to the gates of the stockade. His feet simply pounded the earth without thought, as if somehow independent of the fact that his heart was bursting out of his chest, until the nightmare was far behind him and the huge pine logs that represented his salvation towered over him. The mindless rhythm was fuelled by a chant repeated over and over under his struggling breath, the words of which he was barely conscious: *I'm sorry... I'm sorry... I'm sorry...*

AT THE GATES, the men had gathered – breathless, soaked from the storm, their weapons dark with the blood of their enemies. Bjólf beat upon the massive timbers with the pommel of his sword, then stood back and squinted up through the stinging flecks of rain at the watchtower.

"Open up!" he bellowed.

Behind Bjólf and his men, all was now silent. But before them, beyond the rampart, voices could once again be heard raised in argument. Among them, though almost drowned out by the chaotic bickering of numerous unidentifiable men and women, the familiar tones of the crewmen Bjólf had ordered to stay at the gate, now raised in anger.

Gunnar and several other of the men on the outside of the stockade looked anxiously at the dark line of trees, aware that there was fresh movement there. But before Bjólf could raise his voice again, a head appeared at the top of the watchtower. It was the old man, Klaufi.

"Open the gates, old man!" called Bjólf.

"I cannot," said Klaufi. Bjólf stared back up at him in disbelief.

Klaufi merely shrugged. "It is forbidden to open the gates without the express permission of..."

Bjólf's curt reply cut him off. "Whatever gods you follow, you'd better start praying to them, because unless you open these gates right now..."

It was Klaufi who interrupted Bjólf this time, even as the sounds of the distant death-walkers in the edges of the wood crunched and crackled in their ears. "My hands are tied. I must abide by the laws laid down by the council of the hall of... of..."

His voice trailed away. But it was not words that had stopped him. Down below, Bjólf's eyes blazed with a furious flame, his sword raised at the end of his muscular arm, its point directed at Klaufi's neck as if to take the old man's head, the wrath on his darkened face so palpable, so extreme, that the old man felt it might somehow strike him dead with a mere glance.

"Open these gates, you old fool," rumbled Bjólf, his voice cutting through the dying storm, "or, by the gods, my final act upon this earth will be to hack them to splinters and watch the dead tear the living flesh from your wretched, worthless bones."

At that, Gunnar gave a terrifying roar and charged at the gate, sinking his axe into the timber with a shuddering crash that sent chips of wood and bark flying. Klaufi stepped back in dread as the watchtower swayed. Godwin came forward next, axe held high... then Thorvald... then ten more axes with stout arms and strong backs behind them, ready to batter the gates to oblivion.

Before they could strike, another pale, alarmed face appeared above. Halldís. She was panting, breathless.

"They're our guests!" she cried at Klaufi. "Our allies! For Freyja's sake, open up!"

There was a clatter and a rumble behind the timbers, and the gates swung open. Bjólf's men poured in, casting hateful glances at the mob that had assembled there. A space cleared around the warriors.

Kjötvi stepped forward, his good ear bloodied. "They tried to stop us," he said. Farbjörn, Arnulf and Hrafning were close behind, each of them showing the signs of having been in a struggle. "Things got a little heated," continued Kjötvi. "We stopped short of using weapons. But some were not so considerate." His hand went to his right ear, which, Bjólf could now see, had had its top third sliced off, making it now almost a perfect match for the other. Bjólf looked around at the suddenly quiet crowd, baffled by this turn of events.

Hrafning read the look in his eye. "It was him stirred them up," he said, and nodded towards a pale figure that lurked at the back of the motley throng. Bjólf just had time to catch sight of the sickly, self-satisfied features of Óflár before he melted away into the shadows.

"Would you like me to gut the little weasel?" muttered Gunnar. But Bjólf – cautious Bjólf – raised a hand to stop him.

Others from the hall arrived – at their head, Frodi pushed through to the front of the crowd, looking on mortified and apologetic. Here, at least, a man with some sense of honour, thought Bjólf. The crowd then parted for Halldís, down from the watchtower, who wore a similar expression, though perhaps tempered by other, more complex feelings as she looked at Bjólf. She stepped up to him.

"Do not blame them," she said. "They have lived in fear for too long, for reasons that you now begin to understand."

"Yes, I begin to," said Bjólf, his voice hard and unsympathetic. He turned his back on her and faced his men. "We leave at first light."

Halldís stared at him in disbelief, and, stepping forward, grabbed his arm and spun him around. "You cannot leave." There was urgency – even yearning – in her voice.

"Can I not? I am master of my own destiny."

"But your task here is not done," she pleaded, a note of anger entering her voice. "You came to help us."

He took a step toward her, forcing her to back away from him. "We are not the men you sent for. We never were. Our coming here was pure chance. Our leaving, however, is a matter of choice."

"You accepted our hospitality," muttered Frodi, glowering. "We thought you honourable men."

"Think what you like," replied Bjólf. He would get over Frodi's accusations. But Halldís' despair stung him. He turned again. "We will sleep tonight wherever we are welcome." He gestured to the gate. "Out there, in our ship if we must."

"No!" said Halldís. She checked herself, then let her gaze fall, despondently contemplating the churned mud at their feet. "You are still our guests. You have my father's hall."

At this, the old woman Ragnhild suddenly lurched forward from the crowd, her arms raised in a weird gesture, her eyes rolling back in her head, a long, loud groan escaping her lips. Bjólf was ready with his sword but, to his surprise, she then pulled a small soft leather bag from inside her gown, tipped the contents upon the ground and fell to her knees. With her face still raised to the heavens, she passed her hand over the small, white tablets of bone that lay scattered in front of her. Runestones.

"Is the old woman a runecaster?" asked Gunnar, frowning at this unexpected outburst.

174

"Our seer is dead," said Halldís. "But Ragnhild has the gift."

The old woman pulled at her hair until it hung about her wildly, wailed once more, then cast her eyes over the scattered runestones.

"I see it!" she moaned. "The hidden purpose of the women at the well, the immortal *dísir*. It is clear, our salvation comes in the shape of a ship. I see it marked out in flame! Upon it are the great warriors from other lands who will deliver us. The enemy will be destroyed, the curse wiped out, and the victors shall live forever as esteemed heroes to us all!" She looked up at Bjólf, a great smile spreading across her face. "You will not leave us. Your fate is here, Bjólf son of Erling. You and all your men. And it is good!"

Bjólf looked her in the eye for a moment. "Let me show you what I think of fate."

And with that, he turned and walked away.

# CHAPTER TWENTY-FIVE

## THE LEAVE-TAKING

"WHAT DID YOU, as a man of religion, make of that?" said Bjólf to Gunnar as the crew strode off to gather their possessions.

Gunnar thought about his answer for several moments as they ran the gauntlet of bemused villagers. "Frankly?" he said, finally. "Utter bollocks. If that woman has the gift, then the emperor of Byzantium can wear my arse for a hat."

Bjólf smiled. "Don't hold back, Gunnar. Tell me what you really think."

"I think that the sooner we're out of here, the better off we will be."

Bjólf clapped him on the shoulder. "For once, big man, we are in total agreement."

Back at the hall, the men passed out the mail, armour and remaining weapons that had been stowed in the small, dark antechamber at its entrance. All understood that, this night, whatever the etiquette of the hall, they would sleep with their weapons close at hand. No one interfered with their activities. Halldís was nowhere to be seen, and all the others maintained a discreet distance. Atli, still shaking from his ordeal, looked forward to a few hours of warmth and sleep by the hall's great hearth and some of the leftovers from the feast.

Bjólf looked over those who were injured. Thankfully, all were minor wounds. The one significant exception was the horrible wound upon Jarl's neck, where the female death-walker had taken a piece of him. That would require Magnus's expert eye. In many respects, Jarl had been lucky; the bite had stopped just short of the parts that would have threatened his life. But, although Jarl refused to show it, Bjólf knew that the ragged tear had left its victim in excruciating pain. And then there was the question of this strange pestilence. Had it been passed to Jarl? Bjólf did not wish to think about that for the moment. Jarl had maintained a kind of dogged, forced good humour since they had returned to the safety of the stockade, as if he too wished only to put it from his mind.

Bjólf turned from him. "Magnus?" he called. "There's a patient for you here." But the old monk was nowhere nearby. Bjólf sighed impatiently and scanned the low-lit interior of the hall. "Magnus?" he called. But there was no reply. No movement.

Others began to look around. Only gradually did they realise that Magnus was not among them.

"Has anyone seen him?" called Bjólf, his sense of unease growing. "Has anyone seen him since we came back through the gate?"

No one had.

They searched for hours beyond the stockade wall, all the while watching and listening nervously for more of the shuffling, vacant ghouls. Having learned the lesson from their earlier encounters, each man went about his melancholy business in silence, thankful that the rain had abated. But for a distant scuffling or groaning carried on the breeze, there was no more sign of the death-walkers that night. Yet all secretly feared what they might find.

The sky was beginning to lighten when they discovered him. It seemed he had doubled back in an attempt to outflank the lumbering enemy, and while clambering over a large outcropping of rock near the left bank of trees had fallen into a cleft in the grey, moss-covered stone. He lay awkwardly in the narrow, grave-like gap, his temple smashed and bleeding, his eyes rolled back in his head, his breath barely perceptible. He had fallen victim not to the death-walkers, not to his own valour or to some rash, foolhardy act, but to nothing more than a meaningless accident.

They took him to the hearth, tended his wounds and kept him warm. Fjölvar knew a little of the healing arts, and did what he could. Halldís sent her most learned practitioner – a crook-backed woman with a knowledge of herbs – but herself remained distant. The cruellest irony was that the only one who really knew how to deal with such a grievous wound was Magnus himself. Magnus the Healer. Magnus the Gentle. Magnus the Wise. There was knowledge in him that would be forever lost.

Bjólf sat with him for the rest of the night. Atli, though exhausted and craving sleep, sat up too, Magnus's shallow, rasping breaths marking the time until they were to leave.

In his long and colourful career, spanning more voyages than he could recount, Bjólf had experienced all manner of farewells. Some were joyous and celebratory, some marked by tears and anguish. A good number were accompanied by the battle-roar and clatter of weapons, while yet others were silent and stealthy, watched only by the plashing fish and the ravens that croaked among the dawn treetops.

But never had he known a leave-taking so bleak, so dismal.

The villagers, for the most part, remained in their homes. Bjólf and his men – kitted out much as they had been for their dramatic arrival the previous day, but now curiously drained of the pride and bold defiance that had once inspired in them – set out in silence beyond the stockade, largely unregarded. Four men carried the unconscious Magnus between them in a makeshift bier. Though all knew it, none spoke of the fact that he was dying. All loved the old man too much to admit it.

It was not until they were upon the path leading down to the muddy harbour that the full extent of the previous night's carnage became clear. All around them, from one bank of trees to the other, dozens of bodies – or parts of bodies – littered the ground, all hacked and hewn and in various horrid states of mutilation and decay, a ghastly, stomach-turning stench hanging about the place, too heavy for the morning breeze to carry off. Twisted limbs stuck up into the air, some in tortured gestures. Rocks and grass and mud were occasionally stained with the black ichor, the gentle undulations of the landscape jarringly pockmarked here and there by shapeless heaps of gore, or denuded bone from which the flesh had slipped or been slashed. It was as if, in that one night, the dead of ages had been hauled shrieking from their graves, wrenched apart and scattered about to be picked at by birds and beasts. But there were no beasts to pick at this flesh, and not a single bird sang.

The fog had lifted. The sun shone. But all served only to make the horror the more immediate, the more inescapable. The final atrocity was the fact that what little had remained of Salómon and Eldi from the previous night had now completely disappeared – taken by whom, or what, none could tell. Of the others – Grimm, Lokki and Hrolf – nothing more was ever seen again. The night had swallowed them. As they made the final approach to the ship, through bone-strewn mud and water, all tried not to imagine the fates of their fellows, or shuddered visibly at the unwelcome thought.

As the last of the rainwater was bailed, the oars were thrust out and the vessel rowed into the river where it was turned slowly downstream, Grimmsson's rowing boat towed behind. Bjólf stood at the stern, noting with a bitter pang of despair the gaps in the rowing benches, doggedly refusing to turn back towards the stockade. Had he done so, he might just have made out the solitary figure of Halldís upon the rampart, a blue cloak wrapped tightly around her against the cold morning breeze as she gazed at the gradually departing ship, a look of empty desolation upon her face. But it was the certain knowledge that she alone was watching that kept Bjólf's back turned on the village of the daughter of Hallbjörn.

It remained so until long after the place was gone from view.

# CHAPTER TWENTY-SIX

## THE RESURRECTION AND THE LIFE

THEY HAD BARELY departed when Magnus finally gave up the ghost.
For hours afterwards they followed the winding course of the river
in silence, the wind in their faces. The channel became broader, the
turns longer and more meandering, and here and there it began to
fork off into other tributaries, some of which were near-choked
with overhanging trees and creepers. But, bit by bit, the banks
became more favourable to the presence of men; the vegetation
thinned, seeming to spring forth with a more youthful vigour. No
longer the impenetrable, primordial murk of the cursed land they
had left behind, but fresh and inviting, the penetrating sunlight
clearing the airy forests of the dank moulds and fungi that had
weighed so heavily upon the air of that weird domain. To port,
far beyond the trees, the land rose to craggy, mountainous uplands
whose jagged tops shimmered in a hazy morning mist. Beyond
them, Bjólf surmised, lay the steep-sided fjord which led to the site
of their encounter with Grimmsson's ship. Yet nearby, the banks'

edges were shallow and inviting, the grass lush, the soil dark, the trees lofty yet not oppressive, their branches filled once more with the songs of birds.

It felt like emerging from a nightmare, and yet, even this began with the end of a life.

Looking down upon the neatly wrapped corpse of Magnus, Bjólf called out to his crew.

"Heave to!"

Thorvald leaned on the tiller. The men shipped the oars, and Finn threw out the anchor. They would land here and rest a while. Perhaps hunt some game. And, most of all, they would give Magnus a decent burial. He, at least, would be properly laid to rest. It would not quite be the funeral he deserved – no array of rich accoutrements to accompany him to the next world (in truth, Bjólf was uncertain what warrior trappings, if any, were appropriate to the Christian heaven). But the spot was tranquil and beautiful, with dappled sunlight and scattered clumps of fragrant herbs here and there – the very ones the old man had once so carefully gathered to ply his craft – and Bjólf knew that, to Magnus, this would be worth more than all the wealth and ceremony of a king.

With the ship safely anchored a short distance from the shore, Bjólf took his place upon the steering deck, the body of Magnus at his feet, and turned to his men.

"I am no religious man, but Magnus followed the White Christ, and while I profess no knowledge of gods or their ways, it is only right that we honour him in his own manner, out of love and respect for the man we knew." A general mutter of approval passed through the assembled company. "But also, I wish to pay him my own tribute, this last time. There are others for whom I would like to have done the same, others we have lost. I cannot stand over their bodies and speak words of praise at their deeds. We have been denied that right. And so, my words over this, our most recently fallen, go out in honour of them all." He paused for a moment, head lowered, thinking carefully about the form of his words.

"Magnus was a great friend. A fearless man and a generous one, whose skills in healing we all have had reason to thank over the years. Some of us live today only because of him." There were nods of assent. "I remember when we first found him, locked in a filthy cell, drunk and baying for the blood of his abbot – branding him a coward and a hypocrite in the foulest possible language..." Another laugh, more raucous this time. "This was not what I had come to expect of a Christian monk. The very next moment, he was telling us where the abbot's silver was hidden and begging to be taken away from that hell-hole. Somehow I sensed we had found – what can I call it? – a kindred spirit. He began as our guest, became our friend. Our teacher. Such were the qualities of the man..." Bjólf cleared his throat, looked suddenly self-conscious and uncertain, then pressed his flattened palms together awkwardly in an unfamiliar gesture. This was to be, he hoped, how Magnus might have wanted it. His eyes sought out Odo amongst the men crowded on the deck. Odo nodded discreetly to confirm that Bjólf was doing it right.

"Man comes from earth, and returns to earth," Bjólf began, hesitantly. He'd heard parts of the sacred book from Magnus many times before, but now he was starting to wish he'd listened more closely. It all seemed to jumble together in his head. "We commend his soul to... to... the hall of Christ..." Was that right? He recalled that Christ and his men were sailors, but what else? He searched his memory, trying to find somewhere in it the sound of Magnus's voice. "Long may he feast there... at the... last supper of his God..." A groan came from somewhere. Was his attempt at this really that bad? He pressed on, regardless. "And revel in that heroic company... until the great day of his... earthly resurrection." Yes, now he remembered. A familiar phrase popped into his head, as if Magnus himself had uttered it in his ear. He spoke it triumphantly: "The Christ told his men, 'I am the resurrection and the life'..."

As he spoke the words, a second, greater groan came from the deck. With it was a sound which seemed utterly incongruous – the slow tearing of fabric. Before Bjólf could grasp what was happening, the front few rows of the crew recoiled suddenly, crashing into those behind, and an ungainly white shape seemed to loom out of nowhere. It staggered drunkenly before him, shreds of stretched and rent linen unravelling and falling away from its face as the thing within emerged like a moth from its silken cocoon.

Magnus. And not Magnus.

Bjólf was momentarily paralysed, not with fear, but with disbelief. Others seemed similarly stricken. In the weird, still silence that followed, the eerily frozen company stood tense and motionless, expressions of horror and incredulity upon their faces, as the ghoulish figure wearing their friend's features swayed uneasily before them, its arms still part-swaddled by the remains of its wrappings. Its head turned stiffly, twitching, taking in its surroundings like a ghastly newborn. Its feet shuffled and it lurched suddenly around to face the body of men. At the sight of them – of this great feast of flesh – the expressionless mouth lolled open, spilling drool upon the gnarled wood of the deck. From it came another horrible, imbecilic wail.

Shrunk against the gunwale, half-slumped in horror, Atli scrabbled backwards at the sound as if to put more distance between him and this new nightmare. Next to him, the old, rusted spare anchor – the very one Háki the Toothless had swung with such crushing effect at the jaws of Grimmsson's men – shifted noisily at his elbow and fell flat against the boards. At the sound, the dead parody of Magnus turned, baring its teeth, and lunged at the boy.

Atli flung himself out of the creature's way as several men – snapped out of their reverie – jumped forward in an attempt to restrain it. As they did so, its arms finally sprang free of its linen bindings and flailed about wildly, catching one or two across the face. They reeled back, but more waded into the fray, grabbing at it in a disordered melée of shouting and thrashing. The thing turned on anyone that came near, fearless, thoughtless, punctuating the uproar with the sharp clatter of its teeth snapping at their flesh.

Many now had weapons drawn; seaxes and knife-blades flashed in the sunlight. Yet many who would not have hesitated under other circumstances – who had survived past battles only because of their lack of hesitation – were suddenly afflicted by a crippling doubt. This was Magnus. Wise Magnus. Gentle Magnus. Was he alive after all? He walked. He moved. Could he not be crazed with fever? Might he not be saved? Even as the ghastly, pallid mockery lurched before them, evoking all the horrors of the previous night, misplaced hope stayed their hands.

Bjólf stepped forward, then, sword drawn. "Get back!" he called as he strode towards the wild brawl, blade raised and ready over his shoulder. The men immediately scattered, knowing their captain would not wait to strike his blow. The creature whirled around, saw his approach, and even as Bjólf swung at it, flew at him with no regard for its own welfare. The sudden move caught Bjólf off guard; he tried to redirect his blade as it sang through the air, and caught the creature across its raised arm with a clumsy strike. The thing staggered and crashed against him. Bjólf fell as its severed arm – still moving – thudded on the deck next to him, splashing thick, foetid fluid across his face.

The thing was still on its feet, looming over him. Some of the men, the spell broken, had snatched up spears and poked at the writhing figure. But its eyes were fixed upon Bjólf. Ignoring the spear-points, it cried out again – a hollow moan of blind, ravenous hunger. Drool dripped upon Bjólf's chest.

Gunnar, meanwhile, had grabbed the nearest thing to hand – the iron chain that had come aboard with Grimmsson's treasure chest. He swung it around his head in a great circle, its heavy length clinking and roaring in the air. The others stepped back at the sound, and he made his move. The iron links caught the thing a heavy blow on the side of the head, wrapping around its neck, and Gunnar hauled the creature towards him with a roar and threw loops of chain about its body, pinning its arm against its chest. He spun the creature around and looped the chain through itself before pulling it tight at its back. "Finish it!" he cried out, gripping the thrashing ghoul from behind in a bear hug. Thorvald broke from the crowd, his heavy axe in his hand.

Then, just when it seemed it was over, the fiend smashed its head back into Gunnar's face. He staggered back, letting go his grip, blood pouring from his nose. The thing teetered sideways, away from Thorvald, its remaining arm wriggling free again, the long chain dragging after it.

CROUCHED BY THE gunwale, Atli looked up once more at the thing that had been Magnus, stumbling above him. This time, his mind was clear. This time, it would be different. Out of the corner of his eye, he had seen Bjólf scramble to his feet. A look passed between them as Bjólf hefted one of the oars. Atli understood. "Hey! Over here!" he cried. The creature whirled around and made for him once more. Atli did not move this time, but pressed himself hard against the gunwale until the very last moment – human bait for the monster. In moments the thing was almost on him. As its hand grasped for his face he dropped, curling himself into a ball. The full weight of the oar, swung with all Bjólf's strength, cracked against the creature's back and sent it flying forward, stumbling over Atli and tipping head-first over the side.

The weight of its iron bonds dragged it swiftly beneath the surface. As the loose chain rattled along the deck, Bjólf caught hold of it and wrapped the end around the brace cleat. The chain pulled tight, and Atli peered tentatively over the side, into the churned, weedy water that had swallowed the creature. But of Magnus there was now no sign.

Bjólf clapped Atli on the shoulder with a grateful nod, even allowing himself a hint of a smile. He did not say anything. But that silent recognition meant the world to the boy.

Gunnar approached, shaking the dizziness from his head. He scooped up some water from the river and splashed it over his face and beard, then spat, and snorted the remaining blood out of his nose noisily.

"You should know better than to put your face in the way of someone's head," said Bjólf.

Gunnar simply made a gruff rumbling sound deep in his throat, one of his more subtle means of expressing annoyance. He wiped his big forearm across his mouth, and then stared at the few tiny bubbles that broke the surface, a dark and brooding look upon his face.

"Kylfing. Gøtar. Oddvarr. Now Magnus," he said. "They were all dead, of that there can be no doubt. And yet…"

Bjólf raised his hand, silencing the big man, and turned and leaned on the gunwale, staring at the place where the still quivering chain disappeared beneath the water.

"We've all seen it now," he muttered, gazing into the impenetrable, green-tinged depths, his expression dark. "The dead return." He sighed deeply. "I needed to see it with my own eyes. That is my own failing." Gunnar shrugged, as if this were not such a bad failing to have. Bjólf spoke slowly, in calm, even tones. "This was how Grimmsson's ship died. The ones you saw in the woods, they not only attacked his crew; they took the pestilence aboard. Passed it on."

He looked along the length of the *Hrafn*, and amongst the men spied a solitary, motionless figure sitting slumped, head hanging, his face pale and with a clammy sheen of sweat.

"Watch Jarl," said Bjólf.

He searched further, found another whose eyes were fixed upon the same subject, as they had been since departing the vale of

Halldís and Hallbjörn. "And watch Einarr too. His wits have been shaken since last night. Who knows what master he follows now." Gunnar, his heavily browed eyes scanning the ship, gave a curt grunt of acknowledgement.

"But what of Magnus?" he said after a long pause. "He suffered no bite. No wound at the *draugr*'s hand. And Kylfing and the others, too..."

"It is among us," Bjólf said, nodding slowly, his voice grim, resigned. "As with the dead of Hallbjörn's clan – they leave their graves regardless of the manner of their death. It is in the air. In their blood. In us. Now we carry this curse with us, wherever we go." He turned to Gunnar. "There is no escape, old friend."

Gunnar stood in silent thought, then exclaimed defiantly. "Pah! So what if death stalks us? When did it not? Nothing is changed. We do as we have always done – fight to stay alive!"

But Bjólf was not cheered by the words. He spread his hands out before him, reviewing every mark and scar, as if suddenly baffled by his own flesh. "We're dead already."

# CHAPTER TWENTY-SEVEN

## THE END BEGINS

ATLI CREPT AWAY from Bjólf and Gunnar, simultaneously appalled and numbed by their words. They had not known he was listening, had not even noticed him lingering there. That was the one advantage of being the least among the crew. Yet the knowledge had not helped. Instead, it had crippled him. He wandered the length of the ship not knowing what to think, let alone what to do. Here he was, starting out in life, yet already marked for death, doomed never to rest, never to ascend to the great halls of the warriors.

All about him, men muttered darkly. They had not been party to the same exchange, but they were not fools. Many had already drawn the same conclusions. Here and there, strange stories sprang up. They spoke in hushed tones, huddled in small groups.

"Kylfing used to say that among the Rus they told of a night-time blood-sucker," whispered Farbjörn to those gathered around him. "It was said a cursed man, or one who died in disgrace might become one, and that the affliction was passed on by its bite."

At these words, all eyes slid sideways to where Jarl sat. He stared vacantly at the deck, making no movement but the occasional febrile shiver. None sat with him.

Though doing so gave him a sickening feeling of shame, Atli gave the man a wide berth as he passed.

"My cousin has sailed far and wide out in the west," said Skjöld the Icelander to another small knot of men. "He says there is a deadly disease out there in the icy wastes in which the victim comes back to life for a time and can divulge secrets about the future." Several around him nodded as if they knew this to be the truth.

"We should have asked Magnus," said one, shaking his head. "We have squandered a valuable opportunity."

"What's the point?" scoffed Njáll dismissively. "Our future is clear enough." But few shared the Celt's cheery fatalism.

At the far end of the ship, another man sat alone. Einarr stared the length of the vessel, two swords upon his lap – his favoured blade, and an old notched weapon of his grandfather's – both of which he sharpened with a steady, obsessive purpose.

IT FELL TO Bjólf to finally break the sombre mood. Stepping up to the steering deck, he addressed the crew, his message straightforward, the words brusque and practical. "We rest now. Go and hunt. Then we'll eat and drink ashore." Pausing for a moment, he cast a cautious eye upon the forest, and added: "Keep your weapons about you. Tonight we sleep aboard ship."

None argued the point.

A rope was swiftly set up between the ship and the shore by which they could ferry themselves back and forth in the boat, and within only a few hours, men were returning from the woods with raised spirits. The hunt had been good: there were game birds of all kinds – pigeons, plover, lapwings and grouse, as well as several duck and a wild goose. Some had trapped hares, and Fjölvar, by a stroke of good fortune, had almost walked straight into a deer. Thanks to his skill with the bow, it was soon destined for the spit. Hazelnuts, berries, wild celery, nettles and a variety of herbs had been gathered, too – but the greatest prize was brought home by Úlf, who emerged red-faced and covered in stings, proudly holding aloft the crushed remains of a bees' nest, dripping with that most luxurious of commodities – honey. His arrival drew a cheer, and as Thorvald set about making the fire, a few men even began to sing as they sat and plucked the feathers from their dinner.

It was then that Finn, seeing Bjólf alone, approached him. "I beg your permission to stay ashore tonight," he said. Finn's mood was sombre and subdued, even by his own cool standards. But Bjólf recognised the look in his eye, a look that had come upon him before at times of trouble or doubt.

"You have it," he said.

"You have not asked me why."

"You have your reasons."

Finn allowed the faintest of smiles to flicker across his thin, straight lips, gave a brief nod, and made for the boat.


BACK ON THE *Hrafn*, Atli was crouched upon the deck. He had been charged with scrubbing the boards clean of the gore that had been spilled upon it. Had, in fact, been abandoned there until the job was done. Exhaustion from lack of sleep had nearly got the better of him. The sound of the rowing boat hitting the side of the ship made him jump out of his reverie. Watching quietly, he saw Finn step aboard and, approaching his sea-chest, draw various strange objects from it. Chief among them was what, at first, appeared to be a large wooden bowl, but proved to be a drum, the skin painted with all manner of strange images and symbols: birds and beasts and stylised figures of men, and a host of bizarre, spindly signs and characters at whose meaning he could only guess. Finn tapped its taut surface with his finger. It rang out a clear, resonant note. Seemingly satisfied with its condition, he rummaged further in his chest and drew out a small bundle of cloth, in which were wrapped a metal ring and a smooth length of animal bone. He wrapped them up again carefully, and placed both bundle and drum in a skin bag which he slung over his shoulder. As he turned to make his way back to the rowing boat, he caught sight of Atli. The boy looked away and scrubbed fiercely. When he looked up again, Finn was towering over him. For a moment, each looked at the other. Then Finn spoke in quiet tones.

"I go to listen to the earth spirits, seek their guidance. For that my feet must be upon the earth. I do not know what they will say, or what they will ask of me. But if I do not come back, tell them this is what I did. That I did not leave willingly, but acted out of love for this ship." Atli nodded, wide-eyed. With that, Finn turned and left.

All ate well that night, but, few slept soundly. From the dark shadows of the shore, the hollow sound of Finn's reindeer-skin drum beat its lonely, melancholy rhythm on through the dark hours. Most aboard understood what that meant, though none would speak of it. And beneath them, somewhere in the weedy waters, another sound – one that Atli recognised – further disturbed their restless slumber. It was the never ceasing *scrape-scrape-scrape* of Magnus's fingernails clawing against the wood of the hull.

THE MORNING – SUNLIT and beautiful as it was – brought a new and unexpected horror. So withdrawn had he become from the rest of the crew that none could remember for certain when Einarr had ceased to be among them. A search of the shore at first yielded nothing – then Finn appeared from the woods, looking haggard and drained, and directed them to the spot.

"I kept the wild beasts from his body," he said.

In a clearing, beneath a tall pine, Einarr's lifeless, bloody corpse lay. Hanging from a branch high above was a length of rope, and at its end a curious contrivance formed of two swords. Each was lashed to the other close to the hilt, their blades uppermost, like a half open pair of scissors. A short way up, another length of rope was twisted around the crossed blades to prevent them parting further, and it was to the middle of this that the line to the branch had been tied. The lower part of it and much of the tree were splashed with blood. Einarr had evidently placed his head between the blades, tightened the rope behind his neck, and jumped from a lower branch. It had decapitated him instantly, like a pair of shears snipping off a flower head. It was, for him, the only certain solution. Finn had heard the sound, and stayed with the body until morning, when the boat would return.

Bjólf surveyed the scene with a mixture of pity and contempt.

"What do you want done with him?" said Gunnar.

"Leave him to the birds," said Bjólf bitterly. "Nothing we can do will bring any honour to this."

Bjólf then went and spoke with Finn for some time, away from the others. Gunnar watched Bjólf's face as he responded to Finn's muttered words, listening intently, and wondered what it was that passed between them.

When they returned to the ship, news came that Jarl, too, had passed. None had checked on him during the night or made efforts to tend his wound. As Bjólf approached the pale body, its expression haunted and tortured even in death, he saw that the crew maintained a wide space around it – and not, he knew, out of respect. Without hesitation he took up Godwin's axe, swung it high in the air and brought it down upon Jarl's neck. His head sprang from his body and rolled towards their feet, spilling fresh gore upon Atli's carefully scrubbed deck.

Bjólf leaned on the axe and looked each one of them in the eye. "I would expect any of you to do the same to me." He handed the axe back to its owner. "Set his body in the boat and let the river take it. He was a man of the sea. Let him return there in peace." And he headed towards the prow.

"What now?" called Thorvald.

"Now we go back."

"Home?" came a hopeful voice.

"To Björnheim and the hall of Halldís."

There was consternation among the men. Even Gunnar looked at him in surprise. Bjólf stood upon the foredeck, facing his crew.

"Finn! Tell them what you told me."

All eyes turned to the Saami shaman. He spoke in a clear voice. "Our future lies with Halldís and the men of the black ships. There can be no doubting it."

The grumbling of the men surged again; some in protest, others suddenly less certain. Many believed implicitly in the power of Finn's magic. Bjólf raised his hands to silence them once more.

"I speak with no spirits. No gods. But for what it's worth, I am of the same opinion." There was further muttering of discontent, but Bjólf raised his voice again. "This tyrant Skalla, and his men, they are the source of this scourge. But they also possess its secret." He paused as the men became suddenly silent. "A secret that we can take from them."

So that's it, thought Gunnar. He has a plan.

"We cannot fight the power of a black wizard!" called one.

"He is no wizard," spat Bjólf, angered at the words. He strode back and forth as he spoke. "The white powder. The clear liquid. Halldís spoke of these things. Skalla controls his death-walkers with them, just as Magnus used herbs to heal. And Magnus was no wizard." There was a murmur of agreement. "Skalla is just a man. And if he can control this pestilence, then why not we?"

Bjólf turned to Finn once more.

"Tell them..."

"The spirits showed me a vision of their island fortress split apart and consumed by fire."

The murmuring grew in volume again.

"Do you still doubt that we can do it?" Bjólf called out, as if daring them to believe it. "Do you?" He drew his sword and ranged its glinting point before them.

"Leave now if you wish. You're all free men. But for good or ill, this ship sails south." He pointed southward with his blade, then swept it over their heads, arm outstretched, his voice rising with vengeful fury as he spoke. "The secret lies within that fortress. Bow to this curse if you like. But that's not my way. I mean to fight it, to fight until my muscles tear and sinews snap, to cut out its stinking black heart and see that stronghold ruined and in flames!" Some of the men roared their approval. "At the very least, I mean to do some good before I die." His voice grew quiet again, his face grave. "If you find that meat too rich for your tastes, go now, and let no more be said of it."

Gunnar drew his sword and raised it silently, slowly into the air. Without hesitation, Atli drew *Steinarrsnautr* and did the same. Njáll and Godwin joined them. Then Fjölvar, Odo, Thorvald, Úlf... One by one each man raised his blade aloft, every one showing his pledge, until the deck was a forest of glinting steel. Bjólf raised his own sword in salute, and as he did so a sudden breeze moved the gilded vane upon the mast, turning it southwards.

"The wind is with us," called Bjólf. "Raise the sail! To the south, and Skalla's ruin!"

A great cheer erupted. Immediately the men dispersed, each to his task. Shouts went up all over the ship, and men hauled on lines, muscles standing out like whipcords. The yard was heaved up the mast, the great sail unfurled, the great black image of a raven filling the sky above them.

As the rush of activity continued Finn approached Bjólf, and spoke to him in quiet tones. "You did not tell them everything, about what the spirits revealed."

"They showed you victory," said Bjólf. "That's all I need to know."

"They also said that none of us would leave fjord of the black fortress for a thousand years."

Bjólf looked Finn in the eye, then without a word turned and strode towards the tiller where Gunnar stood, staring indecisively at the chain that was still wrapped around the brace cleat.

"What about him?" said Gunnar, a note of indignation in his voice. "We cannot just leave him to writhe and flail in the depths for eternity. It is Magnus! Our friend!"

"Magnus is long gone," said Bjólf. And with that, he unfastened the chain and let it slip over the side. He watched it disappear like a snake into the water as the men made ready to turn back to the land of the death-walkers, and their grim appointment with Skalla.

# PART THREE

## *RAGNARÓK*

# INTERLUDE

SKALLA SAT IN the great hall's late gloom, elbows on his knees, one hand held against his wrecked left eye. He felt strangely detached from all that had happened to him – oddly unmoved by his injury, or the loss of half his sight, even as his good eye watched the blood which soaked his sleeve and oozed through his half-closed fingers, drip into a thick pool upon the beaten earth of the floor. An image of a clawed hand flailing towards his face flashed through his mind. He shuddered at the resurrected memory of its bone scraping against his.

That feeling, too, would fade, in time.

Twelve nights had passed since the first one came. The creature had been drawn by the sounds of their feasting, bitter with envy, perhaps, at the pleasures of honest meat and ale and the promise of lusty embraces that it was now denied; enraged by the voices joined in song, the joy of fellowship, the celebration of life. It was a life-hater from the misty margins of this world, of neither earth nor Hel; a lost traveller between life and death who had no lord and bore no arms and was immune to the bite of human blades. Dead, and not dead. A hate-filled monster. A demon.

Such was the opinion of his master. It was, so Skalla had begun to realise, calculated to cast the conflict in a more heroic light.

To him, the act had no more heroism than the killing of a rat. What was certain was that this guest had come with a wholly different kind of feasting in mind. At least, thought Skalla, it displayed a sense of humour – if sense it had at all. He had reason to doubt that, though. It seemed to him they were driven by only the basest instincts. He had observed their movements the past several nights, as one invader had become two, then five, then seven... He had watched as the first of them to invade the hall had struck the guests through with shock and dread, how its bloody assault upon the nearest of them had happened before any knew how to respond, and how all had made repeated, futile attempts at restraining it, having no weapons to hand, while the woman Arnfrith had screamed over and over in confused horror, begging them not to harm her late husband. That man had been killed by some beast whilst out hunting, they said. Now they knew better.

He had watched each successive night as the clamour of feasting had drawn more of them, the dead of previous nights returning as if in some nightmare, and wondered at the dogged refusal of Hallbjörn to admit weapons or to quit the hall, even when his guests were dwindling in number and those that persisted were getting eaten alive.

And he had watched, especially, during that last desperate fight, when the *draugr* had proved too numerous for the newly-posted hall-guards to repel, seeking confirmation of his conclusions before taking action. And even then, his actions were by way of an experiment – a confirmation, or otherwise, of a theory. The crushing blows to the heads of three of the fiends with the heavy iron poker – the same one with which he had tended the fire for so many years – provided the confirmation he sought. Each of their skulls had been smashed outright with a single impact, felling them immediately – the last achieved in spite of his grievous wound.

The fact that it had also saved his master's life was pure coincidence.

"You have served me well over many years," said Hallbjörn. "And never more loyally than today. You fought when others fled." He turned, walking in a small circle, avoiding a patch that had been churned to red mud in the struggle. "Perhaps it is time to talk about your future."

"Future?" said Skalla.

It was something he had had little reason to think about. He had trained himself to avoid it over the years. What had been the point? How was his wretched future to be any different from his wretched past, consisting as it did of the same tasks, the same hardships, the same endless succession of days?

"About your *freedom*..." added Hallbjörn. He spoke with great gravity, emphasising the final word as if it were a potent charm, and carried in its utterance some magical, transformative power.

"Freedom," repeated Skalla. He rolled it around in his mind, muttered it again, as if considering it from different points of view might somehow endow it with life. It remained as dead as earth. The notion, after all, was meaningless. It seemed as though every free man assumed the idea would mean so much more to a lifelong slave such as him. They were wrong. "Freedom to do what?"

Hallbjörn laughed, a note of irritation in his voice. "Why, to do whatever you wish. To remain here. Or to make your way in the world, if you so choose."

To remain here. To work exactly as he had been working, no doubt. Or to venture out there, to what? With what? What kind of choice was that? It was, thought Skalla, the kind of generosity that only a wealthy man could think worthwhile;   a gift that, to one with nothing, meant nothing. An act of benevolence that, in truth, gave more to the giver.

But then, perhaps there was something out there that had caught his interest, after all. Something no one could have expected. And something of which Hallbjörn was unlikely to approve.

"What would you have me do?"

The question clearly pleased Hallbjörn. "We must go to the source of this pestilence and stamp it out," he said, his voice suddenly charged with a stern gravity. The voice of destiny, thought Skalla. The voice of an imagined saga, told in an imagined future around this very fire. "I *ask* that you join me in this quest."

So that was it – the great honour that Hallbjörn was now bestowing upon him. To fight and die for his jailer.

In truth, Skalla had been thinking quite a bit about the source of this pestilence. Since the great firestorm, the night it all began, he had overheard increasingly wild stories about the mysterious island in the fjord and the dark, magical powers that had begun to emanate from it. Skalla did not believe in magic, even as he had watched the dead of the clan of Hallbjörn stagger back into the hall, the marks of their deaths still upon them. In them, he saw no curse. Just another process to be understood. He knew the world for what it was: dead matter, mindlessly shifting in space, grinding the pathetic creatures that scuttled between its cracks with as little thought as a millstone gives a weevil; a relentless chaos of struggle and death, from which only the deluded sought escape through desperate belief in the beyond. Skalla had never had the luxury of such childish notions. Creation was material to be used, held at bay, bent to one's will. Only then could fleeting pleasures, brief moments of satisfaction, be wrung from it.

And what did he care whether dark or light? Two sides of the same coin. Dark, light, day or night – he was equally a slave whichever held sway. The lash raised the same weals, whether brandished by a good man or a bad.

But power – that which dictated whose hand was on the lash... that interested him greatly. It was something he had hardly known. Yet, for that very reason, he felt he knew it more keenly than any of the pampered, overindulged free men who passed him by each day; men who, through years of familiarity, failed to even register his presence. That, too, could prove an advantage.

Yes, there was a power growing upon the island, that was certain. He had seen it challenge Hallbjörn in his own hall, shake his authority to its roots, turn the laws of life and death upon their heads, bringing fear to those who had for so long fancied themselves fearless. It had struck ruthlessly, coldly, without passion or anger and with no regard for etiquette or honour. And for that reason, Skalla knew, it would win. In the past twelve days Skalla had become aware of an entirely different future from the one that, until now, had seemed inevitable. In his mind's eye he now saw something he thought never to see: the fall of the power of Hallbjörn in this land, and the rise of another.

Skalla looked up at Hallbjörn, removing his red, blood-slicked hand from his torn left eye. He saw his master wince at the sight of his injured face, then hastily regain his composure, his kindly, benevolent expression. The reaction gave Skalla a curious glow of satisfaction. He had never before cared how he looked. No woman would look at him, not even the slave girls from whom he had once forced brief, empty pleasures, before such things had ceased to seem worth the effort. But they would all notice him now. Perhaps even fear him. And fear was the greatest power of all.

This would be his way, now. Where others saw a curse, Skalla would find opportunity. And the greater opportunity – the one that had begun to emerge out of the fog over the past few days – finally stood before him, clear and unassailable.

"Odin gave an eye in exchange for wisdom," he said, holding Hallbjörn's gaze. "Perhaps, now, I too see the future more clearly. See what must be done."

"Good." said Hallbjörn, smiling. He turned and went to the high seat, and from behind it drew out a sword in a gilded, richly embossed scabbard. He turned and approached Skalla, carrying the sword before him with great reverence, laid flat across his upturned hands. Its hilt and pommel were of gold, with fine cloisonné inlay of garnets and blue millefiori glass, its grip made of alternating rings of silver and whalebone. This was a great sword from the old times, the only battle-blade permitted in the great hall. But this one ventured into battle no longer. Even in the desperate conflicts of past nights, it had remained sheathed. It was a sword of ancestors, meant for the giving and taking of oaths, upon whose blade – and the blood it had spilled – such oaths were made inviolate.

Hallbjörn, still smiling, drew the great blade and, laying its scabbard gently upon the ground, held the sword before him towards Skalla. Only gradually did Skalla grasp the nature of the honour that was to be bestowed upon him. He was to be given his freedom, and the opportunity to swear his allegiance to Hallbjörn. To be given the status of a warrior.

To Hallbjörn's surprise, Skalla reached forward and took the sword by the grip. Without expression, he swung it from side to side, judging its weight in his hand. Hallbjörn half laughed, frowning at his slave's ignorant action, went to correct him. Before he could do so, Skalla swung the blade with all his strength, severing the old man's head. The expression on its face as it left his body and bounced sizzling into the fire was one of utter disbelief.

Yes, it was a good blade. Sharp enough. It would serve him in his new purpose.

This new power would need men. An army. And an army would need a captain. So why not him? They cared not for status or protocol. But he had to move quickly, before another saw the chance. He would gather others around him – slaves, like himself, who had suffered under the yoke of the old ways. They would accept his authority. He would exploit their bitterness and resentment, fashion a force of men to offer to the new regime that was rising in the fjord, and in doing so turn the tables on their masters.

Skalla glanced down without feeling at the headless body of the man who had once owned him. Taking a step back from the spreading pool of blood, he looked up at great beams of the hall that would one day be his, and, sheathing the great sword in its magnificent golden scabbard, shoved it roughly through the worn, dirty leather belt fastened about his greasy tunic and stalked off into the night.

The first blow of the new order had been struck.

# CHAPTER TWENTY-EIGHT

## THE RETURN OF THE RAVEN

THE SAILING WAS good; their passage swift. Beneath the great raven – bulging before the wind, wings outspread – their expressions were grim. But, as they were carried southwards towards their fate, there was a growing defiance upon the brow of each and every man. They had witnessed much in the past few days – seen a possible future presented to them in the grisly fates of their less fortunate comrades. But, with their quest now set, they were now determined. Swords were sharpened, axes honed. They would not end like Magnus, or Jarl, or Einarr. They would fight until they were victorious, or until death took them. And each man silently pledged that he would not leave another of his fellows to suffer the living death.

When they once again stood before Halldís and her court, with Bjólf at their head, they were very different men. There was no pretence now. They came fully armed and armoured, sweeping aside protests as they entered the hall.

"We come to war," Bjólf had said, "and go nowhere unless equipped for war."

Halldís had allowed it. That tradition, noble as it was, had cost them enough lives.

"We thought you lost to us," said Halldís. Her voice was cold, but Bjólf fancied he detected more than a hint of irony in it. Well, he could hardly blame her for that.

"It seems things once thought lost have a habit of coming back."

"Some more welcome than others." She paused, keeping him guessing another few moments. "We are glad at your return." Her expression warmed, a flicker of a smile crossing it – even, he thought, something mischievous, flirtatious. "Tell us, what was it drew you here again?"

"We have a new purpose," he said. She raised her eyebrows, questioningly. "Before we came merely to trade, knowing nothing of your plight."

"And now?"

"We come to fight. To destroy the black ships and put Skalla in the earth. To fight our fate. The fate that afflicts us all."

She held his gaze for a lingering moment, knowing now that Bjólf's crew laboured under the curse of undeath that, even as his ship had been leaving, she had hoped they'd escaped.

There were murmurs of approval at Bjólf's bold announcement. Ragnhild beamed with joy. At Halldís's shoulder, Frodi held Bjólf's gaze and nodded slowly in satisfaction. At last, it seemed, the two men had come to an understanding. Bjólf was glad to have regained his respect.

Then a pale, joyless figure stepped forward from the rest, regarding Bjólf and his men with a sideways look. Óflár the Watcher. Óflár the Patient.

"You seriously believe you can alter the course of fate?" he said. His voice was thin and reedy, its tone as pinched and mean as his person. He extended his long, skinny hand in the direction of the distant harbour. "Why not try to change the course of this river while you're at it?" Several members of the court sniggered at that.

"I have seen the course of a river changed," responded Bjólf calmly silencing the doubters. "I have also seen blocks of stone piled high as mountains in the deserts of the south. And a great wall, as high as three men and twenty *sjømil* long or more – the whole width of England. Men did these things. Men who did not shrink from challenge. Who did not sit comfortably at home, who did not amount to nothing merely because they refused to question what was thought impossible."

Óflár's milky eyes narrowed to slits. His supporters among the assembled throng shuffled their feet uncertainly as he passed before Bjólf in silence, then circled and stalked slowly back. "You have great confidence in your powers where before you had none," he said, then turned on the rest of the crew as if probing for signs of weakness. "Is this the view of you all?"

Gunnar cleared his throat and shrugged. "My noble captain and I do have rather differing views on the nature of fate," he said.

Óflár allowed himself a thin smile at this. The big man's tone changed as he fixed the pale figure before him with glowering eyes. "But better to fight than to cower."

Óflár's pale fists clenched. Frodi did not attempt to hold back his smile.

"Are you with me?" called Bjólf to his crew.

"Aye!" came the shout – strong and clear, all voices as one, the sound ringing about the rafters of the great hall.

"You have your answer," said Bjólf.

Seething, his mouth downturned like a spoilt child, Óflár slunk back into the shadows.

Halldís stepped forward then. "We cannot avoid what fate places before us," she said. "Yet I believe that an intelligent man may moderate what fate brings, if he is clear in his mind and is prepared to seek the help of friends."

Bjólf nodded in acknowledgment.

"You said that Skalla had power over his death-walkers," he said. "We mean to take that from him. It is the one hope for the salvation of us all – my crew and your people."

Frodi raised his eyebrows, impressed at what he heard. "It will be a hard fight," he said.

"That is the only kind of fight we understand," responded Bjólf with a half-smile. "But we need to learn all we can about our enemy. Numbers, weapons, the kinds of men they are..."

"We can tell you all we know," said Frodi. "But you may be able to see some of that for yourself, and sooner than you think."

Bjólf looked from Frodi to Halldís, a frown upon his face.

"Skalla comes to collect his tribute once a month, after the first day of the full moon," explained Halldís. "And it is full moon tonight."

Bjólf and Gunnar exchanged glances. They would need to plan quickly.

"When does he come?" asked Bjólf.

"Midday. When the shadows of the stags upon the gable point their horns at the well."

"What strength?"

Frodi spoke this time. "Always one ship with at least twenty men. Several armed with crossbows. Fearsome weapons."

"Yet those behind them are poor warriors, for the most part," added Halldís. "No match for your men. But..."

"But" – Frodi took up the point – "they have their *draugr* berserkers..." He hung his head and sighed. "Against them, I am afraid, there is little defence."

"Everything has its weakness," said Bjólf. "Theirs is a white powder that Skalla carries about him." He allowed his eyes to linger upon Halldís for a moment, then turned to his crew. "We shall lie in wait, watch from the forest's edge. See what we can see. Take them if we can." He turned back to the mistress of the hall. "Perhaps we can force this to a swift conclusion."

At this, Frodi stepped forward. "If we are to fight, you can add my sword to those of your men."

More came forward then, each pledging to stand with Bjólf. He nodded and smiled in grateful acknowledgement. True, the men were old, but their will was strong, and they knew their enemy.

Gunnar grunted. "And what if more of those death-walkers come sniffing around while we're crouched among the trees?"

Bjólf looked at him with fire in his eyes. "We point them at Skalla," he said.

# CHAPTER TWENTY-NINE

## SKALLA

ATLI PEERED OUT nervously from the thick tangle of undergrowth, his sword drawn, the smell of sweat, rotting wood and rank estuary mud in his nostrils. At first he had laughed when he saw the men smearing the stinking mud upon their helms; then Gunnar told him it was to prevent their position being given away by the glint of metal, and he had swiftly followed suit. That was his first lesson of the day.

Ahead of them, beyond the trees, the harbour was a picture of peace. It had been that way much of the morning. The grisly remains of the slaughter of the death-walkers had been cleared, and now the sun shone down, the grey-green water sparkled, and the wind sighed in the trees. Only the total absence of birdsong attested to the abnormal nature of the place.

He shifted to relieve the cramp in his foot, and cursed as he caught his thumb on a bramble thorn. To the left of him, Godwin gave a nudge and raised a single finger to his lips. Atli reddened, and stuck his thumb in his mouth.

The harbour, as yet, was empty of life, devoid of threat. But there was still the forest. What lay in there, and what might emerge, none could say for certain. Had they destroyed all the *draugr* that night? Most of them? Or were they merely the first – the advance guard of a vast, stumbling army of blood-hungry flesh-eaters?

Atli tried to imagine how many had died here since the world began, to picture them all returning – hundreds, thousands of them. How far back could this curse reach, he wondered? Years? Generations? Did it have the power to animate even the dried up bones of ancient ancestors, whose ways in life would now seem strange?

He looked behind him, past the great huddle of crouched and armoured men, into the depths of the forest where no sunlight penetrated. He had lost count of the number of times he had done that today. Gunnar, immediately on his right, caught his eye, and pointed forwards. Atli blushed again, and turned back towards the harbour. Of course, nothing could approach them through that great thicket without announcing itself, and the death-walkers were hardly models of stealth. But Atli's nerves were already getting the better of him. The waiting was becoming unbearable; he wanted to piss, but did not dare, he felt dizzy and sick, his heart pounding in his chest, his stomach clenched into a ball, every muscle in his body as tight as a harp-string and ready to snap. He had come through the long night of the death-walkers. But this was different. This, if it came to it, would be his first real battle.

He tried to banish all such thoughts from his crowded head, and focus solely on the task, on the empty scene before him. Part of him wished for the black prow of Skalla's ship to come soon and end this torment. Another wished it to be put off as long as possible.

PREPARATIONS HAD BEGUN immediately their meeting in the great hall had concluded. The older volunteers among Halldís's people had exhumed their long-idle weapons, and set about honing them back to life. Some trained and sparred, trying to coax dim memories of battle back into their limbs. At Frodi's suggestion, Bjólf had set Úlf to thickening their shields with a double layer of boards – protection against the crossbows whose power Frodi knew only too well.

The greatest task had been that of concealment of the ship. Some had argued for simply mooring it downriver, away from the fjord, from which all assumed Skalla was to come. But Bjólf was against it. What if this one time, for reasons they could not anticipate, Skalla were to come from the other direction? Some suggested hauling it ashore, into the stockade – but all knew that even over level ground, that was a back-breaking task. Fjölvar and Finn were in favour of hiding it in the thick vegetation of one of the half-choked inlets they had passed. But if they were going to do that, suggested Bjólf, why travel so far? Why not do the same thing right here? He pointed out the huge trees that draped their branches into the water on the north side of the harbour, opposite their proposed vantage point. Might not their ship disappear behind those?

A hasty survey showed it to be possible. Without delay, the men removed tents, sea-chests and weapons from the ship to the stockade. Only the great box of booty remained, stowed below deck. Bjólf did not trust their hosts that much just yet, and it was more than an afterthought that had him set Finn, the stealthiest among them, the task of keeping watch on Óflár. With the inner branches cut away, the mast was lifted from its housing in the mast-fish and lowered, and the ship carefully floated behind the huge, overhanging screen into the great cavern of tree and leaf. After a few hours work – and some judicious dressing of the branches – it was as if the *Hrafn* had never existed.

That night, Bjólf and his men had pitched their wooden-framed tents in the clearing before the hall – a great circle of them around a central fire of spitting pine logs. Haldís had food brought, to which they added some of the spoils from the previous day's hunt. Still, it was a modest feast compared to that night downriver.

"They are keeping it from us," complained Finn as they sat chewing bread around the crackling blaze, the bright painted colours of the tents glowing in the flickering light. "The good food," he explained, seeing the question upon Bjólf's face. "I have seen it, when I followed Óflár. He went to a large store-house, to check something. So I made it my business to check it too." He swallowed a tough gobbet of bread, gesticulating with the remaining piece as he spoke. "Food. Everywhere. Grain. Dried meat. Whole carcasses of mutton and beef hanging. They have deceived us!"

"It's no deception," said Bjólf. Finn frowned.

"Tribute for Skalla," explained Gunnar. He spat a piece of gristle into the fire and dug at his teeth with a finger. "It's what is to be collected tomorrow. Not destined for our table, nor that of Halldís."

Finn bit at his bread again, disconsolately.

"What else did he do?" asked Bjólf.

Finn shrugged. "He is a very boring man. After the store house he went to another hut and fed a bird in a cage. He put it on his arm, then watched it fly about. Then he went home and drank alone."

"Clearly a man whose company is in great demand," quipped Gunnar.

"Keep watching him," said Bjólf. Then they had turned in, to gather strength for the next day's encounter.

IT WAS FJÖLVAR – far out on the right flank and closest to the point of approach – who heard them first. The whispered message was passed down the line, as very shortly Atli heard them too. It was the same sound he had heard the day the *vikingr* came out of the fog. The steady dip and heave of oars, the clunk and creak of wood against wood. He strained to see past the closely-packed helms ranged to his right, through the foliage to the river. But he could make nothing out. To their left, up at the stockade, a shout went up. Someone in the watchtower had seen them first. Atli had a moment of panic at not being able to see their enemy and leaned forward, and Gunnar hauled him back.

Then the black ship slid into view.

It was long and lean, its timbers so dark they appeared pitched inside and out, the stark figurehead not a thing carved of wood, but the great, horned, empty-eyed skull of an aurochs. And, behind it, standing high upon the prow – there could be no doubting it – Skalla. He was clothed head to toe in black, the tunic of thick leather and covered with blackened, interlocking plates of metal; a foreign, unfamiliar style of armour. Above the angry scar that slashed through his dead left eye, his helm gleamed with the sheen of black flint. But the fine sword at his waist was sheathed in gold.

Up at the stockade, the gates had opened, and from them now issued a rabble of spindly figures: a ragtag band of people from the village, carrying Skalla's spoils, headed by Halldís and two elderly armed guards, whose presence, thought Bjólf, could be little more than symbolic.

"The exchange will be swift," whispered Frodi. "Skalla does not waste time on pleasantries."

As they watched, the oars were shipped, the vessel run up almost to the water's edge and a long gangplank extended to the shore. Skalla strode down it then, followed by four black-clad men. They positioned themselves at the edge of the grass, unnervingly close to where Bjólf and his men lay hidden. Frodi had been right – Skalla's followers were not the most fearsome specimens of manhood. But what they may have lacked in physical presence, they made up for with their formidable weapons. The crossbows that were slung about them were like nothing any of them had ever seen; awesome in appearance and flowing in design, the material black and gleaming like carved obsidian.

Halldís stopped a short distance away, the nervous villagers placing their cargo on the ground before her. She did not bow her head in welcome as was her usual custom. Her expression today was cold as stone. Skalla gave an abrupt signal, and several crewmen scurried down the gangplank and set about loading the goods. No word was spoken.

BJÓLF LEANED IN close to Gunnar's ear. "I count twenty-five men at most. If we hit them fast enough..."

Gunnar gripped his arm. Immediately, Bjólf saw the source of his alarm. A second ship had drifted into view – identical to the second, but for the ram's skull upon its prow. Bjólf read the agitation upon Halldís's face, sent desperate thoughts in her direction, whispering to himself through clenched teeth. *Don't look around... don't look around...*

Halldís stared straight ahead. The second ship sat back in the harbour, its dark crew scrutinizing the transaction upon the shore.

"It's still us against twenty-five if we're fast," whispered Gunnar; trying, for the moment, to put the crossbows out of his mind. "By the time the others got to shore..."

It was Skalla who silenced him this time.

"Your face gives much away," he said, regarding Halldís. His voice was hollow, empty of expression. In the trees, hands tensed around weapons. A passionless smile creased Skalla's face. "You wonder why we come in such numbers."

"You do as you wish," replied Halldís, struggling to sound indifferent.

"Yes," said Skalla. "I do." He removed his gauntlets and turned around slowly as the last of the cargo was loaded, presenting his back to her. "I have heard that a ship came here. A ship with many warriors."

Bjólf cursed under his breath.

"Someone has betrayed us..." hissed Gunnar. He glared at Frodi. Frodi looked back at him in shocked bemusement.

Halldís maintained her composure. She stood in silence for a moment, as if weighing alternatives in her mind. Finally she spoke.

"It's true," she said. Skalla turned to look her in the face, surprised by her words. "We killed them," she continued. "Poisoned their food, cut their throats as they slept and burned their bodies. Perhaps you saw the smoke?"

Skalla stared at her in amazement, then a hoarse, rasping laugh escaped him. "You really are full of surprises. You certainly have far more about you than your father ever had." Skalla fingered the pommel of the gilded sword as he spoke. Halldís bit her lip, refusing to be drawn. "Since we are forced, in these harsh times, to dispose of our dead before our dead dispose of us, there is no evidence to verify your story." He sighed. "Convenient." His eyes bored into her, searching for weakness, and then he turned away, suddenly. "Well, it seems you missed one..."

He waved his black gauntlets, and two of his men heaved a third, heavily muscled figure from the ship onto the gangplank, dragging him ashore by the ropes that bound his wrists. Every one of Bjólf's men gaped in astonishment at Helgi Grimmsson. They shoved him forward, and he staggered and fell to his knees, a stone's throw from where Bjólf was concealed, his face beaten and bruised.

"This is the only one we have encountered alive," said Skalla. "We found him wandering in the forest. So far he has proved most unco-operative."

He prodded Grimmsson with his boot, and Grimmsson spat upon it, the spittle mingled with blood. Skalla laughed again and turned back to Halldís. As he did so, Grimmsson looked up, and for a moment seemed to catch Bjólf's eye, deep in the undergrowth. Bjólf, staring back in disbelief, felt the hairs on the back of his neck prickle. Yes, it was true. Grimmsson had seen them. He gripped his sword and shield, prepared in the next moment to hear their presence proclaimed, for desperate fighting to erupt, the advantage of surprise utterly lost.

But something quite different happened.

As he held Grimmsson's gaze, he saw the big man, his eyes blazing, give a brief but urgent shake of his head, then tear his attention away. It was distinct, but subtle, such as Skalla and his men would not notice from behind.

"What was that?" whispered an astonished Gunnar.

Bjólf could hardly believe it himself. "He was warning us. Warning us not to attack."

"But why? They know we are here."

"No," said Bjólf. "They're not certain."

As they watched, Grimmsson staggered to his feet, and, turning, lurched towards Halldís. "You killed them, you bitch!" Halldís reeled in shock at the outburst. Skalla hauled on the rope, pulling Grimmsson back from her as one would an unruly dog.

"He seems to know you. I believe this one may be their captain. An unfortunate loss; he could have served my masters well. But I need to make an example."

He signalled once again. Two men hurried ashore and drove a stake deep into the ground near where Halldís stood, securing Grimmsson's rope to it with what seemed excessive care. Others, meanwhile, heaved three great, black oblong boxes down the gangplank, dragging them to within a short distance of where Grimmsson was now bound.

Grimmsson spat again in contempt, taunting them, a crazed look in his eye. "You'd better kill me well, Skalla, or by the gods I'll come back and bite your pox-ridden bollocks off!"

That defiance was soon to be shaken. With nervous hands, the men had prised off the lids – some visibly recoiling from what was revealed inside – and now retreated hastily to the refuge of their ship.

From his vantage point, Bjólf could not see what lay within. But Grimmsson could, and across his face flashed an expression Bjólf never imagined he would see upon his old rival; a look of uncomprehending horror.

Skalla drew a small flask from inside his tunic, and called out to the villagers. "Stand back, or you will all die."

They did not need telling twice. Halldís withdrew hurriedly.

Others simply turned and fled towards the stockade. Skalla threw a clear liquid from the flask into the boxes, one after the other, then backed slowly away towards the ship, watching intently.

In each box, something stirred. There were groans. A thud. A weird, deep growl – half-human, half-beast. The sound of nails clawing against wood. The first of the boxes shuddered violently, then jumped as if from some powerful impact. And from it, bit by bit, moving awkwardly, rose a huge, hulking figure of a man. At least equal to Grimmsson in size, its body was thick and muscular, but as grey and dead as the grimmest of the death-walkers. On its chest it wore a battered leather hauberk, scored and stained by battle, and here and there, the bloodless, green-tinged flesh showed signs of wounds that had been crudely repaired with stitches of rough, yellowed thread. The sutures strained and pulled the flesh as the creature stood and flexed its massive arms, a low rumble in its throat. A close-fitting helm obscured most of its features – but red eyes glowed from within the shadows, and a gaping mouth hung open in the tangled, gore-spattered mat of its beard. It wore no sword, this warrior, and carried no shield. But around its waist was a heavy chain, and from its right hand hung a battle axe of immense proportions, held in place by two iron nails.

So awe-struck was Grimmsson by this ghastly figure, that its two companions were on their feet before he realised – each as big as the first and in the same close-fitting helms; one in a ragged, rusting half-coat of mail, the other hung about with what had once been the whole skin of a wolf. The first had the wooden shaft of a great hammer nailed to its palm. The second had no weapon familiar to a warrior, but to the bones of both hands were bolted vicious iron claws.

The first looked about, sniffed at the air, turned a full circle with an unsteady gait as if not yet awake, and stopped, facing Grimmsson. Bjólf's rival could stand no more. "Come on then!" he bellowed at them, making as if to attack, heaving so hard on his rope that the stake threatened to pull free, his voice charged with renewed contempt.

It was the last coherent sound he ever made.

The first of the berserkers made a loud snort like a bull, and with a sudden burst of ferocious speed, like wild dogs let off the leash, all three flew at Grimmsson.

Flailing fists pummelled and tore, teeth snapped and snarled, and blood and gore was flung about with such savagery that in moments the living man was reduced to splintered bone and shapeless shreds of glistening, pulsing tissue.

Skalla stepped forward, dipping his hand into a small, black lacquered box, which hung on a cord about his shoulder. All three of the ogres turned at the sound of his approach, parts of Grimmsson still hanging from their champing mouths. Showing no emotion, Skalla stood his ground as they turned upon him, and in one swift movement flung a spray of the white powder across their faces. Instantly, as if felled by elf-stroke, the three colossal figures stiffened and crashed to the ground, dead as a ship's carved figurehead.

Bjólf, Gunnar and the rest looked on in shock and awe, the smell of fresh, hot blood and torn flesh carrying on the air. The attack was over so fast, the destruction so complete, that none yet knew how to react. A sword blow, the impact of an axe, the stab of a knife – these things they understood. But for such utter, instantaneous devastation to be wrought upon a living body... It was beyond their comprehension.

Skalla snapped his fingers. His men – no less terrified, with appalled expressions on their faces, one retching – crept back reluctantly and, faces averted, began to load the lifeless, blood-soaked hulks back into their boxes.

Some distance away, Halldís finally dared to put her hand to her face. A spot of Grimmsson's blood came away on her pale finger. She swayed, her face drained of colour.

Skalla looked around, almost as if he had expected some intervention, then faced her again. "Well, perhaps you told the truth after all," he said, nodding slowly, his cold eyes upon her. "I will not underestimate you again." With that he turned, preparing to leave, then again changed direction, as if having one last thing that he wished to say. "Oh, I nearly forgot – if they are all dead, then they won't be needing their ship, will they?" He signalled to the captain of the second vessel, out on the river, and from it a hail of flaming arrows was unleashed upon the great overhang of trees, within which was hidden the *Hrafn*.

Gunnar leapt up in fury, his axe ready to split Skalla's skull, but Bjólf grabbed his belt and hauled him back down before he could give their position away. He shook his head despondently. "Even if we could take them and their berserkers, the other ship would make it away and warn the rest."

Gunnar slumped back, defeated. As they watched, the great trees burst into flame. Beyond their branches, Skalla's arrows had already ignited the sail, and the hungry blaze now leapt and licked along the planking of the deck.

"It's just a ship, Gunnar," whispered Bjólf, still restraining him. But both knew he did not believe it.

Without another word, without looking back, Skalla strode up the gangplank and the black ships departed, leaving undreamt of ruin in their wake.

Bjólf and his men finally crawled from their cramped hiding places, spirits crushed, horrified beyond measure at the sights before them. A few instinctively rushed to the ship, splashing into the water with the thought of effecting some kind of rescue. But it was all too late. All were turned back by the intense heat of the blaze, whose eager shoots now reached to the very tops of the trees. The branches upon which the fiery tendrils climbed crackled and spat and fell burning into the water, a huge column of thick smoke billowing above. Reflected in the steaming water, the blackening shape of the *Hrafn*'s elegant prow stood like a silhouette in the great roaring torrent of flame – its timbers, marked with the deeds of ages, steadily consumed, its memories forever lost.

Bjólf hauled off his helm and let it drop to the ground, barely able to comprehend what had happened. His mind kept spinning back to the tantalising moment when the powder had been there, right before them, almost within their grasp; the moment before everything was suddenly snatched away.

"I should have been on board," he muttered, the flames from the fire reflecting in his eyes. "I always thought it would be my funeral ship."

Lacking the words to ease his friend's torment, Gunnar poked at the edge of the circle of mangled flesh with his axe. "Grimmsson saved us. All those years of sniping and fighting, and he saved us. Why?"

Bjólf shrugged, tearing his eyes from his dying ship. "Honour amongst thieves." He looked back upriver, in the black ships' wake. The wind gusted, changing direction, carrying the smoke across the sun and throwing his face into shadow. "Perhaps because he had encountered something truly evil, such that our similarities suddenly seemed more important than our differences."

Halldís approached, her face drawn. She looked up at Bjólf, her hand upon his arm, mouth open but empty of words, shaking silent tears from her eyes. The sight of this man crushed by defeat was almost more than she could bear. He took her hand, drawing comfort from the contact, and gave a forced smile of gloomy resignation.

"We must leave," she begged. "The noise will have attracted death-walkers."

In silence, the men trooped back to the safety of the stockade. Last of them was Bjólf, who hung back just long enough to see the exposed ribs of the great old ship devoured by the flames.

# CHAPTER THIRTY

## KING ÓFLÁR

As THEY HAD trudged up the hill and on through the village, thoughts of the day's events had begun to consolidate in Bjólf's mind. He had not remained defeated for long. Despair had turned to melancholy, melancholy to bitterness, and, by the time they reached the great hall, to a murderous rage.

"We were betrayed," he snapped as he strode back and forth before the mead benches, his sword still in his hand. Its blade swept through the air as he spoke. Even his friends were keeping a respectful distance from him now.

"But who?" said Halldís, exchanging a look of deep unease with Frodi. He turned and stared into the hearth, his face dark and brooding.

"I know on whom I would place my wager," he muttered.

"But, more to the point, how did they pass the message?" added Gunnar. "No one here would go by land, and we know none went by boat."

"Their information was scant," said Godwin, "or many of us would doubtless be dead by now, torn apart by their berserkers."

"They had the chance," nodded Frodi.

"But they did not take it," frowned Bjólf. "They did not know everything. Grimmsson was able to mislead them. They were warned – about us, about the ship – but did not know what else might have passed." He rubbed his chin, and looked up to the rafters as if somehow seeking inspiration there. *Come on, Thor... Odin... anyone...* he thought. *I've neglected you all these years, I know, but I'll take any help I can get, whether you exist or not.*

A vivid childhood memory came to him, then, quite unbidden: of his uncle's hall – a far more modest affair than this – and of the sparrows that used to nest among the beams. During feasts, they would swoop down and steal scraps from the tables. In time, they became so tame they would even take food from Olaf's huge hand. He smiled at that ridiculous image. The old man loved those birds. Such a thing could not happen here, in this lifeless realm. He had not seen a single bird since they had arrived.

Then he turned, fixing Finn with a look of frightening intensity and pointing at him with the tip of his blade.

"This bird that you saw Óflár feed," he said, his voice like thunder. "He let it fly free?"

"Yes," said Finn, shrugging.

"What kind of bird? A hawk? A hunting bird?" He did not think Óflár the kind to have a pet.

"No... Eating bird. What do you call it?" He flapped his arms and imitated its sound. "Coo-coo-coo!"

"A pigeon!" exclaimed Gunnar. The men looked at each other in sudden comprehension.

Bjólf turned, brow furrowed in fury, fingers clenched so tight around his sword grip his knuckles were white, and stormed out of the hall, leaving the great door swinging behind him. Moments later, he was back again. He strode up to Halldís and grabbed her by the hand. "Show me where Óflár lives!" he demanded, and charged out once again, dragging Halldís behind him.

"This should be interesting..." said Gunnar. All hurried after them.

Óflár took his time answering the irate pounding at his door. When he did so, he opened it the merest crack and peered out, suspiciously. "What is the...?"

That was all he had the opportunity to say before Bjólf kicked the door in, smashing Óflár's face and sending him flying back against a wooden pillar. As the pale man lay whimpering pathetically, snorting like a pig through his crushed, bleeding nose, Bjólf strode into the house, grabbed Óflár by his greasy hair, and dragged him out into the courtyard. He did not stop, but passed by his waiting crew and continued on towards the stockade gate, the snivelling screams of his writhing baggage drawing more and more people from their homes.

"Nothing to worry about," Gunnar reassured them. "Just sorting out a little rat infestation."

Bjólf, his anger growing, tugged harder, causing Óflár – bumping along the ground on his skinny rump, his hair almost wrenched from his head – to shriek all the more.

At the gate, the one-armed blacksmith, who was boiling nettles in a pot over a small fire, saw him coming, Halldís hurrying behind him, and the best part of Bjólf's crew behind her. Bjólf did not look like he was going to stop. Jumping to his feet, uncertain what to do, the blacksmith looked from Bjólf to Halldís and back again.

"Open the gates!" she called. The blacksmith and his fellow gatekeeper – a stout older man with no front teeth – fumbled with the heavy bar. Bjólf dumped Óflár on the ground and strode over to the blacksmith's bubbling pot.

"What is this?" he barked.

"Er... s-stingers," stuttered the blacksmith as they heaved the beam from the gates. "An infusion for my... Wha – ?"

But before he could say any more, Bjólf snatched up the pot, strode back to the wriggling form of Óflár and emptied the boiling contents into his lap. Óflár howled, pungent steam rising from his groin. Bjólf looped his arm through the pot's handle, took hold of Óflár's thin locks once more, and, with an expression of fury and disgust, marched out of the gates, dragging his screaming captive down the path to the harbour, where flames still licked at the jagged, sunken carcass of his ship.

HALLDÍS STOPPED AT the gates. None stepped past where she stood. Gunnar looked at her, questioningly. "Do you want us to..." The sentence ended in a kind of half nod towards the receding figures.

Halldís shook her head. "Let him deal with this in his own way."

"I don't understand," whispered Atli, embarrassed by his own ignorance. "What did Óflár do?"

Gunnar gave a grim laugh. "Pigeons are not only for eating," he said. Atli, still confused, looked from one face to another.

"Messages, boy," said Godwin. "They also carry messages."

ALMOST AT THE water's edge, Bjólf hauled Óflár into the very centre of the circle of gore and released his grip. Óflár fell face first into human blood and offal, then recoiled and cried out in shock and revulsion, slipping in the slime, covering himself in it.

'This is your anointing," said Bjólf, a manic look in his eye, and strode about him. "Now prepare to ascend your throne!"

Grabbing him by the scruff of the neck, he dragged the wailing, writhing Óflár towards the stake, sat him roughly against it, and trussed him up with the ragged, blood-caked rope that had once bound Grimmsson.

"This is your mantle!" he bawled in Óflár's ear, pulling the bonds tight.

Óflár screamed in torment, his returning senses finally beginning to grasp the full horror of his situation. He struggled feebly and looked about in panic. At the edge of the forest, upon the northern side, close to the water, could now be seen three death-walkers, their gait jerky and uneven, drawn from the forest by the sounds of death, the smell of blood.

Bjólf held the pot aloft and hammered hard upon it with the hilt of his sword. It rang out loudly like a crude, muffled bell.

"Come one, come all!" he cried. "Attend the court of King Óflár the Great!"

On the south side, now, another death-walker was visible. Bjólf turned and bowed to the whimpering, pleading creature at his feet. "Your majesty," he said, and jammed the nettle-pot roughly upon Óflár's head. A strange, humourless smile crossed his face. "You wished for a kingdom of your own. Well, now you have it. This is your kingdom." He gestured wildly with his sword blade. "And these your subjects!"

Óflár stared wild-eyed at the flames, the blood, the empty-eyed creatures that now stumbled towards him, sobbing and kicking ineffectually, like an infant. Bjólf straightened, staring down at Óflár with contempt. "I leave you to their wise counsel." With that he turned, and walked away, back to the stockade, where the distant screams were finally lost in the wind.

So ended the brief reign of Óflár, son of Hallthor.

# CHAPTER THIRTY-ONE

## OUT OF THE ASHES

FOR HOURS AFTERWARDS, Bjólf sat brooding in the watchtower, staring out towards the vast, blackened hole at the forest's edge, beneath which the embers of the ship still glowed. None dared approach him. Even brave Klaufi, whose watch this should have been, would not go near. An anxious Halldís had asked Gunnar to keep an eye on his friend. He hardly needed telling to do that, but he reassured her he would. Bjólf's men, meanwhile, lurked outside their tents in a state of dejection. Cheated of the opportunity to strike at Skalla, their only other means of attack now taken from them, they sat around the fire, dazed and directionless, and waited – for what, they knew not.

Then, when the smoke had finally ceased to rise, Gunnar looked towards the tower and saw Bjólf gone. Atli was sent clambering up the ladder, and found nothing but a knotted rope secured to the support and lowered to the outside. Off in the distance, he could see Bjólf trudging past Óflár's stripped bones, heading for the vessel's charred remains.

Some time passed before Bjólf was seen again. He called out at the gate, and when admitted marched in without a word, soaked through, a sack over his shoulder. Gunnar could not tell for certain what it contained, but it was something large and rounded in shape.

"We thought you had gone for the treasure," he said, striding alongside his captain and eyeing the sack with a curious frown.

"That can stay at the bottom of the river," said Bjólf. "No good to us here."

"Hmm," Gunnar nodded. "Probably all melted into one great lump, anyhow." Bjólf did not reply. "So, er... what's in the bag?" Gunnar tried his best to sound casual, but acting was not his strong point.

"You'll see."

When they reached their encampment by the great hall, Bjólf dumped the sack on the ground. His men gathered without any word needing to be spoken. Halldís and Frodi, deep in conversation with Godwin and Fjölvar, cut short their discussion and hurried over, Halldís forcing her way to the front.

Bjólf looked around at them all and smiled briefly at the company, then tucked his thumbs into his belt and began.

"We know now what this Skalla is about. He has formidable weapons, that much is clear. But our will is the stronger." There was a mutter of approval. "You are aggrieved at having been robbed of the chance to stand against him. I know that. You want nothing more than to heft your weapons at him and his kind. I know that too. He thinks us destroyed. That is in our favour. Now the time has come to make our attack upon him."

With that, he upended the sack, and a big, heavy lump of wood thudded onto the ground. Charred, sodden with river water, but still sound and clear in shape – the dragon's head from the *Hrafn*. Bjólf picked it up and held it before him. "She has passed through fire. But she will sail again."

A murmur passed through the men. "But how?" exclaimed Gunnar, wondering, for a moment, whether his old friend had finally gone mad.

"We need more than a figurehead to carry us," said Njáll.

"Our ship is ash and embers," added Godwin. "Our only means of attack gone!"

"No!" said Bjólf, his eyes gleaming. "There is another..."

The men stared at each other in bewilderment, dumbstruck.

"Grimmsson's ship..." said Atli. He had spoken aloud without thinking, without realising he was doing it. The men looked at him in amazement.

"Grimmsson's ship," said Bjólf with a slow nod of his head, grinning broadly at the boy. A buzz of excitement suddenly gripped the crew; they chattered feverishly, some even laughing, enlivened by new possibilities.

"It was tethered," said Fjölvar. "It should still be there..."

Godwin nodded. "The death-walkers have no interest in ships. We know that much."

"But what if Skalla's men have discovered it?" said Kjötvi.

Úlf shook his head. "They knew of only one ship when they came today."

"We must act quickly," added Bjólf, "and get to it before it is found."

"How?" said Odo.

"We walk." Bjólf pointed past them all, towards the far end of the village, and the dark trees that lay beyond the stockade. "It lies southeast of here." He looked at Halldís. "A small bay, marked on one edge by a great boulder, half in the water."

"Ægir's Rock," She nodded. "I know it."

"How far?" asked Gunnar.

She shrugged. "A day. I can direct you. To the island in the fjord, too."

"But... the *forest*?" said Eyvind, a note of doubt in his voice. They had learned to fear the place in the last few days.

"The going would be hard," acknowledged Halldís. "The forest is dense, and the death-walkers wander its shadows."

"But they are lumbering beasts," said Gunnar. He hefted his axe. "We can handle them."

"Those 'lumbering beasts' wiped out Grimmsson's entire crew!" said Kjötvi.

"And Grimmsson's crew, we must assume, have joined their ranks," added Godwin. A few muttered their concern.

"But they were not prepared," said Bjólf. "Nor were we, that first night. But we know our enemy now."

Thorvald, who had survived the long vigil upon the ship when so many had perished, stepped forward, nodding. All fell silent. "We fared badly in our first encounter. But we learned quickly. They are slow, their behaviour simple. They do not hide the sound of their approach. On open ground, they can be easily seen. In the forest, easily heard. We have this one chance. My vote is to go."

Thorvald's words carried the weight to convince the doubters. "So, we have a plan!" announced Gunnar with delight, and gave his captain an almighty slap on the back.

"Gather provisions," called Bjólf. "And sharpen your blades. Tonight we sleep, and dream of wanton women. At first light we march to Skalla's ruin!"

# CHAPTER THIRTY-TWO

## THE STRANGER AT THE GATES

THE NEXT MORNING, the men assembled outside the great hall, fully armoured once more, strenghtened shields and bags of provisions upon their backs, helms hanging from their belts, and every weapon they could carry strapped to them. The preference was for heavy blades and clubs; few trusted to stabbing weapons on this trip. There were thirty of them in all, including the boy Atli, whose burden on this occasion was even greater than the rest. Bjólf trusted any one of them with his life, but it was a sobering thought, too often on his mind, that when they had first come to these shores, they had been forty strong.

A handful of men from Halldís's retinue had volunteered to join the raiding party, as Bjólf had expected they would. He admired the courage and determination of these men, all in the twilight of their years, and, despite being doubtful about their suitability for so arduous a mission, accepted them graciously. They had suffered under Skalla for years; this, he felt, was their right. Their addition brought their numbers up to thirty five. Frodi was to stay, under strict instructions from Halldís, though it was clear that it rankled with the tough old warrior. A shame, thought Bjólf; he suspected this one would have proved a fearsome addition to the warband.

With a face like thunder, infuriated at having been denied a place – but kitted out for battle to honour those who were going to the fight – Frodi arrived with two stewards to escort Bjólf and his men to the gate on the far, landward side of the stockade. From here, they were to head into the forest along an old herding path, then strike out south-east for the shore of the fjord – and, they hoped, Grimmsson's waiting ship. Bjólf looked around, expecting to see Halldís nearby. He could not imagine that she would not be here to see them off. Yet it became clear that, for reasons known only to her, she had not come. Though he did not show it, his heart sank at the realisation.

Little was said. With curt nods of acnowledgement on either side, they set off, passing through an as yet unfamiliar part of Halldís's domain. Here, the houses and farmsteads were more scattered, the land increasingly dominated by agriculture. Penned animals and enclosed pasture jostled with a patchwork of cultivated fields in which were grown every kind of crop. Not a scrap of land was wasted. Yet, despite the impression of plenitude this gave, the skinny peasants who watched wide-eyed as the glittering band of warriors tramped past showed that this land, reduced as it was by the limits of the stockade and the demands of Skalla, struggled to sustain them.

Before long, they had reached the far boundary of the stockade wall, beyond which the dark edge of the forest loomed once more, appearing now more vast and threatening than ever. The old south gate, though clearly once the twin of the western entrance that opened to the harbour, now presented a very different demeanour. It stood like a monument to their self-imposed imprisonment, every aspect of it speaking not so much of neglect – though neglected it had certainly been – but of fear. It was impossible to tell when anyone had last dared to pass this way – it could not have been longer than the few years that the stockade had been in existence – but already the forest had begun to reclaim the great boles that had been so insolently torn from it. Invading ivy had forced its way between the trunks, its clinging fronds winding their way around the whole length of the wall, and around the gate itself had crept up the outside of the watchtowers, choking the lookout posts and tumbling over the top of the barrier in a great green wave, bringing with it a tangled profusion of briar, holly, elder and hazel. This whole section of the wall was dark with shadow, and it was only gradually, as his eyes adjusted to the gloom of this forgotten corner, that Bjólf became aware of a figure pacing slowly back and forth at the foot of the left tower, arms folded, head bowed and obscured by shadow.

At first, Bjólf assumed him to be a guard. But what was the point of that? No one came this way, and there seemed no possibility of ascending the watchtower. Besides, although his stature was modest, his dress and equipment were far beyond anything Klaufi or the blacksmith had to offer. Over a green tunic and brown leggings was a shimmering coat of mail, at his waist a richly decorated sword and a fine helm with gilded fittings, on his back a red shield bearing a sacred *valknut* motif inscribed in black, the knot of the slain: a symbol of Odin, and of battle. This man, whoever he was, was no peasant. He could only be another volunteer, reasoned Bjólf, yet none that he had seen were so youthful.

As they approached, the figure turned, unfolded its arms and stepped forward. The face – and the figure – were suddenly startlingly familiar. Halldís. The eyes of all the men widened at the sight. None of them had ever seen a woman dressed in such a fashion. The entire concept was outrageous. But, Bjólf had to admit, she wore it well. Halldís walked up briskly, giving Frodi a look somehow caught between defiance and apology, as if steeling herself for an argument whilst simultaneously hoping she might brazen it out.

"What is this?" Frodi demanded, suddenly stepping into the role of patriarch. Halldís, in response, immediately became the headstrong daughter.

"I'm going with them," she said, her head high, her tone resolute. "That is why I requested you stay, Frodi – to oversee things in my stead."

"But... you cannot..." blustered Frodi, his face red with indignation. "It's... inappropriate. And I made a promise to your father..."

Halldís stood her ground. "My father is dead. Were he here, he would do exactly as I am doing. I rule his hall now. This is my duty."

Frodi, for the moment, was lost for words – Bjólf could not be sure whether because he lacked a suitable argument, or was merely shamed by the fact that a slip of a woman was going to battle while he stayed at home. The *vikingr* captain smiled to himself and stepped forward, folding his arms and rubbing his chin and regarding Halldís with an air of careful consideration.

"Your duty it may be," he said. "But this is my raid, and all here are under my command."

She held his gaze, knowing she was indeed at his mercy, quietly fuming at the thought as she stepped from foot to foot. "You need me," she said. "I promised to show you the way."

"I assumed you meant a map."

"I am the map."

Bjólf gestured to the small party of local men who had joined them. "I'm sure any of these gentlemen could do as good a job in their own land." One of the volunteers began to nod enthusiastically at this, then thought better of it as his mistress shot him a withering look.

She stood for a moment, frowning like a truculent child, unable to counter his argument. But behind the angry defiance, he could see, was a look of desperation – one that fervently implored him to let her do this.

"Give me one good reason why you should come," he said.

"Because my people are worthy of it. Because I have a score to settle with Skalla. Because I am at least equal to an old man or a boy!"

Bjólf shrugged. "All good reasons," he said. "You are free to join us if you so choose." She looked triumphant, relieved. Her instinct was to throw her arms around Bjólf. This time, she restrained herself.

"What?" protested Frodi. "I cannot allow it!"

"You cannot prevent it!" she replied.

"Then it is my duty to accompany you – to protect you. Nothing can induce me to stay."

"Someone must stay, Frodi," she said, a note of pleading in her voice. "The people –"

"Will carry on as they have always done, whether we are here or not," he interrupted. "Cooking, chopping wood, tending crops and cattle, they don't need us for that. They never have!" She looked momentarily outraged at the suggestion. He tempered his tone. "If we succeed, then their future will be saved. If we fail, and never return... why, all are doomed, and what difference then?"

Halldís said nothing, casting her eyes down to the ground. It was clear to all that the debate would be resolved only one way. Having argued her own case with such passion, Halldís could hardly deny Frodi his place.

Bjólf smiled at Gunnar. "The more, the merrier," he said.

The big man did not look wholly impressed.

"Thirty-seven," said Bjólf in his ear, reassuringly. "Almost back to full strength."

Gunnar frowned and muttered to himself. "Some old men, a woman, and a boy..."

And so the huge, moss-covered bolt was heaved from the gate, the thick tangle of vines and creepers hacked away. Slowly, falteringly the great gates were hauled apart; the siezed, swollen hinges resisting, the last of the creepers clinging to the damp, heavy wood.

Their first sight was a dispiriting one.

Against the right hand gate, as if its owner had expired where he stood whilst clawing to get in, was a human skeleton. The bones were wrapped and intertwined by twisting, grasping tendrils of ivy, which formed about them a weird, surrogate flesh. Who this once had been, and where they had come from, none could tell. Gunnar prodded at it with his axe. From a cavity in its skull a shiny brown centipede scuttled. "Well," he said with a sigh. "At least this one isn't still moving."

Ahead of them, beyond the opening, stretched the long forgotten path, its edges blurred by a profusion of growth that had crept from the forest on either side: bracken, black hellebore, patches of spindly hemlock, and here and there the clustered red berries of cuckoo pints and the collapsed remains of gigantic foxgloves. Above, what had once been completely open to the air had now grown over, the branches meeting and forming a bridge across which the riotous vines had already begun to find their way, threatening to turn the trackway into a gloomy tunnel of branch, stem and leaf.

Underfoot, along the mossy, rutted trackway itself, bindweed had cast a choking web, slowly strangling the few flowering plants that dared to poke their heads through it. Nonetheless, the way ahead was clear, and the obstacles few. The going on this part of the journey would be good. What it would be like when they finally had to plunge into the dark trees that loomed up on either side, they could not guess.

As the warriors passed beyond the gates, Frodi turned back to his two anxious stewards. "Bar the gate firmly behind us," he said. Then, before turning away, added: "Hope for our return, but do not wait for it."

With these gloomy words, the huge, bone-wreathed gates closed behind them with a dull thud, and the party began its long march to a distant and unknown fate.

# CHAPTER THIRTY-THREE

## THE STRANGER AT THE GATES

IN SPITE OF the forbidding presence that pressed in upon either side – or perhaps in defiance of it – the mood of the travellers was bouyant. The steady rhythm and sense of purpose, grim though it was, had lifted their spirits, and for much of the morning – walking two or three abreast, with Bjólf and Gunnar at their head – they set a brisk pace, encountering no other living creature, not a sound of movement other than the creaking and cracking of the great old trees. The only reminders of any kind of human presence were the small, grey way-stones that punctuated the route at regular intervals, half-hidden by the invading bracken. Halldís, who followed close behind with Frodi and Atli, paused to scrutinise each one as it appeared, noting the markings upon them – signs that meant nothing to Bjólf – often crouching to scrape off a coat of moss or lichen. One of these, she said, would indicate their point of departure from the path.

All had agreed that the wisest course of action was to move as silently as possible through the trees. For much of the way, the only noises to be heard were their footfalls and the clink of mail and weapons – sounds that they knew would not carry far in the dead, baffled air of the forest. After a time – with the death-walkers, for the moment, all but forgotten – they began to relax into the journey, enjoying what simple pleasures were offered: the sharp, fresh smell of foliage as it was crushed underfoot and the dappled sunlight that filtered between the gently swaying branches. Now and then, someone would gently hum a tune in time with their step. They even began to allow themselves hushed conversations.

"So," muttered Gunnar, leaning in towards Bjólf. "About this farm…"

Bjólf looked at him quizzically.

"The farm," repeated Gunnar insistently. "To retire to."

"Ah," said Bjólf with a nod. "The farm."

"I can see it in my mind's eye," said Gunnar, going off into a reverie. "Cattle and pigs. Good dark soil. Fresh green pasture. A clear stream running through it, coming down from a mountain. A big solid barn and a big solid woman at the farmhouse door."

"It has a distinct appeal."

"But where is it? That's the part that's frustrating me."

Bjólf shrugged. "Denmark?"

Gunnar wrinkled his nose and shook his head. "Full of Germans."

"Norway then? Vestfold?"

"I have a price on my head, remember?"

Bjólf sighed at the memory. A costly night's drinking that turned out to be. He returned to the problem at hand. "Obviously not Sweden."

"Obviously."

"Iceland?"

"Too far."

"You're not making this easy for yourself."

Gunnar gazed off into the distance. "I always fancied England. Good soil. Nice climate."

"You and ten thousand other Norsemen. The English are more likely to welcome you with an open grave than open arms…"

Gunnar sighed. Before he could speak again, Bjólf halted him with a hand upon his chest. Behind them, the rest of the party stopped short. Up ahead, some distance away, was a figure. Gunnar blinked hard; uncertain, at first, whether he was seeing right. But there was no doubting it. Standing in the middle of the path, staring at the ground where the ferns emerged from the left edge of the forest and turned slightly away from them, was what appeared to be a young woman; naked, pale, motionless but for a gentle swaying, as if she were just another of the trees being rocked by the wind.

"Is she one of them?" whispered Gunnar.

"If she is not," replied Bjólf, "she is a long way from home." He could not imagine what terrible circumstances – what madness – could have driven anyone here in such a state.

Bjólf turned, and, signalling to Fjölvar, motioned him forward. "Have an arrow ready," he whispered. Fjölvar nodded, and took his bow from his back. Bjólf advanced towards her in slow, creeping steps, making his footfalls as light as possible, all the while trying to maintain a clear line between the girl and Fjölvar's bow.

But for the slow swaying, she did not move as he approached. Her flesh, though pallid, appeared entirely unmarked; her long red hair hung loose down her back and over her face and breast, occasionally shifting as it was caught by the breeze. By Bjólf's reckoning she was little more than twenty summers old. He had by now convinced himself that she must indeed be the victim of some other tragedy, some other derangement of mind, and, being close, was about to speak out to her when, thanks to his own wandering attention, something snapped beneath his foot. Her head whirled around.

Now there was no doubt.

Her red-rimmed eyes, once beautiful, were as cold and colourless as a fish, her blue-lipped mouth lolling open. Around her neck, he now saw, was the blue-black mark left by a rope. She lurched towards him, her lips curling back as if about to utter some inhuman cry, when Bjólf felt Fjölvar's arrow hiss past his cheek and her head jolted suddenly back. She stood motionless for a moment, the arrow in her eye pointed skyward, then crumpled awkwardly to the ground.

It was a grim lesson to them all. The members of the party moved forward and, one by one, crept quietly past her body. Fjölvar averted his eyes as he passed, somehow more affected by this than any of the previous clashes. Halldís, too, shuddered as she looked upon her and felt the image burning into her memory. Though trying to resist the thought, she could not help but see herself in this wretched figure. Her in another life, with another fate. She did not want to believe that it was a fate that perhaps awaited her still.

"Do you suppose she did that to herself?" mused Gunnar as they walked, gesturing to his neck. Bjólf said nothing, and focused his attention on the path ahead.

After that weird encounter, all were greatly subdued – reminded of what lay ahead and wary of what still lurked nearby. It seemed the uncanny emptiness of the forest closer to the stockade – normally a source of unease, but today a cause for cheer – could no longer be relied upon. Twice afterwards they heard, from somewhere amongst the trees, the melancholy groan of some dead, wandering thing. They maintained their silence, and kept on moving.

It was not long after that Bjólf noticed Halldís, crouching at one of the way-stones with their indecipherable runes, sigh deeply and give the forest beyond a lingering, apprehensive look. It was the look he had been waiting for. She stood and turned to him, but he already knew what was coming.

"This is the place," she whispered, then indicated a spot just along from the stone, no more than a vague thinning of the dense foliage. "There was a path here, but it will be difficult to follow. We must maintain a course south-east – or we will never find our way." Bjólf signalled to his men and peered into the dark interior, where no sun, no guiding light, seemed to penetrate.

Then he drew his sword and, slicing through the clinging, tangled vines, plunged into the dank, all-enveloping darkness.

# CHAPTER THIRTY-FOUR

## IN DARK TREES

AT FIRST THE way ahead seemed impossible. Even in the cleft where the old path had once passed through, a thick profusion of thorny twigs and decaying brambles, piled almost shoulder-high, clung and clawed at them as they stumbled forward into the darkness, the sharp points scratching flesh, catching onto belts and scraping against metal. Their blades caught as they swung to hack it down, and when they struck at it, the thicket sprang back at them, raising a rank mildewy dust that stung their nostrils and made their eyes stream. Many donned their helms to protect their heads and eyes from the lash of the vicious, thorny briars that arched unseen and whipped about them as they moved.

Then, quite suddenly, the dense, woody thicket seemed to relent. The clinging knot of vines dwindled. The snarling, grasping thorns thinned. The way ahead cleared. Bjólf stumbled forward, unimpeded but almost blind, hand held out before him, his toes catching on exposed tree roots. With each step, unseen things crunched underfoot.

As they moved deeper in and their vision adjusted to the gloom, they found themselves in a strange netherworld. The impression was of having entered a vast, subterranean network of green-tinged caverns. From the huge trees – of immeasurable age – spread a floor of gnarled, contorted roots beneath their feet, and a twisted, vaulted canopy of living wood above their heads.

Here, it was too dark even to support the thorny guardians that lined the forest's edge – but, around the twisting roots, the collapsed skeletons of their ancesters littered the woodland floor, some still writhing along the ground with the semblance of life, others, far older, mouldered and decayed almost to dust. It was these brittle remains that snapped and crunched beneath their feet – but here and there, Bjólf could now see, there were also intertwined the whitened bones of small creatures – the tiny, jewel-like skeletons of shrews, the skulls and backbones of rats. Lying undisturbed where they had fallen, they attested to the utter deadness of this place.

There would be no fresh game eaten today.

When it had teemed with life, bears and wolves had been masters of this wood. Then, when some troubled instinct had driven them away, foxes and badgers had held sway – and, when they too withdrew, their prey had briefly flourished. Now, not even the smallest of furred or feathered creatures chose to make its nest here.

In their absence, other, tinier creatures had taken hold, the last inheritors of this doomed realm. Among the branches, their principal predator – now master of the forest – had built a vast and elaborate empire; everywhere about, between every bough and twig, were the webs of spiders, sticking to the warriors' faces as they advanced. They had grown huge and fat in their unchallenged domain, and swayed heavily at the centre of their silky, fly-dotted homes as the party pushed past, or scuttled off to the safety of the trees where the warriors' passing left them torn and wrecked.

Above them, where only the slightest chinks of clear light occasionally penetrated, the towering trunks of the trees swayed and twisted with the passing wind, their gnarled, interlocking boughs emitting eerie creaks and strange melancholy groans, as if speaking to one another in some long-forgotten language. What they spoke of were strong winds passing somewhere up above, yet beneath the canopy, the air was as still as a tomb; flat, heavy and lifeless.

Into it, charging the atmosphere with their rank odour, great yellow brackets of fungi projected, and vivid red toadstools dotted with white thrust up their poisonous heads in profusion – the only colours that disturbed the unremitting browns and blacks of this weird kingdom.

Bjólf could not tell for how long they silently picked their way through this oppressive underworld. Time seemed to stand still. Death-walkers, if they did penetrate this far, might wander forever and never see daylight – or else end up pinned amongst the thorny brambles of the forest's edge like one of the insects trapped in the great silvery skein of spiders' webs.

They did not stop to eat or rest in this forsaken place. Some of the party chewed on strips of dried meat as they went, each according to their hunger, none able to tell now whether the time for eating was due or had long since past. Even so, the going that day seemed painfully slow. For as long as they could, the party had kept to where the covering of forest floor appeared thinnest, believing this must be what remained of the old path. But after a time, even that subtle distinction utterly disappeared. Finally, Halldís stopped and looked about in confusion and panic, her sense of direction gone, the silent labyrinth of trees seeming to stretch out equally in every direction, offering no clue to their place on the earth. She suddenly was struck by the fear that they had wandered in circles, and would forever be hopelessly lost. In the gloom, Bjólf saw her agitation, and understood.

"Kjötvi!" he called. Kjötvi the Lucky limped forward, his expression, as ever, one of anxiety. "South-east," said Bjólf.

Kjötvi frowned and looked about, squinted up at the distant glimmers of light up above, then ahead. He gave a sniff, and made a casual gesture. "This way."

Bjólf smiled at the astonished Halldís, and all continued on, with Kjötvi now at their head.

The first sign that Kjötvi's instincts were correct came from an unexpected source. Fjölvar, who was now leading with Kjötvi, stopped suddenly and dropped to his knee. Up ahead, in the semi-darkness, a different shape – the shape of a man. It was big, this one, dressed in a fine red tunic, broadly belted at the waist. Like the woman on the path, it stood swaying, head bowed, apparently without purpose. Was this what the death-walkers did, wondered Bjólf, when they could not scent human flesh?

Gunnar stepped forward, hefting his axe. "Time I had a go," he said, and, without hesitation, without waiting for a reply, started his swift approach. With his axe raised above his shoulder, he accelerated towards his target, bounding forward, his feet picking deftly from root to root in steady rhythm. Bjólf smiled to himself. The big man could be surprisingly nimble when there was a need.

The death-walker had hardly raised its head before Gunnar's axe crashed down upon it, splitting its skull wide open. The figure reeled forward against a tree and slid to earth, leaving the glistening contents of its head splattered upon the trunk. As he approached, Bjólf saw Gunnar turn the figure over, frown at what he saw, then turn it back onto its face.

Gunnar said nothing as he rejoined the others, but, as they continued on their way, he sidled up to Bjólf and spoke to him in hushed tones.

"Something you should know. That one I just killed... I killed him before." Bjólf frowned at him. "A crewman of Grimmsson's. I drove my spear through his heart during the fight at the fjord."

"Are you certain?"

"The spear-point was sheared off in his chest. Still in him. I'd know it anywhere."

"Then we must be close."

"But if we're close, where are the rest of them?" said Gunnar.

Bjólf said nothing. Gunnar had not expected an answer. But he understood. For now, he would keep this to himself.

As they continued to advance, encounters with isolated *draugr* became more frequent. All were dispatched swiftly and ruthlessly; only one had managed to utter a sound before Úlf's mace smashed its head to oblivion, and if any of its fellows had heard its call, they were left far behind. Unsettling as this development was, most felt it a welcome diversion from the seemingly endless torpor of the dark forest, and they understood that it also meant their destination was near.

Another welcome change came over their surroundings as they trudged resolutely on. The trees became less dense, the light stronger, the ground softer underfoot, cushioned now by a carpet of damp leaves. Quite suddenly, it seemed, they looked around and found the whole of the forest had changed about them; the thick, ancient boles of oak and ash had given way to tall, straight trunks of pine and golden-leaved beech, through which shimmering sunlight filtered. The air had changed, too; fresh, now, with the sharp, pleasing scent of the pine needles that they crushed underfoot as they passed. All around, the forest floor was speckled with tiny flowering plants. Spirits were raised, and their pace quickened as they strode out, confidence in their mission growing once more.

The warband moved differently now the landscape allowed it, with Finn and Eyvind up ahead scouting the path, and the rest in a close-knit group behind, keeping the scouts in sight. No death-walkers had been seen for some time, and the sun – which showed it to be late afternoon – was slanting low through the trees when a whistle went up from Finn. The men halted and dropped to their knees, but Bjólf saw Finn turn and wave him on. He stood, leading the party towards the spot where the two scouts now stood.

They were at the edge of a wide open space, their attention fixed on something ahead. As he approached, a great clearing opened up before him. Devoid of trees but dotted with old, rotted stumps and ragged patches of gorse, it was carved in two by the course of a small stream – barely more than a ditch – which cut a deep groove across the space from their far left to the distant right corner. What had caught Finn and Eyvind's attention, however, was what was standing in a bare, sandy patch of ground right in the middle of it, a little way back from the stream. Upright, motionless but for a familiar swaying motion, its back to them and its head on one side as if idly contemplating something upon the ground, was another death-walker, its stark shadow making a long, dark mark across the scrubby soil.

But this was unlike any of the creature they had seen so far. It was a surreal, unthinkable figure – from head to foot so utterly dark and featureless that it appeared as if merely some bizarre extension of the shadow it cast. At first, struggling to make sense of what he saw, he thought it might be a Moorish man, like the dark-skinned traders with whom he had dealt in the southern sea – perhaps a member of Grimmsson's crew. But that couldn't account for the impossibly pitch-black hue, the weird uniformity of it, nor the fact that the entire surface of its body seemed to be moving.

As Bjólf looked on, a strange feeling of disgust rising in him, the man's skin seemed to constantly shimmer and shift in the sunlight, as if it were bubbling.

"Gods," said Gunnar beside him. "What now?"

Eyvind took a step forward, his sword drawn, then paused to look back at Bjólf. Bjólf nodded his assent. "Stay sharp," he said. "Take no chances."

Eyvind moved slowly, silently towards the strange vision. As he drew close, the party saw him shudder, and stop. He looked back, an expression of hideous bemusement upon his face, then turned to the figure once again, his blade raised in readiness.

"Hey!' he called. The figure did not move. Eyvind called to them over his shoulder, a note of baffled incredulity in his voice. "You need to see this."

Bjólf motioned for the others to move up behind with him. "Stay together. Watch the trees," he whispered. As he approached close to where his scout stood, the explanation – the truth that Eyvind had found so indescribable – became horrifyingly clear. The entire surface of the man's body was covered in millions upon millions of black ants – crawling, moving, clinging to his body and to each other in such profusion that no hint of the man beneath – if man it were – could now be discerned.

"You ever seen anything like that before?" muttered Eyvind.

Bjólf could only gaze in horrified astonishment. He looked momentarily at Halldís, her hand held across her mouth in revulsion. When he turned back, Eyvind was reaching toward the figure, about to prod it with his sword point.

"No!" exclaimed Bjólf. But he was too late. A horde of the ants had immediately swarmed up the blade and onto Eyvind's hand. "Ouch!" he exclaimed, laughing nervously, swatting at them. "They bite!" But the laugh rapidly died away, became a cry of pain, as fresh blood ran where they had taken hold. Flecks of blood flew from his swatting fingertips, and the black mass that covered the death-walker suddenly surged outward from its feet, flowing across the sandy ground like a glossy liquid and up over Eyvind's legs. He screamed in horror as they swarmed into his clothes, over his face, into his hair, covering him in a manic, teeming, blood-hungry carpet of black.

As all the others stood powerless, paralysed by shock and confusion, one man stepped forward to help; Arngrimm, the volunteer from Björnheim who had so enthusiastically supported Bjólf at the gate. He reached out instinctively to Eyvind.

"Don't touch him!" shouted Bjólf. Though only moments had passed, Eyvind had already collapsed to his knees, his hands clasped helplessly to his head, his flesh being stripped from his bones before their eyes. Arngrimm stopped half way between Bjólf and Eyvind, looking from one to the other, suddenly realising his mistake. But before he could rectify it, the black swarm was on his boots, rising up his legs and working its way into every opening and crevice. He turned and tried to run, his face red, his eyes wide in panic. Bjólf and the others backed away rapidly, looking around for some means of escape from this new enemy.

"The stream!" called Atli. "Cross the stream!"

The boy led the way, his burden bumping against his back as he ran, and without hesitation the rest hurried after, hurling themselves across the narrow strip of flowing water and running for all they were worth. Arngrimm, struggling desperately to follow, stumbled, his legs giving way. As Bjólf looked back over his shoulder, he saw the black insect horde swarm over the old man, covering his eyes and flowing into his open mouth until his strangled cries were finally silenced.

# CHAPTER THIRTY-FIVE

## NIGHT GUESTS

FOR SOME TIME they ran, past the clearing and on into the scattering of
tall pines beyond. They had just started to slow when Halldís finally
called out for them to stop. She was supporting one of the old men
from the village; he was sweating profusely, panting in hoarse, gasping
breaths. It had been many years since he had been called upon to run
while kitted out for combat.

"Rest!" called Bjólf.

The party halted; the old man slumped gratefully to the floor. Few
of the rest seemed keen to do the same. Many of them poked about in
the loose carpet of pine needles with their sword points, reluctant to sit
upon it, or swiped at their clothes nervously and scratched at themselves.
They could hardly be blamed. Every step, it seemed, brought some new
terror, some undreamt-of threat. Atli sat on his baggage – which he was
finally now able to drop – and looked up as Bjólf wandered over to him.

"Good thinking, little man," the captain said, clapping him on the
shoulder.

Atli smiled at the acknowledgement. Then, after a moment of thought, he said: "So, when do I stop being 'little'?"

Bjólf looked back in surprise. Some of those within earshot laughed aloud. Atli held his gaze unflinchingly, and for the first time, perhaps, seemed not a boy, but a man.

A smile creased Bjólf's face. "Maybe today. Good thinking, Atli, son of Ivarr..." Then he pinched Atli's arm. "Though you could always do with a bit more muscle."

Gunnar laughed. "Atli the Strong!"

Some of the men chortled at the irony. It seemed to be the way these nicknames worked, either describing the one distinguishing attribute of the individual – Two-Axe, Long-Beard – or stating something that was the complete opposite of the truth – Kjötvi the Lucky, Atli the Strong. Atli didn't mind. He knew how it was meant. To give a name, even in jest, was their way of showing him respect – of showing he was one of them. He was happy to laugh along with his comrades.

It served another purpose, too. To help him put from his mind an image that he had carried with him from the clearing. As they ran, he had looked back. On the ground, collapsed just short of the stream, was Arngrimm – or, at least, the shape of Arngrimm, still writhing and twitching beneath the shifting, devouring shroud of black. Behind him, in a disordered heap, lay what remained of Eyvind. Now mostly abandoned by the insect horde, he had been reduced to a lifeless skeleton, the low sun that, moments before, had shone upon his smiling face now glancing through the gaps between his stripped bones. And then – somehow, the most horrific sight of all – there had been the lone death-walker. Now bereft of its covering of frantically milling legions of ants, the ghastly state of its flesh was now fully revealed. The skin had been entirely removed, and beneath the body had been bored and reamed by a million tiny mouths, leaving some parts barely covered, and others, that had not pleased them, almost untouched. The head was stripped of features – the nose eaten away, the ears gone, only dark, dry pits for eyes. Its teeth and ribs shone white in the sun, and along its limbs, exposed tendons were visible, stretched like wires. And yet – and it was this that made Atli shudder – it still stood, swaying gently, waiting for its now destroyed and useless senses to pick up the scent or sound of prey.

\* \* \*

As THEY GATHERED themselves and continued through the towering pines, Gunnar again caught up with Bjólf, who was walking with Halldís ahead of the main group. She look pale and distraught at what she had witnessed. Although Gunnar and Bjólf and the others were no less appalled, they at least had developed their own ways, over the years, of dealing with such hideous events. Gunnar looked at Bjólf, uncertain whether to speak. Bjólf encouraged him with a nod.

"Have you ever seen ants attack the living like that?" said Gunnar.

"No," said Bjólf.

"Poor Eyvind..." Gunnar shook his head, then cast a glance at Halldís. "You might have warned us you had such pests in your forest."

Halldís shot him a fearsome look. "Do you really think I would have kept silent about such a thing? There are no such creatures... and we also lost a man, every bit as fine as your 'poor Eyvind'!" With that she stalked off ahead, leaving Gunnar irritated and bemused.

"They had feasted upon the flesh of a death-walker," said Bjólf, "and so had become of its kind. That is why they so hungered for human flesh."

Gunnar took a moment to absorb the implications.

"It is spreading to the beasts, Gunnar. We must be more vigilant than ever – and thank our luck that no larger creatures remain here."

Gunnar fell into silent, gloomy reflection as they trudged on their way.

As they went, Bjólf began to notice decaying stumps where trees had once been felled, and even occasional indications of well-worn paths. There were signs of habitation here, though how recent, he could not tell.

They did not have to wait long. Quite suddenly, the way before them opened into a broad, grassy glade, its earthy colours glowing in the low, early evening sun. Worn trackways led through it, and at its heart, casting a long, deep shadow, stood a small, solid farmhouse built of pine logs and, opposite, a great old barn. An abandoned cart stood to one side. It was an uncanny feeling, happening upon signs of such ordinary life in the middle of so forbidding a forest; a haven of normality in the midst of a nightmare. Bjólf hoped it was yet another sign that they were near their goal.

Clearly there was no life here now. No smoke rose from the house. There was neither sight nor sound of any animal. Tall weeds grew through the wheels of the cart, and the hay in the exposed loft of the barn was honeycombed with long-deserted rat-runs. Nevertheless, Bjólf felt comforted by the familiarity of the scene.

When he looked at Halldís, however, her expression was downcast. "What is it?"

She frowned, digging deep into her memories. "I know this place – from my childhood. It is Erling's farm."

"A fiercely independent old man," added Frodi. "He built all this himself. How, I cannot imagine."

Bjólf smiled and looked around. "Erling. That was my father's name."

Halldís sighed. "We are further south than intended."

"Can we not correct our course?"

"Easily. But it means our progress has also been slower than I thought."

Bjólf shaded his eye with his hand and peered towards the sun, already dipping below the tops of the trees. "How far is it? Will we make it before dark?"

Halldís shook her head, gloomily. Bjólf thought to himself, and looked about, then turned back to them, his mood remaining resolutely buoyant. "Then fate has favoured our party, blessing us with a roof under which to spend the night."

"I thought you did not believe in fate," said Halldís.

Bjólf gave her a broad grin. "When it turns my way, I don't fight it."

Before the light had faded, Bjólf and his men had set about clearing and securing house and barn for the night. Both had seen better days, but to the weary travellers, they were luxurious.

The only argument had been over who took the house, and who took the barn. Those in the house would have the additional comfort of a fire – something they could not have risked in the open air – but the dwelling could accommodate no more than a dozen at most. Bjólf had insisted that Halldís and her people lodge there, and that they at least be joined by Atli, Kjötvi, Gunnar and Godwin – the former two because they had served them well that day (and, Bjólf knew, were less robust than the rest); the latter because they would provide good protection for the others. Bjólf himself would join the men in the barn.

And here the argument began. Led by Njáll and stoked by Fjölvar, the men, fighting back mischievous smiles, started to suggest that Bjólf's place was in the house, that he had things to look after there, that the house offered the warmth he needed. Bjólf, refusing to get drawn in, mortified at such comments in front of their noble host, attempted to steer the conversation back to the matter in hand. But the men, seeing him on the run, would have none of it – surely he would be needed to stoke the fire during the night, they asked?

Halldís was not slow to pick up on the innuendo. She feigned haughty offence before him, but, seeing Bjólf's embarrassment, was soon sniggering along at his expense. When he finally realised that she was colluding in the joke, he caved in and accepted his lot, to a cheer from the crew. Afterwards, much to her further amusement, several said a polite "good night" to Halldís – one or two even apologising with rather touching sincerity for their crude behaviour. She thanked them, keeping as straight a face as possible.

Huddled around the glowing hearth, leaning against the thick pillars, they talked and ate their simple rations and laughed into the night – their trials, for the moment, forgotten. One by one, as the food and the warmth of the fire worked upon them, they succumbed to sleep, until finally Bjólf realised he was the last awake. Gently drawing a thick sheepskin more snugly around the slumbering Halldís, he gazed upon her features for a moment before settling himself down for the night. As he drifted off, the last thing of which he was aware was the voice of Úlf, raised in gentle song, wafting from the barn.


BjÓLF AWOKE TO a sudden crash.

Leaping up, bleary-eyed, he whirled around, his sword already in his hand. The interior of the house was still in darkness, but for the fire's dim glow, but he could just make out Gunnar's shape at the window. The shutter was flung wide open, and, slumped through it, Gunnar's axe still in its head, was the figure of a man, his long, neat braids of hair hanging like thin ropes. Even in this gloom, Bjólf could recognise the grey, lifeless flesh of a death-walker.

"It's all right," whispered Gunnar as the others stirred. "I think it's just a stray one." He went to heave his axe from its bony cleft, but as he pulled, instead of the blade springing free, the whole head came away from its body. Gunnar stood for a moment, a blackly comical figure, staring quizzically at the head still stuck upon his axe. "I just need to deal with this," he said, and made for the door.

He had just swung the door open, and was standing with his foot upon his late victim's face, working the axe free, when a look towards the barn made him stop dead.

"Gods..."

"What is it?" whispered Bjólf, stepping up beside him. But now he could see for himself.

Filling the open space between the house and the barn was a numberless multitude of pale, ungainly figures – some mindlessly jostling each other as they crowded into the courtyard, others, in one and twos, still staggering out from the trees to join the tottering throng. Most had been men, well-dressed and powerfully built: Grimmsson's crew. Some were dragging broken or twisted limbs, listing awkwardly to one side or showing other strange contortions that spoke of terrible wounds to their bodies. Others, with no apparent mark upon them, shuffled forward like sleepwalkers. But all were relentlessly focused on the same goal – the place to which all their faces were turned, all their bodies pushed, and all their paths led: the open door of the barn.

A knot of them crushed clumsily in at the doorway, others pressing in behind. Many had evidently already made it inside. From within there were sounds of struggle. A crash. Urgent shouting. Then a scream. The sounds elicited a chorus of moans from the lifeless multitude. Some reached out. Others that had been wandering with little sense of direction now picked up their pace, and started to stagger directly for the source of the pain, the source of food. As they watched, a death-walker flew suddenly backwards out of the barn, an arrow in its neck, bowling several others over. More surged forward to take their place, their sluggish frenzy growing, their bodies funnelling doggedly, unrelentingly into the barn's dark interior, until it seemed the place would burst at the seams.

"Well, now we know what became of Grimmsson's crew." muttered Gunnar.

"We must do something," said Bjólf, the desperate plight of the two dozen trapped men ringing in the night air.

"But what?" said Gunnar in despair. "We cannot fell them all!"

Bjólf turned back into the house and began flinging things about wildly, Halldís, Atli and the others shrinking back from him in alarm. Finally he turned to Gunnar, having found what he sought: three torches, their tops soaked in pitch. "You remember how

Ingjald the Ill-Ruler treated the Swedish kings who feasted in his hall?"

Gunnar nodded.

"Find your way around the back and get our men out any way you can," said Bjólf, placing his helm on his head. "Take Godwin, Atli and Kjötvi with you. I'll take care of the rest."

Gunnar and the others hastily threw their gear about them and broke from the door, heading off into the darkness far to the right. Bjólf, taking one of the torches, thrust it into the fire until the flames took hold, then stood poised at the door, sword in one hand, torch in the other.

"What of us?" said Halldís.

He turned to her, the torchlight illuminating his face, glinting off the metal. "Stay here with Frodi and his men, and make no sound. You will see soon enough whether I have succeeded."

And with his flame roaring in the wind, he was gone.

# CHAPTER THIRTY-SIX

## INGJALD'S STRATAGEM

As HE RAN, his bag weighing heavily upon his back, Atli's mind flashed back to the terrible night before the stockade. But this time was different. This time, fear was no longer his enemy. Moving in a wide arc, they passed swiftly and silently behind the last of the death-walkers, that flocked mindlessly towards the sound and scent of death. Now and again a straggler appeared before them, emerging from the trees, slowed in its progress by some grievous, ugly wound. The axes of Godwin and Gunnar dealt with them.

Soon, they stood at the rear of the towering barn. Within, an arm's length away on the other side of the wooden wall, they could hear the cries of their fellows, the scrape and scratch as they fought for their lives.

Gunnar did not hesitate. "Watch our backs," he said to Atli and Kjötvi, and he and Godwin immediately set about the barn's thick planks with their axes.

Splinters flew. Inside, men heard the blows, and shouts went up.

A section of plank flew free. Gunnar stopped his axe short just in time to avoid slicing through the arm that sprang though the gap.

"Stand back!" he bellowed, his cry echoed by the muffled, desperate voices inside.

They set about the planks once more as the limb was hastily withdrawn, chopping through the wall, chunks of wood flying, pulling off another length, then the piece above it, until there was a rough opening half as big as a man.

Njáll appeared through the gap, red-faced and sweating. "Took your bloody time!" he said, and dived out onto the ground.

More followed. One by one they were hauled out of that death-trap, then, as the hole was broken wider, they came bowling and wriggling out two at a time, the cries and groans of the death-walkers growing all the while, the walls creaking and shaking from the pressure of the undead host within.

All could see a moment of crisis was approaching. "Fetch the cart!" called Gunnar. Atli, Kjötvi and several of their rescued shipmates ran to the old wagon and heaved it around the corner. "When I give the word, push it against the opening."

"There's people still alive in there!" said Njáll, smashing a ghoul with his mace as it appeared suddenly in the gap, moments after Halfdan had flung himself through. Death-walkers were pressing at the ragged hole now, plugging it with their own unwieldy bodies, their arms flailing and grasping, Godwin barely holding them at bay with a broken plank. "Whenever you're ready..." he called out. The surrounding walls bulged and groaned under the pressure, threatening to give way.

"We cannot wait," said Gunnar, then muttered under his breath, "May their spirits forgive me..." At his command they rolled the cart hard against the barn, and the last means of escape was blocked for good.

BJÓLF, MEANWHILE, HAD been attending to the more daring part of the plan.

As he had stood in the doorway of the farmhouse, it had been clear that stealth alone could not help him. Fire was his greatest weapon, but it also ensured that his approach could not be hidden. His attack would require speed. As he watched, death-walkers were still cramming themselves into the barn, as if desperate to fulfil their part of his plan. But at least twenty more stood between him and the barn door, scattered across his path. There would be nothing for it but to run the gauntlet of the creatures, forcing his way past them before they had time to respond.

He squinted into the darkness, trying to read the features of the barn door itself, then scanned the open hay loft high above. He had to time it exactly right. The attempt could not be allowed to fail; there would be only one chance.

Suddenly, the moment of decision was taken from his hands. When he lowered his eyes, they met the face of a straggling death-walker turning directly towards him, its attention caught by his flame. It let out a weird, urgent moan, and others turned at its cry, joining it. It was now or never. He spoke his parting words to Halldís, then charged, his torch flaming behind him.

There was no time for finesse. Head low, shoulder forward, he slammed into the first walker, his helm smashing into its teeth, sending it flying. More turned at the sound of the impact. He swung his sword around, catching the second across the side of its neck, sending its head off at an impossible angle – a killing blow. It dropped like a stone, but directly towards him, its full weight catching his legs as it fell, sending him sprawling. The torch spun out of his grip, landing at the feet of another figure; a great bearded lump of a man in a studded leather jerkin. The creature stared at it blankly, then resumed its course towards the meat, oblivious to the flames now licking up its leg. Others, closing in around him, trampled the torch, stamping it out, and Bjólf's hopes were extinguished with it.

He scrambled for his sword, grabbed it by the grip, but something gripped his ankle – the first one he had struck, but failed to finish. He kicked out at it, as the bearded, burning figure lumbered towards him from the other direction, its flesh crackling as the flames now engulfed its body. If he could only regain the torch, relight it from the death-walker's flames... as he pulled, struggling to rise, a death-walker still on his leg and the hulking inferno almost upon him, another grim-faced ghoul – its leg horribly twisted below the knee – suddenly loomed over him, one putrid hand grasping his shoulder strap, the other clawing at his face.

Then, when it seemed all was lost, the thing jerked inexplicably, its head toppling from its body. The collapsing death-walker revealed a figure behind it – torch in one hand, gore-stained blade in the other, mail shimmering in the flame's light. Halldís. Before Bjólf could respond, there was another crunching impact. The grip on his ankle was relinquished – then a rough hand reached down and hauled him to his feet, and Bjólf found himself face to face with Frodi. The old man turned suddenly, delivering a shattering blow to the burning ghoul, sending him tottering away and crashing into two more. He grinned at Bjólf, the light of his own torch flickering upon his face. "An intelligent man may moderate what fate brings, if he is prepared to seek the help of friends..." And with that he turned again and cracked another of the creeping death-walkers across the temple.

Bjólf looked about him. Alongside Halldís and Frodi stood their three volunteer companions, a youthful zeal rekindled in their eyes, all with swords drawn and ready. Halldís stepped over the twitching bodies towards Bjólf. "We know of Ingjald, even in Björnheim," she said, and thrust her torch into his hand.

Together they turned, the fighters from Björnheim forming a flank on either side of the torch-bearer, forcing their way forward through the staggering *draugr*. The fighting was fierce; Frodi was in his element, joyful at tasting battle again. Halldís, her expression set and grim, struck out with no less vigour, never hesitating, her sword blade biting with ruthless precision. With the way ahead clear, two of the men ran forward, slamming the great barn door shut, putting their shoulders against it as they jammed the bolt into place. Bjólf stepped forward, took aim, and hurled the torch high into the hay loft.

All stepped back, keeping in a tight defensive circle – waiting, hoping, for the fire to take hold. Bjólf took the second torch from Frodi, in case it should be needed. For an agonising moment it seemed the flame had died, but as they watched, the glow in the loft began to grow and spread.

"I pray to the gods that Gunnar has done his job," said Frodi, one eye on the barn, the other on the dim figures that still lurked about them in the gloom.

"Trust Gunnar," said Bjólf.

The flames caught rapidly, leaping out of the loft and up to the gables, swiftly spreading the length of the barn.

Bjólf turned from the fire. "More death-walkers will come. We must make for the forest. Find the others there."

Frodi nodded, and he and his men started for the far side of the clearing. Bjólf flung the torch at the last of the approaching ghouls, sending one tottering backwards, and turned to face Halldís.

"I thought I told you to stay put," he said.

"I make a point of questioning everything I'm told to do," she replied.

Bjólf grinned, his eyes glinting in the growing light of the fire, and, grasping her hand, ran with her towards the trees.

# CHAPTER THIRTY-SEVEN

## ÆGIR'S ROCK

THE MOMENT THEY had seen the flames take hold, Gunnar and the main party of men had plunged into the dark forest, the great roar of the blaze and the last unearthly, hollow moans of its victims echoing after them. Finding the farm had been a strange twist of fortune – one that had allowed them to destroy a whole host of the creatures at a stroke. Yet Gunnar knew that among those horrible sounds carried on the night air were the final cries of men they had failed to save. Having to leave before daylight had been a wrench, but all knew they were safer in the trees; the blaze, now visible from all around, would only draw more of the flesh-hungry fiends, and in the forest they could at least hear them coming.

What proved far harder was holding the party together in the chaotic gloom that reigned there. Gunnar's party had entered first, through a parting in the forest's edge – perhaps once an old path. Soon after came Frodi and his men, followed, some way along, by Bjólf and Halldís. But their hopes of mustering once in the forest were soon dashed. Just a short way into the trees, the woodland once again began to thicken, the boles and roots become more massive, the tangle of foliage more impenetrable. Some blundered into death-walkers and became separated from the rest. Unable to rely on fire, they soon found themselves staggering in an inky blackness with only their ears to guide them, uncertain what might lay behind the footfalls close by, unwilling to call out for fear of attracting the attentions of the wandering dead.

For what seemed an eternity, Bjólf and Halldís, their hands never relinquishing their grip, crept forward through the dark, listening intently. Early on, they had often heard the crack and swish of movement off to their left, where they believed the others to be. Sometimes, it could clearly be distinguished from the slow, shuffling motion of the death-walkers. At other times, the distinction was not so clear. When he could, Bjólf had altered their path towards it, or at least tried to keep it close while navigating his way by the brief, bright glimpses of the sky. But, despite his efforts, the sounds only became increasingly distant, or sometimes baffled his senses entirely, seeming to come from all directions but that which his rational mind told him should be right. Finally, he abandoned his dependence upon them altogether and pressed forward according to his instincts, all the time fighting against the thought of becoming like the lost, directionless death-walkers, doomed to wander this place for eternity, and hoping against hope that the shore of the fjord lay before them.

Though almost blind, he could sense that Halldís, resilient as she was, was close to exhaustion – something he also knew she would never admit. His mind was racing, weighing the possibilities, trying to calculate how much longer they could reasonably continue, when, with no warning, a great expanse of clear sky suddenly opened up before them. They staggered to a halt, staring up. The wind had risen during the evening, clearing the cloud, and the whole dizzying night sky that arced above them was dusted with countless stars. Amidst the needle points of light hung the huge orb of the moon, its ghostly light illuminating a small open glade before them, casting their cold shadows upon the grass. Just ahead, filling nearly half of the tiny clearing, was a grey, flat outcrop of rock, rising towards the far end and falling sharply away where the forest once again took over. Bjólf crept slowly towards it as if in a dream, suddenly feeling his own exhaustion wash over him. "We can rest here," he said: "Death-walkers cannot climb."

She did not argue the point. He helped her up onto the rock, then heaved himself up, threw off his helm and the shield from his back and slumped beside where she lay, her body limp, already possessed by sleep. His hand found hers and closed around it. For a moment, he lay with his eyes wide open, his back to the mossy rock, listening to her quiet breathing and staring up at the impossible abundance of stars – too tired now to make sense of whatever they might once have told him. For a moment he had a vivid memory from his childhood, of lying on his back looking up at the night sky, feeling as if the whole universe spun around that one spot. He thought, fleetingly, that he should stay awake, and on watch until morning. Then he let his eyelids close, and a deep sleep took him.

He awoke suddenly to bright sunlight, his head pounding. Only gradually, as he blinked in the sun's unkind glare did he realise that Halldís was no longer at his side. He gripped his sword and whirled around in panic. But it was certain; he was alone on the rock. Cursing his weakness, staggering to his feet, every bone and muscle aching, he climbed to the highest point and looked about desperately. Nothing but the tall trees of the forest greeted his eyes.

"Hey!" The voice made him start – so much so, he almost toppled from his lofty vantage point. When he looked around, the smiling face of Halldís had appeared above the side of the outcrop.

"What in Hel's name are you doing sneaking around like that?" said Bjólf.

"Come on," she said, extending her hand. "I have something to show you."

Grabbing his gear and scrambling down into the grassy glade, he was led into the trees on its far side where, he could see, the vegetation had already been freshly beaten down. They followed the path, and within moments the trees had dwindled once again, the unmistakable smell of open water met his nostrils, and ahead, to their left, rising above a mountainous tangle of briar and elder, was a great dome of grey-brown stone.

Halldís pointed. "Ægir's rock," she said. Bjólf grabbed her and spun her around – weapons, armour and all – laughing triumphantly.

She beamed as her feet came back to earth. "They say the sea-giant Ægir settled down to sleep one night and was disturbed by a pebble under his back – so he picked it up and threw it inland. And here it came to rest!"

With another shout of delight he grabbed her hand and ran forward, both of them almost tumbling down the steep, tangled bank to the foot of the huge boulder. Within minutes, panting with the exertion of the climb, hauling her after him, they had found their way up onto its great curved brow. As they walked forward to its highest point – the great, dark forest that had so tested them to their left, the great expanse of the fjord and its far shore stretching away to the right – a most welcome sight was slowly revealed before them, one that made them shout again with joy: down below was the small bay they sought; there, still tethered, a little way along, was Grimmsson's ship; and milling about on the shore were Gunnar, Frodi, and the crew.

"What kept you?" called Gunnar, waving.

# CHAPTER THIRTY-EIGHT

## BLACK SHAPES

THE REUNION WAS an exuberant one; the men in resolute mood. The discovery of the ship, upon which so much depended, had greatly lifted their spirits. The vessel itself was in good order. The sky, too, was clear, and there now rose a brisk northerly wind to speed them to their destination. Preparations for the journey had begun before Bjólf's return – all eager for the moment of retribution. Now, all the elements were finally in place for their hammerblow against Skalla.

But not all the news was good. As the crew busied themselves ashore, getting their gear in order for the battle that lay ahead, Bjólf walked the length of the ship alone with Gunnar, and broached the subject that had been troubling him since his descent from Ægir's Rock.

"I see many faces missing from our company," he said. Gunnar nodded, a grave expression upon his face. "How bad is it?"

"Bad," said Gunnar. "Five did not make it out of the barn. Egil. Farbjörn. Guthmund. Sigvald. Kari."

Bjólf's frown deepened. "And the rest?"

"Olaf, Ketill and Ragnar were lost in the forest. Ran into a pack of those creatures in the darkness. Skjöld survived to tell the tale. But..."

Bjólf looked up at Gunnar. "But..?"

The big man's expression grew darker. "He had been bitten When we awoke this morning, he had gone, his sword and armour abandoned by the shore. Hakon and two of Frodi's men also remain unaccounted for. What has become of them, we cannot tell."

Bjólf stood by him at the gunwale, the grey-green water lapping at the timbers. "I make that twenty-one of us now," he said. "That was a costly tactic, back at the farm."

Gunnar shrugged. "Without it, many more of us might be dead."

"Can we still do it?" Bjólf seemed suddenly struck through by doubt. "The men are strong, but is that enough? After all this, I can hardly believe their hearts are still in it."

"Wrong. They are more determined than ever. Change our fate or die trying, that's what we vowed to do. That's what we will do."

Bjólf smiled. "That is what we always do."

"We will make this Skalla pay," said Gunnar, his voice suddenly hard as steel. "For lost friends. For everything. Every one of those deaths will be added to his account."

Bjólf turned and looked back along the length of the ship; a vessel built for war. Yes, Skalla would feel the full heat of their wrath. He slapped its thick timbers. "So, now we have this great tub to contend with..." It was not quite what they were used to: Grimmsson's ship was far younger than the *Hrafn* – cruder in build, longer, and narrower across the beam, with fixed thwarts that served as rowing benches. It also had certain decorative features that were not entirely to Bjólf's taste: the red sail, the iron spikes, the upper three strakes painted yellow, blue and red. But since Björnheim and their first sight of Skalla, he had begun to feel rather differently about the arrogant, vain Grimmsson. Perhaps these affectations were not so bad after all. Grimmsson had saved Bjólf's crew at the expense of his own life, and furnished them with their most awesome weapon – a weapon with which they would strike with deadly speed at the very heart of their enemy. When they did so, it would be for Grimmsson too.

"We've loaded stones for ballast to make her steady in the water," said Gunnar. "It was the one modification needed, with there being so few of us. Other than that, she's ready to go. Everything was in place when we found her – it was as if her crew had simply vanished.

"Let's just make sure our fate is happier than theirs," said Bjólf, and turned towards the gunwale on the landward side, catching sight of Halldís amongst the busy throng at the edge of the trees. Then, just as he was about to jump ashore, something strange caught his eye. Glimpsed at the very edge of sight, something of which he was barely aware, it made him pause. He turned southward, towards their destination, then stepped back from the gunwale, taking in the length of the shore stretching away to his right. Shielding his eyes against the sun, he could see, some distance away, a curious, blurry flicker in the sky immediately above the trees – like smoke, he thought, or the heat haze above a fire. As he watched, he realised it was gradually drawing closer, sticking close to the edge of the trees, becoming more solid as it neared – a texture formed of many different movements. Black shapes. The breeze dropped for an instant, and he thought he heard a strange confusion of hoarse, lonely cries – then the wind once again whipped the sound away.

"What is that?" he said.

Gunnar squinted along the shoreline. "Hmm. Just a flock of birds. Rooks or ravens." He made to go ashore, but stopped himself as he suddenly realised what he had said, turning back to Bjólf with a deeply furrowed brow.

"How can that be, Gunnar?" said Bjólf, a note of urgency creeping into his voice.

Gunnar wrestled with the question as the chaotically swarming flock, its harsh, throaty cries now clearly audible, drew rapidly closer. "It was a raven led us here," he ventured.

"To the inlet, yes," said Bjólf. "But have you seen or heard a bird the whole time we have been near Björnheim, or this part of the fjord? A single one?"

Gunnar stared back up at the approaching black cloud. "Why do they move so strangely?"

Bjólf moved towards the gunwale, his sense of unease growing. "Get everyone into the trees – now!"

He leapt ashore, Gunnar hard upon his heels. "Get under cover!" he called. "Into the trees!"

For a moment, several of the crew stopped and looked at him in bemusement. Then the black mass of ravens fell upon them.

Everyone scattered, heading for the cover of the forest, swatting frantically at the air as the black, ragged shapes flapped and croaked about them. Spiked beaks and claws stabbed and tore, catching in their hair and clothes as they ran. The ravens attacked without fear or caution. Here and there, the crew grabbed at the struggling creatures and flung them roughly away. Some immediately took to the air and resumed their assault; others, broken, fluttered and flopped wildly upon the ground, or scuttled and hopped randomly about, pecking at their feet. Their movement on the ground was twitchy and erratic, like crazed, diseased livestock. In the air they darted more like bats than birds, but their eyes, like those of the death-walkers, were utterly dead; their one clear purpose to pick at living flesh.

The warriors had soon plunged in amongst the trees, where the ravens' attacks foundered upon branches and brambles. But they did not stop. Many caught in the tangle of briar and ivy and flapped and jerked convulsively, hung like moths in a web. Others broke through and hurtled about in their mindless quest for blood.

Bjólf rapidly located Halldís in the dark tangle. With a nod, she reassured him she was unharmed. Like many others, she had donned her helm to protect her head and eyes, but they were struggling to wield their weapons against the creatures in the close confines of the wood. They couldn't stay here. If the ravens were anything like the death-walkers, they would relent only when the source of food was entirely exhausted.

When the creatures had first approached, they had clung to the shore, seeming reluctant to venture over the water. Bjólf could only hope that this reluctance was stronger than their craving for flesh.

"We have the get to the ship!" he cried. "Hold your shields high, and grab whatever gear you need on the way!" Swords drawn, he and Halldís took a deep breath and broke from the trees. As they battered against his shield, Bjólf swung his sword wildly, smashing them out of the air. Others followed suit, swiping with axe, sword and mace, splattering blood, and sending squawking, scrawny, bundles of tattered black feathers bouncing in all directions and littering the floor.

Bjólf hurled himself into the ship, hauling Halldís after him. By ones and twos, the rest of the crew clambered or flung themselves over the side.

"Raise the sail!" bellowed Bjólf, loosing the reefing lines as the croaking mob fluttered and beat about his head. Men flew to their tasks, heaving the yard up the mast. The wind began to fill the sail.

As the ship moved, the attack seemed to abate and a few of the crew cheered in relief. But just when it seemed the crisis was at an end, Bjólf heard another cry go up and saw someone pointing. From the port gunwale he could see, half crumpled on the shore, the figure of Kjötvi. Slowed by his injured leg, he had been mobbed by the main body of ravens, which all but smothered him as he lay hunched in a ball among the twisting roots, his arms protecting his head.

Before he could make a move, Bjólf saw another figure leap ashore. Hrafning ran to his friend, a wooden stave in his hand, cutting a swathe through the swarming multitude, batting them this way and that like in a game of Stick-Ball. He beat them off the fallen man, heaving him to his feet as the birds flocked around his head, wading into the water and finally delivering him to the ship. The ailing crewman was hauled aboard and Bjólf could see that where Kjötvi's right eye had been, there was now no more than a gaping, bleeding hole.

They reached for Hrafning, but he hesitated. Looking away, along the shore, he turned from the ship, waded to shore, and ran along the waterline.

"What's he doing?" said Bjólf. "If he delays any longer, he'll have a swim on his hands..."

The sail was now fully hoisted and bulging in the breeze. As soon as they were clear of the bay, the full force of the wind would take them. Bjólf threw off his helm and mail, about to head back onto the shore, when Gunnar restrained him.

"The line!" said the big man. And Bjólf saw it; in the water, the line that Gunnar had left ashore during their encounter with Grimmsson, that Bjólf himself had tied to the spike on the ship's prow. As he watched, Hrafning, swamped now by the ravens, struggled to where the line lay anchored drew his knife and sliced through the rope. It sprang free and he collapsed, weighed down by the massing bodies of his attackers. The crew could only watch him die, as the ship caught the wind, turned from the shore and was drawn inexorably away from the last resting place of Hrafning, son of Róki.

Though it had hardly been the start they had imagined for the voyage, they were at last under sail, and drawing closer to their goal. Kjötvi, oblivious to his own injuries, was devastated by the loss of his old friend, but all about him, the men muttered words of deep admiration for Hrafning's final deed. While there had been many deaths, this one, at least, had some purpose. It was selfless, heroic. From a barrel of mead discovered amongst Grimmsson's stores, they drank a toast to his memory, all satisfied that Hrafning's place in Valhalla was assured.

As they did so, Gunnar edged up to Bjólf, speaking in confidential tones. "About Kjötvi..."

"I know what you're thinking," replied Bjólf.

"Those ravens drew blood. Will he be all right?"

Bjólf shrugged. Who could know in these strange times? "If anyone will, it's Kjötv. But keep an eye on him all the same."

Stepping up onto the prow, relieved to once again have the timbers of a ship beneath his feet, Bjólf looked at the figurehead – an ugly, oddly elongated, impossible to identify creature painted green and red. There was one more thing to be done.

"Boy!" called Bjólf.

Atli gave no answer, but looked about him. "Did someone let a boy on board?" he said. A guffaw went up from the crew and Bjólf took the point.

"Noble son of Ivarr," began Bjólf again with a bow. "If you would be so kind as to grace your captain with your esteemed presence..." His tone suddenly shifted. "And you better not have lost that bag I gave you."

Atli approached, dumping the heavy bag upon the deck in front of him. "If I had lost it," he said, "I could not have shown my face again."

From the bag, Bjólf drew the scorched, finely carved dragon's head that he had salvaged from the smouldering wreck of the *Hrafn*, and climbed high in the prow. Within minutes, he had lopped off the old gaudy, figurehead and crudely nailed the *Hrafn*'s in its place.

There was a cheer as he stood back to admire his handiwork. "Now," he called out. "Does anyone know if this ship has a name?" All looked at each other blankly. In all their deaings with him, none had taken enough interest in Grimmsson to find out his ship's name.

"A ship must have a name!" called Gunnar.

"How about *Naglfar*," called Thorvald. "The ship that takes the doomed warriors to the final battle at Ragnarók!"

There was laughter at that, it was the kind of grim humour that had kept them all sane over the years.

"I have a better idea," said Bjólf. He filled his mead horn and raised it aloft, standing high before the full sail. "*Fire-Raven*!"

"*Fire-Raven*!" they cried back, and all drank in its honour.

# CHAPTER THIRTY-NINE

## GANDHÓLM

WITH GOOD WEATHER and the wind in their sail, the majority of the crew suddenly found themselves bereft of purpose. For the first time in what seemed an age, there was nothing that demanded to be done – nothing to guard, no one to fight, no threat of death.

It was, Bjólf knew, the calm before the storm. Something for them to savour. He sat with Haldís near the stern, his shipmates scattered about them, but while others relaxed, his mind was still working, running ahead to the challenge that lay before them. It was no more than a series of practical problems to which solutions needed to be found – problems that could be broken down, worked out, ultimately solved. The only issue was, these problems would cost lives.

"Tell me," he said to Halldís, "who are these mysterious masters who Skalla serves?"

Halldís sighed, looked out across the water. "No one knows," she said. "We have had dealings with them, of course. My husband,

Hunding – he went there, negotiated with them, brokered the first truce." She fingered the black and red braided bracelet upon her wrist. "That is where this came from." She looked downcast for a moment, then gathered herself. "But even he did not see the masters themselves. Skalla is their only intermediary. Some say they are gods."

Gunnar looked at Bjólf, but Bjólf gave no response.

"You have said little of Skalla himself," he said after a pause.

"There is little to say," said Halldís. "Little that I wish to think about."

"But you spoke of a score that you have to settle," said Bjólf. "This is personal for you."

Halldís stared down at the deck again. "Because of him, my husband is lost." She looked Bjólf in the eye, shrugged with feigned indifference. "Don't worry – I know full well he is dead, although for months I held out hope. But that is not the main reason. Skalla murdered my father."

Gunnar raised his eyebrows. "You kept that one quiet."

"Can you blame me? Do you know what it's like to live with the shame of your father having been killed by his slave?"

Gunnar puffed out his cheeks in amazement. "Skalla was a slave! This just gets better and better."

Bjólf glared at him. Sometimes he thought the big man spent too much time on board ship and not nearly enough among regular people.

Halldís took it in her stride. "It is what made him so dangerous. He had nothing to lose. No rule to follow but his own."

"Tell me of this island fortress – the island Skalla's masters inhabit," said Bjólf.

"We've always called it Gandhólm – the island of sorcerors."

"You say you've *always* called it that?"

"Of course," said Halldís with a frown.

"What are the odds?" said Njáll with a laugh. "An island called 'the island of sorcerors' which becomes a home to sorcerors."

"It's fate," nodded Gunnar. Bjólf glared at him again.

"Maybe Skalla's masters chose it because they liked the name," chipped in Godwin.

"No, no..." said Halldís, frowning more deeply, her expression one of confusion. "Do you not know? Did no one tell you?"

All looked blankly at each other, then back at Halldís.

"There *was* no island before the masters."

It was left to Bjólf to speak. "Perhaps you'd better explain what you mean by that."

Halldís looked about at the puzzled, expectant faces, cleared her throat, then began.

"IT WAS FIVE years ago, about this time of year. Things were quite normal then, as they had been for generations. Then, one night, without warning, all the animals about Björnheim began to bleat and whinny and crow as if some terrible disaster were about to befall. They kicked and bit at their stalls, and just as suddenly fell silent again. The sky lit up, as bright as daytime, but white, like lightning. The ground shook with a terrible roar, as if the earth were turning itself inside out.

"Then the flood came. A great wave, surging along the river. Our dwellings in the village are upon a hill; they survived. But the other farms in the lowlands were not so lucky. Those who lived to tell the tale said the water was hot, as if boiled in a cauldron. That it brought with it strange things. Within days the floodwater had abated, but from that night, Hössfjord had a new island."

"What?" exclaimed Gunnar. "It just rose up one night, right out of the water?"

"Or fell from above," said Halldís.

"An island that fell from the sky? This is madness! A story of a rock thrown by a giant is one thing. But this..."

"I have no explanation for it," said Halldís. "I can only tell things as they have happened."

Gunnar stared at the ground. "I know what you will say, Bjólf, but it certainly sounds like sorcery to me."

"I do not believe it," said Bjólf. "Will not believe it. Where is the evidence?"

Gunnar, still staring at the deck, spoke in a low, quiet voice. "Berserker warriors, raised from the dead?"

"If they are sorcerors, why not destroy us with a wave of the hand? Turn us into toads? And why does the pestilence also afflict Skalla's men? They are no sorcerors, Gunnar – or, if they are, they are very bad ones."

269

Gunnar fell silent.

Bjólf questioned Halldís further about the fortress – its strengths and weaknesses – but her knowledge was soon exhausted. It remained an enigma, even to her; a mystery that left Bjólf troubled by the multitude of unanswerable questions it raised. Suddenly it had struck him that he was rushing into battle against an enemy of completely unknown powers, and unknown potential – something his uncle had always warned him against. But what choice did he have? Their future, whatever it was, now hurtled towards them with an unstoppable momentum; a confrontation in which all questions would ultimately be answered, everything finally revealed.

WHEN THE AFTERNOON sun was in the sky, Halldís went and stood up on the prow, her attention focused intently upon the left bank of the fjord. She had told Thorvald to keep in close to that shore – only that way, she said, could their approach remain hidden from the ever-watchful eyes of Gandhólm. Then, up ahead, the fjord seemed to bend sharply to the left, its further reaches obscured by a long, projecting spur of land off their port bow. When she recognised the place, Halldís jumped down from the prow, her disposition suddenly agitated.

"Put in here," she said, pointing to a thin, sandy strip in the crook of the promontory. "The island lies immediately beyond this spur."

At the signal from Bjólf, Thorvald leaned on the tiller. The sail was dropped, the mooring lines thrown ashore.

"We reach the far side overland, through the trees," said Halldís as the gangplank was hastily extended. "Then you will see it for yourself."

# CHAPTER FORTY

## THE GROVE OF DEATH

THEIR APPROACH WAS lined with tall, densely-packed trunks of pine and birch, the soil beneath their feet loose and mealy. On the face of it, these were undoubtedly more pleasant surroundings than the forests near Björnheim, but all were aware that they were in the realm of the black guards now. As they marched, drawing inexorably closer to the source of the evil that had afflicted them, the dead, portentous silence of the place began to weigh upon the company. Halldís, especially, became increasingly withdrawn and anxious.

Her mood infected them all. The forest was open to the sky above, but they were hedged around by the massive trees and the gigantic, primordial fronds of bracken that loomed in between. They were on their guard, alive to sounds of movement, but none came. There was no bird, no scurry of squirrel or shrew, not even the buzz of an insect – only the ceaseless sighing of the trees above them. It was a weirdly sorrowful sound, as if the entire forest were in mourning for the passing of its own life. For a time, in that strange realm, it was as if they were the last animate creatures upon earth – so much so, some even found themselves longing for the shambling presence of the undead.

The sight of a figure ahead made Gunnar start, and the company froze about him. Grey and skeletal, dressed in colourless rags, it stood motionless, framed by the trunk of a huge, rough-barked pine, its lipless mouth grinning without expression, its empty sockets regarding them in hideous silence. Bjólf made a movement towards it. It did not react. As he crept slowly forward, he saw that it was pinned to the tree by a series of rusty iron spikes – one protruding between the edges of its bared teeth. This was no death-walker – at least, not any more. It was the first sign of life they had encountered since their arrival here.

As they moved beyond that grim guardian, the soil became more gritty and dessicated. The monstrous ferns suddenly subsided, revealing that all around, as far as the eye could see, the forest floor was strewn with human bones. In stunned silence they picked their way past until the field of grim relics finally dwindled – none daring to point out the fact of the absence of even a single human skull. The bodies had been decapitated, the heads removed, by whom, and for what purpose, the troubled company could not tell.

None were sorry to leave that place.

Gunnar, intent in taking his mind off these gloomy matters, sidled up to Bjólf as they walked.

"I was thinking..." he whispered.

"Be careful with that," said Bjólf.

"About when this is all over. About that little farm somewhere..."

"Ah yes, with the barn and the woman."

"I was thinking, maybe Ireland."

Bjólf nodded appreciatively. "Very green. Lots of rain."

Gunnar shook his head. "But then I thought: too boggy."

Bjólf sighed deeply. "How about Scotland?"

"It's practically Norway these days."

"The Frankish kingdoms?"

"Maybe, but that would mean living among Franks."

"Normandy?"

"Bunch of fanatics."

"Russia then?"

"Full of Swedes."

Bjólf sighed again. "Sorry, old man, I'm running out of countries."

Gunnar raised his arms and let them fall in exasperation. "You see? It's hopeless. There must be somewhere out there a man can live in peace. All I ask is a small, sturdy house with a..." He fell silent. Ahead of them, just visible through the trees, as if his words had summoned it up, was a stout-beamed dwelling in a clearing. All drew their weapons. Shields came off backs.

Beyond the cover of the trees they could now see a whole complex of buildings, roughly arranged around a dusty courtyard of dry, barren earth, a circular space at its centre scorched and blackened. Dead leaves and ash blew across it. Somewhere, a door creaked in the wind. Everywhere there was an atmosphere of abandonment.

Bjólf signalled silently to his men; a nod briefly to left and right. Without a word, two groups, headed by Godwin and Finn, split off and headed out wide on either side. It was the tactic they had employed at Atli's village, and at many villages before that.


ATLI LOOKED AROUND in surprise, uncertain what he should be doing, baffled at the way the men seemed to know Bjólf's intentions without being told. By the time he had realised what was happening, they were already gone. His place – by default, it seemed – was with Bjólf, Halldís and the rest.

They approached the courtyard slowly, warily, passing the open entrance of the timbered house as they did so. Gunnar investigated with silent efficiency, shaking his head as he emerged. Through the open doorway, as they moved on into the open space beyond, Atli glimpsed the same signs of long abandonment that had been evident back at Erling's farm. They kept moving, the only sound the wind gusting through empty spaces, punctuated every now and then by one of Finn or Godwin's men as they investigated the dank interiors upon either side.

The buildings themselves were strange to Atli's eyes. Some had evidently once been ordinary farm outbuildings, probably of the same age as the abandoned house, but had since been crudely adapted or expanded, sometimes employing materials that he could not identify. There were flat, square roofs; iron rods held together with wire and metal pegs; patches of rust grinning through crumbling plaster and peeling paint; featureless partitions of wood that had warped in the wet and were splitting apart; ragged, thin materials hanging in shreds over open windows. Although these ugly features were clearly more recent than the buildings upon which they had grown, they gave a bizarre impression of more advanced decay. The mere sight of them filled Atli with a feeling of dread.

Ahead, he could now see that the large, blackened area had been the site of an immense fire – perhaps a succession of fires. Strange, lumpy remains – part-consumed fragments of wood, odd bits of twisted metal, and what looked like charred bits of bone – were strewn about its ashy centre, seemingly covered in a dark, oily residue. Bjólf stepped carefully into it, felt the ground, and picked his way back out. Finn and Godwin emerged from the last of the outbuildings and shook their heads.

Bjólf picked up speed, moving towards the two larger buildings that lay directly ahead of them. One looked to be a huge barn – long, like Halldís's hall, but with an entirely straight roof and constructed from thick boards through which the wind whipped and howled. To the right of it as they approached, directly opposite, was a smaller and very different kind of structure; low, squat and square and built of uniform grey blocks, with slits for windows. Bjólf stood in the wide gap between the two, looking to one, then the other, then ahead towards a further, smaller clearing beyond, lined with trees. As he caught up with the rest of the company, Atli peered through the huge open doors into the vast, dark space of the barn. At the far end was another doorway, also open, beyond which was dense forest – yet far enough from the opening to admit a dim light. The interior seemed to be divided up into stalls – for animals, he supposed. Whatever they were, they were now long gone.

Opposite was the door to the grey, squat structure, and different from almost every other door Atli had seen here in two important respects: with its heavy planks and thick iron straps it appeared substantial enough to contain wild beasts. And it was closed.

Bjólf looked at Gunnar. "What do you think?"

"I'm trying not to," said Gunnar. "This place... It's like nowhere I've seen. And it has a bad smell."

Bjólf nodded and said to Halldís. "Do you know this place?"

She merely shook her head, her expression troubled, as if the little she knew from the last few moments were already more knowledge than she could bear.

"Well..." began Bjólf. But before he could say another word, a sound made all of them turn. It was the chink of metal on metal, clear and distinct, from somewhere behind the heavy, closed door.

Bjólf approached slowly and silently, and put his shoulder to the door. It resisted, but shifted a crack. Not locked. Gunnar and the others stood with weapons and shields ready. Bjólf shoved with all his strength. The great door scraped half open before grinding to a standstill. Inside, all was black. The sound came again, louder this time. The air that wafted from inside was heavy with the stench of death-walkers.

Bjólf began to creep inside, Gunnar following close behind. Atli had moved up close to Bjólf, and found he was next in line. He faced a choice: follow behind Bjólf and Gunnar, or stand back and let Fjölvar or Halldís pass. He clenched his teeth and plunged in.

Inside, their eyes quickly adjusted to the gloom. Ahead was a straight corridor with several doorways off it, about which rubbish was scattered, and here and there pools of water into which an occasional drip fell. The *chink-chink* came again, echoing from somewhere deeper inside. As they crept on, they saw that the doorways – through which the only light filtered – were not all wide open as they had initially assumed. Their doors were fashioned from bars of iron: some half open, some seemingly locked shut, but all coated with a fine film of rust. Each chamber had a single slit for a window. Some had damp straw upon the floor, and others were entirely empty; in several, chains hung from the walls. That was the source of the sound they had heard.

IT CAME AGAIN, now much closer. Bjólf raised his weapon, moving between the last two doorways. The door to the right – of heavy wood, like the first – was wide open. Beyond was a very different kind of space from the other chambers; still dark, but expansive, cluttered with furniture, at its far end a great, baffling, bulbous shape like a vast, enclosed pot that, as far as Bjólf could see, appeared to be constructed entirely of blackened metal.

The sound came again, directly behind him. He whirled around, sword ready. As he advanced into the opposite room, he heard a shuffling. Another *chink-chink*. The chamber, like the others, was dark, a shaft of daylight piercing through the slit in the wall, blinding him now to what lay in the deep shadows. He sensed a presence to his right, and turned to face it. For a moment he stood motionless, listening intently, trying to make his eyes penetrate the darkness, to make sense of it. From within the room, out of sight, came a weird, low cry that chilled him to the bone. A cry that was like two cries, in an eerie chorus. Then, with sudden violence, a figure lurched forward out of the gloom, flying at his face. He leapt back – it stopped dead at the limit of its chains, in the full glare of the light, the taut links ringing in the clammy, sickening air.

Bjólf reeled back all the way to the far wall. Seeing his reaction, Gunnar stepped in, ready to fight, followed closely by Atli and Halldís. All gaped at what they now saw. "Gods..." whispered Gunnar, a quiver in his voice.

That it was a death-walker was clear enough. Its flesh was grey and in an advanced state of putrescence – at certain points (its manacled wrists, its damaged knees, the fingers of its clawing hands) turning to the black slime that had become all too familiar. In its empty hideousness, its face, too, confirmed all their expectations of such a creature – the dead, fish-like eyes, the expressionless, lolling mouth, the collapsed, decaying wreck of a nose – all slipping away, by slow, inevitable degrees, from the skeletal foundation beneath.

What raised the sight to a new level of abomination, however, was not any aspect of its deteriorating condition. It was the way in which it had been altered. There, next to that rotting, vacant face – also, impossibly animate, yet with flesh that seemed somehow closer to the bloom of life it had once possessed – was a second head, the neck sewn crudely into a cleft at the side of the first, the stretched, wrinkled flesh, all along the join, glistening and dripping a pustular yellow. And whereas the first face conveyed nothing but the expected blank emptiness, the second, it almost seemed, stared back at them with its own expression of pained horror.

It began to utter another cry. Before it could complete it, as if unable to tolerate the sound, Gunnar stepped forward and smashed it down with two decisive blows.

For a moment, they stood in shocked silence. Then, slowly, as if by some instinct – as if in need of answers to the questions that now troubled them – they moved one by one into the last of the rooms: the large chamber opposite.

The cluttered interior was dominated by a number of broad, flat tables, some of which were darkly stained, others covered with strangely-shaped objects – tools of metal, containers of ceramic and glass, some broken. Rarely, if ever, had Bjólf seen such a wealth of glass in one place. Other detritus lay scattered about the floor, unidentifiable in the gloom.

Slowly they moved through this alien environment, trying to grasp its purpose – or perhaps, simply, trying to believe it. After all, there could be little doubt as to the cause of the dark stains on the great, slab-like tables. Ahead, the huge iron ball loomed. As they approached, the stench of the place – already unbearable – intensified. From its top, a kind of chimney extended up and through the roof. At its front, they now saw, was a thick iron door into its interior. Inside, traces of ash. And, Bjólf thought, bits of bone.

Atli stepped forward and peered into the large, trough-like container to one side of the great cauldron and started back in revulsion. It was filled with severed limbs in various states of decay.

Bjólf looked at Gunnar, his expression dark. "We should leave this place," he said.

"I agree," said Gunnar.

But as they turned to go, Halldís caught Bjólf's arm. "There's something in here," she whispered. They stood in silence, not daring to move, until they heard a movement, somewhere back near the door, in the shadows. They looked, but could see nothing. Again it came – a strange, scuttling sound. It was heavy. Large. Yet, in the shadows – less murky here than in the previous chamber – no figure could be detected.

Gunnar turned this way and that, trying to follow the sounds. "It must be an animal," he said.

"But there are no animals," said Bjólf.


ATLI, HEARING ANOTHER scurrying movement, turned to his right, peering along a row of benches. There, appearing from around the corner of one of the tables, was a low, large shape. He tried to shout out as he looked upon it, but could not. Instead, he simply pointed, staggering backwards, a strangled, incoherent cry escaping his lips.

It was enough. Bjólf, Gunnar and Halldís were around him, blades raised in readiness as the thing crept into the light on its awkward limbs. Where they expected to encounter the face of some wild creature, they saw in its place another once-human visage, another lost soul.

It took all of them a few moments to comprehend what they were looking at. At first it seemed it must simply be an injured death-walker, crawling forward upon its hands. Then the ghastly truth became apparent. The thing had no legs – nothing, in fact, below its waist. But grafted to its torso, in the same crude manner as the two-headed monstrosity in the previous cell, and carrying it along like some grotesque, oversized insect, were two more pairs of human arms. Sensing living flesh, it suddenly gave a hideous cry and darted forward with a horrible scampering motion, its teeth bared. Bjólf and Gunnar set upon it without hesitation, smashing the thing with axe and sword until it was unrecognisable.

They did not linger in that place any longer. All four of them hurried back into the daylight, gasping for fresh air.

Halldís wiped at her brow, deathly pale. "Someone... *did* that to it..." she said, falteringly. "Some human hand..." But such horrors were beyond words.

Atli, his head spinning, wished only to put as much distance between that building and himself as possible. His legs wanted him to run. Instead, he stumbled away as far as he dared, towards the entrance of the great barn, trying to pull himself together, his stomach heaving.

As he returned to his senses he looked about him, peering the length of the huge building, with its rows of stalls on either side. He walked in, looking at the vacant cells as he passed, the freshening wind a welcome relief. They had seemed like they were intended for animals. That was what they all assumed. But were they? He did not know any more. It seemed the distinction between human and animal, once so clear, was suddenly foggy and obscure. This, then, was the masters' ultimate achievement: the annihilation of humanity.

He turned, realising he should get back to the warband. But as he did so, a dark shape – silhouetted in the open doorway at the far end and framed by the foliage beyond – caught his eye. It was familiar and unfamiliar; something he immediately recognised, but which felt entirely out of place.

A dog.

He turned back and squinted at it, trying to make out its features, wondering how on earth it could have survived all this. It staggered forward as if exhausted, its head low, then stopped. Perhaps there was hope after all. Perhaps there was life here, fighting back. As he watched, another, almost identical shape appeared, its movements similarly stiff and slow. He smiled to himself, debating whether he should go towards them, bring them back to show the others.

Then three more padded slowly into view.

Atli felt a chill run through him. He cursed his idiotic mistake.

Not dogs. Wolves.

He began to back away from them, suddenly struck by the terrible memory of the ravens at Ægir's Rock, not wishing to turn his back. But as he did so, one moved forward. The others did the same, their movements loping and awkward, and then all of them broke into a run. Before he turned, he just had time to see their red eyes, their matted fur, their gaping, ragged wounds, before hurtling headlong back towards the doorway. He could hear them now, pounding behind him, drawing closer, a low mournful moan coming from the throat of each one. Ahead, one of the double doors blew closed, slamming in the wind. Atli put on a last burst of speed, knowing that wolves would be faster, hoping that death had at least slowed them. With their yellow-toothed jaws snapping at his heels, he flew through the open doorway and onto the ground.

As he did so, a shield struck the leading wolf in the face, sending it backwards. The doors closed violently on the neck of the second, which struggled and howled, before a foot booted it back and slammed the doors shut. Atli looked up to see Bjólf towering over him, his shoulder against the doors, the creatures snarling and scratching in a frenzy on the other side.

"Don't wander off," Bjólf said, and shut the bolt. Then he turned to Fjölvar. "Go and close the other door," he said. "There's enough to think about without these prowling around." And away he walked.


HALLDÍS, MEANWHILE, STOOD pensively at the edge of the second clearing, considering what now lay beyond. There were no more buildings, no more features of any kind, save the opening of a rough pit in the dry, gritty earth a little way ahead. Past that, the dirt gave way to grass and weeds, a narrow dock with a jetty, and a thin line of trees – the last barrier that stood between them and the fjord. Beyond, across the gently rippling water, sparkling in the sun, she could just make out the dark shape of the island. Gandhólm, island of the sorcerors. Island of Skalla, and of Skalla's masters. As she stood, her future before her, her past behind, she suddenly felt overwhelmed by a deep, all-encompassing sense of despair. Suddenly, she wished only for her tears to flow without end, for her throat to give unrestrained voice to all her for torment, for her legs to give way and the earth to swallow her up so she might sleep forever. She fought to dismiss it, telling herself it was merely horror at all the horrors she had seen. But it would not be so easily dismissed. For the first time, she found herself wondering whether she would ever see her home again, whether, after all this, things could ever go back to the way they had once been.

"We made it," said a voice beside her. It was Frodi.

"This is only the beginning," said Halldís, staring into the distance.

"We will make an end of it," said Bjólf, emerging from the knot of men with Gunnar at his side.

"One thing," muttered Gunnar, a deep frown upon his face. "Where are the death-walkers? The normal ones? I thought this forest would be crawling with them."

"Perhaps even they cannot stand this place," said Bjólf. Deep down, however, the question was also troubling him. Standing next to Halldís, he turned to look upon her delicate face – and saw her frowning.

"What is it?"

"Do you hear something? A kind of rattling?"

Bjólf listened. "Atli found some pets in the barn," he said.

"No," said Halldís. "From over here." She walked across the clearing, Bjólf following close behind. As the wind changed, they heard a strange, ceaseless noise, like hard rain upon the deck. No, more like lots of hollow objects being knocked together. But it was impossible to place precisely. She veered towards the pit, and Bjólf followed. The sound grew louder. They drew up to the edge and peered down, Gunnar and the others closing up behind them.

At the bottom of the pit, deeper than the height of a man, a mass of human heads were piled up, covering its floor, their jaws still snapping, over and over, in a never-ending quest for flesh.

Halldís swayed. Bjólf steadied her, drew her back.

"Is there no end to this?" muttered Gunnar from the pit's edge.

"We will make an end," said Bjólf grimly.

Then, from the far edge of the clearing, Finn hissed a warning. A black boat was coming.

# CHAPTER FORTY-ONE

## HEIMDALL'S EYE

IT HEADED DIRECTLY for them; a long, thin-prowed rowing boat containing perhaps a dozen black-clad men.

"Can they have seen us?" said Njáll.

"If they'd seen us, they'd have sent a ship," said Gunnar.

There were hurried tactical conversations, and then the men rapidly dispersed amongst the trees and beyond the edges of the nearest buildings. Atli found himself crouched in the bracken with Fjölvar and four others at the far side of the clearing, near the jetty. Directly opposite, across the clearing, were Bjólf, Gunnar, Halldís, Frodi and Finn, with two other groups positioned further ahead. They had the advantage of surprise, but they had also seen the black crossbows glinting in the low sun. They would have to hit them hard and fast.

None knew for certain what kind of man they faced. They had seen little of them, save Skalla himself, and that example made them wary. Atli sensed the tension in those around him. He gripped his seax, staring at the earth, trying to keep his breathing slow to counteract his racing heart.

The last few moments of the boat's approach were excruciating. For what seemed like forever, they crouched, waiting, seeing and hearing nothing. Eventually, voices could be heard; the clunk of oars; the scrape of something heavy being heaved off the boat; a whine of complaint; low laughter. Atli could not get a clear view of the dock, without moving, but his ears told him that they had landed. A moment later, they walked into view – two in front, crossbows loaded and held before them. Five more followed, some with spears. Four more of the black-clad warriors carried a large, unwieldy sack between them, and two more crossbowmen brought up the rear. Only four of those deadly weapons in total. That was good.

Atli listened to them talk and joke quietly. All seemed cautious, nervous even, but their chatter showed they were trying not to appear so. They did not expect trouble. Atli counted thirteen in all. It appeared they had left their boat entirely unmanned. A fatal error.

Fjölvar pulled back his bow and drew a bead on one of the crossbowmen. Across the way, Finn would be doing the same. He did not even hear the arrow fly, just the dull *thunk* as it struck the lead man. Before any of them had a chance to react, the second crossbowman had been felled by Finn. The four with the sack looked around desperately, panic in their eyes, before finally gathering the presence of mind to drop it and draw their swords. One of the two remaining crossbowmen swung around suddenly, looking directly where Atli was hidden, but Fjölvar's second arrow cut him down as he raised his weapon. The other, unexpectedly, turned and ran for the boat, leaving his fellows in a turmoil of indecision behind him. He got three steps before Finn's arrow struck.

That was their signal.

The two groups closest to the dock, to the rear of the black guards, attacked first. Atli could not remember willing his legs to run, but somehow found himself hurtling out into the open with Fjölvar and the others. Opposite them, Bjölf's company charged from cover, striking with terrifying ferocity. The clash of battle surrounded Atli on all sides, the black guards huddling in a state of terror as the different groups closed in around them.

For a moment, Atli had no target. The others – faster, more decisive – had taken them all. He turned, and found himself face to face with a black guard who had managed to break away from the melée, sword in hand, eyes wide. Between this man and the boat, there was now only Atli. The boy froze. He knew he had to act, that no one would come to his rescue this time. But he felt his strength drain away, his limbs turn to blubber.

But then he saw something in the other man's face that changed everything. Fear. Paralyzed though he was, he had struck terror into this man. The realisation hit him like a lightning bolt. Atli was suddenly emboldened. In his mind, he knew he had already won. He felt his strength return. The man, in sudden panic, flailed his sword wildly and ineffectually, and Atli deflected it easily with his shield and struck. The seax's sharp point pierced the leather armour and slid between the man's ribs. Blood spilled in the dust. He choked, and fell. Atli stood over the body – stunned, but alive.

In moments, it was over. Not one crossbow bolt had been fired, not one sword blow or spear thrust successfully landed on the members of the warband. Without pity, without ceremony, they began picking over the bodies and hauling them into a heap. None showed any desire to investigate the large sack they had dropped.

"So much for the might of the black guards," said Gunnar contemptuously.

As THEY BUSIED themselves, Bjólf stood at the limit of the trees, staring out, for the first time, at the fabled fortress and its island. The dark, lumpen shape sat squatly in the water, its outer edges rough and muddy and broken – crumbling cliffs of earth from which protruded great roots and twisted lengths of metal. At its western end, facing the fjord, was a crudely constructed harbour where the black ships and other, smaller craft sat. From there, paths wound through the muddy chaos to the weird structure of the fortress itself, obscured behind an elaborate stockade of thick logs, with ramparts and watchtowers, black-painted, like the ships. At its hidden heart, it was topped by a tower of unfathomable design, from the top of which spikes and spires stretched skyward. Surrounding the whole island, some distance out in the fjord, a row of great wooden stakes stood up from the surface of the water – a continuous barrier, punctuated only by two roughly-constructed turrets ouside the harbour.

There was something horrid about the scene – something utterly out of place. Bjólf recalled Halldís' tale about the island's creation. He knew it was impossible, but looking at it now, he could give the bizarre story more credence.

"One still kicking here!" called out Njáll suddenly. A man – his eyes wide with terror, his hands held defensively before his face, writhed and whimpered at his feet. "Not a mark on him. Must've just gone down when the fighting started, pretending to be dead."

"Bring him over," said Bjólf.

The guard looked up at Njáll, pleading over and over, his hands shaking. Njáll looked at the creature for a moment in utter contempt, and then grabbed him by the back of his belt, dragged him to a tree near the dock and tied him to it with a length of mooring rope from the boat. He shook his head disdainfully as he strode away.

Bjólf and Gunnar spent some time questioning their jittery captive. It had not taken much persuading to get him to talk – much to the disappointment of Finn, who had volunteered to help loosen his tongue. In fact, at times, the man had seemed embarrassingly eager, as if believing that he might somehow befriend them, and thereby secure his release. They happily encouraged him in his delusion.

From him, they had learned the times of the watches, the rough layout of the lower levels, and the important fact that there were no more than fifty armed guards within the castle walls at any one time. But beyond this – more from the man himself than anything he had directly said – they had also formed a valuable impression of the fighting abilities of those men, and been encouraged by it.

There remained, however, the question of their equipment – which, in many respects, seemed greatly superior to their own. Among the objects taken from the crew of the boat were several objects that none among Bjólf's company could identify, chief among which was a solid black container on a shoulder strap, which, when opened, contained another, largely featureless black cylinder of unfathomable purpose and baffling design.

"What do you make of this?" said Gunnar, passing it to Bjólf.

Bjólf turned it around in his hands, felt its weight, pushed and pulled at one end, which was oddly tapered. To his great surprise, when he pulled, the thing extended – a slimmer black shaft slid out from inside the first, then a yet smaller one from inside that, until the object was nearly three times its original length, as long as a sword blade.

"Clever," said Bjólf, nodding. He held it by the slimmer end, swinging it lightly. "A weapon?"

"It's heavy enough," said Gunnar.

Bjólf frowned, shaking it more vigourously from side to side. "Hmm. But is it strong? I wouldn't put my faith in it in a fight." He turned. "Godwin?" He tossed it to the Englishman.

"Never seen anything like this," he said. "What is this material? Not metal." He tossed it to Fjölvar.

"Not wood either," said Fjölvar turning it over. "Feels like bone." He tossed it to Úlf.

Úlf scrutinised it closely, sliding the parts back into themselves. "Not bone. Not like any I've seen. But this is fine craftsmanship. Arab, maybe." He tossed it back to Bjólf.

"Well, let's ask its owner." Bjólf turned to the tree, against which the guard still writhed fruitlessly in his bonds. He stopped as he saw Bjólf approach, a look of terror in his eyes. Bjólf presented the black object to him, holding it a finger-length from the man's quivering nose.

"Speak," he said.

The guard looked about him nervously, finally summoning the courage to speak. "We call it Heimdall's Eye," he said, his voice clipped and edgy. "It helps us see long distances."

Gunnar guffawed. "Really? Well, I suppose more than a few weeks in this place would send anyone crazy."

"It's true," said the guard pleadingly, his knees shaking. "I have no reason to lie."

"You have every reason to lie," said Bjólf.

"I – I cannot explain it..." stammered the guard. "I do not have the art. But I can show you..."

Bjólf drew his seax, eliciting a whimper from the guard, who closed his eyes in panic. When he opened them again, his bonds were cut, and Bjólf was holding the heavy black rod towards him. The guard let out a shaky breath and, relieved at not having been killed, looked about him for a moment, and then bolted for the trees.

Gunnar sighed and picked up the black crossbow. The bolt flew, striking the guard in the left shoulder as he was halfway across the clearing, the impact spinning him around. He began to fall forward, staggered, took a few more awkward steps, then picthed sideways and fell headlong into the yawning black mouth of the pit. The sound of snapping jaws suddenly increased in intensity, only momentarily drowned out by the guard's final, terrified screams.

"Good shot," said Bjólf.

"Hmm," Gunnar grunted irritably, frowning at the crossbow. "I was aiming for his head."

"If this is the calibre of man we're up against, we've only to shout 'boo' at them," said Njáll. "I thought that one was going to piss his pants."

"Well then..." said Bjólf, his eyes seeking out Atli among the men. "Son of Ivarr, you're the brains of this outfit. See what you can make of 'Heimdall's Eye'." And he tossed him the strange black object.


FOR SOME TIME, Atli sat cross-legged, toying with the strange device, puzzling over its strange materials, its obscure purpose. There were markings on the slimmer end, which rotated, but after endless fiddling it seemed all he could make it do was extend and contract, just as the others had done. Could it perhaps be some sort of measuring device, he wondered? But that hardly seemed to fit with what the guard had said.

He had just given up on it when his own frustration provided him with the answer. As he threw it down onto the gritty soil, a black disc popped off one end and rolled away from him. He grabbed at the loose piece in mortification, hoping no one had noticed, thinking he had broken the precious treasure, but when he looked more closely, he realised that the cupped disc was merely some sort of cover for the wider end of the rod, which was now revealed as having, set a little way back within it, a circle of thick, impossibly smooth glass, its surface curved like a cow's eye. *Like an eye*, thought Atli. *Heimdall's Eye. To see long distances.*

At last, it was making some sense. He turned the object over hurriedly, tried the thinner end. A second, smaller cap popped off, revealing another glass disc beneath. As he held the object up now, extended its full length, he could see that it was somehow hollow, that light passed through it from one end to the other. He held it up to his eye – and got the greatest shock of his life. As clear as if they were within touching distance, he suddenly saw figures of black guards moving about before him. He jumped back, dropping the thing, and blinked ahead of him. The guards were gone. Or rather, they were there, through the trees, upon the island, but now so distant as to appear like ants upon an ant hill. He picked up the object, tentatively, and peered through it again. Immediately, the distant view was magically brought closer. For a moment he he feared that he might also appear closer to them, that *they* could see *him*. But he soon dismissed the notion as foolish. He was still sat here, upon the bank, behind the trees. But then, if they had other devices like this... He scrambled to his feet, and ran off to Bjólf with news of his discovery.

"HEIMDALL'S EYE..." SAID Bjólf, peering through the device as they crouched at the edge of the wood. "Well, it seems our captive was telling the truth after all. Now we know to stay well out of sight, and also that they may easily see us coming." He turned to Atli. "Good work, once again. You have earned your passage, son of Ivarr."

"But what other marvels might they have?" wondered Gunnar, squinting past the trees towards the distant, grim island.

"Whatever they may be," said Bjólf, "they'll be ours by sunrise."

He scanned the uneven surface of the fortress – partly in deep shadow now, with the sun sinking low in the west – taking in its strange features, then switched his attention to the curious barrier that surrounded the island, far out in the water. He could now see that the two distinct structures on the barrier were watchtowers, and that they flanked a pair of crudely constructed gates. Clearly they could be opened from the towers to allow the black ships access to and from the fortress harbour. But what was it all for? "That endless row of stakes in the water," he said, passing Heimdall's Eye to Gunnar. "Tell me what you see."

"Hmm," Gunnar grunted. "Defences of some kind. Wooden pilings, most likely weighed down with rocks. Looks like thick rope nets strung between them, holding the thing together."

"But not strong enough to stop a ship, travelling at speed," said Bjólf.

Gunnar looked at him through narrowed eyes. "Not *stop*... no, I wouldn't say so..."

"How long do you think we have before those men are missed – enough for them to come looking?"

Gunnar shrugged. "Hours, probably. But night is drawing in. No one is going to head out until daylight."

Bjólf stood suddenly and looked at the boat that had brought the black guards, then back in the direction that the Fire-Raven lay. "We attack before dawn, in darkness," he said. "Soak the sail of the ship. As wet as you can make it. Gather dry firewood and pitch. And someone bring me some rope."

"What's the plan?" said Gunnar.

Bjólf looked out towards the monstrous grey-brown island in the middle of the fjord and the black castle that sat perched atop it like a dark, ugly crown. He thought for a moment of the unspeakable horrors that they had witnessed here, and of the dark power in the fortress that had perpetrated them.

"We're going to arrange a funeral," he said.

# CHAPTER FORTY-TWO

## THE LAST BATTLE

TRANI STOOD HUNCHED in the rickety lookout post, shivering in the cold night air. He hated this watch. It was always cold out over the water, but at night it really got into your bones. No amount of moving around, it seemed, could keep the chill out. Not that there was exactly much room for movement, and he wasn't sure the structure would take it even if there were. No matter how many times Skalla impressed upon them that it was one of the most important jobs on the island, it still felt like a punishment.

He cursed Skalla's name under his breath, then began humming a tune his fellows had made up in honour of their leader. The words mostly focused on the fact that Skalla ate babies for breakfast and had no testicles. Trani sniggered to himself, trying to warm his hands on the flame of the torch. At least he had that. Trouble was, even if you stood up close your face ended up roasted on one side and still frozen on the other. Why could they not simply have put another bracket for the torch on the other side, so it was possible to swap it over every once in a while? As it was, the only way around the problem was to turn and face the island, which defeated the object of him being there. He could not allow himself to do it – though, in truth, he was more afraid of Skalla finding out than of any potential intruder sneaking up behind. There had never been any intruder. Why would there be? No one would want to come here.

True, there had been talk of a crew of *vikingr* being seen somewhere. That, supposedly, was the reason for having the watch extended through the night. But the word was they were all dead now. And even if they weren't, they would be soon. No one could survive out there without the masters' protection. He shivered at the thought.

Never mind. The sun would be up soon and the boat back to relieve him. Then breakfast. He stared into the darkness. A weird mist had rolled in from the north over the past few hours, with the salt tang and the chill of the sea. Now great whisps of it were being whipped towards him on the wind like wraiths. As he looked, he thought for a moment he saw an orange glow somewhere out there in the impenetrable gloom. He wiped his eyes and yawned. He'd been out here too long.

But no, there it was again. A dim light, directly ahead.

He thought, at first, it must be a fire out on the promontory, where the fjord turned northwards. But surely it couldn't be. Who could possibly be out there? Something Reim had said when Trani had arrived to relieve him at the watch suddenly came back to him. "There's a boat due back," he'd said. "Keep an eye out for it." Trani had forgotten all about that. To be honest, he had assumed Reim must have been mistaken. But now...

The glow was growing in intensity, seeming to flicker. A trick of the fog, thought Trani. He looked back to the island, then forward again. It couldn't be from the shore. It was too far out. For a moment he pictured that lost boat, still inexplicably out there, only now returning. He kept his eyes fixed on it, watching it get bigger. Without warning, the fog thickened and the glow disappeared completely. Maybe his mind really had been playing tricks. Ghost stories told by his fellows started to play on his mind – of strange lights that guarded tombs or hovered where treasure lay. In vain, he tried to banish them; he didn't want to think about that sort of thing. It was bad enough being out over this dark water, knowing what lurked below. Anyway, it was gone now. He kept staring at the spot ahead of him, where it had been, just to be sure. But there was nothing.

With a shiver – not from the cold this time – he looked back to the island. "Come on," he muttered to himself, looking longingly for the relief boat. "I'm going to catch my death out here..." When he turned back, his eyes were met by a vision from Hel.

Emerging from the swirling, wind-blown fog at terrifying speed, as if from nowhere, was the towering, spiked dragon-prow of a great death-ship – its grinning figurehead bearing down upon him, silhouetted against a blood-red sail, its whole length lit up by leaping, roaring flames. As Trani stared, open-mouthed, unable to comprehend the impossibility of the sight, the ship ploughed straight into the watchtower, sending it crashing into the dark, icy water with a horrible groaning and cracking of splintering wood, before forging on over it. The final shock – the final unthinkable revelation – was the sound that reached his ears in the moments before the heavy, barnacled hull crushed him down into the haunted, freezing black depths. It was the hoarse, otherworldly baying of wolves.


THE BURNING SHIP did not stop. The wind from the north pushed it on, its flames reddening the sky. The gates fell; the second tower collapsed, dragging with it a whole section of the barrier. One by one, all along its great length, the stakes began to topple. In the harbour itself, a cry went up, but the scurrying guards were utterly powerless to halt its inexorable advance. They could only watch in terror and disbelief as the great ship, flames now leaping the full height of the mast, smashed past the moored black ships, igniting their ropes and sails, rammed into the jetty, splintering it to kindling, and finally, carving the first decisive battle scar into the stronghold of the masters, drove its bows high up onto the island's wrecked shore. As it shuddered to a halt, those within sight – to their horror – saw leaping from its deck crazed, red-eyed, ravening wolves, their bodies aflame, their limbs convulsing, their hideous jaws snapping and tearing at anything that moved.

From the rampart, Skalla watched as the beasts – half consumed by fire, their restraining ropes burned through – took his men apart. Flames leapt, lighting up the whole of the harbour. He did not know where the ship had come from, nor who was behind the attack, but it did not matter now. Somehow, he had always known this day would come. If the fire-ship was meant as a diversion from a main attack, then it had more than done its job. The barrier was in a state of collapse, and all knew only too well what that would mean. He must leave those outside to their fate. They would provide his diversion.

He turned to the panic-stricken lackeys who cowered nearby. "Seal the main gate," he said. "Muster my personal guards. And prepare the berserkers."

WHILE THE WESTERN shore had erupted into fiery chaos, upon the eastern side of the island, all was quiet. Guards stood at intervals upon the stockade, nervous for news of the assault upon the other side of the island, their numbers depleted by the emergency, until now, they barely had sight of each other in the early morning gloom. There was a hiss, and a muffled cry, and one fell out of view. Then another. A third black-clad figure jerked suddenly at the sound of a dull impact, choked, then toppled over the rampart. By the time the iron hooks were thrown over the edge of the stockade, there were no guards left alive to witness them. Moments later, a force of warriors – eighteen in number – stood battle-ready upon the rampart, helms, blades and armour glinting in the light of its torches. The time for vengeance had come.

The bold strategy had unfolded exactly as planned. But it had not been without obstacles. Kjötvi, against all the odds, had showed no further ill effects from the raven attack (although he now sported an eye patch, fashioned for him by Úlf from a black guard's leather armour). But Folki had fallen without warning into a shivering sickness, his skin pale, a cold sweat upon his brow. Investigation revealed a bite upon his calf, from the night at Erling's farm. Whether Folki had known and chosen to keep it quiet, or had simply been unaware of the wound in the heat of battle, Bjólf did not know or care to ask. All were aware what it would mean. Folki had insisted on staying behind in the grove of death, knowing he was now a liability. Eybjörn, the last survivor of Frodi's men, had volunteered to stay with him. He had said he was too old to make the climb over the stockade wall, but Bjólf knew the real, unspoken, reason he was staying was so he could give Folki peace after he passed. What future it left for Eybjörn himself, none could say. Of all the deeds Bjólf had seen these past few days, this was perhaps the bravest.

The black boat, packed to capacity, heavy with weapons and mail, sat low in the water. Once the *Fire-Raven* had been set on its course, aimed at the distant torches of the harbour, Úlf and Thorvald – the last men aboard – had dropped into the black boat with the others, and thrown a torch into the great pyre upon the ship's deck. With all enemy eyes on the fire ship, they had rowed in darkness to the far side of the island, cut through the rope netting of the barrier and slid the vessel between the stakes entirely unobserved.

Now, from the ramparts, Bjólf surveyed the challenge that lay ahead. Inside the wooden stockade lay a wide open space, dotted with untidy huts and dwellings of all kinds. Here and there, an isolated figure hurried past, responding to the distant emergency. Beyond stood the formidable inner wall of the fortress. Blank and grey, constructed from the same blocks as the squat building upon the mainland, the square, featureless edifice loomed around the hidden heart of the castle, obscuring everything but the strange, spiky tower that sprang from within, its uppermost spire just beginning to catch the first rays of the sun as dawn broke over the distant mountains. This wall was a very different matter from the first; too high for their grappling hooks, with no guarantee of what lay on the other side. They would have to fight their way in.

Slowly, cautiously, they worked their way around the parapet, keeping low, those with bows and crossbows keeping an eye out for any who might raise the alarm. With all attention focused on the disaster in the harbour, none below even thought to look up. As they neared the western end of the island, the clamour of activity ahead intensified. Soon, the harbour itself was in view. Down beneath them, in the fortresses outer ward, Bjólf could now see black-clad men beetling about, barring the stockade's main gate – some hurrying back towards the western end of the grey edifice. There must be a second gate there; and from the way the men were moving, it must also be open. They had to move quickly.

Bjólf gestured ahead to a wide stairway leading down to ground level. But before they could move, Fjölvar nudged him and pointed past the rampart to the glow of the harbour. At first, it seemed that Skalla's men had barred the gate while a large number of their own were still outside it – a curious fact, to be sure. Then he saw that most of those outside the gate were not black guards. Surrounding them – swamping them – was a host of ragged, grey figures, their appearance gaunt and cadaverous, their movements hideously familiar. Some of the guards were fighting, some fleeing desperately back towards the gates that now shut them out. Others had already been overwhelmed, their screams carried on the wind. And, as Bjólf watched, the ranks of the death-walkers were growing, a seemingly endless, swaying army of wet, beslimed figures emerging slowly from the water.

At last, the significance of the barrier became clear.

But there was no time to waste. The sun was rising. Soon, they would no longer be able to rely on darkness to hide them. Waving his warband on, Bjólf hurried down the gloomy staircase, where they mustered in a tight group between a stable and a forge, its hot smell filling their nostrils. A passing black guard – who carried with him an air of authority – stopped at the sight of them, and opened his mouth as if to issue an order. Then a frown crossed his brow. Before he could raise the alarm, Gunnar put a bolt through his neck.

The time had come. At Bjólf's signal, they surged forward silently, weapons raised, shields together.

The guards they encountered had little idea what hit them. Almost immediately, the first three unfortunate enough to be in their path were struck down, before the warband turned the corner, heading for the inner gate, and smashed into the main group of guards, splitting them apart and sending them flying, faces and bodies bloodied. From the heart of the raiding party, those with bows and crossbows scanned the parapet, picking off their counterparts before any of them could ready their own weapons. Now and again a bolt would slam into a thickened shield – one glanced off Thorvald's helm – but once the archers' positions were revealed, Bjólf's bowmen were soon on them.

As the guards panicked and dispersed, the warband split apart to take them down one by one. Resistance from the ill-prepared enemy was weak. Revenge was exacted upon them with ruthless and bloody efficiency.

\* \* \*

FROM THE GREY battlement Skalla looked down upon the slaughter coolly. Finally, his enemies had announced themselves. "Get more crossbowmen on them," he said. "And lower the inner gate."

The guard hesitated. "But our men will be trapped out there, with the invaders. Shouldn't we...?"

"Do it," snapped Skalla.

He knew the outer gate would not hold the advancing host of death-walkers forever. Eventually, the wooden gates would give out and they would flood the outer ward. Well, let them have it. The inner gate was stronger. Once it was closed, neither the death-walkers nor the invaders would breach it. They would be trapped together. What would happen afterwards, with the undead pressing in on every side, he neither knew nor cared. Let the masters puzzle that one out. He wondered, vaguely, if they were watching from their sanctuary within, hatching plans of their own.


"REGROUP!" CRIED BJÓLF.

The warband drew back into a tight formation, the last of the uninjured guards fleeing, another limping desperately after them. All around, black figures lay crumpled, some still moving or crying out, others rent apart by terrible blows. Ahead of them now, with no obstacle in their way but the dead, was the open mouth of the inner gate. Beyond that, a walled courtyard, and within, just visible, a group of perhaps a dozen men facing them, weapons drawn and faces set. They did not move or flinch. Behind them, other figures were moving heavy objects into place. These men were of a different order from those they had thus far encountered, but there was to be no going back.

As Bjólf watched, a heavy portcullis of iron began to descend over the mouth of the inner gate. He immediately began the charge forward. The moment he did so, a rain of crossbow bolts hit them from the battlements of the grey wall. Ingolf and Aki fell immediately. The rest were pinned down, crouched beneath shields.

"Knock them out! Knock them out!" cried Bjólf, trying to spot the crossbowmen.

But he knew what had to be done: they must press forward,

whatever the cost. Without hesitation, he ordered the charge. Halfdan caught a bolt in the arm and fell as the rest surged forward. In moments, his body was shot through with bolts.

But the tactic paid off. In a few steps they were almost up against the descending gate, too close for the crossbowmen to fire upon them. The black guards within began to move forward, while above them, they could hear the crossbowmen hastily repositioning themselves, their commander barking orders urgently. But it was the turn of Bjólf's crossbowmen and archers now. They fired into the courtyard, felling four men and scattering the rest out of their line of sight.

The way was momentarily clear, but the portcullis was already barely at head height. Without stopping to think, Gunnar threw down his shield and shoved his shoulder beneath the great gate. Had he applied more consideration to the matter, he might have questioned whether he could hold such a huge weight of iron, but it was too late for that.

"Some help here?" he called gruffly.

Úlf and Odo added their great shoulders to his. Their bodies strained, their faces reddened – the gate slowed, but did not halt. Gunnar, the tallest, could feel his shoulder being crushed, his legs about to give way. "Can't hold it for long..." he said.

"Cover me!" said Bjólf, and dived under the gate, shield held high. Fjölvar and Finn followed, their bows ready. The moment he was through, bolts thudded into his shield from above, but Bjólf was too fast. To the left of him, close by, stood two astonished men struggling at a great wheel, the thick shaft at its centre wound around with the great chain that raised and lowered the gate. He was on them so fast that one of the black guards' own crossbow bolts hit the nearest gatekeeper in the leg. Finn's and Fjölvar's arrows flew, and from the inner parapet of the courtyard, two crossbowmen fell. Others scurried out of the line of fire.

Gunnar and the others were crushed to their knees now. Bjólf battered the remaining gatekeeper with his shield and hauled on the wheel with his whole weight. The gate stopped dead – but from the archways around the courtyard, members of the elite bodyguard now emerged from their defensive positions. Filippus and Arnulf, both armed with crossbows, squeezed under the gate and fired off two shots, taking one down and injuring another. Finn leaped forward and added his weight to the wheel. It turned. The gate rose. Gunnar, Úlf and Odo were freed, and the rest of the warband flooded in. Bjólf locked the winch, took up his shield, and drew his sword. All armed themselves, throwing down anything that was now a hindrance to combat: ropes, hooks, cloaks, food.

There followed a savage eruption of hand-to-hand fighting as the two sides tore into each other. It was impossible, now, for the remaining crossbowmen to fire without risk of hitting their own men, and they abandoned their posts on the parapet to join the fray. Freed from threat, several of Bjólf's men discarded their shields in favour of their preferred method of fighting: an axe in each hand for Thorvald, a combination of axe and sword for Gunnar, and for Godwin, the familiar, single, long battle-axe.

Fearless as they were, the inner guard of the black castle lacked the experience of the *vikingr* crew, their slave heritage soon becoming apparent. They fought hard, but wildly – angrily; Bjólf's men, seasoned by many a battle, kept cool heads and conserved their energy whenever they could, watching, waiting for the moment to strike. When they did, rarely did a blade fail to strike its mark. Four fell within moments of the first violent clash, each taken down by single blows. Godwin's axe swept in a wide arc, destroying anything that crossed its path. Gunnar and Thorvald looked unstoppable, striking fear into even the bravest of the black guards. Odo's heavy two-handed sword did not allow his opponents to even get close, cleaving through mail and leather as it struck. By contrast, the sword of Filippus – long, curved, and lighter than its Norse counterpart – flashed at ferocious speed, inflicting terrible wounds upon the unprepared enemy. Atli and Kjötvi followed close behind, finishing them off where they could.

In the very centre, forcing their way forward, keeping steady pressure on the foe, Bjólf, Halldís and Frodi fought side by side, battering with their shields and hacking at those that challenged them. Blood and sweat flew. Teeth and bones cracked. The enemy's shields splintered; their black helms were cleaved in two. Within moments, it seemed, this hammerblow – which had left Bjólf's warband without a single serious injury – had reduced the defending army to a bloodied, disordered handful of men.

Just as victory seemed assured, there came the blast of a horn, and the last few defenders suddenly retreated towards the far wall of the courtyard, leaving Bjólf and his fellow fighters standing.

As the black guards fled, they revealed a single figure in the open space before the warband. He stood alone before them, without fear. Skalla, the horn still at his lips. At his waist, hanging from a cord across his shoulder, the lacquered container of white powder, and at his feet, seven huge, black boxes.

For a moment, Bjólf and Skalla regarded each other in uneasy silence. Then, Skalla spoke.

"Who are you?"

"I am your death," said Bjólf.

Skalla stared, then chuckled quietly to himself. "You and your men are admirable fighters, to be sure. But am I permitted to know the reason for my death?"

"You are not," said Bjólf. "Let your death be as meaningless as your life."

Skalla glowered at him. "Why you?"

Bjólf shrugged. "Because I can."

"You think so? I do not."

"Then I will!" cried out Halldís, pulling off her helm, her hair flying free. An expression of genuine shock crossed his face.

"Now it becomes clearer." he said. "But still I have my doubts. You see, your will is weak. You could have killed me ten times over as we stood here, but you did not."

"Your crossbowmen could have taken us down as we stood," countered Bjólf. "But they did not. Why? Because they do not act except under orders. They have no thought, no loyalty, no will. And you were distracted by your need to find reasons. By the vain belief that your life has meaning, even though whatever meaning it once had you have long since squandered. You are the weaker."

Skalla did not smile this time. "I think you underestimate the seriousness of your situation," he said. His good eye flicked above the heads of the warband, past the portcullis to the distant outer gate. In the silence, Bjólf became suddenly aware of the distant groans of death-walkers – hundreds of them, risen from the depths of the fjord. The outer gate creaked as their decayed bodies pressed mindlessly against it. "Surely you know this was a suicide mission? The *draugr* are at the gates. Its timbers will not hold them."

"What do I care?" said Bjólf. He pointed his sword at Skalla's heart. "We do not go back. We keep moving forward until we are stopped."

Skalla shrugged, turned to the side, and drew a small flask from inside his hauberk.

"Which brings me to the other reason for my skepticism..." And before they knew what was happening he had flung the clear liquid into two of the great, coffin-like boxes. "If this is to be Ragnarók, in which both sides are destroyed," he said, annointing another three in rapid succession, "then so be it." He tossed the fluid across the last two faces, then retreated hurriedly to a heavy wooden door at the far end of the courtyard.

The first of the boxes twitched. Then the second. A thump came from the third. Involuntarily, Bjólf and his warband found themselves taking steps back.

Skalla watched long enough to see the first grey, gruesomely sutured hand rise from its coffin, then disappeared through the door, slamming and locking it behind him. The remaining five guards – two with terrible injuries to their arms and face – realised suddenly that they, too, had been left to the mercy of the undead berserkers, and began to hammer desperately upon the now locked exit. Within moments, the first of the berserkers – Hammer-Fist, one of the ones they had seen destroy Grimmsson at Björnheim – was on its feet. It swivelled slowly, unsteadily, sniffing the air, attracted by the sounds of the guards, the smell of their blood. A second rose. Iron-Claw. As a third revived, clawing at the side of its box, a spiked ball and chain where its left forearm should be, the first two flew into a frenzied attack upon the guards. As Bjólf and the others watched, the two injured men were torn limb from limb as the rest scattered, the courtyard echoing to the horrible sounds. Blood splashed everywhere. From behind them, it seemed the hollow cries at the outer gate suddenly increased in volume. The gates bulged and groaned.

"This will be a hard fight," said Bjólf. Five of the ghoulish creatures were on their feet now. "But they are not invincible. Bring them down. Go for the head."

As he finished, one of the berserkers – Axe-Holder – fixed its red eyes upon Bjólf, and thundered towards him.

Bjólf knew that panic would be their undoing. He stood firm, braced and ready. "Get ready to jump..." he muttered to his comrades.

With the huge figure almost upon him, he dropped suddenly to the floor, behind his shield. The creature stumbled, began to topple, came crashing down like a great tree as the other warriors leapt back. Godwin surged forward again with a bloodthirsty cry, bringing his axe down full force upon the thing's neck. It jarred horribly, flying out of his hands, bouncing off hard metal. The full helm had saved the creature. They were suddenly – disastrously – reminded that these were no ordinary death-walkers. Behind these, buried somewhere deep within this ghastly place, were twisted minds.

The creature tried to struggle to its feet, its mouth gnashing and wailing, its arms and axe flailing madly. Bjólf hacked at its leg with all his strength and it collapsed again. Atli, hardly thinking about the danger, leapt upon its back. It reared up, reaching blindly for him, and he grasped the edges of its battered helm, heaving at it, and was thrown to the floor. But the helm was still in his hands. Godwin, hefting his retrieved axe, his eyes burning with anger, swung again. This time, it did not fail him; Axe-Holder's head flew from its body. He shuddered and lay still, twice dead.

Now, they had a strategy. Two more came at them, one with a length of chain swinging from its arm, the other with a trident in place of its right hand.

"I'll take the one on the right," said Gunnar.

Almost before he had uttered it, Fork-Hand was upon him. He dodged and swung around, catching it on the back of the legs with both axe and sword. It fell, but its weapon slashed Filippus in the throat as it went down. Filippus collapsed, gore pouring from him. The creature grasped at the bleeding body ravenously. Thorvald hacked off its arm with one of his axes, and the creature slumped to the ground, face down in Filippus's blood. A horrific slurping sound issued from the fallen creature. Úlf stepped onto its back, hooked the spike of his cavalry axe under the edge of its helm, and heaved it up as Gunnar brought his axe crashing down upon its neck.

Meanwhile, Chain-Wrist had come lumbering towards the remaining warriors. With a cry of "Mine!" Arnulf jumped forward and dropped to the ground at its feet, emulating Bjólf's tactic. But the huge figure, defying expectation, came to a sudden stop, and before Arnulf could move, brought its fists crashing down upon him. There was a terrible cracking sound, and with a roar Arnulf's body – for he was dead immediately – was hoisted above its head, its hands literally tearing him in half as blood and gore cascaded over its open mouth. Halldís leapt forward, and with all the power she could muster thrust her sword point in the small of the creature's back. The blade went deep and the berserker crumpled from the waist down. With its arms and chains whipping ever more wildly and the shock of Arnulf's death still fresh in their minds, the others rained down blows upon its armoured head until its helm was beaten shapeless and all movement had ceased.

There was a moment's respite. Across the courtyard, the remaining guards had managed to bring down Iron-Claw, but Hammer-Fist had smashed one of their number to a pulp and had the forearm of another between its teeth. The man half struggled, half dangled from its jaw, screaming in torment as his fellow guard scrabbled desperately at the door.

The remaining two berserkers – Mace-Arm and Sword-Wielder – had turned their attention to the warband, and now came smashing into them. In the desperate struggle for survival that followed, with the warriors still reeling from previous assaults, strategies were momentarily forgotten. Sword-Wielder ploughed into a knot of men, sending bodies flying as it struck. By some miracle, all avoided its notched, rusty sword blade, but before any could act, it had grabbed Thorvald and sunk its teeth into his shoulder. He gave a great cry, but did not fall. Others leapt upon the creature, hacking and stabbing at it, but to no avail. Thorvald staggered backwards, taking the creature with him, its teeth clamped around his collarbone, crashing against the wall. Njáll and Finn chopped the creature's legs from under it, bringing it crashing to the ground with Thorvald on top, its sword blade sweeping past the dodging feet of his desperate defenders, its free hand clawing at the flesh of Thorvald's flank, ripping out a great chunk. Somehow, even in his agony, Thorvald managed to draw his seax from his belt. He forced it between his chest and the neck of the berserker, gripped the end of the blade with his other hand, and with all his strength drove the edge of the blade forward against the creature's throat, sawing from side to side. Putrid, oily ichor flowed from the wound, and the creature slumped, inert. The grip was relinquished. Thorvald rolled onto his back, blood pouring from his shoulder and side.

Mace-Arm's assault, meanwhile, had been no less devastating. With the spiked ball-and-chain swinging, it had charged at Odo, who had tried to defend himself with his sword. The chain had wrapped around the blade, the barbed head just clearing his face, but Mace-Arm had then pulled back its arm violently, yanking Odo's sword from his grip and sending it spinning off into the far wall with a ringing of metal. It swung wildly again as swords and axes struck at it, its second pass smashing Odo across the jaw, sending blood splashing across the three men flanking him. He fell, the side of his face a mass of wrecked flesh and bone. Surrounded on all sides now, it swung around in circles, undecided where to strike, keeping all at bay as the deadly spiked weapon hummed through the air in front of their faces.

Their only hope was to disarm it.

Bjólf stepped forward, then, thrusting his shield into its path. The ball struck, the impact almost knocking him off his feet, but the strengthened wood of the shield held, the spikes embedded firmly in its boards. He hauled on the chain, trying to drag the creature off balance. Instead, it lunged for him. He side-stepped, hauling on the chain again, spinning it around, and the shield came loose, its boards split, but Bjólf wound the chain around his forearm, gripping it with both hands, still dragging the creature in a circle as it tried to launch itself awkwardly towards him. He spun it around again and again, pulling with all his strength on the chain, hoping to fling the creature off its feet.

Then, something unexpected happened. Bjólf saw, at the creature's shoulder where there was a crude row of stitching, that the flesh was starting to pull apart. The stitches stretched, snapped, unravelled; the wound widened, and with a great ripping and popping of joints, the creature's body and arm separated, sending it staggering awkwardly towards the gate. It stumbled over a crumpled body and crashed to the ground. The other warriors were upon it immediately, exacting revenge for Odo, for all the losses they had suffered. Its helm was ripped off, its head destroyed.

At the far end of the courtyard, Bjólf now saw that the single surviving guard had somehow succeeded in opening the heavy door – how, he could not guess. It opened further, and he had his answer: within were two of his fellows, gesturing eagerly for the desperate man to enter. But he seemed unwilling to abandon one of his fallen comrades, and was pulling at his collapsed body, even though it was clear to all that he was utterly dead. As the guard dithered,

Bjólf shouted to his men. "The door!" he said. "We must get to it before it closes again."

But between them and it stood the last remaining berserker, his attention turned from the guard and focused fully on the warriors.

Hammer-Fist.

For a moment it stood in that bloody, corpse-filled arena, head low, eyes burning at Bjólf, a steady, snorting breath coming from its nostrils like a bull making ready to charge. Behind it, the guard – still not having been persuaded to leave his friend – was being physically hauled through the gap in the door.

"Keep it busy," said Gunnar. And before Hammer-Fist could make a move, he charged at it with a mighty roar. Almost equal to the berserker in size, he slammed into it, sending it spinning, and thundered on past, jamming himself in the door as it shut against him. A struggle immediately ensued between him and the retreating guards, as they heaved on the door from the far side, and he lashed at them through the gap with his sword. The thing, meanwhile, bellowed horribly, almost as if angered, and flew into a frenzy, pounding towards its attacker.

They had to distract the creature long enough for Gunnar to secure the door.

"Hey!" called Bjólf.

The thing did not react. He ran after it, shouting – then hurled a throwing axe, embedding it in its back. That got its attention. It swung around and, without hesitation, lowered its head and charged at him full tilt, arms and hammer flying as it came. Bjólf stood in the path of the oncoming giant, no trace of a plan in his head. He backed away, made ready to leap, vividly recalling the fate of Arnulf, knowing it would have to be at the very last moment.

Suddenly, the creature jerked and fell forward, its face ploughing into the ground, and came to a standstill at Bjólf's feet. He looked around in shock, and saw Halldís standing behind him, a crossbow in her hand. Then he turned back to the felled berserker. Her crossbow bolt stuck in its forehead, piercing its thick helm.

Bjólf allowed himself a smile. They had done it. They had defeated the masters' most powerful fighters.

His sense of victory was short-lived. They heard Gunnar suddenly cry out. Finn, Fjölvar and Frodi were already racing to his aid, but as they hurried towards the door, they saw him knocked to the ground, limp and bloodied, his helm rolling away in the dirt. His body was dragged roughly through the dark gap, which slammed shut, its bolts shot on the far side. Bjólf pushed past the others and hammered his fists against the door in rage and frustration, but it would take more than fists to get them past the barrier.

Exhausted, but knowing they must fight on, he stalked back to take up sword and shield again, and as he did so happened to glance at Halldís. She looked past him, up high towards the parapet, and her expression darkened. He followed her gaze and there, upon the inner rampart, lurking upon the upper level, was Skalla, his cold eye watching.

Bjólf, his eyes ablaze, pointed his sword at Skalla's heart once again – surrounded, this time, by the masters' ruined army. A renewal of his warning, his pledge. Skalla stared back without expression. In fury, Bjólf snatched up the huge head of Fork-Hand by its hair, its face smeared with Filippus's blood, and with a defiant roar hurled it at Skalla. He dodged as it bounced against the wall, leaving a dark stain, and backed away slowly.

"Your ruin is coming," called Bjólf, his thoughts now only of vengeance, his whole being, spurred by Gunnar's fall, like some primal force of doom.

"Why wait?" said a voice at his side, and Halldís let fly a second bolt from her crossbow. It struck Skalla in the left shoulder, spinning him around. He cried out and staggered, disappearing back through another doorway, into the shadows.

Bjólf lowered his gaze and glared at the thick door ahead of them, somewhere beyond which – dead or alive – he knew his friend Gunnar lay. He turned to the others. "Chop it to splinters."

Godwin, Úlf and Njáll set about the door with their axes, chips flying, its heavy bolts rattling as their blades battered against it in a persistent rhythm, echoing about the space within.

ATLI, MEANWHILE, STOOD in a kind of daze, staring at the torn and twisted bodies that lay on every side, at the reddened blade in his hand. His feelings surprised him. He did not feel sickened; he did not feel afraid. He felt only gladness at being alive. Here, surrounded by so much death, perhaps only moments from his own, being alive had never meant so much. Then a sharp cracking sound made him glance back past the open portcullis towards the outer gate. It bulged inward, the great bar across it now half broken, showing pale wood where it had split, bending as the pressure from the massed death-walkers increased.

"We have a problem..." he said. Bjólf saw it and, urging the others on as they cleared the way ahead, he dropped his weapons and turned his attention to securing the way behind, heading back towards the winch and the half-open portcullis. But as he stepped past the crumpled bodies, something caught his foot. Bjólf stumbled and fell to his knees, cursing his clumsiness. When he looked up, he saw Hammer-Fist rising, staggering to his feet once more, the crossbow bolt still embedded in his skull, his red eyes half rolled back in his head, but the semblance of life not quite gone out.

Bjólf scrambled to his feet, the thing lumbering unsteadily after him, close on his heels. Its hammer caught him on his shoulder, sending him flying. Something snapped. In moments he was back on his feet, searching desperately for a weapon, when the creature's hand gripped his arm. He struggled, pulling in all directions – the grip tightened...

Atli snatched a grappling hook up from the ground and swung it at the towering figure's head, a length of rope trailing behind. Hammer-Fist shuddered and staggered to one side, relinquishing his grip on the *vikingr* captain. It gave Bjólf a second chance at life, but the creature was not stopped for long. Now, in fury, it turned towards Atli.

THE BOY WOULD not last a moment in the hands of the creature. Bjólf looked around desperately, grabbed Odo's great sword and swiped at the thing's head; the sharp pain in his left shoulder barely registered. Metal clanged against metal. It staggered, its anger growing, and turned back to Bjólf. He hit it again, backing towards the winch, luring it on, one eye on the outer gate, just moments from bursting open. Half blind, it lumbered forward.

"Come on!" he cried, suddenly aware as he spoke that he was echoing Grimmsson's last words. As it kept on towards him he battered it around the head again and again, each blow more desperate than the last, but doing no more than slowing its relentless advance.

Behind him, a sudden great crack, and groan and crash of wood, told him that the outer gate had finally given way. A chorus of chilling moans – hundreds of voices merged together into a single ghastly sound – filled his ears. He did not dare turn. In the next moment he stumbled against the winch, almost fell, scrambled back past it. Beyond the inner gate he could see the host of death-walkers advancing, just moments from surging into the courtyard where the warband stood, watching in horror.

Hammer-Fist, sensing weakness, lurched at him, crashing over the spindle of the winch, its arms flailing past the taut portcullis chain. Bjólf saw his chance. He looped the trailing rope around the creature's neck, around the portcullis chain, and pulled it tight. It thrashed and struggled, unable to right itself, blind to what was happening. He looped the rope again, twisting it around the chain, then kicked away the lock on the winch.

The portcullis came crashing down, cutting the first of the death-walkers in two, the rattling chain hauling the writhing Hammer-Fist up high into the air, smashing its head into the great stone lintel that spanned the gate. It dangled, swinging, revolving slowly, lifeless at last, the crossbow bolt driven deep into its poisoned brain.

Bjólf heaved himself to his feet, walked past the clawing hands of the death-walkers that now filled the outer ward, their bodies pressing against the iron gate in their futile quest for flesh. He said nothing, but merely slapped Atli upon the arm in gratitude as he passed, wincing at the pain shooting through his own shoulder. He took up his sword and shield.

As he did so, the wooden door at the far end of the courtyard caved in, reduced to firewood.

Bjólf turned then to Thorvald, who lay slumped against the side wall, his face pale and sweaty, his mail and tunic soaked with his blood. Kjötvi was tending to him, but stood back as Bjólf crouched by Thorvald's side.

"I'm done," said Thorvald weakly. Bjólf nodded solemnly, his jaw clenched. They had known each other far too long to dress it up. "I never thought it would end like this," he added. "To be honest, I didn't think it would be this interesting." Both laughed, Thorvald blanching in pain as he did so.

"We can't leave you," said Bjólf.

Thorvald nodded. "I know what you're saying. You're asking whether I want someone to finish me off, so I don't get up again, like one of them." He gestured towards the gate. He shook his head. "I wouldn't wish that task on any of you. Just leave me one of those." He pointed at the crossbow in Halldís's hands. She nodded at him, began drawing it back ready to take a bolt, fighting back tears as she did so.

"Make sure you don't miss," joked Njáll. "You're shit with a bow."

Thorvald smiled. "Go!" he said, waving them away like a parent shooing children. Then his face darkened, a look of pleading mingling with the pain in his face. "Go..."

Bjólf turned his back on Thorvald for the last time, passing through the silent company until he stood before the dark entrance – the goal that had been so hard won.

"Now we finish it," he said, and walked inside.

# CHAPTER FORTY-THREE

## THE DARK CASTLE

INSIDE, ALL WAS black. With no means of lighting their way, they crept forward, along a straight passageway, constructed, as far as they could tell, from the same uniform grey blocks. Occasionally they passed open doorways – all dark, all as dead and empty as the buildings on the mainland. They stumbled upon objects – some familiar, some unidentifiable, all apparently dropped in haste, perhaps only moments before. Ahead, they fancied they could sometimes hear movement, echoing distantly, as if from some deep cave, some great, labyrinthine space. And another sound – harsh and insistent, like a single note blown upon a horn, but somehow empty, repeating mindlessly, over and over. Then, there was a flickering light, dim at first, but, like the sound, growing in intensity as they moved forward, its source far ahead, where the passageway seemed to come to an abrupt end.

The end proved to be a junction with another passageway, that stretched away on either side. But this was unlike anything they had ever seen. The walls were smooth and white, the floor hard and of an shiny, unidentifiable material, the ceiling flat and featureless and as square and smooth as the floor and walls, entirely lacking any visible means of support. Along its centre, they now saw, ran the source of the flickering: a line of light – neither firelight, nor daylight, but some other sickly illumination that had no clear means of production. It stretched the full length of the long passageway in both directions, unbroken, but here and there, sections of the line flashed intermittently like a guttering flame. For a moment they stood, uncertain which direction to take.

A sound of running footsteps off to their left made the decision for them.

As they passed along the passage, more doorways came within view; some rooms dark, others brightly lit. One contained nothing but rows of beds. Another, angular, spindly tables and chairs, and the remains of a foul-smelling meal, recently abandoned. They moved on, the insistent sound ringing ever louder in their ears, never varying, never stopping. It was, thought Bjólf, like the sound of insanity.

Up ahead, three black-clad figures, laden with unidentifiable objects, emerged from a doorway. Seeing the approaching warband, one dropped everything and fled, leaving the others standing in shock. Bjólf flew forward with the others close behind. They hacked down the two guards where they stood. Fjölvar raised his bow to bring down the third, but Bjólf stopped him. "We follow," he said.

The trail led them to a wider corridor with many more rooms leading off it, and at the end a doorway that looked to be made entirely of glass. None could imagine how such a thing could be made, or why.

From a side room came a crash. They followed the sound.

Inside, there were benches like those in the grey, squat building, many of them covered with glass containers, things made of shining metal, weird instruments out of some delirious nightmare. Cowering in a corner was the one remaining guard, Bjólf recognised him as the man who had eluded them in the courtyard. He stepped up to him, putting his sword point to the man's throat.

"Skalla," he said.

The guard pointed a shaking hand in the direction of the glass doors. Bjólf withdrew his sword, not wishing to demean its blade with this man's blood, leaving him to his miserable life.

Beyond the glass doors was darkness, but for a weak pool of light in the chamber's heart, and a scattering of strange, small dots of light – some green, some red. The doors themselves – if such they were – offered no means of opening. Bjólf nodded at Godwin, who stepped forward, spat in his hands, then swung his axe at them. They shattered in a great explosion of glinting shards, scattering across the floor like gemstones.

Bjólf entered first. Ahead, there was another door, some unknown material this time, smooth and featureless. To their left, in a dark corner, completely in shadow, he sensed a movement. There was harsh breathing, and a cough.

"Why did you come here?" came a hoarse voice. It was Skalla.

"I told you my reason," said Bjólf.

"Some pointless revenge? What am I to you?' He paused, coughed again. "Or perhaps I should ask what *she* is to you..."

Halldís stepped forward, her sword raised. Bjólf held her back. He could just make out Skalla's feet now, just beyond the pool of light, where he was slumped against the wall. But he could see little more, could not see whether he had a weapon trained on them.

"Are you dying?" said Bjólf.

Skalla gave a grating laugh. "Perhaps. It's so hard to tell these days."

"Then I will not waste time. The black box you carry around your neck. You still have it?"

"For what it's worth."

"Give it to me."

"And if I do not?"

"Then I will take it."

"So why even ask?"

"Because now, at the last, I wish you to know why we came." He stepped forward, into the light. "To destroy you. To destroy your masters. And to wrest from your dying hand the remedy for the living death."

A strange, throaty sound came from the shadows. At first, Bjólf thought Skalla had succumbed to his wound. Then he realised, as the sound grew, that it was laughter; deep, resounding, uncontrollable laughter, broken only by a bout of painful coughing. "You did all of this, for that?" chuckled Skalla. He laughed again. "Here! Take it!"

The black box skittered across the smooth floor to Bjólf's feet. Halldís snatched it up, opened it, peered at the contents.

She frowned, sniffing at what she saw, then touched it with a fingertip and raised it tentatively to her lips. A look of disbelief came over her. "S-salt..."

"Yes!" laughed Skalla. "That is what you all fought for. That is what you all died for. A box of salt!" There was a movement. "You'd better have this too." From the shadows, the flask slid across the floor, the same Skalla had used to awaken the berserkers. Bjólf snatched it up, tipped its contents into his hand. Water. Plain water.

"It's a trick," said Bjólf. "This is not the remedy."

"You fools! There is no remedy! No respite, no rescue, no escape."

Halldís swayed, suddenly dizzy. "You lie. The white powder... we have seen it work..."

"On the berserkers... of course! Because my masters made them that way. To be controllable. But they are different. It will not stop the living death that is all around us. Not even the masters can stop that."

Beyond the end door came a thump. A scratching. Sounds of movement.

"What is that?" demanded Bjólf.

"My masters. They shut me out. Left me to my fate." He gave a cynical chuckle. "I cannot blame them for it. I would do the same."

The sounds intensified. There was a sudden hiss, and the door slid open, flooding the chamber with light. In the doorway, silhouetted, stood a huge figure. For a moment all stared, blinking at its half-familiar shape, struggling to focus against the glare. Then, with a roar, it flew at them.

The door slid back, plunging them back into near darkness. Bjólf grabbed for the black box – but as he did so, the huge warrior swatted it out of Halldís's hands. It clattered on the hard floor, its contents scattered among the glinting fragments of glass. Staggering backwards, Halldís drew her sword. The creature's swiping fists struck it from her grip, sending it spinning past Atli's head, then battered her shield, splitting it with one blow. She smashed against the wall and slid to the floor, as the members of the warband, as one, fell upon the hulking creature. In the confined space, in the dark confusion, weapons were as much a danger to their fellows as to their enemy. They set upon it instead with their bare hands.

It had no weapon of its own, this one, but all knew that once its fingers grasped them, they would be torn apart. Úlf and Frodi held one arm fast, Njáll and Godwin the other, and with others grabbing its legs they wrestled the roaring, thrashing thing onto its back. Bjólf stepped into the pool of light, standing over it, his sword drawn. Atli, knowing his part, jumped forward, heaving at the gleaming helm upon its head, ready for the killing blow. It flew free suddenly, sending Atli sprawling back onto broken glass.

None were prepared for what they saw. Sword raised and ready, Bjólf found himself looking down upon the face of Gunnar, or what had once been Gunnar. His eyes were wild and red, his blue-tinged mouth foaming, and there was no trace of recognition in his features. Yet, distorted though they were, the features were still familiar, still his friend.

Bjólf hesitated. In shock, the others – for an instant – unconsciously loosened their grip. The creature immediately leapt forward, grasping at Bjólf, sending him flying, his hands slashed by the scattered shards as he fell. It stomped forward, glass crunching underfoot, towering over him, and, with a ghastly cry, reached down and gripped Bjólf's helm. He felt the metal begin to buckle between its huge hands, about to crush his head. In a last desperate move, he grabbed at the floor, felt the grainy texture under his fingers, the sting in his wounds, grasped at it, and flung it in the thing's face. The creature stiffened. Bjólf rolled out from beneath it as it crashed lifelessly to the ground.

All the party stood dazed, no sound but their panting and the harsh note of alarm that still sounded all around them. Halldís climbed painfully to her feet, looking upon the scene with an expression of growing horror. It seemed to Bjólf that her defiant spirit flickered, that her strong heart – feeling, passionate, human – now teetered on the brink of what it could take. But at least she was alive.

As he threw off his helm, a deep thud from the far room suddenly drew his attention. Then a *clunk* which seemed to reverberate through the whole of the floor, as of something heavy being moved. When he looked, he saw for the first time that the sliding door from which Gunnar had emerged had not completely closed. All along one side, a sliver of light broke through. At the bottom of it, wedged in the gap and keeping the door's edge from the frame, was a beautifully decorated golden scabbard.

"Open it," ordered Bjólf. Godwin and Úlf stepped forward. Others joined them, shoving axes, sword grips, anything they could find into the narrow gap, heaving against it.

"My contribution," coughed Skalla as they worked on it, his features now dimly visible in the light. "To help you to your goal."

Bjólf glared at the shadowy presence. "Why would you, of all people, wish to help us? To betray your masters?"

Skalla gave a shrug, heard more than seen. "Because it pleases me. Because I tire of them. Of life."

In response to a final, mighty effort, the door suddenly hissed open, illuminating the room. Skalla lay propped up in the corner, his breathing rough, his black leather armour wet with his own blood, the bolt protruding from his shoulder, and in his limp hand, lying upon the floor, the fine, gold hilted sword of Hallbjörn's ancestors.

Halldís stared at the precious blade for a moment; a blade she had thought forever lost. Memories stirred. He looked back up into her face. She met his gaze with cold eyes, at the man who had destroyed everything she had known and loved, helpless before her. She could not remember how many times she had wished for such a moment. Staring fixedly at him, she advanced slowly. Skalla nodded at the inevitability of it, almost laughed. She bent over him, took up her father's sword from his weakened hand, then turned and walked away. Without a word, Atli took up the gold scabbard and passed it to her. She sheathed the sword, and put it through her belt.

"You do not wish him dead?" said Bjólf.

Halldís shrugged. "I wish it. But what good is there in it?"

Bjólf nodded, then, turning to Skalla, grabbed him by his hauberk and hauled him to his feet. "Well then," he said, "you can come and meet the masters with us." And with that, he dragged him into the next room.

It seemed that in stepping through the doorway they had finally left behind everything that was familiar to them. None could relate anything here to the world they knew, even those with experience from years of voyages. Apart from a single, strange table or bench to one side, the room was featureless – so featureless that it was hard to see it as a real place at all. It seemed as if it were somehow half-finished – a weird, transitional zone between this world and another, as if whatever strange gods had created this corner of the universe had become distracted, and left it, forgotten, unstamped with any clear identity or purpose.

Every surface was as white and smooth as ice, as if all composed of the same impossible substance, a sickly, oppressive light that seemed, inexplicably, to filter from the high ceiling itself, with no clear source. And there, directly ahead – the only distinct feature in the whole scene, set into the white rear wall and almost as high as a man – was what appeared to be a huge circular shield, forged from steel, its metal shining in the light. All was so strange, so inhospitable, so hostile to life, that there was not one among the company who did not now feel the same deep dread that had afflicted Atli among the decaying, alien edifices in the grove of death.

That the room was empty was immediately apparent. Where the masters had retreated to was not.

"Where?" demanded Bjólf. Skalla nodded towards the great disc of metal in the far wall.

Bjólf understood now that it was some kind of doorway. As he approached, dragging Skalla with him, the lights flickered and dimmed. One by one, the glow from the devices along the benches fizzled out until only a few points of light remained. Skalla looked about him. "They are trying to shut you out," he said. The explanation meant nothing to Bjólf, but he sensed urgency in the words.

"Open it," he said, shoving his captive forward.

Skalla slumped against the wall next to the great metal door, staining it with his blood, his breathing laboured. "Yes, why not," he said with a humourless laugh, coughing.

He raised no latch, reached for no key. Instead, he pulled off his gauntlet and jabbed a finger repeatedly at a strange metal box upon the wall, from which glowed a tiny red light. It emitted a series of unpleasant, high-pitched sounds as he did so. "They do not know that I know this," he said. The fact seemed to amuse him.

The red light changed to green. There was a heavy *clunk*, and, with a deep hum, the huge steel door swung slowly open, bathing them in light.

# CHAPTER FORTY-FOUR

## MEETING THE MASTERS

ATLI HAD ALWAYS thought the worst nightmares were those that came in the dark. He had imagined the darkness filled with shadows, with the threat of unknown, indeterminate creatures, half-hidden or perhaps never revealed, grasping at him from the gloom. With demons, with shapeless monsters, with the hands and voices of the dead. Now he had witnessed these things, seen sights with his own eyes that eclipsed all his most terrible imaginings. For a time, he had begun to believe there were no nightmares left.

The new nightmare – the undreamt of horror – came in cold, sterile light, reflecting off every dead surface, eating into his eyes, into his depleted brain. The shadowless light of the masters' final refuge.

Inside was a fevered, searing vision of ugliness whose weirdly ordered, clean surfaces only made it seem the more delirious, the more utterly insane. Along either side of the room, on starkly white, featureless benches, stood strange things that hummed, and buzzed, and gave off a dead light. Above them on one wall, in cabinets made entirely of glass, were row upon row of vessels – some, like great glass urns, filled with noxious-looking liquids in which were suspended human heads, hands, foetuses and unidentifiable body parts, their lifeless flesh grey and pallid. Here and there, empty eyes stared out, dead mouths lolled open.

At the back of the room, the space opened out into a circular space in which more banks of lights – more than could be counted – blinked and glowed and flicked on or off, arrayed on surfaces in which, here and there, shapes and even pictures – tiny, phantasmic images of people – crackled and moved, as if forever imprisoned behind glass, trapped, like the dead flesh in the great jars, but somehow alive, like shrunken human cattle.

Upon the left side, coming into view as they passed, was a sealed chamber behind glass. Inside, attached to a gleaming metal table, which had been angled upward to give the clearest possible view of what lay upon it, was a man. His body had been cut open, the covering of flesh pulled open by metal clamps, its whole surface pierced by long, steel needles, held in place by complex, shining apparatus. The revealed organs within, still pulsating with life – or whatever now passed for it – were attached to hundreds of tubes through which unnaturally-coloured fluids flowed. Before their horrified gaze, the heart beat, the lungs pumped, and upon his face, the eyes flickered, the mouth moved, seeming to appeal desperately to them from a silent world beyond pain.

None could doubt it now. It was from here that the pestilence had come. It was from here that had spread the unfathomable, inhuman intelligence that had wrought those ghastly creations in flesh – of the dead and the living.

But it was not just these sights, or these thoughts, that so horrified them. It was some other, indefinable quality about the whole of that nauseating interior – this world without shadows, in which everything was revealed, everything too sickeningly evident. The entire room seemed to hum with a kind of dull, aching malignancy that hated life, that sought by degrees to crush and mindlessly consume the spirit. The very air around them – stale and dead, like warmed air spent by corpses – made them feel sick, as if poisoned. It was a place in which life had become an irrelevance, an inconvenience – an anti-world, its physical being so drained and exhausted of humanity that not even its hollow ghost remained to attest to its one-time existence, and merely to look upon its dead matter was to know utter despair, to taste in the mouth the creeping canker of a death beyond death, to feel – as if a shuddering, tangible thing – the ultimate doom of the entire race.

Atli had not thought anything could be more terrible than those ghastly things they had encountered in the grove of death. He had been wrong.

AND THEN THERE were the masters.

As Bjólf had advanced through the opening door into their cursed realm, there had been shouting from within – feeble, terrified voices exclaiming in a strange jabbering language. There was sudden movement, and a loud, repeated, sharp noise – like a log crackling in a fire, but of deafening volume, leaving their ears ringing. He strode towards the circular end chamber, towards its source – an angled, metal tool, the tube-end still smoking, the mechanism now clicking uselessly in the quivering, pallid hand of one of the masters. If this object ever had any dark magic, it was now used up. Bjólf wrenched it out of his weak grip and flung it to the floor.

In front of him, cowering in a corner, his hands raised as if to protect his face, was a small, feeble-looking man in a white coat – his thin, pale, wispy hair barely visible upon the shiny flesh of his barren, balding head, his smooth, pulpy flesh as colourless as a sickly infant. In front of his watery eyes, barely distinguishable from the rest of his bland, characterless face, were two discs of glass, held in place by a fine metal frame. Bjólf plucked them off him. The man whimpered as he did so. He examined them briefly, peered through them onto a blurry world, and, seeing no further use for them, flung them on the floor. The man scrabbled about for them on his hands and knees like a frightened rodent.

Some distance away, behind a solid, white bench, identically dressed, cringed three more puny, pale, smooth-skinned men.

Bjólf turned to Skalla, a look of sickened contempt on his face.

"*These* are your masters?"

"They wielded great power once," said Skalla, a note of apology in his voice.

"I had many reasons for leaving my home, but having great power was never one of them. So why did they leave theirs?"

"It's... complicated..."

"Do I strike you as a stupid man, Skalla?"

Skalla looked into Bjólf's steely, indefatigable eyes, then scanned the bloodied, battle-worn faces that were now arrayed so incongruously in those strange surroundings – faces that spoke of an unconquerable spirit, of a fierce loyalty that Skalla himself had never known.

"No," he said, "you don't." Then he sighed. "Their land is... here. And not here. It cannot be reached by any ship."

"I have no patience for riddles. Speak plainly."

Skalla narrowed his eyes, thought for a moment, then, nodding slowly, began again. "They come from another time. From a future a thousand winters hence. Their world is doomed – overrun with the *draugr*. They fought the pestilence, sought a cure." He shrugged. "Unsuccessfully...

"But they had also devised a means of escape. A mechanism, powered by a great furnace deep beneath our feet. They say it has the power of the sun. Their world fell about them. And so, they flung themselves from it, back here, to an age long before – before the world fell, before the pestilence. They meant to buy time, to continue their work, to find the remedy you yourselves sought..." His voice dwindled to nothing.

Bjólf looked at Halldís, as if seeking some confirmation or denial. She merely stared at the floor, fallen into a withdrawn silence, as if lost to him. For a time all stood saying nothing, the whole chamber seeming to throb with a weird energy that made their guts churn.

It was Halldís who spoke first. "They brought this disaster upon us," she said, her voice low and charged with a mixture of anger and despair. "Their own future was lost, and now their selfishness has doomed ours. There is no remedy. No hope. No respite." She turned and wandered desolately towards the back of the chamber, away from the others, as if seeking only solitude.

"I do not believe it," said Bjólf. "Will not believe it. The future is not set. They have proved it. If they can change things, why not us?"

"How?" asked Halldís, despairingly. "All this might and power..." She reached out and ran her hands across a surface of glass, gazing distractedly at the red-painted metal shape that lay beneath. "They thought they had mastered it. But it has mastered them."

As she stood there, one of the feeble, white-coated men began to chatter urgently at Skalla.

"Shut him up," said Bjólf to Godwin. The Englishman hefted his axe.

"Wait!" said Skalla. Godwin halted. Skalla listened intently to the man's prattling, then turned to Bjólf. "He wishes her to move away from where she is standing."

"You understand their language?" frowned Bjólf.

"Of course," said Skalla. Then, still listening, he raised the brow above his good eye, and chuckled to himself. "Oh, that's good! That lever, the red one behind the glass. It appears that it will send them – this whole place – back to where it came from."

Bjólf could only stare at him in astonishment.

"He is now telling me that I should not divulge these things to you," said Skalla. "But because he never bothered to learn *our* language, he does not know that I already have."

"Such a simple thing can banish all this?"

"As they came, so can they leave. It has been set this way since the beginning. So they could escape quickly if things went wrong."

"And, even now, they have not done so?" said Halldís in disbelief.

"Christ in Heaven," muttered Njáll. "How much more wrong does it need to go?"

Skalla shrugged. "I believe nothing now would induce them to return to that place. It has become too terrible a memory. They call it 'Hel.'"

Bjólf recalled the way Magnus had used that word, how he had spoken of it not merely as a land of the dead, but a place of eternal torment.

"We could send them back, whether they like it or not," he said.

"And ourselves with them," said Skalla. "There's the catch."

Bjólf looked contemptuously at their surroundings, at the square images on the bench before him, showing the death-walkers swarming about the perimeter of the fortress. "What's left for us here?" He took a step towards the lever and smashed the glass with his fist. The white-coated men jabbered in panic as he did so, seemingly trying to appeal to Skalla. Skalla raised his hand to Bjólf.

"One more thing..." he said. "When Gandhólm is torn from this place, this land will be devastated in its wake. For miles around, all life will be utterly destroyed."

Bjólf hesitated.

"As far as Björnheim?" asked Halldis.

"Further."

It meant the end of everything she had ever known. Her friends, her family, her father's hall, the pastures she had played in as a child. Everything the pestilence had touched.

"Then the infection will be cleansed from this world," she said, and with sudden clear purpose took Bjólf's hand in hers and placed both upon the lever. One of the white-coated men leapt up, rushing at them, shouting incomprehensibly. Skalla swatted him to the floor, leaving the man's soft nose gushing blood.

Bjólf looked into her eyes, then back at his men. From every one of them came an almost imperceptible nod.

"See you in Hel, Skalla," he said.

They pushed on the lever, and everything around them erupted with blinding light.

THEY EMERGED THROUGH grey rubble and choking dust into an alien world.

The sun hung low in the blood red sky. What remained of the fortress sat on a great raft of soil and rock, pitched at a queasy angle like a grounded ship, like a huge clod of earth stuck roughly back in the place from which it had been wrenched. The ships, the harbour, the wooden rampart and all sign of the death-walkers from the fjord had been scoured from existence. Beyond, there were no trees, no sign of green.

In the distance, to the east, a great white structure spanned the valley – a wall of impossible dimensions. Other huge, strangely shaped edifices – some broken and collapsed – dotted the landscape. The fjord itself had disappeared entirely, as if boiled dry. The hard grey covering that the ground had now acquired was buckled and broken, pierced through with pipes and twisted metal and, as far as the eye could see, scattered with the chaotic heaps of rubble and wrecked machines. Where the soil was bare, it was cracked and scorched. It was as if the entire land had been laid waste.

Yet, even now, Bjólf had not abandoned hope. Brushing salt from his old friend's eyes as they had made their way out through the twisted corridors, Bjólf had found that Gunnar was not completely inert, but would stand where he was put, and would walk forward when pushed or pulled in that direction. He had bound him about the waist with a chain, and now hauled him along after them, whether hopeful that he may be restored, or out of pure sentimental attachment, none could tell.

As the ragged company of scarred, weary survivors stepped out onto the great, devastated plain, Halldís looked about her in despair. "How does one carry on in a world like this?"

"Fight," said Bjólf. "Stay alive."

"We do not even belong in this world," said Frodi, appalled at the sights before him.

"Then our fate is truly our own," said Bjólf. He looked about at the tangled chaos. "There must be somewhere out there a man can live in peace," he said, momentarily lost in memory. He looked back at Halldís, then. "And a woman."

"Perhaps we can find a ship," said Atli.

"Or build one," mused Úlf. "I assume they still have forests here."

"Perhaps there is a cure somewhere out there," ventured Kjötvi.

Godwin shrugged. "It could definitely be worse."

As they spoke, from somewhere in the blasted landscape of twisted iron and rubble came a long, low groan. The sound was taken up by other voices, spreading like a pestilence; a chorus of melancholy moans. All around, there were stirrings. Movement. Shuffling.

"What now?" said Skalla.

Bjólf spat into the dust, and drew his sword.

# THE END

# STRONGHOLD

**PAUL FINCH**

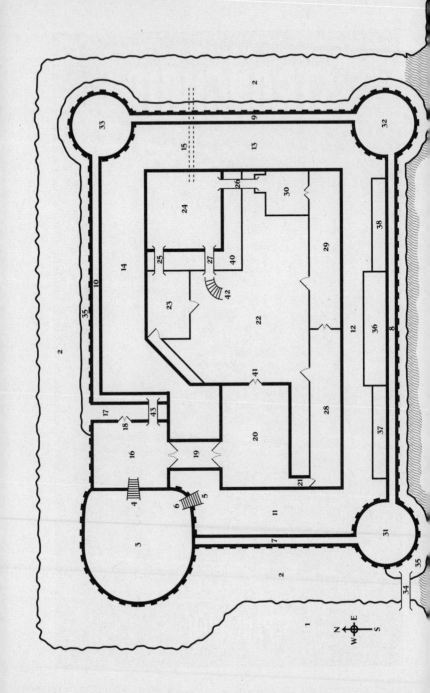

# GROGEN CASTLE KEY

1. Western bluff
2. Outer moat (dry, 30 ft deep)
3. Barbican (60ft high)
4. Stair (between Barbican and Gatehouse)
5. Stair (between Barbican and Bailey)
6. Postern gate
7. West curtain-wall (50 ft high)
8. South curtain-wall (50 ft high)
9. East curtain-wall (50 ft high)
10. North curtain-wall (50 ft high)
11. West bailey (outer courtyard)
12. South bailey (outer courtyard)
13. East bailey (outer courtyard)
14. North bailey (outer courtyard)
15. Keep sewer (subterranean)
16. Gatehouse (multi-levelled interior, 70 ft high)
17. Entry passage
18. Main gate
19. Causeway (20 ft above bailey)
20. Constable's Tower (multi-levelled interior, 100 ft high)
21. Inner Fort wall (80 ft high)
22. Central courtyard (also called 'inner ward', contains numerous sheds, shacks and outbuildings, serving as stables, servant quarters, hospital shelters, etc)
23. North Hall (non-fortified, multi-levelled interior)
24. Keep (multi-levelled interior, 150 ft high)
25. Gantry drawbridge (connecting North Hall to Keep, 90ft high)
26. Gantry drawbridge (connecting baronial state rooms to Keep, 90 ft high)
27. Keep drawbridge (20 ft above courtyard)
28. Barrack house (non-fortified, multi-levelled interior)
29. Great Hall (non fortified, multi-levelled interior)
30. Baronial state rooms (non-fortified, multi-levelled interior)
31. Southwest tower (multi-levelled interior, 100 ft high)
32. Southeast tower (multi-levelled interior, 100 ft high)
33. Northeast tower (multi-levelled interior, 100 ft high)
34. Southwest bridge
35. Berm path
36. Old stable block
37. Support scaffolding
38. Support scaffolding
39. River Tefeidiad
40. Keep moat (dry, 30 ft deep)
41. Ramp (down from Constable's Tower into courtyard)
42. Keep outer stair
43. Gantry drawbridge (connecting Gatehouse to north curtain-wall, 30 ft above entry passage)

Note: The castle kitchens and refectory are located on the ground floor, running beneath the barrack house and the Great Hall. The castle chapel is a cellar, located beneath the kitchens. None of these are visible from this perspective.

# CHAPTER ONE

## 1295 AD

IT WAS EARLY March, but spring still hadn't arrived. The woods to either side of the River Ogryn were not yet in flower. They were black and tangled, laced with grey mist. Within a month the river would be foaming and thundering, swollen with melt-water from the heights of Plynlimon, but for now it was an icy trickle, meandering down the shallow valley, zigzagging between tumbled rocks and fallen branches covered with frost.

At the head of the valley lay a mound of weapons. For the most part they were swords, axes and spears, though there were also improvised farm tools – scythes, flails, reaping hooks. The majority were tarnished and chipped, their hafts or hilts bound with fleece and homespun linen. If they'd been honed to sharpness, it had been done inexpertly; many of the blades had a keen edge but had been thinned to the point where they were brittle. Others had already cracked and broken.

Even so, it was agonising for the Welshmen to surrender them. They passed the mound in their ones and twos, grudgingly discarding their implements, throwing surly glances at the group of mounted figures watching from close by. The foremost of these was a woman sitting on a roan mare. She was of early middle age and extraordinarily handsome, green eyed and feline in her beauty. A hooded coat of white fox fur shielded her from the chill winds, and her long red tresses were bound with a copper circlet. She was Countess Madalyn of Lyr, a noblewoman of high standing in this region. When Powys had been a kingdom in its own right, her family had held its eastern populace in thrall, but, with fair governance and courageous leadership, had stirred loyalty rather than resentment. Now that Powys was a dominion of the English Crown, she was viewed with less affection. Her passion for her people was not doubted, and some regarded her fondly as a living embodiment of happier days, but many either mistrusted her as a collaborator or saw her as a pawn in a greater political game over which she had no control.

Countess Madalyn's daughter, Gwendolyn, was mounted alongside her on a milk-white pony. She also was clad in luxurious furs, and though fairer even than her mother, more slender of build and with an elfin prettiness, in truth she was little more than hogannod; an inconsequential girl, who would some day inherit the countess's title and lands but probably none of her spirit. The passing Welshmen paid her no heed, though when it came to the third mounted figure they either glared at him with open hatred or spat at his horse's feet.

He was Corotocus la Hors, marcher baron of the English realm and Earl of Clun. He was a trim, broad-shouldered man in his late thirties, handsome with close-cropped brown hair, a trimmed beard and moustache, and piercing blue eyes. Fully girt for war, he wore a crimson tabard emblazoned with his heraldic black eagle belted over his suit of black mail, a cross-hilted longsword at his hip, and a thick bearskin cloak at his shoulders. His horse, Incitatus, was a black stallion, sleek and powerful, maybe sixteen hands to the withers. Like its master, it had been born and bred in a crucible of war. As the Welsh trudged past, it tossed its mane at them, snorting and pawing the rutted ground.

"These fellows of yours don't know when they're beaten," Earl Corotocus observed. "I'll give them credit for that."

"They weren't beaten, my lord," Countess Madalyn said. "They surrendered voluntarily."

Neither spoke English as their first language, but, despite their lilting accents, it was the easiest way for the Anglo-Norman lord and his Welsh counterpart to converse.

"Then they aren't stupid either," he replied. "Though they could mind their manners."

"You surely don't expect them to welcome English dominance in their land?"

"If I'm honest, my lady, I have no expectations. I'm here purely to exercise my duty. If I were to falter in that, King Edward's mighty hand would crush me as surely as it would crush you and all this peasant race you claim kinship with."

Countess Madalyn glanced round to where Kye, her personal bodyguard, stood watching her back. An immense, bear-like fellow with a dense black beard and brooding countenance, he had been instructed from the outset not to rise to English provocation. He nodded his understanding of this order.

"Feeling the way you do, my lord, I'm grateful, but surprised, that you accepted the truce," the countess said.

Corotocus shrugged. "Peace terms must always be taken seriously when the alternative is laying siege to a bastion like Grogen Castle. Something tells me these fellows would not have fled it as quickly as the Breton sot assigned to hold it against them."

Grogen Castle, only twenty miles from here, had been abandoned by its royal castellan without a blow struck in resistance to the Welsh army who'd encircled it. Its puny garrison of Breton mercenaries had spent more time drinking and whoring than preparing for war and, when the time had finally come, had discovered that they'd lost all appetite for the hardships of battle. This was in stark contrast to the Welshmen now trailing down the valley. Despite having some mail shirts between them, they were mainly clad as foresters – in hose, felt boots and hooded woollen jerkins. Yet they were a rough, hardy sort, dark eyed and sullen of brow. They were all shapes and sizes; some were young, some old, but they had a vigour and robustness that the average English peasant lacked. Corotocus knew why. The main industry in this part of the kingdom was sheep rearing rather than rood-work. This was physically demanding work carried out on a mountainous landscape of coarse pasture and tumbling, boulder-strewn valleys. The simple act of moving from place to place built up great reserves of strength and stamina in the natives. On top of that, their barbarous tribal customs had toughened them in other ways, and they'd had no option but to grow used to the cold, wet gales howling in from the Irish Sea.

"I'm glad you understand," Countess Madalyn said. "It's very important to these men that you realise they didn't give up the castle because they are frightened of a fight. After Prince Madog's defeat at Maes Moydog, I was able to persuade them that the cause is futile. That it would have meant another prolonged war of annihilation and that, even if they were victorious in the end, the result would be burnt homes, ravaged farmland, famine and pestilence."

Corotocus nodded. "You did right. You are a good mother to your people."

His household champion trotted up from behind, a swarthy Aquitainian knight, whose brutish face was bisected down the middle by an ugly cleft. The relic of a deep scimitar wound incurred many years earlier, this had now left him with features that were weirdly asymmetrical, one eye slightly higher than the other, his mouth slanted, his nose, what remained of it, horribly crooked.

"That's the last of them, my lord," he said.

"You're certain, Navarre?"

"Four hundred men in total have surrendered their arms and are returning to their homes."

This appeared to be true. No more Welshmen now appeared. The last handful was already fifty yards down the valley.

"Good," Corotocus said. "Du Guesculin!"

Hugh du Guesculin, his chief herald and banneret, rode forward. Like Navarre, he wore mail and the earl's household livery. He also carried the earl's gonfalon – a long pole from the top of which the black eagle billowed on a crimson weave. But he seemed less of a warrior. He was portly, with a clipped moustache and dainty manner.

"My lord?" he enquired.

"Begin the punishment."

Countess Madalyn glanced at the earl, puzzled. He smiled coldly. Du Guesculin summoned a page, who put a hunting horn to his lips and blew a single, clear blast.

"Kye!" Countess Madalyn said.

The gigantic bodyguard hurried forward, his mail coat clinking under his leather corselet. He had a spear in one hand, a kite-shaped shield in the other, and a sharp scramsax tucked into his belt. But he didn't get a chance to use any of these. Navarre, who had quietly dismounted, stepped up from behind him and stuck a dagger into the side of his neck. The giant sank to his knees, eyes goggling. He clutched at the jutting hilt, blood bubbling through his fingers. Gwendolyn screamed in horror. Countess Madalyn didn't at first see this. She was distracted by a wild shouting, and now stood in her stirrups to peer down the valley.

Why were feathered shafts whistling back and forth through the frigid air? Why were Welshmen dropping where they stood?

Then she saw the English archers. Having donned leather over their mail as camouflage, they emerged in packs from the trees on either side. The graceful curve of their longbows, as they were strung and drawn with professional speed and precision, was as distinctive as it was terrifying.

"Earl Corotocus!" she cried. "What is this?"

"War cannot just be extinguished, my lady, like a candle you snuff, or an ember you put your foot upon." Corotocus mused. "Though putting one's foot down is an apt phrase at this moment."

The Welshmen in the valley ran in all directions, but arrows flew with unerring accuracy. Like fleeting streaks of light, their steel heads buried themselves in flesh, muscle and bone. Very soon, the valley bottom was dotted with the wounded and dying. Some of those still standing attempted to forge to the valley sides, where they could grapple with their tormentors. But the crossfire was so thick that they were riddled with shafts and dropped like human pincushions, or, if they managed to make it, received a knife in the ribs or the crushing blow of a war-hammer to the top of their skull.

Countess Madalyn watched through tear-blurred eyes.

"You traitorous pig!" she wept. "You gave us your word."

"One does not give one's word to country oafs and expect to be taken seriously, countess. These men are outlaws. They lived as such, and will die as such."

Some Welshmen struggled back towards the valley head, as though to retrieve their weapons. But Navarre and others of the earl's personal mesnie greeted them with laughter and double-handed sword strokes, lopping their legs from under them, sundering their necks at the shoulder. More knights, these mounted, appeared at the lowest end of the valley, where the open, tussocky sward made it safe for their horses. Most wore the earl's red and black livery, but there were others, tenant knights from his wider demesnes, who sported personal devices on their surcoats and shields. It made for a colourful scene as they cantered back and forth, lowering their lances to skewer the Welsh as they ran, or hacking them down with longswords and mattocks. Some fell to their knees and begged for mercy – but were simply ridden over, their bodies torn and trampled by smashing, iron-shod hooves. One stout fellow attempted to grab the lance of a knight decked with blue and white chevrons. The knight released his weapon, but circled around, drew his battle-axe and clove the fellow's cranium.

Even those lying injured were not spared; hunting spears were flung at them as riders galloped past. One older Welshman, his jaw hanging shattered and left eye dangling from a crushed socket, crawled to the river's edge, only to have his face pressed under by a hoof until he drowned. Owen Anwyl, the disinherited Welsh noble who had first seized Grogen Castle, was spared the butchering blade, but buffeted again and again by horses and struck with the hafts of axes and the pommels of swords, his visage streaked with gore from his lacerated scalp. Eventually a halter was looped around his neck and tightened, and he was hauled around the valley on his back.

Countess Madalyn shrieked as rude hands were now laid on her. It was Navarre, his lopsided face written with goblin glee. He dragged her from the saddle and threw her to the ground. She struggled, but could not stop him plucking the pearls from her throat or the rings from her fingers. When she spat and clawed at him, he punched her – not hard enough to knock her unconscious, though his fist was like a bone mallet inside its rawhide glove. She was left stunned by the blow, only vaguely aware that her daughter was also pulled screaming from the saddle and divested of her jewels.

After that, the two women were violated.

Countess Madalyn's fustian gown and the fine silk under-tunic were torn wide open, and her breasts exposed. She winced as Navarre kneaded them like two lumps of dough, sobbed aloud as he feasted on them, suckling, biting, chewing until her blood flowed.

Earl Corotocus and Hugh du Guesculin sat through it all, unmoved. As Corotocus surveyed his triumph, he summoned his page and accepted a chicken drumstick and a goblet of mulled wine.

In time, the carnage drew to a close. Spiked maces, caked with brains and bone fragments, still crashed onto heads and shoulders. Flailing hands were still severed at the wrist, but few Welshmen were left on their feet. Tiring of the sport, Corotocus's knights took those few surviving and hanged them from the surrounding trees. One by one, their gibbering pleas were lost in gargled chokes.

At the sight of this, Countess Madalyn wailed like a baby, but she was struck dumb when she saw her daughter, every scrap of clothing now stripped from her body, trussed with rope and thrown over the front of her horse like a deer. Holding her rent garments together with one hand, the countess tried to intervene, only to be knocked to the ground by Navarre. Laughing, he jumped up behind the captive girl and slapped her naked buttocks.

"Your daughter will be held as surety for your good behaviour," Earl Corotocus said. "At some point in the future, if this land remains at peace, it may please me to marry her to a henchman of my choice – someone I can rely on to treat her in the manner to which she will soon become accustomed."

"You whoreson!" the countess hissed, kneeling upright, her emerald eyes burning with outrage. "You goat's whelp!"

"Insult me all you wish, my lady, but understand one thing. There is more at stake here than the pride of your piffling people. I am lord of the Clun March, but I am more than just a name. In France, I was charged with defending the king's Gascon possessions. We were overwhelmed by sheer numbers, but the king heard about the destruction I wrought on his foes, how my men and I slew hundreds, thousands. He was grateful, and I was rewarded with lifelong investment not just in this – the most difficult corner of his realm – but with lordships all across Wales. Be under no illusion, I intend to hold my possessions and, in due course, to expand them. But these constant revolts are becoming tiresome. I cannot have the king suspecting that his trust was misplaced. Du Guesculin!"

"My lord?" the banneret said.

"Du Guesculin, by my reckoning, there are twenty villages between here and Grogen Castle. Lay waste to them. Torch the houses, scatter the women and children, hang the men and boys. And make a good show of that, du Guesculin – I want gibbets on every hill and every crossroads, each one laden to breaking point."

"Of course, my lord."

"Earl Corotocus, you will pay for this!" the countess snarled.

"Countess Madalyn, we all pay in the end."

Before he left, he made a special example of Owen Anwyl, having his hands bound behind his back, his legs broken with a pollaxe, and then suspending him by the feet from a tree-limb at the highest point of the valley.

# CHAPTER TWO

THE CASTLES THAT King Edward built in Wales after his first war of conquest, some twenty years earlier, had formed a stone collar intended to choke the spirit of native resistance. Designed by the master military architect, James of St. George, they were each one a towering, impregnable bastion, a glowering fastness that came to dominate and oppress the land for miles in every direction. Their very names had now become a byword for invincibility: Conway, Ruddlin, Flint, Harlech.

Grogen Castle was no exception.

It stood on the north shore of the River Tefeidiad, right on the water's edge, and was approachable only from the west due to hilly moorland and thickly wooded terrain in the north and east. It consisted of an outer curtain-wall, some fifty feet high, a fortified Gatehouse, a Barbican, a Constable's Tower, and an Inner Fort, the walls of which stood eighty feet. Inside the Inner Fort were the main buildings – the halls, kitchen, barrack-house and the final defensive structure, the Keep. When Corotocus's men first came in sight of Grogen, there were mutters of awe – due as much to its appearance as to its size. In England it had become the fashion for wealthy nobles who owned privately licensed castles to paint them in glowing colours – white, blue or red – so that they shone from the leafy landscape like objects in fairy tales. But King Edward's Welsh castles were different animals. They were military strongholds so bereft of adornment or luxury that the Welsh poet Euan the Rhymer had described them as 'spikes of Hell thrust out through Cymru's fair hide.'

Grogen fulfilled that vision perfectly. It was comprised entirely of grey granite cemented in huge blocks. Its colossal walls and towers were sheer and bleak, and fitted with projecting upper gantries, which were massively crenelated and equipped with swinging timber panels from behind which an avalanche of stones, darts and boiling oil could be launched. Its only windows were narrow slits through which arrows could be shot and javelins thrown.

However, much more of a shock to Corotocus and his men was not the pitiless nature of this fastness, but the many figures manning its awesome defences.

"What the hell is this?" the earl swore, reining his horse at the front of the column. He slammed his visor open. "Du Guesculin, what in Satan's name is this?"

The banneret lifted his wide-brimmed helmet and, shielding his eyes against the early-morning sun, focussed on the figures dotting the top of the curtain-wall and the parapet of the Barbican. At this distance it was impossible to discern who they were, but there were plenty of them and their blades and helmets glinted.

Others of the earl's men now rode up, among them William d'Abbetot, his chief engineer, Captain Garbofasse of his mercenary battalion, and Craon Culai, who commanded a company of the king's infantry attached to the earl's retinue for the duration of the war. They were equally surprised and, having been assured that the castle was theirs for the taking, not a little alarmed.

"Someone tell me what's happening here!" Corotocus bellowed. He rarely allowed himself to get angry in front of underlings, but now he'd lost face. His cheeks reddened, there was froth on his lips. "Did some of Anwyl's dogs stay behind? How could the bloody place have been reoccupied when he only abandoned it yesterday? Someone explain this to me!"

"Why do none of them move?" Culai wondered. A tall, thin man with pinched features, he seemed spooked by what he was seeing, and it was indeed an eerie sight – the figures on the wall were silent and motionless. Too motionless, some might say, to be living men.

"Are they dead?" Garbofasse asked.

"Neither dead nor living," came another voice. Ulbert FitzOsbern, an older knight wearing a red and blue harlequin mantel over his mail, cantered to the front of the column. "My lord, most likely they're scarecrows."

"Scarecrows?" Corotocus said.

Ulbert nodded. "I saw this done often during de Montfort's rebellion. Castles expecting siege but held by only a handful of troops, would create scarecrows – dummies stuffed with straw – and prop them on the battlements. Given an iron cap and a spear each, it looked to all the world as if the place was strongly garrisoned."

Corotocus laughed loudly, partly to conceal his relief. "Of course. That Breton wastrel de Brione only had a few men. When he heard the Welsh were coming, he'd have panicked. Once again Ulbert, we're grateful for your wisdom and insight." He regarded his other lieutenants sternly. "It comes to something when a homeless knight, an errant wanderer who is only with us to pay off his family's debts, provides a solution while the rest of you stand around like frightened children."

They hung their heads, abashed.

There was still, of course, the possibility that this could be a trap. The earl's force might approach the castle's main entrance thinking it safe, only to be struck by a deluge of missiles. So lots were drawn and ten men selected to go forward. The rest of the army, six hundred in total, arrayed itself on the western bluff to watch.

While to the south Grogen Castle was bordered by the deep, broad flow of the Tefeidiad, it was surrounded on its three other sides by a moat, which had been hacked from the living rock on which the fastness was built. This moat was about ten yards across and thirty feet deep. During the spring thaw, mountain streams emptied into it from the north, but at present it was dry and filled with rubble. The only way to cross over it was via an arched stone bridge at the castle's southwest corner. Having managed this, an enemy force would be required to follow the 'berm' path, a narrow footing running between the base of the south-facing curtain-wall and the inner edge of the moat. This turned at the castle's southeast corner, passed alongside the east-facing wall and the north-facing wall, until finally reaching the main entrance, which was set between the Gatehouse and the north-facing wall in the castle's northwest corner. By this time, of course, the enemy would have been subjected to prolonged attack from overhead as it was forced to circle the entire stronghold.

As the ten chosen men readied themselves, donning not just their helms and shields, but additional plating on their elbows, shoulders and knees, the rest of the army waited. Among them were Ulbert FitzOsbern and his twenty-two year old son, Ranulf.

One of the duties the father and son had been given was to guard Countess Madalyn's daughter. Partly of their own volition, but also at the instigation of Father Benan, the earl's chaplain, who thought it unseemly that Gwendolyn should be naked among so many men, they'd loosened her bonds and given her a cloak to wrap herself in. Though streaked with dirt and tears, she sat upright on her pony, taut with anger but determined to maintain her dignity. When Ranulf offered her a drink from his water bottle, she didn't lower herself to reply.

"It's your choice," he said, turning back to the castle.

The FitzOsberns were tall, well-built men. Age had wizened Ulbert's neck and thickened his paunch, but, thanks to countless clashes in battle and tournament, his son was flat bellied, barrel-chested and stout of limb. He had grey eyes and a lean, square jaw. When he pulled back his mail coif, he shook out a mop of sweaty, straw-yellow hair; sure proof that his family – though they'd intermarried many times with Norman stock, hence their surname – had its origins in Saxon England.

Navarre galloped up to them, his horse chopping turf as it slid to a halt.

"The girl rides with the vanguard," he said.

"Why?" Ranulf asked.

"Isn't it obvious? To lessen the chance of attack."

"I thought the idea was to draw an attack… if there's to be one."

"Earl Corotocus wishes to lose as few men as possible, FitzOsbern. But he needs to know what we're facing. With the girl as a human shield, we'll likely draw a non-fatal response."

Ranulf glanced unhappily at his father, who shrugged.

"Ranulf FitzOsbern," Navarre said in a sneering tone. "I wouldn't like to think you were about to disobey Earl Corotocus."

Ranulf handed over the reins. Navarre rode away, leading

Gwendolyn's pony behind him at a fast trot. The girl sat stiffly, but now looked frightened. She glanced back at Ranulf and his father as if suddenly thinking them a better option than whatever lay ahead.

"Earl bloody Corotocus," Ranulf said. "Corotocus? Where did he get that name? Doesn't it sound like a demon to you?"

"It sounds more Gaelic," Ulbert replied.

"The Gael people would be insulted... those that haven't been slaughtered." Ranulf's voice tightened with disgust. "I've never seen such savagery as in the last few days."

"He treats his English subjects the same way."

"His English subjects can appeal to the king."

"And would the king listen? You know the law of the March. Men like Corotocus thrive here because the king needs brutes to control the border."

"That doesn't excuse him.

"Agreed. By any standards, his atrocities are perhaps... over elaborate."

"Atrocities to which we're a part, father."

"We're excused, Ranulf. We're here through fealty."

"Fealty?" Ranulf shook his head. "We agreed to pay our debts by fighting for him."

"Which we have done, many times."

"Yes, and which I'll gladly do again. Show me armed opposition and I'll fight it now. But I'm tired of terrorising the weak and helpless."

"You should watch what you're saying, boy," another knight said as he walked by, leading his horse. He was Walter Margas, one of Corotocus's tenants. By all accounts he'd done well in the earl's service, but he was now an old, embittered fellow with watery eyes and a grizzled grey beard. His wore a distinctive surcoat of blue and white chevrons but, with his potbelly and bandy legs, he didn't cut a striking figure. "Rogue knights like you are ten-a-penny. The earl could dispense with you tomorrow, and he wouldn't lose a wink of sleep."

"And as for cowards like him," Ranulf said when he'd gone, "do we really want to fight alongside them?"

Ulbert chuckled. "Would you expect to find Margas alongside you if there was real fighting to be done?"

"Father, this isn't a joke."

"Then you must make it one!" Ulbert snapped, turning impatient.

Despite his mild manner, Ulbert was in his mid-fifties and a battle-scarred veteran. He'd served more lords than he could remember, several of whose reasons for waging war were less than worthy and whose methods of prosecuting it were, in truth, appalling. But he'd learned through long experience that taking a moral view was a waste of energy and emotion – all it would do in the end was prevent you sleeping at night, and in wartime you needed your sleep. Thus far on this expedition he'd tolerated Ranulf's distaste for the earl's techniques, but now he feared that it might bring trouble for them.

"We're in Earl Corotocus's service for a term of seven more years – on oath," he reminded his son. "With luck we'll spend the remainder of those years in this castle, doing nothing more than waiting and watching from our guard-posts."

"Seven years... holed up in there!"

"Some men would be glad. The whole army of Hell couldn't get at us in there." For some reason, Ulbert shuddered at that thought.

Below them, meanwhile, the small vanguard of ten men and one woman proceeded down the grassy slope to the bridge, the earl's gonfalon fluttering above them. Still, the figures on the battlements were motionless. The rest of the earl's host lapsed into silence as they watched. Nervously, the vanguard crossed the bridge, rode around the castle's southwest tower, which was cut with numerous, slanted vents so that missiles could be poured onto the bridge from close range, and advanced along the riverside berm. No attempt was made to interfere with them, and gradually the other troops began to relax.

"So far so good," Ranulf said.

Ulbert didn't reply.

The vanguard reached the far end and, when it turned at the castle's southeast corner, vanished altogether. Long minutes followed, which became half an hour, and then an hour – before a rider returned to view, galloping pell-mell across the bridge and up the hillside.

"It's open, my lord!" he cried. "The main entrance is open! Grogen Castle is ours!"

"And the garrison?" Corotocus shouted back.

"As you said, sir... straw men. Effigies."

"So now it was Earl Corotocus who said that," Ranulf observed.

"Of course," Ulbert replied.

The earl marshalled his host, and, with a beneficent air, led it downhill.

His household retainers rode directly behind him. After these came the royal contingents: detachments on loan from King Edward's own Familiaris Regis – the men-at-arms under Craon Culai, the crossbows under Bryon Musard, and the longbows under Davy Gou. After these marched a Welsh sub-chief called Morgaynt Carew – he and his small group of discontented warriors didn't like the English, but had worse grievances against Madog ap Llywelyn, the architect of the uprising. The tenant knights from the earl's estates followed and then came the men on oath, the likes of Ulbert and Ranulf. At the very rear came Garbofasse and his mercenaries, a motley band of cutthroats and outcasts. They wore few colours, but were heavily mailed and carried a vast assortment of weapons, everything from falchions to mauls and morningstars, from halberds to broadswords and scimitars. Garbofasse himself was a brutish giant, with long black hair and famously disgusting breath. In the twenty villages Corotocus had sacked, it was these men who'd partaken most – burning cottages, raping women, revelling in the bloodshed as if bred to it from birth.

"I'd be happier without these scoundrels at my back," Ranulf grumbled as he steered his horse downhill.

"Better they're on our side than against us," his father replied.

The berm path was an unnerving experience. All the way along it, they were acutely aware of the projecting walk fifty feet overhead, and its many 'murder holes' through which all types of objects could be dropped upon them. The curtain-wall rose like a sheer cliff to their left, its skirted base narrowing the path until only two horses could move along it abreast. With a shallow slope into the river on the right, this wasn't unduly perilous, but when they turned the southeast corner and found themselves alongside the moat, it was a different matter. The column hugged the curtain-wall as it processed. Those on the outside, man or beast, only needed to stumble or slip once and they'd plunge thirty feet onto jumbled rocks.

When they finally reached the castle's main entrance, it was an immense gateway recessed to one side at the end of a deep entry passage. Proceeding down towards it, one could still be attacked from overhead via the Gatehouse battlements or via the curtain-wall, which bounded it on the left. However, the gate itself, a massive oaken structure, faced with iron, was open, and the portcullis behind it had been raised. They rode through, their hooves clattering in the long, vaulted tunnel, and then out and along a timber causeway, which passed twenty feet above the bailey, a yard hemming in the Inner Fort. At the south end of the causeway stood the Constable's Tower. This was a miniature castle in its own right. In shape if not size, it reminded Ranulf of the great Tower erected on the north bank of the Thames, but again its gate was open and its portcullis raised. They rode through, passing along another vaulted tunnel and out into the precincts of the Inner Fort, descending a ramp into the central courtyard where, among many thatch and wattle out-buildings, an entire stable block was located.

With their squires and grooms scampering ahead to provide berths for their animals, the knights and men-at-arms shouted and jostled as they dismounted, the sounds of which echoed to the high ramparts. Only slowly and with much good-natured disorder, did they fall into their separate companies.

Last into the courtyard, moving at a leisurely pace as always, rode Doctor Zacharius. With him came the covered wagon filled with salves and herbs and medicines, driven by his assistant, Henri.

Zacharius, a prized surgeon, was a youngish, clean-shaven man, with long dark hair, green eyes and a wolfish countenance. Even now in the midst of campaign, dressing well was important to him. He wore a blue serge gamache, a brown felt hood with scalloped shoulder-pieces, bright yellow hose and blue, long-toed boots. By contrast, Henri was a pallid, tremulous youth wrapped in a dark, woollen cloak spattered with roadside mud. The general feeling, though no-one knew this for sure, was that Henri was one of the doctor's numerous illegitimate offspring, though in this particular case, given that he was being taught the surgeon's skill assiduously and thus preparing for a career of his own, he was probably the outcome of a liaison with a high-born lady.

"Place is completely empty – no serving wenches, not even a scullery maid," Navarre said, approaching the doctor on foot. He chuckled. "Could be a barren spell for you, Zacharius."

Zacharius smiled as he dismounted. "But at least it will end when I leave this place. When will yours end, Navarre?"

Navarre's cockeyed smile faded. "My lord says you have the pick of these buildings for your personal quarters and your infirmary. If anyone disputes your decision, you have his authority."

Zacharius nodded as if he'd expect nothing less.

Navarre scowled as he turned, leading his horse by its bridle.

"Reached the limits of your power, Navarre?" Ranulf wondered, having just emerged from the stable and overheard. "Again?"

"No man is fireproof, FitzOsbern," Navarre retorted. "Anything can happen to any one of us at any time. You'd do well to remember that."

He led his horse away, Ranulf gazing after him, thinking that their incarceration in this place was likely to be even more onerous than he'd first thought.

# CHAPTER THREE

EARL COROTOCUS OPTED to put his headquarters in the Constable's Tower, for this controlled both the main entrance and access to the Inner Fort, and therefore the entire stronghold. Above its entry tunnel, there were various rooms. All were functional – made from cold, bare stone and bereft of wall hangings or furniture, though they had hearths where fires could be kindled, and bales of straw and piles of fleeces to provide bedding. Word soon came that the storehouses in the central courtyard were filled with grain and barrels of fruit and salted pork. There were also kegs of wine and cider, and a deep well in the kitchen, from which a pail of fresh water had already been drawn.

One by one, the earl's lieutenants were allocated their positions. Garbofasse and his mercenaries were to take the Gatehouse, and the earl's household knights the Constable's Tower. The royal contingents would be spread through the castle, the crossbows in the southwest tower, the men-at-arms along the curtain-wall, the longbows to any vantage point of their choice. Carew and his Welsh malcontents, deemed less trustworthy, were assigned to the Barbican, a low but heavily fortified tower just west of the

Gatehouse, where they could man the castle's main piece of artillery, a huge stone-throwing trebuchet, but where, more importantly, the earl could watch them. Lastly, the earl's tenant knights would reinforce the defenders on the curtain-wall.

"That leaves us, my lord," Ulbert said, speaking not just for himself and his son, but for three other indebted knights – Tomas d'Altard, Ramon la Roux and Gurt Louvain.

"Take the curtain-wall on the south side, overlooking the river," Corotocus told them dismissively. He was seated at a long table in the Constable's Tower's main chamber. A map of the castle and its surrounding environs had been found in a chest, and lay unscrolled in front of him. "Bed in the barrack house in the Inner Fort. Rotate your sleeping arrangements with the others. I never want less than half the garrison on watch."

Ulbert bowed and retreated.

"And the girl, my lord?" Ranulf asked. "Do we house her in the barracks too? I'm sure there'll be a side-hall or ante-chamber where she can have some privacy."

"She can have her privacy in the Keep."

"The Keep?" Ranulf said.

As the final refuge, the Keep, a gargantuan square edifice, was perhaps the grimmest part of the castle. It stood in the northeast corner of the Inner Fort, taking up almost a quarter of the central courtyard. It had its own moat, which could only be crossed at ground level by a drawbridge, or ninety feet in the air by two gantry drawbridges connecting to it from the North Hall and the State Rooms. It had few windows; its precipitous walls, which were much thicker than any others in the castle, rose unbroken for an incredible one hundred and fifty feet. It was unimaginable that anyone should try to storm such a structure. But it was equally unimaginable that anyone, save the lowest felon or most dangerous rebel, should be imprisoned inside it. There'd be little light in there, even less clean air, and probably no sanitation. The girl would be completely alone, for none of the men would be stationed there unless the castle's outer defences fell.

A few seconds passed, before Earl Corotocus glanced up from his map. "Ranulf, is that disapproval I hear?"

"How could I disapprove, my lord, of such a fair and Christian-minded judgement?"

All around the chamber, where a number of the earl's men were still loitering, breaths were sucked through gritted teeth. Father Benan, who had been kneeling in prayer before a corner table with a crucifix etched on the wall above it, looked around and gaped. Ulbert stepped forward, thrusting Ranulf out of the way.

"Apologies my lord. My son is a fool who often speaks out of turn."

Corotocus pushed his chair back. He regarded them both coolly.

"You're right, Ulbert. Your son is a fool... but at least he tells me the truth. I'd rather have men around me who are honest in their feelings than toadies who simper and scrape." He stood up. "Ranulf, walk with me."

Ranulf glanced at his father, who averted his eyes.

The earl took a spiral stair, which led out onto the Constable's Tower's roof. Some of his household were already up there, using bellows to pump life into a brazier. Others hugged themselves in their cloaks. At this height, the wind gusting from the peaks of the northern mountains was edged with ice. Ranulf found himself gazing over a rolling, densely wooded landscape, much of it still shrouded with mist.

"You understand, Ranulf," Corotocus said, walking to the western parapet, "how empires are built?"

Ranulf followed him warily. "We're building an empire, my lord?"

"You find my methods abhorrent." Corotocus posed it as a statement rather than a question. "So do I. That may surprise you, Ranulf. I don't like what we're doing here any more than you, but unfortunately we can't choose the necessities we face in life. Only two things can control a recalcitrant race – strength and more strength. Not just the strength to defeat them on the battlefield, but the strength to do what you must to suppress them afterwards. Never underestimate a people's self-pitying spirit, Ranulf – it can be a great motivator. Likewise, don't be fooled by these claims the Welsh make that they are different from us, that they're a separate nation who have earned the right to self-rule and an indigenous culture. The native English thought the same when first they were conquered, but it wasn't long before their world was consumed whole and, in the long run, made better for it. In any case, how have these Welsh earned the right to self-rule? They were as tyrannised by their own lords as they ever have been by ours. They've staged revolts against their princes, they've waged civil wars, their mythology is filled with blood and treachery."

"With all respect, my lord…" Ranulf was cautious about voicing too much concern. He knew Earl Corotocus's reputation for meeting dissent with an iron fist – he'd seen it for himself, he'd been part of that iron fist. But, for now, the earl was calm, almost genial. And why shouldn't he be? He'd captured his main objective without losing a single man. "With respect my lord, that doesn't make what we do here right."

"'Right'?" The earl seemed amused. "What is 'right'?"

"The code tells us…"

"The code is a fantasy, Ranulf. Invented by frustrated French wives who dream of replacing their ancient, worm-riddled husbands with handsome young lovers. You are a fully girded knight. Tender in years, but you earned your spurs in battle. You've already seen enough to know that wars are not won by fair play or courtly gestures."

He put a fatherly hand on Ranulf's shoulder.

"Ranulf, Edward Longshanks is a king who would be Caesar. Once this war is won, he will march against the Scots. He intends to rule the whole island of Britain, from the toe of Cornwall to the Wood of Caledon, from Wight to Northumbria. But right now he is watching the Welsh March. This is a troublesome region for him. If we who are appointed to guard it can curb this menace once and for all, he will be more than grateful. There may be better rewards here than simple relief from the debts we owe." He moved away along the battlements, only to stop and glance back. "But Ranulf… I will not dangle this carrot indefinitely."

Suddenly there was steel in his voice.

"They tell me you and your father played no part at the River Ogryn." His expression hardened. His blue eyes became spear-points. "They say you spared lives in the villages we razed on the road here. Very gallant of you, Ranulf. But that may have been a mistake. As things are, I am your lord. I'd prefer to be your lord and your friend, but I can just as easily be your lord and your enemy. Listen very carefully… if I will not sacrifice my fortune and glory for these vermin that call themselves Welsh, I certainly won't sacrifice it for an upstart boy."

Ranulf said nothing.

"Do we understand each other, sirrah?"

"Yes."

"I didn't hear you."

"Yes, my lord."

\* \* \*

HALF AN HOUR later, Ranulf locked Gwendolyn in the Keep. He found the largest, airiest room for her that he could, but it was still damp and filthy, filled with decayed straw and rat-droppings. He turned deaf ears to her tearful pleas. As he walked away along the cell passage, he refused to look back at her white hands clawing through the tiny hatch in the nail-studded door.

When he ascended to his post on the south-facing curtain-wall, his father was already there, sharing the warmth from a brazier with Gurt Louvain, a rugged looking northern knight draped in a green, weather-worn cloak. Two of the scarecrows had been flung to one side. They were hideous, soulless objects – sackcloth suits stuffed with rags and bound to stick frames. Their faces had been made up with streaks of what looked like dung or mucus. Weirdly – probably because the Breton troops had been bored – some of these faces were smiling exaggeratedly, almost dementedly – like caricatures from Greek or Roman drama. It gave them a sinister air, as if they knew something the English didn't and were delighted by it.

"How long must we rot in this hellhole?" Ranulf asked of no-one in particular.

Ulbert shrugged. "Until the king deems the rebellion quelled. And the longer that takes, the happier I'll be." He indicated the land beyond the river, its dense conifer wood receding into the blanket of mist. Nothing moved over there, neither man nor beast. "Look at that. Isn't that beautiful?"

"Beautiful? I see emptiness."

"Exactly." Ulbert shoved another log into the brazier. "No-one for us to kill, and more importantly, no-one to kill us."

"That's because there's no-one left."

"Don't fool yourself, Ranulf," Gurt Louvain said. He was a doughty man, but his bearded face was icy pale. Anguished by the slaughter they'd wreaked over the last few days, he'd developed a nervous twitch. He glanced at the silent trees beyond the river, and the shadows between them. "There's always someone left."

# CHAPTER FOUR

ALMOST TWO FULL days passed before Countess Madalyn reached the secret hafn, and by then she was a wreck.

Famished, frozen and faint with pain and weariness, she tottered down a path winding steeply between groves of silent alder. Below her, the hafn – or 'hollow' – was filled with mist. Its trees were twisted stanchions, the spaces between them strewn with rocks and stones. Footsore and filthy, still clad in her ragged, bloodstained garb, she stumbled forward until, at the north end of the hollow, she came to a sheer cliff face. It was hung with rank vegetation, but had split down the centre. At the base, the fissure had widened into a triangular cavity just large enough to accommodate the body of a small man.

The countess regarded it warily. Her eyes were sore with weeping. Unbound, her hair hung in a flame-red tangle, giving her an appearance of madness, but she wasn't so mad as to go blundering into a place like this without hesitation. After several agonised moments, she cursed her lack of options, dropped to her knees and crawled into the aperture. On the other side, a passage that was little more than a rabbit-hole led through the rock. It was a cleft rather than a bore; its sides ribbed and jagged, its narrow floor deep in razor-edged shingle. She scrabbled along regardless of scrapes to her hands and knees, unconcerned that her torn clothes snagged and tore again. At length the passage opened into a cavern filled with greenish light, the source of which she couldn't identify.

She descended a flight of crudely cut steps. The walls in here were inscribed with ancient carvings – spirals and labyrinths, the shapes of men and beasts cavorting together. Reaching level ground, the steps became a paved path weaving between steaming pools. Overhead, water dripped from the needle tips of innumerable stalactites. Ahead, three figures stood on a raised dais. Countess Madalyn walked with a straighter posture; she groomed her hair with grubby fingers – anything she could do to regain a semblance of dignity.

The figures wore hooded white robes, girded at the waist with belts of ivy. The central one held a knotted staff, yet he wasn't old. His face was broad, pale and clean-shaved apart from a black goat-beard, which fell from his chin to his belly. His eyes were onyx beads: unblinking, inscrutable.

"The Countess of Lyr honours us with her presence," he said, his deep tone echoing in the vaulted chamber.

For all her dirt and blood, Countess Madalyn stood proud before him. "I haven't walked half naked for ten miles just to be flattered, Gwyddon."

"Has your god finally abandoned you?" he asked.

"Nor did I come here to discuss religion."

"Then what? Politics?" Gwyddon gave a sickle-shaped smile. "At which you are clearly a novice to be so easily outmanoeuvred by a marcher baron, when the rest of the world knows the marcher barons are nothing but brute-butchers, the blunt edge of Edward's anger."

"Don't lecture me, druid!" Her voice was a strained croak. "I've been trying to broker a peace for our people while you and your pagan rats hide in holes in the ground!"

Gwyddon's smile faded. To either side of him, his fellow priests, older men with white beards and wizened faces, frowned at her blasphemy. There was a chorus of whispers, and the countess realised that others were close by – men and women, children too – all acolytes of the ancient religion, huddled in the shadows beyond the misty pools.

"Bring the countess some food," Gwyddon said loudly. "Bring her a cloak as well. And a chair."

"I want none of these things," she retorted.

"Nevertheless, you will have them. We may be pagans, but we are still respectful of rank."

Three figures scurried up, recognisable as slaves by their shaved heads and the brand marks on their brows – though whether male or female it was difficult to tell. One laid a cloak of ram's fleece over the countess's shoulders. The second produced a wooden chair, onto which she lowered herself painfully. The third brought a table, and placed on it a bowl of steaming rabbit broth and a flagon of mulled wine. Up until now the countess had ignored her gnawing hunger, but the mingled aromas of sweet carrots, boiled cabbage and succulent braised rabbit-flesh almost overpowered her. She struggled not to fall on it with gusto, though she didn't actually stop eating until she'd scraped the bowl clean, at which point she drained the flagon in a single draught. The wine was rich, spiced with orange and ginger. And it was hot – a heady warmth passed through her cold, battered body.

Gwyddon watched without comment.

"You've heard what happened?" she finally asked.

"Of course."

"Ill tidings travel quickly in Wales."

"In Wales is there any other kind of tiding?"

"What King Edward is doing makes no sense." She shook her head, as bewildered as she was still horror-stricken. "Does he expect to win people over when he appoints someone like Corotocus and gives him a free hand? How does he think he'll gain his subjects' love?"

"You are mistaken in thinking that he wants their love," Gwyddon said. "In these far reaches of Britain, he is content to have their fear."

"You don't seem disturbed by that."

"Why should I be? As you say, we are rats living in holes. And who drove us here? Not the English, not the Normans – the Welsh."

"Pah! In other countries you'd have been exterminated."

"We'd have been exterminated here had Christian monks had their way. Only the sympathies of certain noble families ensure our survival. Your family for instance, countess."

She stood up abruptly. "Don't mistake me for someone I'm not, Gwyddon. I don't sympathise with heathens."

"So why tolerate us in your domain?"

His voice was deep, melodious. He peered down at her, his eyes glinting. The emerald vapour writhed around his tall, enrobed form like a brood of ethereal vipers.

"I... I..." Countess Madalyn was briefly entranced by the vision. "I... don't believe in slaughter."

"You didn't believe in slaughter once," he corrected her. "Why else are you here now?"

"They've taken my daughter."

"I know."

The countess was even more bewildered. How could he know about that? How could he even know about Corotocus's deception? Word of the disaster would travel, but she had come straight here, walking stiff and lame like one dead, but tarrying neither to talk with folk nor to look back over her shoulder. She'd taken short routes through dark woods and hidden valleys that were known only to a chosen few. As her anger ebbed, the countess was increasingly aware of the mystery in this strange, subterranean realm. Its ceiling was speckled with a million tiny lights, like stars in a miniature cosmos. The images on the walls appeared to have moved or changed since she had first seen them. The air was heavy with intoxicating fragrance.

"M-my daughter is all that matters to me," she stammered. "I won't stand by and allow her to be abducted."

"And yet there's nothing you can do. Most of your own warriors went to serve Madog or Anwyl... and now lie slain."

"Can you help me?"

"Ahhh, so we get to the crux of it."

"Don't play games with me, Gwyddon! You know why I'm here."

"It will cost you."

"Cost me?"

"We have no country, Countess Madalyn. No sense of people. Your plight is unfortunate, but of no great concern to us. If your nation was driven en masse to the chopping block and beheaded one by one, my chief regret would be the waste of so much sacrificial blood."

"And how much will it cost me?" She appraised the gold moon-crescent pendant on his breast, the gem-encrusted rings on his fingers, the silver dragon-head pin clasping his robe. "I'd imagine the greater the supplicant, the higher the price?"

"How much do you offer, countess?"

"If you can guarantee the safe return of my daughter..." She faltered briefly, but steeled herself. "If you can guarantee the safe return of my daughter, and the destruction of Earl Corotocus... I will give you half my wealth, half my lands. And protection for you and your sect for as long as there's breath in my body."

He smiled thinly. "Not enough."

At first Countess Madalyn thought she'd misheard. Only in fables and folklore had such a reward been offered.

"Not nearly enough," he added.

"You ask me to beggar myself?"

"I ask nothing of the kind. You can keep your earthly goods, if they mean so much to you."

"In God's name, what do you want?"

He pursed his lips, which, now that she was close to him, looked redder than blood. "No more, countess, and no less than an equal share in the power your victory will bring."

"Power? I seek only the return of my daughter."

"And the destruction of an English marcher lord."

"I only ask that because I know I'll have no choice."

"Countess Madalyn, you will have no choice come what may. If Earl Corotocus dies they'll send someone else, and you'll need to destroy him as well. And the one after that. And the one after that."

"What are you asking... that I start a full-scale war?"

"How many more of your villages must they burn? How many people must they hang? Full-scale war is already upon you."

"The uprising has been crushed with horrendous loss of life. If I were to start another now, it would mean an apocalypse for Wales and its people."

"Your people need only a leader – a proper leader. Someone fearless and respected. You could fill that role, countess. Just as Boudicca did twelve centuries ago. The difference is that, unlike Boudicca, you will have me – and I will ensure that the apocalypse falls on England."

"How?" she asked.

"Allow me to show you."

# CHAPTER FIVE

DOCTOR ZACHARIUS WAS born the younger son of a wealthy merchant in Bristol.

Initially, he did not promise much, though this only lasted a short time. Despite an indolent youth and an alarming lack of interest in the family shipwright business, he soon showed an aptitude for learning. In response to this, his father sent him to a monastery, so that he could train for the priesthood. But, in various ways, Zacharius blotted his copybook with the holy fathers, and, after much soul-searching, his father took him out of the Lord's care and paid for him to attend the medical school of St. Gridewilde's at Oxford University.

The beneficiary of a generous stipend, Zacharius here became a renowned frequenter of taverns and brothels, but at the same time embarked, at last, on a serious course of study. He was fortunate in that his personal tutor, a Franciscan friar, who had once been a devoted student of Canon Grosseteste, taught medicine without mysticism and introduced Zacharius to a Latin translation of the Kitab al-Tasrif, an Islamic treatise dedicated to the science of surgery, an in-depth analysis of which, though he didn't realise it at the time, would raise the young medical student far above the level of the common garden barber-surgeons, whose butcher-shop clumsiness had given the surgical arts so bad a name for so many decades. Zacharius was so inspired by this venerable tome that, on completion of his studies, he paid from his own pocket to have a personal copy made.

His first position after graduation was with the Premonstratensian abbey-hospital at Titchfield, in Hampshire, where, though he was regarded as an all-round skilled practitioner, he particularly excelled with the surgeon's knife. When a novice at the abbey – a nephew of the abbot no less – was brought in from the fields with a severely broken leg, Zacharius, taking his cue from the Kitab al-Tasrif, performed a delicate invasive operation, opening the damaged limb cleanly, repairing the shattered bone, then sewing the wound up and applying splints, and all while the casualty was insensible through a herbal-induced anaesthesia. Within a few months, the novice had completely recovered, with almost no ill effects.

The abbot was so impressed that he spread the word, until it reached the ear of his cousin, Earl Corotocus of Clun, who was in search of a medical expert of his own. When Earl Corotocus offered him a post, Zacharius at first resisted. His cell at Titchfield Abbey was different from those of the monks, who were given to asceticism – he had a carpet, a divan, a roaring fire, tapestries on his walls, shelves lined with books. Compared with this luxury, life in a military environment was not so attractive. But, of course, there were still certain things that Zacharius could not have at Titchfield, which Earl Corotocus could provide in abundance, primarily wine, women and song.

For these reasons alone, and no others, he finally joined the earl's household. Of course, not everybody approved.

"Why are you preparing your infirmary in the open air?" Father Benan wondered.

On Zacharius's instruction, servants had now helped Henri move barrels of water and sacks of grain from several outhouses in the central courtyard in order to make space for beds, though these outhouses were little more than straw-thatched shelters with neither walls nor doors to keep out drafts.

Zacharius glanced up from where he'd laid out a central table and was in the process of arraying his instruments. "My dear Benan, the rooms in this fortress are noisome and stuffy…"

"It's Father Benan," the priest interrupted.

Zacharius smiled to himself. "If any patients are admitted to my infirmary while we're here, Father Benan, the best thing they can have is fresh air."

"But it's only March. And it's cold."

"In which case we bed them with warm blankets and place braziers filled with hot coals alongside them."

Benan chewed his lip uncertainly. He was a youngish man, but plump, with a pink face and, despite his shaved cranial tonsure, long, white-blonde hair cut square across the fringe. Though he mistrusted scientists in general, and Zacharius in particular, he secretly shared the doctor's penchant for foppery and good living. Even now, in the midst of a war, he wore white silk gloves adorned with his rings of office, and a white silk tabard over his hooded black robe.

"You don't intend to open a hospital for local sick people?" he asked.

Zacharius laughed. He well knew Benan's 'High Church' views on this sort of thing – namely that it was important to alleviate suffering wherever possible, but that pestilence was God's punishment for sinfulness, and that to combat it could be seen as a form of heresy. On previous campaigns, in an effort to win the hearts and minds of a local populace, Earl Corotocus had thrown Zacharius's service open to local peasants and villagers, at his own expense – much to Father Benan's chagrin.

"My question was a genuine one," the priest said.

"So was my response," the doctor replied. "You think after what we've done in this land, anyone would come here? Even if their bowels were riddled with worms, their limbs rotted with leprosy?"

Benan chewed his lip. There was no riposte to so valid a point. He eyed Zacharius's surgical instruments. Apparently the doctor had commissioned their manufacture himself, again paying out of his own private funds. They included forceps, a scalpel, a bone-saw, a curette, a retractor, and a curved needle. To Benan's eye, they looked less like instruments of medicine and more like implements of torture. Of course, in his heart of hearts, he knew that Zacharius meant well, despite his lecherous proclivities, and that these menacing items had no more to do with the Devil and heresy than the swords and spears wielded by the earl and his soldiers, but these were confusing times to be a priest.

"I hope you have cause to treat no-one while we are posted in this castle," he finally said.

Zacharius shrugged. "So do I. But for different reasons than you, I think."

Benan was affronted. "My concern for the welfare of men's souls is more important than your concern for the welfare of their bodies."

"That is a higher philosophy, Father Benan, that many of your fellow clerics no longer share." Zacharius fixed him with a frank stare. "First of all, the Church itself educated me in these arts. The Franciscans at Oxford encouraged me all the way. At Titchfield it was the same. But even among those few who objected, it's amazing how quickly a man's principles can be put aside when he himself comes down with a sickness."

As always, Father Benan left Zacharius's company frustrated rather than irked, nervous rather than righteous. He returned to the castle chapel, which was located beneath the kitchen, and sandwiched between the barrack house and the Great Hall. As befitted a functional military outpost, it was little more than a subterranean chamber, built from bare, grey stone and austere in that typical Norman style. The altar table itself was a slab of granite. The pews were stiff, wooden things, embellished neither with carving nor cushion. There was no presbytery here, not even a sleeping compartment containing bedding. He'd seen no altar cloths, no silver candlesticks, no precious vessels of any sort; no doubt, if there had been some they were now in the grasp of the Bretons or the Welsh.

The contrast between this place and his sumptuous residence at the earl's great castle on the River Severn near Shrewsbury could not have been more marked. There, he had had a huge four-poster bed with blankets of feather down, servants at his beck and call, good food, good wine, silver plates to dine off if he wished. The chapel there was lined with white plaster and inlaid with frescoes telling tales from the Bible. There were statues on pedestals, holy inscriptions in the footways. The thuribles and chalices were of white gold; the altar was bathed daily in the reflection of a huge stained glass window, which depicted the Saviour ascending to a deep blue heaven, his noble brow crowned with roses.

What did Benan have for a window here?

A cruciform slit high in the east wall, through which sunlight might occasionally find its way, though only via a series of connecting shafts. Even during daytime it provided almost no illumination.

The dour environment matched the priest's mood. Yet again, he knelt at the altar and prayed for guidance, though he was increasingly worried that this was a vain hope. Earl Corotocus, though a valued member of the royal court and a steadfast defender of the faith, was a cruel and violent man. He kept a great house and ran orderly estates, he undertook the most dangerous missions in the name of his king, but there was nothing Christian in the way he conducted his campaigns – they lacked both chivalry and magnanimity; he was rarely generous to those he defeated. Not only that, he employed a man like Zacharius, whose sins were deemed tolerable because of his uses, and yet whose uses were also of questionable virtue. And, of course, Benan himself was no saint, no martyr. He hung his head in shame as he prayed. He never spoke out against the earl's excesses. He rarely questioned Zacharius any more for fear that the doctor's glib tongue would tie him in intellectual knots.

The earl's army was in a poor moral state right now, Benan reflected. They had crushed the Welsh easily, without losing a single man, without incurring so much as a minor flesh wound. That had seemed very unlikely given the initial circumstances of this uprising. A number of English-held castles had been besieged or, in the cases of Hawarden, Ruthin, Denbigh and Grogen, captured. The town of Caerphilly had been burnt to the ground. To have then entered the fray and triumphed so easily, it was tempting to say that God was on the side of Earl Corotocus. But deep down inside, Benan had a nagging fear – based as much on common sense as on clerical instinct – that the exact opposite was true. And that God would very soon prove this.

# CHAPTER SIX

"Countess Madalyn, what do you know of the Thirteen Treasures of Britain?"

At first the countess was too distracted to respond. They had emerged onto a barren hillside. After the green fog of the cave, she was disoriented by the glaring daylight. There was also a stiff, raw breeze. It wasn't as bitingly cold as it had been earlier, but her body ached with fatigue and she hunched under her fleece.

"Thirteen Treasures?" she said. "Artefacts… artefacts from myth?"

"Not myth, my lady… history." Gwyddon strode on. "Wondrous weapons of war gathered by the founder of my order, Myrlyn, as protection for Britain after Rome's legions were withdrawn. Yet, one by one, in the darkness and chaos of those strife-torn ages, all of them were lost. All except one. This one."

He came to a halt. Countess Madalyn halted alongside him.

In front of them, a large circular vat made from something like beaten copper was sitting on a pile of burning logs. Two younger priests used poles to stir the concoction bubbling inside it. There was a noxious smell – it was sickening, reminiscent of burning dung.

Foul, brackish smoke rose from the vat in a turgid column. When the countess came closer, she saw a brown, soup-like liquid, all manner of vile things swimming around inside it. At this proximity, its hot, rank fumes were almost overpowering.

"This effluent?" she said. "This filth...?"

"Not the filth," Gwyddon replied. "The thing that contains it."

"A cauldron?"

"Not just any cauldron. You've heard of Cymedai?"

She looked sharply round at him.

He smiled. "I see that you have."

"This is the Cauldron of Regeneration? But that is only a legend."

"Certain details concerning its origins are legend. Not all."

She appraised the cauldron again. There were no eldritch carvings around its rim, as she might have expected, no images or inscriptions on its tarnished sides. It looked ordinary, in fact less than that. It might have been something she'd find covered in cobwebs in a cellar or the cluttered corner of an apothecary's shop.

"It was never the property of two ogres living in a bottomless lake," Gwyddon said. "Its creators were never roasted alive in an iron building that was actually a giant oven. But there is some truth in the story. It was brought here from Ireland to keep it from the Irish king Matholwch, who sought it for his own. Once in Britain, it was given to the care of Bendigeidfran, who was slain resisting the Irish invaders. It was, as the bards tell us, broken in that fight, but it was later repaired and hidden again. For centuries its whereabouts remained a mystery, until Myrlyn located it. Since then, it has passed from one generation of our order to the next, always in safekeeping."

He spoke fondly, and with his usual eloquence. But Countess Madalyn was fast becoming weary.

"I come to you with a genuine grievance, Gwyddon. I offer you a fabulous reward. And you mock me with this!"

"Mock you, countess?"

"Both you and I know that this is some harmless cooking pot."

"Indeed?"

He clapped his hands, and a young slave stepped forward. It was one of those who had served Countess Madalyn earlier. In full daylight, she identified him as a boy, though, by his cadaverous face, emaciated frame and the brand-mark on his forehead, which looked to have festered before it finally healed, servitude had been cruel to him. The mere sight of the wretched creature touched her motherly nature. Christendom forbade human slavery, and now she understood why.

Gwyddon, of course, had no such scruples. Reaching under his robe, he drew out a bright, curved blade and plunged it into the slave's breast, driving it to the hilt, and twisting it so that ribs cracked. Blood spurted from the slave's mouth. He sagged backward on his heels, but only when the blade was yanked free did he drop to the ground.

For a long moment Countess Madalyn was too aghast to speak.

"Have I... ?" she eventually asked, her voice thick with disgust. "Have I quit the company of one devil only to be wooed by another?"

"Everything I do has a purpose, countess."

"Everything Earl Corotocus does has purpose..."

"Wait and you will see."

Gwyddon signalled and one of the acolytes from the cauldron came forth with a ladle. Gwyddon took it, knelt, and carefully drizzled brown fluid over the slave's twisted features. When the ladle was empty, he handed it back, rose and retreated a few steps, all the time making some strange utterance under his breath.

Nothing happened.

"Master druid," the countess said. "As a Christian woman, I cannot..."

He hissed at her to be silent, pointing at the fresh-made corpse.

To her disbelief, she saw a flicker of movement.

Though the blood still pulsing from its chest wound darkened and thickened as the beat of its heart faltered and slowed, the body itself was beginning to stir. There was no rise and fall of breast as the lungs re-inflated; the eyes remained sightless orbs – unblinking, devoid of lustre. But there was no denying it; the slave was struggling back into a ghastly parody of life.

First it sat upright, very stiffly and awkwardly. Then it climbed to its feet with jolting, jerking motions, more like a marionette than a human being. The undernourished creature had been stick-thin and ash-pale before, but its complexion had now faded to an even ghostlier hue. Its mouth, still slathered with gore, hung slackly open.

Gwyddon's acolytes muttered together in awe. The chief druid himself seemed shaken. He licked his ruby lips. Sweat gleamed on his brow.

The corpse stood there unassisted, as if awaiting some diabolic command.

At length, Gwyddon came out of this daze and snapped his fingers. An acolyte rushed forward with a towel so that he could wipe his crimson spattered hands.

"This... this is not possible," Countess Madalyn stuttered, circling the grotesque figure. "How can he have survived such a wound?"

"He didn't," Gwyddon said. "He's as dead as the iron that slew him."

She waved a hand in front of the slave's eyes – they didn't so much as blink. Gingerly, she prodded him with a finger. Even through his blood-drenched tunic, she could tell that his flesh was cooling. She prodded again, harder – the slave rocked but remained upright, staring fixedly ahead.

"This is hellish madness," she breathed.

"This is the Cauldron of Regeneration," Gwyddon said. "As the Mabinogion states, it makes warriors of the slain."

"Warriors? This vegetable! This mindless thing!"

"Could he be more perfect for the task? He'll follow any order, no matter how fearful. He'll feel no pain, no matter how agonising. He'll commit any deed, no matter how atrocious."

"And he can't be killed?"

"Countess, what is already dead cannot die a second time."

"I don't believe you. This is druid trickery."

Gwyddon regarded her icily, and then re-drew his curved blade and spun back to face the slave. With a single overhand blow he hacked into the fellow's neck, not just once, but twice, thrice, in fact over and over, cleaving through the sinew. The countess stumbled backward, a hand to her gagging mouth. But Gwyddon hacked harder and harder, blood and meat sprinkling his robes, blow after butchering blow shearing through tissue and artery and, at last, with a crunch, through the spinal column itself.

With a thud, the head fell to the ground.

The slave remained standing. From his feet, his own face peered upwards, locked in the grimace of death, yet somehow with a semblance of life.

Even after everything she'd been exposed to, Countess Madalyn was nauseated, faint with horror. Only amazement at the seeming miracle and the importance of retaining her aristocratic bearing kept her from running shrieking. Again, she circled the mangled figure, though it took her some time to gather coherent thoughts. Enormous but terrible possibilities were presenting themselves to her.

"If he's a warrior, why didn't he try to resist you?" she asked.

Gwyddon found a clean corner of the towel, and dabbed it at the blood dotting his face. "I raised him, and therefore I am his master. He will not attack me. He cannot attack me."

"If this is true, why have you waited so long to bring this weapon to our notice?"

He shook his head at such a foolish question. "Whose side should I have rewarded with it? The Norman-English, who covet Welsh land and seek to make serfs of its people? Or the Welsh and Irish, whose Celtic Christianity is a harder, more barbarous brand than anything found east of Offa's Dyke."

She turned to face him. "So why give it to us now?"

"I don't give it to you."

"Why do you offer it?"

"As I say... now the Welsh have a figurehead. Someone who isn't driven merely by lust for plunder, like Gruffud. Or by personal ambition, like Madog."

"And, of course, someone who is sympathetic to the old ways?"

"Of course. After what you've witnessed today, how can you fail to be?"

Countess Madalyn looked again at the mutilated slave. She knew she was viewing something that couldn't be, yet her eyes did not deceive her. Even truncated, with his head at his feet, he stood rigid to attention. She prodded his chest, his back, his shoulder. He remained standing. She circled him again to ensure there wasn't a pole at his back.

"You've resurrected a murdered slave, Gwyddon," she finally said. "An impressive feat of magic. But can this thing on its own – this ruined, headless cadaver – prevail against Corotocus's knights? Can it resist his slings and catapults?"

"It won't be on its own."

"And how long will it take to raise an army of these horrors, with one cauldron, and one potion? This thing will have rotted to its bones before you're finished. In God's name, we'll all have rotted to our bones."

"Normally perhaps," Gwyddon said. "But I think we're all about to benefit from a change of season. There's a hint of spring in the air, wouldn't you say?"

Two more of Gwyddon's acolytes now approached the cauldron with sticks and stirred its contents vigorously. Thicker, even more noxious fumes swam into the air. Gwyddon tracked their upwards path. The sky was pregnant with grey cloud, much of it already tainted by the smoke that had risen steadily since the brew was first heated. The countess recalled her earlier thoughts that the wintry chill had lessened, that the frost was melting – and now the first drops of rain began to fall. Polluted rain, as was clear from the brown smears it left on the druids' white robes. Rain which, when she cupped it in the palm of her hand, looked and smelled like ditch water.

A bolt of lightning suddenly split the sky over Plynlimon; thunder throbbed like a thousand battle-drums. The rainfall intensified until it was teeming, a waterfall pouring from Heaven. Gwyddon's acolytes fled to find shelter, but not Gwyddon himself. He was lost in a reverie of prayer, his arms crossed over his breast, a clenched fist at either shoulder. His eyes were closed, his broad, bearded face written with ecstasy as the water streamed from it.

THE RAIN DIDN'T just fall over Powys; it fell all over north and central Wales, thrashing on mountain, forest and valley.

The narrows tracks linking the region's hamlets had already been churned to quagmires by the passing of Earl Corotocus's army, but now became rivers of slurry. The charred shells of the cottages and crofts shuddered and sank in the deluge. Those Welsh who'd survived the earl's passing hid, weeping and gibbering, under any cover they could find. And those who hadn't survived, those whose ragged forms adorned the gibbets and gallows on every road and ridge to the English border, started twisting and jerking in their bonds. To the north, on the tragic field of Maes Moydog, the mountain of Welsh corpses, cut and riven and steeped in blood and ordure, was also washed by the rain – and slowly and surely began to twitch and judder. In the chapel graveyards – even those graveyards that were long abandoned and overgrown – the topsoil broke and shifted as the rain seeped through it and the green, rotted forms crammed underneath slowly clawed their way out.

# CHAPTER SEVEN

THE SKIES OVER Grogen Castle were black with swollen clouds. Torrents of rain poured, drenching the mighty walls, flooding the walks and gutters. Even indoors there was no respite. Cold, wet wind gusted through the rooms and tunnels, groaning in the chimneys, extinguishing candles, whipping the flames in the guardroom hearths. Rainwater dripped from every fault and fissure.

In the Keep it was too dark almost to find one's way. Ranulf ascended from one level to the next, with a loaf, a bundle of blankets and a water-skin under his right arm. In his left hand he carried a flaring candelabra; an oil-lamp hung from his belt. He added a little fuel to each wall-sconce he passed and put a candle flame to it, creating a lighted passage, though all this really did was expose the cockroaches scurrying across the damp flagstones and the bats hanging from the arched ceilings like clusters of furry fruit.

When he unlocked the door to the cell it was so heavy that he had to heave it open. Gwendolyn was sitting in a far corner, knees clasped to her chest, her back rigid. The only window was a high slot, too narrow for a human to pass through, and deeply recessed

– it must have been ten feet from the start of its embrasure to the finish. Even in bright sunshine, it admitted minimal light.

"I've brought you this," he said, placing the lantern at the foot of the steps, and lighting it with a candle. "I'll replenish the oil every so often."

Gwendolyn didn't reply. She looked pale, her pretty features smudged with dirt and tears. Her hair, once like spun copper, hung in grimy rat-tails.

"I've also bought you these." He laid the blankets down, walked over and offered her the loaf and the water-skin. She still said nothing, gazing directly ahead as if seeing neither him nor his gifts.

"You need to eat, my lady."

"My lady?" She seemed surprised, before giving a cackling laugh. "I see your bachelry still deceives itself with Arthurian pretension?"

"You need to eat."

Reluctantly, she took the bread and water. At first she only nibbled, but soon capitulated to her hunger, tearing the loaf apart with her teeth and fingers. Ranulf glanced around the cell. The filthy straw gave it the stench of a stable. Water ran down its black brickwork. Having seen the quarters allocated to the men in the barrack house, there were few facilities at Grogen that were much of an improvement on this. Though of course the men hadn't been violently abducted, stripped naked, beaten and sexually assaulted.

"I don't suppose..." he said. "I don't suppose it would do any good to apologise?"

She looked up at him, again surprised. "On behalf of whom – yourself, or the bloodstained madman you serve?"

Ranulf wasn't sure how to respond.

"Let me spare you the trauma of trying to answer," she said. "You're right, it won't do any good."

"I'm not happy about what's happened here."

Ranulf wasn't quite sure why he'd admitted that. Before coming up into the Keep, his father had reminded him that the girl was nothing more to them than a prisoner, the spoils of war, a pawn in a greater game. It was unfortunate for her, but there were always winners and losers in the politics of strife. Ulbert had concluded by strongly advising that whatever was going to happen to Lady Gwendolyn would happen, and that their first duty was to themselves and their family name. They mustn't allow "futile sentiment" to endanger their cause.

Yet, if the prisoner was aware that Ranulf had taken a risk expressing sympathy to her, she was unimpressed.

"I'm sure your unhappiness will be great consolation to those who've died," she said. "Or who've been maimed, or left destitute."

"I understand your anger. Earl Corotocus is a pitiless man."

"And those who willingly serve him? What are they?"

"We don't all serve him willingly."

She smiled, almost maliciously. "Spare me your conscience, sir knight. If it's torturing you, I'm glad. You'll find no absolution here."

"To make things easier, I can only suggest that you comply with the earl's wishes." He retreated towards the door. "No matter how distasteful you find them."

"Comply with the earl's wishes? I think you mistake me for someone else. I will do no such thing, not least because in a very short time the earl and you murderers he calls his retainers will all be dead." Ranulf waited by the door as she laughed at him. "You think this fortress will protect you, Englishman? Welsh vengeance is about to fall on you people with a force you can't imagine."

"Your spirit does you credit, my lady. But don't hang your hopes on how easily the previous garrison here was overwhelmed. To call them 'foolish sots' would be an insult to both fools and sots. Earl Corotocus is of a different mettle; a monster yes, but a soldier through and through. His mesnie has been hardened by battle over many years. In addition, they're nearly all English-born. From birth, they've been raised to view the Welsh as the foe over the mountain, as an enemy existing purely to be crushed."

"Foe over the mountain?" Like many who obsess that they are oppressed, Gwendolyn found it difficult to grasp the concept that her oppressors might feel they acted from a just cause. "What have my people ever done to you? *You* are the aggressors! You always have been!"

"When I was a child, miss, I lived on the shore of the River Wye." Ranulf mused. "I grew up hearing stories of how Prince Gruffud burned Hereford, the capital city of that region, and slew its entire population."

"That was nearly two-hundred years ago."

"King Edward has learned from the mistakes his forebears made. He won't tolerate hostile states on his borders."

"We're not hostile to you."

"Even neutral states must be viewed as hostile. Better to have a wasteland at your door than a tribe of barbarians whose loyalty your enemies can buy for a few cattle." He shrugged. "At least, that's the king's view."

"By the sound of it, it's a view you share."

"I understand the reasoning, even if I disapprove of the methods."

"Well in that you've set me a good example." She smiled coldly. "When my kinsmen get hold of you, forgive me if I understand their anger and merely disapprove when they tear you apart between their horses."

There was a sudden echo of voices from the passage. Ranulf withdrew from the cell, closing the door and locking it. At the next corner, he met Navarre carrying a flaming torch, and one of Garbofasse's mercenaries.

"Where did you put the Welsh slut?" Navarre asked.

"Who needs to know?" Ranulf said.

"Murlock needs to know, if he's to look after her."

Ranulf looked at the mercenary properly. Murlock was a brutal, bearded hulk, several inches taller than most men, his massive, ape-like frame crammed inside a steel-studded leather hauberk. When he grinned, fang-like teeth showed through a mass of dirty, crumb-filled whiskers.

"You're no longer the official jailer here, FitzOsbern," Navarre explained. "I thought you'd be pleased – one less onerous duty for you."

"And this whoreson is taking over?"

"The earl asked Captain Garbofasse for a man whose special skills fitted the task. Garbofasse nominated Murlock."

In the Welsh villages Corotocus had attacked en route from the Ogryn Valley, Garbofasse's mercenaries had taken a lead role in terrorising the populace; setting fire to cottage roofs, slaughtering animals in their pens and raping women and girls. Murlock, for one, had barely been able to keep his breeches laced. But he hadn't just raped them, he'd sodomised them, he'd beaten and kicked them, and made them watch as he'd personally tied the halters around the necks of their husbands, brothers, fathers and sons, and hoisted them up until they swung and kicked in the smoke-filled air.

Ranulf fixed Navarre with a disbelieving stare. "Are you out of your mind?"

"Are you out of yours, FitzOsbern? I wouldn't like to report that you've objected to yet another of the earl's orders."

"This boor... this animal, will *hurt* her."

Navarre shook his head soberly. "No. He's under orders to be gentle."

Murlock gave a snorting, pig-like chuckle, and Ranulf launched himself forward, grabbing the fellow by the Adam's apple and slamming him back against the wall.

In the same second, the tip of Navarre's dagger was at Ranulf's throat.

"Yield now!" Navarre snarled. "Right now, or I'll slice you open like a pear."

Ranulf didn't yield; not at first. He leaned on Murlock harder, mailed hands clenched on his windpipe, squeezing. Murlock's breath was caught in his throat. He couldn't breathe, yet he was grinning. His teeth showed like rotten pegs; his piggy eyes had narrowed to murderous little slits.

"You think I won't?" Navarre said. "I warn you, FitzOsbern... you know the earl likes nothing better than to make an example of one of his own. Nothing has made him more feared."

Ranulf finally stepped back, glistening with sweat, breathing hard. Gasping, Murlock sank to his haunches.

"You're swimming against a tide that will overwhelm you, boy," Navarre said, withdrawing his blade.

Ranulf turned and stalked down the fire-lit passage.

"FitzOsbern!" Navarre called after him.

Ranulf was ten yards away when he glanced back.

"The key, FitzOsbern! A cell door is no use without its key."

Ranulf took a long, heavy key from his pouch and dangled it from his fingers. "Come and get it."

Murlock lurched along the passage. He reached for the key and Ranulf dropped it into his palm, but then grabbed his wrist, yanked him forward and met him on the point of the chin with a club-like fist. Murlock was hurled sideways, caromed from the wall and collapsed to the floor, where Ranulf kicked him in the guts, dropped onto him with his knees and pounded his head and face, knocking out his teeth and smashing his nose like an over-ripe plum.

"That was nothing personal," Ranulf hissed into Murlock's ear. "Just a lesson I learned at the abbey school in Leominster. Prior

Barnabus taught it us each morning with a willow switch – in case we transgressed during the day and he wasn't around to witness it. So be warned, you harm a single hair on that girl's head and this isn't even a hint of what awaits you."

Ranulf straightened up, kicked the fallen mercenary once more, for good measure, and glanced around. Navarre was watching intently, his mouth frozen in a half-snarl.

"Don't look so outraged, Navarre. I gave him the key, didn't I?"

# CHAPTER EIGHT

EARL COROTOCUS'S MILITARY might was the envy of his fellow magnates.

As controller of a troubled corner of the kingdom, he already had rights to maintain armed forces that went far beyond his normal feudal obligations. In addition to this, as one of the foremost barons of the realm, descended in direct line from Roland la Hors, one of the original Norman warlords who'd descended on England like a pack of rapacious wolves in 1066, he had greater influence than most and even greater wealth. His estate comprised innumerable fiefs, castles, honours and titles, every one of which could be used to generate additional soldiery and military funding. Very quickly and perfectly legally, he could put a private army into the field that was almost of a size to challenge the king himself. The warriors he had at Grogen were only its spear-tip.

He was also a student of the most modern methods. Where Earl Corotocus was concerned, battle could no longer be left to the wild chance of heroic charge over level field, nor a single combat between picked champions. Though both the Church and the knightly code frowned on him for it, he had an avowed belief in the usefulness of irregular forces, in hit and run raids, in assassinations and ambushes. His personal household was supplemented with warriors drawn from far beyond his demesnes. Not trusting exclusively to such fanciful, out of date devices as homage and fealty, the earl would willingly take scutage from those less able of his vassals, and use it to obtain quality swords and lances from much further a-field. Hence the presence in his mesnie of paid war-dogs like Navarre, originally from the Aquitaine, and the employment of free-companies like Garbofasse's band who came from all parts of the country and were largely felons and cutthroats.

Yet the most feared section of the earl's military power was provided neither by knights nor mercenaries, but by machines. He'd long studied Greek, Roman and Saracen documents brought back from the East. He'd read detailed books written by the master siege-breaker Geoffrey Plantagenet, and now regarded machines not just as the key to destroying enemy citadels and strongholds, but as the ideal means to inflict vast casualties on enemy forces. Even before his campaign in Gascony, where the fighting was so bitter that all rules of gallantry were dispensed with, Corotocus had been collecting these monstrous contraptions – sling-throwers, ballistae, arbalests – either capturing them, purchasing them or having them custom-built. He now possessed three mangonels that any king or emperor would have been pleased to have in his arsenal, and which he'd christened *War Wolf*, *God's Maul* and *Giant's Fist*. These were gigantic counterweight catapults, which could hurl immense grenades fashioned from rock, lead or iron over huge distances. He'd also acquired a scoop-thrower, similarly designed to the mangonels, but with a broad bucket for discharging masses of smaller projectiles such as fire-pots or heaps of chain and rubble.

All of these siege engines, and many others like them, were now en route to Grogen Castle, disassembled and packaged in over a hundred wagons, travelling west along the Tefeidiad Valley. The earl had initially summoned them because he'd expected that he'd need heavy weapons to strike the castle walls. In the event, they were no longer a necessity, but it had seemed sensible that the equipment should still be brought. Of course this hadn't allowed for the weather.

It was now late at night and the rain had ceased, only to be replaced by a cold, wraithlike mist. The forest tracks had turned to quagmires and, with loaded wagons sinking to their axels and horses to their fetlocks, progress was torturously slow. The infantry guarding the artillery train were also having trouble. Each man carried his personal supply pack in addition to being well armed and wearing a thick mail hauberk. Thus heavily burdened, they'd been marching three days, were already footsore and exhausted, and now had liquid mud to contend with. While it was misty between the trees, the sky had cleared so it was also ice-cold. Men and horses' breath smoked as they trudged along. Every piece of clothing was wringing wet. Every boot or shoe squelched. The black mud coated everything.

Two men were perched on the driving bench of the foremost wagon: Hugo d'Avranches, a portly old knight, who served as quartermaster at Linley Castle – one of the earl's smaller bastions, but the place where the bulk of his artillery was usually stored – and Brother Ignatius, a young Benedictine, who served as Hugo's clerk. Another of the earl's knights, Reynald Guiscard, famous for his quick temper and mane of fiery-red hair, but prized for his self-taught skills as an engineer, came cantering up from the rear.

"God's blood, d'Avranches!" he bawled. "How could you bring us along a road like this? The wagons are tailing back for miles."

These weren't the first angry words they'd exchanged in the last few hours. Brother Ignatius sighed, anticipating yet another loud, futile argument.

"Do you think there are any proper roads through this wretched country?" d'Avranches growled.

"You should have found something better than this! The earl gave you maps!"

"I can't read a bloody map in the bloody dark and the bloody pouring rain!"

"No, and you're too old and bloody blind to read one in the bloody daylight as well, aren't you! But you're too worried about keeping your precious position to let anyone bloody know about it!"

"Name of a name!" d'Avranches swore. "I'll not be spoken to like that! Come near me, my lad, and you'll feel my gauntlet!"

Both men were among the highest ranking in the earl's circle of tenant knights, each sporting the prized black eagle crest on his crimson livery, but they rarely saw eye-to-eye. Guiscard leaned forward from his saddle, deliberately putting himself in swatting range.

"If you'd given as much effort to watching what you were doing,

Hugo, as you do to talking out of your backside, we wouldn't be in this predicament!"

"I'll not be blamed for the weather!" d'Avranches howled. "You blasted tyke!"

"My lords, please," Brother Ignatius said as patiently as he could. "Please. We can't be more than five or six miles from the castle."

"Except that we're on the wrong side of the river," Guiscard retorted. "Because this dolt insisted on fording it back at Nucklas."

D'Avranches swore and brandished his whip. "The earl's first message said that it was best to travel south of the Tefeidiad because the bulk of the rebel forces were north of it!"

"And his second message detailed the Earl of Warwick's victory at Maes Moydog," Guiscard replied, "and his own victory at Ogryn Valley. They're beaten, for Christ's sake!"

D'Avranches grunted, unable to deny this.

As the earl's official quartermaster, his priority was always to protect the heavy weapons. Corotocus had once said: "If men's lives are forfeit, it's a sacrifice I must live with. Men can be replaced. My mangonels cannot!" But on this occasion d'Avranches knew that he'd been over-cautious. Now on the south side of the Tefeidiad, the next point at which they could ford the river again was a good five miles west of Grogen Castle. Which meant they weren't five miles from their destination, as Brother Ignatius had suggested, but more like fifteen. In addition, there was still the possibility that, after the afternoon's rainstorm, the river level would have risen and the ford might not be useable for some considerable time.

"Maybe we should camp here?" Ignatius said.

Guiscard glanced around. He'd been thinking the same, but wasn't happy at the prospect. The wagon train snaked far back through the darkness, making the erection of even a temporary stockade impossible. They were in a forest, but ironically there wasn't much cover. High ground rose to the south and sloped away to the north, but it was thinly treed.

"Up to our knees in sludge and dung," d'Avranches complained. "It'll hardly make for a comfortable night."

"If the Welsh are beaten, there's nothing to stop us lighting fires," Ignatius said.

Guiscard was undecided. He wheeled his horse about. They were still relatively close to the English border, but there was something about this place he didn't like. The woods were eerily silent even for March. There wasn't a hint of wind, so the mist hung in motionless cauls between the black pillars of the trees.

"Is there a delay, my lord?" came a gruff but tired voice. It was Master-Serjeant Gam, who'd plodded up from the rear.

"Aye," Guiscard said. "Send the word. We bivouac here."

"Here, my lord?" The seasoned old soldier sounded surprised.

"I doubt we'll find anywhere better on this road. Tell the men to pitch their tents among the trees, but in circles, with thorn switches for cover. Draw lots – one in every ten to stand on guard duty. Four-hour shifts. Make sure you find decent picket points, Gam. We don't know that the enemy's *completely* defeated yet."

The serjeant nodded and stumped away, only for Ignatius to suddenly point and shout. "Ho!"

They glanced south, to where the silver disc of the moon hung beyond the ridge. Two twisted tree trunks were framed against it.

"I thought I saw something," Ignatius said. "*Someone.*"

"Someone?" Guiscard asked.

"He was against the moon. Coming over the rise."

"Probably a stag," d'Avranches said.

"It was a man. Look... *another!*"

This time they all saw the figure. It was tall, rail-thin, and it came quickly over the rise and descended through the darkness towards them. Another followed it, moving jerkily. This one too vanished into the murk. The crackling of wet undergrowth could be heard as the figures drew closer.

"Beggars?" d'Avranches said.

"In the middle of a war?" Guiscard replied. His gloved hand stole to the hilt of his longsword.

"Refugees?"

"And they'd approach an English baggage-train?"

"We should have sent outriders," Ignatius said in a small voice.

"When we give alms to the poor, you can tend to *our* business," d'Avranches advised him. "We'd have lost all contact with outriders in that storm."

"No, he's right," Guiscard said. His voice rose as he spied another two or three figures ascend over the rise. "We should have sent outriders. *Alarum! Alarum! Master-Serjeant, your trumpeter if you pleee...*"

His words ended in a hoarse shout, as he was dragged from his saddle.

D'Avranches and Ignatius were at first too startled to respond. Guiscard shouted incoherently as he wrestled with someone in the muddy ditch on the north side of the road – which, it occurred to them, meant that danger was not just threatening from one side, but from *both*.

Ignatius now spied flurries of movement ahead of them. The point-footman, who'd been carrying a lantern on a pole as he marched at the front of the column, had been knocked from his feet. The pole stood upright in the mud, its lamp swinging wildly, only partly revealing two ragged shapes that were setting about the footman like wolves on a carcass.

"Good God!" d'Avranches said, focussing on dozens of forms suddenly streaming through the misty woods towards them.

Cries began sounding along the road behind. A carrion stench pervaded the entire column. Ignatius stood up and peered back. It was difficult to tell what was happening, but figures seemed to be wrestling between the wagons and carts. Horses whinnied. Someone gave a gargled shriek. Ignatius looked towards the moon – more and more shapes were coming over the rise: tattered and thin but moving with strength and purpose.

Alongside the wagon, Guiscard got back to his feet. He hadn't had time to free his longsword from its scabbard and his shield was still strapped to his back, but he'd managed to draw his dagger and plunge it into his opponent's breast before rolling the body away. However, there was no respite. Another twisted shape lurched at him through the gloom. Guiscard drew his sword and pulled up his coif. In the brief half-second before this new foe attacked, it passed through a ray of moonlight, and he glimpsed its face – its mouth yawning open and glutted with black slime, its eyes hanging from its sockets on stalks. What looked like a rope noose, its tether-end chewed through, was tight around its neck.

Guiscard struck first, swinging his sword in an overhand arc, splitting the abomination from cranium to chin. It still grabbed hold of his tabard, and he had to strike it again, this time hewing through its left shoulder before it overbalanced and fell. He raised his sword a third time, intent on chopping it to pieces, only to be halted by a searing pain in his right calf. Gazing down, he saw his first assailant, the one he'd thought stabbed in the heart, biting through his tough leather leggings. Thrusting his sword down, Guiscard transfixed it via the midriff and leaned on the pommel heavily. With a wet *crunch*, he sheared through its spine and pinned it to the mud, whereupon, rather than dying, it commenced a wild, frenzied thrashing.

Guiscard staggered backward, stunned. There were shouts and screams all around him, along with a weird, inhuman moaning. The stench had become intolerable – thick, putrescent, redolent of burst bowels, stagnant waste. He was leaped onto again, this time from behind. He flipped his body forward and threw his assailant over his head. But more of them ghosted in from the front and side. He unslung his shield and slammed it edge-on into mouth of the nearest one, but the thing only tottered. Guiscard's coif was then ripped backward; cold, mud-covered fingers rent at his hair. He tried to spin round, but hands were also on his throat. He was dragged back down to the mud, where he was unable to use his sword. He unsheathed his dagger again, but it was wrested from his grasp. He hammered at them with his gloved fists, but it made no difference. Fleetingly, a face peered into his that was little more than raddled parchment; its nose was a fleshless cavity, its eyes shrunken orbs rolling in bone sockets.

On the wagon meanwhile, both Hugo d'Avranches and Brother Ignatius were rooted to their bench. They pivoted around, helpless to move or say anything.

"They can't die!" a man-at-arms screamed as he went haring past. He made it several yards into the trees before he was bludgeoned with a knobbly branch. He sank to his knees, only to be overwhelmed by more dark, stumbling figures.

Ignatius shook his head dumbly. He didn't know what he was going to do. He didn't know what he *could* do. But then a weight fell on him from behind. A ragged shape had scaled onto the back of the wagon and scrambled over its canvas-covered cargo. The sheer weight of it bore him from the bench and into the mire.

As a rule, Ignatius didn't like to fight. He felt it incompatible with his vocation. But as scribe and accountant to a professional soldier, it was impossible to avoid the occasional confrontation. He'd prefer not to be wearing mail over his black burel; he'd prefer not to be carrying the cudgel, the round-headed iron club by which clergymen were permitted to wage war. But he was glad of both now. The thing that had him down was cloaked by darkness, though a sickening reek poured off it. It ripped at his throat with bare hands that were slimy and flabby. He kicked at it, making good contact, though of course this was with a sandaled foot rather than a boot or sabaton, and the assailant would not be deterred. Ignatius grabbed the cudgel from his belt and smashed it across his foe's skull, which flew sideways at an angle that surely betokened a broken neck. The thing's grasp was weakened and Ignatius was able to push it off and scramble up.

It was still too dark to see what was happening. Strangely, there was no clangour of blade on blade or blade on shield, but the woods were filled with gruff shouts and agonised shrieks, and always that eerie dirge of moans and mewls.

Stammering the Act of Contrition, Ignatius tried to climb back onto the cart, only for a hand to catch his mail collar and yank him backward. He fell again into the mire. He couldn't see his attackers properly, though they were ragged and wet and stank to high Heaven. The skirts of his robe had flown up and, though he always wore under-garb in winter, this was made of thin linen and was easily torn aside. The next thing he knew, a hand that was hard like wood but as strong as an eagle's talon had gripped his genitals. Ignatius screamed in outrage, but another of them fell on top of him, smothering him with a torso that was like sticks under rotted leather.

Teeth snapped closed on his manhood like the jaws of a steel trap.

Ignatius's shrill squeal, as his maleness was torn from its root, pierced the night. Such pain and horror briefly gave him new strength, and he was able to throw off the figure smothering him, only to see that yet another was standing astride him, silhouetted by the moon. With skeletal arms it raised a heavy stone above its wizened head, and slammed it down onto his face. Blow after mighty blow crushed the monk's youthful features, flattening his tonsured skull until a hideous porridge of blood and brains oozed from his eyes, ears and nostrils.

On the other side of the wagon, Guiscard, caked in mud and filth, was being rent slowly apart. His mail had protected him to some extent, but now they lay on him in a heap, gnawing at his scalp, numerous pairs of claws trying to throttle him. Only with Herculean efforts, did he throw a couple of them off, and kick himself around in a circle to try and scramble back to his feet – but that was when the wagon began to move. On the driving bench, d'Avranches, white-faced with shock, was snapping the reins like a madman. Unnerved by the pandemonium, the horses ploughed forward, the wagon's heavy wheel passing over Guiscard's right leg. Bones exploded as the limb was crushed. Guiscard's ululation was deafening, but d'Avranches didn't hear it. He kept on snapping the reins.

All Guiscard's other cuts and sprains sank to insignificance as he rolled in the treacle of blood, mud and brains. He barely responded as his assailants swarmed back over him, fleshless fingers pinching his tongue, trying to rend it from his mouth, a stinking maw clamping on the side of his face and, with a vicious jerk, gouging out his left eye.

D'Avranches himself didn't get far. The wagon rolled perhaps ten yards before running into deep ruts. For all his whipping and cursing the animals, and for all their strenuous efforts, they made no further progress. Drawing his sword, the aged knight jumped down, but immediately turned an ankle and fell on his blade, snapping it in two. He clambered back to his feet, managing to draw his mattock and bury it in the skull of a figure lurching towards him. It tottered away, taking the mattock with it. D'Avranches's ankle-joint was on fire, but the urge to survive numbed it just enough for him to stumble off along the road. The pole-lantern was still planted a few yards ahead. The point-soldier who'd been felled lay next to it, his crimson innards scattered around him. Those responsible had moved on to attack the wagon train, but of course there were others – many others. D'Avranches hadn't reached the light before he sensed their contorted shadows skulking from the undergrowth to either side, tottering onto the road ahead.

Sweat-soaked and gasping for breath, he halted beside the light. He stared around, but from every direction they were pressing towards him.

He puffed out his chest and thrust back his shoulders. He might have run a few paces when panic overtook him, he might have left his comrades to die, but now he was about to die himself, and he would meet the challenge resolutely – as he'd always been determined to. He drew his final weapon, a small crossbow. Cranking the string back and fitting a dart onto the stock, he took aim. Though aged and corpulent, with legs bandied beneath his immense gut, Hugo d'Avranches was still a knight in the service of Earl Corotocus of Clun and King Edward of England, and he would make sure these rapscallions knew that.

But when they came into the light, it was a different story.

When he saw their cloven skulls, their smashed jaws and eyeless sockets, the clotted brains that caked their blue-green faces, the ribs showing through their worm-eaten rags – his courage failed him.

They were inches away from falling upon him when d'Avranches placed the crossbow at his left temple, and shot its lethal dart deep into his own head.

# CHAPTER NINE

RANULF WAS IN the castle kitchen, with a hunk of bread under one arm and a bowl in his hands, when Hugh du Guesculin caught up with him. After the events of the last few days, Ranulf wasn't particularly hungry, but he now had a full night's watch duty ahead and knew that he had to get something into his belly. In addition, the game broth, which Otto, the earl's corpulent Brabancon cook, now ladled into his bowl from a huge, steaming pot, smelled delicious.

"I've been looking for you," du Guesculin said.

Ranulf didn't at first respond, even though, with nobody else in the kitchen, du Guesculin could hardly have been addressing anyone else.

"FitzOsbern, I said..."

"I hear you," Ranulf said, picking up a spoon.

Du Guesculin smiled in that usual self-satisfied way of his. Stripped of his mail, he now wore comfortable clothes: green hose and a hooded green tunic, with long, unbuttoned sleeves. He had donned a dagger at his belt in place of his sword. He'd even brushed his bobbed black hair and clipped his short moustache; all the more remarkable given that he was sharing the earl's spartan accommodation in the Constable's Tower.

"I hear you've formed quite an attachment to our prisoner?" he said.

Ranulf shrugged. "Then you hear wrongly."

"Ahhh... so you object to being replaced as her personal jailer because you deemed that an easier tour of duty than standing sentry on these walls?"

"At least I'd be out of the weather." Ranulf made to move through the archway into the refectory, but du Guesculin stepped into his path.

"Except that I don't believe a word of it, FitzOsbern."

Ranulf feigned shock. "You don't?"

"I believe that you feel sorry for the girl, or guilty about the way she's been treated, and are now concerned for her welfare."

"What you believe or don't believe is of no importance to me."

Ranulf pushed his way past and sauntered down a flight of four steps into the refectory, a low, vaulted chamber, lined with benches and long tables, but currently empty due to the lateness of the hour. He sat, tore his bread into pieces and, one by one, began to dunk them in the broth. He tried not to show irritation when du Guesculin sat down across the table from him.

"You really dislike me, don't you, FitzOsbern?"

"I don't have any feelings about you at all."

"Do I disgust you?"

Ranulf smiled. "You don't really want me to answer that question, do you?"

Du Guesculin pursed his lips. "You consider that you're not part of this tragic affair, is that right?"

"I wish I wasn't."

"How noble of you. But let's not conveniently forget the past, FitzOsbern. You are only in the earl's service because you yourself are a murderer."

Ranulf eyed him coldly, but continued to eat.

"Don't be embarrassed about it," du Guesculin added. "There are few men who reach your age in the order of merit without making... shall we say 'errors of judgement'. Even fewer reach Earl Corotocus's age. Tell me, what did you think of his wife, Countess Isabel?"

"I never met her," Ranulf said, wondering where this was leading.

"She died a considerable time ago, of course. Now that I think about it, well before you joined the earl's mesnie." The banneret hooked his thumbs under his straining belt in an effort to get more comfortable. "Contrary to popular legend, it was not the earl's dark moods that drove Countess Isabel to her early grave. In fact, he was very devoted to her. When they married, she had few prospects. She was the daughter of a landless troubadour, who came to England during the reign of Henry III. She brought no title, no dowry. It was a love-match, you see. Earl Corotocus hoped to raise a family with her – to have many children. Unfortunately, it didn't work out that way. Four times she failed to deliver a living child. The final occasion was the death of her. Earl Corotocus was devastated. He never tried to marry again, and his entire personality changed. He became a colder, harder man…"

"What are you trying to say, du Guesculin? That having failed to build an empire of the heart, Earl Corotocus sought to build an empire of land?"

"Something like that."

"And why are you telling me all this?"

"I thought I should give you some insight into his character."

Ranulf laughed as he dunked more bread and crammed it into his mouth.

Du Guesculin watched him carefully. "And into mine."

"I don't need insights into your character, du Guesculin. I know it perfectly well already. You're the earl's device, a mechanism, a thing of cogs and wheels rather than flesh and blood."

"How eloquently you speak… for a rogue knight without a penny to his name."

"You can thank my mother for that. At her insistence, I was taught much more than the skills to bear arms. Many lessons I learned at her knee, du Guesculin. I loved her deeply. When she died, I too was devastated. But I didn't become a tyrannical savage."

"Again, how noble of you. You're too perfect, FitzOsbern. It's almost a pity to sully your angelic thoughts with harsh practicalities, but I shall do it anyway, as we all will benefit. You're aware that the Welsh girl we hold is lawful heiress to most of Powys, the largest province in Wales?"

"Of course. And?"

Du Guesculin chuckled. "You may be a fierce warrior and a learned speaker, but you clearly lack a political grasp. Think about this. Earl Corotocus already holds the March, and a number of disparate lordships on both sides of the Welsh border, but they are dotted here, there and everywhere. Were he to be made undisputed lord and master over all of Powys, he would control the entire middle section of Wales, its absolute heartland. Think of the potential of this. There would be no more scope for rebellion running the length and breadth of the country. In fact, there would be no scope for rebellion at all. The border wars would end."

"And would the people of Powys serve the earl willingly after the things he's done here?"

"What matter? They would still serve him – willingly or unwillingly – because they would have no choice. Oh certainly, there would be hostility. But you know the truth about Wales – their own princes have been as cruel or incompetent, or both, as any Anglo-Norman lord imposed by the Crown. In time they would acquiesce, and the earl could relax his stranglehold. Life would become easier for everyone."

"They might not acquiesce so quickly if they perceive that he has wrested the province by force from their rightful liege, Countess Madalyn."

Du Guesculin smiled. "This is the clever part, FitzOsbern. Perhaps there is no need for him to wrest it by force… if he can acquire it by marriage."

Ranulf shook his head with slow disbelief. "You mean to Lady Gwendolyn?"

"No, of course not – to her invisible twin sister! Who else do you think I mean?"

"The king would never agree to that."

"Of course he would. The king is in the process of fully incorporating Wales into the realm. And he'll use any method available to him. If that means investing one of his most loyal vassals with a significant portion of it, why should he even hesitate?"

"Countess Madalyn would never agree."

"What does that matter?"

"Lady Gwendolyn would never agree."

"Ah!" Du Guesculin raised a finger. "That is where you play *your* part, FitzOsbern. If you have genuine feelings for the girl, perhaps it would suit all of us if you were to, shall we say, 'advise her where her best interests might lie'?"

"I see. And where do you play *your* part?"

Du Guesculin puffed his cheeks at the burdensome task that he himself faced. "I need to convince Earl Corotocus. He has no patience with these Welsh. He sees them as outsiders, barbarous brutes. He'd want to spend as little time here as possible."

"In which case he would appoint a seneschal to rule his Welsh lands for him, no?"

Du Guesculin made a vague gesture. "Quite possibly."

"And that, du Guesculin, is where you *really* play your part?"

"I have served his lordship faithfully for twenty years. Is it not time I was rewarded?"

Ranulf gave a wry smile. "If I'm not mistaken, you have extensive lands around Whitchurch, with matching estates at Oswestry?"

"You are not mistaken, FitzOsbern. But Wales is new territory, and much wilder. I think there will be a greater degree of autonomy."

Ranulf laughed. "You mean you can rule like a great nobleman? Maybe even take a title? Count of Lyr? What about Earl of Powys... how does that sound?"

Du Guesculin stiffened at the mocking tone. "What I propose is perfectly reasonable."

"Why don't you just go the whole hog, du Guesculin? Travel to Rome, make up some scandalous lies about your own wife's lack of fidelity, get an annulment, then return and woo the Welsh girl yourself?"

"I've explained the situation," du Guesculin said, standing up. "From this point it's up to you. As things stand, the Lady Gwendolyn is our enemy and our hostage. Becoming her friend would not be the wisest course. The earl already has half an eye on you as someone he doesn't fully trust. On the other hand, were you to make your relationship with the girl profitable to us, things could be very different."

"Different for whom?"

"You and your father have nothing, boy. When you are released from the earl's service, assuming you survive that long, you will still have nothing. I, however, may have important posts to fill here in Wales. Why not think about that?"

He strode from the table.

"Du Guesculin!" Ranulf called after him.

Du Guesculin turned on the steps.

"Du Guesculin, what do you not understand about the meaning of the word 'atrocity'? These people hate us with a passion that you apparently can't conceive."

Du Guesculin shrugged. "Hatred is one emotion that can be bought and sold, FitzOsbern. Some day, I will prove that to you."

# CHAPTER TEN

THERE WAS NO cockcrow to announce the dawn.

Ranulf first became aware of it when a finger of light crept along the eastern horizon. He and Gurt Louvain had held the night watch together and were on the south curtain-wall, gloved, hooded, wrapped in their cloaks and crouched against a brazier, which was now virtually dead. They'd barely spoken during the long, slow hours. Similar small groups were dotted at regular intervals around the entire circumference of the castle. They too were muted; as silent as the effigies the company had found on arriving here. Some of the weird mannequins still lay on the wall walk, though most, having unnerved the men with their mocking expressions, had been torn to pieces or hurled down into the bailey.

Gurt muttered something about the morning coming at last. Ranulf grunted an acknowledgement. He laid his sword against the embrasure and lifted the timber panel to peer out. The only sound was the soft ripple of the river as it slid by in a glassy sheet. The woods on its far shore were still in darkness.

"I don't know about you, but I'm ready to sleep," Gurt said. He was pale, sallow faced, and clearly younger than Ranulf had first thought. His unshaved whiskers and the dust and dirt of the campaign had for a time masked his youthfulness. His tall, solid physique and strong Northumbrian accent had also made him seem older.

"How did you end up in the earl's debt, Gurt?" Ranulf asked.

"Well," Gurt replied, "it wasn't easy."

He chuckled. Ranulf chuckled too. It alleviated things a little.

"I was squired to John de Warenne."

"The Earl of Surrey?" Ranulf said, surprised.

"Yes."

"Quite a character."

"And a great tourneyor." Gurt became thoughtful. "He taught me a lot. When I was knighted, he attached me to the household of his senior tenant, Walter Bigod."

"Another legend."

"And another great tourneyor. We fought at all the major events – London, Northampton, Dunstable. I did well personally. Or so I thought. In truth I didn't really understand the value of money. My sister was married to a landed knight in Yorkshire. He died not long after they exchanged vows. Hugh of Cressingham, the king's grasping treasurer, was my sister's overlord. He sought to claim the escheat and turn her out. I stepped in and offered to buy the fief as a smallholding, using my personal fortune. Those were the actual words I used, 'my personal fortune'."

He smiled bitterly.

"I was naïve. There was little land attached to that fee – a few roods, a couple of plough-teams, a fishpond. Barely enough to keep the cottars alive, let alone we two and the families we both hoped to have when we found spouses. Eventually I offered to sell it back to Cressingham. In fact, I offered it to him as a gift if he would provide for us in some capacity. But he wasn't interested. The estate had acquired debts. That was when Earl Corotocus stepped in, proposing to settle what we owed and take charge of the property. He had lands close by, and saw our estate as a tactical purchase. If I'd known that, maybe I could have struck a harder bargain. As it was, I was grateful to have the financial millstone taken off me. In return for that favour, my sister became his ward and I was bound to seven years military service."

"Seven years?" Ranulf said. "I didn't see you in Gascony."

"I only began paying my dues last January. Already I'm regretting it. Does it get any easier campaigning with Earl Corotocus?"

Ranulf snorted.

"How about you?" Gurt asked. "What do you owe him?"

"What don't we owe him?" Ranulf shook his head. "My family lost everything in the blood feud between Bohun of Hereford and Clare of Gloucester. That was quite an unpleasant affair. Hereford and Gloucester had never been easy neighbours. In fact, they fought over just about everything. But the real conflict broke out between them over the castle of Morlais. It was a bitter squabble, which turned repeatedly into open violence. Raid followed raid. There were brawls in taverns, brawls on the highway, kidnappings. My father was Hereford's vassal, so he played a full part. The king eventually had them all arrested – that was in 1292, and the charge was waging private war. The two earls were fined heavily and had land confiscated by the Crown. My father and selected other knights, who'd declared for their overlords, were disinherited. Overnight, we went from landed gentry to destitution. My mother was ill at the time and unable to stand the shock."

"I'm sorry," Gurt said.

"It happens. She had the sweating sickness and might've died anyway. The main thing is, with mother dead, my father became errant again. He took me out of squiredom and knighted me himself. Like you, we fought in the tournaments, but as privateers. We did moderately well – made enough to live. But later that year, at Clarendon, father's destrier was wounded in the thigh and lamed. Not only did we take nothing from the tournament, our earning potential was halved. Desperate, we travelled to Wayland Fair, where we put every penny we had into buying father a new horse. It was a fine specimen, and even at that hefty price we thought it was a bargain. Then, three days later, we were accosted in a tavern by one Philip de Courcy, nephew to the Bishop of Norwich. He said he recognised the horse. Claimed it was one he'd had stolen not three months earlier, and accused us of theft. Father was outraged, but also worried. We were landless knights, nobodies without protectors – and this was a capital offence. So we demanded trial by battle. We two, father said, would fight de Courcy and any three of his knights, either in pairs or all at the same time. We would prove our innocence before God. Perhaps realising that, with our lives at stake, we were very serious about this matter, de Courcy took the latter option. Even so, it was a one-sided affair. Up to that time, I imagine de Courcy had bullocked his way through life on the strength of his uncle's name. Two of his men were wounded and withdrew from the fight early, and then de Courcy was killed. It was my blow that struck him. With this very sword."

Ranulf lifted his longsword from the embrasure. Like most battle swords, it was functional rather than handsome. Its two-edged blade had been honed many times, but was still chipped and scarred. Its great cross-hilt was bound with leather.

"I cut through his aventail and severed his windpipe." Ranulf re-enacted the fatal swipe. "*My* blow, but father said that if there was any blame, *he* would take it." He relapsed into brooding silence.

"There was blame attached?" Gurt eventually asked.

"Of course, even though we had many witnesses. The contest was fought on an open meadow outside the town, with the reeve's full permission. But the bishop, who also happened to be sheriff of that county, was enraged by the outcome. He had us arrested and imposed a massive wergild. There was no possibility we could pay it. It looked like death for us. But word of the incident had now reached the ears of Earl Corotocus, who was en route to Yarmouth with his army to take ship to Gascony. Always on the lookout for 'special soldiers', as he called them, he was happy to pay the fine for us."

"And how long have you been returning that favour?"

"To date it's been three years. We have seven remaining."

Gurt looked puzzled. "You might have lost the war in Gascony, but surely you took booty? Couldn't you have bought your way out by now?"

"Father has never wanted to."

"Your father would rather serve? He seems a mild man."

Ranulf stood up, stretching the cramp from his chilled limbs. Again, he lifted the panel. Milky daylight was flooding across the Welsh landscape. White vapour hung in its fathomless woods.

"In his old age, father's become introspective. 'Forget the tournament', he says. 'Earl Corotocus fights *real* wars. That's where the plunder is. When we've served our term, we'll be wealthy. Our lives will be restored'."

"And I thought he wanted to while away this war in the safety of Grogen Castle?"

Ranulf shrugged. His father had become a conundrum to him. Even though only a few years had passed, it was difficult to compare the pale, withdrawn figure that Ulbert FitzOsbern now was with the laughing, brawling, golden-haired seigneur who'd once welcomed all guests – whether bidden or unbidden – to his stockaded manor house at Byford, who'd always ridden in his overlord's vanguard roaring like a demon, twirling his battle-axe around his head. Regret, guilt, a sense of failure – they could do strange things to even the toughest man.

"It's hardship, misery… penance for the loss of our home," Ranulf finally said. "To father, this service is something we deserve. Something we must work off through blood and toil, though under Earl Corotocus it's usually someone else's blood."

"And that doesn't worry your father?"

"Not as much as it once did. Once, he was a moral man, a strict adherent to the code. Now he is focussed purely on 'cleaning his slate', as he calls it."

Gurt was about to reply when they heard a curious noise. At first they weren't sure what it was or where it came from – it echoed over the river and into the forest on the south shore. They glanced around, puzzled. Slowly, it became clear that what they were hearing was a voice calling out – but a fearsome, pealing voice, eerily high pitched.

"Eaaarl Corotocus!" it seemed to be saying, though the distance and the acoustics of the castle's outer rampart distorted it. "Eaaarl Corotocus!"

Gurt leaned through the embrasure. All along the curtain-wall, the other sentries were doing the same. As one, they looked unnerved.

"It's coming from somewhere to the west," Ranulf said.

From their position, they could just make out the south edge of the western bluff. The Inner Fort and the towering edifice of the Constable's Tower masked the rest of it.

"Eaaarl Corotocus!" the voice called again. It sounded female, though there was nothing sweet or gentle in it.

"What the devil's happening?" Gurt wondered.

Ranulf offered to go and see, suggesting that Gurt stay at his post. Gurt nodded, buckling on his sword-belt.

The quickest access down into the bailey from the curtain-wall was afforded by a mass of support scaffolding, which had various ladders zigzagging through it. Ranulf scaled down one of these, and followed the bailey around the outskirts of the Inner Fort until he'd reached the castle's northwest corner, at which point he climbed a steep flight of steps and passed through a barred postern onto the Barbican. From here, he entered the Gatehouse and traipsed back along the Causeway to the Constable's Tower. In total it was a ten-minute walk, and he still had to ascend to the roof of the Constable's Tower, by which time Earl Corotocus had been wakened from his slumber.

The earl, clad only in boots and leather breaches, with a bearskin cloak swathed around his muscular torso, was by the western battlements. He looked uncharacteristically tousled, though marginally less so than Hugh du Guesculin, who had also thrown on a cloak but still looked ridiculous in a full-length woollen nightgown. Navarre, more predictably, was already harnessed for war in his mail and leather. This applied to several other of the earl's household knights, who had been posted here and had shared the night watch between them. Of Corotocus's lieutenants, only Davy Gou, captain of the royal archers, and Morgaynt Carew, the Welsh malcontent, were present. At the north end of the Causeway, Garbofasse and his mercenaries watched from the top of the Gatehouse.

"Eaaarl Corotocus!" the voice came again, just as Ranulf emerged onto the roof. "Earl Corotocus, I know you are in there!"

"Good God," the earl said with slow disbelief.

Ranulf joined him by the battlements. On the western bluff, several figures were ranged a few yards apart. One was on horseback and positioned further down the slope from the others. By her shape, she was a woman. She wore flowing white robes, and had long, flame-red hair.

"Is that the Countess of Lyr?" du Guesculin asked, astonished.

Ranulf leaned forward, but there was no mistaking her. The early morning murk had cleared, to leave the sky cloudless and pebble-blue. The other figures were men. They also wore white, but their hoods were drawn up, showing only their beards

"Eaaarl Corotocus!" the countess cried again, her strident tone echoing. "You are a liar, a thief and a murderer! And I am here to tell you that your tyranny will not be endured. Neither in this land, nor on our border."

Ranulf glanced at the earl. Corotocus was stony-faced but listening intently.

"Earl Corotocus, you and your garrison will vacate Caergrogwyn! After that you will vacate the march. But before you do any of these things, you will surrender your arms and armour, and any plunder you have taken from my people. You will also return my daughter, Gwendolyn. Be warned, if she has been harmed in any way, the price for you and your men is death."

"Feisty bitch," Carew muttered.

"She's got spirit, I'll give her that," Corotocus said. He turned to one of Gou's archers. "You, fellow? Can you strike her from here?"

The archer took off his broad-brimmed helmet and shielded his eyes. "She may be out of range, my lord."

"Try anyway." Corotocus turned not just to the other royal archers present, but to bowmen from his own company. "All of you. A purse of gold for the first man to hit her."

The bowmen set about their task, flexing and stringing their longbows, and letting fly. But it was impossible. First, they had to clear the bailey yard, then the outer curtain-wall, then the moat, and after all that the countess was still high on the bluff, from which she watched their efforts with studied silence. One by one, the goose shafts whistled harmlessly into the abyss.

"We have ballistae in the southwest tower," du Guesculin said. "Any of those will knock her from her insolent perch, my lord. I only need have them brought up here."

Corotocus shook his head. "It's not worth the trouble."

"My men have the trebuchet on the Barbican," Carew said.

"Why waste a valuable missile?"

"We should send someone out there," Navarre snarled. "She's insulted you in front of your men. She must face the consequence."

"Insults don't trouble me, Navarre. The men will stop listening after a while. Let her rot out there."

The earl made to go below, but the countess called again.

"Eaaarl Corotocus! Your silence does you no credit. You are a coward who hides behind his king's walls rather than faces his enemy in the field."

"Away, woman!" he shouted back. His face had reddened slightly. "Be thankful your daughter hasn't become my soldiers' plaything."

"That would be very like you, Earl Corotocus," she replied. "To vent your wrath on a helpless child. Just as you vented it on Anwyl's men after first tricking them into disarming themselves. Do you ever stand and fight, lord of the realm? Have you ever won a battle with bravery alone?"

Corotocus was aware of his soldiers listening along the castle's western walls. They knew he was a fierce warrior and skilled commander, but they also knew that he paid no heed to the customs of chivalry. Maybe, for the first time, some of them were wondering about the apparent non-courageousness of this policy.

"Let me go out there." Navarre begged. "I'll silence the hag."

"It might be an idea after all," Corotocus said. "Too many rabble-rousers go unpunished these days."

"Who are those people with her?" Ranulf wondered.

"Whoever they are," Navarre said, "they'll share her fate."

Ranulf turned to the earl. "My lord, before we attack, might I speak to her?"

Corotocus raised an eyebrow. "You think you can do better than I?"

"With respect, you deceived her once. She might find it difficult to trust you."

Navarre spat. "We don't need her to trust us! She should be hanged and quartered, as Prince Dafydd was."

Ranulf ignored him. "My lord, pacification should follow conquest. Isn't that always King Edward's will?"

Corotocus shrugged. "Try if you wish."

Ranulf turned and shouted: "Countess Madalyn!"

"Who speaks?" she called back.

"An English knight."

"Once you'd have been proud to wear that title."

"Whore," Navarre muttered.

"The war is over," Ranulf shouted. "It makes no sense to start it again."

"This war will never be over until Earl Corotocus and his like have ceased to threaten my people."

"You seek further destruction, madam? Madog's rebel army has been vanquished."

"You may break our bodies, English knight, but you will never break our spirit."

"Countess Madalyn... there will be more deaths."

There was a brief silence, before she replied: "Only yours."

"That's what you get for reasoning with ignoramuses," Navarre stated. He turned to the earl, pulling on his gauntlets. "I'll bring you her breasts, my lord, so that you can play *jeux de paume* with them."

Corotocus nodded.

"I wouldn't be too hasty, Navarre," Ranulf said. "Look."

Additional figures had begun to appear on the bluff, not just from the wooded area above the countess, but all along the western ridge. Within a few moments there were several hundred of them, but more continued to swell their ranks.

"Dear God," du Guesculin breathed. "Who are they?"

Navarre's angry self-assurance had faded a little, but he still sneered. "They don't look much like soldiers."

It was difficult to tell for certain. Over this distance, the gathering force was comprised of diminutive figures, none of whom could be seen clearly. There was the occasional glint of mail or war-harness, though most seemed to be wearing peasant garb, and tattered peasant garb at that. One or two – and at first Ranulf thought he was hallucinating – seemed to be naked. This sent a greater prickle of unease down his spine than their overall numbers did. There was now perhaps a thousand of them, but still more were appearing.

"From the north too, my lord," someone shouted.

Everyone looked, and saw processions of figures crossing the high moors to the north of the castle. They were thinly spread, moving in small groups or ones and twos, and, in many cases, limping or stumbling as though starved or crippled. They resembled refugees rather than soldiers, but all together there must have been several thousand of them. By the time they joined the countess on the western bluff, they'd be a prodigious host. Although the English held this bastion and were armed to the teeth, they were suddenly outnumbered to a worrying degree.

"Still think you can buy and sell the Welsh people, du Guesculin?" Ranulf muttered.

Du Guesculin couldn't answer; he had blanched.

"They're still only peasants," Navarre scoffed.

"If so, they're armed," Ranulf observed.

"What are scythes and reaping hooks to us?"

"I see real weapons," Carew said.

Most of the ragged shapes were carrying implements, and though many of these looked to be little more than clubs or broken farm tools, others were clearly swords, axes, poll-arms.

"Where the devil did they get their hands on those?" du Guesculin said.

"Our artillery train maybe?" Ranulf glanced at Crotocus. "Wasn't it expected to arrive last night?"

The earl didn't reply, but regarded the gathering horde with growing wariness.

"My lord, this is some riff-raff," Navarre protested. "They won't assault this castle. How could they possibly expect to take it?"

"What is that ungodly stink?" someone asked.

A noxious smell, like spoiled meat, was drifting on the breeze.

"Pig farmers, ditch diggers," Navarre said. "Which is all they are."

"That, my lords, is the smell of war," the earl said abruptly. "Muster your men, if you please. Prepare for battle!"

# CHAPTER ELEVEN

BELLS RANG THROUGHOUT the castle for most of that morning. Clarions sounded in every section. But Countess Madalyn waited in silence on the western bluff, as did her army, its disordered ranks eerily still. By eleven o'clock, the walls of Grogen Castle were bristling with swords, spears and arrows knocked on strings; every defender was fully mailed. Even the grooms and pages had been called up and given blades. And yet still nothing happened.

Ranulf, on the south curtain-wall, with Gurt to his right and Ulbert to his left, wondered if this delay owed to some previously unseen notion of Welsh chivalry, but he soon dismissed the idea. More likely the countess was waging a mental attack before the physical one. She was letting it be known that she had no concern about whether the English were prepared to receive her or not; that she was undeterred by their readiness, their armour, their weaponry. The battle would only commence when she decided, for it was she, not Earl Corotocus, who was dictating this day's strategy.

Of course, Earl Corotocus was never one to waste an opportunity. While the countess dallied, he'd prepared his defences to their utmost. Though his personal artillery wagons might not have arrived, the castle had several engines of its own, and these were quickly marshalled. On the Barbican, Carew and his men, under the direction of William d'Abbetot, prepared the trebuchet, swivelling it round on its colossal timber turntable so that it faced the western bluff, then stockpiling rocks and lead weights, some as heavy as four hundred pounds. It took three of them to load just one such missile into the sling, and half the company to pour sweat as they lined a dozen more in the trough. They also set aside a pile of 'devil's sachets' – linen sacks, loosely tied with lace, each one containing ten smaller boulders, a payload that would spread mid-flight and cut a gory swath through massed infantry. At the entrance to the Gatehouse, meanwhile, the gate was locked and chained, the portcullis drawn down. Behind this, a fire-raiser was brought into position. This was a fiendish device: a massive steel tube mounted on two wheeled carts. At one end, a gigantic pair of bellows allowed its crew to expel wind through it at great force. At the other, which flared like a trumpet and, with a deliberate sense of irony, had been carved to resemble the gaping mouth of a Welsh dragon, a cauldron was suspended and filled with lighted coals, sulphur and pitch. When working at full capacity, great billowing clouds of flame could be expelled by it, engulfing anyone who managed to tear down the outer gate and attack the portcullis.

In the southwest tower, there were four levels of ballistae. The lower two comprised polybolas, immense crossbows designed to project large single bolts and fitted with windlasses and magazines so that they could discharge repeatedly and quickly. The upper two levels contained lighter weapons, archery machines constructed with cradles from which sixteen clothyard arrows – fitted either with barbed or swallow-tailed heads – could be shot at the same time. All these frightful devices were built into the actual fabric of the tower, in specially designed rooms containing masses of scaffolding, and angled at a downward slant so to discharge through horizontal ports cut into the outer wall. On the normal parapets on the top of the other towers and turrets, and on the curtain-wall, every archer and crossbowman had ample time to accumulate bushels of arrows. The rest of the men provided themselves with other, less sophisticated missiles – stones, spears, javelins, grenades made from interwoven nails and spikes, and barrels of naptha – a highly flammable mixture of oil and resin, which they could pour on the heads of their assailants.

Father Benan was visibly unnerved by these preparations. He'd seen war before of course, but had previously stayed clear of the actual battlefield.

"I shall return to the chapel and sing a mass for the preservation of our souls," he said, crossing himself at the sight of so many axes, mattocks and cleavers.

"Sing one for the Welsh first," Corotocus advised him. "I'll soon be sending a hundred-score of them to God's hall of judgement.

But if the Welsh were daunted by the sight of the rearmed stronghold, there was no sign. In fact, Ranulf didn't think he'd ever seen as quiet or composed an enemy. Only as the noise of the English activity – the clanking of mail-clad feet on steps and walkways, the clinking of hammers, the rattling of chains, the shouting and the banging and bolting of iron doors – faded, did he realise that no sound at all issued from the vast army outside, except perhaps for a distant low moaning, which more likely was the wind hissing on the wild Welsh moors. There was no beating of drums, no blasting of horns, no guttural roars as the various companies psyched themselves up for combat. Yet neither did he think he'd ever seen so drab a band. He didn't expect glorious heraldry, but few banners or standards flew. The predominant colours were greys and browns; many of the enemy sported nothing more than filthy rags. And, of course, there was that foul fetor, which had got steadily thicker until it now seemed to have settled over the castle in a malodorous shroud.

"How many of them, would you say?" Gurt wondered. "Ten thousand?"

"Even ten thousand wouldn't normally be enough to assail a fortress like this," Ranulf replied. "But..."

"But?"

Ranulf couldn't explain.

"Don't worry, I know," Gurt said. "Sometimes emotion alone will win the day. You can only tyrannise a population so much before it turns on you like a tiger."

"Are you a student of treason as well, Master Louvain?" Walter Margas wondered, walking past them towards the nearest ladder. Despite his age and world-weariness, he was still an efficient eavesdropper. "You two are made for each other. You should get a room in a tavern sometime where you can whimper your sedition together."

"Are you leaving us, Walter?" Ranulf asked. "Surely not? Not when the battle's just about to start?"

Margas's wizened cheeks coloured. "Perhaps you'd rather I defecated up here on the parapet?"

"I'd rather you got back to your post. You can drop your guts with everyone else, when the fighting's over."

"Are you calling my courage into question, sirrah?"

"You were very active on the River Ogryn, as I recall. Riding against unarmed footmen. These odds are less to your fancy, I take it?"

Margas's lips tightened with rage. "When this is over, FitzOsbern, I'll report you both to the earl. You'll find he takes a dim view of those who spread defeatism."

"If you're hiding in the privy, how will you know when it's over?" Gurt asked.

Margas was visibly furious. Spittle leaked into his unkempt beard – but there was nothing else he could do. Aware that others were listening and watching, he trudged back along the wall to his post.

"Useless sack of puke," Gurt said under his breath.

"He likes his cowardly butchers, does Earl Corotocus," Ranulf added.

"If you gentlemen would concentrate on the day," Ulbert interrupted them, "I'd be obliged. There's movement afoot."

To the west, large numbers of the Welsh host were suddenly shambling – *shambling* was the only word Ranulf could think of – down the bluff towards the southwest bridge. There was nothing military about it. They descended in a mob, stumbling, jostling each other. In appearance they were lambs to the slaughter, for they marched neither behind shields nor beneath a protective barrage of missiles.

On the Constable's Tower, Navarre laughed.

"This is going to be too easy, my lord."

Corotocus said nothing, but watched carefully.

The southwest bridge was extremely narrow, and had neither barriers nor fences on either side of it. It had been constructed this way deliberately so that visitors to the castle – whether welcome or unwelcome – could only file across it two at a time, and all the way would be in danger of falling off. The southwest tower, which directly overlooked it, didn't just contain the ballistae, but had been allocated to the crossbowmen, and these were the first to strike. Their bolts began slanting down. The rest of the defenders watched expectantly for the Welsh to start dropping, and for a resulting pile-up of bodies as those behind tripped over them. But this didn't happen. The Welsh crammed onto the bridge regardless of the deadly rain.

"They call themselves 'royal archers'?" Gurt said. "They haven't hit a damn thing!"

Ranulf was equally confused. The king's crossbowmen were supposedly elite troops, highly disciplined and skilled.

"Village bumpkins couldn't miss from that range," Ulbert said.

The downward slope of the bluff was log-jammed with figures, all pushing mindlessly forward. They were hardly difficult to hit. The crossbows in the southwest tower were now joined by longbows stationed further along the curtain-wall, these too in the hands of expert marksmen from the royal house. Sleek shafts glittered through the noon sunlight as they sped from on high, though no obvious carnage resulted. However, it was soon clear that they actually *were* striking their targets, as indeed were the crossbow bolts – but the targets kept on coming. The first few had reached the other side of the bridge and were on the berm, at the very foot of the southwest tower. Those defenders at that part of the castle marvelled that there seemed to be women among them. Not only that, but a lot of the Welsh were already bloodied, in some cases heavily as though from severe wounds. Bewilderment and fear spread among the English. Several of the Welsh visibly bore the broken shafts of arrows. One half-naked fellow appeared to have been transfixed through the chest, yet still he hobbled over the bridge.

On the Constable's Tower they could do little more than shout encouragement to their bowmen, but they too were baffled by what they were seeing.

"They must be better armoured than they appeared to be," Navarre said.

Corotocus didn't respond. His heavier weapons now spoke for him, the polybolas projecting their terrible four-foot missiles, the archery machines unleashing showers of arrows, the shafts of which rattled onto the stonework of the bridge, riddling those figures caught in their path.

The effects were satisfyingly ghastly. With their bodkin points and wide, fin-like blades, the ballista bolts drove clean across the bridge into the massed throng on the other side, ploughing bloody alleyways. There were roars of delight from the castle walls. For a brief second the bridge was no longer crowded – ten or twenty figures had pitched over the side into the moat, falling thirty feet onto the rocks below. Some remained on the bridge, but had been felled where they stood. Yet it wasn't long before this latter group got back to their feet, despite their horrendous wounds. One's head had hinged backward, hanging by threads of sinew. Another had been sheared through the left thigh – incredibly, almost comically, he recommenced his advance by hopping. The laughter slowly died on the castle walls. Even the archery seemed to falter in intensity. Ranulf's hair prickled as he sighted one fellow coming off the bridge who looked to have been pierced by an arrow clean through his skull.

Inside the southwest tower, it was a chaos of dust, sweat and flaring candle-light as the ballista serjeants bawled at their crews to work harder. Frantic efforts were made as magazines were spent and new ones fitted onto the sliders, as winches were worked to ratchet the catgut bowstrings back into position. With repeated, ear-dulling bangs, each new missile was unleashed as soon as it could be placed. There was no attempt to aim. Because of the angle of vent in the tower wall, the projectiles were always shot cleanly onto the bridge. And again they wrought horrible carnage, slicing figures in half, gutting them where they stood. One bolt hurtled across in a black blur, pinioning a Welshman through the midriff, carrying him with it, pinioning another, carrying him, and even pinioning a third – three men like fish flopping on a spear – before it plunged into the midst of their countrymen on the far side. The archery machines sewed the ground on both sides of the bridge with arrows. Countless more Welsh were caught in this relentless fusillade, many of them hit multiple times – through the arms, through the body, through the legs – and yet still, though reduced to limping, seesawing wrecks, they proceeded across.

"This is not possible," Gurt shouted. "There should be a carpet of corpses by now. I don't see a single bloody one!"

On the Constable's Tower, Earl Corotocus summoned a nervous squire.

"Take a message to Captain Musard in the southwest tower, boy. Tell him that, Familiaris Regis or not, if he and his men don't start *killing* these brainless oafs, I'll send them outside with sticks and stones to see if they can do a better job that way."

When the message was delivered, the bombardment on the bridge intensified. The air whistled with goose-feathers. The Welsh crossing over were struck again and again. Dozens more were knocked into the moat, hurtling to its rocky floor, and yet, like those who'd fallen before them, always scrambling back to their feet no matter how broken or mutilated their bodies. They even tried to climb back out, and with some degree of success. A feat that seemed inhuman given that the moat walls were mostly sheer rock.

Ranulf glanced sidelong at his father. Ulbert had lifted the visor on his helmet; always stoic in the face of battle, it was disconcerting to see that he wore a haunted expression.

Many Welsh were now progressing eastwards along the berm, intent on circling the castle and approaching the main entrance at its northwest corner. This meant that the defenders on the curtain-wall were also able to assault them.

Lifting the hatches in the wall walk, they had a bird's eye view of the enemy trailing past below, and so dropped boulders or flung grenades and javelins. It had negligible effect, even though numerous missiles appeared to hit cleanly. The sheer force of impact hurled some Welsh into the river and the current carried them away, though even then they writhed and struggled – albeit with broken torsos, sundered skulls, eye-sockets punctured by arrows. Ranulf saw one Welshman clamber back out from the water, only to be struck by an anvil with shattering effect, blood and brains spattering from a skull that simply folded on itself – and yet he got back to his feet and continued to march. Gurt saw another struck by a thrown mallet; the mallet's iron head lodged in the upper part of the fellow's nose, its handle jutting crazily forward like a rhino's horn – and yet the Welshman, who already looked as if his lower jaw was missing and whose upper body was caked with dried gore, trudged onward.

No agonised screeches or froth-filled gargles greeted the defenders' efforts. There was a sound of sorts – that low moaning, which initially the English had mistaken for the wind. Now that the Welsh were so close, it was clear they themselves were the source of it. But it wasn't just a moaning – it was a keening, a mindless mewling; utterly soulless and inhuman.

At the southwest bridge, more and more Welsh fighters poured over to the other side. Inside the southwest tower, the ballista serjeants yelled at their men until they were hoarse. Bowstrings snapped under the strain and were urgently replaced; the cranks and gears of the war-machines heated and heated until they couldn't be touched. Captain Musard came down again from the tower roof, now frantic. He threw himself to the vents to look out. The enemy should have been lying in heaps on both sides of the bridge. They should have been cluttering the bridge itself. The moat should have been running red with their blood, stacked with their mangled corpses. But it wasn't. Each new salvo darkened the sky. The impacts of missiles slamming into bone and tearing through flesh were deafening. Yet always the Welsh came on. Musard watched, goggle-eyed, as a trio of limping Welshmen crossed the bridge in single file, skewered together on the same length of shaft. He ordered them cut down, butchered. He vowed death for any bowman who failed to strike them. One after another, darts and arrows found their mark, embedding themselves deeply but not even slowing the demonic threesome.

By now, the foremost of the Welsh attackers had reached the point of the curtain-wall where Ranulf, Ulbert and Gurt were stationed.

Ranulf saw one who had lost his left arm, left shoulder and much of the left side of his torso. It had presumably been torn away by a ballista bolt – jagged bones, bloodied and dangling with tissue, jutted out – yet the creature still marched. More to the point, he wasn't even bleeding. The air around him should have been sprayed crimson. Ranulf was so entranced by this unreal vision that when his father clamped a mailed hand onto his shoulder, he jumped with fright.

"Fire!" Ulbert said. "Ranulf, wake up for Christ's sake! We must use fire!"

The call went along the battlements, but only slowly. Barrels of naptha were wrestled forward, but many defenders were in such a daze that they might have tossed them over as they were. Ulbert had to shout to prevent the precious mixture being wasted.

"Timber!" he cried, pushing his way along the walk. "We need timber too, down on the berm. We must form a barricade and ignite it. Bottle them up along the path and we can burn them all as one."

Only a handful of men responded. The others gazed with disbelief at the torn, battered figures below, some disembowelled, their entrails dangling at their feet, others dragging partly severed limbs. Many were human porcupines they were so filled with arrows. Yet they moved on in a steady column.

"Timber!" Ulbert bellowed, having to cuff the men to bring them to their senses.

The only timber available was a derelict stable block in the bailey. Three burly men-at-arms clambered down ladders and broke it up with hammers and axes. Soon, bundles of smashed wood were being hauled up the wall by rope.

"Down there!" Ulbert shouted, indicating a spot about thirty yards ahead of the Welsh force, which at last was being hindered by the avalanche of stones and spears.

The wood was cast down until a mountainous pile had been formed, blocking the berm. Several barrels of naptha were poured onto it, but firebrands were only dropped when the first Welsh reached it. The resulting explosion was bright as a starburst. The rush of heat staggered even the defenders, who were fifty feet above.

Despite this, and to Ranulf's incredulity, the first few Welsh actually attempted to clamber *through* the raging inferno. A couple even made it to the other side, though they were blazing from head to foot and, finally it seemed, had met their match. First their ragged clothing burned away, followed by their flesh and musculature. One by one, they sagged to the ground. Equally incredible to Ranulf was that none of them tried to dunk themselves in the river, the way he'd seen the French do in their camp on the Adour when the earl had catapulted clay pots filled with flaming naptha right into their sleeping-tents.

Behind this burning vanguard, more Welsh fighters were advancing. Some attempted to circle the conflagration, but again they stumbled into the river and were swept away. Others, at long last, began to display a notion of self-preservation. They halted rather than blundered headlong into the flames and, as Ulbert had predicted, were bottled up along the berm, cramming together for hundreds of yards. Naptha was sluiced onto them all along the line and lit torches were applied, creating multiple downpours of liquid fire. There was nowhere for the Welsh to run to, even if they'd been minded to. Many of them – too many to be feasible – stood blazing together in grotesque clusters, melting into each other like human-shaped candles. The stench was intolerable, the odour of decay mingling not just with the reek of ruptured guts and splintered bones, but with charring flesh and bubbling human fat. Yet only slowly did they succumb, without panic or hysteria, collapsing one by one. Thick smoke now engulfed the battlements, though it was more grease and soot than vapour. The defenders' gorge rose; cloaks were drawn across faces. Walter Margas, his blue and white chevrons stained yellow with vomit, staggered around like a dying man.

When the smog cleared – and it seemed to take an age – all that remained on the path below was a mass of black, sticky carcasses, twisted and coagulated together, yet, unbelievably, bodies still twitched, still attempted to get back to their feet. Unable to see this latter detail, those on the Constable's Tower cheered. They were watching the bluff, where the remainder of the Welsh host was finally holding back from the bridge, perhaps having realised that further attempts to circumnavigate the castle via the berm were futile.

On the curtain-wall there was less euphoria.

"Two hundred," a man-at-arms stammered. "We must have accounted for two-hundred there!"

"And if you times that by how *often* we killed them, the number should be closer to two thousand," Ranulf replied.

"This is the work of devils," Gurt said, leaning exhaustedly. Dirty sweat dripped from his face. Ulbert too was pale and sweaty, his red and blue tabard blackened with cinders.

"Just be warned," he said. "This isn't over."

"But if that's the best they can do," Gurt insisted, "try to march around the outside of the castle – which must be over a mile – we can attack them with fire all the way. We'll incinerate the lot of them."

"*Is* that the best they can do?" Ranulf asked. "Or were they just probing? Testing our defences?"

"The latter," Ulbert said. "Now they know that to reach the main entrance, they must first smash the curtain-wall."

"And how will they do that, sir knight?" Craon Culai wondered. He was a tall, lean fellow with a pinched, sneering visage. Captain of the royal men-at-arms, but originally low born, he'd long resented the air of authority assumed by the equestrian class. He lifted off his helmet, yanked back his coif and mopped the sweat from his hair. "Do they command thunderbolts as well?"

He was answered by a deafening concussion on the exact point of the battlements where he stood. Three full crenels and a huge chunk of the upper wall exploded with the force, shards flying in all directions, slashing the faces of everyone nearby. Culai and the three men-at-arms standing with him were thrown down into the bailey, cart-wheeling through the scaffolding, hitting every joist, so that they were torn and broken long before they struck the ground.

It was a dizzying moment.

Ulbert wafted his way through the dust to the parapet and peered across the Tefeidiad. On its far shore, three colossal siege-engines had been assembled, each one placed about thirty yards from the next. Diminutive figures milled around them.

"God-Christ," he said under his breath. "God-Christ in Heaven! The earl's mangonels!"

Ranulf and Gurt joined him, wiping the dust and blood from their eyes. There was no mistaking the great mechanical hammers by which their overlord had shattered so many of his enemies' gates and ramparts. The central one of the three, *War Wolf*, had already ejected its first missile. The other two, *God's Maul* and *Giant's Fist*, were in the process.

Their mighty arms swung up simultaneously, driven by immense torsional pressure; the instant they struck their padded crossbeams, massive objects, which looked like cemented sections of stonework, were flung forth. All of the defenders saw them coming, but the projectiles barrelled through the air with such velocity that it was difficult to react in time.

Ulbert was the first. *"EVERYBODY DOWN!"*

On the roof of the Constable's Tower, Corotocus and his men moved en masse to the south-facing parapet, drawn by that thunderous first collision. They were just in time to see the next two payloads tear through upper portions of the curtain-wall, fountains of rubble and timber erupting from each impact, a dozen shattered corpses spinning fifty feet down into the bailey. One missile had been driven with such force that it continued across the bailey until it struck the wall encircling the Inner Fort. Huge fissures branched away from its point of contact.

The earl's expression paled, but as much with anger as fear. Blood trickled from the corner of his mouth as his teeth sank through his bottom lip.

"Good... good Lord," du Guesculin said. "They've raided the artillery train. Taken possession of our catapults."

"And how are they operating them, this peasant rabble?" the earl retorted. "Have they engineers? Can they read Latin, Greek...

none of my diagrams and manuals are written in Cymraeg, as far as I'm aware."

Had he been on the river's south shore, Earl Corotocus would have had his answer. Already, the three great machines were being primed again. The hard labour – the cranking on the windlass, the retraction of the throwing-arm – was provided by mindless automatons, some in shrouds, others naked, many in rags coated with gore and grave-dirt. They moved jerkily, yet with precision, speed, and unnatural strength. But when there was skilled work to be done – the measuring of distance, the weighing of missiles in the bucket – it fell to three figures in particular.

They too were ravaged husks; heads lolling on twisted necks, gouged holes where eyes had been, organs rent from their eviscerated bodies. Yet Corotocus would have recognised them: Hugo d'Avranches, Reynald Guiscard and, notable in his black Benedictine habit – which now was blacker still being streaked with every type of filth and ordure – the walking corpse of Brother Ignatius.

# CHAPTER TWELVE

FOR THE REST of that first day, the Welsh army stood in silence on the western bluff while the three mangonels did their terrible work. Projectile after projectile was launched across the Tefeidiad. One by one, they struck the upper portion of the curtain-wall or its battlements. The only breaks in this pattern came when delays were caused by the contraptions having to be partly disassembled so that they could be moved on their axes to take aim at different sections.

Wholesale damage was caused. Tons of rubble cascaded into the bailey and onto the berm, burying the dead and maimed of both sides. By late afternoon, the English had lost close to forty men, their shattered bodies flung like so much butcher's meat down through the scaffolding. There was no danger of a major breach being caused – the wall itself was nearly twenty feet thick, its outer face shod with granite, its core packed tight with brick rubble, but the position on top of it was becoming untenable.

A message was soon sent to the roof of the Constable's Tower, requesting permission for the south wall's defenders to withdraw to the Inner Fort. It was rebuffed. As the earl's decision was relayed back, another three thunderbolts struck. One passed clean through a gap already blasted in the battlements, ripping the legs off an archer who was attempting to cross the damaged zone via loose planking. Men scattered in front of the other two, but impacts like claps of doom threw out blizzards of splinters and shards, in which twelve more men were slain and twice that many wounded. One lay on the smashed parapet with his belly burst, his exposed guts hanging down the wall like a mass of ropy tentacles.

"Go and talk to the earl," Ulbert shouted to Ranulf as they crouched together. "I'd go myself, but with Culai dead I'm the only one left here with any seniority. Reason with him, plead with him. At this rate, every man on the south wall will be dead by nightfall."

Ranulf had taken his helmet off earlier because it was so dented by repeated impacts. He tried to put it back on, but it would no longer fit. Cursing, he tossed it away, sheathed his sword, slung his shield onto his back and clambered down the scaffolding.

"Ranulf?" his father called after him.

Ranulf looked up.

Under his raised visor, Ulbert's face was smeared with dirt and blood. He wore a graver expression than his son had ever seen. "Politeness costs nothing. Insolence may cost us a lot."

Ranulf nodded and continued down.

In the bailey, it was difficult to work out just how many men lay dead amid the piles of broken masonry. Several of them had been dashed to pieces, their constituent parts mingled in a macabre puzzle of butchered bone and bloody tissue. Father Benan was present. He wore his purple stole and stood with hands joined in the midst of this gruesome tableau. When he heard Ranulf's footsteps, his eyes snapped open. They were wide, rabbit-like; his cheeks were wan with shock, his brow dirty and moist.

"I'd move out of this place," Ranulf said. "There's more where this came from."

"When... when we first arrived," Benan stuttered, "I offered to hear all the men's confessions. But the earl said it wasn't necessary. That we wouldn't be attacked."

"The earl is not always right. It's a pity it's taken us so long to realise that."

"Dear God!" Benan's eyes were suddenly brimming. "To serve Earl Corotocus and die unshriven? That's not a fate I'd wish on anyone."

Ranulf didn't like to dwell on such things. He couldn't remember the last time he himself had taken confession. "I'm for the Constable's Tower, Father. You should come with me. You're in danger here."

There was a colossal boom as another missile struck the wall behind them. An entire tier of scaffolding fell spectacularly. With a shriek, a man-at-arms fell with it. Benan flinched, but shook his head.

"I must offer a requiem."

"For these scraps of meat?"

"Their souls may yet be saved."

"Father, there are other souls in this castle who could use your prayers. And they still live."

"Go to them. I will join you anon."

Ranulf turned and jogged away up the bailey, though in his full mail it was hot, hard work. He again had to make his way through the Barbican and the Gatehouse, from the tops of which, respectively, Carew's Welsh malcontents and Garbofasse's mercenaries were watching the massed force on the western bluff with a mixture of fear and awe. These two groups in particular faced a dire consequence if taken alive, and the prospect of either that or death suddenly seemed significantly closer than it had done a couple of hours ago.

Ranulf hurried back along the Causeway. By the time he'd climbed to the top of the Constable's Tower, he was streaming sweat and blowing hard. Fresh blood trickled from a slash on his brow. Earl Corotocus was at the south battlements, with various of his lieutenants around him. The rest of his household stood further back, their shields hefted, their weapons brandished. All eyes were fixed on the river's distant shore, and the great war-machines at work there.

"My lord!" Ranulf said, shouldering through.

Corotocus barely glanced at him.

"My lord, you've denied us permission to withdraw from the south wall?"

"That is correct." Corotocus said. He seemed less uneasy than those around him, but there was a tension in his brow. His eyes were keen, blue slivers.

"My lord, you've seen that we're under a very heavy barrage?"

"No-one ever said that fighting the Welsh would be easy, Ranulf."

"Fighting the *Welsh*?" Ranulf struggled to hide his exasperation. "It's come to your attention, has it not, that we're facing more here than just the Welsh?"

"Ahhh… more talk of witchery. It's all over the castle at present. And yet it's so powerful, this witchery, that they've resorted to using catapults – our own catapults, no less – to force entry."

"Either way, my lord, they will soon succeed."

Corotocus turned and looked at him. "Especially if those men I appoint to defend my stronghold have no stomach for it."

"My lord, we are only asking to withdraw to the Inner Fort. It's a more defensible position."

"Return to your post, sir knight."

"My lord, we have nothing to strike back at the mangonels with. In due course they will pound the south wall to rubble. Must all the men there die to prove a point?"

"It would take a decade to pound that wall to rubble, FitzOsbern, as you know. Even with a dozen mangonels."

"My lord, the men on that wall face certain death."

"*Death!*" Corotocus roared, spittle suddenly flying from his lips. "So be it! If they must die to preserve this bastion, they must die. I won't surrender the outer rampart and allow these devils to walk into our precincts unmolested!"

"So you admit they're devils?" Ranulf said quietly. "A rare moment of honesty from you…"

"You impertinent…"

The earl went for the hilt of his sword, but before he could unsheathe the steel, William d'Abbetot appeared, quite breathless. Close to seventy, bald and white-bearded, he was exhausted simply by his journey from the Barbican. Having removed his mail earlier, he now wore only hose and a linen shirt, both of which were clingy with sweat.

"You summoned me, my lord?" he asked.

Corotocus continued to glare at Ranulf, who glared boldly back.

"God's blood, FitzOsbern!" the earl hissed. "If you weren't born of a she-wolf in a pit of marl! How is it you're the only man alive who doesn't fear me?"

"Should I fear you more, my lord, than what waits for us outside?"

"I need only snap my fingers and you'll be thrown to them first."

"And would that serve your purpose?"

"It may be your just desert."

"We're all going to get our just deserts, my lord. Every one of us."

The earl jabbed a mailed finger into Ranulf's chest. "You stay here, FitzOsbern. *Right here!* D'Abbetot?" He turned to the elderly engineer and pointed south, just as two more projectiles made deafening impacts, dust and rubble exploding into the air. "You see our problem?"

D'Abbetot dabbed his damp pate with a handkerchief. "I do, my lord. Once they've broken the battlements on the south wall, they'll do the same on the east and north. It's only a matter of moving the engines. Of course they'll have full control of the berm path long before then."

"Unless we stop them first," Corotocus said. "How serviceable is the trebuchet?"

"It hasn't been used much in recent times, but it's in working condition. A little oil here and there, some replacement hemp..."

"Can you target the bridge with it?"

"The bridge?"

"There is only one bridge, d'Abbetot. In the southwest corner, for Christ's sake!"

"But my lord, if we smash the bridge won't we be trapped in the castle?"

"We'll also be out of reach. The Welsh can't regain the berm if the bridge no longer exists. They aren't ants, are they? They can't fill up the moat with their dead and just walk over the top."

"Especially as they don't appear to be dying," Ranulf put in.

"Well, d'Abbetot?" the earl growled.

"I'll see to it, my lord. Straight away."

D'Abbetot hobbled off.

"Have the bridge down by nightfall and I'll reward you with estates on every honour I hold," the earl called after him. He turned back to Ranulf, still having to restrain his anger. "You're quite a speaker, sir, for a rogue knight. You must have a high opinion of yourself to voice so many viewpoints in such august company."

"Wasn't it you, my lord, who said you'd rather have men who told the truth?"

"Yes, Ranulf, it was. But that doesn't mean I won't kill them for their impudence."

Ranulf pursed his lips. Perhaps it was time to hold his prattling tongue.

"You may hate my cruelty, Ranulf. You may resent my power. You may revile my ambition. But do you know what hurts the most – your mistrust of my abilities."

Ranulf could not refute the charge. His temper had got the better of him, for there was no doubt that breaking the bridge was a clever plan. No matter what demonic powers protected them, the Welsh could assail the castle with missiles for day after day, but if the bridge was destroyed they could make no further gain. They could never physically wrest the stronghold from its defenders. Of course, a prolonged bombardment would still inflict horrendous casualties.

"My lord, if they continue to pound us…"

"It will achieve little," Corotocus said. "Apart from wasting their time. King Edward plans to enter this country through the north, but he won't sit on his arse there forever. Even if he doesn't receive a plea for help from us, he'll come down here at length to consolidate his gains. Let's see how they fare then, against a host of fifty thousand. In any case, once the bridge is broken, I can withdraw all my troops from the south wall. We won't need the outer rampart any more."

Ranulf nodded. Earl Corotocus might be a brute but he'd always been a capable tactician.

"Which brings me back to *you*," the earl said. His lieutenants hovered behind him, uncertainly. Only Navarre looked pleased by this turn of events. "I can't tolerate your constant rebellions, Ranulf, or your petty treasons. So your sentence is death."

Some of the knights hung their heads. Navarre broke into a delighted grin.

"Do you hear me?" the earl said.

"I hear you, my lord."

"You think I can endure this indefinitely, boy? You think I can be defied with venom in the midst of battle, when other men of mine – better men, and more loyal than you – are dying all around? Do you think I *should* endure it?"

Ranulf said nothing.

"Be assured, if I didn't need every man in my command right now, I'd hang you from the highest gibbet in Wales. But don't be comforted, Ranulf. When this war is over, the sentence will be confirmed. And of course you must challenge it. You must claim trial by combat, as is your right. I'll be more than happy to oblige…"

Before he could say more, a shadow fell over them. They glanced up.

A dark but glittering cloud was arcing from the top of the western bluff towards the castle's northwest corner. At first it was like a flock of birds, sunlight glinting on their black, metallic feathers. But then they realised that it was debris – or 'iron hail', to use catapult crew parlance – maybe a ton of it, spreading out as it descended on the Barbican.

Its impact was deafening and prolonged. It covered almost the entirety of the Barbican roof and spilled partly onto the Gatehouse alongside it. Even from as far away as the Constable's Tower, a hundred yards to the south, the clangour of impacts, the chorus of shouts and screams was ear-splitting.

Earl Corotocus moved to the north battlements, the others joining him. Though located on elevated ground, the Barbican wasn't as tall as the Constable's Tower. Subsequently, they had a perfect view of the damage the iron hail had inflicted. The trebuchet appeared to be intact. A good number of Carew's Welsh were milling around it, though many others lay prone as though felled by hammer-blows.

"The scoop-thrower!" du Guesculin shouted. "Dear Lord in Heaven, they've got the scoop-thrower as well!"

"Of course they've got the scoop-thrower," Corotocus replied. "It's the deadliest machine in my arsenal. Would they leave that behind?"

"Why is it trained on the Barbican?" Navarre wondered.

"It's trained on the *trebuchet*, you idiot! If they break the trebuchet, we've no way to demolish the bridge and they can continue the infantry assault."

"Can't we disassemble the trebuchet and move it?" du Guesculin said.

Corotocus snarled his frustration. "There's nowhere to set it up where it'll be out of reach of the scoop-thrower unless we move it to the east rampart, where it will be useless anyway."

"What in God's name do we do, my lord?" Du Guesculin had gone white. Of them all, he had looked most hopeful at the suggestion the southwest bridge might be made unusable and the Welsh held in abeyance. "In the good Lord's name, what do…?"

"Arm the trebuchet!" Corotocus bellowed. "Smash that bridge now, before it's too damn late!"

"D'Abbetot will need Carew and his damn malcontents to help," Navarre said. "But look at the state of them."

Even after one deluge of iron hail, the priority on the Barbican had changed from mutual defence to self-preservation. There was still much shouting and consternation, but something like a retreat was in progress. Numerous wounded were being assisted up the steps to the Gatehouse.

Corotocus bared his teeth.

"Get over there, Navarre," he snarled. "Remind Captain Carew that if this castle falls he and his Welsh malingerers will be singled out for even less merciful treatment than we English. Remind them they are to assist William d'Abbetot, my senior engineer, in any way that he requests, and that this means holding their position until ordered to do otherwise. If any object, put them to the sword immediately."

He turned to another of his tenant knights, a wiry, leathery-skinned fellow in a black and orange striped mantle, called Robert of Tancarville.

"You as well, Robert. And *you*!" Corotocus pointed at Ranulf. "A chance to redeem yourself early."

Ranulf didn't suppose the Barbican could be any worse a posting at this moment than the south curtain-wall. He nodded curtly and followed the other two.

"Let's hope d'Abbetot hadn't already got up there," he said, joining them on the downward stair. "If he's dead, the trebuchet's no use to us anyway."

"Always you expect the worst," Navarre jeered.

"No, I expect the iron hail," Ranulf said. "The worst may be yet to come."

# CHAPTER THIRTEEN

THE BARBICAN WAS another supposedly impregnable feature of Grogen Castle.

Standing just to the west of the Gatehouse, it was a bastion in its own right: a squat, hexagonal tower, filled with rubble so that it was basically a gigantic earthwork clad with stone and fitted around its rim with huge crenels. Its roof was broad enough not just to accommodate the trebuchet, but over a hundred men-at-arms and archers, who could assail, in more or less complete safety, any force attempting to attack the castle's main entrance. The trebuchet itself was powerful enough to shoot clean down to the river, or, thanks to its turntable base, far up onto the western bluff. It was a strong and defensible position for any company of men, but it had never been foreseen that it might be attacked from overhead. When Navarre and Tancarville arrived up there, it was a scene of carnage. The corpses of Carew's malcontents dotted the Barbican roof, while many of those still living clutched bloody wounds as they flowed up the Gatehouse stair to mingle with Garbofasse's mercenaries.

In general terms, Carew's band were poorly armed, clad in hose, leather jerkins and boots. One or two were in mail, and some wore pointed or broad-brimmed helmets, but most lacked shields to shelter beneath, and so the iron hail had taken a massive toll of them. Carew, who had also retreated to the Gatehouse, was better equipped than most. His helmet was fitted with nose and cheek pieces. He also wore a hauberk of padded felt studded with iron balls, but he'd been cut deeply across the neck. Blood gushed from the wound as he sought to bind it.

"Carew, where the devil are your dogs running to?" Navarre shouted, as he and Robert of Tancarville approached with swords drawn.

Carew spun to face him. "Hell's rain has just fallen on our heads! Didn't you see?"

"Hell is where you're headed if you don't get these wretches back to their posts!"

Ranulf now arrived, with William d'Abbetot alongside him. They'd overtaken the elderly engineer on their way here. Ranulf had held back to assist him as he puffed his way up the steep Gatehouse stair.

"You expect us to stand under the iron hail?" Carew shouted.

"The earl expects you to stand until the last man, if necessary!" Navarre retorted.

"And will you set the example for us, Aquitaine?"

"Do as you're commanded. *Now!*"

"You first, you crooked-faced ape."

Navarre raised his sword, but Ranulf stepped between them. "Fighting among ourselves is the last thing we need," he said. "Captain Carew, where do you and your men think you're retreating to?"

"We can still protect the castle entrance if we man the Gatehouse."

"The Gatehouse is also in the scoop-thrower's range."

As if in proof there was a wild shout and another nebulous shadow fell over them. Instinctively, Navarre and Tancarville lifted their shields. Ranulf did the same, but dragged d'Abbetot, who of course was not armoured, beneath his. Carew fell to a crouch, arms wrapped around his helmet. No-one else reacted before the second hail struck.

Every type of missile smashed down: bolts, nails, screws, stones, bits of chain, hunks of jagged metal. Ranulf had a sturdy shield. It was fashioned from planks and linen strips glued together, bound with iron and overlaid with painted leather. It felt as if a giant with a sledgehammer was beating on it and it was all he could do to keep the thing horizontal. When the deluge was over, the shield was buckled out of shape, though it had served its purpose – both Ranulf and William d'Abbetot were shaken but unhurt. Others hadn't been so lucky.

Garbofasse's mercenaries were better armoured than Carew's Welsh, but several of them had been struck. Ranulf saw split scalps, lacerated faces, broken limbs. All around, there were groans and gasps as dazed men helped fallen comrades to their feet. The Welsh, caught for a second time in the hail, had fared even worse. Those climbing the steps from the Barbican had been hit simultaneously by a timber beam, which had shattered three skulls in a row. The Barbican roof was under inches of debris; several dozen lay half-buried in it. Others still on their feet wandered groggily, their helms battered into fantastical shapes. Carew gazed bemusedly at his hands, which were badly mangled, the flesh torn away from several bent and broken fingers.

"God help us," d'Abbetot stammered. "We can't post anyone on the Barbican or Gatehouse under conditions like these. They'll be massacred."

"We need to demolish the bridge," Ranulf said. "That's one thing we *must* do before yielding these posts." He took d'Abbetot by the elbow and forced him down the stair, both struggling not to trip over corpses or slip on treads slick with gore. "How long before the scoop-thrower's ready to discharge again?"

"Several minutes. But that won't be long enough for us." Panic grew in d'Abbetot's voice. "I have to find the range, and that could take four or five shots. And if I can't turn the damn thing around, we can't even aim." They'd now reached the trebuchet, but every Welshman in the vicinity seemed to be dead or critically injured. "For God's sake, FitzOsbern, get someone else down here... we can't turn the damn thing round on our own!"

Ranulf called back to the Gatehouse. In response, Navarre tottered down the steps, with Tancarville close behind. Navarre's shield had splintered and he was bloodied around the face. As they came, they rounded up several of the walking wounded.

"Christ help us!" d'Abbetot moaned. "Look at this!"

Even to Ranulf's untrained eye, it was clear that the first two volleys of hail had done severe damage to the trebuchet. The sling ropes had been severed, the padding on the crossbeam ripped asunder.

"How long to repair it?" Ranulf asked.

"Damn it, I don't know. Have we even got replacement materials?"

"Mind your heads!" someone shrieked.

Yet another shadow fell over them. Again, Ranulf grasped the engineer and dragged him beneath his shield. Tancarville raised his own shield and squatted. Navarre now had no shield. Maybe eight or nine of Garbofasse's mercenaries had joined the remaining ten Welsh still alive on the Barbican roof. Only a couple of these were quick enough to take evasive action. When the next deluge struck, it was mainly stones – of all sizes, from cobblestones, to pebbles, to pellets – banging on iron, cracking on brickwork, ripping through flesh and wood and hide. There were more screams, more gasps and grunts. Ranulf didn't know how many hundredweight of minerals were impacting on his shield as he tried to hold it aloft. His forearm ached abominably, but long before the storm ceased an even more frightening problem arose – for three human bodies also landed on the Barbican.

One came down on the top of its skull, which imploded so completely that there was nothing left of it. The others bounced across the roof like sacks of broken crockery, finally rolling to a standstill. Ranulf had heard about this before, though he'd never witnessed it – the catapulting of diseased or decayed corpses into fortifications. Normally it was an aspect of prolonged sieges, signifying that the besiegers were becoming desperate and would use any means, no matter how ghoulish, to force a capitulation. It rarely happened as early in the conflict as this.

That was when the three bodies began to twitch.

Slowly, Ranulf lowered what remained of his shield. He'd seen much here already that defied description, but what he now beheld set his senses reeling.

A trio of twisted forms rose clumsily to their feet.

They were better armed than the majority of the enemy he'd so far seen. Two were in leather jerkins and leather breeches. One had bare feet but wore gauntlets, while the other was shod with metal sabatons but barehanded; one of those hands had been severed at the wrist. The third figure, the headless one, was naked except for a mail hauberk, which hung down as far as its knees and looked something like a shroud. It soon dawned on Ranulf how appropriate this analogy was – the hauberk was indeed a shroud, for it had been put on the figure after death. They'd all of them been dressed like this after death, for evidently they *were* dead.

Ranulf now understood this fully.

These creatures were dead and yet somehow they were also alive.

The rest of the men on the roof were too preoccupied to have noticed the figures stumbling towards them. D'Abbetot was seated groggily on the trebuchet turntable. He'd been struck in the face by a stone, which had slashed his brow and spit his nose. All of Carew's malcontents had now been floored. Only one clambered back to his feet. Navarre removed his battered helmet and shook out fragments of metal, blood dripping from his brow. Tancarville was on his knees, stunned. Five of Garbofasse's men were still upright, but all were visibly injured.

"The enemy's with us!" Ranulf shouted, unsheathing his sword. Only slivers remained of his shield, so he threw it down. "In God's name, the enemy's here!"

Still the others didn't react. He swung back to face the demonic threesome, now only a matter of yards away. The headless figure was armed with a spiked mace. The one in the gauntlets had landed with a spear, though this had shattered on impact, so it had scooped up a falchion with a curved blade. The third carried a pollaxe which, though it would normally require two hands to wield it effectively, was being brandished in one hand with no difficulty.

They were true visions of horror, these walking dead men. Broken bones ground together as they advanced, white shards protruding through their pulverised flesh. Of their two remaining faces, one had been crushed to the point where a vile sewage of blood and brains flowed from its nasal cavity. The other had been pierced through the mouth by an arrow, the barbed head of which projected beneath its chin, digging into its throat. One of its eyes had been eaten away; the other was a maleficent orb glinting from a cradle of splintered bone.

"Off your arses!" Ranulf shouted, though it was more of a howl. The tough young warrior, who'd known almost nothing but war and strife since he'd first been knighted, literally *howled*. "To arms, I say!"

The three figures approached like marionettes jerking on invisible strings. But gradually they seemed to focus their energy. They became stronger, faster; they walked with a heavier, more determined tread. Even Ranulf, who'd seen them coming first, was mesmerised. He only just raised his sword in time to parry a downward blow from the spiked mace, before retaliating with a huge crosscut, which caught the headless horror across the chest. He failed to cleave the mail, but sent the creature tottering backward, and now at last the other troops realised that the Barbican had been infiltrated.

D'Abbetot's eyes goggled, even though blood was streaming into them. Navarre went for the one-handed monstrosity, thrusting and hacking with all his strength, though it fended him off with unnatural skill, catching him across the chin with the point of its pollaxe, laying open his disfigured face once again. Two mercenaries went for the one in gauntlets. One of them swung a morningstar, only for the chain to wrap around its forearm. It yanked him forward and drove the falchion into his belly, his entrails flopping out in glistening coils. The other mercenary thrust a poniard into its skull, ramming it through the bone into the tissue beneath, but it swept him aside and, snatching the morningstar, looped it around his throat and threw him over its shoulder, snapping his neck. The surviving Welshman came for it with a spear. A massive, two-handed blow took the monster in the midriff, impaling it clean through. Again it showed no pain, no weakness. Neither blood nor mucus spilled from its jammed open mouth. It grappled with the Welshman and, raising its falchion, sundered his battered helm and the cranium beneath. A third mercenary hurled a javelin, which buried itself in the corpse's gaping socket. Now there were two implements protruding from its head. Instead of succumbing, it broke the javelin's haft, grabbed the shrieking mercenary by the throat and thrust the haft's dagger-like shard into his groin. The mercenary's scream became a shrill screech of emasculation.

A few yards away, Navarre clove his opponent through the right shoulder and, with a mighty backstroke, lopped off its head. But it still came on. Only when he severed its left leg just above the knee did it topple over. Ranulf made equal gains, using massive, swinging strokes to fend his opponent to the battlements, where he was able to chop the mace from its grasp, and kick it backward through an embrasure.

Yet, they'd no sooner destroyed the assault party than a fourth avalanche of rubble struck them. On this occasion, nobody was prepared for it. One second Ranulf was standing, blade dripping, the next he was beset from above by rocks, stones and lumps of metal. His scalp and face were ripped open and he took an agonising blow on his collar bone before he was able to pull up his coif and hunker down, his arms crossed over his head. Others followed suite, though not all. Robert Tancarville flailed uselessly at the sky with his sword, and was hit in the face by a coping stone. William d'Abbetot shrieked incoherently as he was hammered to the floor, one missile after another bouncing off him, smashing his hands as he tried to protect his head.

And again there were corpses. This time a couple of them missed the Barbican altogether, crashing down its wall into the moat. But at least eight landed cleanly, and were very quickly upright. They were equally rent and mutilated, but again were clad in mail and leather and armed with every type of weapon.

Ranulf had to push himself back to his feet on the tip of his sword as the horrible spectres lumbered forward, groaning and mewling. He met the first with a two-handed blow that severed its trunk at the hips, but then was grabbed around the head and flung to the floor. He cried for help.

Garbofasse and a dozen more men hobbled down from the Gatehouse roof. All wore crushed helmets and carried bent shields; their faces were gashed and bruised. They were in a poor state to meet seven ravening corpses, and could barely defend themselves as the dead things raised their mauls and mattocks. Navarre was also back on his feet. Like Ranulf, his mail had protected most of his body from the hail's edge, but his face was almost unrecognisable. His sword had snapped mid-blade. Disgustedly, he cast it away, grabbed up a flail and rejoined the fray.

For minutes on end, battle raged across the Barbican. When the cadavers' weapons broke, they tore into their prey with claws and teeth. They rode every counter-blow, though their limbs were hewed, their skulls shattered. One after another, Garbofasse's mercenaries were despatched. One's helmet was struck with such force that his churned brains spurted through its visor. A second was skewered through the midriff with a broken axe handle. A third was beaten to the ground with an iron bar. A fourth was lifted bodily into the air and carried towards the battlements; his spittle-filled shrieks rang aloud as he was flung over. Garbofasse strove at the monsters with a battle-axe in each hand. Ranulf clove one's head cross-wise, slicing through its open mouth with his blade, shearing off the top half of its skull, though it stayed on its feet, foul fluids gargling in its opened oesophagus.

More of Garbofasse's troops limped down from the Gatehouse, only to be met by another iron hail. This was heavier than any thus far. The usual debris was laced with razor-edged flint. Again, the men were slashed and brutalised. Ranulf staggered towards William d'Abbetot's body, belatedly thinking that saving the engineer's life should be a priority – only to see that what remained of him was being pounded like mulch into the rubble. Even those much younger and stronger than d'Abbetot were cut down. Once the hail had finished, only Ranulf, Navarre, Garbofasse and three of his mercenaries remained on their feet; all had been freshly wounded. The only ones unaffected were the corpses. Though torn anew, in some cases reduced to parodies of humanity – grisly effigies of exposed bone and filleted flesh – they came on as before.

"Back to the Gatehouse," Ranulf called.

These Welsh – if they *were* Welsh, and not from Hades itself – could not be slain or hurt. They could march through their own artillery storm, while the English fell under it like wheat to the scythe.

"Back to the G-Gatehouse... *now*!" he stammered. "We can't win this!"

# CHAPTER FOURTEEN

IN THE DISORDER that followed the retreat onto the Gatehouse it was impossible for coherent orders to be issued. Five maniacal corpses still held sway on the Barbican, but attempts to place a shield-wall at the top of the Gatehouse stair and bar their path were hampered by yet another iron hail, which now swept the Gatehouse roof, driving those remaining to the downward hatches. In the cramped rooms below it was a chaos of blood, straw and smoke. Throats were raw with shouts and gasps. Men were slumped with exhaustion, caked in dirt and gore, their tabards and surcoats in tatters.

At last Earl Corotocus arrived, forcing his way through, with du Guesculin and more of his household men struggling along behind. Father Benan, white-faced and tearful, brought up the rear.

"What is this madness, Corotocus?" Garbofasse roared, shoving men out of his way. "A third of my troops are dead and they've barely struck a blow yet!"

"They've struck plenty of blows," Ranulf interjected. "Mainly against women and children. This may be the price of that victory."

Corotocus couldn't respond. He was too startled by the bloodied, battered state of his lieutenants.

"What devilry have you unleashed on us?" Garbofasse demanded.

"My lord," Father Benan simpered, "my lord, this is too terrible..."

"Earn your corn, priest!" the earl barked. "Confess the dying, help Zacharius succour the wounded."

"Those... those men," du Guesculin stammered, his eyes bulging as he recalled what he'd seen from the Constable's Tower. "Catapulted alive onto the... and to fight and kill. It must be some kind of illusion."

"You dolt!" Garbofasse threw a crimson rag into his face. "Are these wounds an illusion?"

"Navarre?" the earl said, turning to his most trusted henchman.

Navarre was seated on a stool, sweating, breathing hard, his scalp and face horribly cut. He could only shake his head.

The earl swung to Ranulf. "What of you? You were hand-to-hand with them, damn it, what did you see?"

Ranulf looked him straight in the eye. "I saw dead men walking like puppets, but wielding weapons like Viking berserks. I saw mildewed lumps of carrion, some still coated with grave dirt, raging at us like barbarians."

"Damn devilry!" Garbofasse swore again. "Damn blasted devilry!"

The word went around quickly. Men who previously had been too weary or hurt now leapt to their feet. There was shouting, pushing.

"Enough!" the earl thundered. "You peasant scum! *Enough!*"

A deafening silence followed. He peered around at them. Fiery phantoms writhed on their wounded faces, on the arched brick ceiling overhead.

"You maggots!" he said. "The whole army of the world's dead may be out there, and they couldn't break these walls!"

"They won't need to break them," Navarre said, finally standing. "Forgive me for speaking plainly, but as long as they have the scoop-thrower we can't man the Barbican or the Gatehouse roof."

"And as long as they have the mangonels," came another voice, "we can barely man the curtain-wall."

This was Ulbert. Despite the fearsome attacks on his own position, news had reached him that a company had been wiped out on the Barbican. He'd come hotfoot to find his son. Though he flinched at the sight of Ranulf's lacerated face, he was palpably relieved to find him alive. He turned again to Corotocus.

"My lord, I needn't tell you, but with the curtain-wall lost, all they'll need to do is walk around the outside and come in through the front door."

"We must break the southwest bridge as we planned," Garbofasse asserted.

"That's now impossible," Ranulf replied. "The trebuchet's damaged and William d'Abbetot is dead."

"We should withdraw," du Guesculin urged his master. "Move back to the Constable's Tower."

Ranulf gave him a scornful look. "If the scoop-thrower can strike the Gatehouse roof, surely you see that it can strike the Constable's Tower as well?"

"What are our losses on the south wall?" Corotocus asked Ulbert.

"About half our strength. The fire barricade on the berm has prevented their assault force circling the castle, but it won't last forever."

Before anyone else could speak, there was a ghastly shriek and a mercenary tottered forward clutching his belly, from which a spearhead protruded. Behind him, there was another shriek. In the dim-lit press of damaged, sagging bodies, it was difficult to see exactly what was happening, but the rearmost hatch appeared to have been forced open and a figure had dropped down. It was now assailing another of Garbofasse's men with a scramsax. Its third blow clove his skull so brutally that his brain was exposed. It then shambled forward, striking at anyone within range. An instant later it was face to face with Corotocus. The earl's eyes almost popped from their sockets. The demonic thing was naked of clothing, but it had been stripped of most of its flesh as well. Muscle tissue hung in shreds. All it had for a face were torn ruins. Multiple arrows transfixed it.

Never had a nobleman, even as steeped in blood as Earl Corotocus, seen any creature as mutilated as this and still apparently alive. His eyes tracked slowly upward as it raised the weapon with which to sunder his cranium. And then the reverie was broken, and a dozen blades stormed it from all sides, hacking, slashing, reducing it to quivering pulp, chopping it to segments, which continued to squirm and twitch on the floor.

"The hatch!" someone screamed. "The damn bloody hatch!" Swiftly, the open hatchway was blocked with beams and planks.

"More of them will land up there," Navarre shouted. "We've no option – we *have* to go up and repel them."

"And face the iron hail?" Garbofasse scoffed.

"We could form a testudo…"

"It's suicide!"

Navarre looked to the earl for instruction, but the earl was still mesmerised by the gory fragments scattered at his feet.

"My lord," Father Benan whispered into his ear, yanking the shoulder of his cloak. "My lord… this is not… this is not the natural order of things."

Corotocus finally came round. "What are you gibbering about? Didn't I send you to your work?"

Father Benan shook his head. He half smiled, though there was an eerie light in his eyes, a form of shock or craziness. "My lord, don't you see what this means?"

Corotocus pushed him aside, and lurched over to where Captain Carew sat hunched against a pillar. "Carew?"

Carew said nothing at all; he merely offered up his hands, both bound with bloody rags and mangled beyond use.

"My lord," Father Benan said, grabbing the earl's cloak again. "You once endowed me with a generous chantry. To sing psalms for your soul. Every day and every night, you said… to protect you from Hell's vengeance in the afterlife."

Corotocus gazed down at the severed head of the thing that had just attacked him. To his incredulity, what remained of its tongue was still moving in the cavity where its lower jaw had been. He stamped on it with his mailed foot – again and again, hacking at it with his heel, cracking its skull apart, flattening it out so that its eyes popped out and a noisome porridge of rotted brain-matter flowed across the flagstones.

Father Benan was undeterred. "My lord, I *cannot* save you." He gave a fluting laugh even though tears spilled onto his cheeks. "Not with all the psalms or prayers in Christendom."

Corotocus turned and stared at him.

The priest shook his head frantically. "You may endow a hundred orders to try and bribe God for over a hundred centuries, but He will not listen. This abomination is a sign that you are past help. That God has turned his back on you… "

"Silence, you fool!"

"Not just on you but on all those who follow you. These unnatural horrors are the price we pay for your crimes against God and Humanity..."

"You snivelling louse!" Corotocus grabbed him by the habit and threw him to his knees. "You *dare* hide your cowardice behind Holy Orders? Somebody whip him! Whip him 'til there's no skin on his back!"

There was hesitation before anyone obeyed, which was a new experience indeed for the Earl of Clun. They'd all heard the priest's words. They all knew in their heart of hearts that the things they'd done in Wales under the earl's command would never find favour with Jesus Christ. But much less would it find favour to chastise one of His anointed prelates.

"D'you hear me!" the earl roared at them. "Punish this dog! This traitor who invokes God's curse on us!" Still they were reluctant. "You mindless children! Are you blind as well as stupid? The witchcraft is outside! Since when did God ever send devils to do His holy work?"

"Since when did the king of England send devils to do his?" the priest said with another laugh.

The earl kicked at him, sending him sprawling.

"Do you all hear this treason? Is this a fitting comrade, who switches his allegiance the moment the enemy is close?"

"My lord," someone protested. "A holy man..."

"What's holy about him? You heard his weasel words. If the Welsh get in, he'll no doubt hasten to tell them that it wasn't him. That he advised against this mission, which, incidentally, we are carrying out on the orders of our lord, the king." He spat on Benan's cassock. "Do not be fooled by these priestly vestments. This turd has shown his true colours. He's a snake in the grass, who would deceive us all. Now do as I say. Get him out of here, scourge his worthless hide."

"You heard His Excellency!" Navarre shouted.

To see the household champion hurt, and yet still strong and fiercely loyal to his overlord galvanised the rest of them. Two household knights came forward and dragged the weeping priest away.

"Back to the business at hand," Corotocus said. "Shore those other hatches. Make sure they can't be broken again."

As the mesnie bustled, Ranulf wondered if the earl was at last losing his grasp of military realities. He'd wasted time punishing a malefactor, and yet a desperate battle was raging outside. He was content to close off the captured areas of the castle rather than try to recover them. There were exclamations about this from the more experienced knights. They pleaded with the earl that the Barbican, or at least the Gatehouse roof, needed to be cleared of the enemy, as the warriors catapulted up there would now be able to enter the bailey. But the earl replied that no more than a handful would manage it. The dead could have the Gatehouse roof, but so long as its interior was held from them, the bulk of the enemy would be kept outside.

"Does he fully realise what we're facing here?" Ranulf asked his father quietly. "These creatures can't just be cut down with a sword-stroke. I've seen that for myself. In that respect, each one of them is worth any ten of us."

"He can only do what he can do." Ulbert replied.

"What?"

Ulbert rarely showed emotion these days, let alone fear or panic. But even by his normal detached standards, he seemed strangely resigned to meeting whatever abhorrence was hammering on the hatchways above their heads.

"He can't just wave a wand to make this foe go away, Ranulf."

"Someone waved one to make them come here."

"Then perhaps, as soldiers, it is part of our duty to find this person and kill him." Ulbert moved away. "In the meantime we must look to our friends."

The earl was still issuing orders, fully in command again. When Ulbert and Ranulf confronted him, requesting permission to return to the south curtain-wall and organise a retreat for the troops still holding out there, he eyed them thoughtfully. Any anger he still felt at Ranulf was probably tempered by the sight of the young knight's facial wounds, which proved more than words ever could that he'd fought hard in his overlord's name. In addition, there were practical considerations. To withdraw from the curtain-wall now would be to grant the Welsh unfettered access to the berm and thus to the castle's main entrance. But to leave men on the curtain-wall would be certain death for them, not just from the mangonels to their front, but from the corpses in the bailey who could climb the scaffolding and attack them from behind.

"That would be sensible," he eventually said. "I don't want to do it with the southwest bridge intact, but it seems the bridge is beyond our reach. Very well. The curtain-wall is to be abandoned, but only temporarily. When the time is right, I intend to recapture it."

Corotocus gave the two knights leave and they descended quickly to the next level, crossing over a narrow gantry drawbridge, which spanned the castle's entrance passage and joined with the north curtain-wall. Thirty feet below them, the passage was deserted, but it was easy to imagine that soon it would be packed with struggling forms, their ghoulish groans echoing in the high, narrow space. The main entrance gate was recessed into the Gatehouse on the left-hand side of this passage rather than at its far end, which made assault by ram or catapult impossible. Theoretically, such a gate was unbreakable, but Ranulf could already envisage these indestructible monsters swarming all over it until they'd torn it down with their bare hands.

On the north battlements, he leaned against a crenel to get his breath. He pulled back his coif; his hair was sticky with clotting blood. Many of his gashes still wept red tears.

"Are you alright?" Ulbert asked.

"I think my nose is broken."

"No matter. It wasn't much to look at."

Ranulf half smiled. "A pity it couldn't have been your scrawny neck."

"Do you want to wait here and rest?"

"No. There are many hurt worse than me." They set off. As they walked, Ranulf said: "Father, have you ever heard of anything... *anything* like this before?"

Ulbert pondered; his face was graven in stone.

"I once heard about something," he admitted. "It was two centuries ago at least. A rumour brought back from the East. Bohemond's crusader army was in peril. They'd won the battle of Antioch, but the nobles squabbled and refused to cooperate with each other, so smaller parties of knights set out for Jerusalem without them. Soon they were starved and parched. They fought their way across an arid, desolate land, hunted all the way by Saracen horsemen. When they reached civilisation, they were more like animals than men. They destroyed the Moslem city of Ma'arrat, where the more demented among them prepared a cannibal feast. Even those who'd retained their sanity joined them, tortured by the smell of cooked meat. The Saracens were so outraged by this crime that they too broke God's laws. Their wizards summoned a dust storm to envelope the crusader army when it marched again. Many were lost in the confusion. Great numbers were taken prisoner. A year later, these prisoners reappeared at the battle of Ascalon. They were naked and skinless, having been flayed, but despite this they marched against their former allies. The story is that they marched under banners made from their own shredded hides."

"That's a fairy story," Ranulf said. "Surely?"

Ulbert laughed without humour. "In years to come people will refer to this as a fairy story. But that doesn't make it any less a nightmare for those of us living through it."

# CHAPTER FIFTEEN

COUNTESS MADALYN SAT rigid on her horse. A long pole with a gleaming steel point was inserted through a pannier beside her saddle. From the top of it, *Y Ddraig Goch*, the dragon of Wales, billowed on a green weave.

It gave her a commanding aura, a queenly air, but those who knew her would say that her posture was just a little too stiff, her gloved hands knotted too tightly on her leather reins. Though her flame-red hair was a famed glory of the Powys valleys, her fleece hood was drawn up tightly. She wore a linen veil, drenched with perfume, across her nose and mouth. She looked neither left nor right, but focussed intently on the gaunt edifice of Grogen Castle.

From this position on the western bluff, it was difficult to see exactly what was happening over there. Palls of brackish smoke still cloaked the side of the fortress facing the river. The wall on that side had been blackened by fire, and massive projectiles were still being hurled across the water at it. With each monstrous impact, stones and bodies flew through the air, though no accurate tally could be made of the English dead. Likewise on the Barbican, which the great scooped throwing-machine located in the wood beyond the crest of the hill behind her had been pounding with showers of broken stone and metal. Consternation had been caused among its defenders, which intensified massively when, in scenes the countess had never thought she'd witness in a thousand lifetimes, human beings had also been flung up there, spinning through the air, turning over and over. In many cases they'd missed the Barbican altogether, falling short into the moat or striking the castle walls. Even those that reached it were surely landing with such force that they'd be broken to pieces. And yet fighting had followed on the Barbican battlements: figures struggling together, the flashing of blades, bodies and body parts dropping over the parapets, prolonged and hideous shrieks.

Of course, even concentrating on these horrible scenes was preferable to watching the mass of dead and decayed flesh shuffling onto the bluff around her. On first arriving here, she'd tried to steel herself, to face the reality of what she was doing. Initially it hadn't been so bad – one stumbling, ragged figure had seemed much like another if you avoided looking at its face. But it wasn't long before she was noticing the various methods by which these pitiful forms had first been sent from this world: the nooses knotted at their throats, the spears that spitted them, the crazily angled torsos where spines had been broken.

In some cases it had hardened her resolve, reminding her in a way words never could of the depredations inflicted on her people. An old man – eyeless, tongueless, waving stumps for hands – made her weep. A young man – naked, a festering cavity where his genitals should be, a beam across his shoulders, his wrists nailed to either end of it, showing that he'd not just been emasculated but crucified as well – made her seethe with outrage. But as one apparition after another tottered past, it became increasingly difficult to focus on the injustice. A naked pregnant woman, her swollen belly slit open and an infant's arm protruding – and twitching – made the countess's gorge rise. A child torn apart by war dogs, and even now in death unintelligibly wailing – as though for a mother that would never answer its cries of pain and fear – made her clamp a hand to her eyes. A few hours later, even more grotesque figures had begun to appear: those who had died *before* this war – the diseased, the crippled, the starved. In some cases they had died months before. She saw stick limbs, worm-eaten ribs, skulls without scalps, faces that were green, faces that were black, faces that were hanging from the bone.

A tide of raddled flesh and filthy, leprous rags now jostled on all sides of her. The stench was unbearable, eye-watering even through her scented veil. She did her best to remain aloof, as Gwyddon and his acolytes were. But she could no longer look at these poor, corrupted husks. If they made contact with her stirrup-clad boots, merely brushing against them, she cringed. Her mount, which had once belonged to an English knight and had seen much battle, had become skittish, revolted by the smell and alarmed by the meaningless, mumbling discord of the dead. Every so often an instruction from Gwyddon – delivered in the hard pagan tongue of ancient times, rather than the melodious voice of her people now – would despatch fresh cohorts downhill towards the bridge. And how relieved Countess Madalyn was to see the backs of these, though always more would emerge from the woods and hills at her rear, and flow into the gaps.

She tried to console herself with thoughts of romantic myths. The histories of the Welsh had always been notable for brutality and malevolence. The fair Rhiannon tricked her fiancé Gwawl into a magic bag, where he was bludgeoned almost to death by her lover Pwyll, only at which point did he finally agree to release her from the engagement. The beautiful Arianrhod, angered that her family had discovered she was pregnant out of wedlock, cursed her own child, Lleu, for the entirety of his life, the ultimate culmination of which was his marriage to the hag Blodeuwedd, who gleefully murdered him. And yet it was no solace really – not *really* – for these were nought but fancies and folklore. *This* was altogether different. These lumbering wrecks, these sad, rotting travesties who once had been resting in God's sweet earth, who in most cases had paid their dues with agonising deaths and yet now had been called to die again and again and again – they were all *too* real.

The worst incident came in the middle of the day.

The largest projectiles so far impacted on the crenels of the castle's south wall and the roars of battle still echoed from the roof of its Barbican. But the countess was weary with it, reeling with the stench of death. In a moment of weakness, she happened to glance to her right. That was all it was – a glance, very fleeting. And yet, inexorably, as though fated, her eyes were drawn to someone she knew. Before she could think, his name broke from her lips.

"Kye!"

Again, fresh cohorts of the dead had been sent downhill to cross the castle bridge and follow the berm path, and her former bodyguard was going with them. Yet, unlike those others around him, Kye seemed to hear her.

He turned slowly – painfully slowly – to look.

Overjoyed, she dismounted and ran forward, oblivious to the carrion shapes that she thrust out of her way. Kye was a typically handsome son of Wales: tall, huge of build, with his great black beard, black bushy hair and piercing blue eyes.

"Kye!" she said again, elated.

She'd seen him struck down, but she must have been mistaken. He'd been struck, yes, but he'd survived. His even features were unmarked by flame or blade, unbitten by worm. He still wore his gleaming mail habergeon and the red leather corselet over the top of it. His eyes seemed to fix on her, their gaze clear and focussed. As she approached, she yanked back her hood and tore off her veil so that he would recognise her.

He extended a hand of friendship. She opened her arms to embrace him.

And then – horror, despair.

For he pushed her aside, and reached instead for the dragon standard in her horse's pannier.

Some soldierly instinct remained in Kye's curdled brain, some vague understanding that, though he was a combatant, he'd come to this place of battle without weapon or insignia. Now he remedied this, drawing the great banner free. Wielding it before him with both hands, he turned around and continued down the hill with his new comrades. As he went he half-stumbled on a boulder and his head fell to one side, lying flat on his shoulder. A crimson chasm yawned in the side of his neck.

Countess Madalyn tottered away, her veil clasped to her face again, now to stem a flood of tears.


BEYOND THE BROW of the bluff, in a small birch wood, stood a gated stockade and within that a pavilion of gold silk decked with the dancing red lions of Powys. Inside this, the rough grass was laid with rugs and carpets, and there was a banquet table on which food and other refreshments were spread. A smaller table bore inkpots, quills and maps of the castle. In a rear compartment, there was a bed with a lighted brazier to one side, and on the other a silver crucifix suspended from a pole.

That evening, when Gwyddon entered, the countess was on her knees in front of this holy symbol, her hands joined in fervent prayer. Tears still streaked her pale cheeks.

"Countess," he said slowly, "might I remind you... the Cauldron of Regeneration, for all that it calls on great and unknown forces, does not signify the conquest of death."

"No, Gwyddon, it doesn't." She was breathing slowly, heavily. Her brow was damp with perspiration, her eyes red with weeping. "It signifies the conquest of *life*, and all that is fine and sweet and good in this world."

"Countess, we can live our fine, sweet lives when the enemy is destroyed. But to do that we need soldiers. And I have provided you with an inexhaustible supply."

"Leave me, Gwyddon." She went back to her prayers, but the druid did not leave. He rubbed at his beard.

"Tell me, ma-am, did your Jesus Christ not rise from the dead to show your people the way?"

"How dare you!" She whirled around. "How dare you mention our Saviour's name in this place! You are a necromancer, sir. This thing you have made is a pact with Satan, for which I fear I will pay with my immortal soul."

"Even if that were true, isn't it a price worth paying when so many others will be saved?"

She struggled to reply. It was difficult to counter this point even if she'd wanted to.

Ever since the Normans had captured England, progressively more Welsh land had fallen under their sway – either as punitive official policy or through the ruthless intrusion of the marcher lords. When they hadn't been seizing titles and territory, the Anglo-Norman barons had hatched schemes and offered bribes, stirring dissent, playing the Welsh princes against each other. Always, they'd sought new ways to encroach. Until at last, Edward Longshanks – the mightiest of all England's mighty warrior-kings – had proclaimed suzerainty over the entire realm, crushing the Welsh in all-out battle, then invoking English law and English custom. Castles like Grogen had been built to strangle the nation, not protect it. So the time for talking had passed

– the most recent atrocities had surely proved this. The only solution was to fight. But fight with what? England was an empire and Wales had nothing.

"The destruction of Earl Corotocus and his murderous henchmen is the only response you can give," Gwyddon said. "It will signal that the sons and daughters of Wales are no longer English chattels, and that to make war on the Cymry is to invite annihilation."

"Annihilation, Gwyddon, is what I see all around me. I beg your pardon if it turns my stomach." She switched her attention back to her crucifix, rejoining her hands in prayer.

Before leaving, Gwyddon said: "I think you need to rest now, my lady. Your distress is quite understandable. War is indeed hell, and this one is no exception. But there is one thing about this war that will mark it out from all the others – it will be short."

# CHAPTER SIXTEEN

THE ASSAULT ON the castle was now two-pronged.

A tide of the dead again forged across the southwest bridge and attempted to circle the stronghold via the berm path. At the same time, with the defenders having abandoned the Barbican, the attackers were able to catapult more and more of their soldiers over that blood-soaked northwest rampart. For every ten of these launched, five or six would be crushed by the impact of landing – often to the point where they were unable to stand – so even after several volleys of corpses had been discharged, only a relative handful, maybe twenty in total, were capable of continuing the assault. But this handful proved to be much more than just a thorn in the defending garrison's side.

With the roof hatches to the Gatehouse sealed, the Welsh corpses stumped through the postern and down the Barbican stair into the bailey. Here they met a few wounded stragglers who'd retreated without orders from the south curtain-wall, and tore them to pieces. Advancing past the Constable's Tower, they were deluged by more missiles, but bore through it without loss, as their comrades had done outside, and entered the southwest tower by its ground floor door. The ballista crews were too preoccupied trying to rain destruction onto the hordes of cadavers crossing the southwest bridge to notice. Only when blades or clubs fell on their backs or heads, or fleshless claws wrapped around their necks from behind did they realise the danger. Their gasps and grunts of effort became screams of fear and rage. They fought back with their spanners and mallets and knives, but the snarling dead fell on them with bestial fury.

The ballista rooms turned to abattoirs as their occupants were mauled and clubbed and hacked to death. The interlopers then climbed to those higher levels manned by the royal crossbowmen. Bryon Musard shrieked orders with froth-flecked lips as the dead clambered into view. They were assailed with every type of implement, but, already raddled beyond recognition as human beings, it made no difference to them. Hatchets clove their skulls, crossbows were discharged into their faces from point-blank range – and didn't so much as hamper them. Bryon Musard died as the bolt he'd just let loose was yanked from the throat of his target, and plunged to its feathers into his right eye. Others were strangled with their own bowstrings, or beaten with their own helmets until their heads and faces were black and purple jelly.

On the topmost turret of the tower, the bowmen, having recovered jugs and pots left by the drunken Bretons, had made naptha grenades. They lit these and flung them down through the hatches as the dead tried to ascend. Smoke and flame exploded upward, but still the dead came. Blazing from head to foot, they continued the fight, slashing the screaming crossbowmen with burning claws, embracing them in their flaming arms, falling over the battlements with them.

With the southwest tower and the ballistae lost to the English, the dead now thronged over the southwest bridge unimpeded. The berm was cluttered with rubble and charred bones, but they proceeded along it at speed. The English on the curtain-wall attacked them with whatever they could, but still had no shelter from the mangonels across the river, and now faced a new danger: on top of the southwest tower, the dead took possession of discarded crossbows and began discharging them. At the same time, those dead who had infiltrated the bailey began to scale the scaffolding or file onto the curtain-wall from the door on the southwest tower.

The troops on the south wall, mainly comprising men-at-arms and the earl's indebted knights, were made of doughtier stuff than the crossbowmen, but were unused to a foe like this. When Ulbert and Ranulf arrived there, having circled around the north and east-facing curtain-walls, they found a scene of total disorder. Wounded men staggered towards them along the parapet, stumbling through a wreckage of broken bodies and smashed timber hoardings. Even as Ranulf and Ulbert watched, three more projectiles came hurtling across the river. These were the so-called devil's sachets, each linen sack bursting in mid-air, raining colossal slaughter on the fleeing defenders.

"Move onto the east wall and the north walls," Ranulf shouted as men pushed past him. "Take up new positions. The mangonels can't reach you there.

"It isn't just the mangonels, FitzOsbern!" Walter Margas shouted, pointing behind him. "Look!"

The dead from the southwest tower were now half way along the south wall, shepherding the panicked defenders ahead of them. They were led by a particularly huge and horrible specimen. It was clad only in a ragged, muddy shift, which came down to its knees. Its bearded face was a sickly yellow. Black rings circled its sunken eyes. An odious red-grey gruel flowed from its flattened nose.

One after another, it grabbed any defender it could and flung him howling over the rampart. A longbow shaft slanted down from the southeast tower. It struck the monster squarely in the chest, but had no effect. Gurt Louvain moved to meet it. Ranulf shouted a warning and shoved his way forward, his father following him.

At first things went well for Gurt. He engaged the gigantic brute fearlessly and, with deft strokes of his longsword, cut off one of its hands and clove through its left knee. The monster struggled to retain its balance. Gurt slammed his shield into its head, but it wrestled the shield from his grasp and struck him with its stump. Gurt staggered backward, tripping over a piece of masonry. The thing lurched after him, intent on slamming the shield edge-down onto his body – only to fall victim to its own side's artillery. Two more barrages of rocks came whistling over the crenels. The one-handed brute, and several corpses behind it, were struck full on and thrown down through the scaffolding. A second later, a sack of quicklime followed, exploding in a choking, blinding cloud, which engulfed much of the central wall and many defenders, including Gurt.

"Gurt!" Ranulf shouted, still blundering forward.

Several men caught in the cloud completely lost their bearings. Shrieking as they thumbed at their blistered eyes, they toppled between the crenels or fell through the scaffolding. Others tripped over each other, falling and blocking the walk. Cursing them one by one, Ranulf hauled them upright and pushed them on towards the southeast tower. When the way was clear, he tore a strip from his tabard and bound it over his eyes. Taking a deep breath, he entered the burning fog, working hand over hand along the shattered teeth of the battlements. When he found Gurt, who was lying prone and shuddering, he hauled him backward.

Gurt had been wounded by flying splinters; blood oozed from his cheeks and even through the links of his mail, but he'd reacted swiftly enough to the quicklime to put a hand over his eyes.

"D-dear Lord," he stammered, swaying to his feet. "What do... what do we face here?"

"Go through the southeast tower," Ranulf said, stripping the bandage from his own eyes, but blinking hot, peppery tears. "Find a new post on the east wall."

Gurt nodded dumbly, hobbling away.

"You go too," Ulbert said, appearing from nowhere. "I'll form this rearguard alone."

Ranulf was startled. "Alone?"

"One man on a narrow parapet is as good as ten."

"Let me do it. I'm younger."

"You have much to live for."

"And you haven't?"

"Don't dispute with me, Ranulf."

"So this is finally it, father? This is the honourable fight you've been waiting for? The fight that will kill you?"

Ulbert smiled and shook his head. "This fight will kill us all in due course. Haven't you realised that? Go. The more of us gather here, the easier targets we are for the mangonels."

Ranulf retreated towards the southeast tower. "I'll wait for you on the east wall," he shouted.

"Forget the east wall," Ulbert said over his shoulder. "Forget the north wall as well. With the bailey penetrated, the whole outer curtain's defunct. Get what's left of the men and cross the gantry bridge to the Gatehouse. That may still be defensible."

"Very well, but don't delay. You only need to buy us five minutes."

"I can manage a little longer than that," Ulbert said.

Ranulf peered at his father's back. The rear of Ulbert's handsome red and blue quartered mantel was cleaner than its front – a sure and perhaps disconcerting sign that this was one seigneur who rarely ran from the enemy. As if in confirmation, Ulbert unbuckled his sword-belt and unsheathed his blade.

"Five minutes is all we need," Ranulf called to him. "Your word you won't tarry any longer?"

Ulbert looked back and smiled – and it was a warm smile, the first one Ranulf had seen from his father for a considerable time.

"My word and my pledge, boy."

Ranulf moved on, herding the remaining defenders ahead of him.

"Which, as they were given under duress," Ulbert added to himself, "mean nothing. *Ranulf!*"

Ranulf, about to enter the southeast tower, glanced back one more time.

"Be true to your heart, lad," Ulbert said, staring at him intently. "In the end, when all has come to pass, it'll be the only thing you can trust."

Ranulf swallowed, before nodding and moving on.

Ulbert slammed his visor down, hefted his sword and shield, and advanced alone. The quicklime was settling and, just ahead of him now, the dead emerged through it, their forms shrouded with white. The first one had smashed hips and walked at a crazy tilt. Only its gaping red maw revealed that it was made from flesh and blood. Formerly a rood-worker, it wielded a hand-scythe.

Ulbert charged at it.

*"Notre dame!"* he roared.

He parried its first blow, and swept its head from its trunk with a single crosscut. It flailed at him with the scythe, but he drove it backward with his shield until it lost its footing and fell through the scaffolding. The next one lunged with a spear. He hewed the shaft, and rammed his blade through its groin – so deeply that he couldn't retrieve it. It went for his throat, but he knocked its hands loose, drew his falchion and stove its skull. It remained standing, so he kicked at it hard, breaking its right knee with his mailed foot; it tottered sideways and again fell through the scaffolding. The third came barehanded, arms spread wide as though to clasp him in a bear-hug. Again he advanced behind his shield, driving it towards the crenels, finally tipping it through the first embrasure. The fourth one, an eyeless, jawless hulk, was equipped with an axe. It smote him on the right shoulder. His mail turned the blade, but the impact was agonising – Ulbert knew immediately that his shoulder was broken. He staggered out of its way, having to drop his shield.

There was a brazier filled with glowing coals to his left. He hurled it at them to delay their advance. The eyeless horror wore a tattered habit, possibly it had once been a monk or friar. It raised the axe over its head, but now the hem of its habit caught flame. Fire licked up its legs and torso, diverting its attention. Ulbert darted forward, plunging the falchion into its chest, grappling with it, lifting it bodily despite the flames, which enveloped him as well and scorched him through his mail, and dropping it over the parapet.

Exhausted and unarmed, he retreated. A quick glance took in the entrance to the southeast tower, thirty yards behind him. It was cramped and chaotic in there – all the south wall defenders had passed through it, but now the archers from the tower's upper levels and roof were flowing down the spiral stair to join the retreat. More time was needed.

Ulbert swung back around, his right arm hanging limp and useless. Lime-slathered corpses loomed towards him. The first, which wore mail but no helmet, had been split from its cranium to the tip of its chin. Both hemispheres of its riven head hung outwards, the eyes several inches apart, the nose entirely divided, only strands of pinkish mucus linking the two halves together. It brandished a spiked club.

Ulbert grabbed an abandoned shield. It was kite-shaped and cumbersome. With his injury it was difficult to manage, and all he could do was raise it as high as possible and try to fend off a series of frenzied blows. Sickening pain spread from his shoulder, filling his aged, tired body, each jolt making it worse. Alongside the club-wielder, a naked woman had appeared with a heavy stone, though she was recognisable as female only by her shrivelled sex organs. In truth she was a thing of sticks, a withered framework to which scarcely a vestige of flesh was attached. With demonic shrieks, she also struck at the shield.

For a brief time her very ghastliness gave Ulbert new heart. These were genuine devils, he realised – denizens of the pit. All his years in the service of self-interested noblemen might now be assuaged. The villages he'd burned, the crops he'd trampled, the livestock he'd stolen, and the many enemies he'd viciously slain who of course were only enemies to Ulbert and Ranulf because the likes of Earl Corotocus had proclaimed them so. And then the Welsh – who they'd hanged and butchered and driven from a land to which their bloodline entitled them more than any number of charters or benefices ever could.

"Nothing I have done in my life is worthy of the title 'knight'," Ulbert grunted as he retreated, the club and stone smashing repeatedly on his shield. "I have failed my wife, my son, my family name and, above all, myself."

His shield flew to splinters. He grabbed up a javelin and hurled it. It buried itself in the chest of the club-wielder, who staggered backward. The fleshless woman came on regardless. Ulbert took her next blow on his forearm, before slamming his mailed fist into her face, crushing her features as if they were carved in turnip flesh. As she swung another blow, he ducked, caught her in the midriff with his injured shoulder and raised her up – though the pain this induced was indescribable. He dropped her through a gap between the crenels, dizzied, almost falling after her. For a second he hung there, gasping. Lifting his visor, he gazed down the burned, blood-streaked wall to the berm, now a forest of arms and heads and raised blades. The howls and shrieks of the damned rose in a hellish dirge.

"I have reneged on my duties to the weak," he cried, "to the poor, to women, to my fellow countrymen, my fellow Christians, and undoubtedly… to God! But all this will be well…"

An arm hooked around his neck, and tried to yank him backward. He jerked himself forward, flipping his assailant over his shoulder. As it fell from sight, he stumbled around. Claws clamped on his throat and attempted to throttle him. They belonged to a gangling thing that was black with rot and clad only in a leather apron soaked with blood. An arrow had pierced it through the back of the head and emerged from its right socket; an eyeball was fixed on the iron barb in a blob of unblinking putrescence.

"All this will be well," Ulbert said again, choking but grabbing the thing's throat in return, and driving its head against the head of its neighbour with such force that both skulls shattered, vile sludge bursting forth. He tore the arrow from its mashed skull, stabbing and hacking as yet more of them surged against him, forcing him backward through the embrasure. He was acutely aware of the abyss behind him, of his strength ebbing, but he stabbed frantically on. "For though I have been worthless in life, perhaps... perhaps with one final deed, I can be worth something in deeeaaa..."

Further words were lost as he plummeted from the parapet, dragging a couple with him by the scruffs of their necks. Six more followed through sheer momentum. For the same reason, Ulbert fell diagonally rather than straight. He didn't hit the berm but the river – though it brought no relief.

Weighted by his mail, he plunged through its green shallows like a spear, and struck the pebbly bottom helmet first. There was a flash in his head, a sound like thunder, and a short but intense spasm of pain in the middle of his back; and then eerie muffled silence, rippling shadows – and nothing.

Nothing at all.

# CHAPTER SEVENTEEN

RANULF WAS THE last of the curtain-wall defenders to reach the northwest corner of the castle, where the gantry drawbridge connected with the Gatehouse. There were one or two behind him, but he waited as they stumbled past. Some were still blinded by smoke or quicklime, others bleeding and limping. All were exhausted, their armour dented, their weapons broken.

Compared to the south wall of course, the battlements of the north wall were undamaged. He stared back along them, maybe two hundred yards, to the tower at the distant northeast corner. The massive structure of the Inner Fort and the Keep prevented him seeing more than that, but there was no sign of Ulbert hobbling in pursuit. Fifty feet below meanwhile, ragged figures had appeared on the north berm, though initially they only came in ones and twos. Every type of mutilation and dismemberment had been wrought on them, but they'd advanced past the east wall without suffering any assault and now would do the same with the north wall, so they were coming on apace. Soon there would be hundreds of them.

He peered again along the north parapet. Still there was no trace of his father. Ranulf was too numb and bone-weary to feel a sense of despair. But the sweat was drying on his aching body, his skin tightening, and inside his chest his heart was slowly sinking. Hope briefly sprang when a tiny shape suddenly emerged from the northeast tower. But another shape appeared behind it, and then another, and another. And he knew that it was *them*.

Mailed feet clumped over the drawbridge behind. A hand touched his shoulder.

"He could still be alive," Gurt said. "Hiding in one of the other towers maybe?"

Ranulf shook his head. "Hiding isn't father's way."

"He's a sensible enough man to know when discretion is the better part of valour."

"Not today, I fear."

They crossed back over the bridge together. Below them, the castle's entry passage was still empty. It was only about twenty feet across, which made it a deep, echoing canyon, though soon, they knew, it would be packed with howling monstrosities. On the other side of the gantry drawbridge, the interior of the Gatehouse was cramped, dark, and stank of smoke, sweat and faeces. The men who'd retreated from the curtain-wall were milling about in confusion. Arguments raged, many of those who'd already sought refuge from the roof insisting that there wasn't room for anyone else. Ranulf glanced behind him again, watching the dead approach along the top of the north wall. Gurt signalled to a man-at-arms to raise the drawbridge. The fellow attacked the wheel with gusto, but found it stiff with disuse.

"Even if he is in one of the other towers," Ranulf told Gurt, "he's as good as dead. In a very short time, these things will infest every inch of this stronghold."

"Except in here!" came a strident voice.

Ranulf turned and saw Odo de Lussac, one of the earl's youngest tenant knights, a freeholder through family ties rather than right of service. He was in a semi-deranged state. His hair was a sodden ginger mop, his lean, pimpled face ash-white. He was grinning, but his eyes were glazed like baubles.

"The Gatehouse is strong," he declared.

Ranulf shook his head. "Its rooftop hatches will only hold for so long."

"We've secured them."

"And when the Welsh bring the earl's mangonels to the western bluff? When they substitute the iron hail with great boulders?"

"The king will come," de Lussac insisted. "They're all saying he's marching from the north. He may only be a couple of days away."

"For all we know, he's already battling hordes of these creatures himself, without the protection of stone walls."

De Lussac's eyes widened with nervous anger. "You're a traitor, FitzOsbern! Navarre is right. You counsel defeatism. You talk as if some unstoppable tide is sweeping the land."

Ranulf tried not to laugh. "Look there!" He pointed through the portal and over the drawbridge. Beyond it, corpses were advancing. "What do you see?"

"I see Welshmen in masquerade!" de Lussac shouted. His tone was shrill, almost hysterical. "I see peasant rabble who have lulled the foolish and the cowardly, such as you, into thinking the ridiculous. I see, I see…"

His words ended in a gargle as a bolt thudded into his open mouth, burying itself in the back of his throat. Gagging, a crimson river pouring from his lips, he stumbled out onto the bridge, from which he plummeted into the entry passage.

"I see one more heriot for the earl's coffers," Ranulf said grimly.

Another bolt flitted past, striking a squire in the back of the skull. There was renewed panic and shouting. White faces, shining with sweat, turned frantically towards the open portal. Ranulf saw that the dead were still ten yards from the end of the north wall, but that three of them were armed with crossbows, which they'd no doubt purloined from the southwest tower. It was incomprehensible – these rotted, mangled carcasses reloading such sophisticated weapons, raising them to their broken shoulders and taking practised aim.

"Hurry up with that bloody bridge!" Gurt shrieked.

"Help me, my lord, please!" The man-at-arms still worked at the wheel, throwing all his weight against it. Beads of perspiration stood on his flustered brow.

Gurt and several others assisted, and slowly, with a grinding of rust, the wheel began to move. But before the bridge could be raised, the first group of dead had stepped onto it. There were four of them in total and beneath their combined weight, the chain-and-pulley system groaned as though set to break. The men on the wheel had to release their grip and the bridge thundered back into place.

"We must clear the bridge!" Gurt yelled.

Ranulf drew his blade and went out there first. Two others followed. One was Ramon la Roux, another of the earl's indebted knights, formerly a landed lord distinctive through the midland shires for his black mantle with its emblazoned white raven. He carried a shield and a battle-axe and wore a tall, cylindrical helm. The other was one of Garbofasse's mercenaries, a huge fellow dressed in studded leather and wielding a massive, two-handed war-hammer. Though twenty feet in length and about six wide, the gantry drawbridge was only one plank thick and flimsy beneath their feet. It shuddered as the dead shuffled across it towards them.

Ranulf spun as he met the first, parrying a blow from its poll-arm and shearing through its left leg, overbalancing it so that it pitched into the abyss. The one la Roux engaged carried an iron-headed club and it smote him on the front of his helm, denting it deeply. He staggered backward, but managed to sink his axe into its left shoulder, cleaving through to the breastbone. It dropped its club and tried to grapple with him. They teetered on the edge until Ranulf struck from behind, severing its spine with a single thrust, twisting his blade around and wrenching it sideways, truncating the horror at the waist. Now the huge mercenary joined the fray, sidling past the knights and knocking the two remaining monsters from the bridge with massive, sweeping blows of his war-hammer.

Soon the bridge was clear, though it would remain so only fleetingly. Wild shouts rang from the Gatehouse, urging them to retreat, to "get back for the love of God!"

Ranulf and la Roux withdrew but, drunk on victory, the mercenary remained and beat his chest, bellowing that he could hold this bridge 'til kingdom come. At which point – with a loud, wet *crack* – he was struck on the back of the head by a cobblestone. He tottered sideways, blood shooting from his nostrils, before falling face-first from the bridge. Ranulf glanced up and behind and saw those dead who'd already taken the Gatehouse roof massing against its eastern battlements. They were ten feet overhead and out of sword-reach, but were now pelting the bridge and its defenders with any missile that came to hand.

"Back inside!" Ranulf shouted, pushing la Roux ahead of him, and having to swat a javelin with his mailed hand, which otherwise would have skewered his neck.

Twenty feet away, more of the dead were reaching the end of the drawbridge, but, as soon as the two knights were back inside, Gurt and his henchmen went at the wheel like things possessed. The bridge rose quickly. One of the dead had placed a foot on it, and subsequently was cast into the gulf. Several more attempted suicidal leaps, hands outstretched, but all missed their mark and followed their comrade to the carrion-strewn flagstones far below. Before the bridge was completely raised, a final crossbow bolt sailed through its narrowing gap and struck la Roux in the left shoulder, punching into his mail. Cursing, he pulled off his broken helm. Normally a gentleman of deportment who favoured short, pointed beards, clean-shaven cheeks and a trim moustache, his face now bristled with unshaved whiskers, and was ingrained with dirt and sweat. Moreover, both his eyes were swollen and his nose flattened and bloodied. The drawbridge aperture closed with a thump and darkness reinvaded the congested space.

Several more torches were lit before it was possible to see who was who. La Roux had slumped to his haunches, clutching his shoulder, from which blood was pulsing. Ranulf knelt to attend him, saying that they had to get him to Doctor Zacharius.

La Roux waved such logic aside. "Damn that!" he said through locked teeth. "Is that it? Is the curtain-wall lost?"

"I think so…"

"And it was a costly sacrifice," came a third voice.

The press of exhausted men cleared to allow Earl Corotocus through. Navarre and du Guesculin stood one to either side of him, each holding a flaming brand.

Corotocus focussed on Ranulf. "They say your father fell?"

"I think that's true, my lord."

"Ranulf led the charge to retake the gantry," someone jabbered. "I saw it myself. His sword was like a thunderbolt."

"I hear this too," Corotocus said with half a smile. "Your father is a sad loss. It will not go without notation in your family's record of service, Ranulf. You may count half your debt to me paid."

Ranulf nodded as he stood up, unable to work out at so fraught a moment whether this was a generous gesture or miserly. Instead, he blurted out something else.

"My lord, we must release the girl!"

Conversation in the crowded room ceased. Corotocus's expression was blank.

"Would you repeat that, Ranulf?"

"Countess Madalyn wishes her daughter returned. I suggest we comply with those wishes."

Corotocus still looked blank. "And if we don't?"

"If we don't, we'll all die in this place. Or worse."

The earl almost looked amused. "Worse?"

The rest of the men listened intently. Flames crackled. From outside came the muffled hubbub of the dead.

"Do these walking corpses serve their new masters willingly?" Ranulf asked, wondering belatedly if it was wise to air this view, but remembering with painful clarity the last words his father had said to him. "I'd suggest 'no'. Are they breaking themselves to pieces on our walls through past allegiance? Again, no. My lord, they've been summoned through sorcery." The earl watched with lidded eyes as Ranulf turned to face the rest of his audience. "We're all in agreement about that. Aren't we? Devilish sorcery. So I ask this: what if the same is done with our own dead?"

The silence intensified as this horrific possibility dawned on the men. Not only might they soon be facing their own slain comrades, but what if they themselves, once cut down, were denied all funeral rites and set to this diabolical work? Wouldn't their very souls be imperilled?

"And to avoid this catastrophe you advocate that we release the hostage?" Corotocus said.

Ranulf nodded.

The earl brooded on this. Still the flames crackled. From beyond the shuttered tower, the howls and groans of the dead seemed to increase. Objects thudded against the hatches.

"You ride well with a lance, Ranulf," Corotocus finally said. "You wield your sword with enviable skill. Yet brinkmanship is not your forte. We have two key bargaining chips here, and you would happily throw one of them away? Does anyone else think that would be wise?"

Several heads were shaken.

"My lord," Ranulf pleaded, "if the girl is so useful a bargaining chip, why not bargain with her now... and save more of our lives?"

"Because of the *second* chip we hold, Ranulf: Grogen Castle itself." The earl faced his men. "The curtain-wall may be lost, but we still have the Constable's Tower and the Inner Fort. Hells, we still have this Gatehouse, which itself can withstand the most ferocious attack!"

"Earl Corotocus!" came a frightened voice from below. "The Welsh are approaching the main entrance."

Corotocus nodded as if pleased. "Come Ranulf. Watch as I send them back to the Hell they've only just escaped."

Ranulf and Gurt followed him down a stair to the second level. From here, they peered through arrow-slits onto the entry passage, which, as Ranulf had predicted, was now crammed with the groaning, jostling dead.

The demented horde beat on the huge, iron-plated gate with limp hands, skeletal claws and every type of blunt or broken weapon, creating a cacophony that grew steadily louder and more frightening. With a single command from the earl, vats were opened on the first level and streams of burning oil vented down. An inferno resulted, the packed dead blazing like human torches – their hair, their flesh, their clothing – yet they pounded on the castle gate with tireless fury. More burning oil was discharged; more of the dead were engulfed. Those at the white-hot heart of the conflagration wilted, sagging to their knees as they were eaten to their bones. Black smoke filled with grease, sparks and vile cinders spiralled into the upper part of the passage.

"Only fire destroys them," Gurt observed.

"And even then it takes an age," Ranulf replied, focussing on one tall, blazing figure, who appeared to have been carrying a banner depicting the Welsh dragon. This banner had now fallen to ashes but the figure was shaking its talon-like fist at the Gatehouse even as flames flared from its empty eyesockets and gaping jaws.

At last, the half-cremated legion had no option but to withdraw. The earl laughed raucously as it left in its wake a mountain of smouldering bones and blackened, quivering carrion. But his laughter faded when it returned half an hour later, carrying heavy chains and hooks.

"Cut them down!" he roared. "Slay them!" Arrows sleeted from the high portals, hitting the scorched figures over and over, but having no effect. "More oil, damn your hides, damn your wretched eyes!"

Yet more fiery cascades were poured from the castle walls, which the dead simply marched through. Again their rent flesh and ragged garb, now besmeared with broiled fat, saw them ignite like living candles. But they were still able to clamber over the charred offal, beat on the gate with hammers and tongs and, thanks to the metal plating having been heated and softened, to secure breaches through which the hooks could be fixed. When they withdrew again, they hauled on the chains in teams, hundreds and hundreds at a time.

"Navarre!" Corotocus bellowed, scuttling down a flight of stairs. "Man the fire-raiser!"

Ranulf and Gurt followed the earl to the first level, which was basically an archery platform overlooking the Gatehouse tunnel. Below them, Navarre and several others were already alongside the fire-raiser, but now, with a torturous rending of wood and metal, the gate fell. They promptly began working on the huge bellows.

With the gate down, the main mass of the dead came flooding back along the entry passage to attack the portcullis, only to be greeted by clouds of sulphurous flame. With more oil cast from above, it again became a scene from Hell's foundry. But several still made it to the portcullis bars, which they gripped with their bare hands. Further gusts of fire swept through them, peeling away their rotted flesh layer by layer, searing the organs beneath until the vile fluids that filled them bubbled. Again, some collapsed. Others that had made it to the bars were fused there, black and sticky effigies melting onto the glowing ironwork. With the portcullis bolted down and impossible to lift manually, the remaining dead attempted to fix more chains, but now Earl Corotocus descended a ladder and joined the fray.

Calling the fire-raisers to halt, he hurried forward with a sword and mattock. As he hacked at the hooks, a vision of grinning, half-melted lunacy tried to grapple with him through the red-hot bars. He plunged his sword into its chest, only to be spattered with sizzling meat. Other men assisted him. With frenzied blows from axes and hammers, the hooks were broken, the chains severed. The defenders retreated and the fire-raising recommenced – gales of flame, like repeated blasts from a furnace, incinerating even those sturdiest of the dead who still clutched at the bars.

By now the stench and smoke had become intolerable all through the Gatehouse. Men staggered down its tunnel and out through its rear entrance onto the Causeway, coughing, choking, rubbing at streaming eyes. Others vomited or fainted. Ranulf was rigid as a board as he strode out among them. Ignoring everyone else, he headed straight for the Constable's Tower.

"Where are you going?" Gurt called after him.

Ranulf made no reply.

# CHAPTER EIGHTEEN

ON FIRST ARRIVING at Grogen Castle and imprisoning Gwendolyn of Lyr, Ranulf took charge of two keys to her cell. When Murlock the mercenary replaced him, he only handed over one of them. At the time he hadn't been sure why. Had he genuinely felt such concern for the prisoner that he might want to come back and check on her welfare? Or was it the case that, right from the outset, he'd viewed her as a possible source of advantage to him?

Either way, as he re-ascended through the dripping darkness of the Keep, its mighty walls having silenced the sounds of battle without, he knew that he must tread warily.

On the Keep's seventh floor, its arched passages opened into numerous cobweb-festooned chambers. In one such, the garderobe, he saw Murlock standing with his back turned, grunting as he urinated into the privy chute, a brick shaft some four feet in diameter which fell right down through the innards of the building. Ranulf slipped past and proceeded along the passage, until he reached the door at the far end. He inserted his second key and turned it. Once inside, he closed the door behind him as quietly as he could.

Gwendolyn sat in the same place where he'd left her, only now she'd brought the lantern over. Its tiny flame illuminated little more than a few feet, though it revealed that she'd collected the blankets and gathered the little dry straw she'd been able to find, making a nest for herself. On his entry, she knelt up, trembling, possibly expecting that it would be Murlock. When Ranulf stepped into the light, she relaxed a little – but only for a second. Despite her earlier threats, his stained mantle, the gashes and bruises on his face, and the blood-clots in his tangled hair came as a shock to her.

"Has he treated you well?" Ranulf asked.

His right hand was clamped on the hilt of his sheathed sword. He knew there'd be a wildness about him, a dangerous gleam in his eye. It was difficult to imagine that he could present a picture of normality after the day he'd experienced. She nodded dumbly.

"And how rational a person is your mother?" Ranulf wondered.

Still distracted by the state he was in, the girl was apparently thrown by this question. "How rational is my...? How rational would yours be, having seen her people massac-"

"Does she want to see more of the same?"

Gwendolyn hesitated before replying. His abrupt tone implied that he was no longer the courteous knight conflicted between duty and compassion.

"By the looks of things," she said, "it isn't my mother's people who need fear massacre."

"This madness has to end, Gwendolyn!"

"You say that now..."

"Be flippant all you wish, girl, but as things are no-one will leave this place alive!" Despite his best efforts, Ranulf's voice rose to a hoarse shout. "And you will roast on a spit before Earl Corotocus gives you up!" He paused, breathing hard. Fresh blood trickled from his brow. "So I ask you again: is your mother rational?"

"That depends on what you propose."

"What I propose is to end this slaughter. What I propose is to exchange the lives of many for the life of one."

"One?" she whispered. "And who is this one?"

"Who do you think?"

She clearly didn't believe him. In fact, she scoffed. "Your overlord? But how could that happen?"

"It won't be easy. A chance will have to arise. But I need to know… is it a risk worth my taking?"

"Sir knight, if you are losing this battle, as I suspect…"

"Don't hang your hopes on that. We're far from beaten yet!" He retreated towards the cell door. "We *may* lose it. But the tide of Welsh deaths will be cataclysmic. Never underestimate Earl Corotocus when it comes to killing. If he dies here in Wales, orders may already have been given to unleash genocide on your people. And by then even *I* won't be around to stop it."

"Better destruction than slavery."

"I'm offering you an easier way out."

"No, you're *seeking* a way out."

"That too."

"Why should we help you?"

"You'll be helping yourselves in the process. You'll be helping mankind."

She watched him warily, wondering what kind of web he was weaving. Again she shook her head. "I don't believe you would hand over your lord and master."

"There was much I wouldn't have believed when this morning dawned." He opened the cell door. "As you wish."

"Wait!" she called. "Wait. I don't even know your name." He ignored her and made to step outside. "If it helps, sir knight, my mother is a *very* rational woman."

Ranulf glanced back; their eyes met. He nodded, closing and locking the door. Half way along the passage he encountered Murlock, who peered at him balefully. Ranulf didn't bother to speak. He didn't even look at the big jailer as he brushed past.

# CHAPTER NINETEEN

PRINCE LLEWELLYN OF Gwynedd and his nobles arrived that fine autumn morning in 1278, to find the road to Worcester strewn with rose petals and lined with cheering folk.

The October sun beat warmly on the freshly stripped fields to either side. The blue sky was filled with swallows and only the fleeciest hint of cloud. Half a mile ahead of the prince, beyond the thatched roofs of the town, towered the cathedral – an almost magical structure built from chalk-white stone, its arches and statues climbing one above the other, tier on heavenly tier, its lofty pinnacles billowing with gaily-coloured banners. Ranulf, who was only five years old, marvelled at the sight of it.

Such a magnificent edifice could not have been more fitting a venue for an occasion like this, which every adult he knew had assured him was not just joyous, but very, very important for all of them.

As soon as Prince Llewellyn and his party crossed the border from Wenwynwyn and entered the realm of King Edward, the sun had broken through the murky cloud of early morning, and the woods and meadows had come alive with bird-song. A troop of royal knights and heralds, clad handsomely in crimson velvet smocks emblazoned with the prancing golden lions, greeted them at Leominster, and escorted them through villages thronging with happy faced peasants, across brooks choked with lily pads, and past fatted cattle herded on the bright green pastures.

It was truly a good time to be alive in the marcher lands and the central shires of England, for today's great event – after so many years of strife – would at last signal peace with the great principality of Wales. It was no surprise therefore, that everywhere folk came flocking across the fields, cheering. Not just the peasants on the land with their hoes and ploughshares, but all the freemen and guildsmen of the towns as well; the merchants, the millers, the clothiers, the bakers, the butchers, the farriers, the fletchers, the saddlers – people from every level of society, all singing the praises of King Edward, whose wisdom and diplomacy had brought about this treaty, and Prince Llewellyn, whose courage and foresight had made it possible. With such an alliance, the dark and ravaging forces of war, once seemingly without end in this region, would be consigned to history once and for all.

Prince Llewellyn and his men were themselves a merry band. Dark-haired, dark eyed and, in the prince's case, wolfishly handsome. They had come to England displaying all their traditional banners and standards – the Red Dragon, the Lions of Gwynedd – but for once carrying neither spears nor shields, nor wearing mail. Instead, they sported wedding-day raiment, the prince clad in hose and tunic of forest green, a cape of gold thread, and a green hunting cap with a silver plume.

In the heart of Worcester itself, the cathedral concourse was also decked for this grandest occasion, the stone square carpeted with flowers. Flags and pennons streamed from posts and rooftops. Monks and lay-brethren of the cathedral chapter scampered hither and thither to ensure that everything was just as it should be. For it was here where King Edward would require Prince Llewellyn to offer homage and fealty to the English Crown, and officially recognise Edward as his sovereign lord. Only after this solemn moment, would the prince and his betrothed, Eleanor de Montfort, ward and first cousin to the king, exchange their vows and a holy mass be sung.

It would be a significant occasion, Ulbert FitzOsbern had advised his young son. Only when it was completed could the feasting begin, though already preparations were in progress for this. On a broad meadow just outside the town, where many ornate pavilions – each one representing some great household – had been pitched, long trestle tables were being laid with cloth and arrayed with cutlery. Minstrels were tuning their instruments, jongleurs testing their voices. Kegs of wine and barrels of beer and cider had been gathered in abundance. The delicious scents from the open-air kitchens wafted even through Worcester's crooked by-ways – succulent cuts of meat, pork and venison, basting in their own juices, wildfowl and chickens turning on spits, vegetables boiling in salted butter, the sweet aroma of baking bread.

Of course, the greatest moment of all would come when King Edward himself arrived, escorting his cousin by her dainty hand. Ranulf's father would himself walk in this royal procession, though only at the rear, as a loyal tenant of the one of the king's great barons. The rest of the FitzOsbern family, like the families of other lesser dignitaries, would be forced to wait with the eagerly watching crowd, though they were afforded some solace by having places allocated in one of several roped-off stalls with raised seating, which were ranged at the front of the cathedral concourse. The common folk would have to make do as best they could, peeking out between these flimsy, flag-draped structures, or watching from the high windows and steep, shaggy roofs of Worcester's tall, timber buildings.

Ranulf, uncomfortable in his white hose, white satin tunic and long, pointy-toed boots, sat close and snug against the warm thigh of his mother and held her gloved hand throughout, though her grip noticeably tightened when Bishop Godfrey emerged from the cathedral door in vestments of purest gold, with a gold mitre on his brow, and a fanfare of trumpeters announced that the royal entourage was at last approaching.

When they entered the great concourse they came on foot, having walked from the castle, where they had lodged for the night. King Edward, who strode beneath a scarlet canopy carried by four servants in purple hose and scarlet tabards, was perhaps the most resplendent figure the young boy had ever seen: six feet and four inches tall, massive at the shoulder and with a true warrior's bearing. He had a rich, but neatly trimmed beard and a shock of reddish hair, on which his crown was firmly set. His long tunic was of rich murrey velvet, emblazoned all over with lions, his serge cloak decked in a similar pattern. Behind him came the usual gaggle of prelates in their episcopal purple, glittering with their rings and chains of office, and then the greatest of the great magnates, each one in their own traditional heraldic garb.

The bride herself was a slim, child-like figure. She wore a chaste white gown, tight at the hips but full in the skirt, and walked demurely alongside her cousin, one hand in his. A white fur cape hung from her shoulders and a veil of white lace concealed her features, though her coiled flaxen-yellow hair was visible inside its silken caul, studded with gemstones.

Ranulf had heard that she was a great beauty, but that didn't mean much to him. He'd only ever known one beauty in his short life and, as far as he was concerned, she would never be surpassed – and that was his mother. That morning, when they'd risen in their pavilion to prepare for the day, she'd seemed more gorgeous to him than he could ever remember. Bright eyed and red lipped, she wore a lilac dress covered by a green cloak embroidered with woodland flowers, and her glimmering raven hair was coiled beneath a babette and tied under her chin with a linen fillet. Even in the midst of the cheering and clapping, the banging of drums, the tooting of pipes and brazen batteries of trumpets, Ranulf remembered how much he adored his mother. He glanced up at her, expecting, as always, that she would beam down at him with all the love and happiness in the world.

Except that this time it was different.

His mother was frowning.

Her mouth was a tight, grey line. Her cheeks had sunk and were hued an unhealthy shade of blue. Her eyes had collapsed like tarnished stones into cavernous hollows. When she finally smiled, her shrivelled lips peeled back from brown peg-teeth clamped in a skeletal grimace...

RANULF SAT UP sharply, his brow damp.

At first he didn't know where he was.

It was dark and cold, rank with the stench of smoke, sweat and burned flesh. Gradually he noted the grunts, groans and coughs and came to sense the many bodies slumped around him, and his awareness of reality returned. He was on the second level of the Gatehouse, huddled under his cloak and lying in a corner between Gurt and Ramon la Roux. It was probably the early hours of the morning, though from somewhere overhead he heard a faint, echoing *boom*.

From midnight onward there'd been a lull in the fighting. The dead had withdrawn from the entry passage, abandoning their attack on the portcullis, which by then was crusted from top to bottom with the twisted charcoal relics of their vanguard. This had afforded the defenders an opportunity to drink some water, cram some bread into their bellies and catch a little sleep.

Another *boom*, deep and hollow, sounded from overhead. Another followed. And another. Suddenly it was relentless, repeating itself over and over again.

Now that the cold had settled into his body and limbs, Ranulf was stiff all over. As he clambered to his feet, his joints ached and creaked. Other men began to stir. With each impact overhead, dust trickled down onto them.

"What is... what is that?" Gurt mumbled.

"Nothing good," Ranulf replied, heading for the stair.

On the third level, he met Hugh du Guesculin, who was carrying a candle and looked ashen-faced.

"They have a battering ram," du Guesculin said in a querulous tone.

Other men were now milling around them in the darkness, muttering and swearing.

Du Guesculin took Ranulf's arm. "Did you hear what I said, FitzOsbern? Those abominations on the north wall – they have a battering ram. They're using it on the gantry door."

"From the north wall?" Ranulf said. "It must be twenty feet across that gap."

"They've cut down a pine and trimmed its trunk. They can easily reach over. Not only that, they've tied ladders together. Improvised their own bridge."

Ranulf moved past him to the door in question. With each impact, it shook violently.

This drawbridge had never been constructed to withstand attack; it had never really been more than an access point between the Gatehouse and the curtain-wall. In due course, probably very soon, it would be smashed – and the dead would push their own bridge over and flow across it. Though many might be tossed to destruction en route, there would always, as they'd repeatedly proved in this siege of sieges, be more of them. At the same time, they would attack the portcullis again. The crew on the fire-raiser would be overwhelmed from within, and the Gatehouse would fall.

At that moment, sluggish with hunger, muddled by fatigue, Ranulf could not conceive of a single strategy to prevent this. And then, with an explosive report, three of the door's central planks fractured inwards.

"Get the earl," he said, jerking to life.

But the earl was already present, standing alongside du Guesculin. It was Earl Corotocus's manner, even in times of extreme crisis, to be grim but never despairing. Yet now, for the first time at Grogen Castle, his mouth twitched, his cheek had paled to a deathly hue.

"Sound the alarum," he said. "Retreat to the Constable's Tower."

# CHAPTER TWENTY

WHEN AN ARMY is prepared to lose thousands upon thousands of its men, or indeed, as in this case, is incapable of losing a single man, the word 'impregnable' no longer applies to any redoubt.

The English bore this in mind as they readied the Constable's Tower to receive the next onslaught. In normal times, the Constable's Tower would have felt far more secure than the Gatehouse. Its parapets were thirty feet higher, and in terms of structure it was altogether more massive, its walls infinitely thicker. It had more vents for oil and pitch and more loops from which missiles could be discharged. In addition, it could only really be attacked from one side. To the east and south it faced into the Inner Fort, the courtyard of which was a good eighty feet below. To the west, it faced into the bailey, which was a hundred feet below. Neither of these immense distances could be covered by ladder or climbing rope – at least, Earl Corotocus's men had never heard of such a thing. But from the north, it was a different matter.

The Constable's Tower's main door was on the north side, facing onto the causeway connecting from the Gatehouse. What was more, the door faced onto this directly, so that a ram could be brought to bear if it got close enough. It would not breach the tower easily: the gate was fashioned from English oak, some ten inches thick, and was ribbed with steel. Behind it there lay a passage beneath a murder hole, another portcullis, and beyond that the fire-raiser, which the English had refuelled. But given the nature of the enemy, nobody felt that these measures provided sufficient protection. What was more, the north wall of the Constable's Tower was only sixty feet high and was a far less daunting prospect than the walls to the south, east and west.

The English did what they could. They gathered new stocks of stones, spears, darts and arrows. They brought up new barrels of naptha. They crowded against the missile-portals and along the battlements, particularly on the north side, overlooking the causeway. Several companies had already been positioned in the Constable's Tower when the earl and what remained of the Gatehouse garrison arrived, but from that moment on there'd been no sleep for any of them. Blunted blades were re-sharpened, shields were patched, new fragments of armour donned. Every man – even if he wouldn't admit it – now looked to his own survival as much as to victory for his overlord.

By first light they were waiting, so tense that they no longer saw the weird Breton scarecrows, which littered the rooftops even of these inner ramparts.

The men had already passed the stage where sweat-inducing fear was an issue. Fear comes before battle rather than during it; it tends to dissipate after the first clash of steel, to be replaced by a duller but more practical state-of-mind in which warriors think purely about necessary actions. One such necessity was that everyone in the castle should now be present. The Constable's Tower was the key to the Inner Fort, and they could not afford to let it fall. Hence, the earl had redeployed every man into this one bastion, no longer concerned about a mingling of his companies or any confusion among his junior command.

Those wounded from the assaults on the Barbican and the south wall lay on its ground-level, wrapped in their bedrolls, gasping and shivering, with nothing to anaesthetise their pain as they awaited transportation to the infirmary, assuming such a luxury would ever come. Father Benan, one who would normally tend to them, was among their number, naked and slumped against a pillar. The only item he wore was a large iron crucifix, suspended by a cord at his neck. He was scarcely able to breathe, so weak was he from loss of blood. His entire body – his back, his buttocks, his shoulders, his arms, his legs – were crisscrossed with crimson stripes.

He was only vaguely aware, when a person came and crouched alongside him, that it was Doctor Zacharius, now with a gore-stained canvas apron over his fine clothes and his sleeves pinned back on forearms equally sullied.

As Zacharius looked the priest over, he mopped sweat from his haggard brow, smearing more blood there. With the few orderlies he'd been given now redeployed to defend the Constable's Tower roof, he'd had to cease working on his patients in order to help his assistant bring as many wounded as he could to the infirmary. Between them, they had improvised a bier by tying a cloak between two poll-arms, but it was still a laborious process, especially since neither of them had enjoyed much sleep since arriving here. But Zacharius, for all his faults, was not a doctor purely for the esteem it gave him. He believed in his vocation and would not shy from the dirt and drudgery of it.

"Benan!" he said into the priest's ear. "Benan, can you stand?"

Benan grunted in the negative, still too dazed by pain and exhaustion to form words.

"Benan, can you can stand and make your own way to the infirmary? I have salves that will help with these welts."

"There are… others," Benan muttered. "Others… worse than me…"

"Benan, some of these wounds of yours need sutures. You may bleed to death."

Bizarrely, Benan smiled, though it was still a picture of pain, his face gray and speckled with sweat.

"Our Lord," he stammered. "Our Lord was… scourged for our sins…"

"Benan, listen to me…"

"I am honoured… by this…"

"Yes, very good. Look, our Lord died, or had you forgotten? Do you want to die as well?"

The priest gave a crazy, fluting laugh.

"Henri!" Zacharius called over his shoulder.

The boy threaded his way across the room. He too was weary and sweating and wore a canvas apron blotched with blood.

"Henri, help me!"

Zacharius took Benan by one of his arms and indicated that Henri should take the other, but Benan grimaced and struggled weakly, until at last they let him go.

"No, there are others. See…"

Benan nodded towards a man seated against the near wall. He was one of Garbofasse's mercenaries and he was dull-eyed with pain. His leather hauberk had been removed to reveal the splintered nub of his collar bone tent-poling the flesh to the left of his neck; its white needle tip pierced through the skin. Beyond him, another fellow, who was unidentifiable he was so covered in gore, slumped with his head hung down. His blood-matted scalp was so deeply lacerated that his bare skull was exposed.

"Look to those… those who need you most," Benan said.

Zacharius hesitated, before nodding at Henri, who moved along and began to examine the casualty with the shattered collar bone. Zacharius meanwhile stood and gazed around the ghastly chamber. The sight of a makeshift field hospital was familiar to him. But this had come unexpectedly. Out in the courtyard, the infirmary was already a shambles of blood, filth and stained bandages. The infirmary beds they'd managed to construct were already filled to capacity. Rent and riven figures lay groaning in the passages between them. But in here it was even worse. The men were huddled wall to wall, wallowing in their own blood. Bowels had voided; there was vomit on the walls. The stench was intolerable.

As Henri attempted to move his patient, whose gasps quickly became shrill bleats of agony, onto the bier, the doctor turned back to the priest.

"I thought God's role was to love us?"

"No," Benan said solemnly. "It's our role to love Him. By action as well as word. That's why we all will die in this place."

"I can see why the earl had you flogged."

But Benan was lapsing back into unconsciousness. "I'm glad he did," he murmured. Zacharius moved away, to help Henri with their next patient. "I'm glad he did, good doctor. It's… my only hope."


THE MORNING WORE on and no immediate attack came.

The English watched in silence from the roof of the Constable's Tower. Ninety yards away, at the far end of the causeway, the dead stared back from the roof of the Gatehouse. They also stared from the curtain-wall which, now that it had been abandoned, had been inundated by them. They crowded along the top of it, all around the castle perimeter, and yet were eerily still. If the English had felt they were encircled before, they knew it for a fact now. The dead on the curtain-wall were actually within bowshot from the west side of the Constable's Tower, but as the archers had seen how futile their efforts had been before, none sought to waste an arrow now.

"What are they waiting for?" Navarre snapped. "A bloody invitation?"

"I'd guess munitions for the scoop-thrower," Garbofasse replied. "They threw so much rubble at us before, they probably emptied their stocks. They'll have to scour for miles in every direction to find a similar quantity again."

"At which point our problems really begin," Gurt said.

There were mumbles of agreement. Men glanced nervously towards the western bluff. It was clear to all that the Constable's Tower could also be struck by the scoop-thrower. If this happened, the men on its roof would be distracted trying to shield themselves, while the dead would advance along the causeway unimpeded.

This was Ranulf's suspicion, and it appeared to be confirmed shortly before noon, when about fifty of the dead emerged from the Gatehouse in lumbering work-gangs, and commenced laying out planks, beams and bundles of rope. The English watched, their sweat-filled hair prickling. Soon there was a prolonged banging of hammers and a droning of handsaws. Under the guidance of a twisted, diminutive figure, streaked with blood and dirt, yet with a distinctive gleaming pate, the corpses had commenced the construction of a tall framework.

"Is that William d'Abbetot?" someone asked, incredulous.

Earl Corotocus remained tight-lipped, but was clearly seething. Others were less angry and more bewildered, more horrified.

"I don't know which is worse," du Guesculin said. "That they know how to do that, or that one of our own is showing them the way."

They'd all come to dread this moment, when their own dead might be raised to face them, though so much horror had befallen them since Ranulf had first voiced concern about this that to many it was just another routine body-blow. More important to Ranulf was the object the dead were constructing. It was almost certainly a siege-tower.

"After the Gatehouse, they appear to have reasoned that forcing entry through the gate itself is too costly. This time they intend to come over the top," he said.

"You credit them with too much intellect," Navarre jeered. "Most of their brains are running out of their ears. How can they reason anything?"

But as the day wore on, Ranulf's thesis appeared to be correct. Whatever power controlled the Welsh dead, it also thought for them, motivating them like great swarms of ants, as though they were all of a single, collective mind. The work-gangs, who were tirelessly strong, and who operated with the smooth efficiency of skilled carpenters, continued to build the siege-tower, which was soon sturdy and massive, and rose section upon section until it was seventy feet tall. At the same time, other work-gangs descended the western bluff, carrying wheels, which they'd clearly removed from carts and wagons, to make it mobile. Others drove a team of oxen, to add brute muscle to the assault. Still more corpses appeared through the Gatehouse carrying heavy iron plates between them. These had clearly been detached from the Gatehouse entrance and would now be hung as fire-proof shielding along the tower's front and sides.

"My lord," Ranulf said, pushing his way through to Earl Corotocus. "It only remains for them to restock the scoop-thrower, and we are in very serious trouble."

"I agree," the earl replied, deep in thought. "Do you imagine they'll opt for another night assault?"

"I doubt they'll be ready in time for that. So if we're lucky, no."

"Lucky?" someone exclaimed. "Is it lucky to have to wait another night before we die and are embraced by that legion of hell-spawn?"

It was a serjeant of mercenaries who'd spoken. He'd already suffered badly through the iron hail. Crude, self-applied sutures were all that held his face together, though his left eyeball was pulped and distended from its broken socket; stinking black humor dripped freely down his left cheek.

Ranulf ignored him. "My lord, I have a plan – but it can only be executed in darkness."

Corotocus regarded him with interest. "A raid perhaps?"

Ranulf nodded. "If a small party of us can get out there and disable the scoop-thrower, it will buy us time... at least for a few days, until they bring the mangonels onto the western bluff and assault us with those."

The rest of the men listened in stupefied silence. Someone finally said: "Are you mad? Out there, where only the dead rule? It's certain oblivion!"

"It's our only hope," Ranulf argued.

"And who would comprise this suicide party?" Navarre scoffed. "We'd draw lots, I suppose?"

Ranulf shrugged. "The rest of you may draw lots if you wish. However, I volunteer to go. In fact, I will lead it."

"Do you have a death wish, Ranulf?" the earl wondered. "First onto the Gatehouse drawbridge. Leader of the forlorn hope. Has your father's demise unhinged you?"

"What I have, my lord, is experience. Remember Bayonne?"

Corotocus recalled it well; his mouth crooked into a half-smile. Others recalled the incident at Bayonne too, though not so fondly. Several of the earl's knights preferred not to dwell on it at all, for it had flown in the face of everything chivalrous they had ever been taught. On that occasion they had been the besiegers rather than the besieged.

It was in the early days of the Gascon war and Bayonne Castle on the River Nive had been captured by French forces. Earl Corotocus led the English army that subsequently surrounded it. The following siege was a prolonged, tiresome affair, both sides suffering from hunger and foul weather. On regular occasions Abbot Julius, of the Sainte Martine monastery high in the foothills of the Pyrenees, had come graciously down and been allowed entry to the castle by the English, to sing psalms for the embattled French. However, the earl's spies soon informed him that Abbott Julius was a cousin of Count Girald, who was commanding the French force, and was passing intelligence about the English strength and disposition. Not only that, he was organising a local resistance movement on behalf of the besieged and offering gold to pirates if they would intercept English galleys, bringing much-needed supplies to the nearby port.

In response, Earl Corotocus despatched a small group of handpicked men, Ranulf and his father among them, who disguised themselves as pilgrims en route to Compostela, and trod the dusty mountain road to Sainte Martine on foot. Only after begging water and a bed for the night, and finally being admitted to the monastery, did they throw off their rags and cowls, to reveal mail, swords and daggers. The monastery was sacked and burned, its lay-brothers slain, its monks – including Abbott Julius – taken as captives of war. A short while later, Earl Corotocus brought these prisoners before the walls of Castle Bayonne, and stood them on ox-carts with nooses around their necks. One word from him, he shouted, and the carts would be hauled away and the brethren left dangling. Inside the castle, Abbot Julius's cousin, Count Girald, had had no option but to signal his surrender.

Though it was well known that Earl Corotocus waged war in the most cunning ways, he was widely reviled for this ignoble act. Complaints were made against him to King Edward even from some on the English side – especially from those paragons of courtly virtue, William Latimer and John of Brittany. King Edward replied that conflict was always a hellish affair, but on this occasion particularly so as it was a straight contest between he and Philip IV of France, one anointed monarch versus another. With the stakes so high, he would not be held accountable for the "improvisational skills of his commanders". A short time later, when Pope Celestine excommunicated Earl Corotocus, King Edward sent an embassy to the papal court at Naples to have it lifted.

"What do you propose?" the earl said.

"Can we talk in private?"

The earl nodded. They crossed the roof and descended into a stairwell.

"I don't know how alert these walking dead are," Ranulf said. "But I don't think we can afford to take chances. Only a handful of men must go – five at the most. I don't even think it wise to take our best. It'll be perilous, and how many will return I don't know."

"All the more courageous of you to offer to lead it, Ranulf." The earl regarded him carefully, almost suspiciously.

"You're wondering if I really have lost my mind?"

"You wouldn't be the only man in this garrison who had."

"My lord, we face an enemy the like of which has never been seen. An enemy that can't be killed. An enemy that threatens our very souls, or so we assume. I'd be lying if I said that I think any of us will survive this siege. Could any man think rationally in these circumstances? I don't know. But we can only do – as my father used to say – what we can do."

"Tell me your plan," the earl said.

"There are plenty of storages sheds in the courtyard. At the very least, we have rope, we have paint, we have barrels of pig grease."

"And?"

"I suggest that whoever goes out there wears minimum clothing. I once heard a tale of how a Roman army was overwhelmed by a Germanic tribe. The Germans came through the benighted forest naked and painted black from head to toe. They were invisible until they struck the Roman camp."

The earl looked sceptical. "And this will fool our dead friends?"

"As I say, I don't know how alert they are. Do they think the way we think, can they even see as we do? But we must prepare as if they can. We must also grease ourselves, so that if they grab us we can still get free. It's all about speed, my lord. So much so that I recommend we don't load ourselves with weapons. We must break the scoop-thrower and get back inside the castle as fast as possible."

"And how would you even get out of the castle, let alone get back inside?

"When I was in the Keep before, I noticed the garderobe chute. It must lead down to an underground sewer. I suspect it passes beneath the east bailey and feeds into the moat. We can exit that way."

"An underground sewer?" The earl raised an eyebrow. "It may be a tight squeeze."

"In which case, the pig-grease will come in useful."

Corotocus pursed his lips as he pondered. "Supposing you succeed, how do you expect to get back inside? Climbing the garderobe chute? How high is it?"

"If we hang ropes down, with knots and loops tied in them, all it will need is for you to have a number of men standing by. The moment we're in position, you can pull us up. We won't need to climb."

The earl now smiled. Irregular warfare was always to his liking. "I think I'm in favour of this plan, Ranulf. But who will you take?"

"Volunteers initially. If there aren't enough forthcoming, as Navarre said... we'll draw lots."

"I want Garbofasse to go with you."

Ranulf tried not to show how much this disconcerted him. "You don't trust me, my lord?"

"I trust the men less. If you get beyond this ring of dead flesh, what's to stop those worthless dogs fleeing for their lives? You'll be there, but you'll be alone. With Garbofasse, you can control things better."

Ranulf had no particular dislike for Garbofasse, aside from him being the leader of a gang of murderers. And the mercenary captain could not really be described as the earl's man the way Navarre or du Guesculin could. But he was hardly someone Ranulf could trust. All of a sudden, the extremely difficult task Ranulf had set himself looked nigh on impossible.

# CHAPTER TWENTY-ONE

THAT EVENING WAS a pleasant one, redolent of spring. Though cold, the air was clear and fresh. The sky was pebble-blue, but faded to indigo as dusk fell, and to fiery red as the sun finally settled.

At the far end of the causeway, the siege-tower was almost completed and as ominous an object as any man there had seen in all his years of war. The dead still worked in industrious and eerie silence. The only sound was the tapping of hammers as wheels were attached to the great monolith. Its front and sides were shod almost completely with iron plate. Where the iron had run out, the gaps were covered by shields purloined from the English. As the last vestige of sunlight melted into the west, a single ray shot across the land and burnished the object with flame. Several of the dead, clambering back and forth upon it like beetles, also glinted as it caught their pieces of mail.

The English watched tensely, expecting the tower to immediately roll forth along the causeway. But though the teams of oxen had now been brought from the Gatehouse, no attempt was made to yoke them in place. Gradually, the hammering ceased, and as darkness fell the dead withdrew into their fastness. A legion of them still watched from the western bluff and droves more remained on the parapets of the curtain-wall. If other monstrosities were still scouring the Grogen hinterlands for munitions, there was no sign of it. All were stiff and still as the mannequins that had first confronted the English on their arrival here. As night descended, and cloaked them from view, even their mewling and moaning faded. Soon, only the stink of mildewed flesh bespoke their presence.

A querulous voice finally broke the unearthly quiet. It was du Guesculin. "In God's name, why don't they take action? Do the dead need sleep? How can that be?"

"Maybe their masters do," Gurt said. "We don't know if they–"

"Is your friend preparing himself?" Navarre interrupted, his voice edged with resentment.

On first hearing about the proposed raid, Navarre had volunteered, but Earl Corotocus had refused him permission to go, saying that, from this point on, he wanted his best men with him at all times. Navarre was even more embittered when he heard that Captain Garbofasse would also be going.

"So FitzOsbern, that whey-faced whelp, and now that damn mercenary oaf get the chance to win fame, while I, the household champion, remain coddled in this castle!"

Corotocus had snorted in response. "Fame is for fools."

# CHAPTER TWENTY-TWO

THERE WAS NO sign of Murlock as Ranulf stole up through the upper levels of the Keep. The big mercenary was most likely taking full advantage of this long, lonely duty by sleeping. As quietly as he could, Ranulf unlocked Gwendolyn's door, slipped inside and closed it again. The prisoner sat bolt-upright as he approached.

"My lady, can you write?" he asked.

"Certainly I can write."

"Then you must write a letter now." He handed her a folded parchment, an inkpot and a quill. "Hurry."

She took the items hesitantly. "I don't understand."

"I'll be leaving the castle just after midnight. There is a target we must destroy. But I will have another purpose. If I can locate your mother, I will plead for a truce."

"A truce?"

"My terms will be simple. If I return you to your mother unharmed, and hand over Earl Corotocus for whatever punishment she deems fit, she must allow the rest of us safe passage back to

England. If you can write a letter vouching for my honesty, I will put it directly into her hands."

Gwendolyn hesitated, as though wondering whether this was some kind of trap, but finally nodded and began to scratch out a quick note.

"How many others are involved?" she asked.

"So far only me."

She glanced up, shocked. "How can I sway her, if only one man is to turn?"

"We have to try."

She put down her quill. "This is an impossible cause, and you know it."

"When men are prepared to make sacrifices, nothing is impossible."

"And will your friends sacrifice their loyalty?"

"In exchange for their lives, yes... maybe. For that's the choice they will face in due course."

She still seemed uncertain, but she recommenced writing. "For all your faults, sir knight, you don't strike me as someone who fears death."

"Maybe I don't any more. But there was something my father said to me before he died..." Ranulf shrugged and waved it away.

"What?"

"Suffice to say, something good must be dragged from the jaws of this catastrophe."

"Will your fellow countrymen define the betrayal of an overlord as 'good'?"

Ranulf couldn't conceal his conflicted feelings about this. The knightly code stated that duty to your lord should be the keystone of your life. Duplicity with the man who had clothed you, fed you, trained you, the man in whose service you were bonded was supposedly a grave sin – even if it was to the benefit of others. Judas Iscariot had handed Jesus to the temple guards because he worried that Jesus's preaching might bring Roman retribution on the Jewish race. It could be deemed that such an act was well intentioned, yet Judas had been reviled throughout eternity as the arch-traitor. And still – Ranulf again recalled his father's words: "Be true to your heart, lad. In the end, when all has come to pass, it'll be the only thing you can trust." And what his heart told him now was that

Earl Corotocus had gone too far. In Gascony it had been slightly different – that had been a bitter war waged against an enemy who would stop at nothing to wrest control of English sovereign territory. But here against the Welsh, for all their oft-professed hatred of the English, it had gone too far. There had been too much blood, too much cruelty, too much terror. Little wonder the dead themselves were now rising in retaliation. And *that* in itself, of course, made all other considerations pale to insignificance.

"You haven't seen what's gathering outside, my lady," Ranulf finally said. "The customs we live by, the canons we've tricked ourselves into believing… they don't mean anything any more. The world has turned on its head. All that's left is the difference between those things we *know* to be right and those we *know* to be wrong."

She handed him the parchment. "Here's your letter. God speed you with it, for the sake of both our peoples."

He folded it, inserted it into a pouch – and froze. Gwendolyn glanced past him. They'd both heard a scraping sound as of leather or metal on the other side of the door. Ranulf looked around too and saw that the small hatch in the cell door was wide open.

Cursing, he raced across the room and barged out into the passage. Murlock was twenty yards off, walking quickly. When Ranulf started to run, Murlock started to run too.

Ranulf caught up with him at the top of the first flight of steps. Just as he did, the big mercenary swung around, striking with his dagger. Ranulf threw himself to one side and the blade flashed past, jamming point first into the wall and snapping. Then Ranulf was onto him. They tumbled down the steps together, clawing, wrestling. At the bottom, Murlock landed on top and for crucial seconds had the advantage. He pinned Ranulf down, clutching his throat with bear-like paws, head-butting him in the face. Ranulf struggled wildly, but only dislodged Murlock by driving a knee up between his legs. Murlock rolled away, gagging.

Ranulf got groggily to his feet. His nose, already broken once, was now broken again. Hot tears blurred his vision.

Murlock tried to crawl away on all fours. Ranulf lurched after him, grabbed him by the hair, yanked his head back and fumbled for his own dagger. Before he could draw it, the mercenary slammed an elbow back, catching him in the ribs. Ranulf was mail-clad but the impact was agonising and the air whistled from his lungs. He tottered backward. Murlock spun around, this time drawing his scramsax and swiping with it. Ranulf dodged away, the keen but heavy edge missing him by inches, clanging on the brickwork.

Ranulf drew his own sword in time to deflect the second blow, forcing the mercenary to step backward to the edge of the next stairwell. Murlock lunged as hard as he could with his blade. Ranulf again parried and smashed his left fist into Murlock's jaw. It was as hard a punch as he'd ever thrown. Murlock's head spun right as bloody phlegm spat from his mouth; his very neck seemed to shift on its axis. Ranulf kicked him again, this time with a stamping manoeuvre on the side of his right knee. Murlock's leg buckled inwards and he gave a shill, bird-like squawk. With Murlock's guard now down, Ranulf hove at him a final time, slamming the pommel of his sword between his eyes.

The mercenary stiffened and toppled backward like a felled tree, bouncing end-over-end from one step to the next, his limbs splayed. When he finally came to rest at the bottom, he was face-down and motionless. Ranulf scrambled down after him. The blood from the mercenary's nose and mouth was spreading in a wide puddle. There was no hint of life in his apparently broken body.

Ranulf sat back on his haunches, panting.

Of course, even in this drear and filthy place, so much fresh blood would need to be cleared away if suspicion was not to be aroused. Ranulf sheathed his blade and got quickly to work. He dragged the body by its feet into a dungeon and dumped it in the dimmest corner, where he covered it with matted straw. Taking two more handfuls of the stuff, he went back outside and began to mop the floor.

"What if someone misses him?" came a nervous voice.

It was Gwendolyn. In his haste to catch up with the jailer, he hadn't thought to lock her in again.

"Go back to your cell," he said, scrubbing up the gore.

"But he'll be missed."

"The only time he'll be missed is when we retreat to this final refuge and, trust me, if we get to that stage it won't matter anyway."

"But I…"

"Go back to your cell!" he shouted. "I'll lock you in anon."

She scurried back up the steps.

"You may not believe it," he said under his breath. "But that's by far the safest place in this castle at present."

He heard her door grating shut as he continued to scrub the flagstones hard, conscious that time was running out. The hour was getting late and he was soon due to meet the rest of the raiding party in the courtyard.

# CHAPTER TWENTY-THREE

THEY MET JUST before midnight in the main courtyard. Ranulf, Garbofasse and four others: a tenant knight, Roger FitzUrz, a household squire, Tancred Tallebois, an archer, Paston, and a mercenary called Red Guthric – a beanpole of a man, with a hatchet face and straggling carrot-red hair, who Garbofasse said was one of his best.

In torch-lit silence, they removed their mail and their leather and their under-garb, until they wore only loincloths and felt shoes. They then rubbed themselves with black soot – heads and hands as well as bodies and limbs and slathered it with pig-grease to hold it in place. The only weapons they armed themselves with were knives and daggers. Corotocus, du Guesculin and several dozen others watched in silence. Doctor Zacharius had come over from the infirmary. A full day having elapsed since the last attack, he had finally managed to get on top of his casualty list, but he was sallow-faced and covered with other men's blood.

"You fellows look like Moors," he said, rubbing his hands on a towel.

There were nervous chuckles.

"They'll smell like Moors too, when they've finished climbing down the garderobe," someone replied, to more chuckles.

"I knew campaigns in Wales were notoriously hard," FitzUrz said. "But I never thought I'd finish up eating shit."

"Enough!" Corotocus said. "All of you listen to me. No matter what your position, for the duration of this mission you are under the command of Captain Garbofasse and Ranulf FitzOsbern, whose errant status is to be of no consequence. Anyone disobeying their orders will answer to me personally on his return."

There were mumbles of acknowledgement.

They moved to set off, but now Zacharius spoke up. "If you can capture an intact specimen, perhaps I can examine it. Even dissect it. It would be an ungodly act, but are these things godly in any way? It might help us to understand how they are as they are."

Ranulf glanced at him. By his expression, the doctor was perfectly serious. Everyone looked to Earl Corotocus, who seemed briefly intrigued by the proposition, though eventually he shook his head.

"This mission is difficult enough already. If it doesn't succeed, we'll be up to our ears in intact specimens."

The doctor shrugged as if it didn't matter. But Ranulf couldn't help wondering about the wisdom of ruling out such a plan. At present, given his own secret agenda, it would be difficult to the point of impossibility to carry such a thing off, but maybe – if his own scheme failed – it was worth bearing in mind for some time in the future.

"You men need to go," the earl said. "We don't know how long these creatures will hold back for."

They took their ropes and tackle and trooped up into the Keep together, ascending from one level to the next without speaking, their thin-clad feet slapping the dank flagstones. Ranulf was fleetingly unnerved, wondering if Murlock's absence would be noticed. But as it transpired, they were all too focussed on their task. Even Garbofasse, Murlock's immediate commanding officer, paid the missing jailer no heed. They at last entered the garderobe and lowered their ropes down the chute.

Almost as one, they looked frightened. Beads of sweat sat on the dark, oily film coating their brows. In the flickering torchlight, the squire, Tallebois, regarded his comrades with eyes that had almost bugged from their sockets. His lips were wet with repeated licking.

"Looks like the entrance to the underworld," FitzUrz muttered, peering down the black shaft.

"From here on no talking unless you're given leave to," Corotocus said. "We know too little about these Welsh dead. Maybe they can hear you, maybe they can't, but it's a chance you mustn't take. Now... God go with you all."

Ranulf wound a rope with a grapple attached around his body, and clambered over the low brick wall rimming the chute. As he did, he wondered at the irony of the earl's last comment. *God go with them?* With the dead rising en masse, ravening for the blood of the living, did Earl Corotocus seriously think the Almighty was anywhere near this place? And after the slaughter the earl had himself wreaked, did he genuinely believe there was the remotest chance the Almighty would look to English welfare during this tragedy?

They made the descent in twos, for the chute was not wide enough to accommodate all at the same time. Ranulf and Garbofasse went first. As FitzUrz had feared, the brick sides were slimy with human waste. If the stench had been bad outside of the castle, down here the men found themselves in a cloying, malodorous fog, which almost suffocated them. They could virtually taste it – not just on the tips of their tongues, but in the backs of their throats.

The climb itself was exhausting – made in complete darkness, with hands and feet rendered slippery by grease. Several times the men almost slid from the ropes. Frequently, they thrashed about in the blackness, bumping into each other, swinging against the walls. When they reached the bottom, the ordure was over a foot deep, though, thanks to the recent cold, neither as soft nor repulsive as it might have been. Ranulf groped around and found the arched entrance to the drain. This was another nerve-wracking moment. If it was too small for a man to fit down, the mission would need to be abandoned. Thankfully, it was about two feet across and a foot and a half in depth, which meant that, though difficult to crawl along, it would not be impossible.

Their next problem was turning around in the narrow space at the bottom of the shaft, but this Ranulf finally managed to do with much twisting and grunting. Pushing his head and shoulders into the drain, with his hands fumbling ahead of him, again finding more brickwork clotted both above and below with human excreta, he felt as though he was burrowing into the stuff, burying himself alive. How far did this drain run for? If he became stuck, would anyone be able to get him out again? Would the earl care enough to try? The only way was to keep going forward. He'd assumed it would slope downward beneath the east bailey and discharge into the moat. That was a mere fifty yards or more, though, now that he was here, his body enclosed by tight, rugged architecture, with progress only possible by worming forward like a slug, even fifty yards seemed like a massive distance.

He wasn't sure how long it was before he smelled fresh air again. He was already wearied to the bone and felt he'd rubbed his naked skin raw. But at last his hands encountered hanging vegetation. The next thing, he was hauling himself out of a vent that felt no larger than a rabbit hole, and falling face down onto steeply sloped rubble. It was still dark, but Ranulf could now sense the night sky overhead, and, compared to the subterranean realm he'd just emerged from, that was something to offer prayers of thanks for.

Glancing up, he saw stars glimmering through a wash of turgid cloud. The floor of the moat was stony and jagged. The vent was rimmed with brick and, as he'd expected, set into the side of the moat. Much soil had crumbled down from above it, and it was half hidden behind hanging weeds. He remained crouched as he waited for the others, glancing up again, scanning the parapets overhead, which at present were devoid of sentinel forms. A grunting and scrabbling noise reached his ears. It was Garbofasse squirming along the drain towards him.

The mercenary captain was larger in bulk than Ranulf, and was having a torrid time. He only made it to the end of the pipe with difficulty. Ranulf had to reach in, take him by wrists, and pull him the rest of the way. Garbofasse had to suppress cries of agony as he was finally released. Even through his covering of soot and grease, the skin on his ribs and hips was scored by the brickwork and bled freely in many places.

"Name of a name," he panted, crouching. "Name of a God damned name, this had better be worth it."

The other four followed over the next few minutes, all emerging in a similarly filthy and dishevelled state. One by one, they crouched, shivering with the cold and now with the wet as well, for in the last few moments a drizzling rain had commenced.

"Where to next?" someone asked.

"We're on the east side of the castle," Ranulf replied. "If we follow this moat around to the west, we'll likely meet those dead who were cast into it from the bridge and weren't able to climb out again. So we need to get out on this side. After that, we circle around to western bluff via the moors to the north."

There were grunts of assent. If anyone disliked the idea of having to circumnavigate the castle out in the open, he didn't voice it. The thought of having to face the dead down here, in the confined space of the moat, was equally, if not even more, horrifying.

Ranulf swung the rope with the grapple, and hurled it. He had to do this several times before it caught on something that could bear their weight. One by one, they scrambled out, finding themselves on open, grassy ground, where each man lay flat to wait for his comrades. By the time they were all together, their eyes had attuned. Ranulf saw a line of trees to the east of them, but to the north a sloping expanse of star-lit moorland. Nothing moved over there, though it was difficult to see clearly beyond fifty yards or so.

"It's a long way to the western bluff," Red Guthric said quietly. "How long until dawn?"

"We have a few hours," Garbofasse replied. "So we'd better not waste them."

They proceeded north in single file, moving stealthily through thorns and knee-deep sedge. All the way, the mammoth outline of the castle stood to their left, but it provided no comfort, for if they should be attacked now there was no easy way back into it. Despite the darkness, they felt badly exposed. Their nerves were taut. The slightest sound – the cry of an owl or nightjar – brought them to a breathless halt.

Only when far to the north of the castle did they turn west, having to thread their way through swathes of sodden bracken, the stubble of which prickled their feet through their felt shoes. Here, on this higher ground, they encountered the first of the dead. A large, heavily-built woman, naked, with flesh mottled by bruising and a chewed-off noose tight around her throat, lay still in the vegetation. Slightly further on, a youth with an arrow through his neck – it passed cleanly from one side to the other – also lay still. The raiders crouched again, waiting and watching for some time, before Ranulf found the courage to approach.

He crept forward quietly and stood surveying the two bodies, neither of which stirred. At length, he summoned the others, and they hastened past.

From this point on, the hillside was strewn with similarly inert forms. Soon, corpses lay so thick that it was like a benighted battlefield. All of them had done this before, of course: walked dolefully among the slain after some catastrophic engagement. All were familiar with the sight of tangled limbs, hewn torsos, faces frozen in death and spattered with gore. On this occasion, though, it was different. For these beings, though visibly rotting in the mist and rain, had been walking around as though alive not two or three hours earlier. Why they were now 'dead again', if it was possible to describe them in such a way, was anybody's guess.

"Maybe it's over?" Tallebois whispered hopefully.

"Quiet!" Garbofasse hissed.

They continued, keeping low, moving as stealthily as they could. But as the great slope of the western bluff hove in from the left, this became increasingly difficult. There was now scarcely any uncluttered ground to walk on. Ranulf found himself edging uphill towards the higher ground, where a cover of trees had appeared. All the way, he fancied the eyes of the dead were upon him. Were they watching his progress? Could they see anything? Did any functions occur in the addled pulp of their brains? Though he didn't say it, he too felt a vague hope that somehow the spell had been broken, and that these dead were indeed dead again. But he doubted it.

Among the trees, the raiders felt they'd be less visible, though to reach that higher point they had to venture even further from the east moat and their so-called place of safety. The west side of the castle made a dark outline in the night. They could just distinguish the rounded section that was the Barbican, and beyond that the upper tier of the Gatehouse. Further south, at the end of the causeway, was the tall, angular shape of the Constable's Tower. A handful of lit torches were visible on its roof. They looked to be an immense distance away, which was not comforting.

Equally discomforting, in its own way, was the wood they'd now entered – not just because there were further corpses scattered between its roots, but because of its dense thickets and skeletal branches, all hung with cauls of mist. If nothing else, however, the party were soon on a level with the top of the bluff, which meant that they couldn't be too far from the artillery machines.

Ranulf halted and again dropped to a crouch. The others did the same. They breathed slowly and deeply, listening for any sound that might indicate they'd alerted sentries, but hearing only rain pattering on twigs and the chattering of their own teeth; every man there was now shivering with the cold and damp.

"We don't know exactly where the scoop-thrower is located," Ranulf whispered. "It must be up here on the treed ground, because it was concealed from the battlements. Judging from its angle of shot, it can't be more than a hundred yards or more to the south of us, but the exact position is uncertain."

"We should spread out," Garbofasse said. "Form a skirmish line. Twenty yards between each man. That way we cover more ground."

Ranulf nodded; this would suit *his* plan as well.

"There's still no movement from these... these things," FitzUrz said. Of the horrible shapes lying around them, some were more decomposed than others, several little more than bones wrapped in parchment. But again, in many cases, their heads were turned towards the raiding party, as though watching them carefully.

"The puppets don't sleep, but maybe the puppet masters do," Ranulf said. "It probably only needs one command to be issued and they'll come raging back to life." He mopped his brow. He was sweating so hard that the grease and soot was running off him in streams. "Form the line. We're moving south... slowly. Keep your eyes and your ears open."

With some hardship in the darkness and undergrowth, they spread out into a skirmish line, Ranulf anchoring it at the north end and Garbofasse at the south, and proceeded again along the top of the bluff. The ground became even harder to negotiate; it wasn't just bulging with roots, but it had been churned to quagmires by thousands of trampling feet. In some cases, the bodies of the dead lay in actual piles, as if they'd been heaped together by gravediggers. Subsequently, the skirmish line extended and warped as the men struggled to keep up with each other. But on flatter ground, they came across the first of the heavy weapons. Many were still in their wagons, unpacked. Several onagers and ballistae had been taken out and were partly assembled, though further corpses were strewn around these. More work-gangs, Ranulf realised with a shudder. This army of reanimated clay could be turned just as easily to tireless labour as it could to war, and of course it never asked for pay. The full extent of the power this gifted its controller was quite chilling.

There was still no sign of the scoop-thrower, though ahead of them, they now sighted firelight. They slowed their advance to a crawl.

In a small clearing, a circle of tents had been raised, with snores emanating from inside them. In the middle of the circle, raised on a mound of hot coals was a large cauldron or cooking-pot. It bubbled loudly as it pumped a column of foul-smelling smoke into the night sky. They halted, wondering what this meant, though each one of them was thinking the same thing: the dead don't need shelter against the elements; nor do they need to sleep, nor to eat warm food.

Ranulf felt a sudden urge to draw his blade, though he knew he had to resist. Glancing down the line, he saw the next man along, Robert FitzUrz, watching him intently, one hand on his dagger hilt. Ranulf shook his head. They weren't here to perform assassinations. How did they know who actually controlled these dead? How would they know they had killed the right people? In addition of course, Ranulf had his own scheme to attend to. He shook his head vigorously.

FitzUrz nodded and passed the message along the line. They continued to advance, skirting around the small encampment, but now with their eyes peeled for the massive, distinctive shape of the scoop-thrower. They'd penetrated maybe thirty yards further on, again having to thread between piles of corpses, when Ranulf spotted something else. Twenty yards to his right, half-hidden by trees, there was a stockade with torches burning on the other side of its open gate. Inside, he made out what looked like a gold pavilion covered with red lions. He glanced left again. Only a couple of the other men were visible beyond FitzUrz. He slowed down so that soon they were ahead of him by several yards. Concentrating on what lay in front of them, they didn't notice that he had fallen behind. He now ceased advancing altogether and, as soon as they'd vanished into the mist and rain, turned and hurried towards the stockade.

When he reached it, he saw that it had a single guard – a living one – on its gate. The guard was young but heavily bearded and, wearing a white gown and hooded white cloak, he looked like a priest of the old religion. He had a curved sword at his belt and a circular shield on one arm, but his spear stood beside him. He looked wet and tired, and was yawning into his hand. Clearly, the last thing he was expecting was some form of attack. When Ranulf lobbed a stone, which crackled in the bushes, the guard turned dully towards it, as if he wasn't quite sure that he'd heard anything. He never saw Ranulf steal up behind, wrap an arm around his neck and throttle him into unconsciousness.

Ranulf took the curved sword before proceeding. It surprised him that there'd only been one guard, though he supposed that with a multitude of horrors to be called on from the surrounding woods, even the most nervous camp commander would feel relatively safe here.

Creeping to the pavilion, he saw a flicker of flame within. He held his breath before entering. This would be the biggest risk of all, but the stakes he was playing for were higher than any he'd known in his entire life. Whichever way he looked at it, there seemed to be no other option than this. Sliding the sword into his belt beside his dagger, he drew the tent flap aside and stepped through.

Beyond, in a small pool of candlelight, a woman sat with her back to him at a small table. Her lustrous red hair, which hung unbound to her waist, revealed that she was Countess Madalyn; there could not be two people in the camp with her distinctive looks. At first she didn't notice the intruder. She was writing what looked like a letter. A number of other documents, already scrolled and sealed with wax, lay alongside it.

When she sensed that he was there, she gasped, spun around and jumped to her feet.

Ranulf knew that he must have made a ghastly sight, though he was surely no worse than the monstrosities that had been lumbering around her for the last few days. He put a finger to his lips, hissing at her to be silent.

"Cry out and call your creatures, countess... and you will miss something to your advantage."

"Who are you?" she breathed, wide-eyed.

She was clearly frightened, but she was angry as well – and why not? She was a great noblewoman, as befitted her impressive stature and fierce beauty. And she was now embroiled in a war for the lives and souls of her people. Slowly, her expression softened.

"I... I seem to recognise your voice."

"We spoke the day before yesterday," Ranulf said. "Just before this battle commenced."

"You were the English knight who advised me that further war was futile."

"And I now advise it again."

He stepped forward. She retreated, but halted when he took the crumpled letter from a pouch and offered it to her. She opened it and read it. Her eyes widened with wild hope.

"You recognise your daughter's hand?" he said.

"Of course. Is she safe?"

"For the time being. I can't say what will happen to her if this siege drags on."

Countess Madalyn glanced again at the letter. "This tells me that you harbour feelings against Earl Corotocus and that you aren't alone. How many do you speak for?"

"At present just myself. But our men are weary and many are wounded. When they arrived here, they thought the war was over. Even the hardiest of them are now losing their appetite for it. What's more, whatever black gate you've opened to summon this hellish horde has left them terror-stricken. Few question the earl's authority thus far. But that state of affairs won't last."

She folded the letter and regarded him sternly. "Earl Corotocus did not hang and butcher my people alone. Why should I spare any of his wretches?"

"Because one atrocity fuels another, countess. Victory for you here will only provoke the marcher barons to make more incursions into your land."

"Then they too will die at the hands of my army."

"That possibility won't stop them coming," Ranulf said. "They won't believe mere rumour. With no-one alive to tell them the truth about what happened at Grogen Castle, they'll bring even greater forces. And with King Edward's might and wealth behind them, they'll soon find a way to tame your festering rabble. The war will go on, an endless cycle of brutality and counter-brutality."

"Interesting to finally hear an Englishman speaking so. Of course, the main change is that now it is you who stares defeat in the face."

"Believe what you wish about me, countess, but you have negotiated peace treaties before. I know you seek a better way than endless violence."

She pursed her lips as she pondered this, before finally saying: "And how do *you* respond, Gwyddon?"

Ranulf was startled when a second figure stepped out of the shadows. He looked like a druid or priest of the old faith. He had broad, pale features, with a long, jet-black beard and eyes like lumps of onyx. He walked with a knotted staff, but looked young and strong, and had adorned himself with ornate jewellery.

"Don't be alarmed, English knight," the countess said. "When Wales belongs to the Welsh again, Gwyddon will be my first minister. No counsel of mine shall be closed to him." She turned to her advisor. "You heard?"

"I did, madam." Gwyddon nodded, never taking his eyes off Ranulf. "And I urge you to tread carefully."

She turned back to Ranulf. "Not only will you return my daughter, but you claim that you will either hand Earl Corotocus to me, or punish him yourself?"

Ranulf nodded, more disconcerted than he could explain by the priest's unexpected presence. He'd faced enemies before, but the hostility emanating from this fellow was almost palpable. The inscrutable onyx eyes never left him.

"And how do you propose to do this?" Countess Madalyn asked.

"I'll need to plan accordingly," Ranulf replied. "But I had to come here first. I had to know if you would be receptive to my offer."

"So you claim to come to us with a plan, though in truth you have no plan at all?" Gwyddon said.

"I didn't say that."

The priest turned to his mistress. "If the choice were mine, the answer would be 'no'. Why should we hear terms from an enemy who has already been crushed?"

"Gwyddon... or whatever your name is," Ranulf said. "The army that King Edward is bringing into Wales has not been crushed, and likely is ten times the size of your miserable host."

"You see," Gwyddon retorted. "He is crafty, this Englishman. Even now, he seeks to elicit information about the progress of his reinforcements." He sneered at Ranulf. "We will tell you nothing. Return to Earl Corotocus and prepare yourselves firstly for death, and secondly for everlasting service in my regiment of the damned."

"Countess, this is madness," Ranulf pleaded. "There is no point continuing this fight."

Gwyddon laughed. "The point is that Wales is on the verge of greatness."

"Wales is on the verge of annihilation," Ranulf countered. "It doesn't matter how long it takes King Edward to get here, or whether he saves *us* or not. In fact, the longer it takes him to get here the better, because during all that time your army will be rotting to its bones."

"And all that time we will replenish it," Gwyddon said. "The more who die, the greater our reserves of strength."

"Is this what you want?" Ranulf asked the countess. "Queen Madalyn of Lyr, reigning supreme over a nation of mindless corpses? Or will it be First Minister Gwyddon reigning over them? I'm not quite clear."

Countess Madalyn's lips trembled as she heard him out, but she said nothing. Ranulf pleaded to her again.

"Listen to me, I beg you. If we return to England, we can tell everyone what we saw here. We can tell the king himself. If all you want is Wales for the Welsh, I dare say you've won it already."

"Until such time as Edward Longshanks invokes aid from the pope," Gwyddon interrupted. "'Holy Father', he will say. 'There are demons in Wales. Instead of directing our crusader armies east, we must send them west.'"

"If that's what you think, shaman, you don't know King Edward very well," Ranulf said. "No foreign armies will ever be permitted onto the island of Britain."

"King Edward does not control the island of Britain."

"As I say, you don't know him very well." Ranulf turned back to the countess. "Madam, however invincible this fellow might have convinced you that you are, it is better to be King Edward's friend than his enemy. Your army of monsters has given you an advantage, so I pray you don't waste it. With might on your side as well as right, isn't it better to talk?"

Gwyddon made to respond, his face written with scorn, but Countess Madalyn signalled for silence. She read her daughter's letter again.

"You speak well for a common knight," she finally said. "But you have no authority to make this treaty."

Ranulf nodded, as though pondering this. And whipped the dagger and curved sword from his belt. "These are all the authority I need!"

The countess stepped back. Gwyddon's eyes narrowed.

"If I was as treacherous as you fear," Ranulf said. "Wouldn't I plunge these blades into your two hearts right now? Instead of vowing to plunge them into Earl Corotocus when I return to Grogen?"

"This is true," the countess said. "He has taken quite a risk to come here. It would be easy for him just to kill us."

"He seeks only to save his men, so they may fight another day," Gwyddon argued.

Ranulf laughed. "After their experiences here, I doubt any of 'my men' – as you call them – would ever glance past Offa's Dyke again, let alone enter Wales. We'll leave our weapons, our booty. I promise we'll march home and harm no-one. Think, madam, how that would help your position once King Edward arrives. I can plead with him on your behalf. Tell him how you punished the criminal Corotocus, but spared the rest of us. Could there be a greater gesture of good will?"

She gazed at him intently, as if he was slowly persuading her. She was about to speak when there came a frantic shouting from outside the pavilion. It was in Welsh, but Ranulf knew enough of the border tongue to recognise an intruder alert – apparently the English were in the camp.

"See how he lies and manipulates!" Gwyddon roared. "See how he buys time for his assassins!"

The countess's expression froze with outrage.

"Ignore my offer at your peril," Ranulf said as he backed towards the entrance. "You've thrown your lot in with a pagan sorcerer. Continue on this path, and who knows – when you get to Hell, you may share your dungeon with Corotocus himself."

He turned and dashed outside, where he met another of the young priests at the stockade gate. The priest had a scimitar in his hand, but was too stunned by the sight of the intruder to react. Ranulf slashed his throat and knifed him in the heart.

Beyond the stockade, there was no immediate response from the dead, who still lay motionless in the undergrowth. But several dozen yards to his right, behind a wall of black and twisting trees, flames were blazing into the night. A great mechanical outline, with a huge throwing-arm, was engulfed in fire. There were more wild shouts. Some were gruff, some sounded panicked. A half-naked figure came weaving between the trunks, stumbling over corpses. It was Tallebois, the squire.

Ranulf dashed to intercept him, grabbing his arm and bringing him to a halt. The squire squawked with fright.

"What happened?" Ranulf demanded.

"We found the scoop-thrower. We brought coals from the campfire and piled straw beneath it. Now the whole thing's burning. We cut its torsion springs as well, broke its winch and pulley-bar. They'll never use it again." Tallebois laughed hysterically.

"FitzOsbern, where the devil have you been?" came an angry voice.

Garbofasse lumbered into view, with the others at his heels. He was slick with sweat, his pale flesh shining between streaks of soot and grease.

"I tried to find the countess," Ranulf said. "How ineffective would the Welsh snake be with its head removed as well as its sting?"

"And?"

"She's around here somewhere, but now there's no time."

As he said this, a terrible voice sounded through the trees to their rear. Ranulf recognised it as Gwyddon's. The druid was chanting discordantly, intoning some hideous spell. As one, the corpses strewed between the trees began to stir, to shudder, to twitch.

"Dear God!" Tallebois screamed.

"Back to the castle!" Garbofasse shouted.

"We'll never make it across the moor," Ranulf said, ushering them downhill rather than back along the bluff. "Head for the river."

"The river?"

"Do as I say!"

But on all sides, grotesque figures were rising quickly to their feet. Paston, standing further away from the others, squealed like a calf as an axe clove his skull from behind.

"This way!" Ranulf bellowed, racing downhill.

The others followed, pell-mell. But it was a chaotic flight. They tripped over roots or were clawed at by spectral shapes emerging from the mist on either side. Garbofasse fell heavily, injuring his knee. Ranulf stopped and turned as the others ran ahead.

"Go!" Garbofasse cried, hobbling back to his feet. "Get away!" He was already hemmed in by mewling figures, so he picked up a longsword and swept it at them with both hands. Two went down, sundered at the waist, but a third, fourth and fifth were soon on top of him. "Go!" he shrieked again, wrestling with them as they snapped at him with their foul teeth.

He managed to invert one and drop it on the top of its head. Another, he ran through with the sword, though it still lunged at him. More joined the fray, bearing him to the muddy ground.

"Go!" was the last thing Ranulf heard the mercenary captain say, though it became high-pitched and incoherent as his larynx was bitten through.

Ranulf ran on down the hill, striking on all sides with sword and dagger. The others were already much further ahead. Even Red Guthric, personally bonded to Garbofasse, scrambled down the slope without looking back – until he too fell. A corpse had dropped on him from a tree. It was a naked stick figure, its skin hanging in empty folds, but it had sufficient strength to knock him to his knees, whereupon it clamped its teeth on the nape of his neck. Ranulf galloped alongside and drove his dagger so deeply between its ribs that its blade was wedged there. The spindly monster dropped Red Guthric and rounded on Ranulf. He slammed his curved sword through the middle of its chest, entirely transfixing it, but still it tried to grapple with him. Leaving both his weapons behind, Ranulf stepped away, stumbling on downhill. Red Guthric was back on his feet and came as well, but on wobbling legs. When another form blundered into his path – this one a bloated mass of swollen, purple flesh – and wrapped him in a bear-hug, he was unable to resist. Helpless, barely able to scream, Guthric was raised and broken across the monster's knee like a plank.

Ranulf ran on. FitzUrz and Tallebois were just ahead but, as the moon slipped behind clouds, they found themselves fleeing through complete darkness. When FitzUrz turned his ankle, it snapped like a stick. He howled as he fell. Ranulf swerved towards him, but before he could reach him another dead thing, gargling black filth but armed with a massive club, ghosted around the trunk of the nearest tree. Ranulf veered away as it commenced to land blow after blow on FitzUrz's unprotected skull.

Ranulf and Tallebois were now the only two left. Both were fleeing neck-and-neck when they skidded out from the trees onto the open bluff to the west of the castle. Vast numbers of the dead were already gathered there and now – as one – turned slowly to face them.

Tallebois slid to a halt, his mouth locking open, his eyes bulging. Ranulf grabbed him by the shoulder and pushed him southwards rather than straight down the slope.

"There are too many!" the squire gibbered.

"Towards the river! Fast as you can!"

Ranulf buffeted more corpses out of their way as they ran. Claws slashed at them; he had to duck a mighty stroke from a long-handled Dane-axe. But the slope was at last dropping towards the Tefeidiad, the moonlit surface of which glittered just below them.

The last fifty yards were perhaps the worst.

"Use your strength, your weight... anything you've got!" Ranulf panted, as the dead closed in again.

Tallebois still had his dagger. When a woman, whose severed head hung down her back on a few sinews, reached out and caught him, he smote her hand off at the wrist.

"That's the way!" Ranulf shouted. He himself had managed to pick up a war-hammer. A corpse stumbled towards him and he swung the mighty cudgel, crushing its cranium. Another came towards him and he smashed its forehead – with such force that a soup of liquid brain matter spurted from its eye sockets.

The river was now tantalisingly close. Though a great mob of the dead were descending from behind, only a relative handful – three at the most – were in front.

"We can make it!" Ranulf shouted.

Tallebois was so racked with terror and fatigue that his voice squeaked. "We'll drown!"

"If you can't swim, just stay afloat. The current will carry us past the castle. We might be able to get ashore on its east side!"

"*Might* be able to?"

"Now you see why we aren't wearing mail!"

The final few feet of slope were steep, muddy and strewn with loose stones. They skidded and tripped their way to the bottom, blundering headlong into the final clutch of corpses. Ranulf hit the first one head-on, barrelling into its chest, catapulting it backward into the river. Tallebois wasn't so lucky. The other two caught hold of him, one wrapping its arms around his waist and burying its teeth into his naked left thigh, the other looping a skeletal arm around his neck, trying to throttle him. With gurgling bleats, Tallebois hacked with his dagger, but it had no effect. The would-be throttler bought its leering visage close to his tear-stained face. He slashed it back and forth, mangling it, chopping it away in chunks, exposing the grinning skull beneath, but not slowing its attack in the least. Its pendulous green tongue quivered as it hung from the chasm where its lower jaw had once been. It raked its bony claws across his chest and belly, drawing five crimson trails through the sooty grease.

And then Ranulf took its legs from under it.

He swept in with a two-handed blow so fierce that both the creature's knee joints were shattered, and the lower portions of its limbs sent spinning into the darkness. It fell thrashing to the ground. The other monster ceased its gnawing on Tallebois's thigh and swung around to face Ranulf. Its nose was missing, along with its upper lip, but its ivory teeth were fully intact and coated with blood. Taking possession of the sobbing squire's dagger, it came hard at Ranulf, aiming a blow that would have skewered him through the heart. He dodged it, spun around and brought the hammer full circle, catching the creature at the base of its backbone, breaking it clean through.

"Into the water!" he shouted, grabbing Tallebois, yanking him to his feet and hurling him over the last few feet of ground into the river.

Before Ranulf followed, he turned just once.

The rest of the revenants were only yards away, looking for all the world like some vast assembly of reeking remains ploughed from a plague pit, yet tottering down through the darkness towards him. The one whose spine he'd just broken was still on its feet, but now the upper part of its body had folded over until it hung upside down – as though it was made of paper.

Shaking his head at the sheer perversity of what he was witnessing, Ranulf threw the war-hammer into the midst of them, turned and dived into the Tefeidiad.

# CHAPTER TWENTY-FOUR

"I SAW GREAT heaps of munitions, my lord. Nails, chains, piles of pebbles from the river shore. *Ahhh…*"

Squire Tallebois gasped as Zacharius inserted another suture through his ripped-open thigh, using a needle that looked like a fishhook. Having washed the filth off with buckets of water from the well, both the squire and Ranulf were now warming themselves at a brazier inside the main stable block. Earl Corotocus, Navarre, du Guesculin and several other senior household knights stood around them, listening to their report. Fiery shadows played on their attentive faces as Tallebois spoke.

Ranulf, who had pointedly said nothing so far, climbed tiredly into his mail leggings. He and Tallebois had managed to scramble out of the river on the east side of the castle, but only with great difficulty. Having met no more of the dead there, they'd needed to clamber back down into the moat and squeeze themselves along the drain. Thankfully, the earl's men had pulled them up the garderobe chute, but by this time they'd been completely exhausted and the last thing Ranulf had wanted was a face-to-face interrogation.

"They were restocking the scoop-thrower, as we feared," the squire jabbered, a vague light of madness in his eyes. "By cockcrow tomorrow, I fancy we'd have been facing the iron hail again. All over again! The iron—"

"But you destroyed the blasted machine?" Corotocus asked.

"Absolutely, my lord. It can't be used any more, *ahhh*…" Tallebois gasped again as a particularly gruesome gash was closed with a single tight thread. "But there is something else. They had also piled up colossal blocks of stone, which looked as if they'd been freshly quarried. The sort a mason might use to lay foundations with."

"And?"

The squire shrugged. "The dead don't build, my lord… do they? Captain Garbofasse thought they were projectiles. He said this meant they were bringing the mangonels to the western bluff. That'd they'd be ready either later today or maybe tomorrow."

Du Guesculin sucked in his breath. "My lord, the iron hail would merely sweep the Constable's Tower roof, but from that close range the mangonels will destroy it! We must retreat to the Keep at once."

Corotocus said nothing.

"My lord, do you hear me? We should fill the Keep basement with supplies—"

"We will retreat to the Keep, du Guesculin, as and when the situation demands it," the earl interjected.

"But my lord, great blocks of stone…?"

Ranulf buckled his hauberk in place, feeling even deeper scorn for the household banneret than he usually did. It was a pity du Guesculin hadn't been so frantic in his concerns when the south wall defenders had had to face these missiles.

Earl Corotocus now turned to Ranulf. "What's your opinion of this enterprise? Did it succeed?"

Ranulf shrugged. "I always said the mangonels would be brought against the west wall in due course, my lord."

"And the scoop-thrower? It's completely disabled?"

"I didn't see that. So I can't comment."

The earl's eyebrows arched. "You didn't see it? How can that be?"

"He wasn't with us," Tallebois piped up. "He went to find the countess."

"You… went to find the countess?" Corotocus repeated slowly, his eyes suddenly burning into Ranulf like smoking spear-points.

"To cut the head off the snake," Tallebois added. "That was what he said."

There was an amazed silence in the stable, broken only by the snuffling of horses and popping of coals in the brazier. Corotocus continued to gaze at Ranulf, a gaze the young knight returned boldly as he adjusted his coif. At last, Navarre stepped forward.

"You expect us to believe, FitzOsbern," he said, his voice a low, ultra-dangerous monotone, "that a man like you, a sentimental fool who'd take the code literally even to the point of his own death, would murder Countess Madalyn in her sleep?" Before Ranulf could reply, Navarre had thrown down his gauntlet. "*This* says differently!"

Resignedly, Ranulf collected his sword-belt from a corner, buckled it to his waist, and reached down for the gauntlet.

"Pick that glove up, Ranulf, and you cross swords with me as well," Earl Corotocus said.

"My lord!" Navarre protested.

"We are *all* of us engaged in a trial by battle!" the earl shouted. "Or hadn't you dogs noticed?" He rounded back on Ranulf. "But you, sir, have some questions to answer. You say you went to look for the countess?"

"The only way for us to survive this situation, my lord, is to parley with her," Ranulf tried to explain.

"And you took that duty on yourself?"

"*You* weren't there."

"You insolent…" Navarre snapped, but the earl raised a hand for silence.

"It wasn't my initial plan," Ranulf added. "But it seemed like a sensible idea at the time."

There was another prolonged silence. Earl Corotocus watched Ranulf very carefully. Thus far unscathed by the siege, the earl's smooth, handsome features were pale with anger, his blue eyes blazed – but, as always, he was in full control of his emotions.

"I take it you failed?" the earl finally said.

"Yes," Ranulf admitted, truthfully.

They continued to stare at each other intently, as if both parties were waiting for the other to give something away.

At last, the earl sniffed and said: "You and Tallebois get yourselves some food, and them some sleep. I want you back at your posts by dawn."

As Corotocus walked back towards the Constable's Tower, Navarre hurried across the courtyard to catch up with him.

"My lord, my lord… FitzOsbern is a traitor."

"I know."

"You should have let me kill him."

"And divide the company in two?"

"He won't have that much support."

"He has more than you think," Corotocus said. "He's ended the iron hail. He's the man who held the Gatehouse bridge, remember? He's the one who warned us that we might soon be facing our own dead. Even the household men were listening to that."

"Sire, you are Earl Corotocus of Clun, first baron of the realm. FitzOsbern is nobody. A former wolf-head, a rogue knight who–"

"The men are frightened, Navarre!" Corotocus snapped, stopping in his tracks. For a fleeting second, he too looked vaguely unnerved. "They are also tired. They don't share our desire to show King Edward that the Earldom of Clun can hold the Welsh at bay." He strode on. "Besides, I'm not convinced that in a straight duel you'd be able to kill him."

"He'd be the first one to beat me…"

"There's always a first one, you imbecile."

They mounted the ramp to the Constable's Tower. Ordinarily there'd be guards on its entrance, but now all available men were on the walls. Corotocus and Navarre's iron-shod feet echoed in the tight, switchback stairwell as they ascended to the battlements.

"In that case, arrest him while he's sleeping," Navarre said. "Bring charges, make it legal."

"Much as I'm loathe to admit it, we need his sword. We need everyone's sword." The earl halted again, thinking. "But from now on, Navarre, stay close to him."

"Of course."

"Watch his every move." Corotocus smiled coldly, as though anticipating a treat. "When the time is right, Ranulf FitzOsbern will learn what it means to defy my will."

# CHAPTER TWENTY-FIVE

IN THE DARKEST and quietest part of the night, with his assistant sleeping in the wagon, Doctor Zacharius made a solo round of his infirmary, checking bandages and dressings, delivering herbal draughts, either to relieve pain or induce sleep. Most of the casualties were at least comfortable, though the air was filled with coughs, whimpers and soft moans. Once he had finished, Zacharius crossed the courtyard to one of the other outhouses, where a copper bowl filled with water simmered over a brazier. First he washed his hands, using sesame oil and lime powder, and then, one by one, cleansed his surgical implements, towelling each one dry and laying them all out on a fresh linen cloth, which he'd spread on a low table.

"Doctor Zacharius?" someone asked from the doorway.

Zacharius turned. One of the earl's knights stood there – in fact it was the young knight who had survived the mission to destroy the scoop-thrower. Zacharius had seen him many times before and, though he had never had cause to treat him and didn't know his name, he had always thought him a sullen fellow.

"Do you really believe that dismembering one of these creatures will help us understand why they are invulnerable to death?" Ranulf asked.

Zacharius continued with what he was doing. "In truth, they aren't invulnerable to death, are they? From what I hear, these things are already dead."

"You know what I mean," Ranulf said, entering.

He'd finished another late meal in the refectory, as the earl had instructed, but sleep had eluded him for the last hour or so – for two main reasons.

Firstly, though he didn't think he could have done much more than appeal to Countess Madalyn's humanity, which was well known throughout the border country, he wasn't absolutely sure. He hadn't known the priest, Gwyddon, would be present. That had caused an unforeseen problem. Likewise, the Welsh had discovered that the English were in their camp sooner than he'd hoped. None of these things had been under his control. But couldn't he have reacted more appropriately? Perhaps he should have killed Gwyddon. Perhaps he should have taken Countess Madalyn hostage? It would have been difficult, but maybe he could at least have tried. Uncertainty about this was now torturing him.

The second reason was Doctor Zacharius and his comments before they had departed – about returning with a captive specimen. Of course, once the mission had got under way that would have been totally impractical, and Ranulf had quickly forgotten it. But now, with the diplomatic door closed, all sorts of wild thoughts were occurring to him. Had he missed another opportunity to turn the tide in their favour? But what did it actually mean to eviscerate something – even something as hideous as these walking dead – to take it apart piece by piece while it writhed and thrashed, purely to learn how it was composed and controlled? Such knowledge was surely not intended for Man; this was what Ranulf had always been told and had always believed. Such things were best left to God – and yet, after what he'd seen here, particularly outside in the rain and the mist, a terrible fear was now taking root inside him. At the end of the day, if God came down to Earth enraged and cast celestial fire on his children, would those children not justifiably seek to escape it – even if it enraged God all the more? Willing martyrs were made of very rare stuff indeed; only now was Ranulf realising this.

"I can't answer your question," Zacharius said, still cleaning his tools. "But put it this way, I don't believe in sorcery."

"Even after everything we have seen with our own eyes?" Ranulf asked.

"Oh, it exists... superficially. But when a man performs acts of 'sorcery', what he's really doing is manipulating the laws of nature in ways not yet known to the rest of us."

"And you think you can learn about such laws by opening the flesh of one of these walking dead?"

"The Greek physician, Hippocrates, was convinced that diseases did not afflict mankind as a punishment from the gods, but because the systems of organs that make up our bodies were for some reason malfunctioning. He developed many remedies through his studies of the human body, often after life had expired. He saved innumerable lives and the human race was no worse off for that. The Roman doctor, Galen, produced countless books containing detailed sketches of human anatomy, which enabled his students to treat a variety of previously serious ailments with simple procedures. My proposal was similar, if not exactly the same – a straightforward investigation, the results of which might benefit us all."

Ranulf pondered this.

"Why do you ask?" Zacharius wondered. "Are you planning to go out there again, when the last time only two of you returned alive?"

"The choice would not be mine," Ranulf said.

"In which case don't agonise over it. The reality..." Zacharius shrugged. "The reality is that I am neither skilled nor experienced enough to reach immediate and accurate conclusions. I would need the assistance of other learned doctors. In addition, it would take time, which we clearly will have less of once the fighting recommences. I would also need a better place in which to work. Somewhere light and dry to tabulate my findings, collate my samples..."

"I don't understand any of these things."

"But you evidently *do* understand that this battle will not be won by the usual means. You proved that not two hours ago."

"It wouldn't take a clever man to realise that."

"No, but it would take a brave one to admit it." Zacharius continued cleaning his implements. "What are you called?"

"I am Ranulf FitzOsbern."

"You're one of the earl's indebted knights, are you not?"

"I am."

The doctor smiled to himself.

"Something amuses you?" Ranulf asked.

"It certainly does. You occupy the lowest of the equestrian ranks, yet you speak to Earl Corotocus almost as an equal."

"At some point I'll be punished for that."

"I've no doubt you will. But he tolerates you for the time being because during this crisis he clearly considers that he needs you. And after what I heard you tell him, about your wise attempt to parley with Countess Madalyn, I would make the same decision."

"It was a poor plan. It failed."

"At least it was a plan. And you have *my* commendation for it, FitzOsbern, if no-one else's."

There was brief silence, Ranulf eyeing the gleaming knives, scalpels and forceps arrayed in their orderly rows.

"Why do you clean those things so thoroughly?" he asked.

"Because I will have to perform more surgeries with them."

"Is one man's blood poisonous to another?"

"Maybe. I don't know for certain, but why take the risk?" Zacharius laid down another tool – a screw-handled speculum, which he regularly used to open and clamp deep wounds in order to remove foreign objects buried inside them. "It may also be that even the smallest speck of filth will cause an injury to fester, and lead to blood disorders and death."

"You have a strong instinct for your profession," Ranulf observed.

"As do you."

"All I do is fight. Any man can fight."

"I can't. Not to your standard."

"But almost no-one at all can do what you do."

Zacharius smiled again. "Don't flatter me too much, my friend. We all have our instincts. That stubborn fool Benan's instinct tells him that only God can save us now. He thus refuses to allow me to treat him. He wouldn't even be brought down here to the infirmary, but insisted on making his own way from the Constable's Tower to the chapel, where there is no bed, no warmth – and he had to crawl on his belly most of the distance, because he's lost too much blood to stand. But that's all to the good, he says. He has to win back the Lord's favour, and the only way to do that is by self-imposed penance."

"You criticise him for it?"

"Not really." Zacharius sighed. "Who is to say that I am right and Benan is wrong? If forced to make a judgement, I suppose I'd always rather men solved their problems by shedding their own blood rather than the blood of others."

"And yet you'd have no qualm about cutting one of these creatures open to examine its entrails... even if it is bound with chains and completely harmless?"

"None whatsoever."

"Some might say that God would object."

"Some might also say that if a man were brought to me with a mangled limb, God would object to my removing that limb in order to save the man's life. Do you think He would, FitzOsbern? When in all the great hunting-chases of England, limbs are regularly lopped for the far less edifying reason of punishing poaching, and yet those wielding the axe are almost never struck down or even castigated by holy Church, as far as I can see?"

Ranulf struggled visibly with his doubts.

"Surely this is not a difficult concept for you?" Zacharius said. "You who this very night has defied the conventions of his own martial world, bypassing your overlord to make what you believed was a correct decision? But don't trouble yourself with such seditious thinking, my friend. I understand your reservation. How many sacred cattle can we slaughter before we have nothing left to defend? Perhaps it's better to return to your post on the castle wall and leave me in my hospital, where we can both stick to our allotted tasks, which..." He lowered his voice until it was almost inaudible. "Which, in truth, will yield the world little."

Ranulf moved away from the outhouse, still deep in thought – only to return a few moments later.

"I can't capture one of these creatures for you," he said from the doorway. "It would be impossible, so there is no point in my even offering to try. But I'll remember what you said for the future."

Zacharius nodded, as if that was as much as he could expect.

"And I will try to get you out of here alive," Ranulf added. "If I can."

"I wouldn't take any more risks if I were you, sir knight. Not on my behalf."

Ranulf shook his head. "You haven't been outside. You haven't seen what we're facing – not up close. The walls of this castle will not hold them for long."

"And more's the pity." Zacharius shrugged. "I'll never enjoy a comely lass again."

"That said, it's not unfeasible that one or two of us may escape. You should be among them."

"Battle my way to safety, you mean?" The doctor smiled. "My dear FitzOsbern, didn't I just tell you; I'm a lover, not a fighter."

"Maybe we can smuggle you out?"

"And would you smuggle my patients with me? You'd need to, because I won't abandon them."

Ranulf felt frustrated. "But what you've said here needs to be understood more widely."

"As I say, there are other doctors more learned than I."

"Doctor Zacharius! This thing that's been unleashed... it won't end here."

Zacharius regarded him carefully, before shaking his head. "You think more deeply than is good for you, FitzOsbern. More deeply than is good for any of us." He had now finished cleaning his implements and began to wrap them in separate bundles of clean cloth. "Go back to your post."

"I fear Christendom faces a graver peril now than ever came from the Moslem desert or the Mongol steppe."

"Then why should I want to survive to see it?"

Ranulf had no immediate answer to that, because it was a sentiment he was slowly starting to share. Zacharius would no longer talk with him. In fact, he would no longer even look at him. So at length the young knight did as he was bidden, and returned to his post.

# CHAPTER TWENTY-SIX

As DAWN APPROACHED there was, for the first time that year, a feeling that winter at last had flown. Despite the chill, an apricot sky began to arch its way eastwards. Suddenly the trees were rookeries of twittering birds, their bare, twisting branches laden with buds and catkins, their roots resplendent as the first spring flowers poked through the drifts of rotted leaf.

High above Grogen's western bluff, in a circle of gnarled and ancient oaks, there was a wheel-headed cross, cut from granite and carved all over with intricate knotworks, which its coat of green lichen did little to conceal. This was where Gwyddon found Countess Madalyn. She was kneeling in silence before the ancient edifice, a veil over her hair, her joined hands wrapped with prayer beads. Gwyddon regarded her scornfully, before dismounting.

"We are ready to resume the assault, countess. This time I recommend that we press it night and day until the English are broken. Give them no respite at all."

She made no reply.

"Countess Madalyn..."

"I am praying, Gwyddon!" she hissed.

Gwyddon stood back respectfully. The countess's horse was tethered to one of the oaks' lower branches. A few feet above it, a pattern of curious notches scarred the side of the tree trunk, bulging and distorted as though thick layers of bark had overgrown some inscribed image. By the looks of it, it had once been a face. There were similar markings on the other trees.

When Countess Madalyn finally stood and removed her veil, Gwyddon was still waiting for her.

"Were you aware this place was once sacred to an older god?" he said. "You Christians supplanted him. As you did in so many of our other holy groves."

"On the contrary," she replied, looking pale and drawn. "We cleansed this place."

"Its air is certainly sweeter than the air down in the valley."

Countess Madalyn grimaced. "The stench down there is unbearable. I couldn't tolerate it any longer."

"Sadly, it's a price we must pay."

"And what other price must we pay, Gwyddon?" She didn't even look at him as she untied her horse.

"Countess, I understand your concerns, but answer me this: would you have your Welsh countrymen die in droves? Because that is the alternative, I fear. Had we attacked Grogen Castle with an army of the living, ten thousand of us, maybe more, would now lie slain."

The countess didn't mount her beast but stood against it, her head bowed. She appeared weary, almost tearful. Her right hand clutched the bridle so tightly that its tendons showed through her white silk glove.

"I see you don't dispute that fact, at least," he said.

"Gwyddon!" She rounded on him, but more with desperation than anger. "This thing you – *we* – have done is an abhorrence in the eyes of God!"

"In what way, madam? Our soldiers know no terror as they are sent to battle. They feel no pain when they are cut down. For all we know, their spirits are already in God's hands. We are merely making use of their remains."

"And in the long-term, Gwyddon, what do we plan to do with those remains?"

Gwyddon had not been prepared for this question.

"The young English knight was right, was he not?" she said. "This army of ours will simply rot. Soon it will be nought but clacking bones. And what then? We make more, as you threatened? Is that your plan? How *many* more, Gwyddon?"

"These husks are a matter of convenience, countess. When we no longer have need of them, we will dispense with them."

"Will we? And will we then compose our armies of living men – those who *do* feel terror, those who *do* feel pain?" She gave a wintry smile. "I see your concern for human suffering is also a matter of convenience."

"And do you think Earl Corotocus would have any of these qualms?"

"Earl Corotocus is one man, Gwyddon." She became thoughtful. "That young knight said there are strong feelings against him."

"And at the same time, that young knight's accomplices destroyed the very weapon with which we were stripping their battlements of armour. Clearly, that was his real objective."

"He could have killed us both. Would that not have been a more useful objective for him?"

"Even if he spoke the truth, the chances are that he's dead. Only a couple of them, at the most, made it back into the castle."

"Nevertheless…" She climbed into her saddle. "We need to speak with them."

"Earl Corotocus will never negotiate unless it's from a position of strength. And King Edward is exactly the same. This is why ruthless individuals like them will always succeed… and why radical means are needed to stop them."

The countess wheeled her horse around. "We've already stopped them. Earl Corotocus and his army can't wreak any more damage. They are trapped."

"As is your daughter, madam."

The countess paused to think. "Would it serve their purpose to harm her now? They know what their fate will be if they do. My decision is made, Gwyddon. We will maintain the siege, but there will be no further attacks unless the English provoke them. In the meantime, I will send messages to King Edward."

"Who even now is entering Wales from the north."

"All the better." She made to ride away. "Let him see our power first-hand."

"And what if he likes what he sees, and tries to claim it for his own?"

She reined her horse, gazing down at him.

Gwyddon shrugged. "Edward Longshanks is a crafty tactician. He has no truck with honourable warfare. As far as he is concerned, victory is all. When he sees what we have done here, he is more likely to be inspired than frightened."

"What exactly are you saying?"

Gwyddon climbed onto his horse. "I'm saying that if King Edward felt you were pliable, he would certainly sit at the negotiating table, especially with such a prize as the Cauldron of Regeneration to be won."

"You think me a fool, Gwyddon? I would never bargain away the Cauldron. In any case, it would be no use to the English without your arcane knowledge. Unless..." She looked slowly round at him again. "Unless that also is available to be won? Would you share your knowledge, Gwyddon? With the English?"

"Under torture, madam, a man may share anything."

"Ohhh, I see." She regarded him with new understanding. Her wintry smile had returned. "So Wales and the Welsh are also a matter of convenience to you?"

"Wales and the Welsh are my future, madam. As they are yours. Thus, I feel we must destroy the invaders utterly. That is the only kind of message King Edward will understand. We proceed with the assault, yes?"

He posed it as a question, though it was clearly more of a statement. As such, Countess Madalyn made no answer.

"One more thing, madam," Gwyddon said, as he turned his horse around. "If it suits you, you may remain here where the air is fresh and the grass green rather than red. After all, there is no longer any reason for you to witness these terrible events. You made your appearance on the first day, as required. Your part in this affair has been played."

He spurred his horse away, leaving Countess Madalyn alone in the grove of mottled oaks.

# CHAPTER TWENTY-SEVEN

WITH THE DAWN came the dead.

Heralded by a dirge of howls and moans, they crammed along the causeway, a hundred abreast, pushing their siege-tower ahead of them, its mighty wheels rumbling on the timbers. The English responded in the only way they knew how, with showers of arrows and stones. But it made no discernible impact. The oxen, to prevent them being wounded or killed by the castle defenders, were being driven beneath the shelter of the siege-tower's ironclad skirts. As the great structure drew steadily closer, it could be seen that assault teams of the dead were already gathered on top of it. Its gantry bridge, perhaps twenty feet in length, was currently raised, held aloft by two leather thongs, either of which a simple blow would have cut. The lip of the bridge was fixed with iron hooks, so that when it fell across the Constable's Tower's stone parapet, it would catch and hold itself in place.

The earl's best fighting men waited for it, armed not just with shields and swords, but with bills, spears and a stockpile of naptha grenades. Earl Corotocus also had an onager brought forward and devil's sachets packed with bricks broken from the rear battlements.

"They must not cross!" Navarre bellowed, as the tower halted in front of them. "Not one of them!"

When the bridge fell, poll-arms were lifted to prevent it making contact, but the first of the dead merely scrambled to the top of it and leapt. At least five plummeted to the foot of the tower, but three landed safely and a savage melee commenced as they laid about them with axes and mattocks. A retaliatory storm of slashing blades soon hacked them to pieces, but not before the poll-men were themselves cut down and the bridge crashed onto the battlements.

"Onager!" Earl Corotocus roared.

His engineers were already in place, and the first devil's sachet loaded into the bucket. But before the lever could be pulled, the dead on the top of the siege-tower let loose a blizzard of arrows and crossbow bolts. Space was immediately cleared, maybe a dozen men, including those on the onager, struck down. Ramon la Roux, already grievously wounded from the fight at the Gatehouse, pivoted around grey-faced, blood oozing between his lips. A missile had pierced his breast to its feathers. He staggered a couple of yards, fell against Ranulf and dropped to the floor.

With gurgling groans, the dead threw down their bows and, bristling with swords, hammers and cleavers, advanced across their gantry. They were mid-way over, when Ranulf threw himself onto the onager's lever. The complex throwing device had been tilted upward on rear support blocks, so that its payload travelled in a straight line, rather than arcing through the air. As such, ten heavy projectiles were now flung clean into the approaching horde. The first few were felled by gut-thumping impacts, their bodies shattered into glistening green and crimson scraps; those behind went toppling over the side. Two projectiles continued through, striking the rear of the siege-tower's upper tier with pulverising force, smashing an entire section of its framework. But fresh cohorts of corpses were now flooding up its timber throat. While men-at-arms hastened to crank the onager back to full tension, Navarre and others lobbed naptha grenades across the bridge. Several struck the dead full-on, engulfing them in flame; others dropped down inside the siege-tower, spilling fire through its joists and beams.

"More naptha!" Walter Margas shrieked, only for a blazing figure to leap down and wrap its arms around him. Ranulf hewed it from its shoulder to its breastbone with a massive stroke of his longsword. But Margas was already horribly seared. He staggered back to his feet, a twisted, drooling wreck, only to be struck in the face by a javelin, which didn't penetrate deeply but laid his cheek open to the glinting bone beneath.

Though entire sections of the siege-tower had now caught fire, the dead continued to clamber up through it and rampage across the bridge. The onager was again sprung. Its deadly cargo was catapulted through the advancing mob. Yet more went spinning from the bridge, but others made it onto the battlements. One of them sent shockwaves through the English by the mere sight of him. He was a giant of a man, naked save for a loincloth, covered in soot and grease, and armed with a spike-headed mace. The flesh across his throat was gruesomely mangled. His face had been bitten over and over, his scalp almost torn from the top of his head, but it was perfectly visible who he was – Captain Garbofasse, late of the earl's mercenary division.

With black gruel vomiting from his mouth, Garbofasse gave a guttural, inhuman roar and, swinging his brutal weapon around, smote the skulls of two of his former hearth-men, dashing their brains out where they stood.

Other corpses lumbered down behind him. One was recognisable as Roger FitzUrz. The other, walking with a bizarrely crooked gait, was Red Guthric.

"Repel!" Earl Corotocus bellowed, advancing to battle himself, his sword and shield hefted.

With a furious clangour, the two forces met, blade clashing on blade, on mail, on helmet and buckler, falchions crushing shoulder-joints, axes biting through foreheads. The squire Tallebois fell at this point, Red Guthric, his former comrade, hurling him shrieking to the ground and striking at him again and again with a scramsax, cleaving him from cranium to chin three times, each breach an inch from the next, so that his head fell apart like a sliced loaf.

"Ladders!" someone cried.

All along the battlements to either side of the siege-tower, crudely constructed ladders were appearing. Ranulf dashed towards the nearest, but a monstrosity had already appeared at the top of it. Ranulf grabbed a spear, and as it tried to climb through the embrasure, transfixed it through its chest, forcing it backward into the abyss. The next one up, he clove between the eyes and across the left hand, severing all its fingers and costing it its grip. It dropped like a stone, knocking off one corpse after another all the way to the bottom. Ranulf was thus able to grab the ladder and push it sideways. It collided with a second ladder, which also collapsed, depositing maybe thirty more of the dead into the wailing mass of their comrades far below.

Earl Corotocus, meanwhile, was engaged in a savage cut-and-thrust with Garbofasse. The earl took blow after blow on his shield, which already was beaten out of shape, but at last made a telling strike of his own, ripping open Garbofasse's unguarded belly so that a mass of glistening, coiling entrails flopped out. Garbofasse seemingly felt nothing. He raised his mace with both hands, only for Navarre, who had despatched his own opponent, to sever his legs from behind, and then hew and hew at him as he lay there, until he was nought but a pile of twitching, dismembered meat.

The interior of the siege-tower was now a raging inferno. The frantic lowing of the oxen trapped beneath it became a shrill squealing as they were burned alive. One or two dead still attempted to scale up through it, but they too were consumed. So great was the heat that the siege-tower's iron skin began to soften and slide loose. With a splintering crash, the gantry bridge, burnt through at the joints, fell onto the causeway.

The ladders still had to be dealt with. Ranulf had knocked down two, but there were maybe ten others. The English went at them hammer and tongs, splitting the skulls and sundering the limbs of those attempting to climb up and, where possible, smashing the upper rungs, so that the ladders fell in two halves. But now there was another threat. In some cases, the dead had started circumnavigating the Constable's Tower, spilling around the Inner Fort via the bailey. What was more, on the curtain-wall their work-teams had erected rope-and-pulley systems and were hauling up scorpions and other bolt-throwers, with which they hurled grappling hooks linked to nets, climbing ropes and more scaling ladders to the top of the Inner Fort walls. At eighty to a hundred feet, these great ramparts would normally be unassailable, but now the English watched agog as the dead hauled themselves up the sheer edifices with comparative ease.

Drenched with sweat and blackened by smoke, Earl Corotocus had to shout to be heard in the midst of this chaos. His efforts were further hampered as flights of arrows swept up from the causeway. While the bulk of the dead now queued in orderly fashion to ascend the ladders, others – those still equipped with bows and crossbows – stood back and launched their missiles. They took particular aim at those English attempting to throw down the ladders. Ranulf, Navarre and others were forced to step back as a stream of shafts rattled through the embrasures. Gurt Louvain was spitted through the palm of his left hand. Cursing, he snapped the shaft and, with clenched teeth, yanked it free. He bound the wound with an old rag, but it had soon turned sodden with gore. Hugh du Guesculin, who had hung back as much as he could during the fray, was struck a glancing blow to the helmet, which made him hang back even further, though he continued to bark at his master's underlings, calling them cowards and curs.

Also shouting like a madman, Earl Corotocus stalked up and down, striking at any corpse that vaulted through onto the battlements and, where possible, sending men to the south side of the tower, where, beyond a narrow gate, the wall-walk of the Inner Fort began. Diverting along this, they were able to cut many of the climbing ropes that had so far been attached. Large numbers of the dead were thus precipitated a huge distance into the south bailey, where they were literally broken into pieces.

But this wasn't the whole of it.

Some of the bolt-throwers had projected their missiles through the arrow-slits on the Inner Fort's south-facing wall. These connected with buildings inside, such as the barrack house in the Inner Fort's southwest corner, and the great hall in the southeast corner. Frantically, small groups of defenders, led by archery captain Davy Gou, hurried indoors. In the barrack house, where most of their bedrolls were spread on piles of hay, several of the dead were already forcing their way through the arrow-slits. It would have been impossible for living men to enter via these horribly narrow apertures, but the dead cared nothing for crushed bones and torn skin. Gou and his men met them in a whirlwind of blades. As throughout the battle, only complete evisceration and dismemberment would account for the intruders, and, long before this was achieved, many an Englishman's throat had been torn, eye plucked, or limbs sheared.

The battle now girdled two thirds of the castle, and raged on in this murderous fashion for the entire day. On top of ramparts now washed with blood and strewn with dead and dying, the English held out as best they could. Whenever one ladder was thrown down, another replaced it. When one marauding band was repulsed, a second would immediately follow. More and more dead archers were gathering on the causeway. Thanks to their capture of the earl's heavy weapons train, they appeared to have limitless ammunition, and with arms and shoulders that no longer tired, with bowstring fingers that no longer bled or blistered, they poured it over the battlements relentlessly.

And all the while cacophonous booms sounded through the structure of the Constable's Tower, for the burnt wreckage of the siege-tower had been hauled away and an iron-headed battering ram brought forth. A band of corpses, maybe thirty strong, slammed it again and again on the central gate. No amount of pelting with rocks, stones and arrows would dissuade them. So immune were they, they didn't even carry shields over their heads.

Down in the courtyard, the infirmary had been swiftly overwhelmed. Zacharius and Henri laboured feverishly in the midst of blood-drenched bodies piled three deep. Having long exhausted their supply of intoxicants, they concentrated on those who required the least painful procedures, moving straight from one man to the next, pumping sweat as they extracted arrow heads and broken shafts, stitched or cauterised gaping wounds, severed shattered limbs with as few clean strokes of the saw as they could manage. The shrieks and gasps rang in their ears.

Experienced as he was, Zacharius was strained almost to breaking point. On previous battlefields, he'd had orderlies to assist him and, if not orderlies, volunteer monks and nuns from nearby communities. Now there wasn't even anyone to hold or tie the struggling patients down. And there was no end to these patients. Beyond the stinking confines of the infirmary, they were scattered like leaves on the cobblestones of the courtyard. More and more were brought down, many in so dreadful a condition that nothing could be done for them.

Ranulf FitzOsbern came shouting and pushing his way in. He was half-carrying and half-dragging one of his comrades, a fellow knight called Ramon la Roux. From one quick glance, Zacharius deduced that la Roux was already dead. An arrow had pierced his chest clean through; he'd already bled so much that his entire tabard was slick with gore – there could scarcely be a drop of the precious fluid left inside him.

"For God's sake!" Zacharius shouted. "I'm not a miracle worker!"

Ranulf shook his head. "There's nothing you can do?"

"Surely you know the answer to that, you damn fool! Haven't you fought enough wars?" Zacharius whipped around to where other maimed soldiers waited to be treated, watching him with harrowed eyes. "Haven't you *all* fought enough wars?"

"He helped me earlier," Ranulf muttered. "I thought I should at least try."

"A nice sentiment. But somewhat misplaced in this pit of Hell!"

Ranulf finally nodded and let the dead weight that was Ramon la Roux slide to the floor.

"Not in here!" Zacharius bellowed. "This is a hospital, not a blasted mortuary!"

Without a word, Ranulf took la Roux by the heels and dragged him outside onto the cobblestones, where he had no option but to leave him among the other piles of dead or dying men.

Briefly, Zacharius followed him out, mopping his hands on a crimson rag. "Dare I ask how the fight is going?"

Ranulf gave this some thought. "No."

"What's that?"

"You asked me a question, did you not? I gave you my answer. 'No'." Ranulf turned and trudged back towards the Constable's Tower. "For the sake of your own sanity, don't dare ask how the fight is going."

It was now late afternoon and just as Ranulf re-ascended to his post, word reached Earl Corotocus's ears that bolt-throwers were assailing the Inner Fort from the east side, a part of the stronghold which, up until now, had not been struck at all.

"We're spread too thinly," he said to Navarre. "We haven't enough men to cover the entire perimeter."

"My lord, if we retreat now the Inner Fort will fall. We'll only have the Keep left."

Corotocus nodded grimly. "Agreed. We must hold at all costs. The king will come. I know he will."

But beyond Grogen Castle, there was no sign of the king. In fact, quite the opposite. For a brief startling moment, Ranulf had a chance to glance out over the Constable's Tower parapet, and found himself focussed on a landscape literally swamped by tides of the dead. For as far as the eye could see, from all directions, their cursed and bedraggled legions were advancing towards the castle. This vision alone might have been enough to send a man mad, but then, if it were possible, something even more frightening happened.

With a collision like a thunderclap, an object impacted in the middle of the tower roof. It was a massive thirty-gallon barrel, which partially exploded and ejected burning naptha in a wide arc, engulfing maybe twenty of the earl's men. It didn't break apart totally, but bounced thirty yards, crashed through a door and hurtled down a spiral stair in which numerous wounded awaiting transport to the infirmary were crouched or lying, immersing and igniting them one by one. A second such missile followed immediately afterwards, this one a colossal earthenware pot. It struck the western battlements, blew apart and spurted liquid flame all along the rampart, swallowing some half a dozen defenders who were cowering there.

Every man still on his feet spun around towards the western bluff, where the three great siege engines, *War Wolf*, *Giant's Fist* and *God's Maul* had finally been assembled. Tremulous prayers seeped from throats already hoarse with shouting and screaming, as a third incendiary came tumbling down across the valley, black smoke trailing through the air behind it.

# CHAPTER TWENTY-EIGHT

Countess Madalyn had often heard it said that King Edward of England was a tyrant.

Her own people had no time for him, seeing only a despot and conqueror who betrayed his own chivalrous ideals with acts of cruelty and barbarism. But the English had a different view of their ultimate liege-lord. They regarded him as a great war-leader, but also as a font of justice. Any man, it was said, no matter how base, could approach King Edward and beseech him person-to-person. The king had reformed the entire legal system in England in favour of the lower classes. He'd installed a *parlement* at Westminster as a permanent institution. Clearly there were huge contradictions in his character. He was a pious Christian who'd already ridden on crusade once and apparently planned to do so again. He regularly sought diplomatic solutions to international crises; in the 1280s he was known as 'the peace-maker of Europe'. But he notoriously detested the enemies of his countrymen, and when he waged war against them it was a ghastly form of total war, designed to terrorise their populace into subservience.

Could she deal with such a man? Would he even grant her an audience, given what he'd done to Dafydd ap Gruffyd, whose rebellion twelve years ago had been rewarded with a particularly torturous fate; Prince Dafydd's body torn with pincers and hanged until half dead, whereupon it was disembowelled and hacked into quarters?

It was an onerous decision that she faced. But as she stood among the trees on the western bluff and gazed down on Grogen, she became increasingly certain what that decision would be.

The three giant catapults that Gwyddon had captured from the English were now in place on a plateau slightly lower down. Again and again, they lobbed huge, fiery missiles, each one of which trailed across the darkened sky like a comet and impacted on the fortifications with a flash like summer lightning. Night had now fallen fully, which gave the entire business a demonic aspect. The sky was jet-black, but at the same time red as molten steel. Liquid fire raged high on the battlements and streamed down the castle's outer walls. Sulphurous smoke, infernally coloured, belched from its arrow-slit windows. A cloying stench of burning mingled with the more familiar reek of decaying flesh.

Countess Madalyn's dead army seemed numberless as it trudged down the slope like some vast herd of mindless cattle, moaning and mewling as they crossed the southwest bridge and followed the berm path, finally entering the castle through its forced-open Gatehouse. She felt numb as she watched them clamber like ants up ladders and ropes, not just on the Constable's Tower, but all around the walls of the Inner Fort. Even from this distance, the ringing of blade on blade assailed her ears. From so far away, the screams of rage and death sounded like the squeaking of rodents, but there was no end to it. The English were still resisting, as the young knight had threatened they would. But surely they couldn't hold for much longer, and when every one of them was put to the sword, Gwyddon's abomination would be complete. King Edward the crusader would then have no option but to fall upon the Welsh as a nation of devils.

Countess Madalyn felt nothing – neither fear, nor remorse – as she turned and climbed into her saddle. Her bolsters were already filled with food and water. She also had a knapsack containing gold and jewellery as proof of her identity, which she concealed carefully among her saddlebags. Drawing a rough, homespun cowl over her head, she kicked her horse forward.

The hillside tracks would be treacherous in the dark. They were narrow, winding, overhung with low branches. But Countess Madalyn knew her native landscape well.

*Her native landscape.*

It pained her to think that way.

The Welsh were an indigenous part of these British isles, but they had their own culture and customs, their own beliefs, their own long tradition of self-governance. Why could their neighbours in England not see that? She knew that it wasn't the English themselves, but their rulers. Ever since the first Norman kings had created their powerful military state, they'd sought control over the entire island of Britain. For all their airs and graces, for all their pretensions to honour and courtliness, they were at heart a rapacious breed.

It frustrated her, maddened her.

And yet here she was, seeking to parley with one of those very same Anglo-Norman kings. In fact, it was worse than that – with one of the most fearsome and warlike kings that had ever sat on the Westminster throne.

Egging her horse on, she tried to shake these fears from her mind. This was about national survival, nothing less. Not just the survival of Wales in the flesh, but Wales as a spiritual nation. Gwyddon's way was the druids' way. She didn't despise him purely for that. The druids, she knew, had been stalwart friends to the Welsh in their battles against the Romans, the Saxons, the Danes. Everyday Welsh life was flavoured with pagan traditions, mostly of the more benign sort. But Gwyddon, in his overweening ambition, had unleashed a horror the like of which Christendom had never seen and could never tolerate. Even if he was successful, what kind of world was he trying to create where the dead commanded the living? And what would the view of the Almighty be – He, who had forbidden sorcery in all its forms, on pain of everlasting fire?

She rode on, more determined than ever to make a truce with King Edward. She was now descending a wooded brae, very steep and slippery with dew. The air was exquisitely cold in that way that only the air in March can be. Her horse steamed; her own breath puffed in moon-lit clouds. The avenues between the trees were damp, black corridors. Now that the roar of battle had fallen far behind, she heard nothing. Her horse continued to find its own way, with slow, tentative footfalls. Only when they reached level ground, did it increase its pace a little, but she resisted the urge to canter, unwilling to create unnecessary noise. She felt a growing conviction that she wasn't alone. She glanced over her shoulder, seeing nothing but the night. The woods had now thickened, dense clumps of hawthorn closing around her. With a thunder of heavy wings, a large owl exploded from a bough just over her head. Shocked, the countess reined her horse to a halt.

The owl beat its way off into the darkness. She glanced around again. Still nothing: meshed branches, deep shadows. Overhead, leafless twigs laced back and forth across a gibbous moon.

She urged her mount forward. Somewhere not too far ahead there was a mountain stream. Now that the spring thaw had set in, it might be running deeper than usual, but there was a footbridge that she could cross. On the other side of that, a canyon led through to open hillside, below which lay the Leominster road.

There was a crackle in the undergrowth close by. This time she didn't halt, but rode on determinedly. She fancied an indistinct shape was moving parallel to her, about thirty yards to her right. If she listened hard enough, she imagined she could hear a breaking of twigs, a trampling of leaf mulch. Her passage was so narrow that thorny fingers plucked at her, snagging her clothes, catching her cowl. Her mount snuffled loudly, as though nervous. She now sensed movement to her left as well as to her right. There was even greater crunching and crackling in the hawthorn. She dug in her heels, urging the horse forward. It began to trot, and she was forced to duck repeatedly as branches passed overhead.

"Easy, easy," she cooed to the animal. "We are almost at the stream."

It was a relief when she actually heard the waterway, babbling over its stones and pebbles. She wouldn't exactly be safe on the other side of it, but at least she could break into a gallop and put significant distance between herself and Grogen Castle.

And then something stepped out into the path in front of her. Even given the events of the last few days, it was the most horrible thing she had ever seen.

It had once been a man – that much was clear. But what it could be described as now God only knew. The right side of it was intact if somewhat discoloured, but the entire left side of it – its arm, leg, torso, shoulder, even the left side of its face – had been eaten down to the gleaming bones; either by rats or decay, or both.

Countess Madalyn had to stifle a scream of disbelieving horror.

The thing didn't lurch towards her. It simply stood there between the hawthorns, regarding her with its single lustreless eye. The moonlight glinted through the bars of its partly exposed ribcage. It was making its way to join the rest, she told herself. Of course it was. They had been drawn here from all directions. That was its only purpose; to join the siege. Somehow or other, Gwyddon's necromantic skill had implanted a sole directive in the worm-eaten skulls of these walking, teetering husks to capture Grogen Castle and destroy its defenders. It would not harm *her*.

So thinking, she urged the horse forward again. There was no room around the semi-skeletal horror, so she expected it to shuffle aside and allow her passage. But it didn't. When she was a yard or so in front of it, she again had to halt her animal, which whinnied and tossed its head nervously.

"Out of my way," the countess instructed in Welsh, though her voice was unsteady. "Out of my way! Don't you know who I am? I am your mistress, the very reason you walk on this Earth. You must obey my command."

It made no move to comply, though it tilted what passed for its head upward slightly, to regard her more closely. She had to fight nausea when she saw a black beetle wriggle out of the gaping eye-socket and scurry down the rotted cheekbone.

"You must do as I say! Move aside at once!"

In response, its jaw dropped to its chest; for a bemused moment, the countess half expected it to drop off entirely. Instead, the creature groaned – in utterly inhuman fashion. It was like the sound heavy wood makes when straining under pressure; a deep, reverberating creak. Yet there were fluctuations in it, alterations in tone. With hair-raising incredulity, Countess Madalyn realised that this thing, this cast-off human shell, was actually trying to speak to her. Slowly, chillingly, the half-groan-half-jabber rose to a peak of shrillness that was difficult to listen to.

Abruptly, the sound ceased, and the thing lurched forward with lightning speed, trying to grab at her bridle.

The horse shrieked and reared and, before the countess knew what had happened, she'd been thrown to the ground. The impact was in the middle of her back, and drove the wind from her. But her pain was numbed by her fear. Shielded by the horse, which careered back and forth, attempting to wheel on the tight woodland path, she leapt to her feet, gathered up her skirts and plunged into the undergrowth.

She ran breathless and blind, regardless that her clothes were torn by thorns. She fought through them all, tears and sweat mingling on her cheeks. She'd known all along that this would happen, that these blasphemous monsters would at last round on the Welsh as well; that they would seek to devour *all* God-fearing things, for theirs was a realm of darkness, devilry and decay. Even as these thoughts struck her, she tottered out into a clearing, from the other side of which more abominations were advancing. What appeared to be a young woman was approaching, a child walking on either side of her, holding her by the hand. The woman's head was missing from her shoulders, and the child on the left, a boy, had possession of it, carrying it in front of him by the hair. That head, though crudely hewn from its torso, was again trying to speak – perhaps trying to accuse her, the countess thought with dismay – the eyes rolling in its sockets, its lips opening and closing frenziedly, though all that emerged was glutinous green froth.

Screeching like an animal, the countess veered to the left, thrusting again through the thorny scrub. She ran headlong into a sturdy trunk, but rebounded from it, scarcely feeling the blow that she took across her chest. New alleys opened, but figures of lunacy were advancing along them. From all sides, she heard a grunting and mewling, a tearing and thrashing of twigs. But now she heard something else: water again, babbling over broken stones.

The stream. And now much closer than before.

Her heart thudding in her chest, she broke from the cover of the hawthorn wood, and found herself on a rocky, sloping bank. The stream lay directly in front of her, patinas of moonlight playing on it in liquid patterns. As she'd feared, it was deeper and broader than usual. She glanced to her left. Maybe a hundred yards away, the arched outline of the stone footbridge was visible. But even as she peered that way, crooked figures emerged from the trees to block her path. A hand alighted on her shoulder. A brief glance revealed the skin loose on it like a rotted glove, with bare bone fingertips pointing out at the ends.

The countess hurled herself forward, splashing into the water to her knees, her thighs, her waist. Even its icy chill couldn't shock her. Her booted feet slid on its slimy bottom and tripped over shifting stones, but she forged her way into the middle without looking back, her dresses billowing around her. The knowledge that she was now on foot, which would increase her journey-time ten-fold, and that she'd now be soaking wet on a raw, inclement night, meant nothing to her. All that mattered was to escape, to drive herself headlong from these nightmares made flesh that gibbered behind her.

The current in the middle of the stream tugged at her remorselessly, several times threatening to knock her under. She whimpered and wept as she fought it, at one point submerging almost to her shoulders. She prayed to the Virgin Mary for fear that God himself would no longer listen, beseeching the Holy Mother to have mercy on her and on her poor, mistreated people. When she reached the other bank, she had to crawl up it, exhausted, her hair hanging over her face in a stringy mat. And yet she knew those things would be close behind her – even now she could hear them splashing their way across, so she had to get to her feet and she had to continue running, though which direction to take from here she could no longer think.

"Alas, not everyone has the belly for war," Gwyddon observed dryly.

Countess Madalyn looked up sharply.

He was just to the left of her, perched on his saddle, a tall, hooded form silhouetted on the star-speckled night. More of his brethren were mounted up alongside him. Several others, also on horseback, approached from behind her. Behind them came the ragged shapes of the dead.

"Think you so?" Countess Madalyn said scornfully, panting as she climbed to her feet. "And yet here *you* are, far from the fury of battle."

"Battles in which men must suffer are a thing of the past, countess. At least... where *my* army is concerned."

"*Your* army, I see." She gave a wry smile. "But then your army can be anything you wish, can it not? Welsh, English... whoever will offer you the power you crave."

"So you're a student of politics after all, madam?" She couldn't see Gwyddon's expression in the darkness, but there was an irreverent sneer in his voice. "A pity you lack the vision to make it your advantage."

"And how long will that advantage last, Gwyddon? When my life finally ends, which will be soon enough in the eyes of Heaven, what advantage will I have when I stand before my maker? Surely you can't imagine that even if your gods control the universe, they would stand for this aberration you've created?"

He sighed. "Still you fail to understand. Whichever god rules this universe, madam – and I applaud your new open-mindedness, even if I'm not surprised by it – the Cauldron of Regeneration was his, or her, gift to us."

Gwyddon brought his horse forward a few paces, so that his face came into the moonlight. His eyes looked up as he pulled thoughtfully at his beard. When he spoke again, it was in a tone of veneration.

"I told you once before that the Cauldron was not forged by ogres at the foot of a bottomless lake. That was just a fable. In truth, its origin came when it fell to Earth from the stars, a glowing lump of unknown metal. Fashioned into its present form for functional purposes, its latent powers were only discovered by accident. Does that amount to sorcery, when it came to us from Nature?"

Countess Madalyn gazed at him, confused.

He smiled as he continued.

"Is the authority with which I control my minions the result of devilish magic, or merely a side effect of the wondrous object's proximity to my person? Like so many heads of my order before me – going all the way back to Myrlyn himself – I have grown up alongside the Cauldron. I have studied it, possessed it, absorbed its essence, made myself one with it... until now my mere thoughts will manipulate my monsters. Ahhh, I see you are shocked. Yes countess, it's true. Those pagan words, the very mention of which has good Christians like yourself cringing in fear... they are mere stage-dressing."

"You have deceived my people!" she hissed.

"When the English are finished, Countess Madalyn, your people will barely exist."

"Then you have deceived yourself."

He shrugged. "By denying to myself a truth that none of us can be certain of? Hardly. In any case, in the same way that you lack the belly for battle, I lack the knowledge for alchemy. It's a fact of life, but it doesn't concern me overly. The outcome will still be the same."

"And what will that be, Gwyddon – Armageddon?"

"Possibly, though obviously that wouldn't be ideal." He signalled to his priests, two of whom dismounted and approached her. "I still seek moderating influences in my life, if you're interested."

"I would rather die," she said.

"My dear countess... haven't you noticed? Nobody dies any more."

# CHAPTER TWENTY-NINE

LIQUID FLAME FLOODED over the parapets of the Constable's Tower. Flights of arrows continued to rattle across its battlements. The dead came too, droves of them pouring up the scaling ladders.

It was a hell-storm, the like of which Earl Corotocus's most hardened warriors had never experienced.

They engaged their enemy on two sides of the tower, slashing with sword and axe as one torn and mutilated form after another came up between the crenels, struck constantly on visor, shield or buckler, occasionally pierced through the hauberk by feathered shafts, and all the time dancing between pools of fire. English numbers had now been thinned disastrously, so that huge, undefended gaps were created. The dead would find these and then they'd be onto the roof properly, causing wild melees that would spill to every corner.

"Ranulf!" Gurt Louvain shouted. The face beneath his helmet was red and streaming in the searing heat; five arrows were embedded in his shield, a fifth looked as though it had transfixed his left arm, though in truth it had only punctured his mail sleeve. "Ranulf, this is madness! We can't hold them!"

Ranulf had just felled another corpse with such force that it had plummeted to the foot of its ladder, taking a dozen more with it. He peered down the sheer, flame-blackened bricks. In normal times, he'd expect to see a mountain of broken, mangled bodies at the bottom. Now all he saw was a compressed mass of shrieking, moaning heads and fists clamped on weapons. It was a similar tale at the far end of the causeway, though he could see that alleys were being cleared as more siege machines were brought forward: an even larger battering ram, equipped with wheels and a head of spiked steel, and two heavy onagers.

"Mind your heads!" someone shrieked.

Another fire-pot exploded in the middle of the roof. Sheets of flame erupted on all sides. Men were enveloped head to foot and ran blazing and screaming between their comrades, buffeting some aside, igniting others, in many cases falling clean through the battlements to a quicker, easier death.

"Gurt, there's nowhere to run to," Ranulf replied, his voice hoarse from shouting, his throat sore with smoke and thirst.

Another scaling ladder appeared in front of him. A corpse was already at the top of it. It was naked, but an iron collar was fixed around its neck and iron manacles around its wrists, revealing that the first time it had died it had been hanged in chains. It carried one such chain now, with which it lashed madly at the two English knights. Ranulf caught the chain and, with a downward stroke, clove the chain-arm at the shoulder. The monster now had only one hand with which to grip the ladder, and Ranulf's second stroke severed that too. When the corpse fell, it again took those beneath it.

Ranulf grabbed the top of the ladder and pushed it. As he did, another wave of arrows scythed across the battlements. One skimmed over his shoulder. Five yards to his left, a mercenary tottered away, spitting blood and phlegm from where a shaft had punched through his cheek. Ten yards beyond him, a tenant knight died wordlessly, struck in the throat.

"There aren't enough of us left to cover this perimeter!" Gurt bellowed. "And even if Earl Corotocus hasn't realised that, the dead will – they'll flow over us like the sea."

Below, more sets of hastily constructed scaling ladders were being passed hand-over-hand along the causeway. In a matter of minutes, the onagers would be within range. Close to Ranulf's right, more of the dead had gained a foothold. They climbed in through the embrasures and fought like dogs with the two or three defenders who opposed them; axes beat on shields, maces hammered helmets, crushing them out of shape.

Sensing that Ranulf was no longer listening, Gurt grabbed him by the collar and yanked him to attention.

"Ranulf, for the love of God listen! You must speak to the earl. Tell him we have to retreat to the Keep!"

Ranulf nodded and turned, only to be confronted by another pack of snarling dead, working their way along the battlements from the west, hacking down all in their path. Tomas d'Altard scrambled away from them, unable to stand because an arrow was buried in the back of his thigh.

"Ranulf, Gurt... save me!" he wept, only for the curved spike of a pollaxe to be swung down and driven through the nape of his neck with such force that its point appeared in his gagging mouth.

"We retreat when we can!" Ranulf said, mopping the filth from his blade and advancing. "Until that time..."


FROM THIRTY YARDS away, Earl Corotocus watched wearily as Ranulf FitzOsbern and Gurt Louvain engaged the latest band of corpses to have mounted the battlements, their blades twirling. Similar fights were raging all over the rooftop, knights and corpses hacking at each other dementedly as they staggered through a wreckage of smashed shields and burning bodies. To make things worse, catapults on the causeway now joined the fray. Heavy hunks of stone and lead were lobbed over the north-facing wall, slamming onto and through the shields of those few exhausted men who still had the strength to raise them.

"My lord!" du Guesculin shrilled, staggering forward, his face stained black with soot, his shield bristling with snapped-off arrows. "It's only a matter of time before the mangonel crews resort to heavier payloads! The Constable's Tower is lost!"

The earl himself bled from innumerable cuts. His once resplendent tabard was scorched and smouldering at its edges.

"And if we retreat to the Keep, what then?" he roared. "It's our last redoubt."

"My lord, they will never be able to capture the Keep. Its walls are one hundred and fifty feet high. No ladders, ropes or throwing machines can assail those battlements."

"He's right, my lord," Navarre said, approaching. Instead of a sword, he now wielded a mattock, its knobbly head caked with brains and human hair. "All the dead in the world couldn't build a pyramid with their own flesh that would reach such a precipice."

"And how long can we hold out in there?" the earl asked. "Are there supplies enough for us all?"

Navarre and du Guesculin glanced at each other. Only half way through the previous day had the earl given orders that sacks of meal and salt-pork and kegs of well water should be taken from the storehouses in the courtyard and placed in the Keep cellars. Neither could answer this question, because the implication was simply too terrible, so Earl Corotocus answered for them.

"The garrison could not last a week on what we've so far managed to store in there, am I correct?"

Navarre wiped blood and spittle from his disfigured mouth. "You are correct my lord. Either way, the majority of the garrison is doomed."

Corotocus looked to du Guesculin. "How many of us remain in total?"

The banneret could only shake his head, sweat dripping from his disarrayed hair. "I can't perform a proper count here, my lord. Of the Welsh who served you – one or two, at most. Of Garbofasse's scum – thirty or so."

"Archers?" Corotocus asked.

"A mere handful."

"And of mine?"

"From the fiefs, less than half – forty. Less even than that from the household."

Corotocus considered. "Send the household men to the Keep," he eventually said. "No-one else."

Du Guesculin looked shocked. "No-one?"

"My household men are the most loyal."

"Your landed vassals are loyal too, my lord."

"My landed vassals have fat fees I can reclaim and re-issue at a profit."

Unaccustomed as he was to seeking approval from his underlings, the earl risked a glance at Navarre, who gave a curt nod. Even in the midst of this horror, with carcasses piled on all sides, du Guesculin was pale-faced as he turned away.

"And du Guesculin!" the earl said. The banneret looked back. "Be furtive, du Guesculin. On pain of your own death, do not cause a panic."


THOUGH THE ENGLISH managed to retake the Constable's Tower roof for a brief time, by knocking down every set of scaling ladders, more were soon being carried forward. In addition, there was the problem of the battering ram.

The great door at the front of the tower was not recessed. This was to give defenders overhead a clear line of attack. But the dead that came against it with their spike-headed ram withstood the hail of stones and spears, though more necks and shoulders were broken than any battering ram party had ever sustained in the history of warfare.

The great door was solid of course, reinforced with ribs of steel. But they pounded it with their unnatural strength and stamina, and at length the ram's steel tip began to tell, tearing holes which the dead could cram their hands into and rend at the timber like wolves at a carcass. Piece by piece, the door was pulled apart, which led to even more frantic efforts above. With nearly all pre-prepared missiles exhausted, coping stones were worked loose from the battlements and hurled down. They struck their targets many times, but to infinitesimal effect. The dead continued their frenzied and tireless assault, regardless of skulls crushed and limbs shattered. They rent and rent at the creaking, splintering edifice. Only when their fingers and hands were ripped away, their arms reduced to slivers of bone in shreds of pulverised flesh, were they hauled backward so that others could replace them. Gradually of course, as new ladders were raised and more and more of their number regained the parapets, this deluge of destruction slowed to a trickle and at last ceased altogether. And finally the door that King Edward's Savoyard architects had never imagined could be broken *was* broken, wrenched from what remained of its hinges and hurled from the causeway. The decayed legion then funnelled en masse into the passage beyond.

Arrows sleeted into them via the murder holes, more stones were dropped, naptha grenades were flung – none of it to any consequence. At the far end of the passage they met the portcullis, behind which the fire-raiser waited. Gouts of white-hot flame billowed through them. Again, they melted like candles or flared like figures hacked from coal. When they threw themselves onto the grille, which soon glowed red with the heat of a furnace, they fried, their liquefied flesh running down its bars in sizzling rivulets. Only when crossbows were passed forward, and bolts discharged through the portcullis itself, one by one picking off the crew operating the fire-raiser, were they able to proceed. With groans of elemental agony, the overheated metal was bent and twisted out of the way and access was made.

The dead streamed through, howling like the devil's Cwn Annwyn, the hounds which from time immemorial had haunted these drear Welsh moors. Only one man was left on the fire-raiser. He was an arbalester formerly of the royal contingent, though few of his companions remained in any part of the castle that he knew of, and even now he fancied some of those he'd lost might be coming against him – not that this was a prime concern. A crossbow bolt had already struck him in the chin, another in the shoulder. Though his blood splashed copiously on the flagstones, he was conscious enough to scream like a child as their skeletal paws grabbed hold of him. Shriek after shriek burst from his lips, his froth spattering their raddled, rotted faces as they carried him to the pot at the fire-raiser's mouth and immersed him head-first in the bubbling mixture that had cut through their ranks with its demonic breath.

Next, they flowed up towards the galleries serving the murder holes. Defenders met them on the stairs with swords and axes. Slashing blows were exchanged. Struggling figures pitched down the stairwell, locked together. But the dead steadily prevailed. When their weapons broke, they latched onto the English with claws and teeth, ripping mail from flesh, flesh from bone. Others of their host, meanwhile, bypassed the battle on the stairs and herded along the main passage to the inner courtyard. Another portcullis awaited them there. Arrows whistled through it from a handful of defenders on the other side, but, unhindered now by fire, the dead fell upon the great iron trellis and began to lift it with ease.

High overhead on the roof, the melee surged back and forth across a carpet of carnage. Blood ran in rivers. Corpse-fires still burned, spreading hellish, stinking smoke. More and more of the dead ascended from the ladders. Ranulf cut his way through half a dozen of them, only to be confronted by William d'Abbetot armed with a club-hammer. In truth, the aged engineer was so mutilated that he was only recognisable by his garb. His face had been smashed to pulp; his lower jaw hung from strands of sinew. Yet still he shrieked like a banshee as he rushed at Ranulf. Ranulf ducked the sweeping blow and ran d'Abbetot through from behind, but of course to no effect. Even with a severed nervous system, the engineer merely turned and sought to attack him again. Ranulf had to wrestle the club-hammer from him and batter him down with one massive blow after another, until he was nought but crumpled flesh and mangled bone.

At which point, a shocking cry went up.

"My lord!" someone cried. "My lord, Earl Corotocus – *the dead are in the courtyard!*"

Every man still living pivoted round where he stood and stared back across the roof.

"We're breached!" Gurt shouted, floundering towards Ranulf, blood streaming from a fresh gash across his forehead. "Ranulf, we're breached! We have to retreat!"

"Where's the earl?" Ranulf demanded.

Other survivors on the Constable's Tower were wondering the same. Over half the garrison had been here at the start of the battle; those who remained were clumped together at the south side, sheltering behind a wall of battered shields. But now there were only a couple of dozen of them, and even allowing for those killed or wounded, that was inexplicable. It was even more inexplicable that Earl Corotocus, Navarre and Hugh du Guesculin were absent, as were several other of the household knights and squires.

"Has the earl fled?" someone asked, by his screechy tone of voice scarcely able to believe it.

"Retreat to the Keep!" someone shouted hoarsely.

"Wait!" Ranulf retorted. "There must be a hundred wounded in the rooms and passages below."

Gurt shook his head. "Ranulf, if we could carry one each, that wouldn't be anything like enough."

Ranulf knew this to be true, but before he could argue further there were muffled but ghastly wails from beneath their feet.

They didn't know it, but the dead from the ground floor had now reached the levels where the wounded lay and were working their way among the helpless, bandaged bundles, pounding them with rocks, stabbing them over and over with every kind of blunted, broken blade.

Gurt grabbed Ranulf's arm. "Ranulf, we have to get away!"

"Mind your heads!" someone squealed.

Everyone craned his neck to look up, and beheld the first of three colossal blocks of stone spinning down through the night towards them.

"Gods!" Ranulf swore. "The mangonels!"

The impacts were shattering. Huge sections of the paved roof imploded, an avalanche of masonry, rubble and splintered timber cascading onto the heaps of wounded and the packs of snarling dead currently ravaging them, burying them all together.

"Now we go!" Ranulf nodded, coughing out lungfuls of foul dust. "Now we unquestionably go!"

# CHAPTER THIRTY

THE KEEP WAS Grogen Castle's most impressive and indomitable feature.

A great, square bastion, it stood in the northeast corner of the courtyard, where it towered over every other rampart and strongpoint. Though joined from the north and the east to the Inner Fort wall, it was girded on its west and south faces by a dry moat some ten yards across, about forty feet deep and filled with jumbled rocks. There were only three ways to actually enter the Keep. High up, there were two gantry drawbridges connecting with it, one from the North Hall, which, as the name suggested, was built against the Inner Fort wall on the north side of the courtyard, and one from the baronial State Rooms, a wattle and timber building raised against the Inner Fort wall on the east side of the courtyard. These two drawbridges, of course, could both be lifted at a moment's notice, presenting attackers from those directions with an impossible gap to cover and a terrifying ninety foot drop to the moat's rocky floor. The Keep's main entrance was the lower drawbridge. This larger platform crossed the moat on the Keep's west side, about thirty feet above the courtyard itself. Anyone seeking ingress by this route had first to ascend a freestanding stone stair, very steep, which terminated at a narrow lip, thus preventing any organised battering ram party from finding a level surface on which to wield their weapon against the drawbridge while it was raised.

As with all defensive sections at Grogen, the Keep's upper tiers were strongly battlemented and cut with arrow-slits and vents for burning oil. This gave it a broad range of attack all across the courtyard. An ordinary army infiltrating this most central ward of the castle would in effect be corralled between high structures and subjected to hail after hail of missiles from defenders perched on unreachable parapets.

But of course on this occasion it was no ordinary army, and the defenders would be few in number and wearied to the point of craziness. And down in the courtyard, craziness, in fact downright insanity, appeared to be the order of the day.

Wounded men who had already shrieked so long and hard that their throats were raw and bleeding, shrieked again as Navarre and two of the earl's men-at-arms picked them up one by one and carried them by the feet and armpits back across the Keep's main drawbridge, hurling them down the steps. In some cases these victims struck the treads first with their backs or hips, while in others they plunged into the courtyard head first, either way landing with bone-crushing force. The last one, who was probably the heaviest, the earl's men gave up on half way, and tossed him over the side into the dry moat.

"What in Christ's name do you think you are doing?" Zacharius howled, as he and Henri came staggering across the courtyard, having wrapped up their instruments and grabbed what few valuable medicines they could carry.

On seeing and hearing the masses of the dead gathering on the far side of the courtyard, the doctor had been forced to abandon his infirmary. The weeping and imploring of those wounded he'd had to leave behind was a torture that he knew he would never forget. And yet now he had arrived at the foot of the Keep, only to discover the discarded bodies of those paltry few that, over the previous hour, he and Henri had managed to place in the safety of its interior; they'd been flung back out again like sacks of meal. He launched himself up the steps, at the top of which Navarre stood waiting, hands on hips.

"I repeat!" Zacharius thundered. "What in the name of Christ do you think you are doing?"

Navarre regarded him coolly. "There's a place for you and your boy inside here, doctor. But not for a bunch of wretches who, while unfit to wield a sword, are doubtless fit to eat our victuals and drink our drink."

"Those men were my patients, you troll-faced dog!"

Navarre smiled; with his misaligned features it was a chilling sight. "I have my orders."

"We'll see about that!"

Zacharius tried to push past, but Navarre stopped him with a heavy, mail-clad arm. "Alas, there's no time left."

"There's time at least to have you punished, you murdering brigand!"

"It's a pity that I couldn't find you," Navarre said and, without warning, he grabbed Zacharius by the throat.

So tight was the grip that Zacharius could not even gag. He struggled wildly, but he was effete, a fop, and Navarre was the earl's champion. Helpless, the doctor found himself being frogmarched backward towards the edge of the drawbridge.

"Alas," Navarre said again. "I searched high and low for you, but time ran out."

Though he was now fighting for his life, there was no real way that Zacharius could resist this brutal foe. And he knew it. But even then he was unprepared to be pushed backward from the bridge and suspended in open space, his feet kicking ineffectually.

Navarre's smile became a deranged grin. "Still glad your barren spell will end before mine, doctor?"

And he opened his hands.

Zacharius's scream broke from his constricted throat as he plummeted towards the rocks far below – it lingered horribly, before ending abruptly with the resounding impact of meat striking a slab.

At the foot of the Keep steps, Henri stood aghast.

Navarre peered down at him, before shaking his head glumly. "And without your master, what use are *you*?"

He turned idly and strolled back across the drawbridge.

Henri was so stunned that all he could do was stand there rigidly, oblivious to the dirge of demented cries drawing closer and closer from behind. Even when, with a rumble of timber and clanking of chains, the bridge was slowly raised, the surgeon's assistant was too frozen with shock to move. Thankfully, the first blow that fell on him was the last thing he knew, the single stroke of a falchion cleaving his skull asunder.

\* \* \*

JUST BEFORE THEY vacated the Constable's Tower, Gurt and Ranulf looked down into the courtyard, but there was too much confusion there and around the foot of the Keep for them to focus on any particular detail. As such, neither of them saw the murder of Doctor Zacharius and his assistant. It was a mesmerising scene, all the same.

The dead were now emerging in droves from the inner gate, which was directly below them, and streaming all over the inner ward, swarming between its rickety structures, including the infirmary, tearing them down, setting fire to their straw-thatched roofs. The few remaining domestics – the servants, grooms and pages – who'd deserted from the defences and been hiding, were hauled wailing into the open alongside the wounded, where they were all set about savagely; being beaten, torn, and dragged across the gore-smeared cobblestones. A party of the dead had ascended the Keep steps, but now stood howling in helpless rage for the main drawbridge had been lifted and stood upright against the facing wall.

With the courtyard so occupied, the only way from the Constable's Tower to the Keep was along the top of the Inner Fort wall. Ranulf, Gurt and the sixteen men remaining dashed along it in single file, having to kick their way through yet more piles of ghastly Breton scarecrows, all the time aware that those dead who'd climbed to the Constable's Tower roof were close behind. At the same time they were struck with arrows from the curtain-wall, which accounted for a couple more of their number. The survivors finally scrambled through a nail-studded door into the upper level of the barrack house. It was lit by torches but rank with the smell of corrupted flesh – for the dead who had clambered through the arrow-slits here and slaughtered many of Davy Gou's small group of defenders were still present. They had now scattered the straw bedding and personal baggage of the earl's troops, searching for additional weapons – large numbers of which they had found.

The two bands were not evenly matched – there were many more of the dead. But of course additional dead were now closing from behind. So the English had no option.

"Butcher them!" Ranulf shouted, leading the charge. "It's the only way!"

# CHAPTER THIRTY-ONE

THE CHAPEL WAS almost completely dark when Father Benan's eyes flickered open. The tiny candle he'd placed on the altar step was little more than a blob of melted tallow. Slowly and painfully, he tried to rouse himself from the latest swoon that he'd fallen into.

It had taken all the strength he had left to crawl here from the Constable's Tower. In addition, he hadn't eaten or drunk even a sip of water in as long as he could remember. Little wonder he'd been in and out of a dead faint since his return here. The welts that covered his plump body were stiff and aching. The cassock he'd wrapped himself with had adhered in strips to his clotted blood, and wouldn't be removed easily. Slowly, he sat upright on the step. His breathing was low and ragged. He hung his head. Despite the chill, sweat dripped from his brow. By the sounds of it, the attack on the castle was still raging. Thunderous impacts and wild shrieks sounded faintly through the chapel's thick walls.

Benan struggled to think clearly. If nothing else, he knew that he had to get back to his feet. Zacharius would be working out there practically alone. The dying would need shrift. Regardless that he himself was maimed, regardless of this devil's brew that he was part of, the priest knew that he had a sacred duty here. But good Lord, it was icy cold and it was so dark. His sole candle lit only the immediate area around him – the stone step and a patch of rush-covered floor.

He used the bare stone table to lever his shuddering bulk upright. Mumbling incoherent prayers, he bent down, picked up the stub of candle and, as carefully as he could, applied its glowing wick to two of the other three candles that were in reach. The light this created was dim, flickering, and cast eerie shadows over the rows of pews and the narrow aisles between them.

Benan was still glad that he'd taken such a ferocious beating. Oh, he doubted God would be satisfied with a few strokes of the whip; Benan's role in the earl's many atrocities would incur a far greater penalty on Judgment Day, he was sure. But at least it was comforting that he was no longer part of the earl's inner sanctum; that in fact he had more in common with those countless, helpless wretches the earl had slain and brutalised in his quest for power.

Then Benan thought he heard something close by – a rattling sound, as if someone had opened the chapel's outer door. He gazed down the nave. The inner door was half hidden in shadow, but it stood open. The passage beyond it was in inky darkness. Benan waited, but nobody announced themselves.

Suddenly he felt a chill down his lacerated spine.

He clutched at the crucifix hanging at his throat – as he had done throughout his chastisement. It was still sticky with blood, but he barely noticed. He listened intently, but there was no further sound – only the distant, muffled roar of the fighting, which, now that he thought about it, seemed to be penetrating the chapel from all sides – including above. Hastily, he lit the last candle, though it added precious little light to the chamber. He turned again to face the door and felt into the pocket of his cassock. From it, he brought out a scapular dedicated to the Mother of Carmel, made of soft fabric and fastened to a cord. It bore images of the Blessed Virgin and the Holy Child.

Benan regarded the celestial duo. As always, their expressions were serene, untroubled, full of love. Yet for a desolate second they seemed remote. Benan felt a terrible pang of regret for his misdeeds. How he suddenly yearned for that heavenly couple to be with him now – in spirit if not in body, just to bolster his resolve.

He turned again to the empty chapel.

If it was empty.

Fleetingly, he imagined that somebody was down there in the farthest recess. Another chill crept up his spine. Determined to stay calm, he took the iron crucifix from his throat. That was when he noticed that a streak of reddish, fiery light had speared along the floor of the passage beyond the inner door. He'd been right after all – the outer door *had* been opened.

Benan backed up until the altar table prevented him going any further.

The flames from the candles were guttering and cast cavorting shapes on the walls. He mopped his brow and held the crucifix in front of him. It felt good in his hands; heavy, like a weapon. Slowly, wondering if he dared do what he now planned to – a proven sinner like him – he raised the crucifix aloft.

"Glorious prince of the heavenly army," he called in Latin. "Holy Michael, archangel, defend us in our fight against the rulers of darkness!"

He imagined phantoms in the empty pews, regarding him silently. His breath puffed in frozen clouds.

"Come to the aid of the people whom God created in His own image and likeness, and bought at great price from the tyranny of Satan. Holy Church venerates thee as her protector. To thee God handed the redeemed souls, to lead them into the joys of Heaven. Ask the God of Peace to destroy all diabolical powers, so that our foes may no longer control mankind or desecrate holy mother Church."

From the entry passage, Benan heard what sounded like the scraping of bone fingertips along the brickwork.

Fresh sweat broke on his brow. It was impossible for those things to enter here, he told himself. Not that they'd respect the sanctity of a chapel – he'd known enough so-called Christians whose lack of respect had led to them force entry to such sanctuaries, and there shed innocent blood and defile innocent flesh (Earl Corotocus, for one). But the only entrance to this holy place was from the courtyard. If the enemy had gained access here, Grogen Castle itself had fallen.

Benan's sweat-slick hair prickled; he clutched his crucifix all the harder. A stronghold like this could never fall – not so quickly. But still those scraping claws came closer. By the sounds of it, there were several pairs of them.

"Saint Michael!" Benan cried. "Carry our prayer before the face of Almighty God, so the Lord's mercies may descend upon us. Seize the dragon, the old serpent, who is none other than Satan, and cast him into the abyss. We beseech you!"

IN THE BARRACK house, the English went at it like madmen, hacking and rending their way into the phalanx of corpses.

Ranulf ripped one gangrenous apparition from its groin to its gullet and a mass of putrid entrails foamed out, the stench of which alone was almost sufficient to knock him unconscious. Gurt's opponent had once been a woman, now its dead skin was mottled blue in colour and bloated out of all proportion. He smote it again and again with his sword as it raked at his eyes, but still it remained upright. His last blow was a murderous downward thrust through the side of its neck, right into the midst of its torso. The thing simply ruptured, like a bladder filled with bile, spraying filth as it seemed to deflate, odious fluids bursting from every orifice.

Other men were not so successful. A mercenary serjeant called Orlac, a doughty fellow by any standards but denuded of his weapons, strove at the creatures with a broken-off table leg. He struck skull-shattering blows on all sides, but four of them eventually overwhelmed him and bore him to the floor, where snapping teeth tore the arteries from his wrists and the windpipe from his throat.

And now the dead from the rear were entering the fray. Two tenant knights turned to face them. But Ranulf roared at them not to act like loons.

"Go forward!" he thundered, clearing himself a path with sweeps of his sword. "Never mind what's behind us!"

Gurt and the others followed, buffeting their way through the narrow gap. And then they were running again, grunting for breath, their mail clinking, their heavy feet thumping on the floorboards. Somewhere ahead, a wide timber staircase swept up to the great hall. As they ascended, they passed numerous embrasures, which gave through to the fire-lit courtyard. Quick, fearful glances showed that it was now totally filled up with the dead, who howled in eerie unison as they tossed the mutilated remains of their victims between them.

When they reached the top of the stair, the doors to the Great Hall stood in front of them. They were partly open. Without hesitation, Ranulf barged through.

\*     \*     \*

"IN THE NAME of Jesus Christ, our Lord and God," Benan cried, throwing his voice to the vaulted ceiling. "We undertake in full confidence this battle against the enemy."

Darkness now filled the chapel like swamp water; things writhed and oozed in its murky depths. An appalling odour seeped through it. From all the surrounding chambers came a thunderous cacophony of destruction.

The priest's forehead ran with sweat. "Let... G-god arise," he stammered, his throat dry. "Let His enemies be scattered. Let those who hate Him flee before Him..."

Slowly, his words tailed off.

His fearful eyes had focussed on a spectral figure, which had just come in from the entry passage and now glided across the bottom end of the church. Benan could not believe what he was seeing. It was a bishop – dressed in Easter vestments: the glorious white and gold tabard glittering, the jewel-encrusted mitre worn at an irreverently jaunty angle. The figure was moving swiftly, but with humility, its hands crossed on its breast. Benan had to look again, his eyes straining in the dimness. The figure's feet hardly seemed to be moving. For a fantastical moment, the priest wondered if some radiant soul had risen to help him. Then he saw it stop by the baptismal font, bend down – and begin to drink.

In great, sickening slurps.

Tears of terror dripped down Benan's cheeks.

"Oh Lord... save us," he whispered.

THE GREAT HALL was a grim reminder of what Grogen Castle could have been in happier, more peaceful times.

In due course, if the land had settled and Earl Corotocus had come to feel at home in the stronghold, this vast banqueting chamber would have been transformed: a fire would roar in its immense open hearth, the floor would be strewn with fresh rushes, the tapestries and battle standards, now fouled and defaced by the Welsh, would be replaced. The mouldering food and broken crockery that strewed the table-tops after that rabble of Bretons had roistered here would be swept aside and a feast fit for a king laid out. A scent of roasted fowl and venison would fill the air. Wine and ale would flow. There'd be singing and celebration, a harmonious lilting of pipes and lutes.

But at present, lit dolefully by the first rays of dawn, the place was a desecrated shell filled with wreck and ruin – and with the dead.

Perhaps thirty corpses were present, having come in through the casements or ascended via the hall's second staircase. Against such odds, no sane man would have progressed even a single step, except that none of Ranulf's band had any choice. An even greater number of corpses were clamouring at their rear.

"Straight through them!" Ranulf bellowed.

But it was an impossible situation. The dead didn't just meet them with swords, axes and knives, but they flung javelins and spears from the minstrel's gallery. Three Englishmen went down before they'd even engaged the foe. Ranulf ducked one missile, leapt onto a banquet table and ran down its full length, vaulting the blows aimed at his legs, striking to the left and right with his sword. Gurt tried to take the same route, but was grappled with by a pack of them. With desperate efforts, he flung his attackers off, picked up a bench and, holding it horizontal, drove them backward. As they fell, he trampled over them, and the men coming up behind chopped at them. But those English at the rear were pressed together in the confusion until too cramped to move, and then hewn mercilessly from behind.

"Ranulf!" Gurt screamed.

Ranulf had reached the far end of the hall. Another passage lay ahead of him. The way, it seemed, was clear through to the baronial State Rooms. But he turned back. Gurt was still using the bench to protect himself, but it was being hacked to splinters. He tried to duck behind it, only for a blow from a mattock to tear the helmet clean from his head.

Ranulf went back into the fray. A corpse hove in from his left. It wore only a loincloth and its body was gashed and slashed all over. A blow from a war-hammer had smashed its rotted face. Its nose was crushed and shreds of black tongue hung through a mesh of mangled teeth. For a weapon it wielded a burnt log, which it had lifted from the hearth.

Ranulf fended off two blows and severed its weapon hand at the wrist. It responded by grabbing his throat with its other hand. He slammed his mail-clad knee into its groin, but to no effect. He beat its skull with the pommel of his sword. The skull broke open. Another foul fetor engulfed Ranulf, making him choke – the exposed brain was like a lump of mouldered cabbage. Still the thing tried to throttle him. Only when Gurt appeared, and, with a single blow, shore its arm at the elbow, was Ranulf released. A second blow took its legs from under it and it fell to the floor, a twitching, limbless half-man.

"You were supposed to be helping *me*!" Gurt shouted.

"Next time remind me not to bother!" Ranulf retorted, only to cry in pain as a set of broken teeth clamped on his left ankle.

"God's bread!" he roared, striking down five times at his persistent assailant, the fifth impact so heavy that his blade cut through meat and bones to the flagstones beneath, and promptly snapped in half.

"Jesus," Ranulf groaned.

The weapon that had seen him through countless battles was now less than a foot long and squared off where it should have been pointed.

"Never mind that," Gurt said. "We have to flee."

The rest of the Great Hall was like a butcher's yard. All the other English had fallen, though the dead still ravaged at their bodies, beating their heads with stones and logs, wrenching their limbs from their sockets, hacking them with every type of blade. Gurt and Ranulf might themselves have been overrun, had someone else not suddenly become the centre of the dead horde's attention.

Though Ranulf had barely noticed Morgaynt Carew during the later fighting, mainly because his broken hands and scattered wits had left him incapable of wielding weapons properly, the semi-demented captain of the Welsh malcontents had run with them from the Constable's Tower. But now, at last, his dead countrymen had their claws on him. Incredibly, Carew still lived despite having been impaled on a spear, which had been thrust into his body via his anus and up through his bowels and innards, until re-emerging from his gagging mouth. His eyes rolled from side to side as they raised him upright, planted him on the open hearth and began piling timber from the broken benches around him.

Even with every other atrocity Ranulf and Gurt had witnessed, this was an astonishing sight. And yet Ranulf was no longer surprised. It seemed to him that, as the battle had progressed, the dead had become more and more like the living – as if whatever demonic force possessed them had grown used to its new mantle. Their grunts and mewls had turned increasingly to screams of fury. They had been organised from the start, but whereas initially they'd lumbered like puppets, soon they'd become faster and more dexterous. Worse still, as this grisly spectacle proved, they were showing increasing levels of vindictiveness. No longer were they mindless vegetables acting on pure instinct. Now, as though sensing all together that in Morgaynt Carew they had a *real* enemy, they gathered around the hearth in a mob, howling in monstrous glee, waving their weapons on high as a firebrand was produced and flame touched the kindling.

Did this reflect the nature of the force controlling them, Ranulf wondered, or in the putrid sludge of their brains, did threads of the worst kind of human emotions still linger?

"Ranulf!" Gurt screamed into his ear. "Come on, while they're distracted!"

Ranulf nodded.

They turned and headed into the next passage. But the dead weren't distracted for long. Even as the two knights ran, a group of corpses broke off in pursuit. Those few that had been poorly armed before were well armed now, having taken possession of swords, flails and maces from their English victims. They twisted and staggered as they came, travelling on limbs that were smashed or pierced, or on stumps from which the feet had been shorn, but they showed frightful speed. Their torn faces, crusted with the mingled blood of their victims and their own clotted mucus, were contorted by the madness of the damned.

FATHER BENAN COULD feel their eyes on him as they advanced like shades through the darkened chapel. The storm in the other rooms had reached a terrifying crescendo, but he continued determinedly with the rite, his body drenched and shaking.

"Behold the cross of the Lord!" he cried, holding up the iron crucifix. "Flee, bands of enemies!"

Still they came, horrible manifestations of the night, the stench of carrion pouring off them in waves so thick the very air swam with it. One by one, they smashed the pews, ripping them up from the stone floor and casting them aside.

The priest held his ground on the altar.

"The Lion of Judah, the stem of David has triumphed!" he shouted, but his voice was lost in the tumult. "God the Father, in the name of Jesus Christ thine son, may thy mercy be upon us all." He had to duck as a something was flung at him. It missed his face by inches. But he had the fleeting fancy that it was somebody's torn off hand.

"We drive thee out, unclean spirits, whoever thou art!" His throat was raw with shouting. "Every devilish tribe, in the name of God and by the power of Our Lord Jesus, be thou uprooted and driven from those fashioned in the likeness of God and redeemed by the precious blood of the divine Lamb."

He made a hurried sign of the cross. But no scream of tortured souls greeted this powerful symbol, no reek of burning flesh. The thing in the bishop's vestments was at their forefront; now that it was close, its once ornate robes looked filthy and had been shredded as though by an eagle's talons. Benan tried to focus on this fiend in particular. Had it really once been a bishop of the Christian church? Had the dark magic that had invoked this army of the dead seeped down into some cathedral crypt, where sacred bones lay in tranquil repose? As it stepped up onto the altar, he moved forward to meet it, hoping to recognise its face and maybe reason with it. But all he saw, when they were almost nose-to-nose, were the startled features of Otto, the earl's portly cook. They had been torn from the Brabancon's head in one piece, and draped bloodily over this abomination's own desiccated visage.

Benan backed away, fighting to suppress a scream.

"Dare no more, malicious serpent, to persecute God's children! May the Almighty God command thee!"

He made another sign of the cross, but now they were filing up onto the altar from his right and his left. One of them, more bones and filth than actual flesh, had bobbed hair, wore a scarlet fustian gown and a fashionable beret with a rolled brim, indicating that high ranks of layity had also joined the unholy legion.

"May God the Father, God the Son and God the Holy Spirit dispose of thee, foul demons!"

With each incantation, he made signs of the cross, but still they advanced. He scrambled around the altar table and limped to a smaller table at the back. Here sat a leather satchel containing his most precious belongings. From inside it, he took a lidded chalice. As he opened it, he continued to pray.

"May Christ take thee in His hands!" He opened the chalice, thumbing out three blessed wafers, and turned back to the invaders. "He built the Church on firm foundations and promised the gates of the Underworld would never prevail against her."

He broke the wafers into fragments and scattered them around him in a semi-circle.

"Thou art commanded by the sign of the holy cross!" He thrust his crucifix at them. "And by the mysteries of the Christian faith. Thou art commanded by the sublime virgin mother of God, Mary, who from her conception has trodden on your crown."

Again, he made the sign of the cross and, momentarily, their advance seemed to falter – but only for fleeting seconds. If such a thing was possible, the expressions on their decayed faces seemed to have changed, from inhuman anger to something like curiosity.

"Thou art commanded by the apostles! Thou art commanded by the blood of the martyrs!"

One by one, they circled around the altar table.

For the first time in his life, despite all that he'd turned a blind eye to in the service of Earl Corotocus, Benan felt his faith begin to ebb. Never had he imagined he would face an enemy like this, though perhaps, in private, he might have said that he could manage it – that with the fist of the Almighty clenched above him he could stand off the hounds of hell. But still they approached.

"We exorcise thee, cursed dragon!" He lifted the cross as high as he could. "And all these, thine apostate followers! By the living God, by the true God, by the holy God!"

Their hands clawed as they reached for him.

"Flee, Satan!" he screamed. "Thou inventor and master of every deception, thou enemy of Mankind!"

As one, they halted.

Benan gazed, blinking, from one to the other. Though they crowded around him, only affording a few feet of safety, an absurd hope suddenly rose in his breast.

Had the ancient rite succeeded? It would have amazed him if it had. Though Benan had scorned Earl Corotocus for his excesses, he'd feared from the outset that his long record of collaboration with the nobleman had damaged him in the eyes of Heaven. He had simply *known* that God would not send his angels down to assist. That Christ would *not* appear by his side, armed with a flaming sword.

And yet the devils' advance had apparently ceased.

Benan glanced down. The fragments of sacred wafer lay in a distinct line between him and them – like a barrier. Not one of them had set foot across it. His heart rate increased; he felt the beginnings of hope.

"We command thee! We command thee..." Benan's voice rose triumphantly, only for his words to tail off again.

For with slow, malicious pleasure, the thing in the Episcopal vestments shook its head from side to side and with a single, deliberate step, crossed over the holy fragments. The others copied it and, raising their claws, took hold of the shrieking priest from all sides.

Benan dropped to his knees. His eyes were screwed shut as multiple dead fingers groped through his hair and over his tear-sodden face. His heart throbbed in his chest, but, with a core of steel that even he didn't know he possessed, he proceeded with the exorcism.

"Make way for Christ, in whom thou couldst find none of thy works! Bow beneath the mighty hand of God..."

He dared to look up at them again. It seemed that every demonic face in creation was peering down at him. Crushed, pulped, rotted, scabrous masks of what they'd once been, and now possessed by some force of evil no man could understand, exuding it like a fog of death.

"Tremble and flee at the invocation of the holy name of Jesus, before which all Hell will shake. At the name of Jesus, to which all powers on Earth and in Heaven are subject, which the cherubim and seraphim unceasingly praise, saying 'holy, holy, holy is the Lord God of Hosts.'"

Fascinated, they ran their hands over his plump, naked flesh. They found his many welts.

"Our help is in the name of the Lord," Benan croaked. "The name of the Lord! God of Heaven, God of Earth, God of angels, God of apostles and martyrs..."

His voice rose to a castrato screech as, one by one, they dug their bony claws into his wounds.

"...who has the power to give life after death because there is no other god than Thee."

And then they ripped, tearing the wounded tissue from his body like fabric from a seamstress's dummy. His keening howl might have shattered the eardrums of anyone human.

"For thou… thou art the creator of all things visible and invisible," he sobbed. "To whose reign there shall be no end. We humbly prostrate ourselves before Thy glorious majesty… deliver us…"

He screeched again as more meat was rent from his bones.

"… deliver us from the infernal host…"

He batted at them with the iron crucifix, until the bishop-thing snatched it from his grasp.

"Hear us, Father. Hear us…"

But his words ended and all that came from his mouth were scarlet bubbles. The white-hot fire that engulfed him was fading, but he had no strength to stand, and they had to hoist him to his feet. His vision was darkening. The end was coming, he knew. Though it hadn't quite come yet, and he was still compos mentis enough to feel wonder that the bishop-thing was now offering the crucifix to his lips.

How strange, Benan reflected, that after everything they'd subjected him to, they were giving him a chance to make good his martyrdom. He leaned forward to kiss the holy symbol, as so many saints had done in the past while bound to racks or nailed to crosses – but the object was withdrawn before he could make contact.

To his pain-fuddled bewilderment, it was lifted up above his eye-line, where he lost track of it altogether, until he felt its cold iron base placed on top of his cranium, in the very middle of his tonsure. Other dead hands now clamped Benan's head to keep it steady. His confusion lingered a little longer, but a whimper of understanding broke from his blood-slathered lips as the bishop-thing began to press the crucifix downward with crushing force, driving it inch by agonising inch through his skin, his bone, and finally into his brain.

The last thing that Father Benan realised, before his world winked out of existence, was that, if nothing else, when he too walked with the dead, the sign of his faith would be planted in the top of his skull.

# CHAPTER THIRTY-TWO

LIKE THE GREAT Hall, the State Rooms, which would normally form private apartments for the castellan of Grogen Castle and his family, had been ransacked; their exquisite furnishings were smashed or stolen, their tapestries and wall-hangings torn down. Welsh profanities had been written in excrement on the whitewashed walls.

The casements here, while not exactly arrow-slits, were still tall and narrow, set in deep embrasures, and had been covered with sheets of tinted horn, though many of these had been shattered, for grapples had been shot through them.

"Which way?" Gurt said, as he and Ranulf entered the first room, breathless.

Ranulf knew that these State Rooms were located in the southeast corner of the inner court and, indeed, casements looking down into the bailey stood in front of them as well as to the right. This meant that, to reach the Keep, they had to head through the arched portal on their left. Before they did, they closed and bolted the door behind them, but almost immediately there were smashing impacts on the other side. Gleaming axe-heads appeared through the shuddering wood.

"That way," Ranulf said, pushing Gurt towards the arch.

"What are you doing?"

"I'll try to slow them down."

Gurt nodded and hurried out of sight. Ranulf turned back to the door, against which a storm of axes and hammers was now raging. Amid the shattered furniture, he found a wrought iron candelabra, the central stem of which was a tall, spear-thick shaft tapered at its tip to a needle-point. He rammed it against the door, wedging its base under the central transverse plank and planting its tip between two floorboards. This braced the door well, though more axe-heads burst into view. Now they were being twisted, worked from side to side in the gaps they had made, cracking the wood, forcing the planks apart. Ranulf backed away. The inside of his mail was awash with sweat. He suddenly felt intolerably tired; every cut, bruise and sprain ached. He turned to follow Gurt – only for something to catch hold of his bitten ankle. Glancing down, he saw an arm extended from beneath an overturned divan.

Another of the dead things now dragged itself into view – or rather, it dragged its upper half into view. It had been severed at the waist, and not by a clean blow either. A jumble of ropy innards slithered behind it, drawing a slug-like trail of crimson slime. Ranulf tried to yank his foot free, but the thing had a firm grip and now sank fingernails encrusted with grave-dirt into the injured joint. Ranulf yelped. Instinctively, he drew his sword and prepared to slash through the offending limb, only to remember that his sword was now a third of its normal length. He cursed.

The monster reached with its left hand and took hold of his sword-belt, by which it hoisted itself to waist height. It was climbing up his body, bringing its face ever closer to Ranulf's – though so caked with mud and blood was that face that only its gaping maw was visible; a maw in which the tongue was alive with maggots, in which only brown shards remained of its teeth.

Ranulf stabbed frantically down at it.

The squared-off sword was still sharp enough to rip repeatedly through flesh and bone, to plough what remained of that countenance to vile jelly. With its left hand, the monster tried to grab his sword arm, but this weakened its purchase on his belt, and he was able to fling it to the floor. Before it could right itself and come after him again – he had a crazy mental image of it running crab-like, balanced solely on its hands – he snatched the candelabra, and thrust it down into the horror's chest, driving the point through its heart, and, with a grinding squeal of wood, transfixing it to the floorboards, where it commenced to thrash and bellow like a maddened bull.

No longer braced, the door shuddered and split even more violently, but the bolt seemed to be holding – at least for the moment.

"*Ranuuulf!*" Gurt's distant voice halloed from beyond the archway. "Where in God's name are you?"

"I'm coming!" Ranulf replied, tottering after him.

He entered a lengthy gallery, which, half way along, turned from stone to timber and thatch and opened on its left hand side, where it overlooked the courtyard. At its far end, he could see the gantry drawbridge connecting with the portal in the Keep's south-facing wall. A figure had just emerged from that portal, walking backward onto the drawbridge. Its grimy green livery revealed it to be Gurt. He was arguing with someone.

"Just wait!" Gurt shouted. "Damn your eyes!"

Ranulf was perhaps twenty yards away when he realised what was happening. The drawbridge, which of course spanned a ninety-foot drop into the Keep's dry moat, was rising slightly. It seemed that somebody inside the Keep was determined to close it. Gurt had clearly argued for it be kept open for Ranulf, but had now had been forced to add his weight to the bridge.

"You damn slave!" Gurt shouted in through the Keep entrance. "Less than a minute is all I ask!" The drawbridge had risen half a foot. Gurt, struggling to maintain his balance, drew his sword and pointed it into the darkness. "I swear, I'll take this out of your hide!"

"I'm coming!" Ranulf cried hoarsely.

Gurt glanced along the gallery and his bloodied face split into a relieved grin.

"He's coming now," he said loudly.

Ranulf reasoned that one of the earl's men-at-arms would be inside there, working the drawbridge wheel. But the fellow who now stepped from the darkness behind Gurt, unnoticed by him, was no man-at-arms – it was Navarre. And he had drawn his trusty dagger. Without a word, he raised it over his head and drove it down hard, ramming it between Gurt's shoulder blades.

Ranulf slid to a stunned and breathless halt.

Gurt had gone rigid; his expression of relief had rapidly transformed to one of bemusement. He half-smiled and tried to speak – though no words came out. With a weak gesture towards Ranulf, he tottered slightly, his knees buckling. But it took a shove from Navarre to help him on his way, pitching him head first into the gulf.

*"Guuurt!"* Ranulf screamed, as his friend dropped from view.

Navarre glanced uninterestedly across the drawbridge towards Ranulf, before turning and walking casually back into the darkness of the Keep.

"Raise the bridge," he told someone.

Five seconds later, Ranulf arrived at the end of the timber gallery, but the bridge had already been drawn up out of his reach, marooning him there. With a heavy *clunk*, it came to rest against the facing wall – a good ten yards away.

Ranulf teetered on the terrifying brink. Far below, the tiny shape of Gurt lay still in the foot of the dry moat. Even from this distance, a crimson stain could be seen creeping out around his splayed green cloak. Ranulf might have gone cold at the thought that this shattered fragment was all that remained of the closest comrade he'd had during the fight for Grogen Castle. He might have gone colder still at the thought that, with all the other indebted knights slaughtered – in fact with all of those not bound in Earl Corotocus's personal *mesnie* dead, including his father – he didn't have a friend left in the world. But he was already cold, deeply cold. Not just clammy with sweat, but chilled to the marrow by the nightmares he'd witnessed and partaken in.

He was so numbed that it was tempting to simply remain here and await the inevitable. There was nowhere else to go anyway. Every ten yards along this timber gallery, a stout post connected with its roof, so it would not be difficult to climb up there. But the roof was of thatched straw, which could easily be penetrated by spears or eaten by flames, and beyond that there was nothing. The only solution it seemed was to kneel and offer contrition for his sins, praying that the end might come quickly.

But Ranulf did none of these things.

Instead, he turned and walked back along the gallery towards the State Rooms. He now understood what had motivated his father during his final years: that the antidote to a wasted life could only be a worthwhile death; that the price of living without honour could only be to die covered with it.

Yet Ranulf did not intend to die.

Not yet.

As he'd fought through the barrack house and the Great Hall, it had occurred to him several times that his demise was nigh and that perhaps he should welcome it as a just desert rather than fear it. But now he consciously and determinedly sought to avoid it – because there was something very important that he had to do first.

He entered the room where the legless monstrosity was pinned to the floor. It remained fixed down, but on seeing him became wildly animated, struggling, grunting, tearing handfuls of flesh from its own torso as it sort to dig the implement out. Meanwhile, the door connecting with the Great Hall had almost been battered through. One hinge had come loose, and great chunks of woodwork were missing. The parchment-faced figures beyond gave shrieks of glee when they saw that Ranulf had returned.

Ranulf ignored them. He righted the fallen divan – a luxurious piece of Italian furniture, with a carved wooden base and thick fleece for upholstery – and shoved it across the floor until it was beneath the first casement through which a grapple and a rope protruded. Climbing up, he was able to reach the grapple and pull it down. It would be typical of his luck, he thought, if another dead Welshman was on the end of it and now came through the aperture screaming and raving. But that did not happen. The rope was limp and he was able to reel in forty or fifty yards of it, before drawing his broken sword and chopping it through.

He coiled it over his arm as he headed back to the Keep gallery, though now, with a deafening crash, the door behind him fell and the dead surged through. Ranulf broke into a run, shedding his mail piece by piece as he did – first his coif, then his hauberk, then his leggings. Each time it was difficult, the straps and buckles caked with blood, vomit, excrement; all the glutinous residue of death. He was half way along the gallery, into the timbered section, when he cast off the last piece. His felt and woollen under-garb was so sodden with sweat and urine – he'd lost count of the number of times he'd voided his bladder during the last two days, having had no time to find a quiet corner – that it clung to him like a second skin, but at least it was light, enabling him to run much faster. However, undressing en route had slowed him down, and a quick glance over his shoulder showed that his enemies were as close as ten yards behind, their dirge of shrieks and moans deadening his ears. Knowing that he had one chance only, he unloaded the rope, took hold of the grapple – three iron hooks welded together – and flung it up towards the top of the gantry drawbridge, which was about a foot lower than the lintel of the portal beyond it.

The grapple caught and held.

Ranulf didn't bother looking round. The dead were right at his back – their stench engulfed him, their claws were reaching for him. With no time to rig a harness, he wound the rope around his hands and threw himself into open space. Their howls of rage turned to groans of despair as he swung down across the gulf.

The Keep wall rushed towards him. He'd intended to extend his legs and flatten his feet, to brace himself for impact, but the rope spiralled and he struck the sheer bricks with heavy force, his left hip and the left side of his ribs taking the full brunt.

Seconds passed as he hung there between Heaven and Earth, his vision blurred with tears and sweat, his wrists burning as they supported the entire weight of his body. Finally he was able to focus again; he peered upward. The flat cliff-face of the wall rose inexorably to a sky now tinged pink by dawn sunlight. The rope from which he hung was a taut sinew, which creaked and twisted. He glanced towards the lip of the gallery. The dead clustered there, watching him, even though some of them lacked eyes and some even lacked faces. So great was their press, that one or two fell, hurtling down. Several, he saw, had axes, spears and knives – all potential missiles. How long before they, or whatever controlled them, realised they could still reach him? How long before his strength gave out regardless?

Young as he was, Ranulf's military experience was already sufficient to guide him through extreme pain and exhaustion. The usual trick was simply to pretend that it wasn't happening, to imagine that your agony was just like any other sensation, something minor and tolerable, until you actually fooled your own brain. This always took an immense feat of concentration, though it was easier to do it when you were lying on a battlefield nursing a wound than when you were hanging by weakening arms over a ninety-foot chasm.

Grunting with effort, he turned himself around and planted his feet against the wall. With his mail leggings gone, he only wore light felt shoes. Their soles lacked grip, but he had no choice. The climb that faced him was thirty feet at least and he couldn't manage that by the strength of his arms alone. His injured ankle felt as if hot coals were being crushed into it as he began the long upward walk, step by unsteady step. His shoulders seemed as though they were being wrenched from his torso, as he pulled himself along the rope. The palms of his hands were scored, blistered, already slippery with blood.

He wasn't long on the bricks. Soon his feet were on the timbers of the drawbridge, but that was no consolation. On this smoother surface, he began to slide and lose his purchase. Wind whistled around the side of the Keep, tugging at him, freezing his sweat. But he pushed on, refusing to think of the perilous drop at his back. He wasn't sure how far he had to go when the first axe buried itself in the wood alongside him. This gave him renewed impetus. A spear stuck to the left, and he climbed all the harder. Now he was focussed on the grapple at the top of the rope, which was suddenly in sight. But the last ten feet were the worst. More missiles were flung, only missing him narrowly. His pain had become torturous – not just in his wracked limbs, but in his chest, where his heart thundered until fit to break, where his lungs wheezed as they dragged in so much air that he thought they would burst.

Ranulf knew he couldn't have gone much further when he finally clawed his fingers over the bridge's upper rim. His back muscles tightened like bowstrings as he hoisted his body up that last foot or so. Sweat poured into his eyes; his limbs were numbed by the strain, which didn't diminish even when he made it onto the top. For a moment he lay lengthwise, gazing back across the gulf. The dead were still watching from the timber gallery. Another of them threw something – a maul, which spun right at him, and might have shattered his skull had it not impacted on the brickwork above his head.

Slowly, shaking as though with fever, feeling hollow and bloodless throughout his body, Ranulf slid beneath the lintel and lowered himself into the Keep by his hands. He hung there briefly – it was still a significant distance to drop, ten feet or more - but finally he let go. He landed on the paved floor with foot-stinging force, dropping to his haunches and rolling.

When he sat up, still gasping for breath, he was in a stone passage lit by torches, which led to a stairway at its far end. There was a recess just to his left, which, as he'd suspected, contained a wheel-

and-pulley system. The crank-handle had now been removed and a steel peg knocked into place, to lock the mechanism. Another room adjoined this, possibly a guardroom.

As Ranulf got to his feet, a figure in a studded leather jerkin emerged, carrying in one hand a scabbarded sword and in the other a large mallet. The figure, Haco, a surly, black-bearded type who served as one of the earl's men-at-arms, stopped dead when he saw Ranulf. He was so surprised that his mouth dropped open.

"Closing our doors a little prematurely, weren't we?" Ranulf said.

Haco threw the sword down, and took a wild swipe with his mallet. Ranulf ducked it, and looped an arm around Haco's neck, quickly walking him backward. Haco gargled for breath, lost his footing and fell. As he did, Ranulf slammed the back of his skull against the paving stones as hard as he could. Haco was left dazed, allowing Ranulf to snatch the mallet from his twitching hand, and apply two swift and fatal blows to his forehead.

Stripping the jerkin from the body, Ranulf donned it himself, cast the mallet aside and picked up the sword. It was a broadsword, heavier than Ranulf's longsword if several inches shorter. It was a less sophisticated weapon, but it would be easy enough to wield. Instead of a sword-belt, its scabbard was attached to a harness, and designed to be carried on the back. Ranulf fastened it into place, adjusted it slightly so that its cross-hilt was in reach over his left shoulder, and moved along the corridor into the depths of the Keep.

He was still fatigued beyond belief, still riddled with pain. But the new task he had set himself would not wait.

# CHAPTER THIRTY-THREE

"NAVARRE!" RANULF SHOUTED, reaching the bottom of the penultimate stairway.

He was almost at the top of the Keep. He'd seen no major evidence of occupation on any of the levels he'd ascended through, which indicated how few men the earl had left. Since Haco, he'd encountered nobody at all – until now. Navarre, who was part way up the stair, turned in surprise. But that surprise didn't last. He grinned and descended again, loosening his sword in its sheath. He had removed his hauberk, but had retained his mail leggings, which were fastened over his homespun shirt with leather straps, so he was nearly as ill-attired for combat as Ranulf.

"FitzOsbern," Navarre said, sounding pleased. "I was hoping you'd get through."

"Damn shame *you* have, when so many decent men haven't."

"They all fell in a good cause."

"They fell because you and our dog of an overlord led them to certain death. And in Gurt Louvain's case, because you murdered him."

Navarre pulled on his gauntlets. "Ah yes, Louvain. Well, I'm afraid he was being awkward."

Ranulf drew the sword from the scabbard on his back. "Then allow me to be the same."

Navarre grinned again. With his bisected face and mangled mouth, it was a picture of demonic evil.

"I'm so glad you said that, FitzOsbern." With a rasp of metal, he too drew his sword, swishing it back and forth in front of him. "Our overlord forbade this once, seeing some possible advantage in keeping you alive. But the time is past for uncertainties of that sort. Doubtless, he also wanted Doctor Zacharius to live, but, when the moment of truth came... well, these free-thinkers are an expensive luxury, are they not?"

"Zacharius? You killed... ?"

"Again, all in a good cause."

Stupefaction seeped through Ranulf like a slow poison. He could barely comprehend what he'd just heard.

"You cretinous oaf!" he roared. "Do you realise what you've done?"

"I know what I'm about to do. I'm about to rid Earl Corotocus of his last dedicated enemy. Compared to you and your nest of traitors, FitzOsbern, those creatures out there will be child's play."

"Navarre, even Corotocus doesn't deserve a madman like you!"

Navarre laughed. "Enough talking, FitzOsbern. On guard!"

They circled each other like cats, each man watching the other intently. It did not go unnoticed by Navarre that Ranulf was breathing heavily from his exertions below, and that he carried himself stiffly. This of course offered an advantage that a champion of Navarre's experience could not resist exploiting.

With a wild laugh, he struck first, jabbing his sword-point at Ranulf's face, though this was a feint. Typically sly, he'd also produced his dagger in his left hand, and this he now thrust at Ranulf's midriff. However, Ranulf saw this, and smashed the sword aside, before striking the dagger from Navarre's hand with a blow so fierce that it sent the weapon spinning into the shadows. Navarre snatched his hand back, scowling. Even tired, it seemed that FitzOsbern's main strengths, namely his supreme hand-eye co-ordination and the blistering speed of his ripostes, had not deserted him.

Navarre, who relied more on sheer power, stepped backward,

but only to regain his balance in order to strike again, this time with a two-handed stroke from overhead. Ranulf fended it off with a mighty *clang*, but the impact dealt his shoulders a jolt that he felt all the way down his body. He realised that his limited energy was flagging already. If he were to survive this contest, he would have to end it quickly.

"You were never going to last through these border wars, FitzOsbern," Navarre scoffed. He struck again, but again Ranulf parried him. "A man with a conscience is a man who is fundamentally weak."

"And *you'll* last?" Ranulf grunted through gritted teeth, striking back swiftly. "You think there's any way out of this spider-hole your master has led you into?"

Navarre didn't immediately reply. Again, the speed of Ranulf's counter-blows had taken him by surprise. His teeth too were now gritted, his facial groove so red and enflamed that it looked set to crack open.

"Loyalty to one's lord is all," he snarled. "Betrayal of that creed merits ignominious death!"

Their blades clashed furiously as the fight spilled along the passage, sweat spraying from their brows, sparks flashing in the dimness. But Ranulf's growing exhaustion was giving his opponent the upper hand. Blow after heavy blow rained down on him. It was all he could do to fend them off, never mind retaliate. At last he was backed against a row of iron bars. Sensing victory, Navarre stepped forward with a demented grimace, and lunged hard at Ranulf's chest – only for Ranulf, with his last ounce of stamina, to step nimbly aside. Navarre's sword-arm passed through the bars and wedged there – just briefly, but long enough for Ranulf to turn and slash down hard, severing the limb at its shoulder.

Navarre didn't have time to scream.

The second stroke took his legs from under him, shearing them at the knees. The third was a downward thrust, delivered as he lay on his back, piercing him clean through the middle of his grotesque face, finally splitting it apart into the two separate hemispheres that for so long it had desired to be.

The sudden silence in that dark passage was ear pummelling. The echoing clangour of blade on blade dissipated quickly in the Keep's far reaches.

Ranulf sank to his knees, gasping, leaning on his upright sword. So tired was he that he thought he would pass out. Sweat dripped from his chin, blood trickled from his numerous cuts, all reopened through sheer effort. Many moments passed before he was able to shift away and fall onto his side. More time passed as he lay there, the painful beating in his chest subsiding with torturous slowness. At length, he looked up and took in his surroundings. From somewhere overhead, he could hear a booming and derisive voice. He knew this could only mean one thing.

Earl Corotocus had entered negotiations.

GAZING DOWN FROM the top of the Keep at Grogen Castle was like gazing from some colossal escarpment. From this dizzying height, the surrounding mountains were more like foothills. The broad flow of the river, sparkling so magnificently in the rising sun, resembled a garden stream. The rest of the castle's ramparts were so far below they looked like an artist's miniature.

But Earl Corotocus felt neither superior nor confident as he stood on this lofty perch. He didn't even feel as if he occupied a strong position. The entire rest of the fortress –its bailey, its walks, its battlements and towers – were crammed with cohorts of deranged, howling cadavers. They were packed so tightly in the courtyard that scarcely an inch of ground was visible. The same was true of the encircling landscape, at least to the north of the Tefeidiad. The western bluff was hidden beneath a tide of human flotsam. On the sweeping northern moor a host was gathered so immense that it seemed without limit. Even if it hadn't struck Corotocus before, it struck him now that an army of the dead was the largest army that could ever be assembled – for on the Anglo-welsh border, in Wales, and in much of England as well, there was no end to those unjustly slain or deprived to the point where death came too early. Even King Edward, with all the arms he could muster, would have difficulty hewing his way through so vast a multitude.

For this reason, if none other, the earl had now decided – somewhat belatedly, he supposed, though he would never admit it to his retainers – to parley. Ninety yards to his west, on what remained of the Constable's Tower roof, stood several recognisable figures: the statuesque form of Countess Madalyn, with her flowing red hair and imperious aura, and the hooded figures of her priestly acolytes. As these self-appointed leaders stared back at him, possibly realising the stalemate they had at last come to, their monstrous followers fell eerily silent.

"I repeat, Countess Madalyn," Earl Corotocus boomed. "Your forces will never enter this last bastion. They will dash themselves to pieces on its walls, or decompose until they are bones and slurry before the slightest breach is incurred."

Corotocus knew they'd understand this. Time was the one thing an army of the dead lacked. The earl's men, who had only been able to stock enough supplies for a couple of weeks at the most, would eventually die famished or parched. But the besiegers would rot. It seemed an even bet which would be the quicker process.

"You cannot storm us!" The earl's confidence grew as he continued to bellow down to them. "My mighty mangonels will make no impact on these impregnable walls, even if you could manoeuvre them into a suitable position. As you can see, the only possible ingress is via the west or south drawbridges. Maybe you think you can batter these down and create bridges of your own, as you did at the Gatehouse? But I defy you to try, countess. In both cases, the buildings closest to these bridges, the baronial State Rooms and the North Hall, are made from timber and wattle, and have thatched roofs. That was a deliberate ploy by the designers of this castle. I need only have flaming arrows shot down upon them and those structures will burn to ashes. Part of your army will be consumed. The rest will remain as they are now, helpless even to get close to us."

The earl looked around at his men. They were huddled behind him, maybe thirty in total. They were a craven looking bunch: wounded, filthy, red-eyed with fear and exhaustion. Knights were indistinguishable from men-at-arms. Even so, they regarded him with awe. They had come into this place knowing it was their last refuge, believing it would only delay the certainty of death. But now their master's words gave them hope. Could it be that he was speaking truthfully? Had he again plucked them from the jaws of disaster?

He turned back to shout again. "Your only option, Countess Madalyn, is to withdraw. Return your army to the soil from whence it came and await the king's judgement, which I assure you will be fair."

He was surprised when the voice that called back was not Countess Madalyn's, but that of a man. It was deep and melodious, with a Welsh accent and a strong note of authority.

"Earl Corotocus, Countess Madalyn no longer deems you a worthy negotiator. All of your former promises proved to be false."

"Who speaks?" the earl shouted.

"You must produce a different spokesman."

"Who speaks, I say?"

"I am Gwyddon, Countess Madalyn's senior counsellor. You no longer have a part to play here, Earl Corotocus. Until you produce someone whose word we can trust, you and your men remain under sentence of death."

"You insolent dog!"

"Which sentence to be carried out at the first opportunity."

The earl rounded on his men, scarlet-faced. "Bring her forward!"

Gwendolyn of Lyr, her head held proudly, was brought out from the bedraggled ranks and led to the parapet, where the earl ordered her to stand in one of the embrasures. She was pushed so close to its brink that her toes curled around it. Once there, he had her hands twisted behind her back and bound to an iron ring set into the stonework. Of course, this small safety measure could not be seen by the figures on the Constable's Tower. All they saw was a girlish figure, naked save for a red and blue harlequin cloak, standing on the edge of extinction.

Again, Corotocus shouted across the courtyard. "You think I won't cast this child down, countess? Surely you know me better than that?"

"Mother!" Gwendolyn called in her native language, certain that none of her captors would understand her. "Do not listen to them. They will not risk it. They have just secured..."

Corotocus himself leapt up alongside her and thrust the tip of his dagger under her chin. "Silence, you little harridan!" His Welsh was imperfect but adequate. "Hold that tongue, or I'll slit it down the middle and leave you with two!"

Gwendolyn clamped her mouth shut, but blinked fiercely, determined to eradicate any tears caused by the gusting wind. She was determined the English would not think her afraid. The earl gazed back to the Constable's Tower, but saw no obvious consternation. Countess Madalyn was close to the battlements, watching intently, but the priest who had spoken – the one called Gwyddon – was conferring with his henchmen, almost casually. Finally there were nods of agreement from the priests, and they wrestled forward two figures of their own, placing them in embrasures as well. By these prisoners' livery – a surcoat of blue and white chevrons and a crimson tabard bearing three golden lions – they were Walter Margas and Davy Gou.

Corotocus and his men were startled to see that any of their comrades had been taken alive, though both prisoners were streaked with char and ordure. They stood boldly, their chins upraised, but shivered with pain and fear. If Corotocus had been close enough, he'd have seen Margas's cheek hanging in a bloody flap, exposing his clenched molars.

"An awkward situation," du Guesculin said quietly.

Corotocus gave him a withering look, before turning to his other men. Two of his household archers were still in possession of their longbows and had quivers containing a few arrows each. He signalled them.

"Make sure your aim is good," he said.

At one time, such a cryptic order would have left them bewildered. But under these circumstances, there seemed no question about what was being demanded of them. Both bowmen stepped forward, knocked arrows and let fly. They had had much target practice over the last few days. Perhaps this explained why both shafts hit cleanly, one striking Margas in the middle of his chest, penetrating to his heart, the other catching Gou in the throat, sinking to its feathers.

The two corpses crashed from the parapet, turning over and over as they plummeted into the courtyard.

There was no word of complaint from Corotocus's men, all of them having moved unconsciously into that dark, soulless realm where the loss of any life is a price worth paying if it might save your own.

"Have you any more for me, countess?" Corotocus laughed. "I have plenty of arrows."

"Such is the reward for blind loyalty," came a weary voice.

Corotocus spun around. Gwendolyn looked too, surprised to hear a familiar tone.

Ranulf trudged forward from the door connecting with the lower levels. His face was haggard, damp with seat. His clothing and the blade of his drawn broadsword were both spattered crimson.

Corotocus in particular looked stunned. He glanced past Ranulf through the doorway behind, at which Ranulf chuckled.

"Don't waste your time looking for Navarre, my lord. He's already in Hell. Which is where you'll soon be."

"Archers!" du Guesculin shouted.

The two bowmen stepped forward, fresh arrows knocked to their strings.

"So this is the great marcher baron!" Ranulf scoffed. "Who, even when his world has come to an end, sends other men to fight for him."

"You betrayed us, Ranulf!" Corotocus growled, pointing a shaking finger.

"That's not how I see it."

"You would have delivered us all to those things."

"No!" Ranulf said, pointing back. "I would have delivered *you*!" He turned to the rest of the company. "Would any man here object to that, if it meant that you would be saved? Are the bonds of fealty so tight that, on this man's orders, you would strike blow after blow against the innocent and then take his punishment for him?"

There was no response.

There were still one or two honourable knights among this wretched band – men who had held vigils, gone on quests, ridden in the tournaments wearing the colours of fine ladies. But all were now grizzled, begrimed, stained over and over with their own gore and the gore of others. They were more like sewer rats than men. Reduced to this forlorn state, perhaps it was no surprise that none seemed willing to side with him. The only safety they knew, and it was a slim one at that, lay with their overlord.

"If you fall defending this stronghold," Ranulf asked them, "what do you think will happen to Earl Corotocus when the king arrives? He may be punished for stirring up a hornet's nest the like of which the world has never seen. But what will that punishment involve? The confiscation of estates? A money fine? *You* meanwhile will be dead! Everyone you ever served with will be dead! Or worse – enslaved for eternity by satanic magic, forbidden entry to God's kingdom."

"You speak treason" someone cried, fear making him angry. "Not just against the earl, but against the king."

There were mumbles of agreement. Others too began to shout and hurl abuse. Ranulf hung his head tiredly. He didn't suppose he could blame them. Most here owed everything they had to Earl Corotocus. They knew no other life.

"He is indeed a traitor," du Guesculin said, venturing forward now that he could see there was no fight left in this rebel. "But he sins not just against the king. He's allied himself to these demons... to Lucifer himself."

Ranulf shook his head with contempt. "You're a liar, du Guesculin. You're the worst liar of all, because you've seen what this madman's cruelty and tyranny has brought, and still you side with him."

"For crimes against God there can be no forgiveness," du Guesculin retorted. "Archers..."

"Wait!" Corotocus shouted. After initially seeming afraid, albeit very fleetingly, he'd now re-assumed his air of lordly confidence. When he spoke again, it was in an even, almost affable tone. "I don't necessarily share that view, du Guesculin. That certain evils cannot be forgiven. God does not share it either."

"My lord, I..." du Guesculin protested.

"Silence!"

Corotocus eyed Ranulf as he walked around him. Ranulf still had his broadsword and could have cut his overlord down at a whim. At this proximity, even two flying arrows couldn't have prevented it. But as always – and Ranulf cursed himself for this – he felt it important to know what Earl Corotocus was about to say next.

"Did you really slay Navarre?" the earl asked. He sounded impressed.

"It was the easiest but worthiest accomplishment of my life," Ranulf replied.

"Hmmm. I understand your feelings. He was a difficult fellow. He always felt challenged by you, of course. At least it's been settled in the honourable way."

"You're out of your mind, la Hors."

"Possibly, Ranulf, possibly."

"You should kill me now, my lord, because when I'm able to I will surely kill you."

"Let's not be too hasty. There's a method even to my madness." The earl put a thumb to his chin as he pondered. "Seeing as you've accounted for Navarre, I'm afraid it now falls to you to complete his final task."

"I don't take orders from you any more."

Corotocus sighed. "I see. Well, answer me this... do you wish what remains of our company to die? Do you wish them torn apart on these ramparts, or trapped in this place until they're forced to feed on each other? Is your hatred of me so irrational that you would sacrifice what's left of your comrades to so ghoulish a fate?"

Ranulf glanced at the rest of the men. Their expressions had changed, the hostility of a few moments ago replaced by an intense, childlike fear.

"There may be one or two worth saving," he said.

Corotocus laughed. "And it won't be difficult for a warrior like you to do it." He moved back to the battlements, looking down towards the Constable's Tower, where Gwyddon and the other druids were still in debate. "As you can see, Ranulf, we've reached an impasse. But I have a plan to break it, one that will save all our lives. Unfortunately, when we leave here... someone will have to stay behind to keep charge of this hostage. Navarre didn't know it, but he was due to be volunteered."

"The generosity with which you reward your servants knows no end," Ranulf said.

"Serving me is its own reward. Or so I'm told. But let's assume that *you* volunteer for this task. It won't be as onerous for you as it would have been for Navarre, you having already made an alliance with these creatures, or at least with their mistress."

"That didn't go quite as I planned," Ranulf admitted.

Corotocus gave him a frank stare. "The alternative is that I push this girl over the edge right now, because she'd be no use to us any more."

Ranulf said nothing. There was nothing he *could* say. Yet again the earl's wiles had backed him into a corner. Pleased, the earl leaned over the battlements and again bellowed to the group on the Constable's Tower.

"You can cease that pointless gabble!"

The druids turned and regarded him.

"There is nothing for you to discuss!" Corotocus shouted. "The situation is perfectly simple. If you try to enter this Keep, the girl will be thrown to her death. If you refuse my men and I permission to leave safely, she will starve with the rest of us. And if you ever again presume to bypass my authority to negotiate with my underlings, she will die under a flensing knife."

They made no reply.

"Am I clear?"

Still they made no reply. Gwendolyn shot the earl a scornful look. Corotocus noticed this, and for a second Ranulf thought that he was going to drive his dagger into her back. But again the earl kept control of himself. In truth, Corotocus, though he could sense his men watching, witnessing this continued disrespect, knew that he was not in as strong a bargaining position as they might believe. He could not keep the Welsh girl standing on this parapet forever. Brave as she doubtless was, she was half-naked, shivering and weak from lack of sustenance. If she collapsed in full view of her mother, even though safely tied, it could have a disastrous effect.

"My terms are these, countess!" he called down. "They are non-negotiable, but under the circumstances I think they are generous. My retainers and I are leaving Grogen Castle. You will have your creatures clear a path for us. That path will remain clear until we are far from this place. In the meantime, your child will remain here on the brink of oblivion. If any attempt is made to interfere with us, she will be pushed to her death. If any attempt is made to halt our retreat along the river – and be assured, from this vantage point we can see as far as the English border – she will be pushed to her death. However, once we have departed safely, the man I leave behind will stand down and you may retrieve your child unharmed."

"I have to give you credit, my lord," Ranulf said. "When it comes to saving your own arse, you're quite the genius."

"I meant what I said, Ranulf," the earl replied. "About liking men who tell me the truth. If you survive this, there's still a place for you at my court."

"I doubt your court will be around for very much longer. Even if you get away from here, what's to stop this horde sweeping over the border after you?"

"The bachelry of England. What else?"

Ranulf shook his head. "I'm not sure even the bachelry of England will be enough."

"Earl Corotocus!" a voice echoed up from the Constable's Tower. It was Gwyddon again. "By the good grace of Countess Madalyn of Lyr, you and your men may leave Grogen Castle. She gives her word that you will not be molested so long as her daughter is safe."

Corotocus treated his men to a satisfied smile. A few managed to return it.

"Then we have our truce." he called back. "But first I have one more demand."

"Speak."

"Our horses. We will not walk from here like yeomen farmers. We will ride out as we rode in, knights."

There was a pause, and then: "That is acceptable."

The earl nodded, turned to his men and pulled his gauntlets on. "Ready yourselves. Take only your weapons. No supplies – those will only weigh us down. Once we're away from here, we can gallop to the border."

There was a slow bustle as it gradually dawned on the men that their ordeal might be coming to an end. A few stood dazed, not totally believing it.

"Move yourselves!" the earl shouted, his voice a whip-crack. "This window of opportunity may be brief."

Ranulf walked to the battlements. Despite the deal that had just been struck, he was surprised to see a long, meandering alleyway clearing through the mob filling the courtyard. It led from the base of the Keep to the ramp entering the Constable's Tower. Beyond that, he could see a similar space being made along the causeway. With a whinnying and clopping of hooves, horses, made skittish by the stench of their lumbering grooms, were brought from the stable blocks and led to the bottom of the steps at the Keep entrance.

"How can you agree to this?" Gwendolyn hissed at Ranulf, her eyes filled with emerald fire.

"It doesn't please you?" He was surprised. "This way, everyone gets what they want."

"Except justice."

"How much justice are you looking for? Most of those men who came here and violated your people are dead."

"And the one who commanded it? What will happen to him?"

Ranulf shook his head, peering over the parapet again. "I'm more concerned about what will happen to me. How much control does your mother have over these creatures?"

Gwendolyn glanced down as well. Only now did she really seem to focus on the army that had come to liberate her; she found it impossible not to cringe at some of the things she saw.

"There's a good chance," Ranulf said, "that once the earl is gone and the Keep thrown open, their vanguard will ascend to this roof before your mother does. Will they listen to orders from you? I find that doubtful."

Gwendolyn shrugged. "You've played your part in this tragedy, sir knight. What will happen to you will happen."

"Well that's encouraging…"

"What in the name of Heaven do you expect?"

"I want Corotocus punished too," he whispered. "It's because of him that my father died and my friend was murdered. If I survive this thing, I would like to be the one who follows him to England and exacts vengeance."

"And I should give you the means?" She snorted with derision. "You think that because you are slightly more enlightened than most English knights, that means I like you? Even for the small part you've played in the disaster that has destroyed my country, I loathe and detest you."

"You little ingrate!"

She turned pointedly away from him.

"Ranulf!" Corotocus said, returning. He'd now donned a full basinet helm with an open visor, and wore a fresh cloak and tabard over his mail. His longsword hung at his left hip and a two-headed battle-axe at his right. "I trust you aren't thinking of abandoning your post while we're in the process of leaving this place?"

"That's something you'll find out for yourself when you try to leave," Ranulf said.

"Very clever," Corotocus sneered. "But I know you, boy. And I know your conscience. If you let this girl loose or even neglect to guard her so that she gets loose of her own accord, there'll be nothing to stop her calling across the castle that she's safe. If we aren't away from here by then, these monstrosities will fall on us like mad beasts."

"My lord, why don't you just leave while your household thinks you're wonderful? Because when you get back to England, they'll begin to realise the depth of your defeat, and then you'll be regarded somewhat differently."

Corotocus chuckled. "Don't make the mistake of thinking this is over, Ranulf." He turned to Gwendolyn. "Nor you, you Welsh harlot! This affair isn't over."

Gwendolyn didn't deign to look at him.

"Your people have won the battle," he said, "but not the war. We'll be back, and there'll be the devil to pay. Now mind what I say, Ranulf. Neglect your duty here and these hell-hounds could fall on us when we're most vulnerable."

"Why tar everyone with your own brush, my lord? Countess Madalyn gave you her word as a noblewoman that you would have safe passage."

"No... Ranulf." Corotocus shook his head pensively. "No. That Welsh wizard gave me his word. I don't know what that means exactly, but it disconcerts me a little."

Corotocus moved away, descending the stair. Du Guesculin and the rest of the household filed quickly after him.

Puzzling over that final comment, Ranulf looked across the courtyard to the roof of the Constable's Tower, where Countess Madalyn stood as she had before against the battlements. She had not moved since he had first arrived here. Neither, as far as he had seen, had she joined the debates of her underlings, though that did not necessarily mean that she hadn't issued quiet commands to them, as she undoubtedly would in normal times. However, for some intangible reason, Ranulf now felt a creeping chill in his bones. Why was she so still? Why had she not led the negotiations herself? It was not Countess Madalyn's way, he was sure, to leave something so important to somebody else. But neither, he thought with a shiver, was it Gwyddon's way.

# CHAPTER THIRTY-FOUR

EARL COROTOCUS UNDERSTOOD the importance of appearance.

The new cloak and tabard he'd donned were thus far unsullied. The black and crimson of his household devices glittered in the dimness of the Keep's interior. He brushed as much grime, dust and blood as he could from his battle-scarred mail. He'd even fluffed the crimson plume projecting from the crest of his helm. When he reached the Keep's lowest level, he strolled fearlessly along the stone passage to its main entrance, his spurs clinking on the flagged floor, one gloved hand clamped on the hilt of his sword. The men – those living, who now cowered nervously behind him, and those dead, who waited outside in silent expectation – had to know without being told that Corotocus was of a superior caste. It was essential he cut a striking figure, so they'd realise immediately that, by his very nature, this was a man untroubled by the events of recent days, a man who took torment and destruction in his stride because it was part of his born duty to do so.

As well as appearance, Earl Corotocus also understood the importance of propaganda.

"The battle is now over and, because of me, you fellows have survived," he said, turning to his household in front of the main portal.

Their faces were milk-pale in the gloom.

"This time yesterday, you were staring annihilation in the face. But now I have bought your futures back for you. Remember that when you are far from this place. Each one of you here owes me more than he could ever repay in a thousand lifetimes."

"They'll gladly devote the remainder of this lifetime attempting it," du Guesculin replied.

Corotocus eyed them sternly, as if daring anyone to disagree. He straightened the edges of his cloak and turned back around. "Lower the drawbridge."

With an echoing rattle of chains, the timber gate was lowered. Daylight flooded in, making them all blink. The reek of death followed, thick as swamp mist; the men choked and gagged. Up until now they had not come face to face with so concentrated a mass of their enemy.

Earl Corotocus's face, however, showed neither disgust nor revulsion. He walked boldly over the bridge, his hollow footfalls resounding across the otherwise silent castle, until he had reached the top of the steps, at which point he halted and gazed down.

The dead gazed back, rank after close-packed rank. Straight away, there were those among them he recognised. Craon Culai, with his body so crushed that only his face was distinguishable; Odo de Lussac, burned almost to a crisp, a crossbow bolt projecting from his charred mouth; Ramon la Roux, an arrow still embedded in his heart. Even Father Benan was present; he seemed to have dressed himself in hanging rags, thick with blood and mucus, until the earl realised that these were actually remnants of his own flesh. Most bizarrely, the priest's iron crucifix protruded from the top of his skull, where it appeared to have been hammered into place. Others were indistinguishable even as human, horrible remnants of men and women who had died by axe, sword, spear or noose, or whose torn and forgotten husks had lain mouldering in the ground for weeks, feasted on by worms and maggots. Every sickly colour in the spectrum was represented: blue faces, white faces, green faces, black faces, yellow faces, purple faces. There were faces without skin, skulls without hair. Were it summer, the earl imagined this ghastly host would be engulfed in swarming flies. No doubt countless such vermin were already hatching from the clusters of eggs lodged in their pulped flesh and yawning sockets.

Despite this, he walked casually down the steps, to where a troop of thirty or so horses was waiting. By good fortune, the nearest was his own black stallion, Incitatus, a powerful battle-steed bred and trained to smash through lines of infantry, though the challenge this time would be to keep the tempestuous brute in a relaxed state. To Corotocus's surprise, the dead had even saddled it for him, correctly. In fact, they'd saddled all of the horses. He glanced towards the stables, and there saw Osric, his former groom, a reaping hook buried in the side of his neck, standing by the open door – as if in death he'd automatically re-assumed the role he'd played in life. Just to be sure, the earl checked that his saddle was secure and that his animal's bit was in place before climbing into his stirrups.

Others of his company were now descending after him, but they were stiff with terror, clinging together like children. Almost invariably, they scurried frantically down the last few steps, grabbing the first mount they could, and vaulting onto its back.

The passage across the courtyard was still open, but looked narrower than it had from above. It would not be easy traversing it with an army of standing corpses ranked to either side. Corotocus peered to the top of the Constable's Tower. The rigid shape of Countess Madalyn gazed down at him, her priests alongside her. There was no conversation between them now. Their attention was fixed unswervingly on the departing English.

"Hurry," the earl said to his men, the last few of whom were traipsing down the steps.

Wheeling Incitatus around, the earl set off first, walking the animal at a steady pace. The passage was so narrow that, at most, they could travel only two abreast. Du Guesculin hastened forward to be alongside his master. Aside from the clopping of hooves and timorous snuffling of brutes, there was no sound at all, which, now that they were so close to their foe, was not surprising – for there was clearly no more life in these beings than there was in strips of hanging leather or piled-up cords of wood. They were inanimate, soulless; genuinely nothing more than mummified carcasses cut from gibbets or ploughed up from burial pits. Except that, as the English passed, their heads slowly turned, tracking each departing horseman one by one.

"My lord, will we face this gauntlet of the damned all the way to England?" du Guesculin said, in a whisper made hoarse by fear.

Earl Corotocus didn't respond. For all his bravado, his mouth was too dry to form words; his back was so straight that it hurt. When he tried to release his hand from the hilt of his sword he found that he couldn't. The fingers had locked in place.

"My lord, I said…"

"I heard you the first time!"

"Will we?"

"Who am I, God? What more to you want of me? I've gained you a free passport, haven't I?"

"A passport to what?" du Guesculin wondered.

# CHAPTER THIRTY-FIVE

"At least untie me," Gwendolyn protested. "There's no blood left in my fingers."

Ranulf, the only other person left on the Keep roof, peered down the wall to where Corotocus and his company were now snaking slowly and warily across the courtyard. He glanced towards her, distracted.

"If I do, you must stay in sight," he said. "Your mother needs to know you are safe."

"You really are a good little English soldier, aren't you?

He bristled at that. "Now you mention it, yes! Just because I sympathise with your position, don't make the mistake of thinking I'd serve every Englishman I know to your vengeance."

"Cut me loose, please."

Reluctantly, he sawed through her hempen bonds with his sword. She stepped back from the embrasure, and leaned tiredly on the left crenel, rubbing at the wheals on her wrists. She still wore only the red and blue cloak they had given her on the first day. The wind set it rippling on her lithe form.

"You must be frozen," he said.

"You finally notice now?"

"Wait here." He turned and, several yards away, spotted the black and red tabard that Earl Corotocus had discarded when he'd changed. It was torn in places and stained with grime, but it was made from heavy wool and at least it could be worn as a proper piece of clothing.

He handed it to her. "If you can bring yourself to wear these household colours, you should find this more comfortable and a little less revealing. Put the cloak back on over the top and you'll be warm enough."

She took the item from him, now looking thoughtful. "You're not too bad a fellow, sir knight. I've decided that I *will* speak up for you."

He shrugged. "Assuming anyone will listen."

She made to remove her current garb, but then saw that he was watching her.

"If you'd avert your eyes please?"

Ranulf was surprised. "You plan to change here and now? Getting undressed in front of your mother's army is probably not the best idea."

"To offend someone's eyes, they need to have eyes in the first place, do they not?"

Ranulf shrugged again, and turned his back. He peeked over the battlements. The earl and his men were half way across the courtyard, the earl riding tall in the saddle. Ahead of them, the ramp leading up to the Constable's Tower door had also cleared. Far above that, Countess Madalyn and her priests watched, unmoving. Behind him, Ranulf could hear a rustling of cloth.

"I fear Earl Corotocus means what he says," he said. "He'll seek restitution of some sort."

"And we Welsh won't?" Gwendolyn replied.

"Revenge and counter-revenge are a recipe for disaster, my lady. They've made life on these marches intolerable for too long already."

"I agree. So we should end it now, no?"

He smiled. "If only that were possible."

"Wasn't it you who told me that, with sacrifice, anything is possible?"

There was a slight inflection in her voice as she said this, a sudden decisiveness, which made him spin around. As he did, Gwendolyn screamed long and loud. Ranulf was stunned by what he saw.

She had donned the earl's tabard, as he'd suggested, but instead of putting the blue and red cloak over the top of it, she had wrapped this around one of the Breton mannequins – and had now flung that mannequin over the battlements. She continued to scream as it fell, at the same time making sure to step well back from the parapet.

EARL COROTOCUS THOUGHT his eyes were deceiving him.

Even though the object seemed to fall unnaturally slowly, its blue and red cloak billowing like sail cloth, there was no doubt what it was. Its legs were splayed, its arms spread-eagled. The ear-piercing scream lingered on the rancid air, only to be silenced when the object vanished into the dry moat. At first Corotocus was numbed to near immobility. When he finally glanced up again, the unmistakeable shape of Ranulf FitzOsbern was hunched over the Keep battlements.

In that astonishing moment, the world came to a standstill for the Earl of Clun and his remaining household. Each one of them was fixed to his saddle, each one swallowed air the way a parched man swallows water.

Corotocus looked back along his procession of followers. To a man their faces were stark white, beaded with sweat, their eyes bugging. If any were conversing he couldn't hear them thanks to the thunderous roar of his own blood in his ears.

As a wail of anguished rage sounded overhead from the roof of the Constable's Tower, the earl banged his visor shut and, putting his spurs to his horse's sides, urged the beast into a furious gallop. The ramp and open portcullis were only twenty yards ahead of him and he was sure that he could make it through. As he did, he glanced over his shoulder. Du Guesculin was close behind, his face shining wet as he spurred his own steed mercilessly. But now corpses were stirring to demonic life, surging in from both sides, trying to close the passage – against which odds, the rest of the men were too far behind to even have a hope. In ones and twos, they were encircled, their horses whinnying hysterically, lashing out with their hooves, smashing the faces and skulls of their assailants but, as always, to no avail. One by one, the riders were pulled screaming from their saddles and hurled to the floor, whereupon axes, spades, clubs, maces, flails and falchions rained on them in a blur of blood, brains and exploding bone fragments.

Corotocus made it as far as the Constable's Tower ramp before a party of the dead blocked his route. Framed in the V-shaped viewing slot of his visor, this group actually resembled soldiers. They wore steel-studded jerkins and iron caps and had pikes, which they tried to lower to form a hedge.

"Incitatus, the field!" he bellowed, his voice sounding brazen from the confines of his helm.

This was a battle cry his steed was familiar with from many occasions in the past. Before the pikes could be arrayed, it had crashed clean through, scattering the figures like skittles. One tried to grab the bridle, but, with a single blow of his axe, Corotocus severed its arm at the shoulder. Another snatched the horse's tail, only to be dragged along behind, Incitatus's flying hooves kicking it continually in the face, reducing it to mulch. Still the thing clung on, and finally, as it had been trained, the animal pivoted around and trampled the hapless passenger into a carpet of shredded flesh and bone. Again, Corotocus focussed on du Guesculin, who was close behind but was having trouble making further progress. The dead were hampering him from all sides. His horse reared in terror rather than ploughing forward, which attracted more and more of them to him.

Pleased, Corotocus spun his animal round again and charged up the ramp, through the arched entrance to the Constable's Tower and along its main passage, where the clashing of his hooves echoed like hammers on anvils. All the way, he fought fiercely with those corpses attempting to hinder him. Gripping Incitatus with his knees, he wielded his axe in his left hand and his sword in his right. None of his dead foes were mounted, of course, which gave him a huge advantage, though again and again they stood in his path and had to be barged out of the way.

Frantic cries for help drew his attention back to the rear, where, incredibly, du Guesculin had also made it into the building. Corpses were still running alongside the banneret, trying to pull him down. One fell beneath his horse's legs, tripping it. The animal skidded on its knees over the cobblestones, shrieking as hair and skin was flayed from its joints. As it righted itself, du Guesculin cried again for his master's assistance, laying desperately about him on all sides, fighting as hard as he'd ever fought. But those dead in the passage who had unsuccessfully attempted to waylay the first rider now switched their attention to the second.

This was the opportunity Corotocus needed, he realised. Spurring his mount, he galloped on towards the open portcullis at the far end. Another corpse stepped into his path – a near-giant bristling with arrows, who the earl was sure he'd personally had lashed to a tree and shot to death at a village not far from here. The giant was swinging a mighty poll-arm around its head, but, with pure knightly skill, the earl wove around the ponderous figure, burying his sword in its cranium as he passed. Now he had only his battle-axe, but this was all he needed. As he approached the portcullis, he glanced into the right-hand alcove where its main mechanism was contained. A wedge had been hammered into the central wheel. The earl flung his axe at it as he hurtled by – and struck clean. The wedge was dislodged and, as he rode beneath the portcullis, its great iron structure, still bent and twisted from the dead army's attack on it, began rumbling downward. Its impact on the cobbled floor reverberated through the entire tower, halting du Guesculin only a few yards short of freedom.

Corotocus glanced around one last time as he galloped along the causeway. Behind the iron grille, he caught a final glimpse of his lieutenant's despairing face.

"My gift to you!" Corotocus said under his breath. "Go and feed on *him*! He'll make a meal for all of you!"


Du Guesculin chopped wildly at the sea of decay that ebbed around him. The portcullis was so warped at its base that he might have been able to slide his body beneath it. But that would have meant having to dismount.

A claw now took hold of his cloak. He cut the tie, shrugging the garment loose, and, with no other choice, drove his animal back into the bowels of the building, still hacking them down, stomping over those that fell, breaking their limbs and torsos, grinding them into the stones, but having to stand in the stirrups to avoid taking blows himself, and now – suddenly – stopping and gaping with horror. For a veritable flood of black and twisted forms was pouring down the passage towards him, their howls a dirge from the lowest level of damnation.

All-consuming terror had now cost du Guesculin his sense of place and direction, so, when he veered his animal to the right through a very narrow doorway, he had no idea that this was the foot of a spiral stair leading to the roof. Of course, when he discovered the truth, there was no turning back.

It was a perilous ascent for a four-footed beast, rising steeply, turning, turning, turning. Around each corner there was another shambling horror to block his path. He knocked each one aside, or smote it down, their blood and brains splattering up the granite walls as his blade bit through them. But always they were back on their feet quickly, and he heard their echoing ululation as they hastened in pursuit. And then, when du Guesculin thought that things could not get worse, he entered that upper region of the Constable's Tower where destruction had been wrought by the mangonels.

Suddenly he was in open rooms crammed with piles of rubble and burned, blistered body parts. Dust clouds still hung here, obscuring almost everything. Crushed, crab-like shapes clambered or slithered towards him over the mounds of masonry. One of these was still able to stand on two feet and grabbed his bridle. Du Guesculin peered down at Gilbert, his own squire, though he only realised this when he saw the grimy red hose and tunic. The boy's face had melted like cheese and hung from his naked skull in loops and tendrils.

The now deranged horse tried to retreat, but its footing slipped, and suddenly it was sliding backward as the scorched floorboards gave way beneath it. Du Guesculin just had time to leap from the saddle as his mount disappeared, screaming, into the dusty spaces below. Twenty feet down, with a shattering *crack*, its spine struck a stone buttress, which sent it spinning, lifeless, into a void of darkness that was filled with the shrieks of the dead.

Du Guesculin, himself teetering on the edge of the hole, turned on his heel just in time to see the apparition that had once been Gilbert lurching at him, hands outstretched. He drove his sword into its breast, but this did not hold the thing back. Gasping, he spun around and stumbled away, tripping and landing on his knees with such force that one kneecap was split to the cartilage. Choking at the pain, he lumbered on. Another stairway appeared through the gloom, this one leading to the open sky.

Du Guesculin sobbed his way up it. At the top, he found himself on the roof, huge sections of which had imploded from the impact of the mangonel missiles. Beyond the first of these crevasses, Countess Madalyn's druids were ranged in a row: pitiless men –

bearded and stern beneath their hoods, their onyx eyes fixed on him intently. On his side, stood the countess herself.

Blubbering spittle, gibbering for mercy, du Guesculin tottered towards her.

"Countess, I beg you, I beg you…"

He dropped to his knees despite the agony this caused him, clasped his hands together and gazed up at her, though his vision was blurred with tears.

"I am Hugh du Guesculin, banneret of Clun, Lord of Oswestry and Whitchurch. I am not without influence. And unlike Earl Corotocus, I can be trusted. Ma-am, listen, please, I beg you. I know King Edward. I can parley for you. I can end this war so that Wales remains with the Welsh, with you as their queen. I can do all this. I beg you, ma-am, listen to me please."

She reached down with both hands and cupped his face, almost gently. He blinked, not understanding what this meant. Slowly, her features swam into focus. They were as handsome and noble as he remembered. But they were also pale and rigid as wax. Beneath her aristocratic chin, a crimson line ran from one ear to the other. When she exerted the necessary strength to drag him to his feet and hoist him into the air, that line yawned open, exposing her sliced windpipe. With eyes of lustreless glass, she strode to the battlements. Du Guesculin's scream was a prolonged, keening whistle as, with one hand at his throat and the other at his crotch, she raised him high over her head.

He continued to scream even when she'd flung him over the parapet, the scream lingering as he plummeted – down, down, down, head first, legs kicking manically, until landing with horrific force on the courtyard floor, where he smashed apart like a beetle under a boot.


FROM THE ROOF of the Keep, Ranulf watched aghast as these events unfolded. But if it shocked him to the core to see what remained of the earl's household torn to pieces in the courtyard, it was an even greater shock to see what happened to Hugh du Guesculin.

Ranulf turned stiffly to face Gwendolyn. She regarded him boldly, her smudged but beautiful face written with triumph.

"No doubt you're enraged?" she said. "Well, now perhaps you understand how I feel. Justice had to be done."

He stalked towards her.

She didn't flinch. "Now that the guilty ones have been punished, this is where it can end."

"Indeed?"

"Indeed," she said. "You'll thank me for it in due course."

Ranulf didn't say anything else, just hit her – not hard enough to kill her, though he was sorely tempted, but sufficiently to knock her unconscious. She toppled through the embrasure, but he caught her by the tabard and pulled her back to him. In the process, he glanced again into the courtyard, where all the earl's men were now dead, their mangled remains being flung back and forth between the howling cadavers. Other corpses, of course, in fact cohorts of them, were already flowing across the Keep drawbridge.

Ranulf didn't wait to see more. Throwing Gwendolyn over his shoulder, he hurried to the top of the stair.

# CHAPTER THIRTY-SIX

EARL COROTOCUS DID not witness the death of Hugh du Guesculin. He never looked back once as he galloped hard along the causeway.

More of the dead were crossing it towards him. But he veered around them. He was no longer armed, but that was of no concern. All that mattered was flight. As the Gatehouse loomed towards him, he was struck by the alarming thought that they might now have closed the portcullis at its front entrance. This goaded him to spur his animal until its flanks bled.

Nobody else obstructed him as he charged in through the arched entrance and up the Gatehouse's central passage. To his relief the portcullis was still raised, though a fresh phalanx of corpses was coming in beneath it. Leaning low, cloak billowing, the earl snapped his reins with fury. Incitatus struck the dead like a streak of black lightning, scattering them on all sides. Corotocus hurtled out of the Gatehouse and into the entry passage. More of the dead streamed along it. He crashed through them one after another, though the main danger here was the charred human fat that seemed to smear every surface. His horse skidded dangerously on it, before righting itself at the end of the passage and bolting eastward along the berm path.

Corotocus might now have been outside the castle, but he was still far from safety. Hemmed against its ramparts by the moat, he knew he had to circumnavigate two thirds of the entire stronghold before he would reach the river, at which point perhaps the most desperate gamble of all awaited him – crossing to the other side in full mail.

The decayed horde was gathered en masse beyond the moat. Their demonic lament rose to a crescendo when they beheld him, but aside from throwing spears, rocks and other improvised missiles, they could not reach him. Small groups were still drifting along the berm in his direction, still seeking to enter the castle. But as long as they remained in these restricted numbers, he knew he was a match for them.

"Incitatus, the field!" Corotocus bellowed.

The mount was now galloping at full speed. Blood streamed from its flanks, not just where the earl had spurred it, but where the dead had clawed at it. Foam flew from its bit; its eyes burned like rubies, as if it somehow knew that these clusters of stick-figures cavorting towards it were responsible for its pain. It clearly relished the collision as, one by one, it bounced them out of its way.

Corotocus yelled with laughter. Occasional missiles hit him, but his mail or helmet deflected them. He rounded the castle's northeast corner, to find more of the dead approaching from the southeast. If such a thing were possible, they seemed surprised to be confronted by the fugitive. Again, he crashed through them, delighted as they were chopped apart beneath his hooves or smashed against the castle's skirted wall. At one point he encountered a dead woman carrying a dead child. Though pale of skin, they were barely marked by the grave. The clothes they wore – the woman's dress, her linen veil and wimple, the wooden clogs on her feet, the baby in its swaddling – they were all spotlessly clean. Fleetingly, they might have been alive, but, even if they had been, the earl would have ridden them down just the same. The woman was catapulted into the moat, losing the child as she fell. They both landed skulls first on the rocks below, their arms and legs spread-eagled. The earl rode on. Directly ahead lay his salvation, but also his deadliest obstacle. The Tefeidiad.

In normal times, to leave Grogen Castle, one would turn at its southeast corner, and follow the berm all the way to the southwest bridge. But beyond that lay the western bluff, from which the vast majority of Countess Madalyn's army were still pouring across. So only the Tefeidiad provided a possible escape.

As they reached the southeast corner, Corotocus reined his beast to a halt, its hooves ploughing furrows in the dirt. He loosened the strap beneath his chin, and threw his helmet off, shaking out his sweat-soaked hair. Then he unlaced his cloak.

The river glided past ten feet below. It was about sixty yards across to the far side. Only small numbers of the dead were visible over there, compared to the titanic horde on the other sides of the castle. But Cotorocus knew the river was too deep at this point for Incitatus to simply wade across. He had no doubt that his horse could swim such a short distance, but could it swim it with an armoured rider on its back? It was a chance Corotocus was prepared to take, because there was no time to remove his mail carapace as well.

He urged his animal to the edge. Breathing hard, lathered with sweat, the spirited beast might have been game for almost anything at that moment – but jumping into a broad, fast moving river? Snorting with alarm, it held back.

"Yaa!" Corotocus shouted, jamming his spurs into his mount's sides.

He could sense more of the dead approaching, both from the right and from his rear. He risked a glance. The dispersed groups that he'd thundered through with such ease had got back to their feet and turned in pursuit of him. Even greater numbers were headed towards him from the direction of the bridge.

"Yaa!" he cried again, goading his steed.

The first of the dead were only a few yards away, reaching out with their fleshless claws, when Incitatus's growing fear overcame its instincts. With a wild neighing, it leapt from the bank. Corotocus clung on as best he could. He knew that his extra weight would be a stern test for the beast, but, encumbered with mail, he couldn't afford to be dislodged.

Initially they both plunged beneath the surface, the icy, brown water closing over their heads. But then they broke back into the air again and, with a truly colossal effort, the horse began to kick its way forward. Corotocus hung onto the reins as the river flowed heavily against him. He tried to float his body as much as possible, but in his mail he wasn't buoyant. They were only a quarter of the way across when the poor animal started to sink, the water rising up its neck and up the earl's body.

"You damn coward, Incitatus!" the earl snarled. "Don't you dare fail me now! Not when we're almost home."

Of course, they weren't really 'almost home'.

Increasing numbers of the dead were appearing through the trees on the south shore. As they'd shown throughout the siege, these rotting cadavers appeared to be connected via some kind of inexplicable 'hive' consciousness. Several times during the siege, it had been remarked on by different men that they moved en masse and attacked together "like ants". In similar fashion, they'd now apparently become aware that the earl was escaping and were scrambling to intercept him. But in reality they were still few and far between on the far bank. Once he was ashore, he was sure he could get through them. From there it was only a day's ride to the English border and through woods and open countryside. No more blind alleys, no more embattled ramparts. Incitatus would make it for him, but, if the proud beast's heart burst asunder in the process, it was a price worth paying.

As if sensing the faith its master was putting in it, the horse renewed its efforts to reach the other side. They were now half way across, the icy flood breaking over their heads, the terrible undertow tugging at them. They'd already drifted maybe fifty yards. Without needing to look, the earl could sense Grogen Castle falling away to his rear.

But the rocks on the south shore were much closer. The trees loomed larger; he could see the spaces between them and the tangled undergrowth.

Then there was a crunching of shingle and the earl's heart leapt again. Incitatus had found the riverbed. The Tefeidiad was getting shallower. Suddenly, the charger was moving with greater strength and purpose. Corotocus alighted himself properly on its back. He tried to sit upright, though the water still came as high as his waist. He punched at the air with triumph – just as something being carried on the current collided with him.

It was below the surface, and at first he thought it was a fallen log or branch. Then he realised the truth. It was a body, so covered with weed and river-mud that it was only vaguely distinguishable as human. Not that it was human in any true sense.

With one hand, it grabbed at the earl's bridle.

With the other, it grabbed at the earl.

Corotocus shouted, but now he had no blade to fight it off with. An even deeper fear went through him when he realised that his assailant was wearing chain-mail and coloured livery – it was one of his own knights.

"Desist, you dog!" he cried. "You traitorous…"

Bracing its feet against the horse's flank, and with a single mighty heave, the dead retainer hauled its former master from the saddle.

Incitatus, weary but at last unburdened, continued on its way, wobbling ashore on foal-like legs, before trotting away to the east, dripping and shivering, unmolested by the ranks of corpses gathering there. A few yards away, Corotocus floundered, even though he was only now in three or four feet of water. His attacker had got to its feet and clamped one hand on his throat. Though hampered by his mail, the earl struggled back gamely. He hadn't come all this way to be thwarted at the final post. He struck his assailant over and over. They wrestled together, went beneath the surface again, broke back into the open air. The earl felt his strength ebbing while his assailant seemed tireless – but it was only when they came nose to nose that Corotocus of Clun suddenly realised the full peril of his predicament.

He froze with fear and disbelief as he stared into his opponent's face. Though smashed and wounded, though bloated from its immersion in the icy depths, and despite the brown river water gurgling from its gaping mouth, that face was horribly familiar.

"Ulbert!" Corotocus choked. "Ulbert, don't you recognise me, your lord and master?"

What had once been Ulbert FitzOsbern clearly *did* recognise Corotocus. For the grotesquely distended lips, which had once spoken only words of wisdom to the nobleman, now curved into a most fiendish grin.

Corotocus shrieked madly, insanely, as his former vassal tightened its one-handed grip on his throat, and, planting its other hand on top of his head, plunged him back beneath the water. And this time held him there.

# CHAPTER THIRTY-SEVEN

WHEN GWENDOLYN OPENED her eyes, her jaw ached abominably. At first she was disoriented, her vision blurred. She tasted blood and realised that she was wringing wet all over.

Confused, she sat up on a bed of damp vegetation. As she hung her dizzy head, it gradually occurred to her that the suffocating stench of death had dissipated. Instead, there was a fresh woodland fragrance. In fact, it was more than fresh. A soft rain was falling.

"The rain?" someone said, as though reading her befuddled thoughts. "Damn it... the rain!"

"What?" Gwendolyn glanced around. "Where am I?"

Her vision swam into focus. There were trees on all sides, many lush with catkins. She was sitting among young ferns, springy and bright green. Ranulf stood a few yards away. He held out cupped hands with which to catch the rainfall. When they were full, he sniffed at them gingerly.

"The rain," he said again. "I think it's in the rain!" He turned to look at her, so dumbfounded that her wakening had made no impact on him. "Have you smelled it?"

Gwendolyn shook her head. "The only thing I can smell, is…"

Her nostrils wrinkled as she detected a slight fetor. But it didn't take long to trace it to her tabard, which was streaked with a foul, sticky residue of human waste. It smeared her face as well. Good Lord, it was even in her hair. Now that she looked at Ranulf closely, she saw that it coated him as well, not that he seemed concerned.

"Where are we?" she demanded.

"A Welsh forest, Lady Gwendolyn." He regarded her sternly, as if finally realising that she'd come round. "The sort of place your druid friends would feel very at home. Do *you* not feel at home with them?"

"The castle, I…"

"The castle is that way." He pointed into the woods behind them. "About two miles, I'd say. I'd have got further, but I've been fighting continually for the last few days, I've barely eaten and even your sylph-like form became heavy after a time. You see, even the most gallant of us knights have our limits."

"You still haven't released me?" she said, incredulous.

"You broke the truce. What do you expect?"

"Are you mad?" She jumped to her feet, though it briefly made her dizzy again. "It was over, it was all over."

"On the contrary. It's only just beginning."

"You poor English fool. My people will keep coming after me."

"It could be you flatter yourself, my lady."

"You think they did all this for nothing?"

Ranulf shrugged. "If all they want is you, go to them. I'm not stopping you. You're not my prisoner."

She looked bewildered. "Then why am I here?"

He tore up a handful of ferns and commenced scrubbing the slime from his clothing. "Believe it or not, I brought you here with me for your own protection."

"What are you talking about?"

"If you hadn't been so busy plotting the death of Earl Corotocus and his household, you might have seen what was really happening back there."

"I'll lie for you," she said, backing towards the trees. "I'll tell them I fled the castle on my own. I'll pretend you are among the dead. It's the best I can do for you."

"Go ahead."

"They may want to know how I escaped."

"Through the garderobe sewer." He threw the filthied ferns away and grabbed up some more. "We used it before to launch a raid. The ropes were still in place. It was not difficult."

She nodded, but was unnerved by his oddly matter-of-fact attitude. "You should return to the English border quickly. It's the only hope you have."

"It's more hope than you have, if you're heading where I think you're heading."

"You're quite wrong about this." She tried to make her voice more confident than she suddenly felt. "I've seen what they are. I know it's hideous, an aberration. But I am Gwendolyn of Lyr. They will not harm me."

"Really? You don't sound too sure."

"My mother commands them."

Ranulf laughed, but it was a wry laugh, lacking humour. "Your mother is merely their figurehead. She can easily be replaced... and sooner rather than later she will need to be." He eyed her carefully. "*You* would suffice in that role as well, I suppose, until such time as you too needed replacing."

"This attempted trickery is unbecoming to a knight, even an English one."

"If you wish to go, go. I'm past caring." He turned and strode off eastward. "Fare you well."

Frustrated and frightened, Gwendolyn hurried through the trees after him.

"You can't expect me to go to England with you?" she said, having to trot just to stay level with him.

"I don't ask you to. The likelihood is that you wouldn't be safe there either. Not for long. None of us will."

"You just resent that the Welsh have found a way to fight back."

"The Welsh!" he hissed, suddenly rounding on her. "The Welsh no longer exist! Did you or did you not see that?"

Despite everything, she was taken aback by his ferocity. His eyes blazed; spittle seethed at his lips. It was as though some intense emotion that he'd been bottling up inside had suddenly burst free.

"T-that's... that's not true," she stammered. "My mother..."

"You mother has *joined* them!"

There was a long, dull silence, during which Gwendolyn's look of slow-dawning horror gave Ranulf no pleasure whatsoever.

"Probably against her will," he said, "though I doubt that's any consolation to you."

"What do you mean she's joined them?"

He strode on. "What do you think I mean?"

She ran after him again. "You're lying!"

"Go back and find out for yourself."

"Are you telling me my mother is dead?"

"I'm sorry to have delivered it so brutally."

"Sir knight, stop if you please! I command it, stop and talk to me!"

Reluctantly, he halted and swung around to face her.

"I asked..." She stumbled over the words, her lovely green eyes brimming with tears. "Did... did you actually *see* this?"

Ranulf didn't need to speak. His harrowed expression said it all. Gwendolyn wept for a moment, though, perhaps remembering her noble lineage, she managed to get hold of herself again with remarkable speed.

"What... what am I to do?" she finally asked.

"What are any of us to do?"

Tears ran freely down her cheeks again, but she shook her head defiantly. "I must still go to my people."

"Then come with me." He pointed towards England. "Like it or not, your people lie this way now."

A few days ago, she'd have endured unimaginable torture rather than admit such a thing. But since then she'd seen for herself the ghoul-like creatures that had brought death to the English interlopers. Though it was from on high, she'd witnessed the ferocity with which they'd beat and strangled and torn their enemies. She'd heard their inhuman groans, their demented screams. Above all, of course, she'd smelled them – the maggot-riddled carrion that passed for their flesh. Did she really wish to ride at the head of so hellish a horde? It was highly unlikely – nay, it was impossible to imagine – that her mother would be willing to do so, for all her rage and anguish at the crimes committed by the English.

When Ranulf walked on, Gwendolyn walked behind him. She had to struggle to control her sobs, which now bespoke pain and bewilderment as much as grief.

"And try not to cry too loudly," he said over his shoulder. "We don't know who's listening."

She glanced at the trees to either side; the only sound from them was the pattering of rain. And yet there were many dark places there.

"Are we not away from danger yet?" she asked.

"This rain is falling everywhere."

"Everywhere?"

"Near enough everywhere. Can you imagine what that means?"

Gwendolyn stopped in her tracks, and looked behind her. The springtime woods were a riot of green bud and pink blossom. Overhead, blue sky broke through fleecy cloud. Mellow warmth had settled on a landscape which only a few days ago had glittered with ice and frost. Somewhere in the woods, the voice of a cuckoo was heard. The season was in full bloom. There was an air of rebirth. And yet – he had said 'everywhere'.

This tainted rain was falling *everywhere*.

Chilled to her marrow, Gwendolyn of Lyr again ran to catch up with Ranulf FitzOsbern. She hardly dared think how many graveyards lay between here and safety. Or where safety, if such a thing existed, might actually be found in this new, nightmarish world.

# EPILOGUE

DEAD BODIES WOULD no longer be a feature of battlefields, Gwyddon reflected as he strolled through the precincts of Grogen Castle, while his army departed north.

Oh, the great stronghold was still a grim sight, its ramparts broken, many of its towers and inner buildings burned to blackened frameworks, its walls and walkways splashed with blood, strewn with arrows, spears, swords, smashed shields, severed limbs. There was scarcely a corner of it where evidence of horrific violence was not on full display. Though he was now completely alone here, if he stood still and listened, he fancied he could hear the harsh song of blade on blade, blade on shield, blade on mail, the cries of anger and pain, the thunder of collapsing masonry as catapulted missiles wrought cataclysmic destruction. The air was still rank. Dust, smoke and soot still hung in ghostly palls.

And yet there were no dead bodies anywhere.

Those slaughtered English who had not been caught in the morning's rain, those who lay inside perhaps or under parapets, had in due course been treated with the cauldron brew. Then they too had risen to their feet and marched north. It was now late afternoon, and apparently King Edward had reached Conway. But for all that he routinely sewed those lands he planned to conquer with spies and informers, he would not fully understand the nature of the enemy that was moving to meet him. Most likely he would not even believe the stories he was being told.

Gwyddon would not be part of this next clash, of course; nor would any of his priesthood. They had withdrawn to their sanctuary under the mountain, and shortly he would be joining them. He anticipated with some confidence that King Edward would be defeated. The king reportedly had fifty thousand men, but the army marching to halt him had already swollen to many times that number, and, as Earl Corotocus had discovered, it was invulnerable to most, if not all, earthly weapons.

The absence of Earl Corotocus from the English slain was a minor irritant to Gwyddon. Those killed in the courtyard had eventually been laid out in a row, so that he could examine them before they were recalled. Though many had been mutilated beyond recognition, Gwyddon had eventually concluded that the earl was not present. His helmet and cloak had later been discovered next to the Tefeidiad, but not his flesh. In itself this was not massively important. One man alone, even one man who could call on substantial powers if he returned to England, would be no great threat. Most likely the earl had died in the river anyway, and his carcass had been washed away. Gwyddon would have liked to know for sure, but it was no disaster that he didn't.

He walked up into the Keep, his footsteps echoing through the dank passages and empty rooms. He entered the garderobe and peered down the black shaft, in which hempen ropes still hung. It was possible that the man who had led his men out into the courtyard had not been Corotocus, and that the real earl had escaped this way. A few others among the English almost certainly had. Most probably, they had taken Lady Gwendoyln with them, for she too had been missing when the final body-count was made. Again, this was no great disaster. Ideally, Gwyddon would have kept the heiress of Lyr alive for as long as possible. She would have become the new symbol of this uprising; the excuse for the insurrection. Around her otherwise completely insignificant person, they could have rallied in vengeance for the 'murder' of Countess

Madalyn. But such concepts as justification and lawfulness were fast becoming unnecessary. As it was, Countess Madalyn made a more than adequate stage-prop. She still rode at the head of the army. In a few weeks' time, when her ligaments were so rotten and her bones so brittle that she couldn't climb onto a horse much less ride one, Gwyddon would have to think of something else. But that was a problem for the future, not the present.

Overall, he was very satisfied with the way the siege had progressed. Even those one or two English who had survived could now be of use. They would return home and spread the word that Grogen, King Edward's mightiest bastion, had fallen within a matter of days, and that Earl Corotocus of Clun, his fiercest dog of war, had been vanquished. The fear and confusion this would cause would be worth more than threats delivered in the Welsh tongue ever could.

And then of course there was the bliss of victory. Even here, in the foulest chamber in the foulest building of the entire castle, Gwyddon was imbued with it, almost light-headed. How could he not feel triumphant; how could he not feel his own glory wrapped around him like a silken cloak? The first blow in the war to end all wars had been struck – and what a blow it was. The enemy was reeling with it. Of course, it was important not to be totally overcome with one's own importance. There was much to do yet if he was to realise his dreams of conquest. But there was no denying that this had been a more successful start to his campaign than he had ever imagined possible.

He turned to leave the garderobe, and was confronted by a shadowy figure standing in its doorway. Gwyddon stepped forward, curious.

It was one of the English. A large, burly fellow, wearing a steel-studded leather hauberk, covered in fragments of straw. His face was black with clotted blood from a brutally smashed nose, his hair and beard thickly matted by it. He was solid on his feet, but very still. He regarded Gwyddon with dull, ox-like eyes.

"Go north," Gwyddon told him. "Join your comrades. The great battle goes on."

The creature responded by hitting him under the sternum.

At first Gwyddon was merely shocked. He thought the creature had struck him with a clenched fist. But then a slow, agonising chill began to ebb through his lower body. He looked downward, and saw the hilt of a dagger jutting from his midriff. He tried to grab hold of it, but there was no longer strength in his arms. He glanced up at his assailant, his mouth dropping open. This creature was indeed English, but not one of their dead.

His vision fading, Gwyddon sank to his knees. Try as he may, he couldn't give voice to the anger he suddenly felt at his own folly. The Englishman now crouched in front of him, took hold of the dagger and yanked it loose.

The druid grunted; his onyx eyes rolled white. But that didn't concern Murlock the mercenary, for whom other men's deaths had been the currency of life since childhood. Pulling the druid's beard aside, he inserted the dagger into the Adam's apple beneath and sliced it neatly from one side to the other. The crimson gout that throbbed forth lasted only a couple of seconds, before the body slumped heavily to the floor. But only when Murlock was sure the druid was dead did he strip the moon-crescent pendant from his throat, the gem-encrusted rings from his fingers and the silver dragon-head pin from his robe.

Murlock examined each item one after another, cleaning the gore from them with his own beard. He smiled, pleased. He'd been deeply unconscious for a considerable time, but his instincts had not deserted him. When he'd first come round beneath that pile of rancid straw, his first aim had been to get even with Ranulf FitzOsbern, but time had clearly overtaken that ambition. Whatever had happened here, the earl's army had been crushed, and the Welsh themselves had now departed. It was not the ideal outcome, especially with those who owed him wages slain. But the upside was that there was nothing to stop him going home.

He wrapped the valuables in a leather pouch and stuffed it under his belt. Before leaving, he flung the druid's body down the garderobe chute, where most likely it would never be found, though first he searched it thoroughly just to ensure there was nothing else of worth that he'd missed.

He chuckled.

It might have been a distasteful habit of his, but whichever war he was fighting in, whether he was on the winning side or the losing side, Murlock had always believed in making his service pay.

# THE END

# DEATH HULK

## MATTHEW SPRANGE

# CHAPTER ONE

THE CRACK OF rope against skin, punctuated by moans rising in volume with each stroke, ripped across the main deck. High above, a lone gull circled the furled masts of the *HMS Whirlwind*, oblivious to the human misery below. The entire crew of the frigate stood silent, watching their Bosun administer the Captain's discipline under the watchful eyes of the officers standing rigid on the quarterdeck.

After another two strokes, the Bosun, a heavy set man with the weight of years at sea in his posture, gathered his rope and stood straight as he looked up at the impassive officers.

"A dozen all done, Cap'n," he said.

"Very well, Mr Kennedy. Cut him down and take him to the surgeon." Captain James Havelock nodded. He remained on the quarterdeck, hands behind his back, as he watched the crew file away to their duties as the flogged man was helped below decks to have his bleeding back treated. Corbin, First Lieutenant of the *Whirlwind*, glanced at his Captain and noticed a familiar twitch in Havelock's hawkish nose.

"Third this week, Sir," he said quietly.

"Indeed. The inevitable price of keeping men on ship while land is in sight. But we all have our orders and poor discipline can never be tolerated on His Majesty's ships."

Corbin stayed silent as he looked across the calm waters of Spithead towards land. Dozens of warships lay moored between the *Whirlwind* and the coast, an assortment of sloops, frigates and mighty ships of the line. The pride of the King's Navy was gathered here quiet, laden with awesome potential and yet utterly useless as they awaited direction.

"Still no word of orders?" he asked.

Havelock shook his head. "None, Mr Corbin. And I fear Bonaparte will not dare face us openly at sea." He gave a small grin. "I always thought the man a lion on land but a coward on the ocean."

"We may still have our day, Sir."

"I hope and pray." Havelock glanced down the main deck at the crew of the *Whirlwind*. Most had dispersed but a score remained above deck to go about the dozens of tasks required to merely keep a warship afloat and ready for battle. "Have a word with Mr Kennedy. He needs to keep a tighter grip on the crew. It does us no good to go through this display for every minor infraction that gets reported."

"I always had the impression you find flogging distasteful, Sir," said Corbin.

"It is not a case of that though, in truth, I find it a necessary barbarism," said Havelock. "It is as much a part of discipline as the drills we put our men through or the constant work required to keep this ship clean and hygienic. A warship without discipline is a liability to the Crown and its Captain not worthy of the title. But crews have their own mechanisms for dealing with minor crimes and a good bosun knows all of them. I can live with the odd scuffle below deck but a flogging each day will begin to work against the morale of the crew. Instead of the even-handed rule of authority and justice, it becomes something else. The Captain turns into a bully, or worse, a tyrant. No, inform Mr Kennedy that he is to deal with matters where he can and only bring the worst offenders to our attention."

"As you say, Sir."

Corbin left to descend the stairs to the main deck where he quickly disappeared below to find the Bosun. Havelock walked to the railings and stared at the other vessels moored close to his own, knowing each Captain was facing the same problems he had. The

*Whirlwind* had been moored at Spithead for less than two weeks and he knew some ships had been here much longer. He did not envy the disciplinary problems they might be facing. Up to now, the Admiralty had seen fit to keep the entire fleet in a state of constant readiness as rumours of a French attempt at invasion rolled across the channel as regularly as the waves. It was plain to every Captain here that the fleet could not remain in this state indefinitely but Havelock was not entirely sure that the decision makers within the Mad House were completely aware of what was happening at Spithead.

Only one remedy could solve the ills of the fleet. Officers and men alike required action. As Havelock had said to his Lieutenant, he could only hope and pray that orders would arrive soon. Either that or Bonaparte decide to invade.

"I swear it's true, right as I'm standin' 'ere!"

"Murphy, you're full of it." The two sailors were shrouded in the darkness of the *Whirlwind's* interior, both slouched across the gun carriage they had been tasked with cleaning. Brush in hand, Bryant leaned over the cannon he and his crew had christened 'Blow Hard' and grinned a toothless smile. "Just how come you heard this anyway?"

"I over'eard the marines talkin' last night," Murphy said with some conviction, scratching at his thinning hair.

"You trust the words of a lobster? Lord, man, they have less to do than us right now – their mouths are running away with themselves."

"Nah, not this one. 'E's just come on board, not more than a week ago. An' 'e's been talkin' to others in 'is regiment – they've just come back from Spain, see?"

Bryant sighed. "Well, that plain just doesn't make sense in itself. If Boney is on the attack, why are they bringing soldiers back to England?"

"Hey, I don't pretend to know what 'appens in the army. They're odd enough as it is. They gotta come back sometime, right? Like a ship goes back to port for refittin' and stuff."

Pausing, Bryant thought for a moment. "No, you can just send supplies to an army, wherever you are."

"Whatever," Murphy said, refusing to be waylaid. "I 'eard 'em talkin'. Boney has raised the dead and they now fight in 'is army. Our boys are facin' walkin' corpses, sweepin' across Spain, if ya please!"

The two men worked in silence for a few minutes as they

laboured over the cannon, each casting a look out of the open gunport towards land from time to time. Murphy caught Bryant's eye as the taller man turned back towards the gun carriage.

"So how long d'ya think they'll keep us 'ere?" he asked.

Bryant shrugged. "All depends on the Lords that run the war. And the French." He smiled. "Still, if you are right about the fighting dead, maybe they'll send us along to the Spanish coast to root them out!"

"Hey, don't joke about it!" Murphy said as he crossed himself. "Them things are real, I swear. I ain't fightin' 'em. Ya can't kill somethin' that is already dead."

Glancing around, Bryant noticed that the conversations of the other gun crews were becoming subdued and he gave Murphy a warning stare. "Keep it quiet, man. You know the Captain doesn't like this talk."

Murphy was ready to argue his point but had the sense to lean forward and whisper. "Okay, look at it this way," he said. "S'pose we get our orders tomorrow and then set sail for Spain, as you say. What are ya goin' to do when we see a French frigate, close to board with 'er and then see a bunch of zombies swingin' over the rails, cutlass and knife in hand? Ya goin' to stand an' fight?"

Standing straight and rubbing his chin, Bryant considered this. "Can zombies swing from ropes? Aren't they all, like, shambling?"

Bryant's sarcasm was not lost on Murphy and the shorter man gave him a withering stare, which was returned with a smile.

"Look, Murphy, you and I have been on this ship for more than a year a piece. The Captain will see us right. He won't go sailing us into anything we can't handle."

It was Murphy's turn to stop and think. "Well, that is very true, my friend. But a Cap'n is only as good as 'is officers and crew. Ain't none of us 'ere whose faced a zombie before."

"That is because they do not exist," muttered Bryant, though Murphy either did not hear him or chose not to, and continued unabated.

"As for the officers, you know what I think about them."

Bryant looked up sharply. "For the love of God, Murphy, hold your tongue!"

Instead, Murphy leaned further forward and whispered. "Corbin, that new Lieutenant? Money troubles. 'Eard it from Jefferies. Signed on to get a big prize – an' ya know what officers who are after the money are like. Might risk anythin' to get it, if there is nothin' for them back at 'ome. An' ya know what..."

A sharp clash resounded across the gun deck as Bryant brought the back of his brush down hard on the rough metal of the cannon, cutting Murphy off. A few curious glances were sent his way but Bryant ignored them.

"Murphy," he said, very seriously. "Imagine all the zombies you want, tell me all the stories you like about the French but never, ever talk about an officer like that. Hell, man, you know what that talk costs!"

Chastened, Murphy went back to work, taking an intense interest in a stain on the side of the gun's carriage.

"And what are you talking to Jefferies for anyway?" Bryant asked. "The man's an out and out thief! And a liar! Take what he says with extreme caution. Better yet, stay away from him! Your life will be easier."

"I s'pose," said Murphy. "Still, ya never answered me. What will ya do when zombies start crawlin' over our deck?"

Bryant sighed. "Well, *if* that happened, I guess we fight. If the Captain tells us to fight, that's what we do. It's what we are all here for." He shook his head. "The Captain won't send us into battle unless he knows we can win. He's too canny for that. The sea is in his blood, you might say."

"Aye, 'e came from the right family all right," Murphy agreed. "Still... hey!"

Murphy was pitched off balance from behind as a large shadow passed through the crowded deck, sending him sprawling beside his cannon. The short man looked up into the twilight of the gun deck.

"Ah, I'm *so* sorry Murphy," said a deep coarse voice that echoed from the wooden walls and ceiling. The work of the nearby gun crews came to a stop as they glanced out of the corner of their eyes towards Murphy and Bryant, anxious to see what was going on and yet not wanting to draw attention to themselves.

"Didn't see you down there. P'raps you should take a bit more care while workin', eh?" The speaker was a large and heavy-set man who, despite the best efforts of the Bosun, looked as if he had not washed for weeks.

"Have a care, Jessop," said Bryant, instinctively lowering his brush to his side where it would not be in immediate view.

"You know," said the newcomer. "I find myself at a loose end. Couldn't 'elp but think that maybe Murphy 'ere would 'ave a few stories about the Frenchies 'e might like to share." He stooped low over the sprawled Murphy. "What about it, eh? What 'ave you 'eard the Frogs are up to this time? Taken over Spain yet, 'ave they? Got some new secret ship that will clobber us good 'an proper?"

Ignoring the few quiet titters from the other gun crews, Bryant moved to the side of his cannon to get Jessop's attention away from Murphy and on to him. Resisting the impulse to push the man's shoulder to get him to turn around, knowing it would likely lead to yet another fight, Bryant instead said "You got nothing better to do, Jessop?"

Jessop adopted a hurt expression. "Hey, no need to come the high an' mighty. I was just askin' Murphy 'ere for a few tales. Nothin' wrong with that."

"If ya lackin' in work, Jessop, I'm certain I can find somethin' for ya to do!" The Bosun's voice lashed across the gun deck like his flogging rope, instantly returning the other gun crews to work. Bryant stood unmoving as Jessop turned round to face the Bosun.

"Ah, Mr Kennedy, I was just on my way when I noticed li'l Murphy 'ere lost 'is balance." He stooped to give a hand to Murphy, who accepted it after a second's hesitation, grinning nervously around the gun deck as he stood to his feet.

"On with ya work, Jessop!" ordered Kennedy. "I don't want any slackin' down here, the Cap'n will be down afore sunset for inspection!"

"Right y'are, Sir!" said Jessop, raising a cocked finger to his brow in salute.

He turned to walk calmly back to his own cannon but brushed Bryant with his shoulder as he went, leaning his weight into the blow. Bryant staggered and immediately flushed with anger. Throwing a punch, he caught Jessop in a right hook straight across the chin with his brush, but the big man instantly flicked his head back, grinning. Ignoring the Bosun's cry for order, Jessop grabbed his opponent by the shoulders and brought a knee up into his stomach, causing Bryant to exhale heavily. Winded, Bryant still managed to reach up with his left hand and grasp Jessop's throat in a tight grip. He maintained the hold as Jessop rained down a solid blow that knocked him to the floor.

Pulling Jessop down with him, Bryant again rammed the heavy brush into the man's face who this time rolled with the hit, and the two of them scrambled for purchase on the wooden floor as each sought to gain an advantage over the other. Jessop strained his neck muscles in an attempt to keep air flowing into his lungs, a task that Bryant was having trouble enough doing himself. Jessop managed to pin Bryant's legs to the floor with one of his own but Bryant twisted again before landing another solid blow. Growling in anger, Jessop responded by heaving the full weight of his body, forcing Bryant to the ground and preparing to rain blow after blow on his opponent.

He raised a fist but, before he could sink it into Bryant's face, his arm was gripped tightly by Kennedy, who dragged him upright and then stood between the two men, bracing them each at arm's length.

"I said that is enough!" he roared.

Jessop's expression was triumphant but Bryant's face showed something close to murderous intent.

"Back to work, Jessop!" Kennedy said. "An' be thankful I don't report ya to the Capt'!" Slouching off, Jessop retreated further down the gun deck where he received a pat on the back from one of his own crew. Shaking his head, Kennedy turned back to Bryant.

"Gods, man, why do ya let 'im provoke ya like that? Ya think I don't 'ave enough trouble down 'ere?"

Rubbing his stomach, Bryant winced. "Sorry, Sir. Won't happen again, Sir."

"Bryant, ya better than this. We all 'ave to deal with bullies like Jessop but ya never, ever throw the first punch. Never! Ya know that if this went before the Cap'n, it would be you for the flogging, not Jessop."

Shame-faced, Bryant just nodded.

"Right. Just reign in that temper. Oh, an' make sure ya do a good job on the gun – I wasn't kiddin' about the Cap'n comin' below later on."

"Kennedy, a moment of your time."

Though he had been aware of high tensions on the far end of the gun deck, Lieutenant Corbin had taken his time climbing down the stairs into the darkness before making his way forward. It was not until the Bosun had passed down the length of the ship, keeping an eye on the working gun crews as he went, that Corbin called out to him.

"Mr Corbin, Sir, what can I do for ya?" Kennedy greeted him.

"More trouble?" Corbin asked, cocking an eye down the gun deck.

"Nothing serious, Sir. Just steam getting let off."

Corbin took Kennedy's arm, drawing him closer as he lowered his voice. "Word from the Captain, Kennedy. Try to keep things running smoothly down here. All these floggings do the crew no good."

The Bosun frowned. "With respect, I know my job well enough, Sir. A fist fight below decks is part an' parcel with ship life. I only bring the worst offenders to your attention and the Cap'n."

"I see. Anything I should know about?" Corbin asked, gesturing down the gun deck.

"Not this time, Sir. See, I don't mind passions spillin' over about the French, or the food, or who stole what from who. It's just the boredom talkin'. But I won't stand for no back chat or insult toward the Capt' and 'is officers. Those would be floggin' words. Ain't no other way it can be."

"Okay, Kennedy. Keep them straight and we'll get you your action."

"Well, they can't keep us moored here forever, right Sir?"

Corbin returned Kennedy's smile. "I am sure we'll be setting sail soon."

CLIMBING THE STAIRS back to the main deck and sunlight, Corbin took a deep breath. He had long since become acclimatised to the darkness and the strange, often powerful, odours below the deck of a ship, but it always came as some small relief when he returned to a place where the wind could freely blow. Only the night before, he had heard Captain Havelock describe the conditions of a Spanish frigate he had once boarded. Such ships might only be properly cleaned when they put into port for refitting and even then it might sometimes be missed. Havelock had spoken of refuse slopping about the lower decks and of air in the hold that was actually lethal if a man were to spend more than a minute within. The ships of the French and American navies were apparently treated in much the same way, with their Captains looking at the fastidious cleanliness of the King's Navy as some strange English affectation. His Captain believed that attendance to hygiene was just as important to the running of a good ship as regular gun drills and, given Havelock's record, Corbin was not about to disagree.

Running his hand along the rail as he walked across the main deck, Corbin marched up to the quarterdeck, where he saw his Captain engaged in observation exercises with the *Whirlwind's* two midshipmen, Buxton and Rawlinson. Both were about fifteen years old and still some way from their Lieutenant's exam, but Corbin knew that Havelock had been impressed by their attention to detail and acceptance of shipboard life. He guessed that by having just two midshipmen on board, rather than the usual gaggle of four or five, a healthy rivalry had sprung up between them which drove their studies on. Taking position at the centre of the quarterdeck, Corbin watched the crew go about their duties as he waited for his Captain to finish the lesson.

After several minutes, Havelock noticed Corbin's regular glances in his direction and set the midshipmen a theoretical navigation exercise that would keep them occupied for some time, before joining his Lieutenant.

"Mr Corbin."

"Sir. I spoke with Kennedy and I am satisfied that he is conducting the discipline of the ship as he should. Only the most serious charges are being brought to us."

"And what is Kennedy's criteria for that?" asked Havelock.

"Disputes between crewmen are resolved by himself. Talk aimed at either yourself or the officers is, umm..."

Havelock smiled. "Try not to take such things personally, Mr Corbin. It is a sailor's God-given right to find fault in those above him." Noticing Corbin had given him a strange look, he continued. "But there is always a line and certain things should never be said out loud, no matter what a man is thinking. The Captain has to be the ultimate authority on a ship and nothing can be permitted to undermine that. I will not pass comment on what a man thinks but if he should make remarks that can be construed as mutinous, that is a fire that must be quenched immediately."

"I think we can rely on Kennedy's discretion, Sir."

"Good. However, I still have concerns about the frequency of these floggings. You do not have to go below deck to sense the tension on this ship."

"The men are all looking for action, and soon. Sometimes I think it would be better if the French just started their invasion now."

"Be careful what you wish for, Mr Corbin!" Havelock said,

laughing. "God and his mistress the sea have a habit of subverting your desires!"

"That may be true, Sir, but I think the French might take one look at the fleet here and sail back home sharp."

Glancing at the assembled warships once again, Havelock had to agree. "However, that is all it is – a display. There is plenty of action to go round, especially for frigates such as the *Whirlwind*. If the French start moving or raiding our ships, likely as not it will be the frigate captains who receive orders first. Spare pity for the officers on board the ships of the line. They were the first to be moored here and will be the last to leave, setting sail only when definite action against the French is expected."

"That is one reason I never found any shame in serving on board a frigate," said Corbin.

"Oh, don't let any of your peers in the Admiralty snub you. For my money, you can keep the glory and prestige of a ship of the line. Frigates, Mr Corbin. They are the true masters of the sea and, without them, the Empire would crumble into oblivion and barbarity. Take a good look at the *Whirlwind*," he gestured towards the bow. "A fine ship with speed of sail and a turn that would humble a vessel half her size. With regular gun drills, she can easily outshoot a French ship of the line and she is nimble enough to keep an enemy on the back foot. What she lacks in heavier and longer-ranged guns, she more than makes up for in speed and agility."

"She certainly is a fine ship, Sir."

"Wait until you have had a full voyage on board her, and you'll say that with some affection," said Havelock, smiling. "The *Whirlwind* is a fine ship and aptly named. She also has a strong crew and a good selection of officers." He gestured to the two midshipmen who had turned back to back so neither could see the calculations of the other. "Look, we even have two of the best midshipmen in the fleet, both eager and attentive. Not always the most obvious traits in lads so young. I am glad I accepted their fathers' recommendations."

"Sir, on that note, I wanted to thank you personally for accepting my commission on board the *Whirlwind*. I do not believe it could have been an easy choice, especially with Wynton and Hague already on ship," Corbin said, referring to the Second and Third Lieutenants of the *Whirlwind*.

Havelock frowned. "Do not try to second guess me, Mr Corbin. I do not judge men out of hand and every one of us can find mistakes in his past. I go by what a man says and what he does. You will have every opportunity to prove yourself on board this ship. As for anything else, well, you know and I know, and that is all that needs to be said about it."

Hanging his head for a second, Corbin tugged the lip of his hat in a salute of respect to his Captain. "Right you are, Sir."

"Good," Havelock said. "Well, that has been said. Now, let us see if our young midshipmen have successfully navigated the Cape, or whether they are on their way to Antarctica. Mr Buxton, Mr Rawlinson, I hope you have completed your task by now!"

# CHAPTER TWO

FOLLOWING THE REGULAR routine of shipboard life, the men of the *Whirlwind* found themselves engaged in their unrelenting chores early in the morning. Some were in their hammocks below decks, having just completed the previous watch, fighting for sleep amidst the continuous noise of their shipmates at work. A dozen men worked on their hands and knees on the main deck, pushing rough stones across a wet deck in an effort to rub it as smooth and clean as their Captain desired, while in the masts more toiled with heavy sails and ropes as the furled sails were checked and rechecked. Most had already partaken of breakfast but the smell of fresh cooked meat with eggs, the one luxury of being moored so close to port, still floated up from the galley.

Below the main deck, more men worked to wash the hold, deploy windsails that would circulate air within the nether regions of the ship, and inventory stores. Warships such as the *HMS Whirlwind* were the most sophisticated and advanced machines of their time, requiring an almost unimaginable amount of man-hours to keep them afloat and seaworthy every day, even while in port.

"Boat approaching larboard!"

The cry from the lookout high above at the top of the mainmast caused Lieutenant Corbin to glance up in some surprise and he walked to the railings of the quarterdeck, extending his telescope. Through the glass, he saw a small rowboat closing with the *Whirlwind*, a team of eight marines straining at the oars while another, a sergeant he presumed, stood at the prow trying to gain the attention of the frigate. A flicker of hope caused Corbin to smile briefly. Of late, the Admiralty had been employing marines to ferry orders to and from the ships moored at Spithead and maybe, just maybe...

"Mr Wynton," he said, getting the attention of the ship's Second Lieutenant, who had been inspecting the results of the crew cleaning the main deck. "Would you be so good as to greet our visitor?"

Though they kept on working at their assigned tasks, Corbin could see every man above deck had at least half an eye on Wynton as he stood to the railings and ordered a rope ladder down the side of the ship. It was not long before men started rising from below decks, suddenly having found an important job to do within ear shot of the Marine Sergeant as he clambered up the hull of the *Whirlwind*.

The Sergeant, his bright red uniform seeming almost out of place among the dark blues of the *Whirlwind's* officers and the rather more varied clothes of the crew, saluted Wynton sharply and then produced a sealed pouch which he gave to the Lieutenant. He then turned around sharply and disappeared down the side of the ship as quickly as he had arrived, leaving Wynton to approach Corbin, who met him down the stairs from the quarterdeck. The younger Lieutenant had a gleam in his eyes, clearly sharing the same hopes as Corbin.

"Keep the men calm, Mr Wynton," said Corbin in a low voice. "No need to get them excited until we know what is in here."

"Right you are, Mr Corbin," Wynton said before turning to the crew, many of whom had halted their work altogether as curiosity overcame them. "Okay, men, no one told you to stop! Back to it!"

DESCENDING INTO THE darkness below deck, Corbin could not keep a slight spring from his stride as he hurried to the stern of the ship and the Captain's quarters. He found himself just as eager to discover if they had been given new orders as any of the crew but resolved not to show any outward indications of excitement. There were some things an officer could not be seen to indulge in.

Noticing no one waiting in the small anteroom known as the coach, Corbin passed straight through to the doors of the great cabin and knocked. He was greeted a few seconds later by Havelock's voice bidding him enter.

Inside, the Captain sat at a large oak table before the large seven-paned window through which streamed the bright sun-lit day, causing Corbin to blink after having just got used to the darkness of the rest of the upper deck. Havelock was scribbling another entry in the ship's log, a leather bound tome sacred to all the ship's officers while the remains of his breakfast lay adrift on the great table. He spoke without looking up at his Lieutenant.

"Yes, Mr Corbin? What can I do for you?"

Corbin could not help but smile as he spoke. "Captain, the marines just arrived bearing a message. Orders?"

Havelock looked up at this news. "Perhaps, Mr Corbin, perhaps. But let us not get ahead of ourselves." Despite the Captain's calmness, Corbin could sense a change in his demeanour as Havelock stood up and walked round the table. He took the offered pouch and broke the seal after a momentary inspection. Corbin had to fight from fidgeting as silence descended on the great cabin while the Captain read the letter, with only the sounds of gulls and the sea lapping against the hull breaking the monotony. Presently, Havelock looked up from the letter and smiled.

"Mr Corbin, our hopes and prayers have been answered!"

"We are to set sail?"

"With the tide on the morrow. And we have a good chance of action – there is a French frigate that the Admiralty needs sinking. Here..." He offered the letter to Corbin who anxiously scanned its contents.

*You are hereby required and directed to proceed without loss of time in His Majesty's Ship under your command to the Cape of Good Hope for the purpose of intercepting the French frigate* Elita, *destroying or taking her as prize.*

*The* Elita *has this past three months sunk or captured sixteen merchant vessels sailing around the Cape and has become a liability to the Empire's continued shipping. She is believed to be under the command of a Captain Guillot, formerly of the Boudeuse. Expect no reinforcements in Southern waters.*

*List of merchant shipping sunk or captured by the* Elita *proceeds...*

"Captain..." he began to ask but Havelock held up a hand.

"There is much to discuss, Mr Corbin, but I believe we would be better off doing that when others are present. If you would be so good as to request the presence of the other officers and midshipmen to my table tonight, all questions can be answered then. In the meantime, make preparations to sail and inform the purser that if he requires anything for the stores, he has precious little time. Ah, and please ask my steward to attend immediately – this will be our last chance to avail ourselves of food from shore and I believe that officer and jack alike will be grateful of a real meal before we start on what we have in the galley."

"Yes, Captain. I'll attend to it."

"Excellent. For my part, I must consult the charts of the Southern oceans and our hunting grounds."

THOUGH LIEUTENANT CORBIN had been careful not to mention any specifics of the *Whirlwind's* new mission, his subsequent orders to the crew and officers left no one in any doubt that the ship was to set sail very soon. Consequently, rumours started to run rampant.

The sceptical were quick to point out that the *Whirlwind*, a single frigate, had been assigned to nothing more than convoy duty, protecting some fat merchants on a lonely piece of the sea that would never see any French flag sailing. The doomsayers scoffed at this, opining that the French had already won the war in Spain and were even now loading up ships ready for invasion of England. The King's Navy would be outnumbered at least three to one and the entire fleet would be at the bottom of the channel within a week. Some of the more optimistic actually liked this idea, cheered by the thought of mere three-to-one odds, and confident that a single British ship could withstand the battering of a half dozen French vessels and still remain victorious. The excitable predicted that the *Whirlwind* was the lead element in a reconnaissance squadron that would hunt down and locate the French fleet, tying it up with a series of dashing and heroic actions until the main bulk of the King's Navy could be brought to bear.

Then there were those like Murphy, who happily adopted the latest rumour they heard, then embellished it. Fleets of French ships suddenly grew extended holds crammed full of dead men walking, ready to be unleashed on England's green soil. Stories of a coming invasion became tales of French soldiers (and their zombies, of course) already landing in Yorkshire and setting fire to entire towns. Rumours of French soldiers sweeping the British out of Spain became an account of how the whole of Europe was under the sway of Napoleon – who had recently been turned into an ever-living zombie.

Each new rumour was as readily accepted as the last but even those predicting doom began to work doubly hard as the long stay at Spithead drew rapidly to a close. The extra ration of rum at the end of the day, granted by Havelock, went down especially well, and most of the crew gathered in a toast to their Captain, whom they wished good health and good luck in the coming voyage.

In the great cabin, the mood was similarly buoyant, as officers and midshipmen ate pork with fresh vegetables in a feast prepared by the Captain's steward, and enjoyed the free-flowing wine. Havelock sat at the head of the table, listening to his officers talk among themselves but though he had intended to have the orders read aloud at the end of the meal, he could sense the growing anticipation of those around him and presently gave Corbin the nod to pass on the words of the Admiralty. The midshipmen and other two lieutenants hung onto every one of Corbin's words as he read the letter but it did not take long for the questions and comments to come pouring in after he had finished.

"With luck, the French will not expect a warship in the area if their spies in Portsmouth are watching the fleet," said Third Lieutenant Hague.

Havelock smiled. "Do not count on that, Mr Hague. It is always best to imagine that French spies are at least as good as those we have in Spain and France. They'll notice us leave all right."

Hague snorted. "Filthy spies. That is no way to fight a war, buried in Portsmouth while counting masts."

"And what about our British spies in Paris and Calais?" asked the Captain jovially. "Those brave and noble fellows who tell us what Napoleon is up to, as they constantly wait for a knife in the back?"

"That's different," Hague sniffed, causing everyone at the table to laugh.

"What do we know of the *Elita*?" asked Corbin. "Have you seen her before, Captain?"

"Once," Havelock said. "While she was in port at Brest. A two-decker, likely very fast. Fourth-rater by our standards. Fifty guns, at least."

The table was silent for a few seconds as they digested this information. According to their Captain, the *Elita* was larger than the *Whirlwind*, with more than half as many cannon again and possibly three times the crew.

"The Frogs are building more ships that way," said Hague. "Able to turn sharply with the wind behind them while carrying enough guns to worry a third-rater. When I was last in London I heard tales of the Admiralty commissioning the design of similar ships. Give it a few years and all frigates will be built that way."

"Are they copying the Americans?" Midshipman Rawlinson asked, his round and youthful face fired by the prospect of action and not at all daunted by the news of their quarry's size.

"In concept, yes," said Havelock. "They are what the Americans call super-frigates, only slightly larger than a ship like the *Whirlwind* and yet packed to the gills with cannon and men. The hull and mast design will be all French though, and so should be respected. Hull and masts are what will keep the *Elita* nimble, rather than having all that extra weight robbing her of agility. Such ships are actually quite impressive."

"But are British ships not superior to those of the French?" Rawlinson asked. "Or those of any other nation?"

Havelock sipped his wine before answering but all eyes were on him. "No. Our crews are better trained and better disciplined. Our ships are kept in better working order – and that makes all the difference. However, ship for ship, you have to assume the French and Americans, even the Spanish, are at least our equals. They have some very clever naval architects overseas." He noticed that not all around the table had been convinced by his words. "Look at it this way. If we capture the *Elita*, she will join the King's Navy – you might even get a chance to serve on her later in your careers!"

This comment, at least, was joined with smiles as each man considered his future after this mission. If it succeeded, their careers were guaranteed for at least a while.

"What about this Guillot, the *Elita's* Captain. Do you know the man?" Corbin asked.

"No. That means he is either new and inexperienced, or he has been away from France for a long time, in which case he might be immensely wise in the ways of the sea." Havelock smiled at his officers. "Take your pick. Of course, it might just be that I do not know of every captain out there flying under the Tricolore!"

"Well, in the coming fight, I would rather be here, on the *Whirlwind*, serving under you, Captain, than this Guillot," said Hague.

"Flattery will only get you so far," said Havelock with a grin. "Still, French captains should have our respect every bit as much as their ships do. You should always go into battle assuming your enemy is at least as smart as you are. The difference between he and I will be marked in our crews. Even though we still use press-gangs, our crews are far more disciplined. Every man knows exactly what to do when the cannon start firing and the wood starts splintering. The same cannot be said for those who serve under a French captain. If you ever find yourself wondering why I have ordered one drill or another, your answer lies there."

"Captain, how do you intend to fight the *Elita*? There must be a way to even the odds," said Hague.

"Well, first we have to find her but that will be a relatively simple matter so long as she continues to hunt merchantmen. As for battle..." Havelock paused, considering. "In a straight duel, she outguns us and probably has heavier guns that can out range ours. We cannot rely on superior manoeuvrability, though in those stakes I would tend to bet on the *Whirlwind*. We must also avoid any boarding action until the *Elita* has been pounded into submission, as she also has sheer weight of numbers on her side. No, we must endeavour to close range as quickly as possible, sailing straight into her guns if necessary, then keep her off balance until the job is done."

"I believe that is what Lord Nelson would do," said Corbin with a smile, causing everyone to raise their glass in salute of the famous admiral.

"I heard that Nelson said a brawl in the ocean is preferable to a straight line duel," said Rawlinson, drawing more than one incredulous gaze from the assembled officers.

Havelock smiled. "Well, there is a bit more to it than that, and far be it for me to criticise such a man as Admiral Nelson, but he does have a tendency to simplify things somewhat. If you have made your approach properly and caught your enemy off guard or without the wind, trained your crew to outshoot his, have officers and midshipmen who will keep the men steady, and have not tested Lady Luck too often in the past – then maybe, just maybe, drawing alongside the enemy and hammering constantly at him will carry the day."

"Is this not a job for two frigates, or even a small fleet?" Second Lieutenant Wynton asked, provoking Corbin to raise his eyebrows at the suggestion being raised out loud. Havelock was quick to counter the thought.

"The Admiralty clearly wants to keep as many ships at Spithead as possible, in preparation for the French invasion. Anyway," he grinned, "we have many counts in our favour. Remember, our crew are, by far, better trained. The *Elita* could have the biggest guns in the French fleet, but they will do them no good if they can only be fired once for every two salvoes we let fly. We will likely be in a position to dictate when and how the battle is fought – we will not even consider engaging unless we have the wind. The *Elita* will have been at sea for many months, while we are fresh. Finally, the *Elita* is worth a great deal of prize money if she can be captured so do not underestimate the effect of that on the efficiency of our crew."

The last comment was met with laughter and not a little avarice, as everyone round the table stood to gain a great deal more than any of the crew. Hague raised his glass to Corbin "Well, that will do us all grand I think, and help some of us out a great deal, eh, Mr Corbin?" He said.

Corbin winced slightly and glanced at his Captain who deliberately avoided eye contact. He sighed. "It is true, Mr Hague, I am in need of funds. A small matter of accrued debts in the service of Lord Ashby and some very ill-advised investments to counter them."

"Gambling?" Wynton asked, suddenly sombre.

"Aye, I must confess Mr Wynton, gambling was the poor route I chose to reverse my fortunes."

"Has happened to many of us," said Wynton. "Unfortunately, gambling tends to work best when you do not have desperate need of money."

"Thems that have the money are those who can make the best stakes at cards," said Rawlinson.

"That's right lad," said Wynton. "And that's a lesson you should remember."

Hague, fuelled by a growing amount of wine, slapped Corbin on the back. "Never mind, Mr Corbin! We have our mission and the prize money is in sight! We have the best ship, the best crew and the best Captain for the job!"

"That much is true," said Wynton. He looked seriously at the other two lieutenants and the midshipmen. "Mark my words, all of you. We have a true seaman in our Captain, it is in his blood. You all heard of the Admiral Havelock?"

The lieutenants all nodded but Rawlinson and his fellow midshipman Buxton looked quizzically at Wynton, wanting to know more but hesitant to voice their ignorance. Wynton picked up on their expressions, and after pouring more wine for everyone, settled back in his seat, shifting to make himself comfortable against the hard wood.

"Well, the Captain's grandfather was also in the navy – made Admiral, he did. Led a squadron of three frigates against a French fleet off Guadeloupe. Now, he was outnumbered, to be sure, with four Froggie ships matched against his. But two of them were also ships of the line, huge great vessels that dwarfed his frigates."

The midshipmen looked incredulously at Havelock and then back to Wynton. "How could he have possibly fought against them?" Buxton asked.

"By all rights, he should have turned tail and ran, right?" said Wynton. "Well lad, that is what makes the difference between the likes of you and me, and a true hero. We might have scuttled off to find a squadron of third-raters and reported the position of the French, letting others do the fighting. But not Admiral Havelock. Oh, no. He approaches them, bold as brass, and they don't know what to make of him. He gets right up behind the two big warships and lets loose, sinking one and detonating the magazine of the other, with his first salvo, I heard. The two French frigates were shocked to inaction and quickly overwhelmed, then boarded. The whole thing took less than an hour and netted all crews a handsome prize."

Corbin smiled at hearing the story retold and he joined in with the applause of the others at its conclusion. He noted, however, that his Captain seemed distinctly uncomfortable listening to the story of his grandfather. Wynton had stood up, taking Corbin's attention as he proposed a toast.

"Gentlemen, I give you Admiral Havelock!"

"Admiral Havelock!" They chimed in, raising their glasses.

"For my money, a man every equal to Nelson himself!" Wynton said, who then noticed Hague's bemused smile. "I'm telling you, Nelson gets the glory these days – not that he does not deserve it – but there are others in His Majesty's Navy who are every bit as worthy."

Corbin grabbed the wine bottle and gestured for Wynton's glass. "Come, Mr Wynton," he said. "Let me refill you. Enough of Nelson, let us get back to the matter of the French quarry we will be chasing!"

Wynton sat down heavily in his seat and offered his glass. Corbin glanced at his Captain from the corner of his eye very briefly and was a little surprised, though gratified, to see Havelock give him an almost imperceptible nod of thanks for having changed the subject. He had not known what gave Havelock any discomfort with regards to his grandfather but Corbin had considered it his duty to ease the Captain's burden, whatever it might have been.

"What guns will the *Elita* be carrying?" Hague said, not catching the exchange between Corbin and his Captain. "How will they compare to our twelve-pounders?"

Havelock coughed, then answered. "Having two decks allows you to mount much heavier cannon behind the lower gun ports, as it balances your centre of gravity – you all remember the story of the *Mary Rose*, right? Classic case of a ship toppling over too far because of the weight of its armament. Still, we could be looking at guns as heavy as thirty-six pounders."

Wynton whistled. "I've only seen guns that large on a ship of the line."

"Well, that is the point, really," said Havelock. "That is why they are nicknamed super-frigates. I could tell you that she won't have many thirty-six pounders – but then I would have to admit that she will also mount twenty-four pounders. There may be a few guns, towards the stern or bow, that match ours but only on the upper gun deck. Make no mistake though, she is a powerful vessel."

"Forgive me, Captain," said Buxton. "But why does everybody here not think that we are beaten before we start? With guns like that, she can start firing long before we can and we should be hit before we even get into range."

Havelock opened his mouth to answer but was cut off by Hague. Corbin stifled a grin as Havelock smiled and waved Hague on, who was completely unaware that he had interrupted his Captain. "Lad, it is never as simple as that. First off, the French have got to shoot straight to hit you at range, which is never a given." Hague started counting off the points on his fingers. "Then, they have to reload, and the Froggie crews are not noted for their love of hard work. Our men will shoot straighter and quicker than them on any day of the week – it does not matter if you have the biggest cannon in the world, if your enemy is constantly pounding at you. Third, you have to point your guns towards the enemy in order to fire. And I'll lay good money that the Captain here will have a surprise or two for this *Elita*."

The evening continued and as the wine began to take its toll on the officers, the muffled singing of the crew elsewhere in the ship prompted them to join in with their own songs, Wynton leading the choruses with undisguised gusto. Finally, Havelock rapped his knuckles on the table to get their attention.

"My friends," he said. "We have a large task ahead of us, though it is one that I have no doubt we can complete, with the honour and dignity befitting one of His Majesty's Ships. We have escaped a long and drawn out wait here at Spithead, and in return, will demonstrate to the Admiralty just why the *Whirlwind* is one of the premier ships of the entire fleet!"

This raised a cheer from all the officers and Havelock had to raise a hand to continue, though he did so with a smile. "Get a good night's sleep, for we have a lot of work ahead of us tomorrow. Mr Corbin, would you be so good as to double-check the watches before you turn in. Whose is it now?"

"That would be Mr Buxton, Captain," said Corbin.

"Ah, that is why you were laying low on the wine, Mr Buxton," said Havelock. "Good man. We enjoy our drink in the King's Navy, but duty must always come first. Very well, I bid you all goodnight!"

As one, the officers all stood and thanked their Captain before leaving. Corbin was the last to reach the door and he hesitated before leaving the great cabin.

"Something, Mr Corbin?" Havelock asked.

Corbin opened his mouth to answer then closed it again, thinking better. He paused and noticed his Captain's raised eyebrows. Closing the door, he turned back to Havelock. "Well, Sir," he said.

"You have doubts?"

"Yes, Sir. A few."

"Well, out with it man. I can spare you a few more minutes," Havelock said.

"Well... I understand that the Admiralty wants to keep as many ships here in readiness for anything the French do. But the *Whirlwind* is a fifth-rate ship. To put it up against one of these super-frigates, alone, seems folly. Do we really have a chance?"

"Oh, we have a chance, Mr Corbin," Havelock said quickly. "There is always a chance. However, I do understand and even, to a point, share your concern. The best ship to send against the *Elita* would be a sprightly third-rater, something that can keep up with her and yet still deliver a knockout blow. Mind you, that is exactly the sort of ship the Admiralty wants in British waters right now."

"I thought we might have been joined by another frigate, at least."

"Yes, that would have been preferable. But those are not the cards we have been dealt, Mr Corbin. We have our orders and must believe the Admiralty has its reasons for sending the *Whirlwind* and no other. It is entirely possible that those orders omitted some interesting piece of information that the Admiralty knows and we do not. Perhaps the *Elita* is ravaged by plague and has become short-crewed. Perhaps she has already been engaged by a British ship and has had trouble making repairs. Who knows?"

"Aye, you are right, Captain. If we were to second guess the Admiralty, we might all go mad."

"Oh, that is certain, Mr Corbin! What goes on in the Mad House, generally, could make anyone doubt their own senses. That said, we can normally trust our orders when it comes to engaging the French. Throughout the long years of war with France, the King's Navy has yet to suffer any truly significant losses." Havelock paused for a few seconds before continuing. "There is, however, something more pressing that concerns me."

When Havelock did not continue at once, Corbin prompted him. "Sir?"

"It is this list of ships that have been attacked, sunk or captured by the *Elita*," said Havelock. "Sixteen in three months? That is incredible good fortune for the French. Either the merchants are lining up to be taken or this Guillot is a very skilled captain. There is, however, one other possibility..."

It took Corbin just a second to see where his captain was heading. "There is more than one ship doing the raiding."

"Very good, Mr Corbin," Havelock said. "Yes, we could be sailing into a small French fleet. And if they are all fourth-raters like the *Elita*, we may be voyaging into a lot of trouble." He noticed Corbin's troubled face and then smiled slightly. "Take heart, Lieutenant. There are plenty of natural harbours along the African coast where the *Elita* may be re-supplying, allowing it to stay on station for an extended period while intercepting all merchants who must sail in the area. It may turn out that we are not even facing a skilled captain, just a lucky one. If that is the case, I think we can be luckier."

"I pray that is correct, Sir."

"You've served on a frigate before, Mr Corbin. You know it takes more than heavy guns and a fair wind to win battles with these ships."

"Yes, Sir. In that regard, I have few doubts. The *Whirlwind* is a good ship with a fine crew."

"And they'll be better by the time we reach our hunting grounds," said Havelock. "Even with the right winds, we will be voyaging for a good six weeks before we will have any chance of sighting the *Elita*. It is my intention to practise the men during that time. As well as sharpening them for the coming battle, it will also help keep their minds occupied during what will hopefully be an otherwise uneventful journey."

"As you say, Sir. Captain, there was one other thing..."

Havelock noticed his Lieutenant's hesitancy and cocked his head. "Yes, Mr Corbin?"

"You seemed a little perturbed when mention was made of your grandfather."

If anything, Corbin thought his Captain looked even more uncomfortable now. "A topic for another time, Mr Corbin," he said, a little briskly. "Check the watches, as ordered, then turn in. I want every man above deck at first light tomorrow. We'll announce our orders to them then, before setting sail. We can afford for the rumours to run wild until then."

"Yes, Captain. Goodnight, Captain," Corbin said, as respectfully as he could muster. Havelock nodded in acknowledgement, prompting Corbin to leave the great cabin and return to the main deck to monitor the changing watch.

# CHAPTER THREE

As THE CREW of the *Whirlwind* gathered on the main deck, the air seemed to crackle with excitement and anticipation. By now every man had heard of the visiting Marine Sergeant and the letter that had been handed to the Captain, and few believed this could mean anything other than new orders with a good possibility of action against the enemy. Regardless of whether they would actually face the French in battle, every man was grateful that their stay at Spithead seemed to be over.

Few secrets could be kept long on board the cramped environment of a warship, but rumours and tall tales could easily subvert the truth when it was spoken. So, though there were men who had witnessed the purser make the final preparations for the long voyage, had even toiled to bring new provisions on board, their calculations or estimations on how long a voyage was expected carried less weight than another sailor who opined that hammering the French in the Mediterranean was their final goal, especially if he said it louder and with more conviction. Not every one was willing to accept what another said at face value, of course, and more than one of the crew bore the marks of a fist-fight as impassioned opinions had spun out of hand during the night.

Nearly three hundred souls made up the full complement of the *Whirlwind*, packed into two decks below the reach of sunlight. Now, they filled the main deck and hung from the main mast, standing shoulder-to-shoulder as they waited patiently for their Captain's address. With so many men gathered in one place, new opportunities for rumour mongering and storytelling abounded, and a quiet hubbub rolled with an irregular rhythm over the deck.

On the quarterdeck, Lieutenants Wynton and Hague stood at attention alongside the midshipmen, overseeing the crew as they too, waited. The Captain and Corbin stood behind them, near the prow of the ship, ostensibly discussing last minute changes and provisions, though it was entirely within Havelock's style to use the time to build up anticipation within his crew. As the muttering of the crew steadily grew in volume, it was clear that any wish to motivate them was working. When Havelock judged the moment right, he shook Corbin's hand and then walked purposefully across the quarterdeck to face his crew. Hands placed in a relaxed manner on the wooden railing before him, Havelock leaned forward slightly as he spoke.

"Men of the *Whirlwind*, your time idling here is over! We are about to set sail! Do you have it in your hearts to fight against the French?"

A loud and raucous cheer immediately met his words, persisting until he raised a hand. The crew fell silent almost immediately, as much out of curiosity for the mission as respect for their Captain.

"That is good! We have been ordered to the South Atlantic where we are to intercept the French frigate *Elita*. We have the permission of the Admiralty to sink her but it is my intention to take her as prize!"

Again, cheers erupted across the deck, this time fuelled by avarice and self-interest. Though most members of the crew would receive a tiny fraction of the prize money for a captured ship compared to any of the officers, it would still likely be far more wealth than they might earn in a year of hard toil anywhere else. This was the reason that even press ganged crew tended to stay on board, once they had become accustomed to a life at sea.

Holding a hand up once more, Havelock regained his crew's attention, wanting to focus them on duty as much as the promise of riches.

"It seems the crew of this French ship believe they are the terror of the waves!" A few boos and jeers greeted this news as Havelock continued. "Thus far, the *Elita* has been responsible for the loss of more than a dozen English merchant vessels, all plundered or sunk. Right now, the crew of that French frigate are laughing at us, if you please!"

Havelock stood up straight, placing his hands behind his back as he mustered all the dignity he could.

"Shipmates, I say to you, that French crew has yet to meet a real English ship of war!" The massed cheer began once again at these words and Havelock smiled at his crew. "They think they prove their mettle by attacking merchant ships with but a couple of small guns! In a few short weeks, we will be in their hunting grounds and then we'll give them something to think about! We'll show them how His Majesty's *Whirlwind* fights, aye, and her crew too!"

The growing cries from the crew threatened to drown out Havelock's words; his eyes flickered across the deck, enjoying the moment, not willing to disrupt their enthusiasm as sailors congratulated one another and punched the air with excitement. Having one more thing to say, Havelock raised his hand and, again, received the rapt attention of his crew.

"Men of the *Whirlwind*, I ask for nothing less than your very best. We will soon be facing the enemy and I do not intend for us to be found wanting. Remember, you serve the greatest Navy the world has ever seen, on board one of its finest ships. Whatever hazards we meet, a Frenchman is but a Frenchman and we have always beaten him! Do your duty! God save King George!"

Havelock grinned openly as the crew responded to his speech with a roar that was almost terrifying in its volume. He turned to Corbin.

"Mr Corbin, would you be so good as to set us on our way?"

The Lieutenant's grin matched Havelock's, the man clearly as eager as his Captain at the prospect of action.

"Aye, Sir, with pleasure."

Havelock watched Lieutenants Hague and Wynton descend to the main deck with the midshipmen as they relayed Corbin's orders and the crew of the *Whirlwind* sprang from their perches to set the frigate in motion.

"Prepare to weigh anchor!"

"Stand by to loose the topsail!"

"Weigh anchor, jump to it!"

"Loose the staysail!"

"Loose the topsail! Put your backs into it!"

As wind began to fill the lowering sails of the *Whirlwind* and the frigate began to slowly pick up speed across the low waves, Havelock paced slowly to the stern of the ship, looking at the coast as it began, gradually, to recede from view. The cry of gulls milling above the masts mixed with the sound of the sea being split in two by the sharp prow of his ship and he breathed deeply, enjoying the familiar saltiness of the water anew as he looked forward to another voyage. He listened to the crew, feeling the natural rhythms of the ship as they went about their work in concert with shipmate, officer, sea and wind. Together, the entire vessel and its complement were like a single organism, one unit that, through him, would do the bidding of King and country. He paced back to the railings above the main deck but his eyes were focussed past the crew and sails, to the sea that lay beyond.

"On our way Captain, no problems reported," said Corbin as he returned to the Captain's side, satisfied that everything on board the *Whirlwind* was proceeding as it should.

"Very good, Mr Corbin," said Havelock but he did not turn to the Lieutenant, simply keeping his gaze on the horizon. Corbin was about to ask a question but noticed the faraway look in the other man's eyes. Picking up the lead, he stood quietly next to Havelock, both with hands behind their backs as they took in the wide panorama of the sea, conscious that the distance between them and land grew by the minute.

Presently, without changing the direction of his gaze, Havelock spoke, his voice almost soft. "You know, Mr Corbin, it is a funny thing."

"Sir?"

"I have faced stormy seas with waves crashing down onto the deck, I have met the French in battle and won, and I have dined with Admirals as they thanked me for a job well done. And yet... it is this moment, just as we set sail, that I have enjoyed every bit as much as the rest. It is funny, that so simple a thing could bring so much satisfaction."

Corbin smiled. "It is the sea, Sir. You have it in your blood. I think we all feel this way when first setting out on a new voyage."

"I pity those who are land bound, all those lords and army officers, no matter how privileged, who will never truly understand what it means to be on a ship like this, now, just as we set sail. It is more than a love for the sea, Mr Corbin. It is the discovery of what lies beyond the horizon, the parting of the veil, the knowledge that where we travel, few men have gone before us. Who knows what awaits us south? Victory? Disappointment? A sound thrashing?"

"Well, victory, I would wager, Sir."

"Aye, I think you may be right, Mr Corbin," said Havelock with a grin. "Gods, I would not be anywhere else!"

They stood together for a few minutes longer, watching the crew master the waves by sail and helm. Feeling he had luxuriated enough, Havelock turned to the Lieutenant. "As soon as we reach the Channel, let us have an hour's practice with the guns, Mr Corbin. We'll start as we mean to go on. By the time we meet the *Elita*, I want us to have the best practiced gun crews in the Navy."

"You'll have it, Sir," said Corbin before he faced the main deck to issue the orders. "Hands to quarters! Mr Hague, run out the guns!"

Once again, the crew of the *Whirlwind* sprang into action again, this time to a very different rhythm.

CLINGING TO THE wooden beams running across the ceiling for support, Bryant steadied himself against the swaying of the ship, taking care not to let the wet stairs send him crashing to the floor of the upper deck. Drenched through, he staggered past his cannon to join a group of men who were already feasting on a meal of beef stew and rum. Reaching behind his collar, he stripped his shirt off and wrung it in his hands, cold water pouring onto the wooden floor. The trickle ran under the feet of the sitting men as it made its way to drainage seams along the side of the deck.

"Rainin', is it?" asked Murphy, causing some of the other men to chuckle at Bryant's misfortune.

Bryant playfully shoved him, causing the smaller man to scramble in order to keep his food on its square tray. "Hey!" cried Murphy. "Just jokin'! An' anyway, look what I saved for you 'ere. Complements of 'is Majesty."

Bryant's eyes lit up as Murphy threw aside a cloth, revealing a plate of stew he had kept by for the larger man. Sitting down, Bryant grabbed the plate with obvious relish.

"Ah, you're a good shipmate, Murphy."

A young man with a mop of ginger hair leaned forward into the circle of the gathered men. Brooks had been assigned to Bryant's and Murphy's gun crew soon after the *Whirlwind* had set sail and, upon revealing that this was his first time at sea, had been taken under their collective wing.

"So, Bryant, is it true that we're already in sight of the African coast?" he asked.

Bryant looked up from his meal with a puzzled look "We've barely been at sea for a week. What makes you think we have already made Africa?"

"I was listenin' to Jefferies and his mates talkin' back there," he said, indicating the stern of the ship.

"Heavens," said Bryant as he rolled his eyes. "What is it with you and Murphy? I keep telling the two of you, pay no attention to what Jefferies says. He may sound as though he knows what he is talking about but he knows as much about navigation as any of the ship's rats. He's barely been on more voyages than you, young Brooks."

Brooks actually looked a little crestfallen at this news. "So where are we then?"

"Somewhere off Southern Spain. I heard the Lieutenant mention something about the Cape of Trafalgar earlier this evening. Perhaps someone here has got a map we can look at?"

He was greeted by blank stares and a few heads shaking.

"Perhaps not," he said, sighing as he went back to his food. Across the deck, casting eerie shadows from the few swaying lanterns placed at strategic positions in the rafters, another couple of gun crews had joined each other for food and some of them had begun singing, clearly enjoying their rum before starting their meals.

"So, Brooks, this really your first time at sea?" A weathered looking man seated to Bryant's left asked.

"Ah, yes, yes it is," said Brooks, vaguely wondering if he was being led down a path. As a new face, and one unfamiliar with the ways of a ship of war at that, he had already faced his fair share of ribbing, though most of it had been good-natured.

"You've been bearin' up well," the sailor remarked.

"Ah, Brooks is a natural born seaman!" Bryant declared. "Got his sea legs within hours!"

"That's good," said the sailor. "But it takes more than holdin' your guts steady to make a good seaman."

"Well give 'im a chance!" Murphy chipped in. "The lad's only been 'ere for a few days!"

"That's fair," conceded the sailor. "You pressed into this, boy?"

"Umm, no." Brooks said. "Volunteered. Always wanted to sail. And do my part, fightin' the French. Besides, if you live in Portsmouth, you're better off volunteerin' rather than waitin' for the gangs to come round."

Bryant reached forward and rustled Brooks' unkempt hair. "A real patriot, this one!" He turned to Murphy, who had started to lean backwards, an ear clearly cocked to a conversation among the group of men behind them. Bryant realised that the sporadic singing earlier had now stopped as the other gun crews talked in quieter tones, with some urgency, he thought.

"Murphy, wind your neck back in!" he said.

"Hush!" Murphy waved him back. "They're talkin' 'bout the Cap'n!"

Bryant inwardly groaned but could not help but bend an ear himself. He quickly identified the hard voice of Jessop.

"Jefferies, yer a lyin' sod, an' we all know it!"

"Hey, listen to what I tell ya, or don't – all the same to me." Bryant had to strain to catch everything that Jefferies said. The man was quickly prompted by the others in his group to continue, despite Jessop's scepticism.

"Like I was sayin', there's a black cloud hangin' over 'Avelock. When I was servin' on the Dorchester an' 'Avelock was nothin' more than a lieutenant, we used to call it 'Avelock's Curse." Jefferies looked about his listeners with a certain satisfaction as he realised he had them hooked.

"What sort of curse is that, then?" asked one.

"Little things at first," said Jefferies. "A man slips an' falls to his death from the mainmast. Someone falls overboard an' no one notices for an hour. Sealed barrels o' pork go bad."

Jefferies took a swig from his metal cup as the others digested this information. "Then the weather turns against us, see, sails start shreddin', French ships start turnin' up when the sea should be clear."

"You survived though," pointed out Jessop.

"Well, yeah. 'Ad a good Cap'n back then."

One of the other men leaned forward, rubbing his chin. "There may be somethin' in this, you know," he said. "We've all 'eard about the Cap'n's grandfather, the great Adm'ral 'Avelock. Well, when I was last in Portsmouth, I over'eard a bunch of old soldiers who had once served on ship with 'im."

"The Cap'n?" Jefferies asked.

"Nah, you fool, the Adm'ral. Anyway, they said 'is great victory in the Caribbean was nothin' of the sort. 'E didn't go into battle against a full French fleet and 'e didn't win in less than hour, as they say now."

"So, what happened?" Jessop prompted.

"Well, an' this is just the soldiers talkin', mind. I 'eard that 'e sailed into a French port that was just launchin' a bunch of colony ships – you know, full of decent folk lookin' to make a life for themselves on one of the other islands. Caught the French nappin' and began sinkin' the colony ships until the French port surrendered. But that didn't 'appen until a lot of innocent women and children were sent to the bottom."

The men around him started shaking their heads. "Dirty business that."

"Dirtier that 'e got made Adm'ral for it."

"An' that the Cap'n can trade on the name – no guessin' that granddaddy's position 'elped 'im get a Cap'n's post," said Jessop. He glanced around the deck and noticed the interest his group had gained among Bryant's men. "Family ties like that matter more to the Lords runnin' the navy than bein' a good officer. You agree, don't you, Bryant?" he called.

Murphy scrambled back to his food, hunching over his plate. Bryant refused to meet Jessop's eye but said "That talk ain't wise, Jessop."

"Oh, really?" Jessop grinned as he stood and took two steps towards Bryant, bracing himself against the low ceiling to steady himself against the ship's motion. "Perhaps you would be likin' to do somethin' about it?"

Bryant turned to face Jessop, giving him a baleful look. "I'm eating. Besides, it won't be me that hangs you for mutinous talk."

A grin crept across Jessop's face as he stared hard at Bryant, who just shook his head and went back to his food, not wanting to play Jessop's game. He glanced up as a newcomer walked towards them. Dwarfed by most of the sailors on the main deck, yet distinctive in his simple dark blue uniform, Midshipman Rawlinson picked his way out of the shadows and walked up to the two antagonists.

"Jessop, good. Please come with me," he said.

"Why?" Jessop shifted his mass as he spoke, so that by bracing an arm against one of the rafters running above his head, he leaned over the midshipman in an attempt to intimidate the young man. Rawlinson blinked, not fully prepared for Jessop's insolence.

"Hobbs has reported some missing property, a matter of three shillings and a bone pipe. We are going to look into your belongings," he said formerly.

"I ain't stolen' nothin'.," said Jessop turning his back on Rawlinson. "'Sides, I'm busy right now. Come back when I've finished eatin', boy."

"Sir!" The smirks of Jessop's friends were immediately cut short by the bark of Corbin's voice, as the Lieutenant stepped into the light from the stairs to the main deck. Though wet through with droplets of water streaming from his hat, his anger was unmistakable. He marched straight up to Jessop, completely unafraid of the larger man's muscles and demeanour.

"You will address Midshipman Rawlinson as Sir!" Corbin said, voice suddenly hardened from his usual manner. "Bosun!" he called.

It took just a few seconds for Kennedy to appear, no doubt already on his way once he had realised what was going on within this part of the gun deck. "Yes, Sir?" he reported, a little breathless.

"Escort Jessop to the brig. In the morning, he will answer to a charge of insubordination. You will then attend Mr Rawlinson as he goes through Jessop's belongings and if the missing items are to be found there, a charge of theft will be added."

Jessop kept quiet but his face showed nothing but pure murderous intent as he glared at Corbin. The Lieutenant refused to back down and instead took one step closer to the man before he spoke.

"And if you carry on looking at me like that, man, I will see you swing from the yardarm!"

Expecting trouble, Kennedy grabbed Jessop's arm firmly but was surprised to find no resistance as he led the man down into the lower deck to the brig. Corbin nodded at the midshipman.

"Okay, Mr Rawlinson, about your business. The rest of you, get on with your food or I may decide the topsail needs replacing – and believe me, that is not going to be an easy job in this weather!"

The threat, however idle the crew may or may not have thought it, proved enough to force their attentions back to the food before them. Satisfied that order had been restored, Corbin walked the length of the upper deck to ensure no other trouble lurked and then returned to his post in the wind and rain above.


HAVING DIRECTLY CHALLENGED a midshipman, Havelock had little choice but to condemn Jessop and force him to answer the charge made by Lieutenant Corbin. He was mollified somewhat by Rawlinson's discovery of the stolen pipe among the man's belongings, though no trace of the missing money had been found – not that anyone seriously expected it to turn up.

Once again, the entire crew of the *Whirlwind* lined the main deck but their mood was far more sombre than when they had last gathered in this way. They all knew they were to bear witness to the punishment of one of their own, and however unpopular Jessop may have proved with many of them, few liked to be reminded that it might only be the grace of God that spared them from a flogging. It was never a case of merely taking your licks, no matter how much a man thought he could face the pain – such men had never undergone the agony of a rope across the back. There was a humiliation to be borne too, the knowledge that the entire crew would be watching while the punishment was served.

Flanked by his officers, Havelock watched grimly as Jessop was brought up from below deck, escorted by the Bosun and two red-coated marines. He knew that, when in command of a ship of nearly three hundred souls, it was inevitable that more than a few bad apples would creep into the crew. Indeed, the press gangs were reported to be working overtime on shore and there was more than a little resentment building up on every ship in His Majesty's navy. Havelock had long ago determined that the iron rod was not the right approach to maintaining order on a ship of war, especially when one had a good Bosun to rely upon who could maintain a tight level of discipline. However, when a man turned his back on an officer, or even a midshipman, action had to be taken immediately. To defy Rawlinson was, when the matter was brought right down to its core, no different than Jessop casting two fingers up at one of the Captain's own commands. That way lay anarchy and chaos. As for the charge of thievery, he was probably doing Jessop a favour by publicly punishing him for it. Theft without comeuppance on any ship was likely to be met by a knife in the dark below deck, or a good shove while working at the top of one of the masts. Havelock had enough on his hands without having to contend with murder as well.

"All hands to witness punishment," called out Lieutenant Corbin, standing on the quarterdeck in full dress uniform, as were the other officers. His hand rested easily on the hilt of the sword at his belt.

Jessop steadfastly refused to look into the eyes of any of the crew as he was marched aft to face the Captain. When he stopped in front of the quarterdeck, he stood proud, staring at Havelock, who returned the look impassively.

"Jessop, you have been charged with insubordination to one of my officers and theft of property from one of your shipmates. What do you have to say?"

"Guilty as charged for insubordination, Cap'n," Jessop said. "And I would apologise to Mr Rawlinson for me manners. But I ain't no thief. That weren't me, Sir."

Havelock cast a look at the rest of the crew. "Does any man here have anything to say on Jessop's behalf?" He was answered by a deathly silence.

"If this man is found guilty of these crimes, the Articles of War allow for a maximum penalty of hanging..." said Havelock grimly. Still no one made a move to speak for Jessop which, given what he knew of the man's reputation, did not surprise Havelock in the least. Kennedy caught his eye and Havelock gave a nod to acknowledge him as the Bosun stood forward.

"Cap'n, I submit that Jessop isn't known as a thief by nature and that 'e has offered a full and frank apology to Mr Rawlinson. I would also like to bring to your attention that, when on duty, Jessop is a good sailor and a hard worker."

"Very well," said Havelock. He realised that Kennedy might be guilty himself of slightly overstating Jessop's case but it was the Bosun's task to defend the crew in any way he could. It was, in part, how he kept their respect and, thus, enabled him to keep discipline. After all, with so many witnesses, there was no way Jessop could have denied the charge of insubordination and an apology was a relatively painless way to avoid harsh punishment. Still, Havelock decided to take his Bosun's cue.

"Jessop, you have been found guilty of both charges. Seize him up," he said.

Those among the crew who were wearing hats took them off

as the marines stood behind Jessop. The condemned man reached behind his back and took off his shirt before being led to the main hatch which had been opened for this purpose. The marines tied Jessop's outstretched arms to the hatch, forcing him to adopt a spread-eagled position as Kennedy removed his own hat and jacket and picked up his favoured flogging rope. Havelock nodded his thanks as Buxton handed him a thin red leather bound book. He took the Articles of War, which he opened and began reading from.

"Article Twenty One – If any officer, mariner, soldier or other person in the fleet, shall presume to quarrel with any of his superior officers, being in the execution of his office, or shall disobey any lawful command of any of his superior officers; every such person being convicted of any such offence, by the sentence of a court martial, shall suffer death, or such other punishment, as shall, according to the nature and degree of his offence, be inflicted upon him by the sentence of a court martial. Two dozen lashes."

He looked up briefly at Jessop, before continuing. "Article Twenty Nine – All robbery committed by any person in the fleet, shall be punished with death, or otherwise, as a court martial, upon consideration of the circumstances, shall find meet. Another dozen, Mr Kennedy."

The Bosun nodded as a marine on the quarterdeck began a quick drum roll, the sound carrying across the entire ship as it echoed off the unfurled sails. When the drum stopped, Kennedy reached back and then struck with his rope, the muffled crack causing most among the crew to wince in sympathy.

At first, Jessop just exhaled noisily with each stroke but after the fourth lash of the rope, blood started to streak his back and he began to grunt through gritted teeth with every blow. As the rope sailed down on his naked back time and again, the lines of blood began to cross one another and then flow freely, creating a crimson curtain that ran down the sides of his body. Finally, and to Jessop's gratefulness, the blows stopped.

"Three dozen, Sir," said Corbin.

"Very well," Havelock said. "Mr Kennedy, cut him down." As soon as the ropes were cut, Jessop sank to the floor, a slight strangled groan escaping his lips as he slumped heavily on the deck.

"Thank you, Mr Corbin," said Havelock. "Dismiss all hands."

"All hands, dismissed," called out Corbin. The crew began to disperse to carry on with their regular duties, though few spoke after witnessing Jessop's punishment. Havelock started walking the stairs to the main deck, musing that, for all his faults, the man had been brave enough not to cry out during the flogging. From experience, Havelock knew that such men could easily be a handful to discipline properly but were often a holy terror when facing a French boarding party. They certainly had their uses. Intending to retreat into his cabin for the rest of the morning to plot the next day's course, Havelock's eyes met with Jessop's as the man was being helped back onto his feet by the marines.

"I'm no thief, Sir," said Jessop, in obvious pain.

This simple statement caught Havelock by surprise and he found himself stopping to regard the man for a second before walking on.

"SAIL TO LARBOARD!"

Havelock spun about from his inspection of the sail team on the forecastle and hurried across the main deck before vaulting up the stairs to the quarterdeck. Seeing Corbin already at the rails with an extended telescope, he hurried past Hague who called up to the lookout.

"Do you see a flag?"

"No, Sir," came the shouted reply. "Too far away!"

Sensing his Captain's approach, Corbin turned from the sea and passed his telescope. "A merchant, Sir. Can you make out its nationality?"

Havelock squinted through the telescope, taking a moment to bring the ship into focus. It was heading towards them at an oblique angle, though he could not see a flag flying – not that he expected to in these waters. Almost everywhere, the sea was nominally considered to be British but with war in the air, this was a disputed area. He tried to make out the arrangement of sails and pick out details from the hull in an effort to ascertain the ship's origin but while he guessed it might originally have had a French architect, the practice of taking prizes in battle meant that a ship could change hands a great many times in its life.

"Run up the colours, Mr Corbin," said Havelock. "We have nothing to fear from that vessel and we should be polite enough to announce our intentions."

"Aye, Captain. Run up the colours!" Corbin called to the crew and watched as the Ensign and Jack were hoisted into the air, fluttering in the stiff breeze flowing over the deck.

Keeping his eye trained on the approaching ship, Havelock finally smiled. "Ah, there you see. She answers – a Portuguese ship. Signal her, Mr Corbin. Have her run alongside us a while. I wish to talk to her Master."

"Let's just hope they can understand British signals," Corbin said.

"Avoid code and she should get our meaning."

Gaining the attention of Midshipman Buxton, Corbin gave the order of signals required to bring the merchant alongside while Havelock remained glued to his telescope. The flags were run up on the *Whirlwind* and though Havelock knew they were in full sight of the incoming vessel, he guessed the Portuguese Master was cursing him at that moment. Merchants had schedules to keep and profits to earn, and were better off not dallying in the middle of the ocean.

It took nearly twenty minutes for the two ships to meet, the Portuguese ship lumbering in a long turn to match the *Whirlwind's* course. The crew of both ships lined the railings, trading greetings and well-wishes while Havelock stood on the quarterdeck, looking down at his civilian counterpart. Doffing his hat in a show of respect, Havelock shouted over the noise of the two crews.

"Hoy there! Greetings from His Majesty's Navy!"

"Hallo, English!" The reply came in a thick accent. He sounded faintly resigned. "*Stella Maris*, at your service."

The Portuguese crew continued to wave their greetings, some struggling to ask questions in pidgin English, interested in the *Whirlwind's* voyage and what weather lay ahead. The British crew on the main deck nearest Havelock fell silent, knowing they would learn far more from their Captain's exchange with the merchant's Master.

"What news from the south?" Havelock shouted across to the Portuguese ship. "Have you sighted French shipping?"

"Three weeks past, chased by frigate!"

Havelock frowned impatiently at the ambiguous answer, irritated that he had to rephrase the question. "Was she French?"

There was a short pause before the Portuguese Master answered. "I believe so, yes. French, yes. We run and escape."

"Have you seen any other warships?" Havelock said and again had to wait while the Master translated the reply into English.

"Warships, no. No French, no English, no Espana."

"Have you sailed from the Cape?" Havelock guessed what the answer would be but wanted to be certain.

"The Cape, yes."

Making a few quick mental calculations, Havelock made some predictions of the Portuguese ship's recent course and back-tracked it three weeks. There was no way the Portuguese Master would have been able to identify the *Elita*. Indeed, if he had been that close, he would have been captured. It was within Havelock's authority to order the merchant to heave to in order for him to talk to the Master face-to-face so he could get accurate navigational information but, being three weeks old, it would have been of marginal benefit. It was enough to know, at this time, that a French frigate was still prowling southern waters.

"Thank you, *Stella Maris*. I wish you fair winds!"

Havelock watched the Portuguese master shrug and then bark orders to his crew to turn his ship away from the *Whirlwind* and back on to its original course. He was probably thanking his lucky stars that the English warship had not detained him longer.

Standing by his Captain to watch the Portuguese ship depart, Corbin asked "Useful information, Sir?"

"As much as it is," said Havelock. "*Elita* or not, we know there was a French presence in our hunting grounds three weeks ago – which means our voyage will likely not be wasted. The closer we get, the better our chances of intercepting her if she makes a break for French waters. However, I now believe the *Elita* is on an extended mission, which means she has her own harbour somewhere on the African coast. With a safe place to refit and re-supply, she could stay on station for months more, until her hold is full of stolen goods."

"Might the *Elita* be periodically unloading her cargo onto French merchants?" Corbin said.

"I considered that. Very risky. There is an excellent chance that such merchants would run into a British ship like us and then the cargo would simply come back into our hands. Still, if the aim was to disrupt supplies from the rest of the Empire rather than simply steal what she can, it might be a valid tactic. Especially if the *Elita* is trading stolen goods with natives for supplies on the coast. Yes, this bears some thought, Mr Corbin."

"Do you have new orders for us, Sir?"

"No, we continue south at our present speed. Depending on how large an area the *Elita* is patrolling we will be in her territory within two or three weeks."

HAVING COMPLETED HIS early morning watch, consumed mostly by the daily chore of cleaning the main deck with the large holystone, Bryant descended the stairs to the upper deck, looking forward to wrapping himself in his hammock for a few hours before being called onto duty again. The crew had long since become accustomed to the idea that they were back at sea once more, their days filled with the regular routines of maintaining the *Whirlwind* and keeping her on course. Now four weeks into their voyage, anticipation had been slowly growing again as the ship neared its destination. Gradually, talk among the sailors had turned away from promises of games of chance, or reminiscing of their home towns, to focus on war with France and her allies. They calculated the prize money the *Elita* and her cargo would bring them and divided it between the crew, taking into account losses borne during the fight (a subject which provoked some heated discussion in itself, as a few of the crew were happy to count off specific individuals as doomed). They then spent time surmising what could be bought with their own share.

The flogging of Jessop had long since passed from the minds of most crew but the man himself had seemed somewhat subdued afterwards, which came as something of a blessed relief to most. Bryant felt the whole atmosphere of the gun deck had changed since Jessop had kept to his own company more often, sparing weaker shipmates his own particular brand of cruelty and bullying. It was therefore of some surprise when Bryant climbed down in the upper deck and found Jessop in a recess beside a closed gun port, holding Murphy up among the rafters, the feet of the smaller man dangling freely as he gasped for air through Jessop's stranglehold.

"You li'l Irish rat," said Jessop. "I take a dozen for your stealin' and you're goin' to just stand there an' deny it?"

Murphy was clearly not standing at all and Jessop's grip had made him incapable of properly denying anything, though he made his best effort to shake his head. Sighing inwardly and preparing for the worst, Bryant marched over to the pair and laid a hand gently on Jessop's shoulder.

"Enough, Jessop! He doesn't know anything."

Jessop jerked his shoulder to remove Bryant's hand, though he did not relax his hold of Murphy. "Back away, this ain't none of your business! You ain't stickin' up for the rat this time!" he said, snarling.

Not wanting to provoke the already angry man but also keen to remove his friend from the ceiling, Bryant stood closer to Jessop, staring straight into his eyes. He spoke calmly and with conviction, wanting to diffuse the situation rather than get into another brawl that could easily be answered by the Bosun's rope.

"By my word, Murphy had nothing to do with the theft. He would not have been able to keep from telling me about it."

Face turning a murderous shade of red, Jessop swore and turned his attention to Bryant. "I'm tellin' you, I was fitted up!"

"I believe you," said Bryant quietly. That admission stopped Jessop in his tracks and he relaxed his grip on Murphy a little. Bryant took the opportunity to continue. "I really don't like you or what you do, Jessop. Take that as a gift. But I know you're no thief. You are too... direct for that."

Thoroughly confused, Jessop looked at Bryant, then at the suspended Murphy, then back at Bryant. Seeing no recourse beyond throwing a punch, a course of action that even Jessop realised would not portray him in a good light with the Bosun, he dropped Murphy heavily on the floor and spat. "Ain't worth my trouble anyway."

Murphy remained on the floor until he watched Jessop stomp away into the gloom. "Ah, me thanks, friend Bryant!" he said, with some forced cheer. "I swear, 'e just came out of nowhere and 'oisted me up!"

"You certain he had no good cause?" Bryant asked.

"Hey, I'm tellin' you!" Murphy said in protest. "I ain't dumb enough to go rummagin' through Jessop's things!"

"Hmm." Bryant considered his friend and then decided that the matter was not worth pursuing at this time. "Come on, I'm tired enough to drop off right now."

Crossing the deck, they found a circle of men, the rest of their gun crew mixing with another, leaning on the cannon as they talked. As Bryant began unfurling his hammock and attaching it to hooks scattered among the rafters, Brooks piped up.

"Hey, Murphy, we were talking about what made us sign up with the *Whirlwind*. How about you?"

To his credit, Murphy actually began to look a little embarrassed. "Ah, well," he began. "You see, it was like this... umm..."

"He was pressed," said Bryant, smiling as he kicked off his thin leather shoes. "Too much to drink one night and then ran right into a gang. Woke up on board the next morning, with more water between him and land than he could ever hope to swim!"

"Aye, 'tis true," Murphy said. "Still, found it wasn't such a bad life. Some good people 'ere. An' the pay ain't bad – well, once you get signed up as a proper seaman an' get off the pittance they give the pressed men."

"What about you, Bryant?" Brooks asked.

"Oh, not much to tell," said Bryant, now beginning to become desperate for the peace of sleep. "Worked as a clerk for my father in his tannery until he made some very bad decisions and went bust. Tried gambling – wasn't so good at that either. Then played against a sailor one night and he told me that, up to a limit, a man joining the King's Navy was absolved of his debts. I was under the limit and, so, here I am. And here I go," he said as he climbed into his hammock. "I bid you keep it quiet, friends, I need sleep..."

"Yeah, me too," said Murphy, reaching for his own rolled hammock as he made a big show of yawning theatrically.

"So, what was goin' on 'cross the way, Murphy?" one of the men from the other gun crew asked. "Run into Jessop again? Thought 'e had calmed all that down."

"Tellin' me!" Murphy said. "I told 'im I 'ad nothin' to do with 'is theft but would 'e listen? Would 'e 'ell!"

"It wasn't you then?"

"I swear to God!" Murphy said "No! Bryant, tell 'im!"

"I'm sleeping," came the muffled reply.

"Well, I knew it weren't Murphy," said Brooks happily, keen to support his friend.

Bryant rolled over in his hammock and hooked open an eye, fixing it on Brooks. "And how, exactly, do you know that?"

Brooks suddenly felt very conscious as all eyes turned to him. "Well, it's obvious, yeah? Couldn't be Murphy."

Propping his head up, Bryant looked straight into Brooks' eyes. "I think you meant something more than that. What is it, Brooks?"

Putting his face in his hands, Brooks rubbed his eyes and sighed before looking back up. He was painfully aware that his over-eagerness was going to have consequences, though whether he would face them or if it would be someone else, he did not know. Still, he mustered the fortitude to continue down this path. "I saw someone going through Hobbs' things."

"Who?" Bryant persisted.

Brooks looked around the deck and leaned forward as he answered in a quiet voice. "Jefferies."

"I might 'ave known it!" Murphy said.

"Keep your voice down," said Bryant in warning. "Brooks, are you sure about this?"

The boy just nodded, but Murphy had already been thinking along his own tangent.

"Eh, 'ang about," he said. "If you knew about Jefferies, why didn't you say anythin' before?"

Brooks shrugged. "It happened so fast. And Bryant, you always told me to keep my head down."

Closing his eyes from a weariness that came from more than a simple lack of sleep, Bryant muttered. "Guess I did at that."

The man from the opposite gun crew leaned back, considering this news. "Nah, doesn't make sense," he said. "Why go to all the trouble of stealin' a pipe, then givin' it to someone else?"

"No, it makes perfect sense," said Bryant, sighing. "Hobbs' pipe was not the only thing stolen. Think about it. You steal a few coins and a pipe. The pipe isn't worth that much and is easily recognisable, so you bury it in someone else's kit and watch them get the flogging as you walk away with the money."

"Oh, that's low," said Murphy.

"Indeed," said Bryant. "You then just make a few veiled accusations, the midshipman gets involved and before you know it, Jessop is having his own belongings searched. Up turns the pipe, then comes the flogging. No defence against that."

"An' no one questions it too deeply, as no one really likes Jessop," Murphy said.

Bryant nodded ruefully. "That's right."

"So what do we do?" Brooks asked, simultaneously a little afraid of what might happen to him and yet thrilled to be part of a conspiracy of sorts.

"You don't do anything," said Bryant firmly as he swung himself out of the hammock. "Nor do the rest of you. I'm going to have a quiet word with the Bosun. What happens after that will be his business."

THE WHIRLWIND HAD endured a short storm as it crossed into southern waters, but the sprightly frigate had ridden the waves in a manner that had warmed Havelock's heart, even as he stood on the quarterdeck, getting drenched from the unrelenting heavy rain and waves crashing against the hull of the ship, while watching his crew expertly handle the rigging and constantly changing conditions with deft hands. His officers, too, had acquitted themselves admirably, matching the endurance of the men under their command as they stood through each watch, ensuring the crew acted quickly but not so fast as to put their shipmates' lives in jeopardy.

The dispersing clouds and calming sea had marked the fourth day of the sixth week since the *Whirlwind* had departed Spithead, and driven on by the recent news imparted to them by the Portuguese merchant, the crew had steadily been building itself into a blind excitement. Many of the crew had learned how to handle the ship with steady hands, learning the ropes as it was called, but few were veterans of battle at sea. Havelock had made sure that his crew had constantly practiced with several gun drills every day since they left England and was now confident that any of his crews could keep to a constant rhythm of three shots every minute for as long as their ammunition lasted. In theory, that was enough to outshoot most French ships of war. However, gun drills were a far cry from having to do the same thing when there was an enemy vessel shooting back, cannon balls crashing through the decks, sending wood splinters flying with lethal force to maim your best friends as an officer stood behind you, shouting at you to reload once again and return fire.

There were a small number on board who had seen action before but many were new to the trade and their real test was to come. That was where the planting of discipline within the crew would bear fruit and Havelock was anxious to see the results of his hard work. For now, however, the crew were growing in eagerness to see a French ship in hostile waters and earn their chance for prize money. That, at the end of the day, was what made the wheels of the King's Navy continue to turn.

Even the loss of a shipmate, normally a source of ill omen and dire predictions, had been met without much negative reaction from the rest of the crew. Just two days previous, during the small hours of the mid-watch, a man known as Jefferies had plummeted from the mainmast into the sea. No one had noticed him missing until the end of the watch, by which time locating a man lost in the ocean might have proved impossible, even if Havelock was of a mind to turn the ship around.

In truth, Havelock suspected foul play, especially as no one seemed to mind the mysterious disappearance of the man who was known to be sure-footed on the masts. It happened, from time to time, an unpopular crewman would have an accident and no one would mourn his loss. Having quizzed the Bosun about the incident, Havelock had received the distinct impression that some kind of sailor's justice had been enacted for a crime that, had it come to his attention, would have merited the death penalty anyway. Certainly, Mr Kennedy had been evasive in his answers, taking each question in turn with a look that strongly suggested that Havelock did not really want to become involved. Having sailed with Kennedy for several years in one capacity or another, Havelock had come to trust and rely upon his Bosun, and this seemed to be borne out by the quiet acceptance of the crew over the death of Jefferies. Maybe Havelock would hear the full story when they returned to port. But probably not.

Though the sea had calmed over the past day, the wind remained strong, filling the *Whirlwind's* sails as it sailed down past the African coast which lay out of sight some distance over the eastern horizon. With his ship skimming through the sea at a fair rate of knots, Havelock enjoyed every small twist and turn transmitted through the hull to his feet on the quarterdeck, feeling the *Whirlwind* literally cut through the water, parting it to leave a long wake behind. He smiled. Calm seas, a stiff wind, an enemy nearby and a double watch of lookouts constantly scanning the horizon for sails. This, more than anything, was what it meant to be the captain of a frigate in His Majesty's Navy. The frigate was, after all, a hunter, able to roam the ocean in search of prey that would leave heavier and more powerful ships of war far behind.

Havelock's musings were wrenched back to the here and now by a cry from the top of the mainmast.

"Sail to starboard!"

Looking up at the men on the mast, Havelock followed the line to where they were pointing, roughly thirty degrees off from the starboard bow. Raising his telescope, he scanned the horizon until he found a familiar arrangement of sails.

"What do we have, Captain?" Corbin's voice came from behind him.

"Frigate, a big one. Two-decker, if my eyes are not mistaken," said Havelock. "Unmistakably French. Sailing across our path."

"She is in our lee, Sir. The advantage is ours."

"Indeed, Mr Corbin. I believe we have found our quarry. Pass the word – beat to quarters. Ready the larboard guns."

Corbin turned back to the main deck and shouted triumphantly to the crew. "Beat to quarters! Jump to it! Run out the guns, to larboard!"

He was answered with a cheer as crewmen leapt to their stations. Those on deck had heard the lookout report a sail on the horizon and the news flashed into the lower decks like wildfire. Along the length of the *Whirlwind's* hull, gun ports were opened and cannon loaded before being rolled out, ready to fire. Marines, under the command of their sergeant, lined up on the main deck, ready for the Captain's order to scale the masts for sniping positions or to otherwise line the forecastle.

"Run up the colours!" cried Havelock over his shoulder, and the dual flags of British nationality were soon flying proudly, announcing the *Whirlwind's* intention to do battle with the French ship as she closed inexorably on its position.

Lowering his telescope, Havelock gazed at the horizon, where the enemy ship was just beginning to materialise out of the haze. Smiling grimly, he spoke quietly to himself.

"We have her."

# CHAPTER FOUR

HAVELOCK'S ATTENTION WAS riveted on the French ship, as were any crewman who had the luxury of standing idle as he awaited orders that would throw him into action. Though the French crew must have spotted the *Whirlwind* long ago, she made no effort to change course and the two ships sailed ever closer to one another for nearly an hour.

During that time, the British crew had plenty of opportunities to think about the coming battle. For many, their previous anticipation gave way slowly to a creeping fear. Memories of crippled sailors leaving battered ships at port percolated in their thoughts, along with stories from the older and wiser hands on board that they had listened to just a few days past. The tales of hardship, of blood flowing across the deck and masts falling to crush sailors beneath did not seem so frivolous now as the *Whirlwind* inched towards its enemy. For many of the crew, the thought of their own mortality was only now just beginning to cross their minds. There was an inevitability about their fate that seemed irresistible.

Not everyone on board had such dark thoughts, of course. On every ship of war there would be those who simply did not believe they could ever die while so young, while others took the idea of the invincibility of the King's Navy and their own national superiority to heart.

For his part, Havelock was enjoying a moment of supreme calmness, as he often did before battle. He knew the French vessel enjoyed certain advantages over his ship but he was also aware of the odds in his own favour. The *Elita* would have heavier guns that could out range his own, but this would be countered by their fast closing speed. He guessed the French would have, at best, the opportunity to fire two salvoes at range before he could respond and he did not intend to present an easy target when they opened up on the *Whirlwind*. It was true, too, that the French had many more guns than he possessed, lined up on two decks. However, Havelock had yet to meet a French crew that could fire as efficiently as well-disciplined British sailors and the biggest cannon in the world would do them no good at all if his men could fire two or even three times while they struggled to reload.

He was painfully aware that the *Elita's* crew greatly outnumbered his by perhaps as much as three to one, but Havelock trusted in his own ability not to be caught off guard by a sudden manoeuvre that would send the French frigate crashing into his own before her crew swept over the railings. A dozen different scenarios played through his mind during the long wait as the *Whirlwind* closed the distance with the *Elita*, imagining stroke and counterstroke as he tried to place himself in the French captain's position and predict just what might be his first move.

The French frigate began to loom high before him and Havelock raised his telescope once more, this time sighting individual crew running about the deck of the *Elita*, following their captain's orders. On the quarterdeck of the ship, he saw the unmistakable uniform of a French captain, also looking at his enemy through a telescope. Havelock resisted the temptation for a cheerful salute and instead contented himself with the thought that while the French crew stirred on their ship, his were standing at attention, calm and collected. What a sight it must have been to that French captain!

Of course, it was equally possible that the French captain was arrogant enough to think the coming battle was a foregone conclusion, given that he had the larger ship. That was something Havelock intended to disabuse him of very quickly.

"Sergeant!" Havelock called, and the red-coated commander of the *Whirlwind's* marines stepped up behind him.

"Sir!"

"Get your men up into the masts," said Havelock. "As high as you can go without falling off. Their own marines are likely to have a height advantage over you, so make sure your men shoot well."

"Yes, Sir! We'll send them Frogs packin'!" The Sergeant stomped off, bellowing orders at the two lines of marines who had stood at attention on the quarterdeck with their muskets held steady in front of their chests since the *Elita* had first been sighted. Jumping to obey, they split into three groups, each heading to one of the tall masts of the *Whirlwind*. Slinging their weapons across their backs and climbing up the rigging, they began to take positions high above the deck, where they would be able to snipe choice targets on the deck of the French ship.

"He has still made no change in course, Sir," said Corbin who, after having performed one last tour of the ship to see all was in order, had returned to his captain's side.

"He will, Mr Corbin, you can be sure of that," said Havelock. "On our present course, we'll sail right behind him and unload a salvo into his stern. He won't chance us crippling him like that. No, he'll make a move, just watch out for it."

The two officers, satisfied that their crew and ship was ready to fight, kept their eyes glued on the *Elita*, straining to see the first hint of a move by the French captain. They did not have to wait for long.

"Sir, movement among the sails," said Corbin.

"I see it – she's coming about!" Havelock said. He called down to the crew on the main deck below him. "Steady, men, she'll get a hurried shot or two at us – and then she'll be ours!"

He almost did not notice the cheer a few of his men gave as he watched the *Elita* begin a steady turn towards his ship. The two light coloured bandings that ran the length of the ship's hull were obvious to his eyes now, each line marking the position of one gun deck. The ship had its larboard side to them but he quickly noticed its gun ports were closed.

"She is going to cut across us!" Havelock said. "Helm, steady as she goes. Aim straight for her until I give the word, then hard to starboard!"

"You see their plan, Sir?" Corbin asked .

"Aye, I do. They are going to try steal the wind advantage from us by reversing their course and coming past us. A fine gambit but easily countered."

As the *Elita* continued its turn, prow pointing briefly at the *Whirlwind* before continuing to move on, its starboard side was revealed. Everyone on deck could see the two layers of gun ports being thrown open before cannon were rolled out. For the next few seconds, time seemed to slow down for Havelock as he watched the guns of the *Elita* slowly line up on the prow of his ship. Then the French ship disappeared in a roiling cloud of thick white smoke.

Havelock heard a couple of popping sounds as cannonballs penetrated the sails above his head but the rest of the shot went speeding past the *Whirlwind* to raise large spouts of water in its wake. This was enough to cause Midshipman Rawlinson to duck. Corbin turned round instinctively to admonish him.

"On your feet, Mr Rawlinson! Where do you think you are?"

Extending his telescope, Havelock made a quick calculation as he watched the French canon being rolled back into their gun ports for reloading.

"We are going too fast, they won't get another chance to fire – Helm, hard to starboard, now! Bring us in line with that ship!"

With a deft twist, the *Whirlwind* responded instantly to the wheel, the crew on the main deck automatically adjusting the spread of the sails to match the command. With less than a hundred yards separating the two ships, they sailed in parallel, each racing the other in an attempt to steal a lead and either take or retain the advantage of being on the windward side of the duel.

"Mr Corbin, if you would be so good as to teach these Frenchmen how an Englishman shoots..." said Havelock.

"Aye, Sir. Gun crews, fire!" shouted Corbin, whose order was immediately relayed by Wynton to the gun deck. The entire ship shook and rolled as the eleven larboard guns fired simultaneously, instantly obscuring the *Elita* with a thick bank of smoke. Havelock caught a glimpse of bright light flashing from the French ship before it disappeared, but before he could shout an order to his crew to hold them steady, the *Whirlwind* shuddered as it was impacted by the *Elita's* broadside.

The cry of men was pierced by flying splinters as heavy shot smacked into the side of the ship. Overhead sails ripped and

Havelock saw one man fall from the mainmast into the sea. He sensed immediately that the damage was light, the French crew having aimed high by waiting until their ship had rolled to one side, as was typical for their captains when trying to demast an enemy.

"We'll win the race to reload, Mr Corbin," he shouted. "Doubleshot the guns. Let's see if we can counter some of their heavier firepower!"

"Aye, Sir. Doubleshot the guns!"

Sailing onwards, the two ships sped forward from their shroud of gun smoke and Havelock was gratified to see his regular gun drills had paid off in terms of accuracy. The entire starboard side of the *Elita* was blackened and pitted, and three large, ragged holes in the hull marked the areas where cannon had been blasted by incoming fire, rendering them useless. Even so, Havelock could not help but marvel at the size of the French frigate, its quarterdeck towering over his own position and the two gun decks appearing even more intimidating at this range. All the more so as, while the two ships raced side by side, it was painfully obvious that she was every bit as fast as the *Whirlwind*.

"Fire at your discretion, Mr Corbin," Havelock said, preferring to leave the cycling of the guns to his lieutenants while he watched, hawk-like, for the slightest twitch from the *Elita* that would reveal its captain's intentions. He did not have to wait for more than a few seconds before the guns of the *Whirlwind* roared again, blanketing the area with smoke. Still, Havelock's ears were becoming re-accustomed to the noise of battle and he heard the distinctive crack and splintering of shot smashing into a wooden hull, even as he heard the cries below deck to reload. He smiled as he saw the damage revealed by the clearing smoke. More French cannons had been put out of commission, and several jagged holes very low on the *Elita's* hull would see it taking on water in hard turns.

Watching the French crew work to recycle their own guns, Havelock saw them roll out their cannon even as the order to do so was relayed on his own ship. He realised then that the French crew, while no match for his in a straight race, were certainly more competent than others he had faced in the past. Wincing in anticipation of the assault, Havelock realised that the *Whirlwind* was to receive the full weight of the French two deck broadside an instant before his own guns could respond. He heard the cry to fire from the *Elita* before it once again disappeared in smoke and he was knocked to the deck by a jarring impact that left him breathless.

ARMS COVERING HIS head, Brooks tried to crawl for cover next to his gun carriage before he was hoisted to one side by Bryant. The gun deck was flooded with a dim light from open gun ports and gaping holes in the hull, dispersed by the smoke that hung still in the air. The smell of spent powder mixed with the almost overpowering stench of blood and sweat while everywhere men shouted orders or howled in pain as they clutched splinter wounds or stumps of limbs.

The sights and sounds of battle terrified Brooks and he wanted to do nothing more than curl into a ball. Squeezing his eyes shut tightly, he moved his hands to his ears but nothing seemed to shut out the terrible noise of explosions and men shouting as they fought.

"Return fire, you British dogs!" Hague shouted through the din, straining to be heard.

Hearing the voice of an officer, Brooks reacted automatically and tried to stand. Wide-eyed, he put a hand out to steady himself against the nearest rafter but then slipped, falling hard on the wooden deck. He was shocked to discover he was soon wet through then realised it was from the tide of blood that was slowly spreading across the floor. He became aware that Bryant had shoved a rope in his hands and was yelling at him to pull.

"Come on, run out the gun lads!"

By reflex alone, born from countless drills, Brooks braced himself against the side of the hull and pulled, sensing the heavy gun carriage rumble past before an immense crack thundered from the weapon, bathing him in smoke once more. Whimpering, he stayed motionless until Bryant hooked an arm under his and lifted him up once more.

"Snap to it, lad," Bryant said. "Not long to go now, we have them on the run." He turned away from Brooks briefly to shout for powder and sighed with relief as a young boy, no more than nine years old or so, came scampering through the death and chaos to deliver a metal box of cloth-bound charges.

"Reload," roared Hague. "Doubleshot!"

Murphy scampered to Bryant to take the charges, instinctively keeping his head low, before springing back to the front of their cannon, beginning the process of swabbing it out to receive a new round. Bryant turned Brooks round to face him and, looking straight into the young man's eyes, sought to penetrate his fear.

"Brooks, you hear me?" he shouted, trying to maintain an element of calmness in his voice. "There's no point trying to hide, lad – there's nowhere they can't get you. All we can do is make sure we fire faster than they do. You with me, lad?"

With a slowness that seemed agonising to Bryant, Brooks blinked and looked back at him.

"Stick by me, I'll see you right," said Bryant. "Now, grab the shot and help Murphy!"

Casting a look around his feet, Brooks quickly found the stack of cannon balls in their brass stay and, lifting one out, carried it round to the front of the cannon, taking great care not to look at the massive French warship that loomed close outside their open gun port.

Behind them, Hague wiped his brow, his silk handkerchief now ruined by sweat and powder. Seeing the gun crews remained more or less firm, he quickly trotted to the rear of the gun deck, taking care not to hamper the reloading of any of the cannon. Seeing Wynton at the top of the stairs on the main deck, he called for the older lieutenant's attention.

"Four guns out of action!"

He watched Wynton nod in understanding as the man turned back to relay this to Corbin. He then turned back to the gun deck and, on seeing the crews were completing their reloading cycle, looked out of the nearest gun port to check the position of the *Elita*. Seeing that it still sailed directly at their broadside and that the roll of the *Whirlwind* was just right, he barked the command.

"Fire!"

Hague had to brace himself against a rafter as the whole ship rolled to starboard from the recoil. Through the dirty smoke, he could see many of the crew on this deck were scared, but was gratified that towards the prow of the ship Jessop's team, at least, was alternating between whooping in triumph and cursing the ancestry of their French counterparts. Their attitude was beginning to become infectious and the neighbouring cannon crew had started to join in.

"Reload!" He shouted. "Steady men, remember, that is only a French ship out there and any one of you is worth ten of them!"

From the far end of the gun deck, Jessop's team responded with more promises of what they would do to the French and even some members of the other crews began to smile in a grim fashion.

Brooks had slipped into automatic in concert with Murphy and Bryant as they cleaned their cannon, loaded it with charge and shot, rolled the carriage out and then fired, before pulling it back to start the process again. He glanced up once to see Bryant staring out of the gun port towards the enemy vessel.

"How are we doing?" Brooks asked.

Bryant hesitated before answering. "Looks pretty even at the moment. Keep firing, lad, that's the key. Those Frogs will soon give up if we can fire more often than they can."

His overly confident words caused Murphy to flicker a questioning look at him. Bryant could only shrug. He knew that the *Whirlwind* had been hit hard but he also realised that while the *Elita* had suffered more crew and gun losses, she could weather the damage far better than they. Even though both ships had suffered in these exchanges, the *Elita* had started with more cannon and crew to service them and she still enjoyed that numerical superiority.

Stunned for a few brief seconds, Havelock did not realise that he was being helped to his feet by Lieutenant Corbin. As soon as he saw he was being aided, he put a hand out, forcing the man to back away. It would not do for his crew to think he had been wounded.

Comforted by the thunderous sound and rocking motion that signified the *Whirlwind's* guns had been fired once again, Havelock cast a look at both the *Elita* and his own ship. The French ship sported several holes in her hull from which cannon had been blasted from their carriages. Breaches lower down the hull had grown in number but, on the ship's present course, rode high enough out of the water not to cause any significant problems to her captain.

Casting an eye to the *Whirlwind*, Havelock saw men lying on the deck and smoke rising up from open hatches. More critically, the top third of the foremast had been shot away, leaving the sail to hang down uselessly. That would cost him some speed and agility. He looked at Corbin.

"Damage report?"

"Complements of Mr Hague, we are down to seven guns against the French," said Corbin. "We are also beginning to take on water in the hold."

"Get a crew down there to begin pumping it out," said Havelock.

He thought for a second. "If we stay as we are, that ship will just overwhelm us by weight of guns. We need to break them, and quickly."

"What are your orders?"

"Get the gun crews to load the starboard cannon but tell them to keep the gun ports larboard open. I don't want the French getting a whiff of this until they actually see what we are doing."

Corbin left Havelock's side briefly to relay the instructions down to Wynton and then returned, a question on his lips. "You are going to cut across behind them, Sir?"

"It is worth the gamble. We trade the chance for a knock-out blow against the possibility of handing them the wind advantage." Havelock said. By making this manoeuvre, he would be placing his ship on the leeward side of the *Elita*, which he was well aware, might be a decision he regretted later.

Looking back at Wynton, Corbin received a nod and reported to Havelock that the starboard guns were ready for firing. Watching the *Elita* intently, Havelock began timing their reloading cycle.

"Let's see if we can catch them off balance," he said, as much to himself as Corbin. As the first French gun was rolled out, Havelock shouted his order.

"Helm, hard to larboard! Bring us behind him!"

Havelock instantly noticed that the *Whirlwind* was a little sluggish to respond, indeed, it felt as if the ship was lumbering as it made the turn. However, it was quick enough to put the crew of the *Elita* on the back foot, as they watched the *Whirlwind* make its harsh turn to sail behind them. Their gun crews were still running out cannon from the open ports on their starboard side, only to find the British ship had disappeared from their view.

As the *Whirlwind* held its course, perpendicular to the *Elita's*, the range between the two ships dropped dramatically and, for the first time, the marines high among the masts found themselves able to target the crew on the deck of the French vessel. The crack of musket fire rang out time and again from above their heads, small puffs of smoke from the guns instantly dispersing in the wind. On the *Elita*, half a dozen men dropped to the deck, either dead or clutching at wounds, while others scampered for cover. To his credit, Havelock noticed, the French captain did not flinch, even though his quarterdeck was the main target area for the marines.

Returning to a straight line course, the *Whirlwind* began to pick up speed again and her crew watched as they sailed within a stone's throw of the *Elita's* stern, her gold-etched name plate clearly visible to all. Havelock almost snarled his next order.

"Mr Corbin, run out the guns. Crew to fire at will."

He barely listened as his order was relayed to the gun deck but watched intently as the *Whirlwind* sailed past the French frigate. From prow to stern, his guns fired one by one as they lined up on the rear of the *Elita*, where she was most vulnerable. Havelock momentarily rued the thought that if he possessed heavier guns, his shots would be capable of passing right through the ship, smashing every deck as the shot travelled the full length of the vessel. However, he quickly put this idea aside as, over the course of twenty seconds, he watched his crew put the full weight of the *Whirlwind's* guns into the stern of the *Elita*. The deck below the elegant great cabin was wrecked almost instantly and everyone on board the British frigate heard the cries of the dying and wounded inside the French ship, even above the thunderous rumble of cannon fire. Havelock was particularly gratified to see the French captain dive for cover on his main deck when he realised just what the *Whirlwind* intended to do.

Propelled forward a few steps by Bryant's heavy slap on his back, Brooks nevertheless managed to raise a smile as he looked out of the open gun port.

"You see, lad?" Bryant said enthusiastically. "You can always rely on the Captain! Caught the Frogs completely off-guard with that one!"

For his part, Brooks was just as happy to now be working on the other side of the gun deck, where the devastation of smashed wood and broken bodies was far less apparent than his last station. However, Murphy was also jumping with excitement and the good humour of the pair was infectious.

One of the last guns to fire in the volley that had wrecked the *Elita's* stern, Bryant had grinned as he closed the firing catch of his cannon. By the time the frigate had floated into view of his gun port, its rear quarter was already a mess, a tangle of wood planks and struts that veiled the destruction within. Knowing that the wreckage could provide little hindrance to his shot, Bryant was left to imagine just how much damage he had dealt to the internal structure of the ship.

"Reload!" The inevitable order came from Hague, the triumph in his voice unmistakable. "We have them on the run now, men!"

Rolling their gun carriage back, Murphy looked out of the gun port as they continued to sail past the *Elita*. When he saw the larboard side of the French ship, he smiled.

"They still 'aven't rolled out their guns!" he cried happily. "We're goin' to mash 'em!"

"They ain't turnin', either!" Brooks shouted back.

"They ain't dead yet," said Bryant calmly. "But we are still better shots and we can still reload quicker than they can. Hop to it, lads, let's get ready to give them another taste of British metal!"

Together, they worked in perfect synchronisation as they readied their cannon once more, even sparing a laugh for the news filtering from forward that Jessop's team had boasted they could reload quicker and shoot straighter than the rest of the gun crews put together.

Having finished loading their cannon, the three of them ran the carriage out of the port and Murphy scrambled past the other two in order to poke his head out of the hatch. He stared at the French ship as it first sailed away from them and then began to turn.

"Oh, she's comin' back for more!" he said.

"Hold your fire!" shouted Hague behind them. "On the Captain's word and not before!"


"She's in a bad way, Sir," said Corbin as they both watched the *Elita* begin to make its turn back towards them.

"We are both in a bad way, Mr Corbin," Havelock reminded his lieutenant. "We are taking on water, have a damaged foremast and many guns on our larboard side out of action. We may have fresh guns on this side but then, so does she. I wonder... Oh! Did you see that?"

Havelock's sharp eyes and experience at sea caught the odd motion of the *Elita* a fraction of a second before Corbin did. Coming about to match the *Whirlwind's* new course, the frigate heeled hard to starboard, the weight of its masts listing it heavily as the rudder steered it through the rolling water. It began the turn as smoothly as Havelock had come to expect but, suddenly, the ship seemed to catch something in the water and he saw some of the crew on board lurch forward as their vessel decelerated suddenly.

"What was that?" Corbin asked. "Surely they could not have struck anything?"

"They might as well have," said Havelock with a growing smile as the reason for the *Elita's* strange movement dawned on him. "We holed her on the starboard side, remember? While the wounds were above the waterline, as soon as she turned and rolled onto her side, they would have been underwater." He sighed. "Her captain won't make that mistake again."

"Can we not use it to our advantage?"

"She might be as slow as us now and will favour starboard turns. Still..." He thought for a second. "Mr Corbin, instruct the gun crews to check their fire. They are to wait for my command."

Corbin was puzzled but obeyed without comment. "Aye, Sir."

He looked quizzically at his Captain until Havelock noticed his attention. Havelock gestured to the *Elita*.

"She has yet to run out her guns on this side."

"Did we hit her harder than we thought?" Corbin asked.

"I don't think so. Our guns are not that powerful, though I fancy her rearward cannon may not be firing any time soon. No. Watch what she does next."

They both stared intently at the *Elita* as the frigate continued making its ponderous turn, swinging round until its prow faced them. Once the turn was complete, the ship righted itself and began to pick up speed, closing the distance between them rapidly.

"She's going to ram us?" Corbin asked incredulously.

"No, I fancy her captain intends to board us. I believe I can put a stop to that though!" Havelock said and raced to the stairs leading to the main deck, climbing down them two at a time. Maintaining his pace, he carried on downwards into the gun deck, where he acknowledged Lieutenant Hague with a nod.

"Listen to me, men!" Havelock shouted to gain the attention of the gun crews. "That French ship means to board us! We have scared her crew with our fine shooting so much, they no longer wish to play!"

He smiled openly as the gun crews cheered, some of them reaching through their open gun ports to shake a fist at the approaching frigate.

"However," he shouted, regaining their attention. "We have better things to do than dally with French sword play! Stand to your guns and prepare to fire! On my word and not a second before!"

The crew leapt to their feet, the gunners standing with a hand on the firing catch of their cannon, all eyes on their Captain. Walking smartly towards the nearest gun crew, Havelock stared out of the gun port, watching the *Elita* as she sailed closer, timing the motion of both the French ship and his own. He noticed the cannon's crew looking at him expectantly.

"You've done well today, men," he said, congratulating them. "What is your name?" he asked the nearest.

"Err, Brooks, Sir, err, Captain."

"Well, stand easy, Brooks," said Havelock, keeping his voice even. "We are going to try a little trick the French often like to play here."

The motion of the waves constantly rolled the *Whirlwind* slightly as it sped across the ocean and it was this movement that Havelock began to time. Satisfied that he had the measure of it, Havelock stood back.

"Ready men, on my word and not a second before..." he said. "Ready... Fire!"

His view instantly disappeared in a wave of smoke but soon cheers from the forward gun deck told him that the hit had been solid. A few seconds later, the stern of the *Whirlwind* had passed out of the cloud and he leaned forward across the cannon again to judge the results. He liked what he saw.

The *Elita* had been hit hard but Havelock's timing had sent the full weight of fire into the frigate's masts and sails. Striking from the front, the combined shot had snapped the *Elita's* foremast like a twig, sending it crashing into the mainmast which now leaned precariously. With sails now tangled and out of trim, the French ship slowed noticeably, leaving the *Whirlwind* to skip ahead freely across the waves.

Havelock put a hand on Brooks' shoulder. "That," he said, "is how we halt a French frigate! Well done indeed, lad!"

The raucous cheers of the collected gun crews followed Havelock as he first shook Hague's hand and then returned to the quarterdeck. He found Corbin waiting for him there, a broad smile on the man's face.

"A fine shot, Captain!"

Casting a look back at the floundering French ship, Havelock had to agree.

"Aye. It was. Thank you, Mr Corbin."

Walking behind the mizzenmast, the two officers stood, arms folded, as they watched the *Elita* recede into the distance. By now its captain was not even trying to keep pace as the *Whirlwind* skittered away, instead taking the time to begin repairs to his masts and sails.

"He'll be stranded for some time, trying to make good the damage you caused," said Corbin.

"True, but we have our own wounds to heal before we can think about going into battle again. One or two good salvoes from that ship and we would have been in serious trouble. Gods, but she can hit hard!"

"We are rigging the foremast now, Captain, and should have near full mobility within the hour," said Corbin.

"Good. She won't be her normal sprightly self until that is fully repaired though. What else do we have to contend with? Has Wynton given you the full list?"

"Minor breach on the starboard side below the waterline. The pumps are keeping pace at the moment but we'll have to stop to patch it. Four cannon knocked off their carriages, Kennedy thinks they are all serviceable. A lot of damage to the gun ports and fittings larboard but it can all be repaired, given time."

"We gave better than we took then. Casualties?" Havelock asked.

"Considering what might have been, light. I'm told seventeen dead or dying, nearly half as many again injured and unable to report for service." Corbin tried to look on the good side. "Still, I think we dealt far worse."

"Yes, but then they can afford to take worse. Another race is about to start, Mr Corbin, the one for repair. If we can patch this old girl up and locate the *Elita* again before she can make good the damage we handed her, she'll be ours. If she beats us..." He trailed off, not wanting to think about facing the larger ship while the *Whirlwind* was still battered.

"What are your orders, Captain?"

"Set course due east. We'll find a natural harbour on the African coast and make repairs. I think we can also take the opportunity to send out teams for water and fresh food – the crew certainly deserve it." Havelock thought for a moment. "Speaking of which, give them an extra ration of rum tonight. They fought well and are worthy of the recognition."

\*     \*     \*

"More than any one man has a right to know," said another sailor in answer. "But I would bet my ration of rum for the next month that the Captain 'as 'em all pegged."

"And what are you reckonin' will 'appen when we next meet them Frogs?" Murphy asked.

"The Cap'n will pull somethin' out the bag," said the sailor confidently.

"Aye, but we have some hard work ahead of us," said Bryant, causing the sailor to nod in agreement.

"What do you mean?" asked Brooks.

"Well, we have plenty of damage that needs fixing, as you can see," Bryant said, sweeping an arm to take in the shattered hull larboard. "But the Frogs have their own repairs to make too. If we can fix the *Whirlwind*, make her battle worthy again and find that frigate before they can do anything meaningful, she'll be ours. They'll probably surrender after the first shot!"

"And if they fixed their ship too?" Murphy asked, a little mischievously.

Bryant sighed. "Well, then, we'll have to start all over again." Seeing Brooks' face fall a little at this, he smiled. "Don't worry, lad. Trust to the Captain. He'll see us right."

"Aye," said Murphy. "I certainly 'aven't 'eard Jessop and 'is mates goin' on about 'Avelock's Curse since the battle."

"Like us, they're all too full of rum tonight," said Bryant, ignoring Murphy's waspish comment about chance being a fine thing. "They'll start off again soon enough. So long as we ignore them, they can't do any harm."

The gathered sailors murmured their agreement. The conversation meandered after that, as they discussed the possibility of re-supply during the voyage and the fresh food it might bring, before Brooks leapt in with an excited comment from the battle and the whole fight was recounted yet another time. It would not be the last time that night.


WITH THE SETTING sun at his back, Havelock luxuriated in the warm evening wind that swept across the deck of the *Whirlwind*. He had already noted the presence of seabirds high in the sky but was nevertheless gratified to hear the lookout announce the presence of land dead ahead.

"We made good time," he said to Corbin.

"Aye, she is a fast ship, even with a few scratches."

"Call all hands on deck, Mr Corbin," Havelock said. "It is time we told them of our intentions. It will also do them good to see land."

Corbin dutifully relayed the order and the other lieutenants and midshipmen descended below deck to stir the crew. They arose in groups and gaggles and Havelock was pleased to see that some were alert enough to see land. Word of this rippled through the assembling crowd and more than one sailor had a smile on his face as he looked up expectantly at his Captain.

Waiting until he received a nod from Corbin that all hands were present, Havelock strode confidently up to the front of the quarterdeck and, in his customary manner, spread his hands on the wooden railing. Satisfied that he had the attention of every man on board the *Whirlwind*, he began his address.

"Today, you have fought in a manner that befits a crew in his King's Navy. I am proud to have each and every man jack of you with us on this voyage! It is no exaggeration to say that we gave the French a damn good thrashing!"

Though they might have expected praise from their Captain, this did nothing to dampen the enthusiasm and excitement of the crew. They responded to his words with an impassioned cheer that Havelock let run long and loud. When they finally subsided, he continued.

"We have proved that no matter what ship the French bring to battle, a good British frigate with a hard-working and disciplined crew will win the day every time!"

Another cheer erupted but, sensing that it might partly be fuelled by rum, Havelock held a hand up to still them.

"We still have work to do," he said. "As you no doubt have already seen, we approach land. We will find a safe harbour and put ashore for repairs. And though there is much to be done, spare a thought for the poor Frenchmen, at sea with no means of making landfall!" The crew gave the appropriate cruel laugh at this. "Through your excellent gunnery, they are far worse off than we! We will see to the *Whirlwind's* slight wounds and then head back west to find our prey. And this time, we shall see her surrender, striking her colours as we approach!"

The volume of the crew's jubilant cries made Havelock both wince and smile. For any faults individuals may have, he knew that, collectively, there was a good crew on board this ship. He gave a nod to Corbin.

"All hands dismissed!"

Before the crew could return to their duties or sleep, depending on which watch they had been placed on, a new voice rang out from the crowd. Havelock quickly realised that it was the Bosun who had called aloud.

"Three cheers for Captain Havelock," Kennedy shouted out. "Hip, hip... " As one, the crew raised their voices in a genuine salute of their commanding officer's skill.

Taken aback, Havelock opened his mouth to say something but found he did not have the words. Instead, he just smiled again and nodded at his crew in gratitude. He turned to walk to the rear of the quarterdeck as his men finally dispersed.

He was surprised to find that tears had started to well up, unbidden, in his eyes.

# CHAPTER FIVE

THE SEA THREW itself against the shore, breakers rearing up as they smashed into the pristine white sand and smooth rocks. The coast looked as if it had never been disturbed by the intrusion of civilised humans. Struggling to climb out of the jolly boat with a modicum of dignity intact, Hague readjusted the long sword at his belt and hopped into the sea, another incoming wave immediately soaking him up to the chest. As he staggered to the shore, he kept an eye on the rest of the crew dragging the jolly boat in, alert for any mishaps that might drag them under but they seemed quite accustomed to the conditions. Hague had occasionally seen sea rise up like this on the tip of Cornwall and had to remind himself that nothing separated him from the raw strength of the Atlantic Ocean on the beaches of this land.

Two other boats had already been dragged up onto the shore and he saw Lieutenant Corbin organise various parties, mixing marines in among sailors where he thought prudent, but giving enough latitude to those he felt worthy of trust. He was surprised to see him assign one man to a party of sailors who were going inland alone, a sailor he thought Corbin had been partly responsible for disciplining earlier on this voyage. Perhaps the Lieutenant thought the others would be a stabilising influence or perhaps he just did not much care for what happened to the man while they spent time here. The last sentiment might not have been one worthy of an officer in the King's Navy, but it was one that Hague could readily identify with. Some men were beyond reach, shrugging off the harshest discipline like water from a duck's back.

As Hague stomped up the beach, leading his rowing party, he listened to the tail end of Corbin's orders as the Lieutenant pointed at his men and then directed them into their groups.

"Do not stray too far and always make sure you are within five minutes' run of the shore," said Corbin. "The wildlife round here may not be used to men and many creatures will bite before asking questions. If you see any interesting insects or snakes, believe me, you are better off leaving them alone. If you see any large predators, back away from them carefully. If you meet any natives you *will* show them all respect. Remember, this is their land and they know it better than you do. Party leaders, you have instructions and you know which direction I want you to head in. Mr Hague, you are with me – I believe you have some experience in dealing with the natives of Africa?"

Hague was caught a little off guard. "Eh? Ah, yes, Mr Corbin," he said, recovering quickly. "But that was some time ago and nowhere near this place." In truth, he had spent part of his childhood in South Africa while his father had run a merchant's agency there and while he had picked up some of the native tongue, he was well aware that the speech varied from tribe to tribe.

"You are the best we have, Mr Hague, and if we encounter any natives we may save a great deal of time if we trade with them."

"Right you are, Sir."

Corbin stared hard at the assembled parties. "Remember what I said about the natives. They may prove to be of great benefit to us. However, keep in mind the only experience they may have had with white men could be with the slave ships of the Americas. So, mind your manners as they may appear less than receptive. Only respond in kind if they prove outwardly hostile. Any questions?"

A few sailors shook their heads, which Corbin took to mean that at least a few of his warnings had hit home. He was on a strict timetable from Captain Havelock, who had remained on the *Whirlwind* to oversee the repairs. Having been given a list of requirements – ranging from a good stock of wood, replenishing that used for repairing the hull, to necessities such as fresh water, food and appropriate wood to be used for brushes – Corbin had split the men on the beach into three separate parties, tasking each with searching for just one of these goods. He was to lead a fourth group with Hague, in the hope of encountering natives and trading with them. With any luck, a little diplomacy would reap more rewards than the entire crew scouring for supplies.

"Very well, then. Off you go and good luck!"

Striking off in four different directions, the landing crew of the *Whirlwind* entered the tree line running along the shore and disappeared from sight.


LEADING THE WAY for his party of six, including two marines, Bryant hacked at all plant life within reach of his broad knife as he struggled to get past a particularly thick knot of branches. He had only been leading his group for little more than twenty minutes and already he felt exhausted. Wiping his brow with the back of his arm, he glanced around.

Though they had seen no wildlife, strange calls that may have come from birds or something else best not imagined, constantly rang out. The shrubs and trees were nothing like he had seen before and he noticed their leaves tended to be thick and rubbery to the touch, though here and there a very exotically coloured flower poked its elaborate petals out of the verdant mass as it strained for just a portion of the sunlight trickling through the canopy. The very air lent an ominous feel to the area, especially for men used to serving on board a ship that, while retaining its own specific odours, at least felt the breeze once in a while. Here, it felt as if the wind never penetrated the trees, and as a result, the air was thick, cloying and very damp.

"This ain't no work for a sailor," said Murphy, and though he wished the small man would stop griping, Bryant could not help but agree. He had never imagined anything like this when he had signed up.

"Be just our bleedin' luck to run into damn natives," said Jessop. "Bad move from the Cap'n, not issuin' us with guns. What are we goin' to beat an attack off with? Sticks?" he asked, twirling a particularly heavy branch that Bryant had cut down earlier.

"I doubt he was wild about the idea of giving you a firearm, Jessop," replied Bryant, without breaking his stride.

"You'll be glad of a decent gun if we get ambushed," said Jessop, his eyes beginning to scout out the surrounding shrubs.

"You're beginnin' to worry me now," said Murphy nervously and his eyes too began to dart from left to right as he watched the vegetation. "Anyway, them marines 'ave got guns. If they see any... I saw somethin' move!" he suddenly exclaimed.

As one, they froze, casting anxious looks about them. Bryant was the first to stir from the spell and shook his head. "You're just jumpy, Murphy, calm down. There's nothing here but us."

"Probably just a pig or something, Murphy," said Brooks, not entirely convinced by his own words.

"Pig?" Jessop asked, his attention caught by the prospect of fresh meat.

"There ain't no pigs in Africa," said Bryant wearily. "Only where civilised folk settle. They have other animals here – buffalo, I think."

"What's a buffalo?" Brooks asked.

"Like a cow. But bigger. I think Hague would know."

"Yeah, an' of course, Corbin takes the one man who knows somethin' about the area for 'imself," said Jessop.

"Officer's privilege." If Bryant had the time or strength to shrug, he would have. He stopped and turned round to face his party. "Look, we ain't going to get attacked, there are no natives here and no pigs. Let's just find clean water, as we were told by the nice Lieutenant, and then we can be out of here. Agreed?"

Even Jessop nodded at the wisdom of this. By now they were all wet through, hot and feeling miserable, each longing for the familiar comforts of the *Whirlwind*.

"Right," said Bryant with some finality. "We'll go a little further and then you'll have to take over here, Jessop."

"Why me?" an irritated Jessop said.

"Because I am getting tired, and for all your faults, you are as strong as anyone else here."

Jessop grunted, perhaps unsure of whether he should carry on complaining or accept Bryant's words as a compliment. As one, they started walking again but stopped almost immediately when a low, base growl echoed among the nearby trees. Murphy began to ask what the sound was but Bryant urgently waved him to keep quiet. None of them moved as they began to look around once more. It was Brooks that spotted it first.

"Up there," he said in a whisper, pointing to a spot among the branches of a tree just a few yards ahead of them. Bryant cocked his head and squinted as he tried to peer through the leaves and saw a flash of dull yellow. Moving very slowly, he moved a nearby branch aside and looked into a pair of blinking golden eyes, narrowing as they considered the new arrivals. Stretched languidly along a thick branch just a few yards off the ground was a lithe-looking cat, its fur dappled with dozens of dark coloured spots. They watched its powerful hind muscles tense as it bared two inch-long fangs and spat at them. It was clearly at least as large as a sizeable dog and seemed a lot more powerful.

"Gods, it's a lion!" Murphy said, beginning to shake in fear.

"Ain't a lion," said Bryant. "They live on plains."

"So what is it?" Brooks asked. "Is it dangerous?"

Bryant was at something of a loss. "Some kind of cat. Probably won't attack if we just go round it."

"I can eat cat," said Jessop with confidence as he strode past Bryant, brandishing his stick. Ignoring the warnings of the other members of the party, he jabbed upwards at the animal, trying to dislodge it from its perch.

At first, the cat simply tried to swat his stick away but it began to hiss violently when Jessop connected hard with its flank. It sprang to its feet and leered down at him, teeth bared just a yard away from his head. Thinking that perhaps there might not have been as much meat on the cat as he had first thought, Jessop turned and skipped back to the safety in numbers of the rest of the party.

Tensing for a split second, the cat launched itself with amazing speed at the man's back. Acting purely out of instinct, Bryant lashed out with his knife but only drew a thin line of blood down the cat's ribs.

Moving with a surprising agility for his size, Jessop had already retreated behind the marines, who now found themselves staring into the piercing eyes of the large cat as it crouched, tensing itself for a leap. The nearest marine struggled to unlimber his musket, fiddling at his belt for the ammunition pouch. With a ripple of honed muscles, the cat threw itself forwards, claws digging into the man's shoulders as fangs sunk into the side of his face and neck. The man screamed at an unbelievably high pitch and fell backwards, pinned under the weight of the animal. Screams turned to a gargle as the cat tightened its grip on his neck and rear claws started raking at his stomach, tearing apart the red uniform to stain it with a darker flow of blood.

The second marine, hesitating only a second as he watched the demise of his squad-mate, dismissed any thought of firing his musket and instead reversed it, swinging the butt of the weapon against the shoulder of the cat. It was a weak and hurried blow, which skittered off the creature's hide with no appreciable effect.

By this time, Bryant had recovered enough to step forward and slash with his knife across the cat's haunches, leaving a deep, bleeding cut. The cat released the dead marine and spun around, spitting as it bared its fangs once again. Bryant locked eyes with the animal and saw that it was gauging him carefully, looking for an opening through which to spring and take him down. Shuddering, Bryant crouched, ready to try beating the cat's reflexes by rolling to one side when it leapt.

He was spared the attack by the marine who, yelling with a primal fury he had managed to find deep within, set about the cat with the butt of his musket. The cat shrunk downwards, trying to escape the blows as he swung and jabbed with the weapon. Seeing the animal otherwise distracted, Jessop jumped back into the fight, hammering away with his heavy stick about the cat's head, knocking it insensible almost immediately. As soon as the animal began to move sluggishly under the repeated attacks, Bryant built up the nerve to approach it once more, burying his knife into the cat's neck. He was rewarded with a brief spray of blood, then the cat fell limply across the legs of the dead marine.

Brooks and Murphy crept back from where they had retreated, staring curiously at the animal, its fur now matted with both its own blood and that of the marine. Bryant, Jessop and the remaining marine looked at one another in some relief, the latter two at first beginning to smile and then laughing nervously.

For his part, Bryant was just angry. "You satisfied now, Jessop?" he demanded. "Is the filling of your belly worth the life of a man?"

Jessop started to shrug but then turned to face the last marine. "Hey, sorry 'bout your mate an' all."

The marine cast a glance at his fallen squad mate. "He knew the risks. Anyway, I won't miss 'im."

Glancing back at Bryant, Jessop had something of a look of triumph. "You see?" he said. "Could 'ave 'appened to any of us. An' now we 'ave what we came for – fresh meat!"

Opening his mouth to argue further, Bryant thought better of it, realising that there was no way to get through to the man. He sighed.

"Have it your way. Let's get this animal strung up to a branch. Jessop, you'll help Brooks carry it back."

Frowning, Jessop looked as if he were about to argue the point but the look in Bryant's eyes made him think that here, alone with Bryant's friends, might not be the safest place to complain. Shrugging dismissively, he began looking for a suitable branch from which the cat could be hung and carried.

EVEN THOUGH FOUR marines and twice as many sailors surrounded him, Corbin still felt distinctly uncomfortable as he watched the dark-skinned natives gather in the clearing. It soon became clear they outnumbered his party by at least four to one and though he might have the advantage of swords and firearms on his side, Corbin did not fancy taking chances with this many armed natives who were, literally, just a spear's throw away.

Whereas the other parties had been sent at oblique angles from the beach into the tree line, Corbin had led his party directly through it and they had chanced upon a trail within minutes. Deciding that it was created by natives rather than animals, Corbin had given orders for them to follow the path. It had not been long before they realised that they were not alone among the thick vegetation as they saw shadows flitting from tree to tree beyond the trail, and, having arrived at the clearing, Hague suggested they wait where they were for the arrival of their hidden escort.

The arrival of the first black face at the edge of the clearing had set all their pulses racing but a slow feeling of dread began to spread throughout the party as more and more dark figures stepped out of the trees. Each brandished a primitive looking spear and was clothed only in a short loincloth with a variety of bones and beads hanging from their necks or woven into their black hair. Corbin was left in no doubt that these people would prove to be utterly lethal if provoked and he could not decide if their expressions were a reflection of mere curiosity or... hunger?

Later on, Corbin would reflect on how well Hague had handled himself during the encounter. Showing no outward sign of fear, the Lieutenant had stepped forward and raised his arms in greeting. He began speaking in a strange tongue that seemed impossibly fast to Corbin.

One by one, the natives overcame any hesitation they had, though they did not relax their grip on their weapons. Three started talking to Hague and the conversation became increasingly animated. After a short time, Hague stopped talking, apparently considering what to say next. After he felt the silence had persisted just a little too long, Corbin slowly stepped up to Hague's side.

"Well, you certainly seem to have mastered the tongue, Mr Hague," he said.

"Ah, yes Sir. Unfortunately, we are talking two different languages," he admitted. "Let me try again."

Turning back to the natives he restarted his negotiations, though Corbin could not help but notice that far fewer words were being used, replaced instead by a lot of gesturing and finger pointing. After a while, it seemed as though some progress had been made, especially when the hand movements pointed to various items the party was carrying and Hague had made motions that indicated eating and drinking. The three natives directly opposite them suddenly seemed to get quite excited and kept gesturing towards the marines that accompanied the sailors. It took Hague a few seconds to work out what it was they were after. Reluctantly, he turned back to Corbin.

"Ah, it seems they want guns."

"Guns? They know what guns are?" Corbin was a little confused. "They know how to use them?"

"These people may have a simpler way of life, Mr Corbin, but they have seen the white man before and are well aware of what guns can do. What do I say?"

Corbin thought for a moment. "Well, what do we get in return?" he asked.

Looking a little apologetic, Hague grimaced slightly. "I am not entirely sure, Sir. I've tried explaining what we need and where we want the goods brought. I think we'll get what we are after and it will be brought to the beach. Frankly, I would rather start haggling within sight of the ship than in this clearing."

"That is a very fair point," Corbin conceded. He sighed. "Well, we can spare the guns, and if they get us what we need, I can't say that we will make landfall here again. Might even give those damned slavers something to think twice about."

"My thoughts exactly, Sir," said Hague, smiling with some satisfaction.

"Very well. Make the arrangements, Mr Hague, then we can leave this place."

Becoming anxious to leave the clearing, and the natives, far behind, Corbin watched Hague conclude his business with some impatience. A small commotion from the men behind him made Corbin turn around to see what the disturbance was, keen not to have anything alarm the natives now they were closing a deal. He saw a marine, not part of his detail and clearly out of breath, being interrogated by a few of the sailors.

Taking care not to make any sudden movements that could over-excite their hosts, Corbin nodded to the natives and walked back through his own men to see what the commotion was about. One of his sailors, sensing the presence of an officer, turned round and raised a curled finger to his forehead in salute.

"Beggin' your pardon, Sir," he said. "This marine's just come from the brush party. Says they found somethin' you really need to see. Won't say what."

Corbin looked expectantly at the marine who had begun to recover his breath, though not his composure. "Well?" he asked.

"Complements of Mr Kennedy, Sir," said the marine. "He told me to find you and to not mention what he had seen." The man did not seem apologetic at all in his evasiveness and he cast a meaningful glance at the sailors in Corbin's party. The Lieutenant quickly picked up on his meaning but was puzzled.

"Okay, stand easy man." Corbin said. "We'll make sure Lieutenant Hague has finished here and is making his way back to the beach. Then I will join Mr Kennedy."

THE STENCH FILLED the air around the trail, a powerful, sickly smell that overpowered that of the vegetation or the sweat of the men present. On the rough soil lay five bloody patches, ripped clothing and raw flesh scattered around them, the odd bone poking up to gleam white among the sodden mess. A discarded musket and tattered red uniform identified one of the patches as having once belonged to one of the ship's marines.

Kennedy rubbed his short beard as he took in the scene. "Bad business, this."

"Who else has seen this?" Corbin asked .

"As soon as my men came across it, I told 'em to get back to the beach. I then sent the marine to find you."

Corbin found himself at something of a loss. "What happened here?" he said, finally.

"Never seen anythin' like it, Sir," said Kennedy. "It's like they've just been ripped apart. Some kind of animal, it must be." He shook his head, unable to imagine what kind of beast could do this. "I've 'eard of attacks by creatures in Africa before, Sir, but nothin' like this. Nothin'."

"Can you arrange for them to be buried?" Corbin asked.

Kennedy replied at first with a bitter laugh. "Well, I can cover what's left, Sir. Not much to be done beyond that."

"Okay, Mr Kennedy. Do your best."

A sharp crack marked the arrival of something large passing through the vegetation, causing them all to spin round. His nerves on edge, the single marine cocked his musket and brought it to bear down the trail.

"Whoa," said Murphy, holding up a hand and smiling. "We're friendly!" His eyes then tracked down to the bloody patches and stinking flesh on the trail in front of him, opening wide as he began to realise what they probably were. Corbin noticed four other men behind him, carrying heavy loads. He hurried to stand in front of them but was too late, for they were soon all gawking at their dead shipmates.

"Did we set up a signal fire?" Corbin asked as he flashed a grimace back to Kennedy. He had hoped to keep this scene quiet. Now, it was unavoidable that rumours would sweep through the ship.

"Sorry, Sir," said Murphy. "We was on our way back to the beach when we 'eard voices."

Bryant stepped forward, trying to avoid staring at the blood and gore as he adjusted the weight of his dead party member across his shoulder. "Lost a marine, Lieutenant," he reported to Corbin. "To that," indicating the dead cat now suspended from a pole.

Corbin shook his head. The death toll of this little expedition was beginning to rise beyond all reason. "We'll talk about it later," he said. "Get back to the beach."

Seeming as if he wanted to say something else, Bryant instead took one more look at the raw flesh before them and then instructed the rest of the party to follow him as they left the trail.

After watching them trudge away to disappear into the trees and shrubbery, Kennedy spoke up. "You think this was caused by one of them beasts, Sir?"

Corbin eyed the dead sailors out of the corner of his eye before facing the Bosun. "I don't see how, Mr Kennedy. Seems too small and it did nothing like this to the dead marine that group was carrying. Do what you can here and then make sure everyone gets back to the beach. We should leave as quickly as possible."

"No arguments from me, Sir."

The midday sun beat down hard on the *Whirlwind*, blinding any man foolish enough to look upwards for more than a few seconds. However, the constant breeze coming from the sea was a blessed relief to everyone working above deck or on the side of the hull. Within the bowels of the ship, anyone unlucky enough to be working just cursed and sweated.

Appearing to be everywhere at once, Havelock moved from prow to stern, monitoring all aspects of the repairs, occasionally making a suggestion to the work teams and, once, rolling up his sleeves to help move a large wooden splint to the foremast before it was hauled up into the sky.

Lieutenant Hague had briefly appeared back on board, asking permission to trade firearms with a native tribe he had managed to locate, though he had also been vague about what they were receiving in return. In the end, Havelock had reluctantly agreed to the exchange, though it went against his grain to trade advanced weaponry with primitives. On balance, however, he had much preferred to win his race to repair the *Whirlwind* and locate the *Elita* once more before the French frigate could make good its own damage. This did not stop him from keeping an eye trained on the beach when the natives emerged with their offerings. He did not have much experience in dealing with such people and had heard of many trades turning rotten in the closing moments. He was glad to have Hague on his crew, who seemed to have at least some affinity with the tribe.

Once the beached jolly boats had been filled with supplies from the natives, as well as wood, food and water from the parties that had been dispatched, they were turned around into the sea by their crews and then oars were plunged into the churning waves as they struggled to fight the initial current and head back to the *Whirlwind*. Havelock waited on the quarterdeck for Corbin to climb up the side of the ship and make his report, though he had already seen through the telescope that less men were coming back than had been originally dispatched.

Corbin was only faintly apologetic in his tone but he gave a full and frank account of the landing as he had seen it, which Havelock appreciated. He regretted the loss of life but paid close attention to Corbin's report of the supplies that had been gained.

"We have some fresh water, as I said, Captain," he stated. "But far more milk, from the natives. Seems that is what they usually drink, not sure what it is from though."

"Best not to ask, I imagine," Havelock said.

"Aye, Sir. The natives were also able to supply us with some kind of cloth and wood, though it will need working by the carpenter," Corbin said. "And they gave us all the nuts, roots and fruit we could carry – that should keep the men happy for a few days. Some fresh meat was brought in by our parties, though I doubt it is enough to go round."

"Officers and crew from the landing parties first," said Havelock. "Anything left can be dished out by the Bosun as reward for hard work."

"As you say, Sir."

"You have no idea what caused the deaths on shore?"

"None, Sir," Corbin said. "I don't know what could have done that. One party lost a marine to some kind of wild cat. We buried him on the beach while waiting for the natives."

"Good. I'll mark the other deaths in the log as victims of an animal attack as well."

"Sir, with respect, I am not sure..." Corbin started.

"Yes?"

"Nothing, Sir. How go the repairs?"

"Well enough, though she'll never be truly right until we can pull into a proper dock," Havelock said, a little wistfully. "The foremast is being supported by a tight splint and we daren't risk a topsail on it."

"That will only drop our speed and mobility a little, Sir," said Corbin.

"I would have preferred not to lose anything when in a fight with a ship like the *Elita*. The odds are close enough as it is. Still, we must play the cards we are dealt. The repairs to the hull and gun ports, at least, have proceeded apace. We have even started on the fittings, fixing the non-essential things. It all goes towards..."

"Sail to starboard!" The lookout cried far above them, breaking Havelock's train of thought.

"Damn!" He muttered and drew up his telescope with lightning reflexes as he stared out to sea, slightly northwards.

"What is it, Sir?" Corbin asked.

"She's back again," said Havelock quietly to himself, before handing the telescope to Corbin and pointing to where he should look.

"This is the third time," Havelock said. "She keeps appearing, in the same place every time. Stays a few minutes and then appears to retreat. Never gets close enough for identification. The best I can do is tell she is a three-master. Can you see anything else?"

Corbin squinted hard but a combination of distance and haze foiled his efforts. "Sorry, Sir, no. Could it be the *Elita*?"

"I don't see how. Repair her masts and sails, then get here so soon? Then again, if it were a British ship, why would she not approach? It's damned peculiar."

"Could it be a companion ship to the *Elita*? Maybe a replacement?" Corbin said.

"That might explain a few things," Havelock said. "I think we have to assume she is indeed hostile, until we know better. I have a bad feeling in my bones about that ship and I am damned if I know why."

"What are your orders, Captain?"

Havelock took the telescope from Corbin and raised it to view the distant sails once again.

"She is already retreating back north," he said. Then, to himself, he muttered. "What is it you want?"

Dropping the telescope, Havelock made a decision. "I don't like this. Prepare to set sail, Mr Corbin, set our course due west until I give the word. The crew can carry on with the repairs as we travel. We'll try to sweep round and approach from behind. If she turns out to be friendly, we'll discover soon enough why they have been playing silly beggars. If she is a French ship, we'll have the windward advantage once again."

"Right you are, Sir," said Corbin as he turned to the main deck to begin relaying orders. "All hands ready! Prepare to weigh anchor!"

THEY DID NOT see the mysterious ship again after they set sail, though Havelock posted a double watch among the lookouts and constantly scanned the horizon himself through the telescope. He had ordered the *Whirlwind* to sail due west with all speed until late afternoon, then changed course to sail north for nearly three hours before sweeping back east and then south to run past the coast. Hoping that he had plotted the manoeuvre accurately, Havelock moved to the prow of the ship where his telescope was never far from hand. If he had done this properly, they would now be behind the ship, assuming it had not spotted them at some point and simply fled the area. As the sun began to dip ever lower in the west, with shadows lengthening on deck, he began to fear that this was exactly what had happened.

From time to time, he shouted up at the lookouts among the masts, as much to see if they remained awake and alert as hoping a query from him might suddenly cause the ship to materialise in front of them. Still no vessel showed itself and Havelock's hopes began to fall. Corbin made regular reports as the crew continued to work on repairing the *Whirlwind* but Havelock knew the ship was already fit for battle. What remained was of a superficial nature only.

Twilight was descending when one of the lookouts gave the cry Havelock had been waiting for.

"Sail to starboard!"

Grabbing his telescope and quickly extending it, Havelock glanced up at the lookout to see where the man was pointing and then followed suit himself. Focussing the glasses, he soon picked out a three-masted ship, sailing west away from them, into the setting sun. He could not have asked for a better position.

"Mr Corbin!" he called, summoning the Lieutenant from the main deck. "Change course to follow her! And order the men to beat to quarters!"

Corbin complied as Havelock returned to his place on the quarterdeck. Around him, the crew of the *Whirlwind* rushed to their positions, manning sail, rope and gun as they prepared to go into battle once again. Orders relayed, Corbin climbed the stairs to the quarterdeck and announced that all crew were ready for action.

"This is perfect, Mr Corbin," said Havelock excitedly. "You might find yourself in a position like this just once in your career!"

"Sir?"

"We are cloaked by the night sky, Mr Corbin," Havelock said in explanation. "While she is silhouetted against the fading sun. Thus, we can approach unseen while maintaining an eye on her at all times. Her captain will never know we are here until it is too late."

"A credit to your navigation, Captain," said Corbin, not without a hint of reverence as he realised the position of superiority in which Havelock had managed to place them.

"Now we can see just who she is," said Havelock. "Lieutenant, run up the colours but order the crew not to light any lanterns. We must not give our position away. Let them chat among themselves for the next hour as we make our approach but when we get close, I don't want to hear a single sound from this ship."

For two hours, the *Whirlwind* closed the distance with the other ship, gratifying Havelock that his was still the faster vessel, even with a damaged foremast. Night was now completely wrapped around the frigate, causing crew moving across the main deck to take a great deal more care when traversing ropes and fittings. Though the western sky was quickly darkening, it was still pale enough for everyone on deck to see the ship before them, growing steadily larger. The entire crew, having at first been disquieted with the news from shore of a few deaths, now held their breath in excited anticipation. Having had the order to beat to quarters, there were not many who did not automatically presume they chased an enemy. The veterans among them knew the position of advantage they had been placed in and appreciated the seamanship of the Captain, their words of praise serving to steady the nerves of younger sailors who still remembered their first battle with the *Elita*.

Havelock and Corbin were once again at the prow, this time seeking to penetrate the growing darkness in an effort to identify the ship they chased. Corbin had already remarked on its large size.

"Aye," said Havelock. "That is a ship of the line, and no mistake.

Third-rater at the very least. Perhaps seventy guns. Maybe more. This does indeed explain a great deal."

"The list of missing merchant ships?"

"Indeed. I always wondered whether the *Elita* was operating alone and now, it seems, we have our answer. This is as much part of our mission as capturing that damned oversized frigate."

"Are we wise to pursue such a ship thus, Captain?"

"We are in no danger at this moment, Mr Corbin," Havelock reminded him. "If she did see us, we are fast enough to sail away before she could make a decent move. That's if she proves hostile. If that is a British ship, we may have found a valuable ally in our mission. If not, it is our duty to do what we can to disable or sink her."

"A daring idea, Sir," Corbin said diplomatically.

"We have complete surprise, and are approaching unseen from the stern. Few of their crew will be alert and we should get several volleys in before any reprisal is possible. We will then make the decision to fight or run, depending on how badly damaged she appears."

"A frigate conquering a ship of the line always makes for a fine tale, Sir!"

Havelock handed his telescope to Corbin. "Now you are thinking like an officer of the King's Navy! Here, see if you can make out any markings. There is a flag flying at the stern but I can't make it out. Can younger eyes do better?"

"I'll try, Sir," said Corbin, holding the telescope aloft and squinting as he tried to focus on the tiny fluttering cloth trailing the ship. He spent over a minute trying to gain a steady glimpse. When he did, he dropped the telescope straight down to his side, clearly excited. "It's French, Sir!"

He looked back at Havelock who now wore a wolfish smile. "Time to make some history, Mr Corbin," said the Captain. "We'll retire to the quarterdeck – but do so down the larboard side of the ship, reminding each man that he must keep deathly quiet for the next few minutes. I'll do the same starboard."

Pacing carefully down the main deck, Havelock stopped every few feet to remind one sailor then another to keep his spirits up but also to keep his mouth shut. Everything depended on silence now, as one errant noise could spark the interest of a lookout on the French warship. While the *Whirlwind* would be difficult to see, its huge white sails made sure that it was not impossible.

With both ships travelling in the same direction, it took nearly twenty minutes for the *Whirlwind* to close range, and still Havelock wanted to get even closer, intending to sail within point blank range of its stern and then heave hard to larboard, sending a volley of cannon fire directly into the rear of the ship, just as he had done with the *Elita*. While his small guns would have a limited effect on the huge ship of war, they would be at their most effective at this point.

During this interminable wait, the crew sweated with apprehension and excitement. They knew the advantage was theirs but, being forced to silence lest they be discovered too soon, each man was locked in his own private thoughts of what might happen in the next few minutes.

Guiding the *Whirlwind* slightly off the French ship's beam in order to avoid his sails cutting the wind from its own masts, Havelock forced himself to relax, not wanting to appear too eager in front of his crew. Quietly, he gave Corbin the order to fly the colours, run out the starboard guns and wait his signal to open fire, imagining the enemy captain to perhaps be sitting down to a fine meal in his cabin, maybe with his officers. They would soon be rudely interrupted as the full weight of metal from the *Whirlwind's* guns came crashing through the huge glass windows.

Yard by yard, the distance between the two vessels shrank, the French ship of the line now beginning to tower somewhat over the British frigate, its three layers of gun decks making the *Whirlwind* seem almost puny by comparison. Yard by yard, Havelock counted down the seconds until he judged the time to be right. He waved to get his Lieutenant's attention.

"Now, Mr Corbin," he said, in barely more than a whisper. "Make the turn, hard to larboard."

# CHAPTER SIX

LEANING FAR OVER with the force of the turn, the *Whirlwind* pulled hard to larboard, sweeping behind the massive French ship of war. Havelock could not help but marvel at the size of the enemy vessel as he ran to the railings of the quarterdeck to get a better view. Looking to his left the windows of the great cabin buried within its stern were level with his position on the *Whirlwind*, though he was a little disappointed that no lights were flooding out of them. The possibility remained, however, that the captain of this other ship had retired early and was about to be roused from bed by a very painful alarm.

He hissed over his shoulder. "Mr Corbin, open fire!"

The order was quietly relayed back until Lieutenant Hague, on the gun deck, received it. He shouted to ensure the order was not misunderstood by any of the cannon crew. They, in turn, had already been primed to fire when they saw the stern of the enemy lying in full view of their gun port. However, the stern of this ship of the line was so vast that they were still able to fire almost simultaneously, with the forward guns blasting away just a few seconds before those at the rear of the *Whirlwind*.

Thunderous explosions and bright light, temporarily blinding those who had become accustomed to the night sky, tore the darkness apart and the familiar smell of spent powder filled the air. Already, Havelock could hear Hague's order to reload float up from the gun deck and then the *Whirlwind's* speed had carried it past the smoke cloud of its guns and he looked eagerly at the enemy ship to see the results of his surprise attack.

The windows of the great cabin had been shattered by the assault and large sections of the stern had buckled under the weight of the frigate's metal. Havelock was somewhat irritated that no cries from the wounded could be heard, nor had any fires started. He passed a few course corrections to the helmsman, sailing the *Whirlwind* on a tight line that kept the French ship in line with his guns, then focussed his attention back on the enemy.

Havelock was somewhat nonplussed to see a lot of figures on the deck of the warship and not a little alarmed when he realised that the huge vessel was already changing its course to match his own. His lieutenant noticed this as well and ran up to his side.

"Were they expecting us, Sir? Is this a trap?" Corbin asked.

Mystified, Havelock shrugged. "Makes no sense. To just stand and take the damage we inflicted if you know what the enemy is up to. And yet, Gods, they reacted quickly! Their lookout must have spotted us right at the last moment – you see they are not yet running out their guns?"

The *Whirlwind's* second volley drowned out Corbin's reply, the bright flashes lighting up both ships. When the smoke cleared, both Havelock and Corbin peered through the darkness to gauge the results of the attack. The side of the French vessel was pitted with holes and powder burns, large chunks of the hull planking beginning to splinter and peel away from their mountings.

"A fine shot!" Corbin said.

Havelock was a little less jubilant and instead wore a puzzled frown. "Have you seen their sails?" he asked, disquieted.

"Sir?" Corbin peered into the dark once more and, gradually, began to realise what his Captain had seen. The sails of the French ship were billowing out as if capturing all the wind for miles around and yet they were ragged, with huge holes and tears stretching across their entire span. The mainsail was split in two, straight down the middle and yet, impossibly, both sides were bent forward as if taking the wind. They should have been fluttering like flags, threatening to tear their neighbours apart.

"Damnedest thing I ever saw," said Corbin. "How is that thing sailing?"

"It shouldn't," said Havelock flatly. "That is impossible. Just what the Hell is going on here?" He thought furiously for a few moments. "It doesn't matter right now. Let us throw another volley at them, then extend and come round their prow – we'll send a shot down their length from the other direction, see if they like that!"

Below in the gun deck, they could hear Hague ordering the running out of the cannon as they prepared to fire once more. The *Whirlwind* raced alongside the larger ship, the frigate's speed beginning to tell as its prow started to push past that of its enemy. Havelock watched as, one by one, gun ports started to open on the side of the French vessel and smiled grimly. There was no way they were going to get every port open for a broadside before he fired again and, hopefully, the *Whirlwind* would have moved past many of the enemy guns before they were given the order to shoot.

It was therefore with some surprise that they watched a single cannon on the warship fire, its loud crack and puff of smoke instantly dispersing into the night. Feeling a slight tremor through the quarterdeck, Havelock realised the shot had impacted the *Whirlwind* on its hull, somewhere amidships. About to make a comment regarding poor French discipline, Havelock was amazed to see another cannon fire independently, then another. Soon, the whole side of the warship was clothed in individual smoke clouds as other guns fired, on their own or, at best, in pairs. A continuous staccato blast filled the air, like the low rumbling of thunder. The effect on the crew of the *Whirlwind* was quite unnerving as they endured not a single massive blast but a continuous salvo that lasted for nearly half a minute, until their frigate was able to make headway past the ship of the line. The incoming attack seemed almost light enough to be ignored and then, without warning, a nearby shipmate would lose an arm, leg or even head as a random cannon ball came crashing past.

Pulling ahead, the *Whirlwind's* crew did their best to ignore the losses and continue the business of sailing or reloading their cannon, enjoying a brief respite from the battle as the frigate prepared itself for a new line of attack. On the quarterdeck, Corbin and Havelock exchanged worried looks.

"Who fights like that?" Corbin asked. "It goes against everything we have been taught."

Havelock shook his head, clearly confused. "I don't know who we are fighting here. Pirates, maybe, who have managed to capture a ship of the line and did not bother to remove the French flag? Somehow it does not seem likely."

"Are we to break off the attack?" Corbin said.

"No. We have hurt them more than they have hurt us. We are still in good fighting form and if they are as ill-disciplined as they appear, we have the advantage." He tried hard not to think about the unnatural way the sails of that ship were moving.

"Is it your intention to swing round the prow and attack them from the other side?"

"No, Mr Corbin. To do so would force us to launch an attack on their undamaged side, starting us afresh, as it were. No, we'll cap the T across their prow, fire, and then turn hard about larboard to come down this side again. We'll present our undamaged guns to their damaged hull."

"Very good, Sir. With your permission?" Corbin asked, indicating that he should leave to relay the orders. Havelock nodded him away and looked back at the French ship again, trying to understand what it was he was fighting.

Once the *Whirlwind* had cleared the enemy vessel's prow by sixty yards, Havelock raised his hand to Corbin, who bellowed orders to turn to starboard, bringing the frigate's guns to bear on the warship's prow. Havelock suddenly coughed, nearly retching, as he struggled to find a handkerchief to shield his mouth and nose. Now they had moved downwind of the French ship, he noticed the vile stench that seemed to pour off its deck. It was like nothing he had experienced before, the odour almost overpowering, a mixture of rotting meat, decay, and the pungent aroma of seawater kept in a bucket for too long. He noticed that the other crew on deck were also suffering from its effects, some running to the far railings to heave the contents of their stomachs into the ocean.

"Gods, what is causing that?" Havelock muttered. He knew the French navy did not value hygiene in the same way as British crews but for them to serve on a ship like that stretched the realms of his imagination. The thought of taking the ship of the line as a great prize seemed somehow less appealing and he knew lots would have to be drawn in order to send a skeleton crew over to man it.

Rocking as it fired, the *Whirlwind* launched another salvo at the French ship as they sailed across its path. Several balls bounced off the curved prow, the thick wood serving as effective armour as it deflected the attacks. Others managed to punch through and the elegant figurehead, a painted sea nymph, was shattered in an instant by a single blast.

"Hard to larboard, Mr Corbin," said Havelock. "Bring us about and ready the starboard guns!"

He heard the gun crews pound across their deck as they ran from one side of the ship to the other, urgently loading the starboard guns before opening the gun ports to run them out. As the *Whirlwind* continued its long, sweeping turn that would send it sailing past the enemy vessel from the opposite direction, Havelock crossed the quarterdeck to see if the opposing captain, pirate or not, would accept another exchange of fire or whether he would try to follow the *Whirlwind* in its turn. Instead, he was alarmed to see the sails of the French ship billow out as if filled with the wind from a hurricane.

The giant ship of the line surged forward with unbelievable speed, its prow splitting the sea in two as it travelled, creating a huge wake behind it. For vital seconds, Havelock was speechless as his mind turned – surely no ship had any right to move that fast?

Dimly, he began to realise what the enemy captain intended and he shouted for Corbin urgently.

"Prepare to be boarded! All hands on deck! Now, Mr Corbin!" He had to fight to keep his voice even, lest he risk frightening the crew.


BELOW THE MAIN deck, the gun crews had been spared much of the strangeness that had perturbed their Captain and, indeed, morale had remained high as they realised they were getting far more shots into the enemy than she was throwing back. Casualties had been light and they had yet to lose a single cannon.

"All hands on deck," shouted Lieutenant Hague, his voice carrying above the sound of men in battle. "Prepare to receive boarders!"

"Here we go," said Murphy, clearly unhappy about the prospect of hand-to-hand fighting.

Brooks looked up worriedly at Bryant who smiled back reassuringly. "Don't worry," he said to both of them, as he drew a cutlass he had stashed next to their gun carriage. "You two stick by me, I'll watch over you."

They raced onto the main deck where they were directed by Corbin to form up behind a line of marines who were already loading their muskets. Beyond the red uniformed soldiers, they could see the French warship closing rapidly, like a leviathan of legend surging from the darkness. Bryant cast an eye about the railings behind him and pulled a heavy wooden peg from its hole, about two feet long.

"Here," he said, handing it to Brooks.

"Belaying pins?" asked Brooks, confused.

"Feel the weight of it," Bryant said. "Almost as good as a sword, trust me."

Murphy chipped in as he drew a small knife from his belt. "If a Frog comes up to you, bash 'im over the 'ead with that. 'E won't get up again, I promise you."

Brooks looked from the belaying pin, to Murphy and then back to Bryant. "I'm not sure I can do this," he said, fear beginning to creep into his voice.

"Course you can lad. If you can fire a cannon while we take fire, you can do this. Both of you, stay behind me at all times. I'll look after you."

All around them, sailors held a variety of weapons, either belaying pins taken from the ship or an assortment of knives, cutlasses and axes they had filched or bought for themselves. The marines, their uniforms and weapons a strong contrast to the sailors behind them, obeyed the orders of their sergeant step-by-step, and now stood ready, muskets braced and ready to open fire on the first Frenchman that dared to climb over the railings of the *Whirlwind*.

"Stand ready, men," called Captain Havelock from the quarterdeck. "Remember, you are fighting Frenchmen and every one of you are worth at least ten of them!"

This served to begin steadying the nerves of sailors who had yet to face a boarding action and the veterans among them smiled viciously at the words. Looking at their faces, Brooks realised that there were many on the ship who actually relished the chance to get to grips with the enemy face-to-face. Oddly, he found that strangely comforting.

"What, in the name of God, is that?" A voice said from somewhere within the gaggle of sailors. A second later, they were all gasping as a powerful stench of rotting decay and seaweed rolled over the deck of the *Whirlwind*. Even the normally well-disciplined marines visibly staggered, their muskets dipping for a brief instant before they responded to the Sergeant who bawled at them for dropping their guard.

Bryant looked over his shoulder to see how his shipmates were reacting. Murphy was making caustic comments about not wanting to be the one who was tasked with cleaning the French ship when they captured it. Brooks just looked green as he clasped his hand over his face.

"Brace yourselves!" Corbin cried as the French ship sailed the last few yards. Veering hard to their left, the warship's prow thundered into the side of the *Whirlwind*, forcing everyone on board to take a step back to steady themselves. With a grinding of wood upon wood it slid down the hull of the *Whirlwind*, snapping rails and buckling planking as it went. The side of the French ship rose at least four yards higher than that of the frigate's and everyone on deck looked upwards, steeling themselves for the Captain's order.

As they watched, a dozen lines with heavy metal hooks were thrown over, falling to ensnare themselves among the rigging, masts and hatches, effectively binding the two ships together. Then, a score of faces appeared at the side of the warship and men began to either clamber down the lines or simply drop to the deck of the *Whirlwind*.

The marines opened fire immediately, dropping several boarders to the deck of the frigate. Their sergeant bellowed an order for them to fix bayonets as a huge planked board suddenly became visible high up on the deck of the French ship. Standing vertical for a few seconds, it was then allowed to drop, smashing into the main deck of the *Whirlwind* with a dull thud that was felt by every man on board. More boarders appeared at the top of the plank and they poured down it unsteadily, using it as a ramp to gain access to the frigate.

"At them, men!" shouted Havelock who, they saw, was already advancing, sword in hand, towards two French sailors who had dropped onto the quarterdeck. "Throw them off our ship!"

With a cheer, the sailors on the main deck advanced, eager to smash in the brains of the nearest boarder. Bryant waved Murphy and Brooks forward, brandishing his cutlass.

Together, they pushed past the marines, who were only just completing their orders to fix bayonets. Bryant deliberately steered them away from the ramp, where he knew the fighting would be fiercest. Instead, he positioned his team to defend the ship against any boarders who still chose the risky route of using the lines or jumping onto the deck. One of the early jumpers stirred before them, obviously just winded from his fall. Bryant smiled confidentially at Brooks and Murphy.

"I'll show you how it's done!"

Stepping forward as the man rose Bryant swung downwards with all his strength, burying his cutlass deep into the man's shoulder. His nose wrinkled as he realised the foul stench that covered the deck of the *Whirlwind* seemed to be emanating from the French crew themselves and he was surprised to feel as if the blade had not passed through flesh and bone at all but something a little less substantial. Any puzzlement was soon forgotten as the wounded man rose to his feet, cutlass still lodged in his shoulder. Swinging an arm in a wide arc, the man caught Bryant in the chest with a terrible strength, sending the sailor sprawling into Brooks.

Bryant looked up in horror and disgust at the Frenchman's face. Crooked teeth leered at him from a lipless mouth, and the man's skin was stretched and sallow, greying as it rotted while still on his flesh. Just a few wisps of mangy hair graced the top of his skull but their attention was drawn to his eye sockets. One was empty, a dark pit of blackness that nevertheless seemed very aware of their presence. The remaining eye dangled by a single cord, bouncing on his sunken cheek as he moved.

"Gods!" Struggling to his feet, Bryant eyed his cutlass, still stuck in the man's shoulder. Steeling himself he leapt forward a step and grasped the hilt of the weapon. He was rewarded by a sudden spear of pain as the man swept an arm at him, this time using nails that had grown into steel-hard claws. Four lines of blood began to stain the shirt around Bryant's stomach but he ignored the injury and heaved at the sword. Begrudgingly, it gave way and he pulled the cutlass free, slowly becoming aware that no spray of blood followed it.

The man swung at him again but Bryant jumped out of the way and brought the cutlass hard over his head, into the forearm that flailed at him. It was severed cleanly and fell to the deck. The man did not even grunt in pain as he lumbered forward to take another swipe with his other arm. Eyes growing wide with horror, Bryant yelled inarticulately, a mixture of anger and horror at what he was fighting.

He thrust the cutlass forward, driving it into the decomposing chest of the man, holding his enemy back at arm's length as his opponent tried to claw at him with the remaining hand.

Knowing that he was about to do something he would likely regret, Murphy edged forward, circling the man who remained pinned on Bryant's cutlass. Raising his knife, he charged the man from behind stabbing down with the blade again and again into his neck and base of the skull. The man seemed to lose strength under this assault and sagged, falling to his knees.

Bryant put his foot on the chest of the man and withdrew his cutlass, then kicked out, sending him sprawling. He followed up and, like a madman, chopped away, cutting into the man's head and chest. After a dozen strokes, he realised Murphy's hand was on his arm, bidding him to stop. Bryant looked down at the cut and rotting carcass that lay before them.

Rooted to the spot, Brooks was petrified. Murphy had some choice words to say; "I told you! Didn't I tell you?" he said, almost triumphantly. "Them French are startin' to use the dead in their armies and now they are 'ere on the sea!"

Down by the ramp, their shipmates had begun to realise the nature of the enemy they faced and the line of *Whirlwind's* sailors began to buckle as men retreated. Their officers called out to hold steady but the sailors ignored them, some running across to the far side of the frigate at full stretch before realising they were trapped on a ship in the middle of the ocean. The fighting dead continued to pour down the ramp in ever increasing numbers, fanning out on the deck of the *Whirlwind* as they sought to engage their living enemy.

"Back, back!" Bryant shouted, hustling Brooks and Murphy back among the crowd of other sailors.

"What do we do?" Murphy kept asking. "What do we do?"

"You fight, sailor!" Lieutenant Wynton roared, as he hacked at an approaching corpse.

"Them's zombies!" Murphy squealed, and his hysteria began to spread to the crew nearest him.

"Fight them or join them!" Wynton cried as he deflected a blow from the plank with his sword and then twisted the blade, sweeping it in an arc to sever the head of the creature, causing it to stumble away and crash to the deck, unmoving.

The wave of walking dead crashed into the living across the deck of the *Whirlwind*, gouging, biting and hacking with claws, teeth and an assortment of unclean weapons. Several British sailors fell under this onslaught, paralysed into inaction by their fear. Their screams served to galvanise the others who began to fight with the desperation of men who realise they have nothing left to lose. All along the line, men fell to the deck, disembowelled by wicked claws or gasping their last breath as a pair of pallid hands choked them to death. Elsewhere, animated corpses were pinned down while their skulls were crushed, thrown over board or simply torn apart by frenzied sailors driven far beyond fear.

Taking his place in the centre of the line, Bryant fought like a demon as he swung and hacked at anything moving that did not have a beating heart. He had quickly learnt that a solid blow to the skull could at least slow a zombie down and a decapitation would stop it moving altogether. Failing that, severing limbs at least made them less effective.

Brooks and Murphy cowered behind him, occasionally lashing out with a weapon when one of the infernal creatures came too close. Murphy guessed his small blade was going to be of limited benefit in this battle and turned to gather a belaying pin in his other hand. Taking care to keep Bryant between himself and any zombie, he batted away any claws or weapons that threatened to hurt his friend while another corpse took his attention. Brooks held his weapon close to his chest, standing rigid as his eyes constantly darted left and right, expecting to see a zombie come stumbling through the line to claim his life at any moment.

Aiming a hard kick into a zombie's knee with his heel, Bryant forced it to the ground, feeling a bone break under his blow. The creature flailed at him with a rusty cleaver but he knocked it to one side and swung his cutlass down hard into the centre of its skull, splitting it apart in a shower of grey putrefying ooze. He glanced at the ship of the line, still locked in an embrace with the *Whirlwind* and saw that another score of zombies were shambling down the ramp. They kept together as a group and stumbled directly towards his part of the line.

"Watch out, here come more!"

Though approaching at no more than a slow trot by human standards, the zombies formed a dense wedge that crashed into the line of sailors, buckling it by their weight alone. Men scattered as the zombies struck out at anything within reach that lived, slashing faces with claws and sinking battered swords into chests, seeming to relish the spurt of warm blood that washed over their cold, dead features.

Bryant fought hard to keep his position but even his efforts had to give way to the inevitability of the zombies' assault. He found himself confronted by a pair of the foul creatures, each armed with old-fashioned short swords, and was immediately forced into a defensive posture, parrying each blade as it tried to sneak in to gut him. Timing his riposte, he waited until one of the zombies stabbed at him again and then swung wildly, knocking the sword to one side. He stepped up to the same creature and slammed it with the full weight of his body, throwing it off balance even as its companion turned to face him. Ducking under its swing, he drove his cutlass upwards, piercing the centre of its face with the tip of his weapon. It sunk in several inches without much effort, the zombie twitching its limbs several times before going limp.

As he withdrew his cutlass, he was suddenly aware of a heavy weight bearing down upon him, before a splitting pain announced the return of the first zombie, sinking its sword into his shoulder. He cried out and rolled away, carrying the creature with him. Twisting his body, Bryant continued his roll until he sat astride the zombie, gagging at being in such close proximity of its foulness. Holding his cutlass across his chest with his off hand on the back of the blade, he drove it down across the zombie's neck, severing its head instantly.

Rubbing the creature's gore and flaking skin off his arms and clothes as he stood up, Bryant began looking anxiously for his friends. He panicked as he realised they were no longer with him.

The rush of the zombie wedge into their line had taken Murphy completely by surprise and he had retreated ahead of them until his flight was halted by the railings at the side of the *Whirlwind*. He glanced longingly at the open ocean and, for a brief second, considered leaping into the dark sea, believing it better to drown than be torn apart by these infernal creatures.

Heavy footsteps caused Murphy to spin round, instinctively raising the belaying pin. The reflex saved him as a knife sailed into the wood. He yelped and took a step away until he felt the railings dig into his back. Three zombies advanced, reaching for his throat. Crazed by fear, he struck out wildly, hitting nothing but slipping on something on the deck – whether it was blood or water, he did not have the presence of mind to question. Falling heavily, Murphy covered his head for protection, his vision filled with the sight of three dead men bending down to tear him apart.

An angry cry, unmistakably human, caused him to peer up with a single eye. The head of one of the zombies flew above him and into the sea as an axe bit through its neck. The weapon was reversed in mid-swing to land a blow straight into the chest of the second as Jessop, consumed with fury and covered in blood trickling from a dozen minor wounds, dove into the fight. The third zombie turned from Murphy to grab at the burly man but he head-butted it in return, sending it stumbling backwards as he heaved upwards with his axe. Carrying the impaled zombie with it, Jessop strained as he lifted the creature off its feet, above his head and over the railings. Having cast his enemy into the sea he spun round to catch the last zombie in the side of its skull, dropping it instantly.

Bending down to Murphy, Jessop heaved the small man to his feet and snarled into his face. "On your feet and fight, you li'l Irish maggot!"

Murphy had seen the man angered before but the pure hatred and deadly intent he saw now were beyond anything he had witnessed in a human being. In spite of his fear, he was very glad that Jessop was on his side and he regained his footing, brandishing his weapons to show the man he was back in the fight. Satisfied, Jessop turned back to the fray, twirling his axe as he sought a new enemy to smash apart.

Murphy heard a familiar voice cry out in desperation and he looked around to see a mop of ginger hair near the mainmast. Pushing through the press of sailors and side-stepping a leering zombie, he raced towards his friend as Brooks confronted another of the decomposing boarders.

Backing away and swinging wildly with his belaying pin, Brooks was petrified as he faced the cutlass wielding zombie, constantly giving ground before its attacks. Nearly tripping on a loose rope, Brooks cried out as he sank to one knee and raised his weapon up in reflex. The zombie hacked sideways, slicing into the belaying pin and leaving only a stump in Brooks' hand. Shouting out desperately for help, Brooks managed to regain his balance and started to back away again, only to find himself pinned against the mast. He closed his eyes, raising the remains of his weapon as he waited for death.

Seeing what was about to happen, Murphy let loose an inarticulate war cry as he jumped forward past a stumbling zombie and then crouched, tensing his muscles and dropping his near useless knife. Leaping upwards, he caught hold of a rope that had broken free from somewhere high on the mainmast, and swinging across the few remaining yards, he let the full weight of his momentum carry forward into the blow he made with his belaying pin. Landing the weapon squarely on the back of the zombie's skull, he shattered it completely and, landing lithely on his feet, he stepped over the corpse as it crashed to the wooden deck.

"Brooks, lad!"

Slowly, Brooks opened his eyes "Murphy? Where did you come from?"

SPORTING A LONG, ragged cut on his left cheek Havelock had been fighting for his life since the French ship had crashed into them. Two boarders had jumped from the side of the larger ship, falling straight to the frigate's quarterdeck. Havelock at first thought they had both broken their necks from the drop, but had been horrified to see them rise, their milky eyes staring at him from deep, sunken sockets as they reached for him with wickedly sharp claws. The flash of bloated, rotting flesh had stalled him for only a brief second before he realised, whatever the nature of the enemy, it posed a very real threat to his ship.

Precise strokes of his sword had at first disabled the zombies, depriving them of their arms, then dispatched them as he learned, like so many of his sailors after the initial clash on the main deck, how to fight these unnatural foes. He had backed away as more creatures started dropping onto his deck like sacks of wheat, before stirring from their fall and advancing. Quickly joined by Corbin and a handful of marines, Havelock had led the defence of the quarterdeck against ever-rising odds.

Now coated with sweat under his ripped jacket, his hat lost long ago and sword wreathed in a sickly grey ichor, Havelock fought side by side with his Lieutenant as another pair of zombies advanced towards them. Only the Marine Sergeant now survived on the quarterdeck and he flanked Havelock on his left side, using his sword as skilfully as either of the naval officers.

Working together, their swords flickered out as one and the two zombies dropped to the deck, their heads rolling for several yards before coming to rest. Already, more zombies were clambering over the side of the ship that towered above them, preparing to drop downwards. Havelock spared a glance to the main deck, trying to gauge the ebb and flow of battle. He immediately saw that, while his crew had taken horrific casualties, they had steadied from the fear of confronting the fighting dead for the first time, and now formed a credible line that held firm against the tide of zombies. Away from this scattered skirmishes took place all over the ship. He took a single glance at the number of unmoving rotting corpses lying on the deck and quickly decided that far more zombies lay within the French ship and that his crew would, inevitably, be overwhelmed sooner or later.

"Mr Corbin!" he called, arresting his Lieutenant's attention. "We cannot go on like this."

"Captain, what are we facing?" Corbin said breathlessly, a hint of hysteria beginning to rise in the man's voice.

"We haven't got time to ponder that now! We have to get away from here, Corbin, do you hear me?"

Havelock grabbed Corbin by the arm and shook him, forcing the man's attention on him. Corbin seemed to waver for a brief second, then locked eyes with his Captain.

"What are your orders?" he asked, to Havelock's relief.

"Gather as many men as you can. Then sever those lines holding us to that ship. Once they are cut, we sail."

He saw Corbin's eyes dart with foreboding to the roiling battle on the main deck. He gave the man's arm another firm shake, forcing Corbin to look at him again.

"Lieutenant, this is very important. If we cannot get away from that ship, we are doomed."

Corbin took a shaky breath. "I understand, Sir. You can count on me."

"Good man. Now, go. The Sergeant and I will hold them here. Their swordplay is no match for ours!"

Taking just a second to gather his courage, Corbin ran to the stairs leading to the quarterdeck and ran down them, two at a time. A zombie had started to climb them to flank the Captain's position but Corbin, bracing himself against the banister, kicked out with his boot, pitching the creature overboard. He spotted half a dozen sailors battling a trio of zombies just ahead and he leapt into the combat, slashing with his sword as he aided them in braining or decapitating the decomposing French.

"You men!" He called "With me! We must cut the lines!"

He could sense the sailors' relief as they realised that, at last, they had some real direction. Some of them even grinned as they gathered their weapons and followed their Lieutenant to the other side of the ship where they set about cutting the lines that bound the ships together, while two of their number stood guard with belaying pins, ready to attack any zombie that strayed too close.

After the nearest lines had been cut, the ships began to float apart and the team moved forward, eager to cut the remaining tethers. Corbin looked up and spied another group of zombies setting foot on the ramp, another wave designed to slowly wear down the defenders and whittle them away to eventual defeat. He shouted to gain the attention of the two men standing guard over the line-cutters.

"The board! Pitch it over the side before they come down!" he said, pointing up at the advancing zombies. The sailors at first seemed dubious about intentionally getting so close to the dead but a further word from Corbin sent them sprinting.

Getting a purchase on the wood, they strained, raising it a few inches from the deck, but the weight of more zombies walking on the board threatened to tear their grip loose. Seeing the danger, Corbin ran over and, skidding to a halt, dropped his sword and grabbed the board to add his own strength to their efforts. Straining together they slowly raised the board and, moving to one side, spun it around so it broke free of its mountings on the larger ship. Board and zombie alike fell into the gap between the two ships and were instantly swallowed up by the sea.

Looking towards the prow of the *Whirlwind*, Corbin saw that almost all the lines had been cut. He began shouting orders that would set them underway but the frigate was already shuddering as it began to scrape past the French ship, as if it were aware that to tally longer would mean its own desecration and eventual corruption.

"Set the mainsail," shouted Corbin and his line-cutters began scuttling up the rigging to obey. On the other side of the deck, men still battled with the dead but they had all sensed the *Whirlwind* begin to move and there was an instant change in their demeanour. Morale improved instantly and those still fighting redoubled their efforts while those who had defeated their immediate foes either scrambled up the rigging or grabbed lines to bring the sails into line, or else prowled the decks, quickly dispatching any zombie that leapt from its ship to the frigate's deck.

In less than a minute, the *Whirlwind* had cleared the hull of the French ship and the last zombie had either been cast overboard or cut into inanimate pieces. Corbin ran back up to the quarterdeck to greet his Captain. He found Havelock stooped over the Marine Sergeant, hands pressed to the man's chest which was stained with a spreading shade of dark crimson. The Sergeant's face was deathly pale, matching that of the zombie that had finally claimed his life with a wicked strike to his heart.

Without turning his head to face Corbin, Havelock asked "Are we all set, Mr Corbin?"

"Aye, Sir. We are on our way."

Regarding the Sergeant for just a moment longer, Havelock laid the man's head gently on the deck and then stood up. "But for a few more moments and he would have lived through this. He was a good fighter, Mr Corbin."

"That he was, Sir."

Walking slowly to the stern of the *Whirlwind*, Havelock looked into the darkness, watching the French hulk lie still and motionless on the ocean.

"We are not pursued," he remarked.

"I don't understand, Sir. I saw how fast that ship closed with us – it was like lightning! Why do they not chase us?"

Havelock stared at the zombie ship until it finally disappeared into the darkness.

"I don't know. I just don't know."

# CHAPTER SEVEN

THROUGHOUT THE SMALL hours until the breaking of the dawning sun above the eastern sky, the crew of the *Whirlwind* often resembled the walking dead they had fought earlier that night. Going about their duties automatically, many were dull-eyed and uncommunicative. The constant banter among sailors was noticeable by its absence and orders from officers were obeyed without comment or argument. Stunned by their supernatural encounter, each member of the crew tried to assimilate, in his own mind, just what had happened, even as he mourned lost shipmates.

Having been ordered by their Captain to make good repairs and return the frigate to fighting fitness, the crew of the *Whirlwind* found their ship to have suffered only superficial damage. The sporadic firing of the French vessel had failed to do much more than smash the rigging of the mizzenmast and dislodge a couple of guns from their carriages. The damage to the crew themselves was more substantial and morale plummeted as men were ordered to clean the deck. Whereas this usually meant hours of back-breaking labour with the holystone, today it saw sailors prepare the bodies

703

of their shipmates for burial at sea, sealing them in sailing canvas, while throwing the corpses and severed limbs of unmoving zombies over the hull. Even then, they had to strain to remove the countless pools of blood from the wooden deck, each a reminder of just how hard they had had to fight in order to survive.

While most of the *Whirlwind's* crew who had been killed in the attack were easily identified, a few were not. In areas of the deck where the walking dead had swept forward quickly, trapping sailors behind their line, there remained only a few gruesome scraps of bloody flesh and clothing, mere puddles where men had once stood. Corbin noted the similarity of these finds to the remains of the crew that had been killed on the African coast, and he mentioned his theories to the Captain. Evidently, the ship of the dead had known where the *Whirlwind* was for quite some time and was not averse to deploying its crew on land.

It was not until this gruesome task had been completed that Havelock allowed his crew to resume their normal watch patterns, permitting those off-duty to find whatever rest they could below decks. There was a brief period of excitement as a call rang out that another zombie had been found on the gun deck, having apparently clambered up the hull from where it had been tossed into the sea, to enter the ship through an open gun port. It had lurked in the darkness of the lower decks until a sailor had strayed too close to its hiding place. Stumbling out of the darkness, the creature had terrified the man, who ran up into the daylight, screaming. A small party of sailors eventually steeled themselves to descend onto the gun deck, where they had dispatched the zombie. A thorough search of the ship turned up no more enemies but it had rattled the nerves of everyone on board even further.

All across the gun deck, sailors who were not assigned to the current watch set their hammocks swinging from the rafters but few actually crawled into them. Most gathered in small groups, speaking in huddled whispers as they tried to come to terms with what they had seen, keeping an envious eye on those who did sleep.

Bryant, Brooks and Murphy sat quietly at a table hastily placed across the centre of the gun deck, the crew of two other cannon opposite them. Conversation was sporadic, each man preferring to keep his own council as they hunched over under the light of a single swinging lantern above them. It was Murphy who broke the silence.

"So what 'ave the Frogs turned upon us?" he asked.

No one answered for a few seconds, then Bryant sighed. "I don't know, my friend, truly I don't."

"I told you they was usin' the walkin' dead – zombies – as sailors!"

One of the other cannon crew stirred at this. "It don't seem credible."

"Trust your own eyes," Murphy said. "What do you think we was fightin' last night?"

"It was the dead," Brooks piped up softly. "Face's rotting – and they didn't go down when you hit them!"

"Not without a solid blow to the head," said the sailor. "I saw one comin' at one of me mates, both arms 'acked off. Still it came forward, trying to bite 'im. In the end, we stuck an axe in its chest and 'eaved it overboard. Not 'fore it got Buxton though. Poor lad."

"And that smell!" Brooks said. "I lived near the factories of Portsmouth and never smelled anything so bad."

"T'was the smell of death," said Murphy.

"It was the stink of something that had lain at the bottom of the ocean for years," said Bryant. "I don't know, Murphy, your idea of the Frogs using the dead to fight this war – there's something wrong there. That ship, I swear, had been dragged from its resting place on the sea floor. It was like, I don't know, a ghost ship or something."

They paused there, mulling over this new idea but were interrupted by heavy footsteps and a curse as somebody walked into a gun carriage. Jessop headed their way but his feet were unsteady. They quickly realised that, somehow, the man had managed to get his hands on a rather large quantity of rum. Given the circumstances, they could not blame him but still grew alarmed when they realised he was heading in their direction. No doubt his own gun crew had retired or else become tired of his banter and he was searching for more company.

Tripping over his own feet, he staggered across to their table, bracing himself on Bryant's shoulder before collapsing on the deck. He grinned as he looked into their upturned faces.

"We showed them Frogs, eh? Dead or alive, British is best when it comes to the sea!" He raised his mug in salute, showering Bryant with the strong smelling drink. Jessop reached forward to ruffle Murphy's hair, though the action nearly unbalanced him. "I even saw you start to fight towards the end, ya li'l Irish maggot!"

"Ah, yeah," said Murphy. He turned back to his friends. "Jessop 'ere, 'elped me out in the fight."

"Just 'elped you out?" Jessop roared with laughter, the volume seeming entirely inappropriate for the subdued deck. Many of those in the hammocks turned to complain but held their tongues when they saw who was talking. He leaned over, placing his face right next to Bryant's. "I'm tellin' ya! Your little friend 'ere was in a bad way. Three of them dead men – three, I tell ya – had 'im pinned. 'E was all curled up, ready to die."

Murphy grinned nervously. "Can't say anythin' against that. Jessop, 'e just comes out of nowhere, swingin' 'is axe. Took care of all three!"

"An' ya got balls after that," Jessop said to him. "Out the corner of me eye, I saw ya save Brooks! Worthy of a drink, methinks!" Jessop swigged from his mug then handed it to Murphy.

Brooks smiled his thanks but Murphy was consumed with Jessop's rum until the mug was snatched away. He smacked his lips but Bryant was less impressed.

"You seem in a good mood, Jessop," he said.

"Well, why not?" The burly man asked. "We won!"

"And, presumably, you do not think it strange, the enemy we fought?"

Jessop seemed ready to answer with more bravado but, instead, he considered Bryant's words. Pushing in between Brooks and Bryant, he sat heavily at the table.

"The other men don't like to talk about it," he said.

"I imagine, like us, they are just grateful to be alive."

"You all think it is some Froggie plot?" Jessop asked.

Murphy nodded but Bryant answered for them all. "I don't think so. Not unless the French have found a way to drag a ship up from the seabed, crew and all."

"It might help if we knew which ship it was," said Brooks.

"No, I thought about that," said Bryant. "The French have dozens of ships of the line, probably hundreds throughout the years – and we don't know how old that ship was. We might have seen her nameplate if we had approached her differently, but it would have been smashed by our first salvo."

"I saw it," said Jessop, with a sly wink. The other sailors around the table looked at him dubiously, prompting him to continue. "True as I'm sittin' 'ere, I saw it. We was the first gun crew to fire – it was untouched before we let rip. I saw the nameplate. Even in the dark, it was as bold as brass."

He seemed to saviour the attention until Bryant nudged him. "Well?"

"It was the *Deja*. Never 'eard of it though."

The sailors all tried to recollect the names of French ships of the line they had run across or head heard tales of but all shook their heads as they drew blanks. Still, as Murphy pointed out, the British and French captured and recaptured each other's ships so often, it was almost impossible to keep an accurate track of names. Jessop, though, had been doing his own thinking.

"Now, 'ang on, Bryant," he said. "You said the Frogs can't raise a ship from the bottom of the sea. An' that makes sense. So 'ow come it was there at all?"

Bryant's look was a little incredulous. "Well, I think that is why they call it a mystery, Jessop. Some kind of ghost ship, you hear stories like this."

"Yeah, but I've been thinkin'," said Jessop. "An' I've never 'eard of a ghost ship firin' at someone. An' I sure as 'ell 'aven't 'eard of a ship bein' boarded by the livin' dead."

Knowing that he would be better off not hearing any more, Bryant nevertheless sighed and asked "So?"

"That Jefferies, thievin' scum that 'e was, talked a lot of nonsense. But I remember 'im talkin' about 'Avelock's Curse. An' it seems to me there is some sense in that."

"It fits with what Jefferies said," Murphy interjected before Bryant could speak. "The men die in droves but nothin' bad 'appens to old 'Avelock. 'E survived just fine. Barely a scratch and, remember, the Sergeant of the Marines died just a few feet from 'im. Must 'ave taken a blow meant for the Cap'n!"

"Don't you start that," Bryant warned Murphy, before he was interrupted by Jessop.

"Think about it," Jessop said insistently. "We're 'ere, in the middle of the ocean. An' we just 'appen to come across a hulk of a Frog ship, crewed by nothin' but the dead. It leads us on, lurin' the Cap'n far from land and then turns on us." He sat up straight, draining his mug before turning back to look at them all, deadly serious. "You know what one cursed man can do to a ship..."

"And you can stop that talk too, Jessop," Bryant said, his voice quiet but stern. Again, he was ignored as one of the other sailors chipped in.

"What're sayin', Jessop?" he said. "You talkin' about the Cap'n 'ere, not some green pressed man or midshipman you can just 'eave overboard when no one is lookin'".

For the first time, Jessop seemed a little uncomfortable, as if the weight of what he was saying was only just becoming apparent to him. He shifted uneasily in his seat and swilled his mug, hoping to find more rum within. "There are ways," was all he said.

"Blow that for a game of soldiers," said the sailor. "I ain't bein' any part of this." He stood up from the table, retreating into the darkness of the gun deck to find his hammock.

"And that's good advice for all of us," said Bryant, standing up himself. He was arrested by Jessop's hand grabbing his arm.

"Think about it," Jessop hissed. "If it comes down to him or us... I say we make a move if that damned ship turns up again."

"What's going on here?" The soft voice of Midshipman Rawlinson surprised them all, his small form stepping into the light of their lantern.

Jessop started but quickly recovered, standing up straight, if a little shakily, and hooking a finger to his forehead. "Nothin' goin' on 'ere, Sir," he said. "We was just talkin'.'"

Regarding them all, Rawlinson seemed to be considering what to do and Bryant wondered how much the Midshipman had heard. He had no idea how long the young man had been on the gun deck, nor whether he had been paying attention to their conversation.

Finally, Rawlinson seemed to make his mind up. "You should be sleeping. You all have your regular watches ahead of you." He regarded Jessop. "I am not going to ask you about illicit rum or smell your breath, Jessop, given what we have all been through. But I suggest you return to your hammock now."

Relieved, Jessop bowed his head and crooked his finger to his forehead again. "Right you are, Sir."

The Midshipman watched them all rise from the table to find their sleeping places, then turned to leave, mounting the stairs to the gun deck. Next to their gun carriage, Bryant helped Brooks tie up one end of his hammock as the new seaman dealt with the other. Murphy, with typical speed, had already climbed into his own but he rolled over to regard his two friends.

"So, if it ain't a ghost ship, what was it?" he asked.

"I really don't know what you call a hulk like that," said Bryant, beginning to feel weary now that he saw his hammock in front of him.

"A ship of death," Murphy mused.

"A death hulk," said Brooks softly, causing the other two to look at him curiously. The name was to stick.


"VERY GOOD, MR Rawlinson. Inform Mr Kennedy and tell him to keep an eye out," Corbin instructed the Midshipman. The news of talk among the crew verging on the mutinous was not welcome but he could not find it in his heart to blame the men. The pitched battle of the night before, that had seen dead men boarding the *Whirlwind*, had rocked him to his core, and it had taken a great deal of effort to portray the image of a calm, disciplined and unruffled officer of His Majesty's Navy. Inside, Corbin wanted nothing more than to return to England with all speed.

Captain Havelock had spent the night personally overseeing repairs and passing an encouraging word where he could which at least some of the crew had seemed to appreciate. He had then spent several hours in his cabin, plotting their next course of action, but Corbin now spied him on the quarterdeck, enjoying the morning air as it swept over the frigate. Vaulting the stairs Corbin joined his Captain, needing to inform him about the state of the crew's morale but also eager to hear of their next destination.

"Lieutenant," Havelock greeted Corbin as he approached. "Are we fighting fit?"

"Aye, Sir. She's battered and scarred but as ready to join battle as she ever was."

"The *Whirlwind* will see us through," said Havelock, gazing at his ship with not a little fondness. "And then she'll carry us back home."

"Complements of Mr Rawlinson," Corbin said to change the subject. "Many of the crew are uneasy about last night. Some are taking matters a little too far."

"Talk of mutiny?"

"Not outright, I believe. But Mr Rawlinson was present during a conversation below decks that made him feel uneasy. I had him instruct Mr Kennedy to keep a reign on things, without letting it boil over."

"Very good," Havelock said. "We must give the men a little latitude today – a flogging would work against us in the end."

"What are your intentions today, Sir?"

"Why, we have two enemies, Mr Corbin, both of whom we have

hurt a great deal, I believe," said Havelock with a grin. "It is my intention to locate one or both, and finish them off!"

"Yes, Sir. I believe I know which one I would rather face," Corbin said.

Havelock winced briefly but quickly recovered. "Last night, the enemy had the advantage of us not knowing what we faced. Now we do and I am confident we can compensate for that."

"Your pardon, Sir, but what do you have in mind? She had a distinct turn of speed about her. We saw that as she came into board us."

"True. But I saw nothing to indicate she was particularly manoeuvrable. So, we use that. Keep to her stern, avoid her prow. It even seems that we have little to fear from her broadsides – their return fire was lacklustre at best. As for the *Elita*, I would be surprised to see her even halfway to fighting readiness. We really gave her a bloody nose."

"That we did," Corbin said, heartened to see his Captain had a firm plan.

"I'll address the crew once they have had some rest. Still I would like to know just who it was we faced last night," Havelock said.

"Ah, yes. More news, courtesy of Mr Rawlinson. He overheard one of the gun crews talking about our first salvo. Apparently they saw the nameplate of the ship before we attacked."

"And?"

"He said it was called the *Deja*. Mean anything to you, Sir?"

Corbin was taken aback when he saw his Captain blink dully at him, cast a look to the main deck, and then back, this time with a more urgent look in his eyes. He leaned forward, talking quietly.

"The *Deja*? Are you sure, man?"

"As reported by Mr Rawlinson, Sir. You have heard of it?"

Havelock's expression was one of utter confusion. "That's impossible," he mumbled, as he pushed past Corbin, not seeming to notice the Lieutenant, walking down the stairs to the main deck before disappearing below and retreating into his cabin. Corbin heard the door shut with a dull thud, leaving him totally perplexed.

Believing that his Captain simply required a little time to digest the news, whatever it might ultimately mean, Corbin patrolled the ship, talking to Kennedy, Rawlinson and Hague, ensuring their duties were being attended to and no other problems were arising. All three reported that the crew, as a whole, were beginning to become surly and while no one had transgressed the Articles of War directly, it could only be a matter of time. As he moved from deck to deck, Corbin became aware of a tension settling on the entire ship. It was nothing he could really put his finger on – just a slight delay in a salute, perhaps, or a sideways look of contempt as a sailor worked on the rigging. He could not help but contrast the attitude of the crew to Havelock's earlier buoyant mood when talking about defeating the two French ships. It was as if everyone knew something he did not.

The ship's bell rang twice before Corbin realised that Havelock had still not emerged from his cabin, signifying the Captain had secluded himself, without word, for over an hour. Concerned, he finally steeled himself to approach the great cabin and, once outside the oak door, rapped on the wood.

No answer came and he knocked again with still no response. Hesitantly, beginning to fear for his Captain's health, Corbin pushed the door ajar and peered inside.

Havelock did not acknowledge Corbin as the Lieutenant entered the great cabin. He was sat at his table, back to the long lead-lined window, turning an old-fashioned sword over and over in his hands as he inspected its blade.

"Sir?" Corbin asked, with some hesitation.

It took a while for Havelock to respond and when he did so, his eyes did not take their intent gaze off the sword.

"What is it, Mr Corbin?" he said quietly.

"Sir, Mr Kennedy and I have some concerns over the crew. Morale, you understand."

Again, it took Havelock some moments to reply and when he did so, it seemed as if he were far away. "Ah, yes, morale. The key to a good ship, Mr Corbin. We must do something about that."

Feeling unsure of himself, Corbin took the liberty of sitting himself down at the table, opposite Havelock. He had never seen the expression on the man's face before. He would have described it as... haunted. He was about to venture another question when Havelock spoke once more.

"My grandfather's sword," he said by way of explanation. "Given to him by the First Sea Lord. Now I keep it in here, a memento to past glories of the old man."

"He was a true hero, Sir," Corbin said carefully.

"Oh, yes. The scourge of the French. Certainly helped my career

711

along, I can tell you. There was no doubt about my finding a ship, even if peace should suddenly break out. Ever since I was a midshipman, having the name Havelock was always useful."

"Sir? Is there something awry?"

With care and a little reverence, Havelock set the sword down on the table. Finally, he met Corbin's gaze and his eyes seemed to clear slightly.

"What do you know of my grandfather's great victory? The one that earned him his admiralty?"

"Very little," Corbin admitted. "But I have heard plenty of stories. How he engaged a fleet of two ships of the line and two frigates off the coast of Africa, sinking one after the other, constantly keeping them off balance. I have also heard people say it actually took place at Guadeloupe and that the port there was sacked as a result."

"People like to gossip. They rarely get it right," Havelock said.

"That is true, Sir," Corbin said. After a brief hesitation, he then asked "Would you care to tell me what really happened?"

Havelock took a deep breath. "This is not something I have ever done, Mr Corbin. As is the way of things, a glory in a family's past rarely holds up to close inspection. However, I believe you have been pulled into something terrible and, as such, you certainly deserve to know the truth. Though I would be much appreciative if this were kept between ourselves, assuming we make it back to port."

"You can rely on my discretion, Captain."

"Only a few in my family and certain members of the Admiralty and Imperial Administration know what I am about to tell you. They would not be pleased to learn that you also know the truth. I accept your word of silence as an officer of the King's Navy, Mr Corbin, but I want you to understand the repercussions possible if you should break that word, for any reason. It would mean the end of your career."

"I understand."

Placing a hand on the hilt of his grandfather's sword, Havelock began to speak. "You were right about my grandfather's victory taking place off the coast of Africa – not far from our current position, if I am not mistaken. Nowhere near the Caribbean. I have no idea how that rumour started. Anyway, my grandfather had not been sent down to this wretched part of the world as we have, with orders to hunt down a commerce raider. No, he *was* the commerce raider. Specifically, he had been tasked with destroying a French convoy en route to the east."

"So there was no great battle?"

"Oh, a battle there was," said Havelock candidly. "You see, that convoy was filled to the brim with colonists. Just men and women searching for a new life overseas, no great silver train or other valuable cargo. However, not even the French are callous enough to risk sending so many people so far without some form of protection. Present with the convoy was a ship of the line, a real bruiser of a vessel, I have been told."

"Just the one?"

Havelock smirked. "Sorry, Mr Corbin, yes, there was just one ship of the line. No other warships were in that convoy. Still, it must be said, the defeat of any ship of the line by a single frigate is an action worthy of recognition and could well aid a promising captain on his way to becoming an admiral."

"Indeed."

"However, the actual details of the battle were kept secret, hence the rumours that grew."

Corbin looked puzzled. "But why? If it was a great victory, why not publicise it?"

"Because hunting down ships packed with colonists is something the British people like to think the French do, not His Majesty's Navy. And also because of the manner by which the ship of the line was sunk. You see, my grandfather's frigate could keep the single warship off balance all right, he had the wind and benefit of speed. So, he could pick off the colonists' ships as he pleased while the larger vessel lumbered after him. Towards the end of the engagement, the French ship deliberately placed itself between my grandfather and the rest of the convoy, leeward and at a terrible disadvantage. This move enabled the remaining colonists to escape but the warship paid for it heavily. Unable to defend itself properly, my grandfather was able to sink it with relative ease – though I understand it did take a bit of time." Havelock mused for a second and then added: "That French captain was the true hero that day, but no one ever got to hear about his selfless courage."

"Ah." It was an unworthy response to the tale, Corbin knew but he had been left confused and not a little deflated at this admission. They sat in silence until a thought crossed Corbin's mind. "Sir, what business has the Admiralty in ordering the destruction of colonists anyway?"

"Happens more often than you may think," said Havelock. "After all, a newly discovered land is just a rock in the middle of the sea until you put people on it. With people come towns, forts, garrisons and trade. On the other hand, hunt colonists and you not only keep land bereft of civilisation. You also delay the spread of French Imperial interests. And you can understand how that very much concerns the Admiralty, not to mention Parliament and the Royal Court."

"I can, Sir, yes," said Corbin. With Britain's trade and Empire dependant on her ships being able to range freely on the ocean, the spread of a rival power across the globe could only mean a curtailing of their domination – and profits. While pondering this, Corbin suddenly realised that the Captain had deliberately left something out. This was confirmed when he looked up at Havelock and saw the man's eyebrows lift in question.

"I appreciate the confidence you place by telling me all of this, Sir," Corbin said. "But why are you telling me now?"

"The name of the French ship of the line sunk by my grandfather was the *Deja*," said Havelock simply.

"No!" Corbin exclaimed, amazed by the coincidence. He then slowly began to realise that Havelock did not think it a coincidence at all.

"You know, it's funny," said Havelock, almost conversationally. "I have been aware of sailors under my command talking about the Havelock Curse for some years now. But I never gave it an ounce of credence until today, when I discovered the name of that bedevilled ship."

"You believe that the *Deja* your grandfather sunk and the ship last night are one and the same? That is ... impossible!"

"I believe it shows a wonderful symmetry. A man commits callous murder in the past and is never made to pay for his crime. The victims, searching for recompense, finally receive the chance to make his descendants answer for those actions."

"This is madness!" Corbin said.

"Really? You saw the nature of the enemy we fought last night. How else do you explain it? Think of it – how many years might they have roamed the ocean, not able to rest until they found my grandfather, not even knowing he was dead? Discovering no resolution, they eventually happen upon his grandson. If you were they, what might you do?"

Corbin shook his head, not wanting to follow where his Captain was taking him. "So you think, what, they disappear into a watery grave every day and rise as the walking dead at night, ship and all?"

"I know not how this works, Mr Corbin," said Havelock flatly. "I am no expert in such matters. Perhaps they never return to the sea floor. Perhaps they have only just risen, sensing my presence. All I know is that I have been called to account for the sins of my grandfather."

"So... what do you intend to do?"

Havelock paused, thinking. "A mark must be set for justice," he said finally.

"Sir?" a confused Corbin asked.

"Come, Lieutenant," said Havelock, standing up from the table and straightening his jacket. "The crew must not be allowed to mutiny. Call all hands to deck. It is time I addressed them."

LOOKING INTO THE eyes of the sailors who stood on deck, hung from the rigging and slouched against railings, Havelock could see a variety of emotions, all of them negative. Bitterness towards him for losing so many crew last night, resentment at being so far from home, fear from facing a nearly unstoppable enemy. There was anger, too, aimed at both himself and the walking dead. That was good. Wherever it was directed, he could use anger, shaping and moulding the crew's fury into a credible weapon.

As a whole, the crew had been notably lax in responding to the order to assemble on deck and now they stood, sullen, a low grumbling forming an undercurrent to the sound of the *Whirlwind's* prow cutting through the waves. Havelock had faced sailors disgruntled with their lot many times in the past but this was the closest he had been to a complete breakdown of discipline and he realised that a single rousing speech would not solve the problem. He had to give the crew something tangible and it had to come soon.

"Men of the *Whirlwind*," he said. Thankfully, enough respect seemed to remain among the crew that the sound of their Captain's voice was still enough to silence them. "We have fought a bitter and dreadful enemy, the likes of which have never been faced by a crew of His Majesty's ships. But we survived! We took their full measure and have lived to tell a tale that will mark our place in history!"

Casting a quick glance around, Havelock noticed that his words had an effect on his officers, but that he was failing to reach many of the crew. He decided to change tack and pursue another course. "But we still have a duty to perform," he continued. "We have discovered the reason our merchantmen have been suffering so badly off the African coast and it is up to us to bring victory to King and Empire. The French have debased themselves by allying with an unholy force, one capable of raising a ship long since sunk. But think of this; that ship has been sunk once and it will be sunk again! We withstood a boarding action from a ship of the line, against an enemy already dead and we beat them! Why? Because we are a British ship of war, and we have no equal on the ocean!"

No cheers greeted him this time but Havelock could see a few wry smiles begin to spread throughout the crew. Whatever their background, there were few sailors in the navy who did not believe in the inherent superiority of the British at sea and a call to duty never went amiss. Now to complete the turning of the tide. The only thing stronger than a sailor's patriotism was his avarice.

"We all have our orders. The frigate *Elita* is still at large in these waters, and a fine prize she will make for all of us! I assure you, she is still hurting after our first encounter and the next match will see us pounding her into submission before swinging over the railings and defeating her French crew. We then sail for home – to riches, fame and glory! My friends, you will all be heroes and many a tavern will fall silent as you recall your time on the *Whirlwind* as you faced the very worst the enemy could muster and yet remained victorious!"

Still no outright cheers but smiles had turned to a few chuckles as the crew began to consider what life would be like back in England with the notoriety a mission like this brought, as well as the lifestyle that could be had for a frigate's prize money. Havelock smiled broadly at his crew, encouraging those who were beginning to leave their fear behind.

"And if that ship of the dead comes for us again," he said, catching their attention. "Well, we will simply send it back to the hell from which it came!"

The crew, he thought, were more resigned to their mission than elated by the possibilities but that suited him. Anything to stave off a potential mutiny served his purposes for now. He was about to instruct Corbin to dismiss the crew when a single voice rang out across the main deck.

"And when will your curse be visited on the rest of us, eh, Cap'n?" The challenge came from a sailor leaning with his back against the mainmast. It was not so much the man's words that angered Havelock as his lazy and uncaring demeanour.

"Mr Kennedy," Havelock roared. "Discipline that man!"

Pushing his way through the crew, the Bosun confronted the sailor, who just smirked at him. Kennedy reached forward and grabbed the man roughly by the shoulder, propelling him forward in front of the Captain.

"A dozen lashes, Mr Kennedy," Havelock said.

Corbin, at his side, leaned forward and whispered quietly, so no one else would hear. "Sir, do you not wish to read the charges and remind the crew of the Articles of War?"

"No need for that, Mr Corbin," Havelock said. "He knows what he has done wrong." He then raised his voice so the whole deck could hear his words. "Proceed, Mr Kennedy."

The crew kept their eyes fixed solidly on the deck as the Bosun's rope rose and fell against the condemned sailor's back, a loud crack ringing out a dozen times. His punishment complete, the man was led below decks, though he appeared strong enough to still walk by himself. Waiting until Corbin gave the order to be dismissed, the crew slowly dispersed, refusing to jump to their posts with any speed. To a man, they all steadfastly refused to look up at any of the officers.

"Damn that man," Havelock hissed to Corbin. "I very nearly had them until he brought on that flogging. Now we have to produce some results and quickly."

"Might it have been wise to spare the flogging, Sir? You said earlier..." Corbin asked.

"Absolutely not!" Havelock turned to face his Lieutenant, a look of shock on his face. "It matters little where we find ourselves. Complete discipline must be maintained at all times, utterly. I cannot have anyone challenging my authority, openly or otherwise. Inform Mr Kennedy; any talk that can be considered mutinous is to be dealt with in the severest manner."

Corbin appeared to hesitate for a brief second but then left the quarterdeck to find the Bosun. Havelock remained behind to consider his next course of action and wonder what fate would next bring for his ship.

# CHAPTER EIGHT

Having set course southwards to take advantage of the prevailing wind, Havelock observed the activities of his crew as they scurried about the main deck. Under their Captain's eye, none seemed willing to speak out but he could only guess what they might be saying below decks, and he chafed at having to rely on his Bosun and junior officers to maintain discipline. They were good men, he knew, but the situation was balanced too finely on the knife edge for him to relax his grip. Crews had mutinied for far less than his crew had faced. If the *Whirlwind* finally returned home, fully intact and with victory, it would be a miracle of some proportion.

The frigate, for all the trials it had been matched to, was performing admirably – he had that at least. Slicing through the waves, the ship seemed to almost enjoy a sense of freedom as it was carried by the wind at speed. Havelock wished he could permit himself to enjoy this moment for this was when the *Whirlwind* felt truly alive but his mind constantly churned over the possibilities of his next encounter at sea.

That he now faced two potential enemies did nothing to raise his spirits and he was caught between suppositions. On the one hand, if he was right about the *Deja*, he was fighting an enemy that had a much more powerful vessel, could not be truly destroyed and was determined to find and sink his own ship. Then again, what if it was part of some French plot and the name of the ship was a mere coincidence? What ramifications might that have on the war at large and the Empire in general? For his part, both the *Deja* and the *Elita* now knew of his presence in these waters and if they were allied, might they not seek to join battle with the *Whirlwind* simultaneously? That was a battle Havelock was certain he could not win.

He had spoken with some bravado to Corbin earlier when they had discussed how to fight the *Deja*. Certainly, he believed he could navigate the *Whirlwind* to stay out of the warship's arc of fire and away from its prow, thus stalling any further attempts at boarding, especially if he had the wind's favour. That alone could not win a battle though and he had to find some way of sinking the ship – but how to sink a ship that had already been raised from the bottom of the ocean at least once?

Though they scoured the ocean for prey now, Havelock had little doubt that he need not search for the *Deja*, as he firmly believed the ship would find him. It should have been his grandfather in this place and this time, of course, but he had benefited from the actions of the past as much as his grandfather had, perhaps more so, given his command history. While other captains languished in port on half pay, Havelock had never lacked for a frigate. He could not help but feel that a final confrontation between the death hulk and himself would somehow complete a chapter of history, allowing someone, somewhere to turn the page.

He was far more comfortable fighting the *Elita*. Though it was, in theory at least, a superior ship, he would stand by the shooting and seamanship of his own crew on any day. If the *Whirlwind* could be coaxed into soaking up a broadside or two from the French ship, he believed he could pound her crew into surrender in return. That victory would be all he needed to bring his crew back into line, as defeating a so-called super frigate would raise morale to the sky and get his men believing they could fight anything afloat, and win.

When it came down to final considerations, the nature of the enemy they faced mattered less than the opinions of a newly press-ganged sailor. He was the captain of a British ship of war and the French could be damned, dead or alive!

Rubbing his chin as he contemplated these matters, Havelock drew his hand across stubble and cursed himself for having been so inattentive. While he might have excused one of his sailors for poor hygiene after the last battle, it could never be accepted from an officer, much less the Captain. At the same time, he was somewhat grateful to have a more earthly concern to deal with. He began to make his way to his cabin when a cry from the lookout arrested his attention.

"Wreckage, to larboard!"

He looked up to see where the lookout pointed and drew his telescope to match the direction indicated, just slightly off line from the ship's course. It took him nearly a minute to spot the debris, just a few shattered pieces of wood thrown about by the gentle waves, and he turned to the helmsman behind to give instructions that would bring the *Whirlwind* closer.

"Two points to larboard, if you please."

As the ship approached the scattered wreckage, sailors began to line the railings, eager to get a glimpse. When on a long voyage, sailors quickly learned to give any new development their full attention. Elevated on the quarterdeck, Havelock had a better view than most and he quickly ascertained that the wreckage was strewn over a wide area, though it represented only a few hull planks and hatches. Presumably the rest of the stricken ship was already at the bottom of the ocean, though he had already caught sight of several bodies floating in the sea. A commotion from the main deck caused him to turn and he saw Corbin order the Bosun to fish something out of the water.

Kennedy hoisted a long hooked pole over the side of the ship and lowered it downwards into the water, his skill and strong arms belying the unwieldy nature of the tool. With a deft motion, the man snared something and quickly drew the pole upwards, hand over hand. Reaching over the railings, he grabbed the coloured cloth snagged on the hook and wrung it dry before passing it to Corbin. Before the Lieutenant had started unfurling the ragged flag as he walked to the quarterdeck, Havelock had already identified the red, white and blue colours as belonging to a Union Jack.

"One of ours, Sir," said Corbin as he mounted the steps up to Havelock.

"It is good news of a form, Mr Corbin," Havelock said. "The work of the *Elita*, no doubt. It means we are on the right course."

"Not the... other French ship?"

"No," Havelock said flatly. "That ship is only interested in one target on these seas. It would not stop for anyone else."

"So who do you think this belonged to?"

"Some poor merchant or trader, probably. I know of no other British warships in the area."

Corbin looked thoughtfully at the flag. "Does this mean the *Elita* is now fully repaired?"

"It need not be completely seaworthy to engage a merchant but, in truth, that is something I have been giving some thought to."

"Sir?"

"We are relatively far from the coast now, especially for a ship that was dismasted in its last engagement," said Havelock. "To make it to some safe harbour after our battle, make repairs, then sail here and sink a merchant vessel in this time? Doesn't seem credible to me."

"You have consulted the charts for possible island harbours?"

"I have but nothing is obvious. However, the charts do not list every small lump of rock in the oceans. We must be cautious about presuming the plans and capabilities of our enemy until we have more information. I am guessing the *Elita* is still hurting from our last encounter but I have no wish to sail into a trap and be sunk."

BROOKS SIGHED GRATEFULLY as he dropped his wooden burden to the deck and held his back as he stood up straight. He had at first welcomed news that Bryant's crew had been tasked with aiding the ship's carpenter in making repairs to the decking on the forecastle. Working at the prow, Brooks had expected to benefit from a constant soothing breeze unsullied by the odours of shipboard life but he had not foreseen the backbreaking labour as the carpenter constantly called for new materials and tools.

He nudged Murphy as he cast a look back down the length of the ship, watching the Captain and First Lieutenant examine the flag that had been hoisted from the wreckage.

"What do you think they are talkin' about?"

Murphy followed his glance and sniffed. "Officer talk. Probably discussin' tactics and the like."

"Which ship do you think they are plannin' to fight?"

"If they 'ave any sense, the Frog frigate."

Bryant joined them, straining to drop his own load of wooden planks as lightly as he could on the deck. "If I know the Captain," he said, "he'll be planning to face the *Elita* but preparing to fight the death ship."

"Death hulk," corrected Brooks.

"Hmm? Ah, yes. Of course."

"So, what are you two plannin' to do if we face them zombies again?" Murphy said, immediately causing his two friends to furrow their brows. Neither wanted to reflect on the events of the last battle but the question served to concentrate their minds.

"The Captain won't let us be caught off guard again," said Bryant. "He's too canny for that."

"Yeah, but we 'ad the advantage last time – can't get a better set-up than we 'ad."

"True, but we didn't know what we faced then. You mark my words, the Captain won't make the same mistake again."

"And if it is the Frogs – the living Frogs – we end up fighting, we'll win, right?" said Brooks with a confident smile.

"It will still be a hard battle, make no bones about that," said Bryant. "She'll pound us with cannon and you best keep your head down, lad. And then, even if we win the duel, the French may not surrender immediately. That will mean we have to board the ship, and there are far more of them than there are of us."

"Ah, Bryant, still grumblin', eh?" Jessop's familiar growl caused more than one of Bryant's crew to roll their eyes.

"I thought you were managing the supplies today Jessop," said Bryant, immediately feeling a little weary.

Jessop shrugged. "The ship still ain't quite right, know what I mean? Not everyone is being watched all the time, an' the officers don't want to make a fuss where it ain't needed. 'Sides, I wanted to talk with you."

Making a show of stacking the planking he had brought to the forecastle, Bryant raised his eyebrows in question, and Jessop stooped quickly to help, lest an over curious officer wonder just what task could be found for four sailors who stood about chatting near the prow.

"Me an' some of the lads 'ave been talkin'," he said and Bryant inwardly groaned, guessing what was coming next. "That last floggin' was unfair. The Cap'n has sailed us into God knows what, and 'e is lookin' for someone to blame. That means us."

"Jessop, I told you before, I'm not interested in any of this."

"Ah, you say that now. You goin' to be playin' the same tune when more dead Frogs come swinging over the side? You goin' to be sayin' that when Brooks 'ere gets 'is throat slit by a walkin' corpse?"

"It won't come to that. The Captain's too good. He has too many years at sea to be put on the back foot for long."

"Maybe you're right," said Jessop, throwing his hands up in mock surrender. "Maybe e'll win all 'is battles, then sail us straight for 'ome, with a couple of nice prizes. 'E does that, an' I'll be the first to admit I was wrong."

That admission drew sceptical glances from Bryant, Brooks and Murphy.

"Then again, maybe it doesn't go the way the Cap'n expects. Maybe the curse catches up with 'im. Maybe 'e isn't thinkin' too straight right now. What then?"

Bryant exhaled heavily. "I can't see it," he said. "Look, we faced the worst possible enemy under the worst possible circumstances. And we are all still here."

"Plenty o' the crew ain't," said Jessop flatly.

"Well, I don't want to seem callous, but men die at sea. The ship is still here though, as are you and I. The Captain saw us through."

"Some might say the Cap'n led us into that battle without thinkin' things through, and the rest of us paid for it."

Beginning to lose patience, Bryant turned to face Jessop squarely. "Look, you've spoken to me about this before and I made my position clear. What is it you are after? This talk is dangerous and I have no intention of being flogged or hung for your loose mouth."

"Well, we 'ave to be careful, sure, if there is a free floggin' for every jack on this ship," Jessop said candidly. "An' if we have to face that Frog frigate an' fight, you won't see me complainin'. It seems to me that a frigate is somethin' worth fightin' for. Plenty o' prize money to go round there."

"Your patriotism overwhelms me," said Bryant. "It has, presumably, occurred to you that your share has gone up now there are less crew to claim it."

Bryant was sickened to see Jessop give half a smile as he rolled this thought around for a few seconds. "That's besides the point," he said. "What concerns me and some of the other lads is that ship o' the dead. We can't be facin' that again. We got lucky last time. Won't 'appen twice."

"I know where you are going, Jessop, but you won't drag me into it."

"I ain't askin' for nothin'," said Jessop. "All I'm sayin' is that you should keep your eyes open, that's all. If that ship appears again, me an' some of the lads are goin' to make a move."

Holding up a hand to halt Jessop, Bryant looked squarely across to the other members of his crew. "Murphy, Brooks, get below for the rest of the supplies."

"Oh, come on, Bryant," said Murphy. "We're just listenin'..."

"Now, Murphy – before one of the officers sees you lazing around." It was Bryant's tone, as much as his words, that caused Murphy and Brooks to reluctantly walk away from the forecastle and disappear below deck. He turned back to Jessop.

"I swear, if any of my men get caught up in what you are planning..."

"Consider them out of it," said Jessop. "I'm just sayin', if that ship appears again, somethin' is goin' to 'appen. We'll be goin' for the Cap'n and Lieutenants first, the Bosun too. An' anyone else who disagrees. But it would 'elp if you were with us. You'll bring a lot of the lads round to our way of thinkin'."

Bryant knew that Jessop was right, at least in part. He had no illusions about his overall popularity on the *Whirlwind*, indeed, he would be surprised if many sailors on board knew him as anything other than the leader of his gun crew. However, he also knew that it might take only a few voices acting in concert to win an entire ship over to the idea of mutiny.

"You haven't thought this through. Have you even begun to plan what happens after that?" He inwardly cursed as he saw Jessop's triumphant smile. Of course the man had a plan, however half-baked. He was far too opportunistic for anything else.

"We will 'ave a fightin' ship an' the entire ocean to hide in. We'll roam the coast and grow rich on merchant pickin's. We'll even just grab Froggie ships if you like," Jessop said. "Look, I ain't askin' for your support and if there's ever a trial, you can rightly say you were against the idea. But if that death ship comes at us again, somethin' will 'appen – that's all I'm sayin'. What you decide to do then is up to you."

"Don't you get it?" Bryant said. "I don't want to know this. I don't want to know what you are planning and I don't want to know when you are planning to do it. The Captain still has my support.

As far as I see it, he has done nothing wrong and will see us through the next battle, and the one after that, and even the one after that, whoever it may be against. We got a tough fight ahead of us, Jessop, I agree on that. But we'll get through it. For the love of God and all that's holy, don't throw your life away by going against the Captain. It ain't worth it."

Jessop smiled. "Well, I don't plan on throwin' my life away, you got that right. Anyway, I told you what's goin' to 'appen. What you do then is up to you." He stood and walked away, passing Brooks and Murphy who had returned with more supplies from the carpenter's list.

"So, what did 'e say?" Murphy asked, ever eager for shipboard gossip.

"Never you mind," Bryant said. "What ever that man says is not worth listening to, remember that – both of you."

Murphy seemed a bit subdued at Bryant's hard words but his ears soon pricked up at a cry from the lookout high above on the mainmast.

"Sail to starboard!"

All three strained their eyes to the horizon but they saw nothing through the far haze.

"Now what?" Bryant said quietly.


ONCE AGAIN, HAVELOCK trained his telescope on the horizon, aware that Corbin stood at his shoulder, anxious to hear what ship was in their vicinity. Though it took him a moment to focus properly, a familiar shape soon coalesced through the lens and he smiled.

"It is our old friend, the *Elita*!"

"Can you spy her condition, Captain," Corbin asked.

"I see three masts, all with sail," said Havelock after a moment's pause. "However, that may mean little. Her condition will become apparent in the next few minutes. She is currently heading towards us and her captain will now be aware of our presence. Thus... ah, there you see. She has turned! She runs!" Havelock lowered his telescope and slid it into his belt. "Mr Corbin, we pursue! Change course to match her and raise the stuns'ls. Our girl will give us all the speed she can!"

Corbin grinned. "Aye, Sir! Raise the stuns'ls and pursue!"

Sailors across the deck leapt to the Lieutenant's commands and soon the *Whirlwind* was sailing with its full deployment, a mass of canvas that captured every breath of wind, causing the frigate to skit across the sea as though it were glass. Already, Havelock could sense the change in the crew's demeanour. It happened every time a ship was about to go into battle but it was all the more poignant now, after his men had faced the supernatural. Here was an enemy that was flesh and blood. One they had defeated before and were confident of doing so again. Nothing could rally morale better than the chance of a captured prize and Havelock intended to pursue the *Elita* until she could be engaged and forced to surrender.

For all the pace the *Whirlwind* could muster, the *Elita* was still some distance away and, it turned out, had a good turn of speed herself. The English ship was clearly the faster of the two but it was also evident that the French crew had managed to make good repair. Havelock began to fear they might not make much progress in the chase before night fell which would allow the *Elita* to escape without battle. However, he was also heartened by the French captain's decision to run rather than fight, for it suggested that his ship was still hurting from their last encounter. Perhaps they had sustained greater casualties than Havelock had supposed or they had many guns out of action.

Members of the *Whirlwind's* crew occasionally whooped and cheered, clearly enjoying the speed. It was quite rare for a frigate's true speed to be unleashed in this manner and even Havelock openly smiled as he felt the motion of the ship under his feet, rising with each wave and dropping slightly after their crest.

He could not shake a growing mood of foreboding though and, every now and again, cast a look over his shoulder at the *Whirlwind's* long wake. The *Elita* could be feigning weakness, of course and if it truly were in league with the *Deja*, then a trap was possible. He kept expecting to see the massive dark form of the death hulk streaming over the sea behind them, but the ocean remained clear.

They remained on a course of south-south-east, as the *Elita* continued to run in an arrow straight line, and Havelock began to wonder if she were not heading somewhere specific. Though her sails were now clearly visible to the naked eye, there was still more than a mile between the two ships and the yards ticked away with agonising slowness. The sun was plummeting fast to the western horizon and Havelock's fears of his prey escaping began to resurface. If night fell while they were still out of range, the *Elita* could easily change course and retreat without his lookouts noticing. However, the lookouts were to surprise him with their next cry.

"Land! Dead ahead!"

"Mr Corbin, with me," Havelock called as he quickly marched to the prow of the *Whirlwind* to get a view unobstructed by acres of sail. The Lieutenant joined him and together they peered forward, soon seeing the small but growing land mass, standing proud but alone in the vast ocean.

"That is where she is heading, Sir," said Corbin.

"Aye, Mr Corbin, I believe we have found her harbour. This is where she made repairs – no doubt they have created their own little piece of France on that island. Not on the charts, of course."

"We won't lose her now!"

"Caution, Lieutenant," said Havelock. "We have little more than three hours before the sun sets. Plenty of time for her to swing round the island and strike out on a new course without us seeing. Still, I think you are right. I would wager she plans to anchor there in some cove that will make an approach difficult, if not impossible."

"Orders, Sir?"

"Continue the pursuit for now, Mr Corbin. Let us see what she is up to first."

The sight of land and, with it, the prospect of landfall, further galvanised the crew as they began to dream of fresh water, fruits and, probably, meat. The island was small, perhaps no more than three miles across, and it looked like paradise. Beaches of white sand gave way to thick jungle which stretched up to a line of tall grey cliffs in its centre. It looked like a land of verdant promise, rich enough to support the sailors of a warship indefinitely.

Sailing past the island, the *Elita* changed course to swing behind the landmass, quickly disappearing from view. The *Whirlwind* now appeared to be very much alone on the ocean but every man on board still tensed for battle.

*Now, let us see what play you make*, thought Havelock. He ordered Corbin to maintain their course, but to keep a greater distance from the island than the French ship. It seemed unlikely to him that the *Elita* would reverse its course with the intention of bearing down on them with all guns blazing but he had not come this far to fall to so simple a trap. A little extra distance as they circumnavigated the island would not unduly delay their pursuit and caution was the watchword of any good captain, he believed.

As the *Whirlwind* skirted the island, all eyes were locked on the beach. Flocks of dark-feathered birds rose from the trees, though none crossed the water to investigate the frigate. No other life made itself apparent on the shore but the whole island appeared inviting, seeming to tempt the sailors onto its sands.

Maintaining a distance of no less than a half mile from the shore, the *Whirlwind* slowed slightly as Havelock ordered the studding sails to be furled, the extra canvas sheets serving no function in the expected battle. Like a hawk, he watched the coastline, keen to see if the French frigate had sailed on or anchored. It was not long before he spied an inlet that marked the entrance to a natural cove, carved from the island by the sea's constant motion. As they sailed past the inlet, Havelock cried out in triumph.

"There she is! Do you see, Mr Corbin? There she is!"

Crewmen rushed to the starboard side of the *Whirlwind* as the ship passed by the mouth of the cove. Lying before them was the *Elita*, already anchored close to the shore, its French ensign flying defiantly in the late afternoon breeze.

"She has trapped herself, Captain," said Corbin but Havelock shook his head.

"Do not be deceived, Lieutenant. Her guns face to sea and she will be a far steadier platform than we. If we try to negotiate the entrance to the cove, she will punish us for it, heavily. Once inside, if we are still afloat, we will find there is little room to manoeuvre. The advantage would be hers. We would be outmatched by both her guns and number of crew." He took another long look at the *Elita* before his ship sailed past the cove and out of sight of the French ship. "We must try another tactic."

"A land attack?" asked Corbin.

"You read my mind. Yes, Mr Corbin, we will find somewhere safe to anchor ourselves, a little further on, then make landfall. The jungle will mask our approach. I doubt we will have the luxury of complete surprise but if we co-ordinate our efforts, the advantage will turn to us, as their crew will be split between ship and shore. If we can deal with those on land without warning to the *Elita*, we may just be able to snatch her before an effective defence can be mounted."

"A bold move!"

"Fortune favours those who make such moves. We'll sail two miles onwards and then anchor. Get the men to prepare the boats."

"Aye, Sir!"

Though no more coves presented themselves to Havelock, he was nonetheless happy to anchor a little way beyond a protrusion of land that snaked a short distance from the rest of the island. The heavy vegetation would serve to shield the position of the *Whirlwind* from curious eyes either on land or the sea, should the *Elita* raise anchor and sail in pursuit of them. Either way, Havelock felt confident enough that a skeleton crew left on board would be able to keep the ship out of the reach of the French should the tables be turned and the attack repulsed.

As the crew heaved the three landing boats to the side of the *Whirlwind*, Havelock called for their attention. He could tell immediately from their anxious expressions that few feared for their lives in this venture. Their captain had presented to them an enemy that was not supernatural in nature and a plan of attack that stood a reasonable chance of success.

"Mr Hague," he said, loud enough to be heard by the whole crew. "The ship is yours. You will take command of the skeleton crew and keep the home fires burning until we return!"

"Yes, Captain!"

"Mr Wynton, Mr Corbin, you will both join me ashore to lead the attack. Mr Wynton, you will land first, taking your men into the jungle to deal with any sentries the French may have stationed. Do so quickly and quietly. Mr Corbin and I will be right behind you with the main body of men. We will join our forces before launching an attack on their beach shelters."

"As you say, Captain," said Lieutenant Wynton.

Satisfied that his officers would act as he had previously briefed them, Havelock turned his attention to the rest of the crew. "Men of the *Whirlwind*, we near our mission's end. The *Elita* lies in yonder cove, stationary and inert, her crew tired and battered. They will have no fight in them! As we march through the jungle to battle, remember you are part of the greatest Navy the world has yet seen. Whether we fight on sea or on land, you have no equal and, indeed, it would take ten French sailors to match any one of you!"

Wry grins began to spread through the crew and Havelock smiled in return. A reminder of the innate superiority of the British sailor never failed to instil courage, it seemed.

"I promise you, in perhaps just two hours, we will be sailing out of that cove on board a captured French frigate. Then, together, we will set sail for home – and our just rewards! Men of the *Whirlwind*, can you find it within yourselves to boot the French off this island and take their ship?"

The roar that answered his words was nearly as loud as that which had greeted his speech at the beginning of the voyage, and Havelock nodded his appreciation. He began to dare hope that their encounter with the death hulk would turn into nothing more than a memory, a tale to be told in taverns that no one listening would seriously believe. If this next battle was won, perhaps everything would be set right.

"Mr Wynton, lower your boat and set away. You have your orders!"

Sailors strained on ropes as the first landing boat was hoisted over the side. Crewmen soon clambered down the ropes to take their place in the small boat, raising the oars before pulling away with strong, confident strokes. Immediately, another boat was swung over the side of the *Whirlwind* and Havelock marched down to the main deck, determined to be the first on board in order to lead his men onto the shore.

Standing at the prow of the boat, feeling it surge forward with each stroke of the oars, Havelock fixed his eyes intently on the approaching shore. Wynton and his men had already landed and, after pulling their boat onto the shore, began to fan out and disperse into the trees as they sought out French sentries. Havelock felt a wave of confidence wash over him. This battle would be his finest moment yet.

# CHAPTER NINE

QUIETLY CURSING TO himself, Murphy picked his way through the jungle, unhappy to be in an environment so similar to his last landfall. The images of crewmen torn apart by some unknown beast constantly ran through his head and he twitched at the sound of every rustle in the undergrowth and snapping of branches. He and Brooks trailed behind Bryant, who moved slowly, trying to keep the men to his right in view at all times so they did not get lost.

The British sailors formed a thin line of three guns crews, with Bryant's team on the right flank next to another crew who were led by Lieutenant Wynton. They moved with care through the vegetation, anxious to stay silent, yet conscious of the main body of sailors who would not be far behind them. So far, there had been no sign of any French pickets but they were expected to be placed far closer to the *Elita's* natural harbour.

Tripping over a vine Murphy reached out to a branch to steady himself, only to snatch his hand back as a sharp pain shot up his arm. He muffled a cry as he looked to the offending plant which, he now saw, was covered in thorns. It seemed to him that every living thing in jungles, plant or animal, were out to ensure human life did not venture too far in. As Bryant raised an arm for them to stop, Murphy found himself eyeing the Lieutenant, who had briefly halted to check his pistol.

"So 'ow comes we never gets the guns then?" he hissed.

"Officers only, mate," said Brooks, equally quietly, though their conversation had already caused Bryant to look back with a frown.

"And I just gets me knives," Murphy complained, reaching down to his belt to check that both blades were where they should be.

"Yeah, but you're pretty handy with them."

"I 'aves me moments."

"Will you two be silent?" said Bryant, so quietly they barely heard him. In any case, Murphy considered the absence of French sentries to mean Bryant's statement was a guideline more than an order.

"Just be glad to fight somethin' that will die when you stab it," he said.

"Well, the Captain didn't seem to think there would be any walking dead on this island – or he would have told us, right?"

"Yeah, that's probably right," said Murphy. "As I always say, you can trust the Cap'n."

Even Bryant turned round to give Murphy an incredulous look.

"Anyways, them zombies won't matter any more," Murphy said, completely unabashed. "As the Cap'n said, we deal with the Frogs, grab their ship, and then it's back to Blighty! No more hangin' around these God-forsaken parts. And that means no more dead Frenchmen to fight."

"Yeah, that would be good," said Brooks, a look of concern crossing his face as he remembered the night they fought the dead.

"Still, I wouldn't mind 'aving Jessop round 'ere right now."

"God lord, why?" said Brooks.

"Well, you can say what you like about Jessop. An' I can say a bit, mind. But 'e ain't 'alf good in a fight. You should've seen 'im fight those zombies. Took three on without blinkin' an eye. I swear, saw it me self. A Frog or ten wouldn't stand a chance against 'im."

Bryant turned back round to confront Murphy. "The Lieutenant made sure Jessop was far behind us which, incidentally, is where I wish you were right now. Jessop has a big mouth that would alert any Frenchies for miles around – just like you are doing now. For the love of God, man, shut up!"

Cowering a little under his friend's words, Murphy shrugged slightly. "No need to be nasty about it," he muttered.

Wynton's group had started to move forwards and Bryant waved for them to match the pace. The jungle was noticeably thinner than that they had experienced on the African coast, so the going was a little easier. Conversely, they could see a lot further, sometimes as much as twenty or thirty yards. Acutely aware that they were on French ground, trying to locate sentries who would be watching for invaders, every sailor crouched low as he moved, taking care to avoid brushing through too much undergrowth. Where necessary, Bryant, along with others who wielded cutlasses or heavy knives, cut through vines and other denser patches of vegetation but only if there was no obvious way around it without losing eye contact with the other groups of sailors. This caused their path to meander somewhat but cutting through even a thin branch created a great deal of noise in a jungle that had grown quiet with the onset of twilight. There was enough light remaining for them to pick out details but all had been warned that night would descend extremely rapidly when on the island.

A flash of movement ahead caught Bryant's eyes and he crouched down, raising his arm in warning. Murphy was about to complain about another false alarm when he too saw something move behind the trunk of a tree, a light blue shade that seemed out of place in the jungle. All three of them stayed low as they peered into the gloom and were rewarded by the sight of a man in French army uniform leaning his musket against the tree as he fiddled with the top button of his jacket – no doubt taking advantage of the absence of officers to loosen it.

Bryant looked at his two comrades, putting his finger to his lips, but they were both alert and prepared for action. He motioned to Murphy to suggest that the small man sneak in an arc to their left, while he and Brooks took a more direct route. Their plans dissipated when sounds of rapid movement through undergrowth were followed by a cry echoed through the trees to their left. Clearly, some of their allies had also located a sentry.

Their man had also heard the sounds of the fight and he grabbed his musket, setting the bayonet as he stared hard into the jungle, trying to decide whether he should run or stay. Bryant decided to make the decision for him.

"Come on, now!" he said to Murphy and Brooks, before jumping up and running at full tilt towards the Frenchman.

The soldier spun around in alarm as Bryant thundered through the undergrowth towards him, leaping over fallen branches and raising his cutlass. A loud shot rang out as the sentry panicked and discharged his rifle, its shot flying well wide of Bryant.

Recovering his wits, the sentry raised his musket to block Bryant's downward swing, then lunged forward, forcing the big man to sidestep as the wickedly sharp point of the bayonet lanced past his ribs. He aimed a side swing at the sentry's head in return, but the man ducked under the blow, thrusting forward with his weapon once more. Bryant was forced to give ground or be skewered and he backed away, crouching on the balls of his feet, ready to dodge another attack.

Waving his cutlass dangerously in a false attack, Bryant caused the sentry to flinch and he took advantage of the opening as the man raised his musket, moving forward with a series of wide, confident sweeps of his blade. Several loud cracks rang out as the sentry desperately parried each blow with his musket, retreating several footsteps as he did so. Then he stopped. Arms dropping to his side, his musket fell to the floor as his eyes glazed over. Bryant was puzzled as the man keeled over, until he saw Murphy behind the body of the sentry, smiling triumphantly as he reached down to wipe his knife clean on the man's jacket.

"Nice work."

"I 'aves me moments."

Brooks trotted up to Bryant's side. "Think anyone heard that?" he asked.

"No doubt of it. This place will be crawling with the French," said Bryant. "Come on, let's find the Lieutenant and see what he wants us to do now."

They trotted in the direction of the first fight they had heard, though the jungle was silent now. Brushing through the branches of a tree whose limbs hung low to the ground, they were confronted by several clubs, blades and a single pistol pointed unerringly at Bryant's head. Lieutenant Wynton sighed as he recognised the men under his command and lowered his gun.

"You found one too?" he asked.

"Yes, Sir," said Bryant, curling a finger to his forehead. "He won't be troubling us."

"Good show. Craggs' crew found two more just a ways from us."

"Begging your pardon, Sir, but what are we to do now? Surely the French heard the shots."

"I agree," said Wynton. "We hold here, wait for the Captain to bring the rest of the men up to us. By my reckoning, night is about to fall and we don't want to be stumbling around the jungle while the French are looking for us. We have dealt with the picket line in this area. With luck, the Captain will be with us before the French start a serious sweep of the jungle."

Movement ahead of them brought their conversation to a sudden halt and they all ducked low. Peering through the trees, they spied another two French soldiers. They held their muskets across their chests, scanning the surrounding area as they walked slowly towards the British sailors.

"Unless, of course, they force our hand," said Wynton as he stood up straight. Taking quick aim with his pistol, he fired, the weapon discharging smoke that carried the thick stench of black powder. One of the soldiers fell to the ground but his companion was already raising his musket.

Bryant ran forward, galvanising several other sailors to follow him. The sight of a half dozen maddened British sailors caused the soldier to falter as he tried to decide which target to point his musket at. Before they reached him, he fired and a man staggered but the rest swept onward to batter and slice the soldier as he desperately tried to fix his bayonet to the end of his weapon. He fell quickly and silently to a heavy blow from a club.

Slower to react than most of the others, Brooks went to the wounded sailor who had received shot from the discharged musket. The man was leaning heavily against a tree, clutching his shoulder. He was obviously in a great deal of pain and Brooks helped him sink to the ground before tearing a strip from his own shirt to help bind the wound. Blood covered the man's body to the extent that Brooks could not see whether the bullet had exited through his back or remained lodged among the bones of the shoulder.

Bryant leaned forward to gauge the man's wound. "You should help him back to the ship, Brooks."

"Belay that," said Wynton, who had also moved forward to join them. "There will be plenty more wounded soon and, besides, the lad'll likely get lost at night. Make the man comfortable, then we move on. The Captain and his men will find him and make arrangements. Besides, we need every hand for the fight ahead."

"Aye, Sir," Bryant said, trying hard to keep the reluctance out of his voice. As well as compassion to the wounded man, he had been hoping to find a reason to keep Brooks out of the coming battle. The boy was not only young, he was inexperienced when it came to life and death fights with the French. He resolved to keep Brooks close by at all times during the next few hours. It might well be the making or breaking of the lad.

Cries and shouts in a foreign, yet familiar, tongue echoed in the jungle ahead of them, growing steadily closer. Loading his pistol, Wynton gave orders for them to spread out and take cover. They would meet any French patrols here until they were joined by the Captain.

THE FALL OF night in the jungle caught Havelock momentarily off guard. He had been aware of the sinking sun, though it was hidden by the tall trees, and the slowly dimming light that forced him to stare hard through the undergrowth to find his footing. Night itself came almost instantly. One moment he was peering through the gloomy wild, then he was calling for men to bring forward torches. The sputtering fire provided enough illumination to proceed with the venture but it cast eerie shadows that moved and jumped at the corner of men's eyes, causing more than one false alarm.

At his side, Corbin monitored the disposition of sailors around them, allowing Havelock to concentrate on the task of reaching Wynton's forward party and then engage the French. Moving as a ragged column, they hoped to ensure none would become lost during the trek, though there was no accounting for a sailor's curiosity at times.

Orders had been given for absolute silence during the march but with nearly a couple of hundred men behind him, Havelock began to fear that the sounds of their approach would alert the French long before they emerged from the jungle, and that was assuming Wynton had been successful in silencing any sentries. If any escaped to get word back to the main French camp, this fight would grow harder still. His only hope then would be that the French crew would be split between those on shore and those still on board the *Elita*. He felt confident that the French captain would maintain a heavy watch on his ship, however, as they had plainly spotted the *Whirlwind* approaching their island and would thus take steps to secure a strong position against attack, either from land or sea. It was Havelock's hopes that in trying to cover all possibilities, the French captain would leave himself weaker overall, permitting the British sailors to fight them piecemeal.

A loud crack resounded through the jungle and Havelock stopped in his tracks, the sailors closest to him following suit. It was quickly followed by several more shots and, straining his ears, Havelock made out the unmistakable cries of men in battle.

"Lieutenant! It seems as though Mr Wynton has found the measure of the enemy," he said to Corbin. "I'll take a dozen men and relieve him. Bring the men up in good order. We'll wait for you to begin the main attack!"

"Aye, Captain," said Corbin, turning round to pick a group of sailors to follow the Captain as he ran forward into the darkness. They had to sprint to catch up with him.

The uneven ground forced Havelock to quickly moderate his pace and he chafed at his own slowness as the sounds of battle grew ever closer. Somewhere ahead, he knew, Wynton was fighting, wondering just when his Captain would bring reinforcements. Two of the men who had joined him bore torches and their light was noticeably less illuminating than the score of torches the rest of his force had carried. He drew his sword, using it to hack down any plant life that threatened to impede his progress, while he carried his pistol in his left.

Several cries from ahead warned Havelock that not only was he close to the fight, but the light from his torches had warned the participants of his arrival. Sparing a thought only for those of his men who had, until now, been fighting a terrifying battle in darkness, Havelock began to run. A bright flash ahead followed by a heavy crack betrayed the position of a musket and he shouted his men forward as he pointed his sword ahead. He was briefly aware of Wynton and a few sailors crouched down behind a fallen tree on his right as he tore past. Leaping over a dense fern, he confronted a surprised French soldier who had his back half-turned as he reloaded his musket. Not giving the man time to recover, Havelock swung down with his sword, embedding it deep in the man's back. Screaming in agony, the soldier fell trying in vain to reach behind with an arm to staunch the flow of blood.

Suddenly aware of several other uniformed soldiers and raggedly clothed sailors around him, Havelock realised he had charged straight into the middle of the French line. His men rapidly fanned out and found enemies to engage and suddenly the jungle erupted with the sounds of an intense, desperate melee. Trees and ferns shook as men rolled or crashed through them, the air was filled with the sounds of wood and metal connecting with one another and, through it all, the cries of mortally wounded men. A sailor, his face stained with grime, leapt out of the darkness with a cleaver, clearly fancying his chances of killing an English officer. Havelock calmly sidestepped the rush, batting the cleaver away with his sword, before reversing his stroke and running the man through the stomach.

As he wrenched his weapon clear in a spray of blood, he stalked towards two French soldiers who were pressing their advantage home against one of his sailors. The Englishman desperately swung with a cutlass, trying to keep the bayoneted muskets at bay but he was giving ground with every stroke. Calling out a challenge, Havelock marched forward, slashing at the nearest and sinking his sword deep into the man's arm. His companion, suddenly finding himself the outnumbered one, backed away. The Englishman's strength renewed at the sight of his Captain entering battle, the sailor yelled as he sprang forward with two clumsy but powerful chops. The soldier parried the first with the barrel of his musket but the second found its target in his skull. Panting, the sailor put a crooked finger to his forehead in salute to his Captain. Havelock smiled and clapped the man's shoulder before moving off to look for Wynton. By the sounds filling the jungle, Havelock could tell the fight was reaching its conclusion and by the number of dead Frenchmen lying on the ground, he was confident of its outcome.

"Captain!"

Havelock saw his Second Lieutenant trotting out from behind the trees, sword as red as his own.

"Mr Wynton, report."

Breathless, Wynton did his best. "Met their first line of sentries, Sir. Dealt with them, but the French got a shot off. Alerted the others. We dug in and met them..."

"Down!" A quick movement caught Havelock's eye and he roughly pushed Wynton to one side, even as he crouched himself.

Raising his pistol, he fired near blindly. A French soldier dropped to the ground, clutching his stomach.

Picking himself off the ground, Wynton dusted himself off. "Damn close," he muttered. Then, a little clearer, he gave a half bow. "My thanks, Captain."

"Need to keep your eyes open in this damnable jungle," said Havelock. The familiar sounds of English sailors on the march reached his ears and he smiled. "Ah, here comes Mr Corbin with the rest of our men. Now perhaps we can push on out of this jungle and into more civilised terrain."

"No arguments from me, Sir."

The darkness of the jungle began to yield more British sailors. Havelock was just glad to see them and he waved to get Corbin's attention. The Lieutenant marched briskly towards the two of them.

"Had some excitement already, I see," he said.

"Mr Wynton accredited himself most admirably, I would say," said Havelock. "Just left us a few to mop up."

Wynton smiled as he greeted Corbin. "Let's just say that the Captain's arrival was most timely."

"Form the men up as best you can, Mr Corbin," said Havelock. "They have the taste of a fight in them now but do the best you can. I want to march on within the minute."

"Right you are, Sir," said Corbin, immediately turning to bark orders that gathered sailors together. Havelock reached into a pouch at his belt and began to reload his pistol. Though the weapon could only realistically be used once during a battle, the last French soldier had reminded Havelock that, sometimes, that was enough.

"You have another fight in you, Mr Wynton?"

"Ready and able, Captain."

"Good. That was the easy part. Now we march against an enemy who, by now, certainly know we are coming."

"Did you hope to come this far unnoticed, Captain?"

"Not really. Our sailors are not trained for this sort of battle. However, we can hope that the French are still unaware of our true numbers or even, perhaps, of our true intentions. Still, it will be a hard fight."

"Not to worry, Sir," said Wynton cheerfully. "You said it yourself. Each of our men is worth ten of theirs!"

Havelock returned the smile. "Indeed I did, Mr Wynton. Now come, let us prove it!"

Men crowded close, filling the surrounding jungle in the flickering light of their torches. Checking that officer and sailor alike were ready, Havelock raised his sword so all could see, then marched determinedly onwards towards the beach and the waiting Frenchmen.

It took nearly twenty minutes before the trees and vegetation started to noticeably thin out and, straining his ears, Havelock could hear the sound of the sea, the waves lapping against the shoreline subdued by their passage through the narrow inlet of the cove. He held up a hand to halt the progress of the march and called Corbin and Wynton to his side as he crept forward, instinctively keeping low. The three men, using the trees as cover, padded forward until they reached the end of the treeline.

Before them, a sandy shore extended some thirty yards to the water, its waves glittering with the combined light of a quarter moon and dozens of French torches and lanterns. On the beach itself, they were somewhat surprised to see several hastily erected wooden shacks, no doubt placed by the French as part of their temporary base. They did not seem sturdy enough to resist a brisk wind but, Havelock reflected, in this climate they served their purpose merely by keeping the sun away from sleeping men. Men ran to and fro within the little village but, before the buildings, a clump of men had arranged themselves in a ragged unit. An officer marched up and down their uneven line, shouting out orders to individuals, making them move forward or back in an attempt to make the unit a little neater.

"Must be a couple hundred of them," said Corbin. "And more among the huts."

"Not many more I would guess," said Wynton.

Havelock rubbed his chin as he thought. "Still a formidable force," he said. "They match our numbers, and they are ready for us. We will have to cross forty yards from this position to reach them."

"I don't see any uniforms," said Corbin as he squinted at the French unit. "If they deployed all their soldiers on picket duty, they may not have many guns. What are your orders, Captain?"

Slowly exhaling before he answered, Havelock considered his options before reaching a decision. "Mr Wynton, take a couple of men and scout out our left flank. I don't want to rush these men and then suddenly find the rest of their crew waiting for us in the trees a little further along. That won't do at all."

"Right you are, Captain," said Wynton, as he scuttled off back into the darkness.

"Mr Corbin, how many marines do we have with us?"

"Seven. Not enough to make a difference."

"It will be enough. They will move up first and position themselves on our right. Order them to hold position. They will act as sharpshooters throughout the fight. No sense in risking our only guns in open battle."

"And the rest of us?"

"We charge," said Havelock flatly. "Tell the marines to open fire as we leave the trees. It will force the French to keep their heads down and buy us a few more seconds of surprise. Then we'll be in amongst them and it will be up to God who wins."

As Corbin ran off to gather their men, Havelock was left alone for a few minutes to study his enemy further. In the pale moonlight, he could see the *Elita*, moored in the middle of the cove, the target of this whole enterprise. She was a fine ship and he was surprised to find himself eager to see how she handled at sea. A skilled captain could do a lot with a frigate like that. He noted the three masts were tall and straight, showing no signs of damage or hasty repair. The Captain guessed this natural harbour had been discovered long ago by the French captain, who had prepared in advance for disaster.

Turning his attention back to the shore, he saw four boats pulled up onto the beach and could even make out the oars piled on the sand next to them. Looking towards the huts, Havelock could not help but smile as the French officer continued to cajole his men into a regular unit. Sailors never made for the best land troops but he fancied the men of the *Whirlwind* would have made a far better representation of themselves. Truly, discipline was the foundation of an effective fighting unit, be it on land or sea, and it was something these French sailors sorely lacked. There was a kernel of truth in the idea that a British sailor was worth ten Frenchmen. The odds were not that great, certainly, but given equal numbers, Havelock would put his money on his men in any fight. Still, the French were not to be underestimated, and their leaders had a habit of rising above the failings of their military to perform some truly remarkable actions. He resolved to not let over-confidence blind him to any surprises the French might have in store. On their home ground, they could be a truly dreadful enemy.

The sounds of breaking branches and hissed curses announced the arrival of his men and Corbin duly appeared.

"Complements of Mr Wynton," he said. "The flank is clear. No surprises there."

"The marines?"

"In position and ready to open fire as soon as we move. We await only your order."

Steeling himself, Havelock took a deep breath. "The best of luck to you, Mr Corbin. Let us be off."

Giving his pistol just one last check, Havelock drew its lock back with a solid click and then, raising his sword, sprang forward at a dead run towards the French. He was aware of the sound of two hundred men behind him surging forward and then the multiple cracks of the marines' muskets sang out to his right. Ahead, he saw a couple of French sailors fall to the fire as others instinctively flinched or ducked. He was gratified to see two more in the rear of the line turn and run, scuttling away to hide in one of the wooden huts.

The indecision of the French line was momentary and as their officer screamed at the sailors for a response, they started to shamble forward, gradually picking up speed. The distance between the two forces closed rapidly and Havelock found himself being overtaken by some of his faster men. Cries and challenges sprang from the lips of men on both sides while weapons were held aloft, ready to deal a killing blow. The twin masses of French and British hit one another with a dull thud that was audible to everyone. Almost immediately, the cries and screams started as men were gutted, brained and battered senseless.

A few metres in front of him, a French sailor leered at Havelock before reaching to his belt to pull out a knife. With a practised flick, the knife flew through the air, forcing Havelock to check his charge and duck as the blade sailed past his head, whistling as it split the air. The sailor was upon him immediately, brandishing a club at Havelock's skull. On one knee and at a disadvantage, Havelock rolled to his left before sweeping out with his sword. The blade bit deep into the sailor's ankle, causing him to howl in pain. Standing up straight, Havelock dispatched the man with one slice to the neck but immediately found himself giving ground and parrying wildly as another sailor, a large man with broad shoulders, swung a cutlass at him with broad, powerful strokes. Recovering from the assault, Havelock quickly found the measure of the man. Though the Frenchman was not unskilled in the blade, he was no match for a British officer instructed in the art of duelling. Turning side on to the man, Havelock raised himself on the balls of his feet and matched every stroke, gradually gaining the initiative as he launched his own attacks. A quick feint to the man's face caused him to stumble, leaving an opening for Havelock to give a savage downwards hack that sliced the man open across his chest.

The momentum of the British assault had already pushed the French unit backwards and Havelock found himself having to run forward a few steps to keep with the front line of battle. Dead littered the beach and, in his quick estimation, most seemed to belong to the enemy. Havelock realised that this might indeed be an easy victory and he suddenly grew uneasy. He felt the hairs on the back of his neck begin to prickle and he wondered if something was not very wrong. Had the French Captain prepared a surprise that would suddenly swing the battle against Havelock? Was he even now watching, biding his time for the perfect counterattack? Havelock could not shake the feeling that someone was watching his movements very carefully. He cast an anxious glance across the battle rolling all around him.

He saw Corbin a few yards away, fighting a thin man wearing the uniform of a French lieutenant. His own officer had half a smile as he fought, seeming to relish the chance to match himself against his counterpart. The two duelled with no little skill, the sailors around them not intruding, seeming to sense this was a fight of honour that none should interrupt.

His attention was distracted by the sight of a young red-headed British sailor yelling in alarm as two men rushed him, each thrashing with a large cudgel. There was a loud crack as the boy swung wildly with the belaying pin he carried, knocking aside the weapons of the two French sailors, more by luck than expertise. Giving ground wildly, the boy looked as if he would stumble and be killed at any moment.

Havelock rushed forward but was beaten to it by a burly man he felt he had spoken to before. The man chopped with his cutlass, snapping one of the cudgels with the blow, before thrusting with his weapon to sink it deep into the sailor's stomach. Shouting a warning to the other sailor before he struck, Havelock landed a solid blow to the man's shoulder, forcing him to drop his club. Another blow dispatched him just as quickly, leaving Havelock to confront the two British sailors. The larger man was clapping the boy on the back, trying to inspire confidence in the obviously shaken lad.

"Good work, Seaman..." Havelock prompted.

"Seaman Bryant, Captain," said the large man, crooking a finger in a hasty salute. "This here is Brooks."

"Watch over him," said Havelock. "We have the advantage over the French and it would not do to lose someone now."

"Right you are, Captain."

Turning back to the battle, Havelock tried to make his way to Corbin, who was still fighting the French Lieutenant. Another sailor tried to claim Havelock's life with a cutlass, forcing him to raise his sword high in a parry. A second Frenchman rushed forward from his right, a wicked looking pike aimed right at his heart. Still straining with his sword to stay the path of the cutlass, Havelock reached across his chest with his left hand and fired his pistol. The shot seemed to catch the pikeman completely off guard and his expression was one of utter surprise as he fell to his knees, then collapsed onto the sand. Striking out with his boot, Havelock connected with the knee of the other sailor, forcing him to back off. He immediately followed up with a well-aimed thrust to the chest that the sailor had no time to parry.

Glancing up, Havelock saw Corbin advance on his enemy with a series of quick cuts that forced the French officer to give ground. A quick flick of the Frenchman's sword missed Corbin's forehead by mere inches as he reeled backwards to avoid the blow but, recovering quickly, he slashed across the Lieutenant's forearm. Blood welled up immediately and the Frenchman was forced to swap his sword to his off hand. His movements became noticeably slower and it took Corbin scant seconds to finish the duel. Bowing slightly as the French Lieutenant hit the sand, Corbin turned to find another enemy but his eyes locked onto Havelock's and he smiled.

"A fine fight, Mr Corbin!"

"Thank you, Captain," said Corbin graciously in return. "It seems we have them beaten. Shall we now finish it?"

"Indeed," said Havelock. As Corbin turned to face battle once more, he caught the Lieutenant's arm. "Have a care, Mr Corbin. We have not won yet. I have a feeling things are not all they seem."

"You think there is a hidden force?" he said. "Mr Wynton reported the trees were clear and those huts cannot hide many men."

"I don't know," said Havelock, suddenly unsure of himself. "It is just... a feeling."

Corbin looked as if he did not know how to properly respond. "Well, we can keep our eyes open, Captain..."

"You are right, of course. Come, our men need us."

Leading the way, Havelock pushed through the body of British sailors that surrounded them. The French had suffered during the course of the battle to the extent that men were having to search for an enemy to fight. The fight had spilled from the open beach to the rickety huts and pockets of French sailors were now on the defensive as they were surrounded by an enemy who could sense victory. A large number of them had formed a loose clump in front of one hut and a number of dead or dying British sailors at their feet proved testament to their ferocity.

Pointing out the French defenders to Corbin, Havelock made his way to the fight, finding himself jostled by his own crewmen as he tried to force his way past them, until they saw just who it was they were trying to push back. Once at the front of the British sailors, he fought alongside Corbin, their blades flicking in and out as much as the tight press of men would allow, catching weapons brought down in overhead blows and darting outwards to catch a man's arm, head or heart.

One French sailor confronted Havelock with nothing more than a knife, its short blade coming nowhere near the length needed to reach past his sword. Havelock almost pitied the man as he finished the sailor with one quick slice across the face. It was then Havelock felt the cold hand of fear grip his stomach. He glanced wildly around, trying to identify the source of his unease but nothing was apparent. Corbin continued to fight next to him and though the Frenchmen were fighting like trapped rats, he saw nothing immediately life-threatening in their attacks.

Feeling something pulling his attention, he risked a quick glance over his shoulder. About a hundred yards further down the beach, he saw the sand begin to rise far more steeply than it did around the huts, creating a small rise before the trees of the jungle. Atop this ground, Havelock saw a single dark figure, standing motionless as it surveyed the battle on the beach. The cold hand of fear gripped his stomach harder as Havelock began to realise – how, he did not know – that the figure was looking directly at him.

Returning his attention back to the fight, Havelock half-heartedly parried a few blows aimed in his direction, wondering if this was what it was like to go mad. He glanced over his shoulder again, expecting his vision to be clear but the figure was still there, faintly malevolent in its inaction.

With no conscious decision on his part, Havelock simply turned and left the fight, his place immediately filled by sailors who had been impatiently waiting their turn to battle the French. It took Corbin several seconds to realise his Captain had gone and he glanced about wildly before catching sight of Havelock's retreating back.

"Captain?" He tried to pull away but the defending French chose that moment to redouble their efforts in an attempt to break free of the battle and head to the boats. Havelock did not hear the call of his Lieutenant as he walked, slowly, from the battle. Moving away from the huts, he kept his eyes fixed solidly on the lone figure, still standing proud and unmoving on the small rise. Though not in a daze, Havelock felt as if his actions now were not completely his own. If he had to put a term to it, he would have said it was a hand of destiny that now moved him and he began to dread the coming encounter, though nothing could have prepared him for what he faced once he climbed the rise.

Feet slipping in the sand as he scrambled up the shallow slope, Havelock kept his eyes locked on the motionless figure that waited impassively for him. He could already tell it was a tall man, with a long sword that gleamed dully. When he closed within a few yards of the figure, a familiar stench hit him with a shock, as if a door had just been opened to an ancient tomb. The rotting stink of the death hulk washed over Havelock, and though gagging, he refused to take his eyes off the dead man. Stumbling up the last few feet of the rise, Havelock stood, confronting the nightmare that had appeared on the eve of his mission's completion.

"Captain Havelock," the thing rasped through a lipless mouth, its exposed and decaying teeth grinning manically. Shocked to hear one of the walking dead actually speak, he could see it wore a ragged and mouldering French officer's uniform of antique design, its braid fraying at the shoulders and chest. The skin of its face and hands was sunken and stretched across bone, though it still seemed to possess an unholy strength.

"Captain James Havelock," the thing said slowly, seeming to relish his name. "I am Captain Dubois. I believe you know who I am..."

"Yes," said Havelock, fighting back his revulsion and fear. "You were... are... the captain of the *Deja*. A warship sunk by my grandfather."

"Ah, that is true," Dubois crooned. "'I was killed, you see, by Captain Edward Havelock as I defended men, women and children who sought nothing more than a better life. Innocents, Captain! But that mattered not to your grandfather. Against all the rules of conduct, morality and common decency, he sent many of them to their deaths and, had it not been for the sacrifice of my ship and crew, would have killed them all."

"I know the story, Dubois."

"Then you also know what I want."

Havelock hesitated before answering. "Yes."

The face of the creature wrinkled in what Havelock guessed might have been a grim smile. "Death has taken your grandfather far beyond my reach but now fate has delivered you, and your crew, into my hands."

Though the stink of the French Captain continued to assault Havelock's nostrils, his confidence grew as he confronted the talking zombie. He realised what might have to be done, even if he intended to make it as difficult for Dubois as possible. "What my grandfather did *was* wrong – and I am willing to answer for his crimes, here and now if you wish. But you will allow my crew to return home unharmed."

"I will do no such thing! One life will not balance the debt, Captain! The souls of my own crew must be satiated and that thirst can only be satisfied by the lives of your men. Justice demands like for like! I only pity that you have so few men with you."

"I cannot permit you to do this," said Havelock, holding his head high. "I have offered satisfaction. If that is not sufficient, you leave me with no choice."

"Satisfaction!" Dubois spat, the spray causing Havelock to flinch in disgust. "You English believe you have the moral right to do as you wish throughout the world. But you are nothing more than dogs who have no understanding of the true meaning of honour. You know of your grandfather's crime and yet fail to comprehend what it was he did. Your grandfather is now dead, after having enjoyed a life of privilege, luxury and high rank bought, in part, with our deaths. Now you are here, within our power. Your life and the lives of your crew will not balance the deaths of my crew or the murder of those we swore to protect. But it is a start, and I'll take that!"

"Then I will stop you. If you mean to claim my life, I challenge you to do it here, and now!" Havelock calmly stated as he raised his sword.

"You miss my meaning, Captain Havelock," said Dubois. "You will die, and soon, be sure of that. But not before I take your ship, your crew and even your humanity. You will *suffer*, Captain. No less is required of you."

"I will not permit this."

"It is inevitable, Captain." Again, the features of Dubois twisted in a hideous smile. "Here, in this place, it is I who have the power. You cannot kill me. You cannot stop me. Your fate was written when your grandfather killed us all!"

There was something in the creature's arrogance and certainty that angered Havelock. "I will see you in Hell first, Dubois!"

He struck forward with his sword, a powerful thrust aimed at the creature's heart. Dubois did not move as the blade sank into his chest, his dead flesh giving little resistance as the weapon burst out between his shoulder blades.

"Do you see?" he mocked.

Havelock cried out as he withdrew his sword and aimed a vicious swing at the zombie's neck. Dubois moved now, with a supple litheness that seemed at odds with his decaying physique or the lumbering movements Havelock had seen in the walking dead on the *Deja*. In a fluid motion, Dubois raised his sword up in the path of Havelock's, halting the blow immediately with a metallic clang that knocked rust and dirt from the creature's weapon. Havelock's arm ached at the sudden stop and he withdrew his sword, pacing to the left as he sought another opening.

Standing motionless again, Dubois merely held his sword outwards, its point towards his opponent. Havelock took a step forward and he chopped and swung in a rapid series of attacks, but each was met with Dubois' own blade, who blocked and parried the assault without moving from his place on the sand.

Sweating now, Havelock tried again, feinting at the creature's neck before diverting his swing downwards, intending to cut Dubois down at the knee. Again, his enemy's sword unerringly met the stroke but Havelock was prepared for this and slid his sword upwards to Dubois' face, hoping to skewer its dead features. This time, Dubois did move, a single step backwards that gave him room enough to raise his sword and once again hold Havelock's blade still.

Havelock strained against the parry, trying to force his sword forward just a few inches so it would at least mark Dubois' face but it was like trying to push against a mountain. He realised his enemy's strength was formidable, and likely sprang from a source deeper and more mysterious than mere flesh, bone and muscle. His stare of hatred was returned by Dubois as the two stood, straining against each other's weapon. Their faces just a few inches apart, Havelock glared into the colourless eyes of the zombie, the long ovals that marked Dubois' missing nose exhaled no breath. Havelock panted hard with effort but though he was still aware of the rotting stink of the creature, he forced it from his mind.

They stood like this, Havelock trying to force his weapon forward, for several long seconds before Dubois seemed to tire of the game and made his own move. A knee shot up into Havelock's stomach, winding him instantly and forcing him to take a few steps back. Dubois was immediately upon him, hacking downwards in an overhead swing that Havelock barely knocked to one side, before thrusting forward. The sword grazed past Havelock's ribs and he felt a sharp sting of pain before twisting out of the way.

Following up on the ground Havelock had given, Dubois chopped and hacked, each blow numbing Havelock's arm as he caught the blade on his own weapon, sometimes just inches from his face or chest. The sandy rise dropped behind him and, concentrating on Dubois' attacks, Havelock missed his footing. With a cry of alarm, he tumbled backwards, landing heavily on the ground.

Shaking his head to clear his vision, Havelock looked up to see Dubois standing over him. He swung wildly with his sword but the blow was met by the French captain's weapon. With a twist of his wrist, Dubois ripped Havelock's sword from his hand, causing it to fly through the air before landing in the sand a couple of yards from them. Stepping forward, Dubois placed the point of his sword on Havelock's chest, the blade pushing down painfully. Havelock looked up defiantly, determined not to show a trace of fear.

"You have your revenge, Sir," he said, his voice steady but laden with anger.

"I have already told you," said Dubois. "You will die last. First your ship, then your crew. Then, at the last, I will come for you."

Fury filled Havelock. He was well aware of the sins in his family's history but he refused to be mocked or played with. With a strangled cry, he rolled to one side, ignoring the pain of Dubois' blade as it pressed into his chest. He stretched for his own sword, spying its hilt in the sand just a short distance away. Grasping it clumsily, he kicked out while swinging the sword in a wicked blow aimed at Dubois' ankle. Both foot and blade met empty air.

Confused, Havelock cast about desperately, fearing a trick or surprise attack of some kind. He jumped to his feet and began to realise that he was alone on the sandy rise. Believing his enemy to have retreated into the jungle, he sprinted for the trees, their branches whipping his face as he tried to hack past them with his sword. After getting his foot snagged in a creeping vine and angrily cutting downwards, Havelock vented his frustration into the darkness.

"Why are you waiting?" he shouted. "I am here! Come and take me if you will! Coward! Villain! When we meet again, I'll send you back to the bottom of the ocean!"

The trees had no answer for him.

# CHAPTER TEN

THE BEACH WAS strewn with the dead and dying, the cries of the latter a piteous lament in the night. Wounded British sailors were guaranteed of at least a little comfort from their comrades but their French counterparts could only hope to raise enough pity for a little water if they spoke English. Stumbling back to the shore, Havelock observed all this in a daze. He saw that his men had gained a good victory but he took no pleasure in it, his previous encounter weighed heavily on his mind.

Already, Corbin had organised parties to ready the French landing boats to make an assault on the *Elita* who, even now, remained motionless, moored in the bay. Havelock observed a few of his sailors lounging among the makeshift huts, already retelling their part in the fight with suitable embellishments. More than a few swigged from bottles as they spoke and Havelock marvelled at the capacity of British sailors to locate drink wherever they may be. This tiny reminder of a normal sea life served to raise his spirits a little, though his mind still whirled with the memory of Dubois' face, the duel they had fought, and the rotting Frenchman's deadly promise.

As he approached the water, Corbin noticed his Captain and trotted over, his face full of concern.

"Sir?"

"Report, Mr Corbin," said Havelock.

The Lieutenant paused, clearly wanting to ask Havelock where he had disappeared to, but duty and discipline overcame his desire. "We have the beach, Captain. We have perhaps a dozen dead, twice that wounded and Mr Rawlinson is badly hurt, but the French came off worse. Some of them fled into the trees when it became clear their cause was lost, and the men say they saw a few run into the water. I have already started preparing the boats for the attack on the frigate. We await only your word."

"Very good, Mr Corbin, the word is given. Pass my compliments to the men."

"Very good, Sir. Err, Sir, if I may be so bold?"

Havelock cleared this throat. "My mistake, Mr Corbin. I thought Mr Wynton had missed a French party in the trees. Probably just a few animals."

"Sir!" Corbin appeared amazed. "If there had been a French party there, you going alone would have been tantamount to suicide!"

"The men were otherwise engaged. As it happens, there were no French, so don't fuss, Lieutenant. Now, these boats – they are ready, you say?"

"Yes, Sir. We have four of them. Orders?"

"You, Mr Wynton and myself will take a boat each, Mr Kennedy can take the last. You go for the bow, I'll take the stern, and the other two boats will support us in the centre. If we time our attacks more or less simultaneously, we have a chance at outmatching the French crew."

"And if the *Elita* weighs anchor and sets sail while we row towards her?"

Havelock shook his head. "She would have left already, the moment it became clear the beach was lost. No, I believe her Captain still fancies his chances. Remember, he likely still outnumbers us and we are about to launch an attack on his home ground. Tell the men to keep their heads down as they row. We *will* come under fire."

THOUGH THE DRINK had already started to flow, it took mere minutes to assemble the *Whirlwind's* crew to heave the landing boats into the water and start the short voyage to the French frigate. Havelock stood proud at the prow of his craft, one foot on its hull, as he checked his pistol. He could hear some of the crew muttering behind him, wondering whether their Captain was brave or foolhardy in presenting a French rifleman with such a good target. For his part, Havelock did not know whether he would live or die that night but after his encounter with Dubois, he doubted he would fall to a shot from a French sailor. Not one whose heart still beat in his chest, at any rate.

"Row!" Havelock said to his men. "Put your backs into it!"

As the pace of the small boat quickened under sweating curses, it veered off larboard, heading towards the prow of the *Elita*. Staring into the darkness, Havelock could make out French crewmen on its deck under the light of lanterns hung on the masts and other fixtures. At this range, he could not see evidence of massed ranks of riflemen, and Havelock found himself hoping that the main body of French soldiers had indeed been deployed on the beach. Even so, his heart fell when several gun ports opened on the side of the ship, their cannon pointing ominously towards his tiny fleet.

He heard a faint cry from the frigate, the order to fire, before a series of massive explosions rent the quiet night, bright flashes quickly subdued by thick, cloying smoke. Huge plumes of water straddled the boats of Kennedy and Wynton who, by approaching abeam to the *Elita*, had placed themselves directly in its line of fire. A quick glance showed that they had survived the initial salvo.

Looking back to see how quickly the crew of the *Elita* could reload, Havelock began to smile. The smoke from the attack hung in front of the frigate, effectively obscuring it from view. He heard some of the crew from the other boats give a short cheer as they too realised that if they could not see the *Elita*, then it could certainly not see them. The soft night breeze did little to disperse the smoke and Havelock began to dare hope they could reach the ship before the French had another chance to fire. He counted off the seconds as his boat made its painfully slow progress forward.

Another roar, accompanied by a yellow-orange flash behind the smoke signalled the French Captain's intention to fire blind if need be. Havelock winced at the deafening noise as the guns discharged just a few dozen yards away. Instinctively he glanced to his right but was this time dismayed to see water, bodies and shards of wood flying upwards. Which of the boats had been lost, he could not tell but he cursed. This attack had been a gamble but he had hoped not to lose a quarter of his strength before the fight had even begun.

"Lord have mercy on them," said one of his rowers, and Havelock could not help but agree. He fervently hoped there would be survivors that could swim to the *Elita* once it was in their hands but, given how the men had packed themselves into the boats, he did not rate their chances.

Seconds after the blast, Havelock's boat entered the rolling smoke, thick enough to force him to raise a sleeve to his nose and mouth to filter out the worst of its choking effects. For a moment, he could feel the presence of the *Elita* rather than see it, the ship's great mass seeming to press down on his small craft. Then, it materialised out of the smoke, its great hull rising high above the water. His eyes following the natural sweep of the hull, Havelock shuddered as he saw the gun ports, mounted one above the other on two decks, imagining the raw weight of fire they would be capable of under a crew as well trained as his.

A sailor poked his head over the side of the hull above, and Havelock swung his pistol upwards and fired as the man cried out a warning. The head disappeared, though Havelock could not tell whether this was because of his marksmanship or if the sailor had simply ducked in time. Two sailors stood up behind Havelock as the boat bumped against the side of the frigate with a dull thud. Swinging ropes, they quickly sent two grapples skywards, expertly hooking them over the railings.

Havelock tucked his pistol into his belt and then leapt forward onto one of the ropes, straining as he hoisted himself up, hand over hand. As he ascended the side of the ship, the French sailor reappeared above him. Instead of crying out for help again, he grinned at Havelock as he produced a knife and proceeded to make a great show of slowly cutting the rope. Swearing, Havelock redoubled his efforts, the muscles of his arms groaning in agony as they protested the exertion. As he shot up the rope, the expression of the French sailor slowly turned from glee to anxiety as he realised that the Englishman might actually reach him. Havelock felt the vibrations in his hands as each strand was cut. Realising he would not reach the railings of the *Elita's* forecastle in time, he waited until he felt the rope start to sag then, with one fluid motion, reached out to the second rope alongside and swung across to a safer perch.

The first rope fell away into the sea before the French sailor realised that there was no longer an English Captain hanging on to it and his expression fell. Havelock had cleared the last few feet of his ascent, and holding onto the rope with one hand, drew his sword and swung it in an elaborate slice that cut through the sailor's throat. Shaking the spray of blood from his eyes, Havelock heaved himself over the railings as the dull clunk of another grapple embedding itself close by signalled that his crew had already thrown a replacement rope upwards. Already, one of his sailors was clambering over the railings to join him and they both looked down the length of the ship as they realised that sounds of battle now filled the air.

Sharp notes of metal on metal, wood on skull and the occasional pistol shot announced the arrival of at least one of his other boats, in the centre of the ship, he guessed, from the press of French crew on the main deck. The forecastle was clear of defenders but it did not take long for someone to shout out a warning that drew a rush of sailors towards him. Moving to the centre of the forecastle to give his men enough room to climb on board, Havelock brandished his sword, daring the first man to attack. Despite his bravado, several French sailors deemed their chances good against an English officer and a gang rushed him, forcing Havelock on the back foot immediately as he twisted and parried their blows.


FEELING HIMSELF SHAKING, from fear or excitement he could no longer tell, Brooks hefted his belaying pin as he searched for an enemy, mindful to stay behind Bryant as instructed. He had followed Bryant up a rope at the stern of the *Elita*, with Murphy close below. The Irishman's quips about the size of Bryant's backside as they climbed had raised a smile but all mirth was forgotten as they heaved themselves onto the deck of the enemy ship. Though the French had concentrated their numbers at the centre of the ship, presumably because they expected an attack where the hull was lowest to the water, they quickly swarmed up to the quarterdeck to meet the assault.

Leading the English assault, Lieutenant Corbin had been the first to set foot on the *Elita* and, skilfully brandishing his sword, immediately set about carving a clear area around the grapples his crew were using to join him. Brooks saw that four corpses already lay at his feet.

Edging forward in Bryant's footsteps, Brooks glanced nervously from side-to-side, wary of a sudden attack from some filthy French sailor. He did not have long to wait, as a man with thick greasy black hair ducked under Bryant's cutlass, skipped to one side and then rushed forward. Brooks felt his heart quicken as he raised his club to meet the man's own and they crashed together with a wooden thud just inches from Brooks' head. Already fired with adrenaline from the fight on the beach, not to mention the nerve-wracking crossing of the cove, Brooks cried out as he tried to hold back the club with his own. Taking a step forward, he kneed the man in the groin, causing him to double up. His weapon now free, Brooks swung with all his strength at the man's skull, the soft crunch causing him to blanch with nausea.

The man sank to the deck and Brooks dashed forward to aid Bryant who, though making good account of himself, was swinging his blade as he tried to keep two more enemy sailors at bay. Brooks swung his club downwards, connecting with the arm of one of them. The man snarled in pain and turned to face the boy, thrusting forward with his cutlass. The sword punched through empty air as Brooks turned back and the man advanced to keep pace.

Seeing the sailor raise his cutlass for a vicious swing, Brooks held up his club to block the blow but icy cold terror began to pump through his veins as the sword sliced cleanly through his weapon. Now defenceless, Brooks stumbled backwards as the sailor leered at him, keen to snatch a quick victory before returning to more competent foes.

Fighting to keep his eyes open while he met his fate, Brooks was as equally surprised as the sailor when a whistle of metal flew through the air between them and a knife planted itself squarely in the man's chest. Before any more thoughts registered in Brooks' mind, he saw Murphy step inside the sailor's guard, pinning his sword arm with an elbow while grabbing his hair and forcing his head backwards. A blade was in Murphy's other hand and he repeatedly stabbed the man in the stomach, blood soon flowing freely as the strength ebbed from the Frenchman. Murphy let him sink to the deck before putting a foot on his chest to pull out his knife. Grabbing the dying sailor's cutlass, he tossed it to Brooks with a wink.

"There you go, lad," he said. "You'll do better with a proper weapon, I fancy!"

Casting a doubtful look at the long metal blade he now held, Brooks tried to remember if Bryant had taught him anything about swordplay. Eyeing the mayhem around him, he shrugged, figuring he could use it as a sharp club, and let finesse be damned.

The English now had their full weight of numbers on the quarterdeck and commanded about half its area. The Lieutenant still led the attack, though even Brooks could see that he favoured his left leg and was beginning to slow down under the exertion. Ever mindful of the young lad in their keeping, Bryant and Murphy stood either side of Brooks and the three friends fought together, forming a tight wedge that the French found impossible to break. Pushing forward, they began to take ground.

Swinging the unfamiliar cutlass, Brooks soon found it much better suited for blocking attacks and though his parries were clumsy, the presence of two competent fighters to his flanks served to keep him free from harm. He also appreciated the weapon's reach and more than once he found himself able to thrust forwards to skewer an enemy who was concentrating his attention on one of his friends. Even if he did not score a fatal wound, the distraction usually proved enough for Murphy or Bryant to finish off the attack. One step at a time, they moved forward across the quarterdeck, aware that the other English sailors were making similarly good progress.

Making their way past the *Elita's* double wheel, they fought, leaving a trail of dead or dying sailors on the deck behind them, until they faced just three Frenchmen who had been driven back against the railing of the quarterdeck. A cry went up behind them as the English sailors realised they had all but taken this part of the ship. One of the French spat at them and redoubled his efforts, forcibly pulling his comrade forward to meet blades with Bryant and Murphy. The third, doubting his chances, put one hand on the railings and threw himself over to drop onto the main deck below.

Brooks tried thrusting forward at the man fighting Murphy, hoping to give his friend a little advantage but the sailor twisted away and knocked his blade sideways, the clash numbing Brooks' arm. Murphy stabbed forward but quickly withdrew his hand as the Frenchman's sword cut downwards, missing his arm by a fraction of an inch. The sailor twirled his cutlass with some expertise, creating a singing web of metal as his blade sliced through the air, forcing Murphy to give ground until the Irishman, refusing to back away further, tossed a knife in the air, caught it by its blade and then threw it directly at the man's head. The cutlass whipped round, knocking the knife aside but the man was too slow for Murphy's second throw, which caught him in the stomach. Grunting, the sailor looked down at the blade, giving Brooks all the opportunity he needed to drive his cutlass into the man's side.

Bobbing his head in thanks, Murphy clapped Brooks on the shoulder, who smiled nervously in return.

"I declare, lad, you are getting the 'ang of this," Murphy said.

Having heard many tales from his fellow crew throughout the *Whirlwind's* voyage, Brooks had heard of the fire that instilled itself in the hearts of men during battle. This was the first time he had truly felt it. He had faced too many close scrapes to be anything other than aware of his own mortality but Brooks could feel something changing inside of him. It dawned on him that, if he could survive this battle, he would no longer be a boy amongst men, but an equal to the rest of the crew. That, he felt, was something worth fighting for.

Bryant still battled his opponent, who had learned enough tricks with the sword to keep the large man off balance enough to halt any finishing blow, and they turned to aid their friend. A cry to his left caused Brooks to glance away for a split second and he saw his Lieutenant near the stairs leading down to the main deck, crouched as he faced a French soldier who wielded a long chain that he swung above his head. Corbin's left arm hung limply at his side and he was in obvious pain. He watched as the chain swung quickly in a tight circle, before it snaked out to connect with Corbin's arm once more. The force of the blow sent him flying to the deck, where he landed heavily. Looking up at his attacker, Corbin vainly raised his sword to ward off the next blow.

Without knowing quite what he was doing, Brooks leapt forward, skipping past Murphy who had already engaged Bryant's opponent, trying to keep the man occupied until his friend could land a telling blow.

Running the few yards between himself and the prone Lieutenant, Brooks found himself standing over Corbin, the French sailor looked at his new foe in some surprise. That did not halt his attack, however, and the chain whistled through the air at head height. Instinctively,

Brooks raised his cutlass to block the attack but was perturbed to see the chain wrap itself round the blade and only his adrenaline-fuelled reflexes saved him as the metal links whipped across his face, drawing a line of blood across the bridge of his nose.

Blinking back tears, Brooks tried to wrench his sword free but his strength proved no match for the larger sailor's, who pulled hard, nearly throwing Brooks off his feet. Deciding not to fight on equal terms, Brooks gave up trying to free his weapon, satisfied that the Frenchman could not use his chain either. Lowering a shoulder, he threw himself forward, catching the sailor completely off guard. He ran into the man, who tripped as he backpedalled, trying to keep his ground. They both experienced a brief second of weightlessness as they fell over the stairs behind them, before landing with a heavy crash on the wood of the main deck.

The French sailor was obviously winded by the fall and Brooks felt giddy from the impact but he recovered quickly. Straddling the man to pin him in place, Brooks rained down punch after punch into his face, smashing his nose and lips until blood began to flow freely. Gathering his wits, the man snarled and grasped one of Brooks' wrists but his own blood made the grip slippery. Wresting his arm away, Brooks spied the man's chain to one side and reached for it, taking a hammer-like punch to the chest for his effort.

Fighting back the pain, Brooks grabbed the man by the hair and wrapped the chain round his throat, quickly tightening the loop before the man could force his fingers under the metal links. Pulling with all his strength, Brooks forced the chain to dig into the man's neck, cutting off his windpipe. Turning red, then purple, the man lashed out at Brooks, who ignored the steadily weakening blows. The last strike was more of a slap across his bloody cheeks as the man finally gave his last.

Panting, Brooks stared into the dead man's face, barely aware of the battle that raged across the entire length of the main deck. He started as he felt someone grab his shoulder, and he fumbled for his cutlass, trying to free it from the chain.

"Whoa there, lad!"

It took Brooks a second to recognise the voice as that of his Lieutenant, and he looked up into the man's face which beamed with delight.

"I owe you my thanks. You are a credit to his Majesty's Navy!"

His heart still racing from the fight, Brooks could do no better than mumble his thanks, but Corbin seemed to understand as he ruffled his hair.

"Now, lad, you think you have it in you to kick the rest of these Frenchies off this ship?"

Brooks finally found his voice. "I'll be right behind you, Sir!"

"Come then!"

His arm still hanging wounded at his side, Corbin rushed into the melee of the main deck with a challenging cry, his sword rising and falling with a new found energy. Brooks stood to follow him and caught sight of Murphy and Bryant rushing to descend the stairs from the quarterdeck. Murphy had an odd twinkle in his eye.

"Saw that, we did!" he said. "You done well there, Brooks. Saved Corbin 'imself from certain death! Only thing better than that would be savin' the Cap'n!"

Bryant smiled widely. "That's right – I'm thinking there will be some favours coming your way when we set sail later, lad!"

Standing, Brooks shook his cutlass free, letting the chain drop to the deck. He tried to shrug off the compliments but a smile forced itself onto his face. He knew he had done well.

"Still," said Bryant. "That will be enough heroics for one day. Don't tempt fate. Stick with me and Murphy from now on, and we'll get through this fight alive." He looked into the press of sailors battling one another mere yards away. "Come, let's make an end of this. We can't let the Lieutenant have all the fun to himself."

"Aye, t'would be a shame 'im dyin' now," said Murphy. "Before 'e 'as a chance to properly thank Brooks!"

UNLIKE THE SMALLER *Whirlwind*, the forecastle of the *Elita* was raised above the main deck, in the same manner as the quarterdeck at the stern. This worked in Havelock's favour, as it allowed him to lead his men in a bloody fight that eventually saw them victorious on the forecastle, having swept it clear of all resistance. A half dozen of the crew that had rowed with him lay on the deck but this part of the French frigate now belonged to them.

Standing at the top of the stairs that led down to the main deck, Havelock quickly judged the state of the battle. Across from him, he saw that Corbin was already leading his men down from the quarterdeck, having successfully taken that ground too. However, in the centre of the main deck, the English were taking a dreadful beating. The French had massed in number there and, with one boat missing from the frontal assault, they had obviously found it easy to attack his sailors as they tried to clamber up their boarding ropes. A few had made it and managed to create a small perimeter that permitted their remaining shipmates to climb on board as well. Once on the deck, they immediately found themselves surrounded by more than a hundred angry Frenchmen eager to exact justice for the slaughter on the beach.

A loud voice called out in French, ordering the enemy sailors to balance the defence, from what Havelock could make out. He quickly found the source of the shout, a tall Frenchman dressed in the fine braided uniform of a Captain. The man had not yet entered battle directly but was directing men with his sword to meet Corbin's flank attack. Seeing another of his sailors fall to a French cleaver, Havelock spied his only chance to gain victory and take the *Elita*.

"Come on!" he cried to the men still on the forecastle as he jumped down the stairs, sword high in the air. They quickly fanned out to engage the French from a new direction, but Havelock made a beeline for the opposing Captain. Just a few yards from the man, Havelock stopped and, saluting with his sword, called out.

"Monsieur."

The French officer turned round to face Havelock, who was struck by how young he appeared. No scars graced his face and his skin appeared to have survived the rigours of sea life without blemish. Havelock might have presumed he was a junior officer, were it not for the uniform and something in his eyes that spoke of both experience and wisdom.

"Captain," the Frenchman said, acknowledging Havelock with a slight nod of the head. He placed his off-hand on his hip in the traditional French duelling pose and raised his sword point forward. Around them the battle seethed, with the British gaining a new vigour now more of them had entered the fray.

"I have the pleasure of addressing Captain Guillot?" said Havelock.

"Indeed, Sir. You have me at a disadvantage."

"Captain Havelock, of his Majesty's Navy."

"I will accept your surrender now, Captain Havelock. Your men are outnumbered."

Havelock smiled. "You will find it takes more than a good thrashing to beat an English crew, Monsieur."

"So be it."

With a grace Havelock found admirable, the Frenchman lunged forward with his blade, its shining edge glittering in the light of the *Elita's* lanterns. With a flick of his wrist, Havelock brushed the point of the sword past him, then reversed the stroke to slash across his opponent's chest. Seeing the strike, Guillot stepped backwards and once again gave Havelock a slight nod.

"You have some skill in the sword, Captain Havelock."

"You will find English officers to be quite well trained," said Havelock, closing the distance between them to lunge himself. Guillot accepted the attack and their blades met with a loud metallic ring again and again, as they made stroke and counterstroke, each sensing in the other an enemy to be respected.

Guillot feinted to the right and, drawing Havelock's guard as he intended, struck suddenly with an upward swing. Havelock jerked his body from the sudden blow but, off balance, he failed to parry Guillot's next attack, which sliced his left thigh. Grunting, he felt the blood start to flow, staining his leggings. Though painful, he did not feel he had been crippled by the blow and he matched the Frenchman's strike with several hard swings that forced Guillot backwards. Each was checked by a skilful block or dodge, but Havelock allowed his rage to guide him for a moment, using his anger to give him strength.

He paused in the assault briefly to avoid a coil of rope snaking across the deck but Guillot was waiting for a respite. Again, he lunged with perfect skill, the point of his blade driving for the centre of Havelock's face. Havelock sensed the oncoming blade rather than saw it and tilted his head to one side. Though he avoided having his skull skewered, the point still dug painfully into his cheek, drawing a deep line of blood that quickly drenched the side of his face. This time, it was Havelock's turn to back off a couple of steps.

Still keeping his off-hand at his hip, Guillot started to circle Havelock, looking for an opportunity to finish the Englishman off. For his part, Havelock started balefully at his opponent, not blinking as he waited for the next attack, determined to force Guillot's hand.

Guillot obliged and stepped forward to launch a series of blows aimed at Havelock's head, shoulders and chest. Had Havelock been observing the Frenchman in a gentlemanly duel, perhaps in London, he might have described those swings as an almost beautiful display of swordsmanship. Here, on board an enemy ship in the South Atlantic, that skill could prove deadly. Purely on the defensive, Havelock parried each attack in turn, not seeking to riposte and turn the tables until Guillot relented.

After a few seconds that stretched into eternity for Havelock, Guillot finally stopped and, once again, stepped back. No longer caring about the conduct of gentlemen in duels, Havelock did not allow him to retreat and instead took two steps up to the man, grabbing his sword arm with one hand. He struck forward with his other hand, smashing his sword's gold-laden hilt into Guillot's face.

Crying out loud in both pain and surprise, Guillot staggered backwards, before tripping over the coiled rope, his sword clattering to the deck. He looked up with an expression that Havelock thought was somewhat disapproving, a line of blood trailing down from a smashed lip. Havelock stood over the man, the point of his sword on Guillot's chest.

"I will accept your parole now," he said.

Guillot sighed and then nodded, slowly reaching for his sword, then offering it to Havelock, hilt first. "*D'accord.*"

"Order your men to stand down."

Rattling out a series of instructions in his own language Guillot commanded his men to drop their weapons and surrender. The British crew cheered mightily as soon as they realised their Captain had been victorious in his duel. Just a few seconds ago, many had been convinced they had been about to die and their elation was genuine and heartfelt.

"Mr Corbin!" Havelock shouted, and the Lieutenant quickly ran to his Captain's side. Aware of blood trickling down his neck and into his tunic, Havelock withdrew a handkerchief from a pocket and held it to the side of his face, trying to stem the flow.

"The ship is ours, Sir," he said. "Congratulations!"

"Save the celebration, Lieutenant, we still have work ahead of us. Make sure the French crew are disarmed and then have them escorted to the shore."

"You are marooning my men?" said Guillot as he stood to face Havelock. "What kind of man are you?"

"Monsieur, I fear your men were too successful in their defence of both shore and ship," said Havelock. "I do not have enough crew to guard them and I fear there would be some among them eager to turn the tables against us while at sea."

Guillot seemed set to protest but Havelock raised his hand before continuing. "However, it is not my intention to doom anyone. You have many wounded on the beach that we could not take with us anyway – your men will be able to look after them. We will supply them with food and water from your own hold and I believe they will be able to forage for anything else on this island. You will return to England with us and, once there, I will ensure the French Navy hears of your crew's location. That is the best I can do for you."

"In light of the wounded on the beach, I find this acceptable, Captain Havelock."

"Good. Mr Corbin, get the French on the boats but make sure they are escorted. We have our own wounded to bring back from the beach, remember."

"Right you are, Sir," said Corbin as he ran off to fulfil his Captain's wishes.

"Mr Wynton!" Havelock called out but this time he was met with silence. Instead, Kennedy approached him.

"Beggin' your pardon, Captain."

"What is it, Mr Kennedy?" said Havelock, though given the Bosun's presence on the *Elita*, he had already guessed the news.

"I saw Mr Wynton's boat sink under fire as we rowed. I've already told some men to keep an eye out for survivors as they take the Froggies back to the beach, but I didn't see any survivors."

Havelock sighed. He had lost men and officers before but this enterprise was starting to demand too high a price. "Very good, Mr Kennedy. Gather a few men and make a quick search of this ship. Watch out for any remaining crew below decks and report to me of her condition."

As men, both French and British, began to scatter across the deck to their duties or off ship to the boats waiting below, Havelock and Guillot were left alone. It was the French Captain who broke the silence between them.

"A fine series of attacks, Captain Havelock," he said. "You will no doubt be commended upon your return to Portsmouth. Or do we go to London?"

"You know I will not tell you that yet. And this mission has had a heavy price."

"*C'est la guerre*," said Guillot simply. He paused, thinking, and then continued. "The name Havelock. Have I heard it before?"

"Perhaps. My grandfather..."

"Ah, yes, Admiral Havelock. The scourge of the Southern Seas, the Terror of the French."

"I am familiar with my own family's history, Monsieur."

"And brave butcher of colonists..."

Havelock gave Guillot a sour look but the Frenchman pretended not to notice.

"Yes, the name Havelock is well known to the French Navy. And now his grandson sails the same seas where those tortured souls met their end. I wonder if you will survive to be feted in England?"

Something about Guillot's tone made Havelock's expression change to one of curiosity.

"Is there something you want to tell me?"

Guillot shrugged. "A man must live with his own conscience, and maybe his family's as well. As I said, we are at war. Then as much as we are now. In any event, it is no longer my place to avenge the deaths of my countrymen."

"I am not sure I understand."

"Perhaps there is nothing to understand. You are the victor and I am but your prisoner."

Havelock was not sure if the man was mocking him. A little frustrated, he pushed on. "Is there anything about the state of this ship you will tell me?"

"I have nothing to hide from you now, Captain. I am a French officer alone on an English ship."

"And?"

"Your first attack against us was most impressive," Guillot said. "A fine demasting shot. I presume that was deliberate. Still, as you now know, we had the advantage of this island which we used to make repairs. You'll find she still sails well, as we had prepared new masts sometime earlier. There are still gun carriages to replace or repair and some regions of the hull are not all they should be. Still, the *Elita* will get you to England, and with good speed. Just don't think of taking her into battle, though I presume that is not your plan, given how few men you have."

"I guessed as much. Most efficient, Monsieur, you are to be commended for your efforts."

"All wasted now, with the *Elita* in English hands."

"As you say, it is war."

Havelock continued to watch the French crew depart the frigate with their escorts, the landing boats slowly travelling to the beach to offload their prisoners and take on British wounded. Seeing his wounds, one crewman offered to bind his leg, and Havelock gratefully accepted. After a few minutes, Kennedy emerged from below decks and, saluting Havelock with a crooked finger, he made his report.

"It's a pig sty, Sir. In fact, I wouldn't keep me pigs in these conditions."

Havelock cast a sideways look at Guillot, but the Frenchman seemed unapologetic.

"We can make her proud during the voyage home," Havelock said.

"It will take the whole trip and then some, and that ain't me grumbling, Captain. It really is that bad. The great cabin is in good shape though and the galley is well-stocked. You'll be eating fine, if you can live with the stink, Sir."

"My least concern right now, Mr Kennedy. Any surprises?"

"Both gun decks are a mess. At a push, we can put up a fight, but I wouldn't want to meet anything more than an armed merchantman on the way back. Didn't see any stragglers but I would want to do a more thorough search later."

"Granted."

"And the hold is a pit of foulness, Sir. Not sure what we can do about that until we put into port. Still, it seems fairly full – should make the lads happy, with prize money and all."

"Then it seems like we have been successful in our mission. Start organising the watches, Mr Kennedy, and then – what is going on there?"

The first boat had returned to the *Elita* and its crew, including Lieutenant Corbin, were just clambering onto the main deck. One of them was drenched in blood and seemed to be raving. Though his shipmates tried to calm him down and attend to his wounds, he refused to be placated.

"The Cap'n, I gotta see the Cap'n!"

Frowning, Havelock spoke quietly to Kennedy. "Bosun, bring that man to me."

The man seemed exhausted and though he had collapsed to the deck, he kept repeating his need to talk to his Captain. Kennedy tried to quieten him down but gave up as the man's protests grew in volume. Instead, Kennedy hooked an arm under his shoulder and, supporting the man's weight, walked him across the deck to face Havelock.

The man's eyes opened wide in relief when he saw Havelock. His face was a wash of blood and Havelock could see he had many more wounds across his body. He was amazed the man still had any strength left within him.

"Cap'n, thank the Lord! They slaughtered all of us, even chasin' us through the jungle!"

"Calm down, sailor," said Havelock, trying to quieten the man down with a steady, even tone. "Go slowly, you are not making sense. Are you saying there are still French crew from the beach who can fight?"

"No Sir, I wasn't fightin' on the beach. I was one of them that was left behind on the *Whirlwind*."

Even before the man's next words left his lips, a now familiar cold hand gripped the pit of Havelock's stomach.

"The *Whirlwind*, Sir. She's gone. Sunk,' he said, beginning to grow hysterical again. "That death hulk, the *Deja*, came speedin' out o' nowhere. It was on us before we could do nuffin'."

Seeing the few crewmen on deck look up sharply at this, Havelock grabbed the man's collar and jerked him hard. "For God's sake, man, keep your voice down!" Thinking hard, he manhandled the wounded sailor towards the quarterdeck and, dragging him up the stairs, faced him directly. He was aware that Kennedy, Corbin and Guillot had followed them.

"Now, calmly – and quietly – tell me what happened."

"Sir, it was dreadful, ain't never seen nuffin' like it. That death ship, it moved so fast. Its guns started blazin' and we felt the *Whirlwind* holed almost straight away. Then it smashed into us and the dead swept over us. We were too few! They just tore us apart, in minutes! Mr Hague was killed first, 'e was tryin' to hold 'em back!"

"There were survivors though?"

"A few of us jumped overboard and swam for the island – the ship was already lost and sinkin', Cap'n, I swear! But the damned zombies followed us!" The sailor panted for breath and swallowed before continuing. "We ran through the trees, tryin' to reach you but they took us, one by one. I 'eard the screams of me mates as they fell. One came at me, but I fought it off. Took its 'ead off, I did."

The man began coughing and Havelock motioned to Kennedy to take him below decks for care. Judging by the state of his wounds, Havelock guessed that he would not last the night. He looked at Corbin and Guillot. The Lieutenant seemed pale as he tried to make sense of the news. The Frenchman raised an eyebrow.

"The *Deja*? That name is also well known in the French Navy, Captain Havelock. Just what is it you have awoken?"

For once, Havelock had no answer.

"It seems as though the sins of the father will face justice after all," said Guillot. "I fear you have doomed every man on this ship."

"Captain Guillot, you will go below deck! I will instruct my Bosun to make you comfortable."

"A man of honour might offer himself in order to save his crew."

"That offer has already been made. It was deemed insufficient."

"Ah, then you already have some measure of the enemy you now face?" said Guillot.

"More than you can imagine."

"I think this is something you cannot defeat."

Havelock was grim. "We'll see."

Guillot seemed ready to argue the point but instead, he shrugged then descended the stairs to the main deck to seek new quarters. Corbin was still silent and Havelock had to shake him by the shoulder to get his attention.

"Lieutenant, assemble the men," said Havelock.

"Sir, the *Whirlwind*..."

"Get a grip of yourself, man! We still have the *Elita*, a larger and more powerful ship. The mission will still be deemed a success by the Admiralty, but we have to leave now! Thanks to that man's ravings on deck, the crew will already know the fate of the *Whirlwind* and what pursues us. I must get them on side, and quickly. Call them to assemble. Now!"

Corbin started to move slowly away but he soon picked up pace and, after having found his voice, called for Kennedy to gather the crew on the main deck. Havelock impatiently waited for them to appear below him and noted that more than a few threw surly looks in his direction. He could not entirely blame them, for the night's expedition had already cost them many friends and comrades, and now they had lost their ship. Corbin returned to his side on the quarterdeck as he began to speak, and some crew were still climbing on board from one of the landing boats, the cries of the wounded punctuated his words.

"Brave sailors of the King's Navy," he said, deliberately avoiding addressing them as the men of the *Elita*. "We have suffered many losses tonight but look at what you have achieved! This fine frigate had a crew that outnumbered us by more than two to one, and yet it is now in our hands. I swear to you, there are perhaps just two or three other crews in the entire fleet that could have done what we have. You are all heroes, the best of what is British and a credit to the nation!"

He paused and a deathly silence hung in the air, broken only by the occasional cry or whimper from a wounded sailor. Most of the faces that looked up at him were expressionless, their owners thoroughly exhausted. Others glared with outright hatred.

"You have heard the... regrettable news of the *Whirlwind* and its demise. I, myself, am saddened by its loss. However, our mission is now complete, and we set sail for England! I have been informed that this ship's hold is full and so the prize money will flow like water when we return home. You will all be wealthy! Now, steel yourselves for one final journey as we make the trip home."

A few weary nods met his words, but otherwise the crew remained silent. Havelock inwardly cursed, knowing he would have trouble with discipline on the voyage home. Even the thought of great riches did little to raise the morale of his crew, and that meant more than one sailor was considering mutiny. The only consolation was that things would get easier the closer they sailed to England and the prize money they were all now due. Of course, he would have to face a court martial for the loss of the *Whirlwind* before any money would be paid, but that was something he would gladly face if he could just make it home safely.

"Mr Corbin, prepare to set sail."

The Lieutenant looked at him quizzically, leaning across to speak quietly.

"Sir, we still have wounded on the beach. We need just a little more..."

"Now, Mr Corbin," said Havelock, looking at him meaningfully. "We have no more time!"

Corbin opened his mouth to say something, then closed it as it dawned upon him just what Havelock meant. He glanced through the night towards the entrance of the cove, half-expecting to see the dark mass of the *Deja* lurking at its edge, waiting to send the *Elita* to the bottom of the sea. Reluctantly, he nodded.

"I understand, Captain." He turned to face the crew. "Prepare to set sail!"

# CHAPTER ELEVEN

TOGETHER, BRYANT, MURPHY and Brooks stared at the wreckage of the lower gun deck, gazing at the smashed gun carriages, dislodged cannon and broken fittings. Their elation at having been given one of the heavy 24 pounders to work had quickly crumbled when they saw their working environment. Murphy had made a great show of clasping a rag to his nose and mouth as they went below decks but they were all staggered to see just how much damage had been done to the *Elita* during its duel with the *Whirlwind*.

"You can see now why the Frogs ran from us," said Brooks.

"Aye, lad," said Bryant. "Only a few of their big guns are still serviceable starboard. One quick turn from the Captain, and they would have been defenceless. And now we have to clean up the mess."

Murphy removed the cloth from his face but gagged and quickly replaced it. "Of all the foulness," he said, his voice muffled. "When did they last clean this ship?"

"It is entirely possible that it has never been properly cleaned," said Bryant, shaking his head in disbelief. "They'll get some ventilation going once we set sail. Until then, you'll just have to get used to it."

"I ain't never gettin' used to this."

Brooks cast a look around the deck, eyeing up the huge guns that dwarfed those he was used to on the *Whirlwind*. He could already imagine the back-breaking work of resetting the heavy weapons back onto their carriages, and further down the deck, he could see two other gun crews debating the task as well. "So, where do we start?" he asked.

Bryant sighed. "Might as well take the nearest," he said. "Look, this one is only dislodged from its mountings. The carriage itself looks fine. Murphy, see if you can find us a good bit of rope. It will be easier winching the gun from the rafters than lifting it with our bare hands."

Murphy scuttled off into the shadowy recesses of the lower gun deck as Bryant bent low over the gun carriage to see if the wood had been split by the weight of its cannon. He became aware of a presence behind him and guessed a member of one of the other gun crews was looking for advice or a favour. He was about to stand up when an all too familiar voice floated down to him.

"Bryant, been lookin' for you, man," said Jessop. "We need to talk."

"I'm busy."

"You 'eard what 'appened to the *Whirlwind*. Too fine a ship to be lost to them dead Froggies. But that is exactly what the Cap'n 'as gone and done!"

Knowing he would regret it, Bryant stood up and faced Jessop, sitting himself on the gun carriage.

"I told you before, Jessop. I know what you are after, and I ain't interested."

"The Cap'n is leadin' us straight to our deaths," said Jessop insistently. "You know it and I know it. We've already lost a good two-thirds of our crew."

"At least." Murphy's voice rang out from somewhere in the shadows.

"At least! You see, even the little Irishman knows it!"

"Jessop, I am serious," said Bryant, pointing a finger towards the burly man. "This is hanging talk."

In return, Jessop rolled his eyes. "An' tell me this, Bryant. Just what is the difference between *possibly* 'anging from a yard arm and definitely gettin' a rusty sword in the gut from a Frog who just don't know when to lie down an' die, eh?"

"I know what you are saying…"

"You want your old mate Murphy to die this day? Or Brooks? What about Brooks, eh, does the young lad deserve to meet 'is end?"

Uncomfortable at having been brought into the conversation, Brooks looked from Jessop back to Bryant, but stayed silent.

"You don't 'ave to do anythin'," said Jessop. "Just a word or two 'ere and there. I got me lads on side but the crew likes you. You'll pull the rest round."

"And then?"

"We'll take 'em by surprise!"

Bryant could not help himself from giving a short laugh. "Jessop, do you really think the Captain ain't expecting something? He has had too much sea beneath him to know something ain't up with the crew."

"Well, maybe," said Jessop. "But it makes no difference anyway. The officers 'ave been dyin' alongside us, an' there's just a few of 'em left. We'll take care of the Captain, and that Froggie officer too. Corbin'll 'ave to go – shame, as I sort of liked 'im. But it 'as to be done clean. All officers 'ave to go."

By now, the other two gun crews had heard what was being discussed and they moved up the deck to lend their weight to the argument. All Jessop's men, Bryant could sense the mood turn dark quickly.

"It's them or us, plain an' simple," said one.

"Come on, Bryant," said another. "The *Whirlwind* 'as gone, an' that death 'ulk is in the area, we know. It's comin' for us right now."

"That's right," said Jessop, bolstered by his support. "We ain't got no choice. We act now, or die today!"

Taking a deep breath, Bryant stood up to stare Jessop squarely in the eyes. "My answer has not changed," he said. "I will not aid a mutiny in any way. But hear me well, Jessop – you are on a fool's errand with your plan. The Captain is smarter than you and, whether you believe it or not, he is tougher than you. If you attack him, he will cut you down. And then make mincemeat of your friends. We all saw how he fought against the French." He cast a meaningful look at Jessop's co-conspirators and was a little gratified that at least a couple of them began to look doubtful.

"Can I at least rely on your silence?" said Jessop, and Bryant saw the man begin to clench his fists, as if he were readying himself for a fight if he heard the wrong answer. Though he was not swayed by the implied threat, Bryant understood well the code upheld among shipmates.

"You are going to regret what you do, Jessop, but I ain't no tell-tattle. Go seek death at the Captain's hands if you must. I won't interfere."

"But I will." The new voice from the near end of the gun deck caused them all to whirl round in surprise. Jessop groaned softly when he saw the lithe form of the Bosun step into the lantern light.

"Ah, I ain't got no argument with you, Mr Kennedy," he said.

Kennedy did not miss a beat as he stepped up to Jessop and prodded him in the chest with a finger. "If you 'ave a problem with the Cap'n, you see me about it first. Get past me an' the Cap'n will hear your complaints."

Bryant moved back slightly as he saw Kennedy was poised on the balls of his feet, ready to react to any move Jessop made. He grabbed Brooks' sleeve and pulled him back as well.

Jessop grinned at Kennedy. "Ah, it don't 'ave to be like this," he said. "You can see what is goin' on, surely?"

"Jessop, you're an ignorant bully, which is a shame, as you 'ave guts and the makings of a good sailor about you. Right now we need every man we got, so get back to your guns and make us ready for battle should that damned ship make another appearance."

"An' if I refuse, Bosun?"

"Then I told you before. You want some o' the Cap'n, you got to get through me first. An' don't you think I won't be enjoyin' it!"

Letting the challenge hang between them for a few seconds, Jessop smirked then half-turned away from Kennedy. He sprang round like a coiled spring, aiming a meaty fist squarely at Kennedy's nose but the Bosun had been ready for the ploy. He ducked under the punch and then exploded into action, launching a series of heavy blows into Jessop's body, the thump of each hit echoing across the gun deck. Jessop exhaled noisily but forced himself to stand up straight, just in time to take a blow to the chin which sent him reeling.

One of Jessop's crew mates took a step to join the fight but was arrested by Bryant's firm grip on his shoulder.

"This is between Jessop and the Bosun," he said.

"Aye, that's right," said Kennedy. "What about it, Jessop? You 'ad enough? You wantin' to be droppin' this matter and gettin' back to work?"

As a reply, Jessop roared and charged Kennedy, ignoring another blow to the face as he crashed into the man. They fell, arms and legs flailing as each sought to get a quick advantage. Jessop's crewmates surrounded them, shouting out words of encouragement. Curiosity getting the better of them, Bryant, Brooks and Murphy joined them, but remained silent.

On the wooden floor, Jessop had hooked a leg across Kennedy's body, trying to pin him down while he started to rain punches downwards. Kennedy took a few blows to the face and chest before catching Jessop's fist in his hand. Raising his head, he bit down on Jessop's hand, getting a howl of pain for his efforts. Distracted by the blood that now flowed, Jessop relaxed his hold on Kennedy slightly, giving the Bosun the opportunity he had been looking for. Jabbing with a knee, he caught Jessop in the side of the head and knocked him sideways before standing up, fists at the ready for another assault.

Jessop rolled across the deck, panting. Too late, Bryant saw a flash of metal on the floor nearby, a short blade that he guessed one of Jessop's friends had dropped. As he cried a warning to the Bosun, Jessop grabbed the knife and stood, turning to face Kennedy with a look of triumph.

Spitting in disgust at the low tactic, Kennedy remained impassive, merely beckoning Jessop on. All too keen to oblige, Jessop charged forward again, stabbing down at Kennedy's chest. Freed from any excuse to restrain himself, Kennedy watched Jessop's movements closely before springing into action again. He caught the descending knife hand, then twisted his body, forcing his back into Jessop's chest. With his free arm, he hooked his elbow backwards into Jessop's face but instead of letting him stagger backwards, he brought the hand still holding the knife down onto his raised knee.

Again, Jessop cried out in pain and the knife fell from his nerveless fingers. Releasing his grip, Kennedy stooped to pick up the weapon but twisted round as Jessop grabbed him from behind. They struggled for an instant before Jessop managed to curl a foot behind Kennedy's leg and, heaving forward with all his strength, threw the Bosun to the floor again with a solid crash.

Backswinging with his free hand, Kennedy caught Jessop across the side of the head, throwing him on his back. In a sudden lunging motion, Kennedy planted the knife firmly in his opponent's chest. Jessop, exhaled one bubbling breath and then fell still.

Leaving the knife in Jessop's chest, Kennedy stood and cast a withering glance at the ring of sailors who had now all fallen silent.

"Anybody else 'ave a problem with 'ow the Cap'n is doin' things?" he said, demanding a response from Jessop's crew. To a man, they avoided his grim stare.

"Thought not," said Kennedy. "Clean that mess up. Then get back to work."

Reluctantly, Jessop's crew started heaving their fallen friend towards an open gun port as Kennedy gave them one last glance and then turned to check on the repair details on the upper gun deck. Bryant's crew slowly drifted back to their own gun carriage, Murphy smiling as he produced a length of stout rope. Brooks was wide-eyed.

"That was incredible," he said. "The Bosun knows how to fight!"

"You don't get to be a Bosun unless you can give as well as you take," said Bryant. "Just you remember that in later years. You never, ever cross the Bosun."


USING THE LIGHT of the breaking dawn pouring through the windows of the *Elita*'s great cabin, Havelock poured over Guillot's navigational charts. He had to admit, they were most complete. Havelock had heard rumours of French explorers and their accuracy in producing maps of the southern seas, but this was the first time he had seen a set first hand. It was little wonder that a French commerce raider could retain an advantage in these waters.

His impressions of the rest of the ship during his brief tour were less than complimentary, and the frigate had pretty much lived up to every stereotype due a French vessel of war. The cabins used by the officers, including the lodgings of the former Captain in which he stood, were luxurious and well-equipped, and he had already heard reports of the contents of the galley which was stocked with preserved foodstuffs that made the *Whirlwind* seem primitive. There was little doubt that his voyage back to England would be one of the most comfortable journeys he had ever made by sea.

Take one step out of the officers' cabins, however, and Havelock was all too aware of the ship's deficiencies. Leaving aside the damage the *Whirlwind* had done to the frigate in its duel, which his crew would have to work hard to repair while sailing, the *Elita* had not been maintained in a manner befitting a ship of the King's Navy.

Structurally, it was sound and the hull had weathered his earlier attacks well, even if the fixtures and fittings had not. The living conditions, however, were terrible and he did not envy his crew who would have to make the best of them until the *Elita* pulled into port and could be stripped down, from stem to stern. The decks had not been regularly scrubbed, refuse had not been disposed of properly, if at all, and the air had been allowed to linger. Havelock knew that more than a few of his crew would succumb to various maladies over the next few weeks

The one consolation would be that, with so few crew on board, they would have a great deal of individual space, a luxury in itself on board a ship of war. They simply had to live with the dreadful stench that seemed to permeate the very wood of the entire vessel.

The disastrous casualties his men had sustained weighed heavily on Havelock's mind as he turned his attention away from Guillot's charts and back through the large windows of the great cabin. The *Elita* had already raised anchor and was now sailing towards the entrance of the cove, leaving the wounded on the beach behind. So many men were being left behind but far more were already dead, shipmates that had looked to him for wise command and reasonable assurance that they would see the green fields of England once more, whether they were volunteers or pressed. Once on board his ship, it made little difference to Havelock how a man came to be there.

The loss of the *Whirlwind* was a savage blow too and, in some ways, it pained him more than the deaths of British sailors. His claims to the prowess of the frigate had not all been bluster by any stretch, for she had truly been a fine ship, quick across the waves and nimble of turn. The speeches to the crew of prize money and great wealth might also turn to dust, for the loss of any ship in the King's Navy inevitably resulted in a court martial for its Captain, with a board ascertaining the circumstances of its loss. Quite what he could tell them about the *Whirlwind*, he did not know. He began to fervently hope that the tales heard in the Admiralty of Napoleon using the walking dead within his armies in Europe might actually be true. It might lend his own story some credence.

As a replacement ship, the *Elita* could do well, he knew. With a thorough strip down and refitting, along with a new crew, the two gun deck frigate would be both fast and powerful, with few equals in her class. Right now, she was a pale shadow of what she could be. He could feel it in her movements beneath his feet, there was something in the way she rode the waves and made sharp turns that just did not *feel* quite right. It would be hard, sailing on board a ship of such unrealised potential for so long.

Thoughts of returning to England might quickly become academic, of course. The jungle-covered island, now beginning to recede behind the *Elita*, seemed idyllic in the growing rays of the morning sun, but Havelock was not deceived. An evil lurked in these waters and he could feel in his heart that a reckoning was coming. The *Whirlwind* had already been claimed, along with most of his crew, and Dubois would no doubt seek to finish his vengeance. Havelock had not been completely unsympathetic to the plight of the old mariners, their souls doomed by the actions of his own blood.

There would have been some honour in a Captain's sacrifice for the good of his crew but Havelock had come too far now to simply roll over and die, and the encounter with Dubois had ended any possibility of making recompense with the dead. He had already resolved to fight the dead captain and sink his ship in return for what had been done to the *Whirlwind*. History be damned, it was time to live in the here and now. Havelock vowed to ensure his crew and the *Elita* made it back to England safely, death hulk or no.

His military mind began to turn over, considering feints and countermoves that may work against the supernatural horror that pursued him across these waters. He still had an agile ship that could keep the lumbering death hulk off balance, though it was no match for the *Whirlwind* in that area. The *Elita* did have potentially greater armament but the big guns on the lower deck especially would take some time to restore to full working order and, in any case, he did not have the crew to man them all. Initiating or receiving a boarding action was completely out of the question. His crew had only escaped with their lives by the skin of their teeth the last time they had met the hulk and with so few of them left now, the battle would be a foregone conclusion. Havelock had few illusions that the hulk still held hundreds of zombies that had not yet been committed to battle.

He knew he could simply hope that the death hulk and its unholy captain would not notice their departure from these waters but Dubois had so far seemed to know exactly where he was at all times. In any case, he had witnessed the *Deja's* straight-line speed and knew there was not a ship afloat that could outrun it, though he was painfully aware that he was still entirely ignorant as to how long the hulk could sustain such speeds. It had not appeared to be entirely dependant on the wind for motion.

The cannon fire of the *Deja* had been notably sporadic in their last battle, which gave Havelock a little hope, as he knew his return fire might be no better. However the report given by the wounded man who escaped from the *Whirlwind* had seemed to indicate that the hulk was at least capable of co-ordinated fire, and this was a very real concern. He might be happy to chance trading broadsides, fancying the accuracy and speed of his own gun crews to be far superior to those of walking corpses, and French ones at that. The balance would lie somewhere between the skill of his gun crews and the heavy 32-pounders that lined the triple gun decks of the *Deja*, which were far larger than the cannon of this frigate. If they could indeed be fired in unison by Dubois, the *Elita* would be shredded into matchwood in minutes.

It all seemed to come down to ifs and buts, leaving Havelock with few real options. Perhaps he could score a series of lucky hits that would hole the hulk and sink it, or dismast it – if it even needed sails to manoeuvre at the sea, which he was beginning to doubt. Maybe he could outwit Dubois and force his ship to ground on a reef or sand bank. However, the waters around this island seemed clear and deep, typical of a land mass thrust up to the surface by volcanic activity. With Guillot's charts he might be able to find a suitable area off the coast of Africa or further afield but he doubted he would be given enough time to sail that far.

Whatever the outcome of their next encounter, Havelock made himself a solemn promise. He would not make it easy for Dubois to find victory and, if possible, he would save as many of his crew as he could. As a gentleman and officer of the King's Navy, he could do no less.

Footsteps outside the great cabin diverted his attention from the panorama outside and he turned before a sharp rap at the door resounded in the small room.

"Enter!" he said, feeling resolve come back into his voice. Thrusting the door open, Corbin appeared.

"Captain. Sail sighted to larboard," he said.

"Is it our old friend?"

"Yes Sir. Looks like the death hulk has come for us."

\*     \*     \*

CLEARING THE STEPS two at a time, Havelock ran up to the quarterdeck, telescope already in hand as he scanned the horizon behind the *Elita*. The jungle island was to their rear larboard quarter but no hulk was in sight. Kennedy waited for both the Captain and the Lieutenant, pointing towards the island.

"Saw 'er as we left the cove, Cap'n," he said. "Disappeared as we rounded the island but she'll be back."

Havelock raised his telescope to view the shoreline but saw nothing but sand and trees. Making a decision, he turned to Corbin.

"Full sail, Lieutenant. Let us put some water between us, and that island. At sea, we have options – here, none."

"Aye, Sir. Mr Kennedy?" The Bosun scrambled down the stairs to the main deck, bellowing orders that unfurled canvas and filled the sheets with wind. The *Elita* soon picked up speed noticeably and, despite his sense of foreboding from the impending battle, Havelock began to feel the old thrill of a fast frigate skimming across the waves.

Damn the hulk, he thought. This would be a fine and well-fought battle, whatever the outcome.

A dark shadow appeared to pass over the island, arresting Havelock's attention. Raising his telescope once more, he saw his enemy. Sweeping from behind the curve of the island's shore, the black hull of the *Deja* surged forward, already turning to face the *Elita*. The arrival of the ship seemed to suck energy from the climbing sun and every man on board the frigate felt a blackness descend upon him, chilling his bones.

Now in broad daylight, Havelock had his first clear look at the ship of the line that had chased him all this way. The sails were ragged and though they looked as if they were filled with the wind, their angle appeared all wrong to him, as if Dubois had not cared how his lines were set. The speed the ship drew from the sails, however, could not be denied and an impressive wake extended from its stern, the water churning from the quick passage of something so large. Casting his eyes forward, Havelock studied the hull, trying not to feel intimidated by the triple line of gun decks that could amass a truly terrible weight of firepower. The painted wood was flaking all down its length, with barnacles and sea plants gracing every square yard. More than a few planks along the hull had popped free of their fixtures, robbing the vessel of any atheistic grace – though they seemed to do little to hurt its performance.

Lining the deck and grasping at vantage points on its masts and rigging were the crew. Havelock thought of them more as a horde, a ragged and decaying mass of zombies that soundlessly gesticulated, seeming to jeer and mock the ship they pursued. Adjusting the focus of his telescope, Havelock studied the *Deja's* quarterdeck, searching for his counterpart, and took a sharp intake of breath when he realised that Dubois was indeed standing there. Rigid, the zombie Captain's attention fixed on the telescope he held in his mouldering hands, Dubois looked straight back at Havelock. As the two stared at one another, Havelock thought he could make out a chilling grin on the face of his opponent. He lowered his telescope before turning to Corbin.

"Are the crew steady?" he asked.

"They will follow your orders, Captain," said Corbin, not quite evading the question.

"Good. We'll let her follow us a little longer, gauging her speed. I imagine she will close range in good order but let us test the theory first. If we can outrun her, we should."

"I heartily agree with you, Sir."

Havelock cast a glance back at Corbin. "Be prepared to fight, Lieutenant," he said. "I fully expect she will overhaul us and that battle will be inevitable."

"As you say, Sir."

"Good." Havelock rubbed his chin, ignoring the stubble he found there as he watched the hulk sailing towards them. Though it had moved with great speed as it sailed round the island, the *Deja* had now seemed to settle in its pace, matching that of the *Elita's*.

That gave Havelock cause to wonder. He had already guessed that the warship did not draw on the same winds as he for its sails. Could it be that whatever supernatural source drove it on was limited in some way? Perhaps it was daylight that robbed the ship and its crew of power, or maybe the remaining crew of the *Whirlwind* had damaged it in some way before they fell.

It was equally possible that Dubois was merely toying with him, of course.

Across the deck of the *Elita*, Havelock saw that his crew went about their tasks with a certain mechanical detachment, and he noted that more than one took strenuous pains to avoid casting a look back at their pursuer. He winced involuntarily as it was suddenly made apparent that the main deck and rigging were conspicuously empty of able bodies. The *Elita* was a larger vessel than the *Whirlwind*, true, but the casualties he had sustained would be a major factor in the fight ahead, and one he would have to contend with if victory was to be secured. The first step, he decided, was to instil some backbone into his shaken crew.

"Mr Corbin, gather all men that can be spared," he said. "I wish to address them."

Corbin, called for order and those on the wooden deck looked up at the quarterdeck, while others still working high in the rigging of the sails dutifully relaxed in their efforts to give the Captain their attention. Havelock stepped forward to the railings of the quarterdeck and looked down at them, hesitating for a moment as he marshalled his thoughts.

"I have met Lord Nelson just once," he said, his statement catching the crew off guard. Expecting to hear another platitude appealing to their own bravery, they leaned forward to hear a tale of the Navy's greatest hero, one who had constantly met and confounded England's enemies. Private stories of the man from officers who met him were rare and always eagerly received by a ship's crew.

"It was perhaps six years ago, while I was First Lieutenant on the *Heracles*." He noticed a couple of nods at this, and recognised two crewmen who had also served on that ship.

"Our ship was part of a squadron that sailed in the Mediterranean, tasked with guarding Nelson's flank as he began his now infamous Battle of the Nile. The night before he sailed to engage the French, Nelson gathered his captains for a fine meal on board his ship, the *Vanguard*, to discuss tactics and stratagems. As commander of the flanking squadron, my Captain, one Thomas Maccalsson, was invited too, and I was lucky enough to be brought along as his escort."

Havelock gave a brief smile as he remembered the evening, the heady company of so many competent Captains, each of them senior enough to command a ship of the line. And then, of course, there was Lord Nelson himself.

"What a place for a First Lieutenant to be!" said Havelock, noting his crew were fixed on his tale. "I kept quiet, as you might imagine, while I listened to the captains talk over a fine roast beef. Ploy and counter ploy was raised and discarded as they argued the best way to achieve victory over the French. Through it all, I watched Nelson. While some tempers frayed, he remained clam, allowing each man to say his piece before moving on.

"Whether it was my fortune or not, he soon spied the quiet Lieutenant at the other end of the table, sipping wine and trying not to be noticed. 'Sir!' he called out to me, silencing the entire company. 'Be you an officer in the King's Navy or not?' I don't mind telling you, as all those experienced eyes turned to me, I was mortified." Havelock noticed a few of his crew chuckling at this image and he nodded candidly. "Aye, there was a time as a young officer when I did all I could not to be the centre of attention." This drew some outright laughs, which Havelock stalled with a raised hand.

"I tripped over my words, amazed that this man, already a legend in the service, was sparing the time to talk to a Lieutenant who would not even be involved in the battle. 'Speak up, Sir!' he said to me. 'Every other man here has told me how he would fight the French and yet you sit there and say nothing! Explain yourself!' Well, how does one respond to that? I tried…

"I started to say that I was but a Lieutenant while every other man present was a post-captain but Nelson dismissed that with a wave. 'Nonsense!' he cried. 'You are a First Lieutenant and hope, I presume, to make Captain one day, with a command of your own, yes? Then explain yourself. How would you fight the French tomorrow?'

"Well, I studied the charts Nelson had laid out in front of us and started to make some noise about drawing up our ships into a line and moving in close to pound the French ships. No doubt I failed on some details and this brought some sniggers from the assembled Captains. I faltered, red-faced, but Nelson rapped a cup on the table to silence them.

"He stood and faced me. 'You need another year or so at sea, lad, but you may show some promise, I'll warrant you that!' Then he said something that, I swear, I will never forget so long as I live. 'Gentlemen,' he said, though he looked at me. 'If you do nothing more tomorrow than place your ship alongside an enemy vessel, you will not go far wrong in my book!'"

Havelock paused as each sailor weighed this in his mind. "As you know," he went on to say, "Nelson won the battle, setting the tone for our Navy's war against the French right up until this day. I won't lie to you men, you all know something of the terrible nature of the enemy that chases us now. And we have all lost friends and comrades. We will soon be in battle against that dark ship and whether we die or are victorious will be down to what each one of us does. But I say this to you; if you do nothing more than carry on firing your gun or stabbing with your blade, you will not go far wrong in my book!"

The crew cheered, a ragged cry that was borne by their small numbers, as Havelock cast a glance back at the *Deja*, still matching their speed behind them.

"Mr Corbin," he said. "A hard starboard turn on my mark, and get the men to run out what starboard guns we have. I tire of being chased. It is time we made an end of this, one way or another."

Taking a deep breath, Corbin steeled himself and saluted. "Aye Sir, a hard turn it is. On your word."

Corbin quickly got the men working again, and as they prepared to adjust the tack of the sails, he looked back at his Captain, brow raised in anticipation. Taking one more look at the hulk, Havelock turned to Corbin and nodded.

"Now, Lieutenant."

Orders rang out as sailors scuttled throughout the rigging and across the deck as they heaved and tied the sails to new positions while the helmsman spun his wheel. The *Elita* lurched for an instant under the strain of the manoeuvre, then her prow lifted from the waves and swung round to face the direction she had just come from, the whole ship tilting as it turned.

"Two points to larboard, helmsman!" Havelock called out, setting a course that would keep the *Deja* on their starboard side.

Now they sailed towards the hulk that had chased them, few crew could avoid looking up from their work to see their enemy as the two ships rapidly closed. However, Havelock fancied that the feeling of certain doom had gone from them. There were perhaps few who expected to win the coming battle, but he thought they might at least trust him not to send them to their deaths unnecessarily.

For several minutes, Havelock and Corbin watched the distance between the two ships slowly shrink. On the main deck, Kennedy nodded up to Corbin, who turned to his Captain.

"Crew reports the guns are ready, Sir."

"Very good, Mr Corbin. Now we will see what this ship is capable of, though she be only half fighting fit."

The *Deja* continued to close until there was little more than a couple of hundred yards between the two ships. The hulk then seemed to rear out of the water, its deck canting backwards as jets of spray were thrown upwards past the prow. It surged forward with unnatural speed, appearing to make a lunge for the *Elita*. Seeing this, Havelock smiled.

"She'll never turn on to us in time, not at that speed," he said. "Mr Corbin, on my word, fire our guns."

Though the hulk had cleared the remaining distance to the frigate, Havelock was right. It was now going far too fast to make any reasonable turn and the *Elita*, travelling slightly off angle to the vessel, would be carried by the wind straight down its flank. As the ships passed within just a few yards of one another, the British sailors got an all too close look at their enemy, the chilling cries of zombies screaming through broken throats made an eerie sound. All made crude gestures at the crew of the *Elita*, seeming to perform a macabre dance as they clawed the air and bared rotting teeth. Havelock eyed the *Deja* carefully, noting the stinking seaweed dressing the masts, the crumbling railings and various forms of sea life littering the decks. He also watched the gun ports lining the hull of the hulk begin to open but he could already see the cannon would not be run out until his ship had passed them by. Keen to strike the first blow, Havelock gave the order to attack.

"Fire!"

The order was relayed down to the gun decks several times before a massive blast and billowing smoke erupted from the *Elita* as the whole ship shuddered with the recoil. Large holes were blasted into the decaying wood of the *Deja*, and more than a few of the zombie crew spilled out into the sea. The cheers of the crew on the main deck were quickly overwhelmed by a staccato series of gun fire, the sporadic shots smashing into the other warship one by one, this time aimed at the upper part of the hull and masts. The dirty sails rippled as shot passed through them and several zombies were annihilated in an instant as a combined quarter ton of metal tore through their massed ranks. Havelock looked quizzically at Corbin.

"What happened there? Why the delayed shot?"

It took Corbin just a second to guess. "Limited crews to man the guns, Sir. Someone must have readied the crewless cannon to fire, running down the deck to touch off the fuses after they had fired the main guns."

Havelock smiled at the ingenuity of his crew. "A pint of rum after the battle to the man who thought of that!" he said. "Still, we won't have enough time to do that again. We'll have to rely on the crewed guns alone."

"Aye, Sir." Corbin stared at the *Deja* as it passed them by. "Did we do any significant damage?"

"The fight is just beginning, Mr Corbin, there will be no miracle shots here. Bring us about behind her stern and tell the crew to fire when ready."

The *Elita* dipped its prow into the water again before turning, a trait that was beginning to irritate Havelock, as it robbed the ship of a few seconds of manoeuvring. Then it swung round beautifully, presenting a broadside to the rear of the hulk, the rotting wood still sporting the marks of their previous duel in the *Whirlwind*. Once again, the *Elita's* few manned guns roared, and this time Havelock was glad to see large chunks of blackened wood blown clear of the *Deja*, one large section of the upper hull spinning gracefully through the air before it landed in the sea with a large splash.

"Reload, Mr Corbin," said Havelock. "Tell the crews to aim at the waterline. We'll try holing her. If nothing else, it should slow her down on the turns."

As the frigate turned starboard once more to this time race alongside the *Deja*, Havelock could hear orders to reload and aim being relayed to the lower decks. It was with some alarm that he saw the gun ports down this side of the hulk begin to open, one by one. However, they did not fire as the cannon were rolled out and instead seemed to be waiting for an order. Havelock gritted his teeth, knowing a full broadside from a ship of the line could be telling, even to an outsized frigate such as the *Elita*.

He was gladdened to hear his own guns were ready to fire and he nodded at Corbin to proceed. Yet again, explosions and smoke poured from the frigate's broadside and the shots found their mark below the triple line of gun decks on the hulk. Spouts of water were thrown up across its length as some of the fire thudded into the hull below the waterline and elsewhere, massive holes were gouged into the side of the *Deja*. Undismayed by this damage, a few zombies leered from their gun ports until an order silent to those on the *Elita* instructed them to fire.

The titanic roar that belched from the hulk deafened Havelock briefly, and he staggered from the concussion while wreathed in filthy smoke. Men screamed as they were rendered limbless or blasted overboard, while wood splinters flew through the air with equally lethal results. Beneath his feet, Havelock could feel the frigate groan under the battering, its wood shifting in ways it had never been designed to accommodate.

Gasping, Havelock staggered to the helmsman who, thankfully, was still on his feet. "Hard to larboard!" he said. "Take us back around!"

The *Elita* seemed sluggish in the turn and reluctant to pull away but once the deck crew saw what their Captain was trying to do, they rushed to the rigging to reposition the sails. Havelock watched their efforts but his eye was quickly drawn to the main mast in the centre of the ship. Likely nicked by a shot from the *Deja*, it had an inch wide crack running vertically up its length. Though it seemed to hold, he knew it would not last long under the strain of the sails as they filled with wind.

"Mr Corbin, furl the tops'l and topgallant. Just keep the mains'l flying."

"Aye Sir, but that will rob us of any advantage of speed."

"Regrettable but if the main mast gives, we may be dead in the water. Literally. And run out the larboard guns!"

Continuing its turn, the *Elita* came about as the crew on the gun decks ran from one side of the ship to the other to run out the cannon that now faced the hulk. Havelock knew that constant switching of broadsides could not be kept up during battle without exhausting his men but he had dared not risk trading shot with the *Deja* after its initial attack. His first instinct was to get out of its line of fire, then to swing back behind it for another attack on the hulk's wounded stern. If he could throw enough metal into that part of the ship, he would not be able to avoid dealing some serious damage. While the last exchange had dealt his ship a grievous blow in terms of men and guns, his more carefully planned attack would hurt the *Deja* in its mobility. At the end of the day, if he could reduce its ability to make sharp turns, he could pound it at a safe distance until the hulk sank to the bottom of the ocean once more.

The hulk continued to sail away from the *Elita*, and Havelock guessed that Dubois was trying to put some distance between them in order to protect his stern. *You have not reckoned on the accuracy of British gunners*, he thought.

Once more the frigate found itself passing astern of the *Deja*, though at greater range this time and in the opposite direction. The larboard guns kicked the *Elita* as they sent more burning metal through the air, and though some shot missed its mark, creating great geysers of water just behind the hulk, others were aimed to perfection. More debris spun off the back of the *Deja* and Havelock eagerly raised his telescope to inspect the damage.

He barked a short laugh in delight as he looked on to see what his crew had accomplished. The stern of the *Deja* was a complete mess now. Though this insult to its Captain cheered Havelock a great deal he was far more interested in the rudder, which had been shot away with the last volley.

Smiling, he waved Corbin over to his side. "We have her, Mr Corbin," he said, passing the telescope. "Rudderless, she is no longer a match for us. We'll stay in her rear quarter and sink her at our leisure. Pass the word to the crew – we'll take no prisoners for what they have done to us!"

"Shall I get more crew to the gun decks? We can increase the weight of fire with more guns being manned,"

"Yes. But make sure the wounded are tended to first. We now have time on our hands."

"Aye Sir." Corbin turned to enact Havelock's instructions but then stopped, standing absolutely rigid.

Havelock noticed the strange posture in his Lieutenant and frowned. "Something, Mr Corbin?"

At first, Havelock could not hear Corbin's whispered reply. The man then cleared his throat and spoke again.

"Sir... She's *turning*..."

"Impossible," said Havelock, though he sounded less than certain. He took the telescope back from Corbin and raised it to the hulk but he could already see the ship was indeed beginning to come about, for the first time seeming almost graceful in its movements.

"How can she do that?" said Corbin but Havelock had no good explanation. Instead, he thought furiously.

"Lieutenant," he said but Corbin continued to stare at the hulk, now bringing its prow to bear on the *Elita*. "Lieutenant!"

The shout stirred Corbin and he spun round, eyes wide. "Sorry Sir!"

"Make sure the larboard guns are ready. We'll give her a blast at point blank range."

"But then she'll be on us!" said Corbin and Havelock could hear a thin strain of hysteria begin to edge into his voice.

"And then we'll fight! We have beaten her once in an attempted boarding, we'll do it again! Only this time, we have been pounding her steadily. Who knows how many of her accursed crew we have destroyed already?"

"Not enough. It will never be enough!"

Havelock began to notice that more than one sailor was looking up from the main deck and he gave them a meaningful glare that encouraged them to get back to work, before he returned his attention to Corbin. He had fought too long and too hard on this voyage to be scuttled by a shaken officer. Taking a step to put Corbin in-between himself and the rest of the crew so no one else would see what he was about to do, Havelock grabbed the Lieutenant by the collar and pulled him within inches of his own face.

"Pull yourself together, man," he said, voice low but laced with an unmistakable undercurrent of threat. "Remember where you are." He held onto Corbin in this fashion until sanity began to return to the younger man's eyes.

"Now, prepare the larboard guns and ready the men for boarding," Havelock said, slowly and carefully as he released Corbin.

"With respect, Captain," Corbin said as he straightened his jacket. "We hole her and she will not sink. We attack her crew and nothing short of placing them in front of a cannon will kill them. We cannot fight this enemy!"

"And what would you suggest we do, Lieutenant?" said Havelock angrily. "That ship will overhaul us if we try to run. What does that leave? Are we to just lay down here and die?"

Corbin opened his mouth but found he had nothing to say in reply.

"No!" said Havelock. "We will stand and we will fight, and if this battle is ever remembered, history will be our judge! I, for one, refuse to go down without my sword in my hand and a pile of enemies at my feet!"

"This is the doom of us all," said Corbin mournfully.

Havelock bit back his immediate response and took a deep breath before speaking. "Lieutenant, I do not require your consent or your hope. All I require is that you obey my orders and fight!"

Slowly, mechanically, Corbin drew his sword and, after a brief pause, raised it in salute to Havelock. His voice was quiet, almost inaudible as he spoke. "I'll fight, Sir."

"Good. Now make the preparations." Havelock spun away and walked to the railings of the quarterdeck overlooking the sea between the *Elita* and the rapidly oncoming *Deja*. He thumped a fist on the wood in frustration, partly at Corbin's loss of nerve but, most of all, because he cursed the fate that had brought both him and his crew to ruin.

He knew Corbin had been right, in his facts if not in attitude. They faced an enemy ship that could not be sunk, crewed by sailors that were all but impossible to kill. What captain had ever been matched against such an enemy before? All he knew was that if they were to die, what mattered was the manner of their departure, whether they died as brave heroes or craven cowards. If only there were some other means beyond fighting or running, neither of which promised success against the *Deja*.

Havelock blinked. Of course there was a third way, an answer to the horror that could vanquish his enemy, sending Dubois and his nightmare crew back to the bottom of the ocean. It was an unthinkable course of action but that, in itself, gave him an advantage. Dubois could not see it coming, for it bordered on the suicidal. He turned back to Corbin who was just descending the stairs to the quarterdeck, a twinkle in his eye as he started to smile.

"Mr Corbin!" he said. "A moment more of your time, I think."

There was something in Havelock's tone that made Corbin frown with curiosity, and he marched briefly back to learn what the Captain had now concocted.

"A slight change in plans, Mr Corbin, a little addition, if you will permit me," said Havelock, beginning to relish his new thought.

"Sir?"

"Ready the boats, prepare to drop them over starboard. Make sure there are enough ropes to get men to board them quickly when I give the word. Then assemble everyone. The guns will fire once, then their crews will join us. I don't want anyone below decks after the volley."

"I understand, Sir, but what are you saying? We should abandon ship? The hulk will just chase us down in our boats."

"Ah, but therein is the beauty of it," said Havelock, smiling broadly now. "There is one more task I would like you to perform. See to it personally, I don't want any of the crew to see what we are doing until there are zombies swarming all over us. You see, I have had an idea..."

# CHAPTER TWELVE

HAVELOCK GAVE THE oncoming hulk one last, disparaging look before he turned to the main deck to set his plan in motion. Corbin had already retreated below to fulfil his duty, though the Lieutenant had looked at Havelock with incredulity as he explained what was required. Corbin had looked set to argue but seemed, at last, to realise that they had few choices left and the unthinkable might be their only salvation, even if it could claim the life of every man on board in the process. Some of the crew, at least, might have a chance of survival.

"Mr Kennedy, my side, if you please."

The Bosun threw the ropes he had been wrestling with to a nearby sailor as they began hoisting one of the boats up into the air in preparation to lower it into the sea. He bounded up to the quarterdeck at Havelock's call, eager to hear the full extent of his Captain's plans. He was to be disappointed.

"Mr Kennedy, I would like you to remain here on the quarterdeck until the Lieutenant returns. He is... completing a special task for me."

"Aye Sir, as you say," said Kennedy. He cast a glance at the hulk, now just a hundred yards away. "Might I be enquirin' as to your intentions, Cap'n?"

Havelock smiled evasively. "Why, Mr Kennedy, I mean to give that unholy ship a damned good thrashing! Now, quick to it, she closes. Give me full sail, Mr Kennedy, I want every ounce of speed we can wring from this fine vessel."

"Full sail? Cap'n, the mainmast is cracked, she won't take much."

"She won't have to, Mr Kennedy, I assure you. But right now, I need speed!"

Without further comment, Kennedy nodded and shouted down to the main deck, where sailors scuttled to do his bidding, racing up the masts to unfurl canvas while others pulled hard at the rigging. Sails dropped down rapidly, the mainmast creaking ominously above the ship as the wind caught the *Elita* and the sheets billowed forwards. The frigate increased in speed noticeably and Havelock walked to the side of the helmsman as he turned his attention back to the *Deja*, now barely forty yards away. Again, its crew seemed to swarm over the hulk's deck, brandishing rusting weapons or vicious claws as they mimed what they intended to do to each and every crewman on board the *Elita*.

"She's goin' to run us down," said the helmsman under his breath.

"Steady, man," said Havelock in reply. "We will snatch the initiative here. Hold her steady for just a moment more, make them think we are ready to meet our fate..."

The *Deja* ploughed through the waves then, with just thirty yards to go, her prow picked up in its characteristic way as the massive ship laid on its unnatural burst of speed. It was what Havelock had been waiting for.

"Now, helmsman," he said. "Hard to larboard! Cut across her path!"

Nearly caught off guard, Kennedy bawled instructions down to the sailors working the rigging, getting them to adjust the sails to the new course as the *Elita* lurched round. Its speed and sudden movement carried it past the prow of the hulk, and a collective howl erupted from the zombies on board, the sound chilling the hearts of even veteran sailors, as they realised their quarry was escaping. Watching his broadside line up on the *Deja*, Havelock grinned as he gave his next order.

"Mr Kennedy, fire!"

A few critical seconds passed as the order was passed down to the gun decks and then the cannon roared, chugging out both smoke and metal as the hulk was pounded. The *Elita*, leaning hard away from the hulk in its turn, fired its cannon at an inclined angle, discharging its anger directly across the deck and masts of the *Deja*, just as Havelock had planned. Corpses, now finally having the life blasted out of them, were hurled clear of the ship in pieces, their limbs and heads scattering across the sea. The *Deja's* foremast lost a yardarm but Havelock now had few illusions that it actually required sails to move across the ocean. His intention was to do anything he could to end the existence of as many of its crew as possible before the next stage of his plan.

As the *Elita* passed abeam of the *Deja* on its larboard flank, Havelock smiled grimly as he saw none of its gun ports were open, and he felt a little gratified that Dubois did not have all the answers, that he could be surprised by a sudden and unexpected move. This would prove to be vital if Havelock were to triumph over the undead Captain.

The *Deja*, its prey running, began to slow down to more normal speeds and began to turn towards the frigate, intending to follow it. However, it still carried a great deal of momentum, and the turn was shallow, making Havelock think that, perhaps, the loss of its rudder *did* have an effect after all.

"Helmsman, hard to starboard," he said. "Bring us right around – reverse our course!"

Though the expression of the man at the giant wheel seemed to flicker between desperation and despair, he followed his Captain's orders with automatic obedience. The sails reset for this manoeuvre, the *Elita* began to turn in the opposite direction, again leaning hard over.

A mighty crack, like thunder, resounded across the *Elita's* deck and Havelock looked up in alarm to see the top length of mainmast begin to sag under the weight of its sails. The fracture running up its height had widened to four or five inches in places and he could see the two pieces begin to move against one another. The mast began to lean forwards noticeably but then checked its movement, and Havelock realised it was being held in place by the rigging and little else.

"Lord, spare me that mast for just one more minute," he said under his breath.

Sailors still working high on the mainmast looked at one another uncertainly for a brief moment and then began scuttling down to the perceived safety of the deck. Others gave it nervous glances as they worked, fearful that the mast would topple at any second onto them.

Emerging from the lower decks, Corbin reappeared, his face grim, followed by the gun crews. He cast an appraising look at the damaged mainmast as he marched to the quarterdeck to join Havelock, shuddering at the damage the frigate was taking.

"You could really feel that break below decks," he said, nodding to the mast. "Will she hold?"

"I pray to God she will – for just a little further," said Havelock. "Is everything set below?"

Corbin gave him a meaningful look. "Aye Sir. It is alight now, four minutes by my reckoning."

"Very good, Mr Corbin."

"Sir, if there could be another way..."

Havelock shook his head. "You said it yourself. We cannot kill her crew; this is all that remains." He slapped Corbin on the shoulder. "Be of good cheer, Mr Corbin! We may yet escape this and send that damned hulk to the bottom of the sea!"

The mainmast once again groaned ominously, but Havelock ignored its underlining of his words. The *Elita* carried through its tight turn and every sailor on board watched the *Deja* as they circled round, until, finally, it was dead ahead of them.

"Straighten her up helmsman, steady as she goes," said Havelock. "Then lash the wheel and join your shipmates on the main deck."

The sailor gave Havelock a fearful glance as he began to realise what the Captain intended to do but obeyed without argument. Kennedy frowned as he looked to the helmsman, the *Deja* and then back at Havelock, it slowly dawning on him too what was going to happen. Corbin just looked sick.

"Mr Kennedy, prepare the men to receive boarders, but keep them away from the forecastle. It won't be safe up there."

"Cap'n," said Kennedy in protest. "This is..."

"You have your orders, Mr Kennedy. I would be obliged if you follow them."

The Bosun gave a quick look at Corbin, who refused to meet his eye. Finding no support, he had little choice but to do as Havelock had instructed.

"Aye, Sir."

The *Deja*, going too fast to turn quickly and being too large to slow down in time, had been outmanoeuvred by the nimbler frigate. After passing broadsides, the *Elita* had managed to turn a complete half-circle inside the hulk's own turning radius so that the frigate was now thundering over the gentle waves at full speed straight towards the *Deja's* side, a reversal of what Dubois had planned for Havelock earlier.

"Come, Mr Corbin," said Havelock, unbuckling his sword belt and letting it drop to the deck as he drew his blade. "It is time to join our crew."

Leading the way, Havelock descended the stairs to the main deck. He began to focus his attention on the fast approaching hulk, not seeing the salutes of his crew or their well-wishes. He no longer thought of duty, or his career, or the court martial he would face for losing two ships on this mission. All that mattered now was the final confrontation with Dubois, and being able to look into those cold, dead eyes as the French Captain realised the tables had been turned and that it was he who was doomed.

The *Elita* sped towards the hulk and several sailors cried in dismay as they saw its gun ports open and cannon roll out. On the hulk's deck, zombies gathered in a throng at the railings, waiting for the chance to leap onto the frigate's deck and begin rending its crew. For their part, the British crew dove for the deck, trying to find any scrap of cover behind the mainmast or coils of thick rope as the *Deja* unleashed the full weight of its broadside into the *Elita's* prow. Only Havelock and Corbin remained upright, the latter out of an officer's duty, the former more from a belief that fate would not snuff his life out just yet.

The upper half of the prow was turned into matchwood in a second, though this did little to slow the metal shot as it blasted the *Elita's* forecastle apart and then sped onwards across the main deck. All around, the air was filled with a deafening howl, flying splinters and the cries of men who lost limbs to the speeding metal. Wails of pain soon gave way to those of terror as sailors saw shipmates decapitated or torn in half by the attack, drenching the living in hot blood.

Corbin was one of the first to die, a heavy 36 pound shot moving at terrible speed catching him in the chest. Mercifully, he felt no pain as his life was snatched away, his body thrown backwards to be pulped by the wooden structure of the quarterdeck in the blink of an eye. To anyone watching, he seemed to simply disappear, leaving a thin red mist of blood which quickly fell to the deck.

Another shot found its mark squarely at the base of the mainmast, severing it in two instantly. No longer having any support within the wooden shaft itself, the rigging gave way and the mast toppled forward, hitting the foremast with a terrible crack. This too snapped like a twig, dragging canvas and rope onto the deck. Lucky sailors found themselves having to fight their way clear of the entangling sails and rigging, while others were crushed by the masts themselves.

His attention so rigidly fixed on the *Deja*, Havelock did not notice any of this, missing even the disappearance of his Lieutenant. He had the presence of mind only to grab a railing as the *Elita* closed the remaining yards to the hulk and smashed into it with an horrendous splintering of wood that seemed louder than even the *Deja's* guns.

Every man on the frigate was hurled forward by the impact as their ship came to a sudden and abrupt halt. The *Elita* had carved its way through the hull of the *Deja* so that what remained of its prow was rooted deep within the lower decks of the hulk. The two ships were locked firmly together, with only the *Deja* holding the frigate upright instead of listing to one side after the terrible pounding it had received. For a few seconds, everything was quiet, with only the lapping of the sea and the grinding of wood upon wood filling the air. Then, a dreadful, inhuman cry came from the hulk as swarms of zombies, hundreds of them, began to throw themselves onto the deck of the frigate in search of the living.

The *Elita's* crew, stunned by cannon and the sudden ram, were slow to respond at first and those furthest forward died cruelly with no chance to retaliate. Others, galvanised by the sight of their shipmates being torn apart, quickly stirred to action. Several, fearing for their lives and believing all was lost, threw themselves overboard, even as Kennedy began shouting at a small group to lower the boats over the side. The rest grabbed whatever weapon lay closest to hand and prepared to fight for their lives.

Canvas shredded and men screamed as they died as the horde of the walking dead poured onto the *Elita* in a seemingly never-ending stream. The sailors were soon driven back into a tightly packed mass around the ruined stump of the mainmast, huddling together for mutual protection as zombies threw themselves into the fray, sweeping round the sides of the main deck to begin encircling the living. Now cornered, a palpable change began to stir in the hearts of the British. Trapped, with nowhere to run, they developed a terrible vengeance, beginning to fight like demons, almost eager to wrench the limbs off one zombie or slice clean through another. Some limbless corpses, still twitching with unnatural life, were hurled high into the air to land in the centre of the sailor's group, where they were torn apart by those not yet pushed to the front line of battle.

"Dubois!" Havelock shouted as he strode forward, separate from the rest of his men. He hacked to all sides with his sword, laying zombies low with each strike, the dead no longer holding any fear for him. He searched for his counterpart, the rotting French Captain whom he had sworn to lay to rest. One zombie, its legs torn free by an enraged sailor, crawled along the deck and grabbed for his ankle. Havelock spat at it and brought his heel down hard on its skull, splitting it open with ease. Grey pulp sprayed across the deck, but Havelock had already moved on to send another zombie's head spinning with one strong swing of his sword. The blade quickly became sheathed in grey skin and flesh, tattered remains of the enemies he had dispatched.

"Dubois!"

One immensely tall zombie, close to seven feet, bellowed intelligibly as it charged the sailors, determined to force their tight unit open, leaving them vulnerable. Heaving a massive wooden plank, perhaps torn from the ruined prow of the *Elita* herself, the creature smacked aside a cutlass raised to parry the blow, sending the weapon spinning across the deck. The now defenceless sailor tried to back away but could take no more than a step before being pushed forward again by the men behind him. He raised his hands in a desperate attempt to ward off the coming blow that would crush him like an insect.

Havelock cut downwards into the knee of the zombie and it buckled instantly, falling to its hands. Another blow severed its head but before the sailor could stammer his thanks and grab another weapon from a shipmate, Havelock had already turned and once again resumed cutting his way through the mass of zombies.

"Dubois!"

More zombies clawed at his face, losing limbs to his sword in the process, before they parted at some unspoken command, intentionally stepping aside before continuing onwards to slaughter his men. Looking forward towards the hulk, Havelock caught a glimpse of the dirty French Captain's jacket as he jumped down to the deck of the *Elita*. He grinned wolfishly. Casting a quick glance back at his men,

Havelock, for the first time, saw how precarious their position was and also realised that Corbin was no longer with him.

"Mr Kennedy!" he called to the Bosun, who was at the forefront of the British sailor's mob, keeping zombies at bay with broad sweeps of his cutlass. Already a small mound of still corpses lay at his feet, causing those behind to stumble on the uneven pile and then fall prey to his attacks. Briefly, their eyes met.

"Get what men you can to the boats!" Havelock said, straining to be heard above the noise of battle. "Your duty here is done."

Without waiting for a reply, Havelock stalked forward, sword at the ready, as he marched to confront Dubois. No zombies made a move to harm him. Behind Havelock, a few men bolted as soon as they heard their Captain's order but, once alone, they were quickly surrounded and torn apart by the zombies.

Seeing Havelock disappear into the fray, Kennedy took command of the sailors, organising them to move, slowly but with determination, towards one of the boats. Taking the lead in guarding the backs of the retreating crew, Kennedy shouted for those nearest to start lowering the boat to the water while he fought to drive the pursuing zombies back, anxious to give his men as much space and time as he could. He heard the distant splash as the boat was dropped into the sea and was soon aware of men leaving his side to dive overboard, before heaving themselves into the small craft. A quick rush of zombies, perhaps stimulated by the sight of living men escaping, caught Kennedy by surprise and he gave a sharp cry as one got under his guard and sank its remaining teeth into his shoulder. He struggled to force its head back but the distraction was all its fiendish companions needed as they bowled the Bosun over, dragging him to the deck. Once pinned under the weight of several moving corpses, Kennedy found himself unable to even raise his arms as claws and teeth started to rend his flesh. His cries of agony were quickly silenced by a large axe splitting his skull in two.

Finding an area of the deck relatively clear of debris from the masts or the battle, Havelock waited calmly for his enemy to join him, confident that none of the zombies still climbing down from the hulk would trouble him. They raced past to catch any crewman still remaining on the *Elita*, any who were too slow in abandoning the ship. Dubois then approached with a limping gait Havelock had not noticed before, his appearance all the more hideous in broad daylight. Havelock did not even bother to salute with his sword, merely holding it at a slight angle, ready to either strike or parry any sudden lunge from the creature that had robbed him of two ships.

"Come, Dubois. I no longer fear you." Havelock's voice was calm and even, now certain in what he had to do. There was now nothing left but to play the final part of the act.

"You have doomed your ship by your own actions, Havelock!" the hateful thing spat. "Your crew lies in tatters and those escaping will not get far, I promise you. Now all that remains is for me to claim your own, worthless, pathetic life."

"Claim it then." Havelock's smile seemed to enrage Dubois. The zombie's lipless mouth gaped open as he howled in anger, while his entire body shook with rage.

"Worm!" Dubois exclaimed, as he lunged forward with his blade, straight for Havelock's heart.

Ready for the opening move, Havelock sidestepped the strike, cutting with a back swing aimed at Dubois' skull. The zombie reacted with equal speed, cocking his head to one side to let the blade pass harmlessly above him. Havelock felt his sword bite for just an instant as it sliced Dubois' ragged ear clean from his head.

White eyes blazing, Dubois advanced, swinging his sword wildly but with great accuracy. Knowing he could not hope to match the zombie Captain's raw strength, Havelock hopped from foot to foot as he dodged most of the blows, attempting to parry only the keenest of attacks, and then just angling his blade so Dubois' weapon would slide away, rather than be held fast. During the assault, Havelock was careful to keep half an eye on any obstructions behind as he was forced to give ground, lest he find his foot caught in a rope or jagged hole punched through the deck. He had little doubt that Dubois was no longer toying with him, that this was, indeed, the end.

Though he seemed to have endless reserves of stamina, Dubois checked his attack for an instant, perhaps wanting to re-examine his opponent to find a point of weakness in the swordplay. Havelock saw his chance and stepped forward to initiate his own series of attacks. Doing his best to avoid meeting Dubois' sword with his own, he made several feints that forced the zombie to manoeuvre in order to avoid being flanked and caught out of position. Their blades clashed twice but Havelock checked his swing each time, knowing that to use his full strength against Dubois would give him nothing more than a numb arm or, worse, a broken blade.

Dubois checked one of Havelock's attacks and then hacked downwards in a powerful blow intended to split him in two. Havelock twisted at the last moment and then lunged with all the skill the dead Frenchmen had shown in the past. Dubois, caught by surprise at the sudden strike, backed off two steps, arching backwards as the point of the sword came close to his desiccated face. He tried to knock the blade away, but Havelock had already withdrawn it and the parry went wide, leaving Dubois open.

With any living opponent, Havelock might have ended the fight right there by delivering another lunge to the heart or stomach, or perhaps sweeping his blade in from the side to dig into Dubois' neck. Knowing such attacks would do little to this creature, Havelock instead cut downwards at Dubois' left hand, which was outstretched and flailing as the zombie tried to keep his balance. Using two hands to drive the stroke down with as much speed as he could muster, Havelock again felt his sword bite, a moment of resistance, before it carried on downwards to splinter the deck.

White-clouded eyes looking a little dumb, Dubois watched as his hand, severed at the wrist, flopped to one side before lying still. He hissed as his attention went back to Havelock, their eyes locking, one with loathing, and the other with something approaching amusement. Screaming, Dubois raced forward once more to attack Havelock with three lightning fast lunges aimed at heart, head and stomach. Ready for the maddened zombie, Havelock once again gave ground, staying out of reach of the sword. His smile bubbled over and he began to laugh.

"Why do you laugh, Englishman?" Dubois said, demanding a response. "You think these pinpricks you have dealt mean anything to me, to one who has spent decades on the seabed waiting for a chance of rightful vengeance?"

"You cannot defeat me, Dubois," Havelock said, still chuckling.

"Your crew are already dead men. And I think you will tire before me in this fight!"

Havelock shook his head with a sad smile. "You have already lost. Victory, today, will be mine."

Stepping forward to renew his attack, Dubois quickly checked himself, stopping as if he were trying to puzzle out just why this enemy, who had already lost his ship and could not possibly win in a straight duel, was so confident. Havelock had no intention of giving him the time to guess and swung loosely with his sword, aiming for Dubois' own weapon. The zombie parried solidly as Havelock had expected and he made a brief show of trying to strain against Dubois' strength. He then took a step forward to place himself under his opponent's guard and, hooking a foot behind Dubois' leg, pushed forward with his shoulder, throwing his whole weight behind the move.

Too late, Dubois saw what Havelock was trying to do and though he backpedalled to keep balance, his foot locked with Havelock's and he fell to the deck, sword clattering from his deathly grasp. He screamed, a wrenching cry mixing frustration and anger as he hit the deck heavily, clawing upwards with his remaining hand to ward off Havelock's inevitable follow through.

It never came. Dubois hoisted himself on his elbows and looked up at Havelock, his rotting skin wrinkling in surprise.

"Why did you not try to finish me?" he said. "Even if you cannot kill me, you might try to hinder me further. Is this some foolish pretence of honour?"

Havelock took a step back, though he kept the point of his sword towards the prone zombie. "I told you, Dubois. I have already won. Now, pick up your sword and continue, if that is your wish. I am quite ready to play this out to the end."

A bone cracked as Dubois got to his feet, then turned to bend down to retrieve his sword.

"You are foolish, Captain," said Dubois. "Now your soul will be claimed for the deep."

"That may be true, but it will not be at your hand, accursed creature!"

Still side on to Havelock, Dubois bowed his head for a moment, enough to make the Englishman wonder what the creature was doing. Then Dubois whipped round, his sword following the line as it split the air with an audible whistle, its blade sailing true for Havelock's throat with all of his supernatural strength. He raised his own weapon to parry the attack and caught the force of the blow completely, staggering backwards several steps from its momentum. Havelock's sword arm fell to his side limply, numb from having taken much of the blow's force.

Dubois did not relent and he stalked forward, shoulders hunched like some predator poised to strike. Havelock took another step back and tried vainly to raise his sword to ward off another heavy blow. Then his world turned black and deafening as his body was blasted into the sky. Before he faded into unfeeling darkness, Havelock heard Dubois' cry, a long, mournful lament of a man who had striven for decades to complete but a single goal, only to find it snatched away at the last moment. His last thought was one of gratitude, to Corbin, for having followed his orders faithfully in setting a fuse to the ship's magazine. Then he thought no more.

The explosion blasted the bottom out of the *Elita*, shredding its hull, before boiling upwards to throw the deck and masts yards into the air. Fuelled by methane created in the filthy hold, fire incinerated the lower decks, gutting the ship utterly. Zombies and dead sailors alike were catapulted skywards before falling into the sea, some at great distance from the floundering ship, raining down into the sea like clumsy blackened gulls diving for fish.

The remains of the *Elita* began to take on water rapidly and it listed heavily, its stern already beneath the water. Its shattered prow locked into the *Deja*, it dragged the hulk with it, the larger ship pulled heavily to one side. The sea flooded into its open gun ports, racing through the lower decks in an inexorable tide that swept the remaining zombies with it, their arms and legs flailing uselessly as they tried to stop themselves being slammed into bulkheads. As the hulk began to fill with water, it listed even more, rolling almost completely onto its side. The sea, now able to flood through the open main hatch on its exposed deck, soon filled the rest of the ship and the *Deja*, robbed of all buoyancy and still locked in the *Elita's* death grip, sank downwards rapidly, returning to its original grave on the seabed.

Within a minute, all that remained of Havelock's last battle was a mass of bubbles where the ships had been as the last vestiges of air were squeezed out of them by the ocean. For a hundred yards in every direction, debris floated to the surface, a mix of wood, canvas, rope and bodies, those recently killed carried on the gentle waves alongside those long since dead.

THE FEEL OF cold water surrounding him, making his clothes sodden and heavy, roused Havelock to a sense of semi-consciousness. His thoughts disjointed and not entirely of this world, he began to dream, of battles at sea in an age before his own, of French armies sweeping across the globe to threaten his beloved British Empire, and a future dominated by Napoleon's imperial court.

He saw legions of zombies decimating a fleet led by Lord Nelson, who fought long and hard against impossible odds as the French invaded England. He saw King George fighting alongside Pitt the Younger in the streets of London, both surrounded by townsfolk as they desperately sought to defend the palace against blue-coated French soldiers. Visions of the old American colonies flashed through his mind, begging for aid from a friendless world as the French swarmed across the Atlantic to claim their territory in recompense for aiding their cause of freedom before everything started fading to blackness once again.

Havelock jerked, violently, as he fought for life. His actions seemed slow and inaccurate, as if he were moving in soup. Fighting for breath, he opened his mouth and found himself swallowing the sea. Panicking, he opened his eyes and discovered himself under water. Dimly aware of light to one side of him, he struck out, limbs flailing as he desperately sought the surface. Throat constricting and lungs bursting, he seemed no closer to open air and, at that point, he almost gave up, ready to let the sea claim his body as he slowly spiralled downwards into the darkness. Then, he heard the echoes of Dubois' mocking voice and he swam with renewed vigour, ignoring the crushing pain in his chest.

Surfacing with a splash, Havelock drew in a huge lungful of air and then started choking. Trying to catch his breath, he cast about the surface of the quiet sea through watering eyes, he saw the dark mass of the *Deja* roll over and quickly disappear between the waves and felt utter relief. Completely drained, he lay on his back, allowing the sea to carry him where it wished as he slowly began to recover.

It took him only a few seconds more to realise that he was not alone in the water, as three of Dubois' remaining crew clawed hungrily through the sea towards him, their sightless eyes fixed on his living flesh. With no more fight in him, with no strength left to give, Havelock took one last look at them and then closed his eyes, beginning to laugh as he waited for the end.

# CHAPTER THIRTEEN

THE SMALL BOAT bobbed gently on the vast expanse of sea, the waves carrying it up and down on the low crests in a continuous rolling motion. Only three men were carried inside, the only survivors of the desperate flight from the doomed *Elita* and, though thoroughly exhausted, they had returned to the scene of the battle in the vain hope of finding more of their shipmates alive and praying for rescue.

At the prow of the boat, Murphy sat, his chin resting on his arms which were folded on the hull. He kept half an eye open for any stranded sailors but, not seriously expecting to find any, he lulled on the border of sleep. Behind him, Bryant pulled weakly at the oars, his shirt in tatters as his torso bled from dozens of scratches from claws and flying wood splinters. Brooks was curled up at the back, nursing a leg injury that was bound with cloth ripped form his trousers. Having been in the frontline against the zombies as they closed in around the mob of sailors on the centre of the main deck, he had fought well but had taken a swipe from a cutlass for his trouble.

"So, where you plannin' on takin' us after this, Bryant?" Murphy said sleepily.

"Back to the island."

Murphy raised his head wearily and scanned the horizon around them, seeing nothing but the endless ocean.

"Can't see no island," he said before sinking back down.

"Think we go southwest from here," said Bryant. "Won't be too long before we see it. We didn't travel far before that ship caught us."

"An' 'ow do you know which way southwest is?"

"It's that way," said Bryant, nodding slightly ahead of them, though Murphy did not bother turning round to see the gesture. However, the Irishman did frown.

"You got a compass tucked away somewhere?"

Bryant sighed. "How did you get to join my gun crew, Murphy? Look at the sun. It is still morning, so take your bearings from that."

"Only morning?" said Brooks. "I feel like I have been fightin' for a year."

"Aye, you fought well, lad," said Bryant. "How's the leg?"

"Still bleedin'. Stopped most of it though. Think I'll get gangrene?"

"Not if we get you to the island quick enough. We'll take a proper look at it then."

"Could still be zombies on the island," said Murphy. "I 'eard they were chasin' our men through the jungle."

"Yeah, but we also got our own men on the beach," said Bryant as he paused in his rowing for a moment. He gave a short laugh. "We even have some of the French to help us there!"

"It was the damn Froggies that got us into this," said Murphy.

"But we'll all be in the same boat on the island." Bryant cast a look about the small craft. "So to speak. I can't see they will be in any mood to fight."

"Then it will just be a case of whose ship turns up first – theirs or ours," said Brooks.

"Aye, possibly, though I imagine some passing merchant has more chance of stumbling across us. Not every vessel at sea is a warship. You see anything up ahead, Murphy?"

"No," he replied, not even bothering to lift his head. Bryant snaked a foot forward and kicked him gently in the back before returning to his oars.

"Oww! Okay, I'm lookin', I'm lookin'!" He made a show of stretching up and looking around the horizon, before sinking back into rest. "That 'ulk went down pretty fast," he eventually said.

"Not surprised with the blast it took," said Brooks. "You see the *Elita* go? Blew men and zombies clear into the heavens!"

"Nice of the Cap'n to warn us about that," Murphy said under his breath but his voice carried in the quiet air. He earned another kick from Bryant for the comment.

"Don't you go talking ill of the Captain," said Bryant. "It's because of him that you, me and Brooks are still alive. And you have to give him credit for staying on board, going down with the ship. Despite the stories, there are not many Captains who would do that."

"No, many of 'em would be the first to push their way onto the boats," said Brooks. After a moment of reflection, he added "He was alright, was the Captain."

"Aye." Bryant continued to row slowly, careful to avoid tangling the oars in any of the debris that had started to float past them. Though fascinated at the amount of wreckage nearby, they all tried hard not to look at the various body parts that were carried on the surface.

Bryant frowned as he squinted into the near distance. "Hey, Murphy. You see that? Over there, movement in the water."

"Umm..." Murphy propped himself up and stared hard. "Ah, Bryant, steer away. Them's zombies, still alive an' kickin'."

"Well, where are they going? Is it one of ours in trouble?"

"Someone in the water. Think they're dead."

"Zombies don't go after the dead, Murphy!" said Bryant. "Brooks, get up here, help me with the rowing – we need to get there before they do!"

Brooks grunted with pain as he moved forward, relying on his arms for support more than his legs. He lifted his injured leg up over the plank Bryant sat upon as he moved into position, before taking an oar.

"Put your back into it, Brooks. I don't want to lose anyone we don't have to."

His interest now caught, Murphy sat up straighter, trying to get a good look at the body floating in the water. "Hey, Bryant. You saw the Lieutenant buy it, right?"

"Blasted by cannon before we rammed the French ship."

"That body's wearin' a uniform – I think it's the Cap'n!"

"Brooks..."

"I know, I know," Brooks said, fighting back the agony of his leg as he pulled back and forth on the oar. He crooked his injured limb to one side, using his good leg to brace against a rib within the boat as he strained to propel the craft as quickly as possible.

Working together, Brooks and Bryant gave the boat a good turn of speed and they closed rapidly on the floating body, trying to steer into a position where they were between it and the zombies clawing their way through the water. As they drew alongside, Murphy cried out aloud that they had indeed found the Captain and he leaned over the side to begin dragging him on board.

Bryant stood up and raised his oar as the first zombie lunged out of the water to scramble onto the boat. A loud crack was carried by the gentle breeze as the paddle of the oar connected with the zombie's head and it reeled backwards, stunned or finally dead, Bryant could not tell. He had already reversed the oar and was driving it downwards onto the skull of a second creature, repeatedly battering it until it stopped moving.

Behind him, a third zombie had thrown its arms over the side of the boat and was beginning to clamber on board, its swollen tongue passing over rotting teeth as it leered at the fresh victims on board. Without thinking, Brooks reached forward and plucked a knife from Murphy's belt before turning round to confront the boarder.

The zombie swiped a wicked claw at Brooks, opening a shallow wound in his arm. Ignoring the pain from both that injury and his leg, Brooks scrambled into the back of the boat, raising the knife. He stabbed forward, driving the blade deep into one of the zombie's eye sockets. The creature twitched violently, then fell still. With a last mighty effort, Brooks shoved the creature overboard, where it started to sink immediately.

As he sank down into the boat, he heard Murphy cry out. "Hey, Brooks, that was me best knife!"

Murphy had only managed to get Havelock's shoulders out of the water and was clearly struggling. After casting a suspicious eye at the water to make sure no further attacks from the dead were likely, Bryant crouched forward to help him. Together, they pulled the Captain onto their boat, noting that, aside from a few cuts and grazes, he seemed to be more or less intact.

After checking to see if Havelock still breathed, Bryant gently tapped him on the cheek, adding a little more force when he was met with no response.

"Captain?" he said hesitantly. "Captain, we're from the *Whirlwind* – the *Elita*. You're safe now. Captain?"

Looking curiously onwards, Murphy was about to ask if the Captain was dead, when Havelock gave a start, and immediately lapsed into a coughing fit. Bryant placed a hand on his shoulder as he began to look about wildly.

"It's alright Captain, you're safe. We are among the living."

"Dear God," were Havelock's first words and he rubbed his eyes as he sat up and tried to catch his breath. He frowned when he saw the other occupants of the boat. "You are the only survivors?"

"Sorry, Captain, yes."

Havelock leaned heavily against the side of the boat and sighed. "I had hoped for more."

"There is no shame in it, Captain," said Bryant with conviction. "I don't think there is another Captain who could have done what you did today.

"'Tis true," said Murphy. "You are a true blue-blooded hero. Captain Havelock, killer of the unkillable, sinker of the unsinkable!"

"And willing to stay on a doomed ship to the end," said Bryant. "You get yourself another ship, Captain, and we'll be the first to sign on!"

Waving back their praise, Havelock thought back to his duel with Dubois, the rigged explosion of the *Elita's* magazine and, finally, the zombies racing through the water to fulfil their Captain's promise of death. He rubbed his temple in disbelief.

"I was to die, you see," he said, causing Murphy to give a curious and perplexed look. "That was what was meant to be."

"I don't think so, Captain," said Bryant with confidence. "Perhaps you should have been killed several times over. But you were thrown clear of the explosion and we were here to pull you from the water. I would say that God clearly preserves you for another purpose."

"And perhaps honour is now satisfied," said Havelock but he did not explain himself to his remaining crew. Settling down into the boat, he allowed his eyes to close as he thought of Dubois and what the French Captain had sought so fiercely.

He hoped Dubois was finally dead, blown apart in the explosion of the *Elita* and that, perhaps, some peace could be found in that rest. Try as he might though, Havelock could not bring himself to believe Dubois was completely vanquished. Maybe Havelock would receive a visitation of a vengeful spirit in the future. After the events of the past few days, he could now believe almost anything was possible. More likely, Dubois was trapped somewhere in the joint wreckage of the two ships, lurking on the sea floor for another chance to strike at the Havelock family.

The truth remained, however, that Dubois had been bested. It might well be that Havelock would, one day, have to face his nemesis once more to again answer for the actions of his grandfather. Perhaps it would be a later generation of Havelock that would be given that onerous task. For now, at least, he believed he could relax and, finally, sleep.

Watching his Captain rest, Murphy cocked his head as he watched an expression of serenity wash over Havelock's face. Looking over his shoulder, and seeing no sight of land, he turned back to the recumbent Captain.

"Bryant says the island is somewhere southwest. Is that right, Cap'n?"

Murphy received no answer. Havelock was already fast asleep.

# THE END

AN OMNIBUS OF POST-APOCALYPTIC NOVELS

# SCHOOL'S OUT FOREVER

SCOTT K. ANDREWS

'The twists and turns keep you reading.' *SFX on School's Out*

*UK ISBN: 978-1-78108-026-9 • US ISBN: 978-1-78108-027-6 • £10.99/$12.99 CAN $14.99*

Lee Keegan's fifteen. If most of the population of the world hadn't just died choking on their own blood, he might be worrying about acne, body odour and girls. As it is, he and the young Matron of his boarding school, Jane Crowther, have to try and protect their charges from cannibalistic gangs, religious fanatics, a bullying prefect experimenting with crucifixion, and even the might of the US Army. Welcome to St. Mark's School for Boys and Girls...

School's Out Forever collects School's Out, Operation Motherland and Children's Crusade, with the short story The Man Who Would Not Be King, an introduction by the editor, interviews, and new, previously unpublished material.

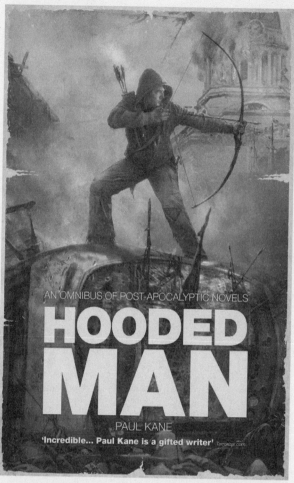

AN OMNIBUS OF POST-APOCALYPTIC NOVELS

# HOODED MAN

PAUL KANE

'Incredible... Paul Kane is a gifted writer' *Terror.co.com*

ISBN: 978-1-78108-168-6 • $12.99 CAN $14.99

When civilisation shuddered and died, Robert Stokes lost everything, including his wife and his son. The ex-cop retreated into the woods near Nottingham, to live off the land and wait to join his family. As the world descended into a new Dark Age, he turned his back on it all. The foreign mercenary and arms dealer De Falaise sees England is ripe for conquest. He works his way up the country, forging an army and pillaging as he goes. When De Falaise arrives at Nottingham and sets up his new dominion, Robert is drawn reluctantly into the resistance. From Sherwood he leads the fight and takes on the mantle of the world's greatest folk hero. The Hooded Man and his allies will become a symbol of freedom, a shining light in the horror of a blighted world, but he can never rest: De Falaise is only the first of his kind.

This omnibus collects the novels Arrowhead, Broken Arrow and Arrowland.